# WHILE WE WERE DREAMING

Clemens Meyer was born in 1977 in Halle and lives in Leipzig. *Bricks and Mortar*, his first novel to be published in English by Fitzcarraldo Editions, was shortlisted for the German Book Prize, awarded the Bremer Literaturpreis 2014, longlisted for the 2017 Man Booker International Prize, and shortlisted for the 2019 Best Translated Book Awards. His collection of stories, *Dark Satellites*, appeared with Fitzcarraldo Editions in Katy Derbyshire's translation in 2020. *While We Were Dreaming* (*Als wir träumten*), Meyer's debut novel, was originally published in Germany in 2007.

Katy Derbyshire, originally from London, has lived in Berlin for over twenty-five years. She translates contemporary German writers including Inka Parei, Heike Geissler, Olga Grjasnowa, Annett Gröschner and Christa Wolf. Her translation of Clemens Meyer's *Bricks and Mortar* was the winner of the 2018 Straelener Übersetzerpreis (Straelen Prize for Translation). She occasionally teaches translation and also co-hosts a monthly translation lab and the bi-monthly Dead Ladies Show. Katy Derbyshire's translation journal for *While We Were Dreaming* is published online at *toledo-programm.de*.

'The cumulative power of [the] well-constructed, pitiless and unflinching dispatches from the underbelly of society is remarkable.... Historical events often pass unnoticed by those living through them, unaware even of how much their lives have been changed. It is Meyer's achievement to capture the profound effects those events had on the lives of those at the bottom of German society.'
— David Mills, *Sunday Times*

'On reading Clemens Meyer's debut novel, it is impossible not to draw the comparison with another coming-of-age-novel, Irvine Welsh's *Trainspotting*. It has the same power, the same narrative virtuosity.'
— Santiago Artozqui, *La Quinzaine littéraire*

'A beautiful debut on friendship, boredom and hope.... Meyer manages to bring to life a hazy and complex period of history.'
— Pierre Deshusses, *Le Monde*

'It is breathtaking in its power, in its harsheness, and tenderness. It reminded me of Jean Genet's *Miracle of the Rose*.'
— Marine de Tilly, *Transfuge*

'A book like a fist... German literature has not seen such a debut for a long time, a book full of rage, sadness, pathos and superstition.'
— Felicitas von Lovenberg, *Frankfurter Allgemeine Zeitung*

'Still a literary revelation fifteen years after its publication. No other book describes the attitude to life of an entire generation in East Germany more authentically and precisely.'
— *Esquire*

Praise for *Dark Satellites*

'Figures from society's margins are at the centre of the stories... *Dark Satellites* throws a perceptive light on circumscribed lives on the edges of Europe.'
— David Mills, *Sunday Times*

'Meyer's snapshots of urban life – a burger bar, a fairground wheel, a neglected train station – are so vivid they make you see your own surroundings in the light of those faraway buildings.'
— Anna Aslanyan, *Spectator*

'Meyer's writing is brittle, laconic, clear, intense – and once again on top form. Short stories are clearly his forte. He finds memorable images for his themes: a dance without music in an unused Russian canteen; a midnight haircut; a man who slides into another identity after a break-in to his home and leaves his briefcase, the last requisite of his old life, in an abandoned shop. Meyer's stories are quiet, tragic and once again populated by ordinary people, for whom he has always harboured sympathies.'
— Steffen Roye, *Am Erker*

Praise for *Bricks and Mortar*

'The point of *Im Stein* [*Bricks and Mortar*] is that nothing's "in stone". Clemens Meyer's novel reads like a shifty, corrupted collocation of .docs, lifted off the laptop of a master genre-ist and self-reviser. It's required reading for fans of the Great Wolfgangs (Hilbig and Koeppen), and anyone interested in casual gunplay, drug use, or sex.'
— Joshua Cohen, author of *Book of Numbers*

'Meyer's multifaceted prose, studded with allusions to both high and popular culture, and superbly translated by Katy Derbyshire, is musical and often lyrical, elevating

lowbrow punning and porn-speak into literary devices ... [*Bricks and Mortar*] is admirably ambitious and in many places brilliant – a book that not only adapts an arsenal of modernist techniques for the twenty-first century but, more importantly, reveals their enduring poetic potential.'
— Anna Katharina Schaffner, *Times Literary Supplement*

'[*Bricks and Mortar* is a] stylistic tour de force about the sex trade in Germany from just before the demise of the old GDR to the present, as told through a chorus of voices and lucidly mangled musings. The result is a gripping narrative best described as organic.'
— Eileen Battersby, *Irish Times*

'A journey to the end of the night for 20th/21st century Germany. Meyer reworks Döblin and Céline into a modern epic prose film with endless tracking shots of the gash of urban life, bought flesh and the financial transaction (the business of sex); memory as unspooling corrupted tape; journeys as migrations, as random as history and its splittings. A shimmering cast threatens to fly from the page, leaving only a revenant's dream – sky, weather, lights-on-nobody-home, buried bodies, night rain. What new prose should be and rarely is; Meyer rewrites the rules to produce a great hallucinatory channel-surfer of a novel.'
— Chris Petit, author of *Robinson*

'This is a wonderfully insightful, frank, exciting and heart-breaking read. *Bricks and Mortar* is like diving into a Force 10 gale of reality, full of strange voices, terrible events and a vision of neoliberal capitalism that is chillingly accurate.'
— A. L. Kennedy, author of *Serious Sweet*

Fitzcarraldo Editions

# WHILE WE WERE DREAMING

CLEMENS MEYER

Translated by

KATY DERBYSHIRE

# CHILD'S PLAY

There's this nursery rhyme I know. I hum it to myself when everything starts going crazy in my head. I think we used to sing it when we hopped about on chalk squares, but maybe I thought it up myself or dreamed it. Sometimes I mouth it silently, sometimes I just start humming it and don't even notice because the memories are dancing in my head, no, not just any memories, the ones of the time after the Wall fell, the years we – made contact?

Contact to the brightly coloured cars and Holsten Pilsener and Jägermeister. We were about fifteen back then and Holsten Pilsener was too bitter for us, so we'd usually drink local. Leipzig Premium Pilsener. It was cheaper too, seeing as we sourced it straight from the brewery's backyard. Mostly at night. The Leipzig Premium Pilsner Brewery was the epicentre of our neighbourhood and our lives. The wellspring of long drunken nights in the suburban cemetery, endless orgies of destruction and dances on car roofs in the Bockbier season.

Original Leipzig Pilsener let loose our bottled blond genie, who grabbed us by the hair and lifted us over walls, magicked cars into flying machines and lent us his carpet to float away on, spitting down on the cops' heads.

Usually, though, those strangely dreamlike flying nights ended with a crash-landing in the drunk tank or on the corridor of the nick, handcuffed to a radiator at Leipzig Southeast Police Station.

When we were kids (are you still a kid at fifteen? Maybe we weren't anymore, that first time we faced a judge, usually a woman judge, or the first time the police drove us home at night and we went to school the next morning, or not, with the 8 from the handcuffs still imprinted on our skinny wrists), when we were good kids, the epicentre of our neighbourhood was the big Duroplast State Toys and Rubber Stamps Factory, where an otherwise insignificant classmate got us rubber stamps and toy cars from his stamp-pad-manufacturing mother, so we never beat him up and sometimes gave him a few coppers, or let's call them aluminiums, 'cause that's what our coins were made of back then. The big factory went bust in 1991 and they tore the building down, and the little rubber-stamp and toy-car fence, his mother was out of a job after twenty years and hanged herself in the outside toilet, so we still never beat the insignificant boy up and sometimes gave him a few coppers. There's an Aldi there now – I could pop in for cheap beer or spaghetti.

That thing about the boy's mother, it's not true. She got a job at a new Shell garage in 1992 and pretended not to recognize us when we bought beer or vodka or korn from her, because it was night and the shops were shut and the walls of the Leipzig Premium Pilsner Brewery were just too high sometimes.

The best thing was, the brewery was there even when we couldn't see it, when we were carrying an old lady's handbag home for her a couple of streets over, or when it was night (I mean those terrible dark nights in winter, when all you see is the lights and you feel so sad), or when we closed our eyes as we drove past. The big old Leipzig Premium Pilsner Brewery was there. We could smell it. It smelled so fucking great, it really did, tangy like hops, a bit like tea only way better. When the wind blew the right way, we could smell it for miles.

And I can still smell it now when I open the window even though I'm far away, but the others don't believe a word of it. And how would they know anyway – I haven't told them – and when we're lying in our beds on sleepless nights, I bite down on the corner of my blanket to stop myself telling tales of those wild times.

On nights like that, I often think of Alfred Heller, the kid we called Fred. He had a face gone greyish blue from all the drinking, like ripe stilton. Fred was a couple of years older than us but he looked fifteen, wore these round glasses like a good little schoolboy, and then he'd joyride stolen or dirt-cheap cars without a licence, around our neighbourhood and all round town. Sitting in a car with him was weird because there was hardly any space, too many beer cans on every surface, and we did the craziest things on our nights out with him. Something happened to us when we got in a car with Fred, something made us lose all inhibitions, we felt this absolute freedom and independence we'd never known before, and we yelled it out; it was like the witch with five cats who lived next door to me had cast a spell on Fred's beaten-up cars. Sometimes we used the rolled-down passenger window as a surfboard, holding onto the roof with one hand. It was like a merry-go-round after a bottle of Stroh 80.

This one time, speeding through the city, wasted Fred let go of the steering wheel and said, 'Shit, I can't hack it no more.' I was in the back, between Mark up to his eyeballs on drugs and Rico, still clean back then, and we couldn't hack it either and we only had eyes for the lights of our city racing past us. And if it hadn't been for Little Walter, who was in the front seat next to a suddenly resigned Fred, and whose life I saved twice in one night, later on (and who still just walked out on us, on another night much later), if he hadn't grabbed the steering wheel and jumped on Fred's lap – slumped down on the driving seat – and brought the car to a halt with a whole load of burnt rubber, I'd be dead now, or I might have lost my right arm and have to do all my paperwork left-handed.

Fred Heller had a brother, Silvio. Silvio didn't have Fred's criminal energy, but he did play chess. The brothers lived together and while Fred & co. were doing dirty deals in the living room, I'd play chess in the kitchen with Silvio. He had his own interpretation of the rules, but I accepted it 'cause (like he told me once as he balanced his bishop on the top of the vodka bottle and checked me from there, or rather checked my king) the Ghetto doctors had fucked him up in the days of the Zone and he only had a few years left to live. There must have been some truth to it because he dragged one leg and his left arm was almost lame. Aside from that, his face would sometimes make these really weird contortions, he'd roll his eyes 'til the whites went green and beat his head against the chessboard (I was scared he might get one of the pointy bishops stuck in his eye). The whole thing impressed me so much that even in winning positions, when my knight was raping his king (by his rules), I'd give up right away, bite the head off my king and stick it in the four-star freezer compartment, run off to Fred & co. in the living room and join in the dirty deals.

The Ghetto doctors fucked him up. Took me a while to work out what that meant, 'Ghetto,' when Fred and his brother were telling their tales. Their parents had given them up and they'd been in a secure facility for kids and teens with behavioural issues for years, in the Ghetto, and Silvio must have had too many of the antidepressants and hush-you-up jabs and messed up his liver and kidneys. Sometimes he talked about experiments, but I don't think that was true. I once asked Fred if he was still in contact with his parents. 'No,' he said, 'my knife gets a hard-on when I see them.' Old Fred probably gets a hard-on when the wind blows these days, 'cause he's in some bastard jail. I don't know what his last trick was that got him put inside, all I know is he was on probation for the umpteenth time and his file was as thick as Meyers Encyclopaedia, and all I know is what I've been told and what's turned to legend, almost, by now.

He was driving around town and the cops were on his tail, it was night and he was at his normal alcohol level, and somehow it suddenly took hold of him. He'd probably planned it as his last big show. Certainly had style. Slammed on the brakes. Turned the car 180. Pedal to the metal. Rammed the first cop car. Rammed the second cop car. Reversed and did the same again. Don't know how many times. They say the cops couldn't get their doors open in the end. Then he got out and stuck his hands up like Billy the Kid, and said: 'I surrender.'

I don't know if the cops climbed out of their concertina cars through the sunroofs but in any case, the first one who came stumbling towards him got a punch in the face that broke his nose, and Fred's been gone ever since. Even though he told me before that he'd never go back inside the Ghetto and he wanted to give up all that crap. And I almost believed him. This one time, see, Fred and me and my old school friend Mark, already up to his eyeballs on drugs even then, we were in a bar and these guys tried to start a fight with Fred (about some old dealings, he said), but he wouldn't rise to it, not even when they tipped beer over his face. And when I reached for a bar stool he said: 'Leave it, Daniel, forget it, this is my business.' The three guys were next to us at the bar and one of them nudged Fred so hard he fell off his stool. His glasses smashed but he put them back on, blinked through the broken lenses and said to me: 'Leave it, Daniel,' and to them: 'I'm not doing a thing, you tosspots, I'm on probation.' He kept on saying it as they pushed him around, and one of them hit him in the face a couple of times. Then Fred pulled out a jack-knife, there was a quick click and the blade stood upright, and he laid his left hand on the bar and rammed the blade through it into the wood. 'You nasty fucking poofters aren't getting me out of here!' They fucked off then and I called a doctor. And before the doctor came and pulled out the knife, which was jammed pretty deep into the wood, me and Fred had a couple of shots of double-distilled korn, while the landlord wiped away the surprisingly small amount of blood. Never in his life had he felt this good, Fred said, with one hand nailed to the bar.

My old school friend Mark, sitting next to us off his head, didn't notice a thing. He still doesn't notice a thing these days, 'cause he's strapped to a bed in some empty white room, in rehab.

Bed. Rehab. My sweet little Estrellita. I sing, I dream, my sweet little Estrellita. She wasn't really called Estrellita but I like to call her that, it means little star in Spanish, and when some arsehole drove into a tree with her in the passenger seat she was in a coma for five weeks, and when she woke up again she was even sweeter than before, so tiny and fragile, and she made eyes at me at least five times over. I can't even remember what colour eyes she had. I must have been in love or something, 'cause she was really a gorgeous little... slut. Walter, also little but not as gorgeous, he told me that and said I should keep my hands off her 'cause half of Leipzig (including him, that dirty bastard) knew every inch of her body, except for the colour of her eyes. And that was how Little Walter saved me from getting the clap and paid me back a bit for saving his life twice in one night.

It was a night like a dream. We were hanging out in our park. I'll soon be walking through it and watching the kids playing there, in the same sandpit we used to piss in, and puking wasn't unusual either. Fred got caught again that night, standing up on top of the brewery wall and handing down the beer crates to Rico, who we called Crazy Rico behind his back 'cause he'd once bitten the tip off our Pioneer leader's nose, back in the Zone days when the guy tried to confiscate Rico's Captain America comic book, and the only reason Rico didn't get kicked out of school was 'cause a few weeks later there were no Pioneers and no more Pioneer leaders either. But it's not true that Rico took a bite out of the cop's nose when he tried to confiscate the beer crate and Rico and Fred. Mark, who was supposed to be helping but was sitting on the kerb juggling pebbles for some drugged-up reason, unnoticed by the cops, Mark saw it and clawed his way past all the spiders and spider's webs to the park, where Walter, Stefan – we already called him Pitbull in those days – me and my clapped-up Estrellita were waiting, all thirsty. We were really crazy thirsty 'cause just before, to start off the evening if you like, we'd slaughtered one of Fred's semi-legal wrecks. Fred said he didn't need the car anymore, and then someone kicked in the door, and then we all ripped the door out together and smashed all the windows, knifed the tyres and all that. I reckon if we'd had the skills of that French guy Monsieur Mangetout, the one from the Guiness Book of Records, we'd have eaten that car right up. I don't know what came over us, we got high on it. Sure, it was the alcohol too, but something inside us went click and switched to insane in the brain. My sweet little Estrellita danced screaming on that car roof, my God, did I love her.

We went insane in the brain again once Mark told us where Rico and Fred were. We wanted to get them out and we smashed up every rubbish bin, traffic sign, park bench and every fifth car along the way to Leipzig Southeast Police Station. The crazy thing was that when we politely kicked the big iron gate and told them why we were there, the cops just said: 'Get out of here, you can come and collect them in the morning.' Even though our yelling, thumping, shouting was loud enough to wake Rico's deaf grandmother, who got a bad night's sleep 'cause Rico didn't come home to her. Rico's arms were behind his back and they pushed him down a long white corridor into a bright white room with a typewriter for writing up the arrest report, suspected theft. We heard him shouting from inside, 'It's OK, I'm fine, we're the greatest!' Like he'd already got used to being behind bars, even back then.

Outside, Estrellita puked on the windscreen of a cop car pulling in, so we took her home right away. And when we got to her building, Little Walter jumped out of a third-floor window 'cause of some bitch who wouldn't fall in love with him and go on a trip to the seaside, and I caught him by the collar just as he was falling, and that crazy bastard was yelling, no, more like babbling, 'I love you, Anja!' as the fabric ripped and Mark leaned way out, no longer in command of his motor skills, trying to pull Walter back in. I can't remember exactly how we all managed not to break our necks, all I know is that Little Walter gave it another try later and threw himself in front of a truck and we stumbled home dazed and confused after I'd plucked him off the road, just before he got mushed to a pulp. It was all crazy, like a nightmare on a hot summer night, thirty degrees.

Not a night goes by when I don't dream of all that, and every day the memories dance in my head and I torment myself asking why it all turned out the way it did. Sure, we had a whole lot of fun back then, but still there was a kind of lostness in us, in everything we did, a feeling I can't explain.

It's Wednesday, and in a minute they'll unlock the door and take me to Doctor Confessor. There's this nursery rhyme I know. I hum it to myself when everything starts going crazy in my head.

The school was on fire. We were on our backs in the stairwell and the corridors, too late to get out. Grenades were hitting the ground floor. Mark came stumbling up the stairs, a sign round his neck saying GRENADE SPLINTER INJURY in big black capitals. He lay down a couple of steps below me.

'Shit, I'm hit,' he said quietly.

'Where?' I leaned my head against the bannisters.

He pointed at his sign. In small print and brackets at the very bottom, it said: ABDOMINAL REGION.

'Grenade splinter in your abdomen, that's your lot,' I said. 'That's like a shot in the stomach, you're gonna cark it. Dead!'

'Nah, they're coming for me any minute!'

'Doesn't matter, you'll get internal bleeding.'

'Shut it, Danny!' He turned his face to the wall. He was so quiet now I could hear him breathing. The bannister rails were uncomfortable on the back of my head and I slid closer to the wall. 'If you had a gun you'd have to shoot yourself,' I said. 'Would you do it?' He didn't answer, probably in pain. Like the guy in the western who shot himself in the head 'cause he knew he wouldn't make it. I was glad there was nothing wrong with my stomach. I raised my head and coughed loudly – I had a couple of burns and smoke poisoning, although there was nothing about the poisoning on my sign. I coughed even louder so they'd hear me and come and get me. Someone ran along the upstairs corridor where Katja was. She'd lain down on a blanket next to the door and when I went to lie down next to her, the stupid medics sent me away. 'Burns and minor injuries on the first and second floor,' they'd said. Katja's sign read: SEVERE HEAD INJURY

(PROBABLE LODGED BULLET). She was head of the Class Council – she'd picked the best spot and the best injury.

'Burns are harmless, they'll leave you to rot here, they don't care. All you need is a bit of water on it.' Mark had turned back around and was tapping at his sign with a grin. 'With me, they gotta cut me open, they have to be quick with me, it'll be the girls from year eleven and then I can rest my head on their tits!' Just then, they really did come down the stairs but their stretcher was occupied by Katja, her head injury sign on her chest. She didn't have proper breasts yet, you could just about see them in P.E. and when she held a speech on Pioneer afternoons and did a nice lean forward. Her head wobbled side to side on the stretcher – Hey, watch it, there's a bullet in there somewhere! She put her hand underneath her head and smiled at me. I gripped my sign and smiled back. The two year eleven girls were wearing brown army shirts unbuttoned over the chest (not that big), their sleeves rolled up and their boots making a lot of noise. Mark was now lying right in front of them in the middle of the stairs. 'Oi, what about me, am I supposed to snuff it here, or what?'

'Come on, mind out the way, it'll be your turn soon!'

'Shot to the stomach, I've got splinters in my belly, grenade splinters, gigantic ones!'

The girls laughed and clambered over him. I watched Katja's head bobbing down the stairs, dangling lethargically off the stretcher again.

'This is such crap, Danny, my arse is starting to hurt!'

'See, who are they leaving to rot now?'

'Leave me alone!' He turned back to face the wall.

'You know what they'll do to me? I've got smoke poisoning, pretty bad. Mouth-to-mouth resuscitation, get it?'

'Rubbish!' Mark righted himself and looked up at me, his eyes wide. 'That's rubbish, isn't it?'

'No, no, believe me, this boy from year six told me, he had the same thing as me last year. Severe smoke poisoning!'

'You're crazy, it doesn't say anything about smoke poisoning, and nothing about "severe" either!'

'Yeah but smoke poisoning's always severe, they don't have to write that down specially. You always get smoke poisoning when you have burns – I was right in the middle of the fire! And they have to do everything exactly like in real life!' I coughed and wheezed and held onto the bannisters.

'So they'll give you the kiss of life, I mean really, and press air into your lungs?

'Right, just not too much air of course, 'cause you're OK really, but they have to practice it. They french you as well, 'cause they have to check you haven't swallowed your tongue, that happens sometimes, see.'

'Danny, you're pulling my leg!'

'No, I swear. Pioneer's honour!' I raised my hand. 'They roll their tongue around your mouth, and maybe they even like it. Right, yeah, they definitely like it. With me, anyway, I know all the tricks, Mark – and then they just can't stop frenching you!'

'And their tits, Danny?'

'Yeah, they're resting on you, you get a good feel of them!'

'Let's swap, come on!' He took off his sign and held it up to my face.

'Forget it!'

'Danny, listen, a shot in the stomach's fine too, they feel up your belly, you get a nice stroking, only the girls do it, you know, they only let the girls do it 'cause they've got more nimble fingers!'

'No, Mark, forget it!'

'Come on, look what it says here: *abdominal region*! Get it, Danny? Abdominal region!'

'I don't wanna swap, Mark, no, I don't want to. Bugger off with your stupid splinter!' I slid away from him to the wall. He crawled after me.

'Hey, wait, no listen, abdominal region, right, they have to check it all out!'

I pushed him away. 'I don't want your stupid sign, don't you get it? It's *my* smoke poisoning! Get off my back with your crappy shot in the stomach!'

'Please, Danny, go on, give it to me, let's swap, we're friends, aren't we?' He grabbed at me and my sign and I slapped his hand away. His other hand was instantly on my jumper, I stood up, kicked at him, and we rolled down the stairs. The string from my sign tangled around my neck, Mark fell on top of me and his knee bored into my belly. 'Mark!' I couldn't shout properly, couldn't get enough air. 'My sign, Danny, give it here! You always want everything for yourself!'

'Mark, please!' He let go at last, probably seeing I was going blue in the face. I took a deep breath. 'You're crazy, man!'

Two legs. Two brown leather shoes. Two trouser creases right in front of my face. I turned away and looked up. The headmaster. Mark rolled off me; the string from my sign was now broken and it fell off my neck as I stood up. 'Name, class?'

'Mark Bormann, 7b.'

'Daniel Lenz, 7a.'

'I know you, Daniel, don't I?' He looked me straight in the eye and I nodded and looked at the wall. 'You do know we've got visitors today?' We nodded. 'So you know we've got visitors today.'

'Yes, sir,' we murmured.

He bent down and picked up my sign. 'You've got burns, Daniel?'

'Yes, sir,' I said, quietly again.

'Well, Daniel, imagine a child in... Nicaragua. You do know what's happening in Nicaragua?'

'Yes, sir,' I said, although I didn't know exactly what was happening in Nicaragua.

'A child with burns waits for help. He waits for trained medics. And he's in pain, so he tries to lie nice and still.' The headmaster knotted the string back together and hung the sign around my neck. 'You're good in class and the Pioneers, Daniel. You know our military defence lessons are very important for our Free German Youth members, so they can learn to help injured children.'

'Yes, sir.'

He took a step aside to face Mark.

'Mark, you do know who's come to visit our school today?'

Mark had one hand in his pocket, and he took it out again. 'The National People's Army, Mr Künzel!'

'An officer of the National People's Army, Mark. Our school has a reputation for our military defence lessons. And our Free German Youth members are relying on your cooperation, and I expect,' he turned back to me, 'I expect you, in future, and by that I mean from now on, to refrain from such disruption and cooperate with discipline.'

'Yes, Mr Künzel,' said Mark.

'Yes, sir,' I said.

He nodded a few times and rubbed his chin, then continued up the stairs. Before he went through the door to the corridor, he turned around again. 'Remember:

discipline, like good Pioneers!' He smiled and left.

'I wish he had a splinter,' whispered Mark, 'no, I wish he had two, right in the belly. From a grenade exploding right next to him!'

'Hey,' I said, sitting back down on my step, 'that stuff about the girls was made up...'

'Come off it, you're just saying that so you get them to yourself.' He squatted three steps down from me and faced the wall. I listened to the sounds around the school building. There were people running on the floor above us, someone somewhere called out, it sounded like 'Is there a fire here?' and it echoed in the corridors, doors slammed. Then a couple more medics came past us, girls *and* boys this time, talking and laughing and paying us no attention, 'cause all the stretchers were occupied.

'This is so crap,' Mark said, and his voice sounded dull – he was speaking to the wall. 'Let them leave us here to rot, the stinkers, let them leave us here all day, I don't care!'

'Not so loud, he's bound to be sniffing around here somewhere, still.'

'Danny, I tell you, if Rico was here...'

'Jeez, Mark, don't keep going on about Rico...'

'Sorry, Danny, I just meant...'

I crawled up a few steps to where I could look out of the window. I saw the medics running across the playground with their stretchers, past the extension, to the sports field. There were big tents set up there, where we were supposed to be treated. I could see them if I lifted my head a little; they were green and when I squinted it looked like a dense forest. I closed my eyes. A door slammed below us and then they came up the stairs. 'Over here,' Mark yelled, 'we're here, come on, get us out of here, can't you?' Two girls came over to me, the same ones as before, and two boys stopped by Mark. 'No,' he said. 'That's not fair,

Danny, tell them!'

'Stop making such a racket!' The boys grabbed him by the head and feet and rolled him onto the stretcher they'd put down beside him.

'Burns.' The two girls leaned over me, one holding my sign. They both had dark hair, almost black. 'Burns aren't that bad, we'll start by cooling them.'

'Smoke poisoning,' I said and slid onto the stretcher. 'I've got real smoke poisoning as well!' The girls laughed and then jiggled me into position, and I looked down the front of their shirts, their breasts not very well hidden.

'Don't believe a word he says,' Mark yelled from one flight down, 'he's lying, he's lying about his smoke poisoning!'

The girls laughed again, then lifted the stretcher and walked slowly down the stairs. I was lying feet-first, looking up at the breasts above me moving inside their shirts on every step. Then we got to the bottom and they carried me across the playground. The two boys went much faster with Mark, almost at the extension already. Next to me, I saw the podium with the stone lectern and the three flagpoles, empty now. The flags were only fastened to the ropes for muster, and then pulled up very slowly to marching music or something. The stretcher swayed, the sun shone, and I shut my eyes. The playground was quiet; someone was sweeping somewhere, probably the school caretaker. My face got warm and the dark space in front of my eyes grew lighter, and there were white dots in it. I laid one hand over my closed eyes. I was tired, fell asleep late the night before. Dad had been out drinking 'til one 'cause he had two days off. I wanted to take a day off school as well but I wasn't allowed, and anyway I saw Katja at school every day, sitting in front of me, and the back of her neck was so beautiful.

'Wakey, wakey!' I opened my eyes. We were in a tent, Katja a few yards away from me on a stool, winding a bandage around her head. No, she was unwinding it and rolling the bandages up as she unwound.

'Your head wound all better already?'

'Oh, Danny.' She smiled and I looked at the ceiling. Nice green canvas.

'Here we are.' The two girls lifted me onto a cot they'd set me down beside. 'Tina, can you get me the burns pack?' Tina was the one whose breasts I'd been lying underneath; she went to a folding table covered in bandages and bags and cases. She picked up one of the cases, with a big red cross on it and a small flame in the top corner. She put the case on the cot and sat down next to me. 'So where's it burning?' she asked, and then they laughed the way only year eleven girls laughed. Tina put her hand over her mouth and the other one blushed. They opened the case and rummaged around inside it. 'I mean, where are your burns?'

'On my leg,' I said, and looked at Katja. She'd finished unwinding her head and she shook her hair, then combed it with her fingers.

'You'll have to get undressed, then.'

'On my neck, I mean, my whole neck's all burnt, no skin left at all!'

'We'll have to take your shirt off, or we can't treat it.' I sat up and lifted my arms. They took off my sign and then fiddled around with me, Tina unbuttoning my shirt.

'Where's Mark gone?'

'Another tent.' Tina's breasts brushed against my chin. I saw Katja's face between the two girls' arms. She looked at me and then turned her head aside.

'Ow,' I said as they took my shirt off; it caught on my ear and they tugged at it.

'Don't be a baby.'

'Don't you be so rough,' I said, loud enough for Katja to hear.

'You wish!' Tina folded up my shirt and laid it next to me on the cot.

'Hey, Daniel.' Katja was standing in front of me. I looked down at myself, checking my vest was clean.

'You mustn't mess around today, Daniel.'

'Yes, miss.'

'Oh, Danny.' She smiled. 'You know what I mean. You have to come along this afternoon, otherwise you'll get a black mark...'

'I'm gonna get a black mark anyway.'

'Oh, Danny...'

Tina and her friend bandaged my neck and then Tina took a little plastic pot out of the case and held it up for me to look at. 'This is what we would have put on there, I mean, if it was real. It's for cooling. And don't scratch your burn or you'll get germs in it and it'll get infected.'

'I haven't got germs,' I said. 'You can take it off again now.'

Katja put her hand on my bare shoulder. The hand was very cool. 'Danny, listen, you have to come this afternoon, you and Mark.' She stepped closer, put her mouth to my ear. 'I know you want to go to the cinema again, Danny, but you have to come, for my sake.'

'Look at those two lovebirds!' Tina's friend clapped her hands and they both laughed.

Katja took a few steps back. There were two frown lines above her nose. 'You can cut your silly gossip! Or I'll tell Mr Dettleff about all your corner-cutting!'

The girls weren't laughing now, they were fiddling around with my neck. 'What a little snake!' Tina whispered. She stuck a safety pin in my bandage. Her breasts brushed against my chin. Katja turned away and walked to the tent flap. 'Hey, Katja!' I pushed the hands and breasts away, got up and went after her. She stopped but didn't turn around, and I stood behind her. I lowered my head and whispered into her hair, 'I'll definitely come this afternoon, definitely!' The bandage dangled from my neck onto her shoulder.

'You promise?'

'Promise.'

'Pioneer's honour, Danny.' She turned her head and looked me in the eye.

'Pioneer's honour,' I said, and then she smiled, pushed the flap aside and left the tent. I'd actually wanted to cross my fingers behind my back, 'cause I'd promised Mark that morning on the way to school that we'd go to the cinema later, but I couldn't do it. *Old Surehand* was on at the Palast-Theater, which Mark and I had seen three times already, which I wanted to watch over and over 'cause of the train robbery at the beginning where Old Surehand shoots through the fuse at the last moment, but that didn't matter now.

I heard footsteps and voices outside the tent. The flap was lifted aside and two girls came in, on their stretcher a boy from year six, who grinned and waved at me. His sign said: BURIED UNDER RUBBLE. They lifted him up and laid him on the cot. I folded my arms over my vest and rubbed my shoulders. 'What are you still doing here? We've got enough to do, look!' Tina was holding a rubber tube with some kind of mask on one end.

'My shirt,' I said quietly.

'Over there.' She pointed at a folding chair and pushed me aside. I unwound the bandage from my neck and put it on the chair, picked up my shirt and put it on. 'Buried under rubble,' one of the girls behind me shouted, 'stopped breathing a while ago!' I tucked my shirt in and went outside.

The sun was shining but it was pretty windy. I walked around between the tents, looking for Mark. Mrs Seidel was standing outside one of the tents. I turned around and walked back but she'd already seen me. 'Daniel!' she called, and I stopped in my tracks. 'Daniel!' I heard her footsteps behind me and turned around. She was wearing her good grey slacks and an army jacket with epaulettes, undone at the top so everyone could see her blue Free German Youth shirt. 'Have you finished your task, Daniel?' She eyed me over the top of her glasses.

'Yes, miss.'

'Good,' she nodded, at which her glasses slipped down to the end of her nose and she pushed them back up, 'then report to the School Council tent. It isn't one o'clock yet.' She checked her watch. Then she nodded again and took a few steps back. 'And, Daniel, I want you to wear your neckerchief this afternoon...'

My hand rose to my collar. 'Yes,' I said, 'of course, Mrs Seidel.'

'Good, Daniel.' She nodded and then went back to the tent. Her trouser legs were too wide, billowing in the wind. 'Daniel!' She'd turned around again and waved. 'Come with me.' She walked up to the tent, me trailing her slowly. 'Wait here.' She pushed the flap aside and went in. I could see a few chairs, teachers sitting on some of them. I drew a rifle in the gravel of the sports field with my foot, then I picked it up, aimed – no, I didn't need to aim properly, it was a machine gun, I just pointed it at the tent and pulled the trigger. Nothing. I'd forgotten to flip the safety catch. I fired off the whole clip through the canvas, the empty bullet casings flying off behind me.

Mrs Seidel came back out. There were two bullet holes

in her shoulder. She was holding an army jacket, which she handed to me. 'Here you are, put this on, Daniel, or you'll catch cold. Why aren't you wearing your jacket, I told you earlier it's chilly outside!'

'I...'

'Hand the jacket back in before you go home.' She adjusted her glasses and returned inside the tent. Someone in there laughed.

I put the jacket on; it was far too big, over my knees.

Someone's hand alighted on my shoulder, a very light touch. Katja laughed. 'It's way too big for you.'

'So? It's what soldiers wear!'

'Hey, Danny, I just wanted to tell you boys to tidy the stretchers away now. You can't go yet, it's not one o'clock.' She pushed up her sleeve and checked the watch on her thin wrist.

'No, Mum,' I said, stroking a finger over the glass of her pretty watch, 'I'm not going home yet.'

'Katja, can you come, please!' A girl from the School Council was standing in the space between the tents, beckoning. Katja turned around. She took my hand and pulled. 'Hey, Danny, go and look for Mark so he joins in as well. I think he might have gone. You have to report to Teachers' Tent Two. Everything has to be by the book today.'

'Yes, ma'am.'

She smiled, then she waved at the girl from the School Council and ran over. 'Daniel,' she turned around again. 'Remember your promise!'

I nodded, then buttoned the jacket up to the top and walked slowly between the tents. A group from year six marched in step past me, and I turned away and put my hands in my pockets. I walked to the wall and sat down on a bench. Some kids were lined up at the very back of the sports ground; I could make out their green uniforms. Now they threw something, little red balls: practice hand grenades. I'd found one once and taken it home with me. I'd painted the ribbed metal with black varnish and now it looked like a real one. I spotted Mark walking by the extension; I could tell him by his yellow jacket. He walked across the playground to the school gate. I wanted to get up and call him, but I stayed put and watched him bend down and pick something up, a stone perhaps or a dropped coin. We were going to meet at the pirate ship at quarter to three, we'd it arranged that morning. Mark walked out of the big gate and disappeared from view.

A couple of boys from 7c passed my bench, that little Walter behind them, dragging an empty stretcher, red in the face with his jacket unbuttoned. He saw me and nodded, then he stopped. 'Hi, Danny, alright?'

'Yeah, I'm alright. Where d'you get the stretcher?'

'They're in front of the School Council tent. We're supposed to tidy them all away, Danny. They go in the extension, in the cellar.'

'Yeah, I know that.'

'You are joining in, Danny, right? You know, the School Council...'

'Yeah, I know.' I got up, nice and slowly, and then I stretched and smoothed my jacket. 'Shall I take one end?'

'No thanks, Danny. I can manage, otherwise it'd look stupid, you get it...'

'Yeah, I get it.' I turned around and headed to the School Council tent.

'Hey, Danny, I'll wait here, then we can go together.'

'Right, OK.'

Outside the School Council tent, a few teachers were standing in a circle around the stretchers. I looked at the ground and walked between them, then squatted by the stretchers and pulled the top one off the pile.

'Always working hard, our Pioneers!'

Two brown leather shoes. Two trouser creases right in front of my face. I held onto the stretcher grip with both hands and looked up. The headmaster laughed, next to him a man in uniform. He looked a bit like Rico's dad, who'd been an officer as well, but this man had more medals on his chest and he was pretty old. One medal had a fist and a flaming torch on it; he must have pinched it from Mr Singer's suit jacket, but now I saw Mr Singer beside them and his medal was still there, along with all the others. I tugged at the stretcher, already rolled up; I stood up and tucked it under my arm.

'That's right,' said the man in uniform. 'You'll make a good soldier one day, won't you?' He patted me on the back and smiled with his mouth closed.

'This is our Daniel,' the headmaster said, and Mr Singer nodded once, twice, three times. 'He was in the talent contest last year, recited a poem. Top marks, Daniel, remember?'

'Yes, sir,' I said. My foot drew a circle in the gravel.

'That's the stuff, Daniel,' said the man in uniform, 'always keep active, always play an active role in the collective. Always stick to it, always lead from the front of the collective! That's a terrific jacket you've got there.' He put his hand on my shoulder and smiled with his mouth closed, and the headmaster and Mr Singer nodded.

'Yes, Daniel,' Mr Singer said in his deep voice, 'you can learn a lot from our comrade the colonel.'

'Keep it up,' said the colonel, and he took his hand off my shoulder, a big heavy hand. 'Here come your classmates.'

'Yes, sir,' I said, 'thank you, sir,' and then I walked off. The boys from 7c came past me, walking very fast, almost running. 'Our Pioneers,' Mr Singer said behind me in his deep voice. I walked between the tents, along the wall. I looked at the grey buildings on the opposite side. A woman leaned out of one of the windows. She had long white hair and was shaking a pillow like she was waving at me.

Walter was still standing all alone on the sports ground. He was leaning on the two poles of the rolled-up stretcher like on a double lance, and now he raised them slightly and stamped little clouds of dust out of the ground. 'There you are, Danny. You took ages.'

'Nice of you to wait.'

'No problem, Danny.' We headed round to the extension, Walter with the stretcher over one shoulder, walking crooked. 'Look, Danny, like a builder.'

'Yeah,' I said, 'not bad.' We went down the cellar stairs, tube lights flickering ahead of us.

The school caretaker was standing at the end of the cellar walkway. 'Left,' he said, 'to the sports compartment.' Walter removed the stretcher from his shoulder. There was a bang.

Shards of glass rained down on our heads. 'Damn!' I ducked. Walter had hit one of the tube lights with his stretcher.

The caretaker came running towards us. 'You little buggers!' he yelled, waving his hands around in front of our faces. 'Jesus, you li-li-little buggers!' He'd always shout that when there was any kind of trouble, he'd wave his arms around and his face would go bright red. I knew he'd calm down again in a minute. The caretaker was alright. Everyone liked him, even though he was a bit funny in the head. Someone told me once he'd fallen out of a first-floor window, years ago, while he was cleaning it, fallen right on his head, and since then he'd been a bit funny in the head and had a stutter, but not a bad one, and only when he got worked up. Another thing I'd heard was that he'd been really handsome before that, the lady teachers had secretly kissed him at breaktime, probably down here in the cellar. Now he had a nose like a boxer and his chin was all crooked.

'You... you li-little bu-bu-bu... Oh well, never mind, I'll put a new one in later.' I brushed the glass out of my hair.

Walter was squatting down, picking up a few shards. 'Sorry, Mr Schädlich.'

'Stop that, st-stop that, kid, leave that Russian rubbish, you'll cu-cut yourself on it. The broom's ba-back there, boy, you sweep it up pro-properly!'

'OK, Mr Schädlich.' Walter stood up and walked down to the broom corner. I jammed his stretcher under my other arm. 'Come on, get on with it, gimme that Russian rubbish!' Mr Schädlich grabbed the stretcher from me and dragged it behind him to the wooden cage with the thousand balls. He chucked the stretcher in there and stayed put in the doorway. 'Want to take a look? I know you boys are always wanting a look in there!' He smiled and moved out of the doorway, and as I passed him he put his hand on my shoulder, just for a moment. I shoved aside the nets of footballs hanging from the ceiling and put my stretcher down carefully with the others. 'Hey,' the caretaker whispered behind me, 'there's table tennis balls back there, a whole bu-bucketful, the good ones, kid, you can take a couple, I know you like table tennis. Five stars, boy, they're all four or five stars!' I heard Walter sweeping up the glass outside the cage. 'Go on, quick, boy, quick, quick, the others are coming. No one nee-nee-needs to see. I won't see a thing, boy. Five stars!' His head was right by mine, shooting me a crooked grin. I walked past shelves, ropes, javelins, red hand grenades, then squatted by the bucket and stuffed a couple of handfuls of table tennis balls in the pockets of my army jacket. 'Competition balls,' the caretaker whispered behind me, 'five stars... You can hit 'em 'til the soup spills.'

'Thanks, Mr Caretaker,' I said, 'cause I knew he liked it when we called him 'Mr Caretaker,' and he smiled and brushed a hand over his crooked chin.

'No problem,' he said. 'They'll just go to rot down here, everything rots down here.'

Footsteps outside the cage; I heard Walter's voice and other voices and I walked outside, past the caretaker. 'Wait... wait a mo, kid,' he said behind me, but I went on walking, 'cause the boys from 7c were standing around Walter with their stretchers. They were laughing.

'Made a mess, have you, pipsqueak?' Walter had stopped sweeping and was resting on his broom.

'Shut it, you wankers!' He couldn't stand being called 'pipsqueak,' it made him really angry, even though he really had hardly grown since he started school.

'Keep on sweeping, pipsqueak, sweep it all up!'

'Piss off – you stink!' Walter shoved the biggest one of them in the chest with both hands. The biggest one was Friedrich, Maik's best friend. He wasn't as strong as Maik the Bruiser, but he was strong enough, and he didn't even move when Walter pushed him. He looked down at him and I saw his cheeks and his mouth moving. Out of his mouth came spit, still hanging on a thread like a spider, then it slapped down on Walter's hair.

'You stupid pig, you stupid disgusting pig!' Walter rammed his head into Friedrich's chest, Friedrich stumbled against the wall, the others stepped back and put their stretchers down. 'Knock him down, Fried!' I ran between them and shoved them aside, Thomas from 7c planted himself in my path, I slammed my elbow against his shoulder and he made way. Friedrich had raised his fist right above Walter's face. He had gigantic fists but he was still a coward, only ever started fights with boys smaller than him. I'd beaten him up once, even though I was a bit shorter than him, but it wasn't easy and it took a long time. Rico had stood by and watched and called out tips for me, back then, while Friedrich and I pummelled each other. Now *I* was standing next to Walter and Friedrich, but Walter didn't stand a chance even if I called out tips – he was just too small. Friedrich was holding him by the throat with his other hand; all he needed was to land one punch and he'd have him. I grabbed his fist. 'Let go of him.'

'What's it got to do with you?'

'Let go of him!'

Friedrich let him go. Walter leaned against the wall, his head down. Suddenly the caretaker was between us, pushing us apart. 'Not OK, not OK, boys. No fi-fighting. Get that Russian rubbish out of here!' He shoved the stretchers with his foot.

'That little cry-baby started it!'

'Do-don't care. Put that r-rubbish away and go home.' Friedrich and the others picked up their stretchers and deposited them in the compartment with the thousand balls. The caretaker went after them, grumbling. 'None of that crap here in my cellar.'

I put my hand on Walter's shoulder. He pushed it away and then wiped his face on his sleeve. 'I didn't mean to cry, Danny.'

'You weren't crying.'

Then they passed us again, the caretaker jangling his keys behind them. 'You'll get your turn!' Friedrich clenched his fist as he went past Walter. I ran after him and positioned myself on the stairs ahead of him. 'Listen,' I whispered in his ear, one hand on his arm, 'you leave him alone in future, OK?' Friedrich stared past me, stepped aside and walked up the stairs backwards. He stopped just before the door.

'Think I'm scared of you? Your Rico's not here anymore, is he, and if Maik, if Maik...'

I ran up and stopped one step below him. 'Maik knows full well Rico sometimes comes home on the weekend... and anyway, I'd keep my mouth shut if I was you, what with that thing in the park, the neckerchief... Rico's training every day now... in there.'

'We'll see, Danny!'

'I'll beat you all on my own, you stupid wanker!'

There was a bang. He'd slammed the door behind him.

'Sorry, Danny.' Walter tapped me on the shoulder, his face still bright red.

'It's OK.' I searched my trouser pockets and gave him a hankie. 'Come on, let's go home.'

We crossed the schoolyard to the main building. Friedrich was already out on the street. Walter watched him go, smiling, perhaps 'cause Friedrich looked so small as he turned the corner up ahead. 'Will you come up with me a minute? I've got to get my jacket.'

'Sure, Danny.'

The main building was quiet now. We went up to the third floor. No injured kids to be seen. Mrs Seidel was standing ahead of us on the landing. 'You can give me the jacket right here, Daniel. I'm heading over to the sports ground anyway.' She was holding a big silver thermos flask.

'But... I can take it myself in a...'

'Just give me the jacket, Daniel, I'm going back to the tent. The colonel's waiting for his coffee.' She smiled and adjusted her glasses with her free hand, then held her arm out to me.

'... but... I can do it myself, Miss.'

'Daniel, the jacket! I haven't got time for this!'

I peeled the jacket off and draped it over her arm. I felt the table tennis balls in the pockets. They moved like tiny animals. 'Daniel, the jacket's all white on the back, you could have brushed it down!' She tapped at the white stripes down the back and glared at me over the top of her glasses.

'The cellar,' I said, 'the stretchers...'

She put the thermos flask down on the stairs and bashed at the army jacket with her free hand. And out they came. The big side pockets didn't have zips and the table tennis balls leapt out of them, pinged off the first step and ponged off the next, down past me. Mrs Seidel gave a shriek, just a short one but very high-pitched. She dropped the jacket, Walter leaned forward to catch it but missed – he was just too small – and the rest of the balls rolled out of the pockets and down the stairs. Walter sat down on a step, now very pale in the face.

'Daniel, where did you get these balls from, where are the balls from?'

'I... the balls are...'

'They're mine,' Walter said quietly and stood up. 'I found them in the cellar, by the stretchers...'

'There's no point in lying, Walter.'

'I'm not lying, Miss, they were on the floor, in between the stretchers, and I thought...'

'So many table tennis balls, Walter! Tomorrow I'll have to...'

'I thought nobody needed them...'

'Don't interrupt me, Walter! I'll have to talk to your class teacher, perhaps the headmaster as well, and your parents too, of course. It's theft of school property, and that means the people's property, Walter! And you,

Daniel...' she peered over her glasses at me, 'why did you go along with this nonsense? You know we'll soon be deciding whether we have to give you a black mark.' She took a deep breath. 'I'm very disappointed in both of you.'

'But Miss, they're... they were supposed to be for the table tennis club...'

'Walter, please, don't make matters worse! You two collect up the balls and put them in my desk drawer. And get a move on, before anyone comes. You know we've got an important visitor!' She picked up the jacket and searched the pockets, but they were empty now. 'I expect you both to take part this afternoon with exemplary discipline,' she said in a very quiet voice, 'to make up for your mistake.' She folded the jacket over her arm and picked up the thermos flask. She gave us a silent stare until we lowered our heads, then she went down the stairs, carefully stepping over the balls and shaking her head. I looked at the balls close to her feet, a couple right up against the tips of her shoes. I saw Walter looking at her feet too; we'd hang a sign around her neck, and Tina and her friend would come by and lift her onto a stretcher and we'd help them carry her, 'cause Seidel was very heavy. But all we heard was her footsteps getting quieter. We were still standing on the stairs, not moving. We looked out of the window and saw Mrs Seidel marching across the schoolyard to the sports ground. The thermos flask flashed in the sunlight and I squinted one eye. Then we gathered up the balls. Some of them had rolled all the way down to the first floor. We ran up and down the stairs a few times until we couldn't find anymore balls. 'I've got nine,' said Walter, 'how about you?'

'Eight,' I said; actually, I had eleven. Walter smiled and then we went up to the classroom. Walter opened the drawer in the teacher's desk and put the balls in there; I fetched my jacket. I kept two of the balls, handing one to Walter. 'For you,' I said. 'So we can play table tennis some time.'

'No thanks, Danny. Better not.'

'Come on, take it, they're the good kind, five stars.'

He looked around and stepped back. 'Thanks, Danny, but I'm no good at table tennis.'

'Alright.' I put it in my trouser pocket. We went downstairs. There was another ball at the top of the stairs to the cellar. I lowered my foot on it until it gave a low pop, and kicked it down. It stopped outside the cellar door, squashed flat and still moving slightly. Walter held the door open for me and we ran out into the schoolyard, past the main building, to the road. 'Hey, Walter, the pirate ship,' I said as we got to the post office opposite the school. 'Want to come to the pirate ship later on?'

He stopped right by the yellow postbox and stared at me, eyes wide. 'Really? To the pirate ship? But Danny, the Pioneer manoeuvre...'

'There's plenty of time. Before, I mean. In an hour or so.'

'But Danny, Mark won't want me there, Mark's bound to be angry.'

'It'll be fine if I bring you along. Come round to my place first. You've always wanted...'

'I have, Danny, yeah. Thanks, Danny.' He put his hand on the postbox and wiggled it around. 'Can I really come with you?'

'Course, Walter. I said so, didn't I?'

We walked slowly. On the bridge at the Silver Slope, we stopped and looked down at the tracks. A diesel engine with four freight cars stopped at the toy factory's loading bay. A couple of men unloaded crates and bustled around.

'Hey, Danny, d'you think they sometimes nick stuff, for their kids, I mean?'

'Don't know. Maybe.'

'Hey, Danny, is it true about Henry, that his mother gets you toy cars and...'

'Who told you that?'

'Just something I heard, Danny.'

'You hear too much.'

'Sorry.'

'No need to say sorry.'

He leaned against the balustrade and drew little houses in the dust with his feet. 'I bet there's loads of stuff in those crates. Cars and stamps and that. What do you like better, Danny, knights or soldiers?'

'Red Indians. I've got loads.'

'Yeah, Danny, Indians aren't bad either.'

'Are you scared?'

'A bit. D'you think we'll get in big trouble?'

'Don't think so, Walter. Don't worry about it. The caretaker will come up with something if they ask him.'

We went on and then Walter had to turn off down his road.

'OK then, see you at my place in an hour.' I reached out my hand to shake on it, and he gave it a long squeeze before he turned and went home.

'Aw, shit, what's he doing here?' Mark was leaning against the mast, one hand in his pocket, the other punching the air.

'Come on, relax, you know Rico wouldn't mind!'

'Rico, Rico! He's not here now... he's... You'll be bringing the whole class along soon, and then there'll be trouble again!'

'I can just go, it doesn't matter, it's fine, I'll just go.'

Walter was next to me, wiping his leg with his hand, and then he moved behind me.

'Rubbish, you're staying, you're staying here!' I turned around and pulled him back over. 'At least there's three of us then! Paul can't always come, and Rico... twice a month, and sometimes he can't make it... It's crap!'

'Tell him, go on, you tell Rico!'

'Shut up, Mark, stop going on about Rico, will you!' I kicked the side of the ship and then walked up to him. I climbed onto the foredeck and looked down at him.

'You started it,' he yelled. 'I don't give a shit!' He ran up front to the bow, clambered through the hatch and disappeared below deck.

I ran after him. I turned around; Walter was still standing by the mast, looking at the ground. 'Come on then!'

He put his hands in his pockets and walked over slowly. We climbed down the ladder. Walter trod on my hand for a second, but I didn't say anything. Not much light came in through the hatch. Mark had lit the three candles. He was sitting on his chest, the one he'd brought along from the rubbish dump, his back turned. Walter gripped the ladder and looked around. 'Crazy,' he whispered.

'Yep,' I said. 'Not bad, eh?'

'And you built it all yourselves?'

'Well, a lot of it was already like this, but the mast was really hard.' Walter walked over to the bottom end of the mast, which was actually a long rusty iron bar that we'd stuck in the ground down here, pretty deep so it wouldn't tip over, which meant it was only partly poking out of the deck, slightly taller than Rico. Rico had got hold of the flag too and fixed it to a fence post, and we'd tied the post to the mast with wire to make it a bit longer.

The flag had a skull on it, drawn by Rico, so we couldn't tell him it looked crap. 'I cut up a sheet, at night, you know, the doors are locked so I can't get out but I've always got a felt-tip handy.' He'd only had a red felt-tip handy, and the skull looked like it was blushing.

'Wow, this thing must have been really heavy!' Walter patted the mast and then gripped it with both hands.

'It fell on my foot,' Mark said, not turning round. 'Cause you weren't paying attention, Danny.'

'That's rubbish!' I said. 'You know it's 'cause your arms aren't strong enough!'

Walter glanced at Mark and then wiped the rust off his hands.

'Your mummy gonna tell you off for getting dirty, is she?'

'No,' said Walter quietly. 'It's for the gummy bears, I don't want to get them dirty.' He pulled a little bag out of his pocket and held it out to Mark, who grabbed it.

'Gummy bears, real Haribos. Where d'you get them?' The packet was already open and he dug his hand in.

'My mum buys them at the station,' Walter said. 'At the Intershop.' Walter's mother was a secretary at the church up in Stötteritz. She'd sometimes get West German money there, he'd told me, and she spent it at the special hard currency shop at the station. He hardly told anyone else 'cause they laughed at him at school for his church. He sat down on the chest next to Mark. I ran over and took a handful of gummy bears; Mark was gobbling so fast the bag was almost empty. The tiny bears stuck together, and sand crunched between my teeth as I chewed them. 'Great bears,' I said, and Walter smiled.

'Hey,' he said, knocking on the wooden wall beside him, 'what did this used to be, how did you make it?'

'Lorry,' Mark muttered as he chewed, 'used to be a lorry trailer. Someone dumped it here. It's ours now.' He reached into the bag again, then stood up, moved aside a few boards from the wall and showed Walter one of the big wheels.

Walter squatted down and punched the tyre. 'It's still got air in it.'

'Course it has, everything's shipshape here. If we want, we can couple the trailer up to a car and drive away. To the sea, to the Baltic, right Danny?'

'Yeah, we could.' I said. I crossed to the stern and looked through the porthole at the buildings and the yard out back, then I went to the opposite wall and looked through the other porthole at the railway embankment. No one in sight.

'Hey, Mark, about the cinema later,' I looked at the barred gate in front of the embankment, 'the cinema...'

'No can do, Danny, right?'

'Yeah,' I said. 'Not today.'

There was a barred gate on the other side of the embankment, behind it the supermarket backyard. Sometimes freight trains delivered flour and beer and chocolate...

'So you do want to go on the manoeuvre, Danny.'

'Yeah,' I said. 'I have to.'

'But we arranged it all, Danny, *Old Surehand*.' He was behind me now, and I turned around to him.

'I'm sorry, Mark, I can't help it.'

'You could have told me earlier, Danny, at school. I haven't even got my Pioneer uniform on.' He reached for my collar and adjusted my neckerchief. 'I thought as much right when you got here, Danny.' He wasn't grumbling, he was perfectly calm, and I looked past him at Walter, who was sitting in front of one of the candles, watching the flame. 'I'm not cross with you, Danny... Well, maybe a bit.' He went to his chest and opened it up. He took out a green shopping bag, put it down by his side and took off his jumper. Then he pulled his white Pioneer shirt out of the bag, unbuttoned it slowly and put it on. 'Come here, Walter, do my neckerchief.' Walter got up and went over. 'I'm not asking you, Danny – you can't do it properly yourself.' He smiled and buttoned up his shirt. Walter stood in front of him and pulled the red neckerchief in place, then started knotting it. 'Got my trousers with me too,' Mark said, and nudged the bag with his foot. 'Brought everything with me except the cap, but I don't need that.' I put my hand in my pocket and crumpled my cap in my fist. 'See, if you don't...' Mark said, smoothing his shirt, 'you know, you were supposed to decide, and I brought along everything specially. I saw you, with Katja I mean, earlier on.'

'Katja,' I said.

'Yeah, with Katja. And I thought...' he put his trousers down on the chest, took the pressed blue Pioneer trousers out of the bag and put them on, 'I made a bet with myself... that you'd still come with me, to the cinema, to the Palast-Theater, Danny.' He did a couple of knee bends and plucked at the trousers, then he stuffed his things in the bag and put it in the chest. 'Lost my bet.' He picked up two bricks and put them on the lid.

'I don't get you two,' Walter said, blowing a candle out. 'They're not that bad. Pioneer manoeuvres, I mean.'

'Rico used to like them,' I said quietly, and I wet my forefinger and thumb and pressed out the flame of the second candle. It was almost dark now, and we went to the hatch where the last candle was burning.

'Yeah,' said Mark, 'back then. That was a while ago, Danny.'

I nodded.

'But the electric rifles aren't bad,' Walter said.

'Proper air rifles are way better.' We were at the hatch

now, and Mark blew the candle out.

'But the landmines,' said Walter, 'all the lovely landmines...'

'Listen,' Mark tapped him on the chest, 'if you want to come back, you'd better shut up.' Walter nodded and we climbed up the little ladder onto the deck. We put the boards over the hatch and a couple of bricks on the boards, and then we left our ship.

The shooting was over. The green lamp at the shooting range for the electric rifles had lit up one last time, a hit, my last shot, six out of ten, not bad at all, and the pop of the air rifles had stopped over in Room Two where the Free German Youth had been shooting. We put the electric rifles down on the tables and went to the door.

'Did you see, Danny? I was really good,' Mark said down in the schoolyard, and he laughed and slapped his chest. 'Almost like Old Surehand! You'll never beat my nine!'

'Who cares about your nine, who cares about Old Surehand?' I wanted to say, but the kids pushed and shoved from behind us and we stumbled on. Everyone bustled around, grouping together: Pioneers, Free German Youth and teachers. There was Mrs Seidel, and next to Mrs Seidel stood Katja, my Class Council head. They put us into groups according to height. I stood in the back row, Mark two rows in front of me. I looked ahead at the little podium, at the Pioneer leader Mr Dettleff, the headmaster Mr Singer, who had just been supervising the shooting ranges, the head of the Friendship Council Mikloš Maray, whose dad came from Hungary, and now the colonel came to join them, his epaulettes looking huge. Marching music sounded from the two speakers in front of the podium; Mrs Seidel turned around to us and put her finger to her lips. The music got quieter, then came screeching and whistling from the speakers that hurt my ears – Mr Dettleff was at the microphone stand, fiddling with it. 'Left face!' A couple of idiots always turned in the wrong direction. 'Eyes front! Forward, march!' The music set in again and we marched. We marched in a square around the podium, and while we were marching three boys from the Friendship Council raised the flags very slowly on the three flagpoles. Someone trod on my heel and I turned around. Year eight were marching way too fast and not sticking to the right distance. Then we'd marched once around the podium and we stopped.

'Right face! Eyes front! At ease!' Another screech from the speakers. 'Pioneers! I greet you with the salute of the Young Pioneers and the Thälmann Pioneers: For peace and socialism: Be prepared!'

'Always prepared!' we chanted, and we touched the thumbs of our outstretched hands to our heads, like shark fins, in the Pioneer salute.

'Free German Youth! I greet you with the salute of the Free German Youth: Friendship!' And the Free German Youth said: 'Friendship!' and a couple of idiots in front of me joined in and laughed; they always did that. 'Dear Young Pioneers and Thälmann Pioneers, dear Free German Youth, I welcome you to our Pioneer manoeuvre "Service for Peace" and I look forward to a successful and productive Pioneer manoeuvre!'

We wandered around Stünz Park. Stünz Park was the biggest park in Leipzig East, way bigger than *our* park where I'd meet up with Mark and used to meet up with Rico. The only park bigger was the Peace Park, and that was way bigger. We walked in groups of three, twenty-one kids and Mrs Seidel. The others were with the

Homeland Education teacher over by the lake. Mark was walking beside me and a bit behind us was Stefan the Biter, who liked me but didn't really get on with Mark. We were the advance party, 'cause Mark had such good eyesight. Mr Singer had told Mrs Seidel that after we'd marched around and saluted the flag as usual at muster, and praised Mark's shooting performance. 'And Daniel also made a positive contribution to the collective with a good performance at the shooting range. If he wants to learn – and I think he does, he wants to learn from his mistakes as well – then he's on the right path.' I didn't know what mistakes he meant, and the right path meant nothing to me either.

'I've got one,' Stefan yelled behind us, 'I think I've got one!' We turned around and ran over.

'Rubbish, that's just a broken shoebox, look!' Mark kicked at it and the shoebox got stuck in a bush. 'Look properly, jeez!'

'Yeah, yeah!' Stefan walked on, pushing a twig along with his foot.

'Don't be so mean to him,' I said quietly.

'Right, Danny, you'll be bringing him along to the pirate ship soon too, will you?'

'Leave it out, Stefan's OK. He's got enough trouble with Maik and his lot.'

'Maik's an arsehole, Danny, you're right about that.' He turned around cautiously, but there was no need to be scared; Maik was off sick, had been for four days now. He was at home in bed and looked terrible – his father had done it. Katja had told me. She'd gone to visit him 'cause she was responsible for the class collective.

'Danny, stop a minute, everyone stop, there's one, I've got a landmine, and there's another one, jeez!' Mark squatted down by a bush and cautiously extracted a cardboard box camouflaged with a few twigs and leaves. Stefan had run to the second box, a few yards away under a tree. It was the same every time – where there was one box there'd be another close by, 'cause they thought we'd be so pleased with the first one we'd overlook the other. I squatted down next to Mark, who opened the lid as I held onto the box. 'Careful, Danny, or it'll blow up!' In the box was a red balloon, and the tips of the nails that pushed through the sides of the box were almost touching it. Mark gripped the balloon with both hands and pulled it out, nice and slowly. Mrs Seidel was standing next to us; I saw her pointy shoes. 'Nice and calm,' Mark whispered, 'any minute now.' A few laughs behind us, and I heard Mrs Seidel shushing them. Mark had the balloon out, the landmine was defused, and he held it up above his head and laughed.

Mrs Seidel said, 'Well done.'

We went over to the second mine, where Stefan hadn't finished fiddling with the box. He'd rolled up his sleeves and gone red in the face, looking up at the clouds in the sky as he felt the balloon. A couple of girls were sitting next to the box, picking up conkers. 'Don't mess it up,' Mark whispered as he looked down at him. Stefan had now extracted the balloon from the box. It was a long green one, with a little tip poking out at the top. 'Look at that stupid willy balloon,' Mark whispered with a laugh.

'Very good,' Mrs Seidel said. 'We'll get lots of points for that.' Stefan shoved the balloon under his jacket, where it moved around like a little dog. Two girls picked up the empty boxes with the nails in the sides. We always took them away with us; Pioneers protected the environment. 'Be careful,' said Mrs Seidel, 'don't hurt yourselves.'

There was a bang somewhere in the bushes. We looked at our balloons but they were fine; Mark and

Stefan were holding them tight. We'd got back into threes and I couldn't see Walter anywhere, but I knew he had something to do with the bang. 'Walter's missing.' A girl was standing in front of Mrs Seidel, and I ran past them to the bushes.

'Daniel, you can't just...' But I didn't turn around, and then I spotted Walter's brightly coloured jacket in among the branches. He was sitting on the ground in front of a landmine box. There was something blue clutched in his hands. I squatted down; the balloon had burst, there was nothing to be done.

'Come on,' I said, 'it's not that bad. Who gives a shit?'

'I'm mending it,' he said quietly, pulling at the rubber, 'I'm patching it up. Look, Danny, here's the hole, it's only little... up there where you blow it up, we'll knot it back together, yeah, Danny?' He looked at me and his eyes were huge. He pulled and tugged at the rubber, and I reached for his hand.

'Stop it, it's stupid,' I said, and I took the broken balloon and threw it in the bushes. 'Stop it, come on, get up!' Walter picked up the empty box and stood up.

'He's crazy,' Mark said, behind me.

I turned around. 'Shut up, Mark!' I yelled. The others were standing in the bushes now.

Mrs Seidel came over to us and stopped to face Walter. 'You mustn't just leave the group like that, Walter.'

'I'm sorry, miss,' – he held out the box – 'it broke. I almost got it out and then it burst on me...'

'Walter,' said Mrs Seidel, 'that's why we're a group, a collective, Walter...' She fell silent and glared at Mark and me over the top of her glasses, and we turned and went to the others. We sat down on the grass between the bushes and watched Mrs Seidel, who was standing in front of Walter so we couldn't see him anymore. She was waving her hands in the air like the music teacher did when we sang. Then she came back over, Walter behind her. He was still holding the empty box pressed to his chest, and I put my hand on his shoulder, but he walked on past me.

We got back into threes and walked on. Ahead of us, we saw the railway embankment and the entrance to the tunnel underneath it. A stream flowed through the tunnel; no one knew its name. It came from the Stünz allotments. A lot of the plots there were vacant and run down 'cause the stream stank so badly. We walked through the tunnel, holding our breath. The tunnel was quite long 'cause the embankment above us was so wide, three tracks, one to the Leipzig East engine shed.

'What a mess,' Mark whispered next to me.

'Shh!' That was Mrs Seidel. She was a few yards behind us, in the middle of the group so she could keep an eye on everything.

'Gas attack,' whispered Mark. He looked at me and grinned.

'Gas attack,' someone whispered behind us.

'Shh!' That wasn't gas, it was Mrs Seidel, who was very pernickety about us doing the exercises right. We were on enemy territory and we weren't allowed to talk. The stream stank and that was the gas attack, every time, every year. No one knew when it had started. A train crossed overhead; there was a clatter and a banging like the tunnel was collapsing, and a couple of girls screamed. 'Shh!' said Mrs Seidel. There was a splash in the stream, usually calm and black. Someone told me once there were rats in the tunnel, water rats. Then we were back outside.

Ahead of us was a patch of grass, a green tent erected on it, and tables outside it with lots of cups on them. 'A field kitchen!' someone called out. And now I saw it too, behind the tent, a few Free German Youth standing around it, handing out plates. We marched over in threes.

'Not so fast,' called Mrs Seidel. 'We've still got our last exercise to do!' She pointed at a group of Pioneers carrying medicine balls, trying to throw them into yellow rings placed on the ground. Most of them missed – the medicine balls were too heavy and only went a short way, then rolled passed the rings. I couldn't help laughing 'cause it looked so funny, the way they twisted and turned when they hurled the balls. 'First the exercise,' called Mrs Seidel, waving both arms, 'the last exercise!' But there was no point, we were all heading straight to the field kitchen and the tent and the drinks. Mark was ahead of me, almost running, his balloon gone, and I turned back for a moment. The balloon bounced across the grass, back to the stream, and vanished between the bushes.

# PALAST-THEATER

Mark had disappeared. He'd run away from rehab and disappeared off the face of the earth. Maybe it was partly our fault, 'cause we hadn't visited him even though we, especially Rico, knew how important it would have been for him. We'd asked around everywhere but no one in the neighbourhood had heard anything about him, no one knew whether he was even still in town or had gone to Berlin where he could score on every street corner; Berlin was a big place. Mark had been gone for over a week and we'd started reading through the police reports and the death announcements they printed in the paper every few days, when Thilo the Drinker came to me and said he knew something, said he'd heard something, and Thilo the Drinker heard a lot when the day was long, 'cause he often hung out on the streets drinking.

'Danny,' he said, 'Danny, I know something. Danny, I've heard something.'

'Tell me,' I said.

'About Mark,' he said.

'Tell me,' I said, and he moved his lips and coughed and ran his hand down the front of his neck. I went down the offie with him and got him a couple of beers and five little miniatures of Goldkrone, and then we sat down on the kerb and drank. 'Tell me,' I said, but he couldn't tell me anything yet, 'cause he'd put the beer bottle to his lips and he drank and drank until it was empty. He took a deep breath and thumped his chest.

'Thanks, Danny, you shouldn't have... I would've told you anyway... so Mark, you know... you remember the old cinema behind the East Woods.'

'Palast-Theater,' I said.

'Palast-Theater.' He nodded. 'Burned down. Couple of

years ago now.'

'I know,' I said.

'So someone... someone saw him there. Inside the cinema.'

'Who? Who saw him there?' I opened one of the miniatures and passed him the little bottle. He jammed it between his teeth and tipped his head back until it was empty.

'Mate of mine, Danny, just a mate.' I jangled the beer bottles in a plastic bag between my feet, then pushed the bag over to him. He took out a beer and opened it with his keyring. He had all kinds of keys on it, though he didn't have a flat of his own; he lived over by the Esso petrol station with some other drinker I didn't know, and didn't want to.

'It was Stefan... Pitbull, I mean.'

'He told you?' I passed him another mini and now he drank more slowly, and his hands were perfectly still. 'Nah, Danny, nah, I just saw him. In the cinema, with Mark.'

'Can't have done.' I knotted the bag and stood up. Pitbull had been to see me just yesterday and we'd thought about how to find Mark. Pitbull was a fucking dealer now, everyone in the neighbourhood knew that, but he was our friend, our brother, everyone in the neighbourhood knew that.

'Danny, no, Pitbull wasn't there, I just said he was. Me, it was me what saw him!' He was getting louder and louder, almost shouting and grabbing at my leg. I sat down again and put the bag between us.

'The thing about Pitbull,' he said, 'Danny... Pitbull's...'

'Fuck Pitbull,' I said, 'what about Mark?'

'He's gone to ground there, gone to ground. Believe me, Danny, that's where he is!'

'Since when?' I took one of the minis out of my pocket and drank it. 'Since... since... don't know, Danny, saw him there two days ago.'

'And you're only coming to me now?' I drank another mini and balanced the last one on my knee.

'Sorry, Danny, sorry, I forgot... didn't think of it. Stupid of me, Danny.' He slapped his forehead and the beer bottle in his other hand trembled and danced, spewing foam down his arm.

'How do I get in there?'

'Through the backyard, you have to go through that way, there's a pile of rubbish right against the wall, Danny, there's a window, boards, move them away and you can get in.'

'Thanks, Thilo.'

I pocketed the mini, picked up the bag and stood up. I walked to the railway embankment; it was afternoon and I had a couple of hours before it got dark. At the corner, I turned back to look. Thilo the Drinker was still sitting on the kerb, his arms wrapped around his knees, his torso rocking back and forth.

'Thilo!'

I saw him turn and wave at me. I still had four beers in the bag, and I put two bottles and the little Goldkrone on the roof of an old Wartburg parked right next to me, then I walked on towards the East Woods.

I stood on the road and stared at the front of the old cinema. The Palast-Theater was on the edge of town, a few hundred yards from the *You are leaving Leipzig* sign. It was a small cinema and it had usually been pretty empty, even in the Zone days, and that's why the guy who owned it set fire to it three years after the Wall fell – that's what people in the neighbourhood said. But the insurance company didn't care what people in the neighbourhood said; they paid up, and the guy packed up and left. And maybe it really was an accident or a blown fuse or something, 'cause in the summer after the Wall fell they showed dirty movies and half the neighbourhood went along to watch *Mutzenbacher, The Story of O., Die Stoßburg* or *Schulmädchenreport,* 'cause we never had that kind of thing in the Zone, and the guy who owned the Palast-Theater made a mint.

I looked up at the name under the roof, which was lit up red on the nights of the late showings, 'Pa ast-Theater' – the 'l' had broken long before the Wall fell. Above the letters were two little windows with broken panes, and the wall around the windows was black. I stepped onto the pavement and stopped outside the entrance. The big brown double door was boarded up, a sign on each side saying *No entry! Parents are liable for their children!* as if the battered, half-burned cinema was more attractive now than back then when the projectionist or the cashier went out to the playground in the East Woods to gather up a few more kids for the matinée showing, 'cause only Mark and me and another two or three drinkers' kids had turned up, and they weren't allowed to run the film until at least ten people were there, there were rules and everyone stuck to them. Next to the door was the display with the listings and posters behind glass, the shards now inside the box and only a scrap of paper left inside it, *Film for* and half an *a*.

I walked around the building to the backyard. The houses next to the cinema were derelict and empty too; no one wanted to live on the edge of town anymore, this far out in Leipzig Southeast, and people in the neighbourhood joked that the East Woods would grow all the way out to the *You are leaving Leipzig* sign in a few years' time. There was the pile of rubbish Thilo the Drinker had told me about, bricks, blackened wood and old furniture, and above the heap was the boarded up window. I clambered up the heap, stumbled and grabbed the boards for support. The beer and minis had been a good investment. A couple of the boards were just leaned against the window and I pushed them aside. It was dark inside; I listened, perfectly still. Nothing. I climbed onto the windowsill and squeezed through the gap. Shards crunched beneath my feet. I took out my original stormproof Zippo and lit it up. I was in an empty room, with only film posters on the wall, and then I saw there was a window in the opposite wall, with no glass in it, and next to it a door – I was in the box office. It still smelled a bit burnt; the fire had broken out on the top floor, in the projection room, and devoured its way down to the auditorium before they could put it out. We'd been drinking in the East Woods that night, Mark, Rico and me, and when we heard the fire engines and then saw the fire's glow above the trees, we ran over there. 'Our cinema,' Mark had said over and over, 'our lovely old cinema.' And now he was here. I replaced the boards in front of the gap as best I could, then traced the wall with my lighter. *Der lange Ritt zur Schule, Crime Busters, Old Surehand.* I stopped. Someone had tried to rip the poster off the wall but it was stuck too firmly – only the bottom half was gone. I ran my hand over the torn paper and then walked to the door. Turned the handle. It was open. I was in the foyer. I leaned over the little ticket counter. 'Two children, please,' I said quietly. The lighter was getting hot in my hand and I flicked it shut. I put the two beer bottles in my pockets and chucked the plastic bag into the darkness, then I crossed the foyer, arms outstretched. Something wooden, must have been the door to the auditorium. I felt for the handle but the door was already opening with a creak. I stopped and listened again. Nothing. 'Mark?' I called out, quietly and then again, louder. 'Mark, it's me, Daniel!' Was that a rattle? 'Mark, mate, it's me, Daniel!' But all was still. Perhaps he was long gone by now, perhaps he'd gone out... I lit my lighter again and walked down the steps to the seats. The rear rows were burnt and the walls were black too. I went forward to the little stage; I could see the ragged screen, the curtain gone. A toilet door was open – I shone my light in and saw a smashed basin on the floor. I climbed up onto the stage and looked out at the dark auditorium. My Zippo was getting hot again so I put it on the floor. There was something there, right in front of the screen. 'Mark,' I said quietly. He was just lying there, not moving. Perhaps he was asleep and dreaming a little dream, perhaps he'd ended it all. I squatted down by him and put my hand on his face. Cold. The sleeping bag and blanket were empty; I picked them up and threw them against the screen.

There was a bag there too, but I didn't want to see what he had in it. 'You stupid arsehole! Where are you?' My lighter petered out and I looked for it in the dark. Warm. I picked it up, jumped off the stage, felt for the first row of wooden seats, folded one down and sat. I lifted my arm into the bright flickering beam of light above me, my hand a black shape right in front of Old Surehand's face as he cocked his gun and aimed and shot the burning fuse off the dynamite stick in the nick of time. 'Stop it, you stupid idiot, put your hand down!' the children behind me shouted. Mark laughed next to me. 'Where are you, you stupid arsehole?' I popped the top off a beer on the edge of the seat and lit a cigarette. I drank a slug, put the bottle on the floor in front of me, took the other bottle out of my pocket, put it down next to the first one and leaned back. I stretched out my legs; the bottles touched and gave a low clink. The drinkers were here. They were sitting somewhere behind me, clinking their bottles and laughing and not interested in *Winnetou 3.* They smoked cheap cigarettes, stank of Handelsgold, and the smoke came all the way to us in the front row, little clouds floating in front of the screen, gun smoke from the shots and the bandits had plenty of ammunition. 'They'll end up setting this place alight,' Mark whispered next to me, 'it's not allowed, jeez!' But the No Smoking rule was probably less important than the Screenings Only from Ten Viewers rule, and the projectionist was probably glad to have found anyone who wanted to watch *Winnetou 3,* 'cause only Mark and me had turned up and he couldn't persuade the kids in the East Wood playground, even though he'd have let them in for twenty pfennigs, 'cause most of them had already seen the film and they probably didn't want to watch Winnetou get wiped out at the end, not again. Everyone cried when Winnetou died in his blood brother's arms, and we'd seen the film a few times as well and we couldn't help crying a bit every time too, and when the time came we bit our tongues and stared straight ahead. The drinkers had come, and the drinkers probably didn't give a shit whether Winnetou carked it, 'cause it was raining outside and they'd have had to go on sitting on their benches outside the supermarket if the projectionist hadn't fetched them. They clinked their bottles and laughed and stank all the way to the front row. But when the time came and Winnetou got wiped out – that murdering bastard was a really good shot – and when Old Shatterhand caught him before he hit the dust and then laid him on the stretcher, the sun set, an army trumpeter blew one last farewell tune, and Old Shatterhand cried too and remembered all the good times and the rides with his blood brother, they suddenly went quiet. 'He's dying,' whispered one of the drinkers, and then he coughed like he was about to cark it as well, 'he's going.'

'It's his friend,' another one whispered, 'his real best friend.' And Old Shatterhand held his brother's hand and looked into the setting sun and then at his brother, and his eyes glinted. I bit my tongue as the drinkers behind us sniffled. 'His friend, his very best real friend.'

'My brother,' Winnetou whispered, though he was barely breathing now.

'His brother,' whispered one of the drinkers, 'it's his brother,' and they coughed even more, 'his only best brother,' and then when it was over and everyone rode off, they kept perfectly still until the lights went up. They stayed in their seats as we got up and went to the exit, their faces red, glinting a little above their shaggy beards, and they looked at the floor.

'Danny,' said Mark.

'My brother,' I said, and he laughed.

I hadn't heard him coming; he was sitting somewhere behind me, and when I flicked on my lighter and was about to turn around, he said: 'No. Please, Danny, turn it off.'

'How did you know it was me?'

'I just knew. Front row, Danny, our cinema, no one else comes here.'

'Thilo the Drinker,' I said.

'What about Thilo the Drinker?'

'Nothing,' I said. 'Want a beer?'

'Roll it over to the wall.'

'Left?'

'Left.'

I laid the bottle on its side and gave it a push. I heard it slowing to a stop, then I heard footsteps walking away again. A seat creaked somewhere behind me, a hiss, and he drank.

'Thanks, Danny.'
'Where've you been?'
'Just out for a walk.'
'Go back. It's better.'
'I can't.'
'Try it.'
'Are you angry with me?'
'No. Maybe a bit.'
'And the money, Danny?'
'That's alright, Mark, everything's fine.'
'No,' he said, 'it's not.'
And he was right, nothing was fine.
'You could have asked,' I said.
'Would you have...?'
'No,' I said, 'not for your shit.'

He'd been round to see me, a few weeks before his rehab. He badly needed a hit, I could tell. But I didn't have anything, he knew that, and he knew I'd trust him when I left the room. But I didn't trust him, I searched him and found my fifty-mark note hidden in his shoe. I wanted to punch his lights out and take him to some doctor so he'd learn to say no at last, but I couldn't punch his lights out, I couldn't do anything for him and I just let him leave.

'I'm sorry, I'm so fucking sorry...'
'No. It was the shit,' I said, 'it wasn't you, Mark.'
'Yeah,' he said, 'it was the shit.'

He was quiet now and I could hear him breathing. I lit a cigarette and his lighter clicked too. 'You still got our Zippo?'

'No,' he said, 'I lost it, I must have lost it somewhere. Wasn't paying attention.' I knew he hadn't lost it, it'd been a good Zippo and he must have sold it for five or ten marks. 'Remember, Danny...?' He didn't want to talk about his Zippo, 'cause I'd nicked it from the Viets selling stuff outside the supermarket a few years ago and given it to him, even though there were plenty of stories going round the neighbourhood about the Vietcongs chopping thieves' fingers off with a samurai sword if they caught them.

'Remember, Danny...?'

'What?'

'The films, the dirty movies, Danny. Back row.'

'Sure,' I said, 'I remember.' The guy on the counter had let us in for a tenner a head once *Josefine Mutzenbacher* had started, even though we weren't sixteen yet, but he'd stopped caring about the rules after the Wall fell.

'Remember,' Mark said behind me, 'remember how horny we were?'

'Course,' I said. 'Especially you. You had such a hard-on you sat two seats away from me.'

He laughed and then he drank, and then he laughed again. 'You were spanking the monkey, Danny, you were wanking.'

'Yeah,' I said, and now I laughed too, 'but you, you were too.'

'Tell me about it!' he laughed louder and louder, and his laughter echoed around the auditorium. 'I shot right at him!'

'Shot at who?'

'The guy,' he yelled, and I heard him slapping the seats, 'the guy in front of me, Danny. Shot my load right onto his jacket, and he didn't even notice!' He laughed and laughed and slapped the seats so hard the whole cinema boomed, and then he was suddenly silent. I took my beer, drank it up and put my fag end in the bottle. 'Good times,' Mark said behind me.

'Yeah,' I said, 'they were. And now?'

'Don't know, Danny.'

'Go back, give it another go, you can do it.'

'Maybe, Danny.'

'How's your arm?'

'Better. I use my leg now.'

I felt like getting up, going back to him, punching him in the face right between the eyes and then dragging him to some doctor who might be able to help him. But I stayed put, looked straight ahead at the screen and lit a cigarette.

'Hey, Danny...?'

'Yeah?'

'How's...?'

'Rico's fine. Got in trouble again, has to go away again soon, but he's fine apart from that. Paul's OK. And Pitbull... Pitbull's a fucking...'

'And you, Danny?'

'Alright. Same as usual.'

'You got to go away too?'

'Not right now.'

'That's good, Danny.' He coughed, and then he sniffed behind me like he was snorting up snot, probably scared to shoot up while I was there, and it was far too dark and it all took time. Once, when we were drinking in Pitbull's cellar, I'd found a syringe on him. I'd grabbed him by the throat with one hand and held the syringe up to his eye with the other, the needle almost touching his eyeball. 'If I catch you fixing I'll kill you.' But I hadn't killed him, I'd never laid a finger on him again, but sometimes I wished I'd tried it, at least, even though it wouldn't have changed anything.

'Hey, Danny...?'

'Yeah?'

He was talking very quietly now, so quiet I could barely understand him, and with pauses between the words; the shit must have been reaching his brain. '...When you were away, Danny, I... I didn't have no one. No one said: "Don't do it, Mark." No one. Why did you just leave, Danny?'

'Leave it out, just fucking stop.' It was always the same when he was high, he always blamed us. Were we to blame? 'Come on, leave it out.'

'Why didn't you guys visit me, Danny?'

'Please, Mark, there's no point. You, it's just you.'

'I'm sorry, Danny, for everything. I'm a piece of shit, I'm so shite.'

'No,' I said, 'no, you're not. Remember when you taught me how to drive a moped?' He cried, and he must have been trembling too, 'cause the seats creaked. I felt like getting up and leaving; there was no point to it all.

'Hey, Danny,' he mumbled, 'they told me there's this pill that can say no, they... they lied, the bastards lied.'

'Remember back in the day?' I said. 'In the warehouse, when we showed the cops what's what...'

But he didn't care, 'I'm so shite, Danny, I'm so shite,' but I just kept on talking, talked about the old days, about Little Walter, about Fred, about the Eastside, about Goldie's bar where we used to drink, talked about the Green Pastures and how much Goldie hated it 'cause we'd sometimes cheat on him and he'd be all alone behind his bar, talked about the old lady and the old lady's apple korn – 'remember how it shone, golden, remember that?' – talked about Pitbull's dog back when Pitbull was still called Stefan, but he didn't answer, so I talked and talked, about Rico who was once Leipzig's best boxer, and how he danced around the ring and was sure to dance again one day, talked about the neighbourhood girls all just waiting for us, talked about Chemie Leipzig who were sure to climb back up the league table, talked and talked until my mouth was dry and I was trembling too and sunk down in my seat. He didn't answer. I turned around and looked into the dark.

'Mark?' I called quietly, 'Mark?' But he didn't answer. I lit my lighter and shone it in his direction. He'd gone. And I guessed, no, I knew, that I wouldn't see him again.

## RAYS

When Mark told me about his parents' microwave oven on the way home from school, I pretended not to care 'cause we didn't have one. The Wall had only just come down, and hardly anyone in our class or the neighbourhood had a microwave.

'So what?' I said. 'What's so special about that, a microwave oven?'

'Jeez, Danny, aren't you listening? You put something in there, something to eat, even soup, and a few minutes later it's done.'

'Like a normal oven, you mean.'

'No, man, not like a normal oven. You can't cook soup in the oven. Way smaller, and way, way faster. It uses rays!'

'Radioactive, or what?'

'You're just jealous 'cause you haven't got one!' He stopped and blocked my path.

'No way, I'm not jealous!' I pushed him aside. 'My mum's getting one soon. From Grundig, they're the best!'

'Rubbish, the Siemens ones are best. Cost the most too!'

'I've got a Siemens calculator,' I said. 'They make really good calculators, but microwaves...' The calculator had been a free gift, I'd got it at the Siemens booth at the trade fair when I went with Rico and it hardly had any buttons, you couldn't even do negative numbers on it, but I didn't tell Mark that.

'Come back to mine,' he said, 'and I'll show you how great it is.'

'What, right now?'

'Yeah.'

'What about your parents?'

'They're at work, aren't they. But honestly, the microwave, you've never seen anything like it!'

'Yes I have, at the trade fair.'

'That's different.'

'Hey, has your dad bought new mags?'

'Yeah, three new ones. I can get them whenever I like.'

'And is your sister in?'

'You want another look at her knickers, eh? No, she's not in.'

'OK,' I said quickly, and I turned away 'cause I was blushing, 'cause I was thinking of his sister's knickers. 'Let's go to yours. But only for the mags, I don't care about your stupid microwave.'

'You say that now. But once we've eaten, it tastes a lot better as well 'cause the rays, you know, they go through much better...' He was already walking off, talking all the while, and I ran after him.

The microwave was a plain white box with *Siemens* written on the front, and the door had tinted glass so you could see inside. The thing looked like a telly, stood on a table next to the cooker, and there was a vase of dried flowers on top of it.

'I thought it'd be smaller.'

'OK, it does look quite big... but the food has to fit inside, you know, it can't be much smaller, it has to have space for a pizza, or a chicken.'

I pulled the door but it didn't open.

'Not so hard, Danny, you have to press here, this button here.' He pressed a square button and the door leapt open. 'That's how to do it, not brute force, you'll break it!'

'Alright, Mark, no need to piss your pants.'

Inside was a flat round glass plate; I turned it, tugged at it and it was in my hand. 'Er, it's come off...'

Mark laughed. 'You can take it out, and you put it back

in again here. I thought you knew all about microwaves?'

'Yeah sure, but they're all different, there's a thousand different makes.'

'Yeah but Siemens, they're really the best. Look at this!' He shoved me aside, closed the door, turned a knob with a scale and a light went on inside. The microwave buzzed and I felt air coming out. Mark fiddled with the knob, a bell dinged once and the door opened again. Mark rested his hand on top of the microwave. 'Not bad, eh? It's all automatic, you can set it for anything. When your food's done the bell rings, so you know... And the door, you can set it for everything.'

'And your rays, where are your rays?'

'Here, they come out of here.' He put his hand inside the microwave. There were two grates in the walls on either side of the glass plate, and behind them I saw two lamps.

'What, they come out of those bulbs?'

'Watch and learn.' He closed the door again and pressed a few buttons and twisted the knob. The microwave began buzzing, the glass plate turned, and the strange light lit up again; this time I looked more closely. 'And in the light,' Mark said, 'that's where the rays are.' My forehead was almost touching the door. 'You can't see them, Danny, they go right through the food.' He turned the knob, the bell dinged, but the door stayed closed.

'Put something in there.'

He opened the fridge. 'Nah, Danny, nothing here, my mum hasn't been shopping yet. No wait, I can put a slice of bread in.'

'Bread! Haven't you got any proper food?'

'Stop complaining, you didn't come round to eat. I just want to show you!' He took a loaf of bread out of the cupboard and cut two slices at the kitchen table. He put them on the microwave's glass plate and set the knob to three minutes on the scale. 'It'll get really brown and crispy, way better than in the oven.' We pulled up two chairs and watched the slices of bread rotating on the plate.

'I can't see anything,' I said. 'We should be able to see something by now, it should be getting brown or something.'

'Just wait another minute.'

'Hey, the mags, weren't you going to get the mags?'

'Yeah, yeah. But look at this first!'

'Come on, it's crap, I thought we could have pizza or something.'

'I can't help it, Danny. My mum hasn't been shopping yet, she was going to...' Ding! The bell rang once, the plate stopped turning and the light went off. Mark opened the door. The bread looked exactly the same as before. He took one slice out and dropped it. 'Damn, it's boiling hot!'

The bread was on the floor; I picked it up carefully. 'It's all soft,' I said, 'and a bit clammy. Not exactly nice crispy toast.'

Mark used a tea towel to take the glass plate out of the microwave. He pressed his finger into the other slice. 'I dunno, Danny, it really is a bit soft. I must have set it wrong. Look, you can set the power here, it must have been way too low...'

'Jeez, I thought you were such an expert. A floppy slice of bread, and that's all I came round for.'

'Oh, come on, Danny, I just set it wrong, these things happen. We've only had it two days, I can't know everything yet, can I.'

'The mags,' I said, and I bit into the bread. 'You were going to show me the mags.'

Mark broke off a bit of his slice and chewed it slowly. 'See, doesn't taste half bad, does it, Danny? The rays go right through it... Come with me!'

I trailed him to his parents' bedroom. He stopped at a little chest and opened a drawer. There was a pile of newspapers but no naked women: *Fussballwoche*. 'Look at these, Danny, they're not bad either.' He pulled a paper out of the pile. 'BFC Dynamo Champions Again' the front cover said.

'Those bloody Berliners,' I said. 'Is there anything about Chemie in there?' He handed me the paper and I flicked through it. Then I put it back. 'Later,' I said. 'Girls first.'

'Right,' he said. 'They're all underneath the football.' He cleared the *Fussballwoche* out of the drawer and there they were, two little piles side by side, and the top two covers featured women baring all.

'Yeah,' I said, 'they're good.'

'The best ones are on top,' Mark said, 'But there's some *Pralines* as well.'

'*Praline*'s not bad either.' I took one pile and Mark had the other. We sat down on the rug. I ran my hands over the breasts on the front cover; the paper was smooth and shiny. 'They're rated eighteen,' Mark said. 'My dad got them from the sex shop over on Mühlstrasse.'

'I know the one,' I said. And I knew it well – it had been a toy shop before and the salesman was still the same one only now he sold different toys, and I often stood outside the window after school and looked at the magazines and videos. There were bras and other see-through underwear in the window too, and even rubber dolls, and once I'd seen a whip but that was soon gone again. Probably some drinker from the neighbourhood had bought it to beat up his wife. Maybe his wife had run off after that and he'd bought himself one of the rubber dolls.

'Look at this one!' Mark held a woman up to my face,

her legs spread so wide she must have been a gymnast. 'Did you know they were so pink? It's crazy, look at that pussy, boy, that's gorgeous!'

'Course I did,' I said, grabbing the mag and holding it tight. 'I knew that. I've seen mags like this loads of times.'

'Have you seen films as well, Danny? Proper porn films.'

'Course. I've seen it all.' Karsten's big brother sometimes watched pornos with his mates. He knew someone who worked in a video shop but they'd never let me watch. 'You're too young,' they'd told me. Karsten said they wanked in front of the telly and they didn't care if the others were watching.

'Do they do proper shagging?'

'Course. They're really wild.' We shuffled closer together and flicked through the mags. 'Look at that giant pair of tits,' I said, showing him a blonde in some kind of paddling pool, clutching a red ball to her belly.

'Nah, they're too big for me.'

'What d'you mean, too big?'

'I just don't like them that big. Daniela's aren't that big either, and I like her, you know.'

'Yeah, but she's only fourteen.'

'So? So am I,' he said; actually, he was still thirteen. I flicked through my mag and then gave it to Mark, and he handed me his.

'Look at that,' I said. 'She's got half her hand up there.'

'Seen it.'

'Jeez, it's so shiny.'

We flicked through the porn mags over and over. There were plenty of copies of *Praline* and *Das neue Wochenende* on the floor too – they were way cheaper than proper porn, only one mark fifty, but the women didn't show as much. It was still enough though. I picked up a *Praline* and flicked through the pages. 'They're not bad either,' Mark said. 'Got good stories in them, about sex and that.'

'Right,' I said, 'but you have to be over sixteen to get them as well.'

'Ever tried?'

'Course, at Rudi's shop, but they wouldn't sell it to me.'

'You have to nick them, Danny. Stick them under your shirt and get out of there.'

'Have you ever nicked one?' I put my *Praline* aside and looked at him.

'Yeah,' he said. 'Once. At Rudi's shop. Rudi's so old he doesn't notice.'

'I don't believe you – why didn't you show me it, where is it?'

'It's... I threw it away ages ago. It was... it was all ragged, Danny.' He grinned.

'And how did you do it? The stealing, I mean. Weren't you scared?'

'Nah, Danny, nah, no time to get scared. You just have to be really fast. Well, maybe a bit. But everyone was talking about them, the dirty mags, you know. And I wanted one. But now,' he laughed and stroked the shiny paper of the magazines, 'now I don't need to nick any, I've got plenty right here!'

I got up. 'Hey, Mark, I'd better be heading home... nearly dinnertime...'

'Wait a tick, Danny, hold on, don't run out on me. You can eat here. We'll make pizza, Danny, in my microwave.'

'But you haven't got any pizza.'

'Have you got a bit of time to spare, Danny?'

'Well...'

'Have you got time or not?'

'A bit, OK.'

'See, Danny? We'll go to the supermarket and get

pizza.'

'Have you got any money? I've only got one mark and a few coppers.'

He picked up the magazines and put them back in the drawer. 'We don't need money, Danny. Your mark will do fine. You will do it, you won't chicken out, you're not a scaredy-cat, are you?'

'No, I'm not scared. You know I'm not. Course I'll come with you.'

'Great, Danny.' He grinned and went to the door. I saw he still had a hard-on. I walked into the hall behind him and put my coat on quickly 'cause I had a hard-on too, and it wouldn't go down.

'Your school bag, Danny, take your school bag with you.'

'What for?'

'You'll see. And take a couple of books out of it.'

I picked up my satchel. I'd cut off the leather straps a few days before and now I carried it like a briefcase, the same as most of the kids in our class. I took out the biology textbook and the maths book – they were the heaviest – and put them next to the telephone. Then we went down the stairs and then across the backyard – it was quicker that way – over to the supermarket at the tram stop.

I took out my one-mark coin and went to the trolleys. 'Hold on, Danny, we'll need that.' Mark fished a small circle of cardboard out of his pocket and put it in the slit on the trolley handle. 'I made it in Art. Gave one to my mum as well. You have to double up the cardboard, though, or it's too thin.' I put my school bag in the trolley. We went in. Mark pushed the trolley. 'Come on,' he said, 'let's get a fizzy drink first, the cheapest.' I picked up two cans for forty-nine pfennigs each and put them in the trolley.

'How much have you got left?'

I calculated. 'Thirty-five pfennigs.'

Mark searched his pockets and pulled out a ten-pfennig piece. 'Forty-five,' he said. 'That's enough for two bread rolls, as cover, get it? So it's not so obvious.' We went to the glass box with the rolls in it and Mark took two out. He even used the metal tongs on a chain.

'What about our pizza?' I whispered.

'Now we'll stroll over to the freezer section,' he said. We leaned inconspicuously on the trolley handle. I kept looking round; the place was pretty crowded 'cause it was about the time people started getting home from work.

We went down the alcohol aisle, a real crush down there, and Mark ran over an old man's shoe. It didn't seem to bother the man though, 'cause he had a trolley full of bottles and he stank like he lived down the alcohol aisle, but then he did call out when we'd long passed him, 'Watch it, you snotfaces!' It must have taken the pain a while to register in his addled brain cells.

'Tramp,' said Mark.

'Drunk,' I whispered.

We got to the freezer with the pizzas and Mark started rummaging around in it. 'Mark,' I whispered, 'it has to say something on the box, that it's for the microwave, I mean, so it'll work. That's what I heard.'

'Rubbish. The microwave can cook anything. You can heat anything up and bake anything. 'Cause of the rays, I told you.' He picked out a pizza.

'Not that one,' I said. 'Brick oven – who knows what that is. Bet it's not nice.'

He put it back and took another. 'One salami pizza. What do you want?'

'Pizza Specialo,' I said, and chose a box from the freezer.

'Looks a bit small, my one's bigger.'

'So?' I said, putting the box in the trolley. 'That doesn't matter, not if it's the special kind.'

Mark looked around. 'Down that aisle,' he whispered, 'by the washing powder, and start opening your bag now.' We pushed the trolley slowly down the washing powder aisle, where it was empty. I opened my satchel. 'Wait,' said Mark, 'there's that old bloke again.' The old man pushed his trolley past us, gave us a dumb grin, and then put a three-kilo box of Persil next to his alcohol bottles. He put on another stupid grin and tucked his shirt down the front of his trousers so far that his hand disappeared and it looked like he was scratching his balls. We stared at our trolley and pushed it away from him.

'Dirty bastard,' I said. 'What a dirty old bastard.'

'I bet he's one of those penis-flashing perverts. You've got to watch out for them, Danny, they lure you home with them and touch you up.' Mark opened my satchel and stuffed the salami pizza between the books. I grabbed my Pizza Specialo; it was freezing cold and stuck to my hand. Mark had walked around the trolley and positioned himself in front of me while I stuffed and pressed, but the box wouldn't go into my bag. 'Jeez, Danny, someone's coming!' I tore my shirt out of my trousers and shoved the pizza under it. Two women walked past us; I did my jacket up. 'Jeez, Danny,' Mark whispered, 'are you crazy, you should have taken more books out, I told...'

'Now who's the scaredy-cat, eh?'

'Forget it, Danny, I'm not scared, no way.' My satchel was still open, and he fastened it shut. We pushed the trolley to the tills. Only one of the three was open and we joined the end of the queue. I took my bag out of the trolley. 'That's better,' Mark said, 'not so obvious.' We made slow progress.

Someone touched my shoulder and I turned around. The old man was behind us. 'I saw you,' he whispered. He stank so badly of alcohol I could hardly breathe, and his eyes glistened. 'Don't worry, lads, I won't tell on you...' My hand clutched the trolley handle and he touched it. I felt the pizza cold against my belly.

'One thirty-eight.' We were at the till. Mark put the bread rolls and the fizzy drinks back in the trolley. I turned around. The next till had opened up and the old man had moved over there. Behind me was a woman with black hair, her breasts bearing down towards me, and as I stumbled a few steps back and bumped into our trolley, she smiled at me. She was wearing tight jeans and I looked at the triangle beneath her belt and then back up at her smile, which might not have been a smile, the triangle and the smile... 'One thirty-eight!' The pizza against my stomach was so cold I couldn't get a hard-on, never again, and I put my hand in my pocket to look for my money. I counted the coins onto the cashier's palm; she nodded, clinked them into the till and handed me a two-pfennig piece. 'Thanks,' I said, pushing the trolley towards the exit with one hand, my school bag in the other. Mark walked beside me.

'Jeez,' he said as we put the trolley back, 'what was up with you? She was giving you a really funny look.'

'I don't know, do I? It was my first time.'

'We're real professionals now,' Mark said with a grin. He poked the card circle out of the slit and we walked back to our road. Once the supermarket was out of eyeshot, I stopped, undid my jacket and pulled the pizza out from under my shirt. There was a wet patch on my vest.

The pizza was soft and we couldn't cut it properly. We'd left it in the microwave for more than twenty minutes but it was no use. We ate it anyway. We put it in a big bowl and ate it with spoons.

'But it did turn around,' I said, 'and the light shone on it, with the rays in it...'

Mark smiled. 'It's not that bad like this, Danny. I must have set it wrong. It's all new, isn't it?'

'Course,' I said. 'Not bad at all. A bit of a change from usual. But let's put the other pizza in the oven, yeah?'

'Yeah, probably better, Danny. And then we'll have another look at the mags. Have I shown you the Girl of the Month? The dark-haired one, she's the best.'

'Yeah,' I said, 'the mags.'

# THE BLACK HOLE

## I. Contact

'I'm in love,' says Walter, who we call Little Walter, 'cause he's really pretty little; only Rico says it's 'cause he's got a little dick. We're drinking in Pitbull's cellar, Mark, Walter, Pitbull, Rico and me. Pitbull nicked some money from his mum and we picked up a crate of beer from the two gays in the off-licence – they even sell us vodka and korn and brandy, 'cause they fancy us.

'Who are you in love with?' I ask.

Walter shifts the empty beer crate he's sitting on closer to me. 'You know the newsagents...'

'On the corner of Kohlenstrasse?'

'No, there's a new one, up by the trade fair.'

'You mean that nasty little place in the Black Hole!' I laugh. We call the area around the trade fair the Black Hole 'cause there are all these vacant houses crumbling away up there, people just disappear there and almost all the streetlamps are dead as well. Actually, it's like our neighbourhood, Reudnitz, and like all over Leipzig East, but over in the Black Hole there are loads of hookers and the little Viet women sell their bodies in the park by the main road and we save up our pocket money and dream of them at night, but in the daytime we're scared.

'It's the nicest shop in the whole of town!' Walter throws his fag on the floor and steps on it. 'Anyway, there's this girl there, I think it's even her shop. I take my mum's lottery slips there for her, anyway, she's beautiful!'

'Big-bucks beautiful! Nothing's for free in the Black Hole, Little Walter!' Rico gets up and goes to the door, fingering his belt.

'Shut it,' Walter whispers so low only I hear it, 'cause he doesn't want trouble with Rico, no one wants trouble with Rico 'cause he loses it fast since he came back from the place, back in the Zone days, but we don't talk about that.

'Not in the backyard, Rico,' Pitbull says. 'I'll get in trouble, it already stinks like an old man's armpit! Go over to next door!' but Rico doesn't answer and he's already out in the corridor.

'They're not into golden showers,' says Mark. He's on the old sofa in the corner, reading the latest *Praline*. We nicked it for Paul, actually, at Rudi's shop, but Paul couldn't come 'cause his mother's locked him in again, 'cause she's scared Paul will turn criminal if he hangs out with us. She doesn't know Paul's got the biggest porn mag and video collection in the neighbourhood, maybe in all of town. It's legendary, even Mark's dad's collection doesn't stand a chance. Everyone in the neighbourhood likes him 'cause Paul's happy to lend them out and sell them and do deals with his videos, but he's still one of us.

Mark puts his empty bottle back in the crate and takes a new one. 'Come on, Little Walter,' he's slurring his words already, 'I bet she's pretty old.' He slaps Walter on the cheek.

'Nah,' Walter says, pushing Mark's hand away, 'she's not old at all, thirty tops, I dunno, maybe even only twenty-six.'

'Golden oldie,' Mark mutters, and that makes me laugh and Pitbull laughs too while he's drinking, his beer foams up and the foam runs down his chin.

'Shut it,' says Walter, 'you're wasted already!'

'No, I'm not,' Mark yells, and pretends to stagger, and slurs, 'Yeah, right, I'm well tight. Can't even walk!' Mark can take his drink but he always drinks way more than us and gets drunk quicker, and then he usually says... 'Anyway, I had four at school already,' Mark says and downs half the bottle in one. Walter lights a cigarette and blows the smoke against the wall. He smokes 100s; they look really long against his little face.

I tap him on the chest. 'So, what's up with her then?'

'None of you want to know anyway, you guys don't give a shit.'

Mark goes back to his corner and starts flicking through the *Praline* again.

'Yes, we do want to know,' Pitbull says, 'carry on, a bit older's a good thing, she'll give you a proper seeing to!'

Walter smiles and leans his head against the wall. 'She looks really fit. I've never seen a bloke there, I mean her boyfriend or whatever. She hasn't got one, I bet, she never gets picked up after work.'

'What, are you following her around and watching her?'

'No, just by accident, man! I go there a lot, don't I. My mum does the lottery Wednesdays and Saturdays. And sometimes I go in for scratch cards and that. But you know what, when I give her my lottery slip she holds my hand really funny, she really touches me, I swear, she's got really soft hands!'

'She's supposed to use tweezers, is she?' Mark calls out from his corner and holds up the *Praline*, 'Now that's what I call pussy!' We stare at the Girl of the Week baring her breasts at us on a double-page spread.

'Let's have a look at that bitch,' yells Pitbull and goes over to Mark, 'cause he loves the Girls of the Week – the whole of last month is on the wall above the sofa, eight breasts so Pitbull doesn't have to sleep alone, and he often sleeps in his cellar. Walter watches him, looks at the girls on the wall and fiddles with his shirt buttons, pulling at them until they almost come off, but then Mark and Pitbull would see his Micky Mouse T-shirt under his shirt, and they'd laugh at him 'cause he loves Micky Mouse even though he's pretty good at hot-wiring cars.

'Go on, tell us more,' I say. 'Do you ever talk to her, does she say anything to you?'

'Yeah, sort of, a bit...' he raises his head and smiles, 'like last week, she asked me if I've got any lucky numbers. She doesn't know they're my mum's...'

'Lucky numbers. Sounds like a good start.'

'You know, the thing is, she's not from round here, she's from over there, from the West, you can tell by how she speaks, like an accent... and... and she told me, as well.'

'From the West,' I say, and I nod and pat him on the shoulder, 'not bad...'

Mark and Pitbull put the *Praline* aside and come over to us. 'What? A wicked bitch from the West, what does she want from you? Don't talk bollocks!'

'It's true!' Walter leans back and drinks a mouthful of beer, then he lights a cigarette. He puts his pack on the table and I take one.

Pitbull sits down on the half-full crate and the bottles make a low clinking sound. 'What if she's taking the piss, or maybe she just wants a dirty affair.'

Walter smiles and scratches his head. 'An affair,' he says, 'wow, an affair...'

Someone comes running down the cellar stairs. The steps sound pretty loud – it's not just one person. We leap up. I grab my half-full bottle. Rico comes in through the door, red in the face, his belt still unbuckled. 'Guys, come quick, there's an old lady over at number 20, she needs coal carrying and she can't do it herself. She'll pay a tenner!'

We run, Rico leading the way. We run up the cellar

stairs, through the hall and into the backyard. It's almost evening, getting dark, and we crawl through a gap in the fence to the next-door yard. The place is full of junk; sometimes we find nice stuff in there. There's an old fridge on the grass and Rico stops and lands a few straight punches and hooks on the white metal. Rico's pretty good at boxing, he wants to go professional one day, and he shows it off all the time. Then we see the old lady. She's sitting on a little bench up against her building, her hands folded around the grip of her walking stick. We exchange glances, Rico nods, and we stroll over to her. She's wearing huge glasses with dark lenses – we stop in front of her but she doesn't see us. 'I almost pissed on her,' Rico whispers, 'and then she goes and talks to me.'

'She wouldn't have seen anything anyway,' says Little Walter, 'when you undid your flies, I mean.' We grin but Rico doesn't even look at him.

He tugs his collar into place, then builds himself up right in front of the old lady. 'Hello,' he shouts, 'we're back. You can open your cellar up now!' He shouts very slowly, with long pauses between the words, as if the old lady's not just half-blind and half-deaf but a bit soft in the head as well.

'Oh, my goodness!' She raises her hands and her stick falls over. 'Here you are, yes. Yes, I can see you now!' She gets up and feels for her stick. Pitbull picks it up and puts it in her hand. She waves the stick around a bit and goes over to the back door.

'She's ready to drop dead, any day now,' I say.

'No, listen,' Rico whispers. 'She's a goldmine, get it? There'll always be something in it for us if we go shopping for her or whatever. And a tenner for the coal, that's enough for a bottle of brandy or two packs.'

'Half a crate,' Pitbull whispers.

'Right. And now multiply that by a month. It's getting cold, winter's coming soon, you get it?'

'It's not that much,' I say.

'Wait and see,' says Rico, 'winter's coming soon,' and I nod, and the others nod too and grin crooked grins.

'Hello,' the old lady shouts, 'where are you, where are you, boys?' She's already inside, holding the door open. We walk in past her. 'It's so good you're here,' the old lady says. She closes the back door. It's dark inside the building and the old lady's standing between us, tapping at the floor with the stick. She stinks. She stinks like Rico went all over her when he pissed against the wall, but with a sprinkle of alcohol on top. Someone flicks on a lighter, it's Pitbull, grinning and showing me his broken front tooth. I spot the light switch on the wall and turn it on. The old lady points her stick at a small door. 'My cellar, there's my cellar. And my coal, boys.' She sways and leans on her stick for balance.

Rico goes to the door and tries the handle; it's locked. 'The key,' he yells, 'we need your key!' The old lady leans her shoulder against the wall, fumbles in her coat pocket and takes out a huge key, with a smaller one attached to it with a wire. I take it and put it in my pocket.

'The small one is for my padlock,' the old lady says, 'so no one steals my coal.' She laughs and coughs, and I turn my head away, 'cause she spits. I hand the key to Rico and he opens the door. We walk down the stairs. 'Fill the buckets up nice and full,' the old lady calls from the top, 'for my coal box. I'm going upstairs now, boys. I live on the top floor.'

'She's not quite right,' says Walter.

'Which one's your cellar compartment?' Rico shouts, turning to the door.

'Nice and full,' the old lady calls down.

Rico takes the key and walks from door to door. 'It must fit somewhere.'

'Here's one lump of coal already!' Mark shoots it to Pitbull, Pitbull passes it back to Mark and they run laughing along the cellar walkway.

'Help,' the old lady shouts down, 'help me, boys, the light!' I turn around; the light's gone out in the stairwell.

Pitbull shoots the coal at the wall. 'Can't she walk up in the dark? She can't see anything anyway!' He takes out his lighter and goes to the stairs. I see his flame in the darkness. He switches the light back on.

'My light,' the old lady screeches. I hear her footsteps on the stairs, getting quieter.

Rico's found the old lady's cellar compartment and opened the door. The whole space is full of coal, a mountain of it almost touching the ceiling and the light bulb, like the old lady wants to live as long as her coal lasts, sixteen winters, and there's a little heap of wood by the door and a chopping block next to it with an axe wedged in it. 'Nice axe,' Pitbull says, and pulls it out of the block and waves it slowly in front of his face, 'almost as good as mine.' He's got a garden axe in his cellar, we call it his 'junior axe' because it's so small, but he still lugs it around with him some nights, 'cause a couple of guys ripped him one time, that's what we call it when the bastards empty your pockets and take your clothes and shoes and all, if they're any good. Pitbull had to walk all the way across town half-naked and barefoot, 'cause he was wearing good clothes that night, he'd saved up for ages for them, and for the girl he was going to see, 'and now there'll be a massacre,' he says, 'if anyone else ever tries it.' He pulls back his arm and almost takes my nose off, then slams the axe into the chopping block.

'Be prepared,' Rico says, putting his hand to his

forehead with a grin. 'Remember? A Pioneer is always honest and helpful.'

We pick up the buckets and chuck coal in them. Rico, Pitbull and Mark walk through the cellar and up the stairs with the full buckets. We hear them laughing in the stairwell. Walter gives me one of his Lucky Strikes, 'cause he knows I like them and I've only got Golden 25s from the Vietcong.

'So, Walter, how are you gonna do it, with your lottery girl, I mean. You reckon it'll work out?'

'Definitely, Danny. You should see the way she looks at me! Women are well into shorter men, I've heard.'

'Could be,' I say. 'Yeah, you're probably right.'

'So I guess I'll catch her when she's closing up, Danny, around six, that's a good time, and take her out for a drink or something.'

'Does your mum ever win anything?'

'Nah. Three numbers now and then, no more than that. But I mean, that'd be it, a big win, we could get out of here, you know...'

I nod.

'And then... and then I could take that girl out, really take her out somewhere, not just some chip shop.'

We stare at the coal and smoke. We put out our cigarettes and flick them away. We hear the others thumping down the stairs. They come in and slam their buckets on the floor. 'Jesus Christ,' says Rico, 'she's got two massive crates up there next to the stove, wants us to fill them up, it's a shitload of work!'

'Time and a half,' I say, rubbing my thumb against my index finger, and Rico smiles and looks past me.

'The whole flat's full of booze!' Mark's holding a bottle of Goldblatt; he takes a swig and passes it on. It's my turn last and the bottle's almost empty. Goldblatt is the cheapest brandy but the drinkers in our neighbourhood swear by it. I chuck the empty bottle in among the coal. Mark and Pitbull squat down and fill up the buckets. Walter picks one of them up and walks across the cellar, all crooked. I want to take two but Rico takes one off me and runs ahead. He likes lugging heavy stuff around, it's good for his muscles, and he needs them 'cause he boxes and he wants to go professional one day. He carries the bucket up to the second floor with his left hand, that's his jabbing hand, the one he softens them up with until he wipes them out with his heavy right. We overtake Walter on the first floor; I put my bucket down for a moment on the third.

'Come on, old fella!' Rico grins down through the bannisters. He bobs and weaves on the staircase like he's in the ring, swinging the full bucket. The old lady's outside her front door. She's still got her coat on, she's resting on her stick. The sign on the doorbell says *Böhme*.

'Come on in, boys.' She starts coughing, coughs like crazy and holds onto the wall. We lug the buckets to the big tiled stove in the living room and shake the coal into the wooden crates.

'Nearly full now,' I say.

Rico nods. 'Looked like we'd need more, before.'

The old lady comes in. 'Thank you, boys. D'you want a wee drink?' She points at the table; there are a couple of bottles on it and a plate with a big chunk of dried-out cheese.

'Later,' I say and pick up my bucket. As we go out the front door I see the old lady taking off her coat in her hallway. She's only wearing a nightshirt. We run down the stairs, making as much noise as we can.

'I'm taking a break this time,' Rico says. 'I've got to train tomorrow or my muscle'll go hard, see.'

'What muscle's that then?' I grin and he boxes my shoulder lightly.

Walter runs past us, swinging his empty bucket. 'I'll be first this time,' he shouts, and we hear him laughing further down.

We're sitting at the old lady's table, drinking apple korn out of teacups. There's a fire raging in the stove, the stove door is open, and we can see the flames playing on the wall. The old lady's wearing a bathrobe over her nightshirt, sitting in a big armchair by the stove and drinking. She's made herself hot grog and the whole place stinks of booze. 'Good work, boys,' she says, and she raises her cup and slurps half of it up.

She's made a whole pan of grog but we're sticking to our apple korn. 'Who knows what's in there,' Rico said, and he's right, the old lady looks like bits drop off of her now and then.

'A proper fire,' the old lady says. 'It's burning really nicely.'

It was a while before the coal took 'cause the old lady didn't have any firelighters left. We tried it with the old chunk of cheese first, 'it's fat, and fat burns well,' Mark said, but the cheese didn't burn well and the room still smells a bit, but the old lady's grog covers it up pretty well.

We wanted to try it with the brandy as well but Goldblatt's not strong enough, only 22 per cent, and the old lady told us off. 'My good stuff, boys, not my Goldblatt, you can't use that, you can't burn that!' It didn't work until Pitbull found a bottle of Stroh 80 in the kitchen, even though we drank half of it. His eyebrows are a bit burnt now but luckily he's got short hair, a number-one crop, so he looks like a hardman and people in our neighbourhood respect him even when he hasn't got his junior axe with him. I get up and check on the fire. The coals are glowing properly now and I close the stove door.

'Your money, boys,' the old lady says, 'you'll get it in a minute, you've earned it, you can go out dancing.'

We laugh. 'Proper banging Techno,' says Mark.

'Oh yes,' the old lady says, and laughs with us. Rico lights up a cigarette. 'No!' the old lady yells. 'Not in here, go out on the balcony!' She starts coughing and holds a towel in front of her mouth.

'I'm going, alright,' Rico says and gets up.

'Hold on, I'll come with you!' I walk after him to the door.

'I'm sticking here with granny,' Mark says, topping up his glass.

'No smoking in my living room, oh no,' the old lady says. 'My Jochen's not allowed to smoke in here either. Only on the balcony.' We cross the kitchen to the balcony. The big pan of grog is on the cooker. Rico wants to flick his ash in there but I push him ahead.

The balcony faces out over the backyard and we look over at Pitbull's building. It's dark outside now, blue light flickering in a few windows. Rico gives me one of his cigarettes; he's only got Golden 25s from the Vietcong as well. We smoke and flick the ash down into the backyard.

'Danny, the poor old lady's gonna croak if she doesn't get anyone to help her out a bit.'

'I dunno,' I say. 'Someone must come over now and then. She said something about a Jochen, didn't she?'

'But Danny, we can earn a bit of money if we come over often, and there's plenty to drink and all.'

'I dunno, Rico.'

'Danny, I bet she's got enough money, I bet she gets a big fat pension, she'll be glad if we come over. A bit of a helping hand, see?'

'What if you don't find anything? And what if she notices?'

'Jeez, Danny, we'll find something, we're almost professionals now.' He grins. 'Only ever a little bit, see? Not everything at once, no, we're men of honour.'

'She's half blind, Rico.'

'That's just it, Danny. That's why she needs a bit of a helping hand, see?'

'Right,' I say and nod. 'She might really be glad of it. Maybe she'd think it's worth it.'

'Right,' Rico says, and puts his arm around my shoulder, 'it is worth it, totally worth it!'

We stare at the buildings opposite with their dark backyards. We flick our fag ends off the balcony, watching the glowing dots until they disappear, and then we go back inside.

The old lady is at the cooker, filling her mug with a ladle. Half of it spills on the floor and Rico goes over to her. 'Hold on,' he says, 'I'll do it.' I see the old lady's hand trembling. She says nothing as Rico takes her cup out of her hand. 'I'll bring it through,' he says. We go through to the living room and the old lady hobbles after us.

Pitbull's gone. 'Where's...'

Mark grins and says, 'He's just having a bit of a look around.'

'So dark in here,' the old lady says. 'Must be getting late.' She gropes for the standing lamp by her chair and switches it on. She pulls a blanket up over her until only her head's poking out.

Pitbull comes in and sits back down. 'Only booze,' he says. 'But loads of it. Nothing else though.'

'Oh yes,' the old lady says, 'my good Goldblatt. Have another one, boys, I've got plenty.' We open up a new bottle of apple korn. We fill our cups and the old lady reaches for the bottle and adds a good dash to her grog. We all raise our glasses. 'I used to go out dancing a lot,' she says, 'in the old days. I'd dance and dance...'

'And dance,' Walter says, and laughs and looks at us, and then he blushes 'cause we don't join in.

But the old lady laughs. 'Oh yes,' she says, 'oh yes,' and she laughs and wobbles her head. 'All night long,' she says and slurps her grog with apple korn, 'until the early hours.' She talks about her husband, who she danced with and who's been dead a few years now, 'gone,' she says, 'just shuffled off, the bugger!' She talks about her son who comes by once a fortnight. 'Jochen,' she says, 'my Jochen's a good boy. He comes and brings me my money and a nice bottle, he always brings me a nice bottle.'

'When's he coming next, your Jochen?' Rico asks.

'Tomorrow, maybe, or later. Jochen always comes round.' She slurps her cup empty, gets up and hobbles into the kitchen.

'Shall we give you a hand?' Pitbull calls over.

'No, no, I'm fine, I can manage.' We hear her rummaging around out there.

Walter gets up, goes over to the unit with the TV and switches it on. 'Lottery numbers,' he says and smiles.

'Not worth it,' Mark says. 'They're shafting you, pipsqueak.'

'You shut it!' He takes a notepad and pen out of his shirt pocket, they're drawing the numbers on TV, I don't watch, only hear the balls rattling, but Walter writes the numbers down.

'Any luck?' I ask.

'Nah,' he says and turns the telly off.

'Bet you get your girl instead, your lottery girl, I mean.' He smiles again.

'What about our money?' Pitbull goes over to the

unit and opens a few drawers. 'She's got nothing, maybe. Look, just crap.' He holds up a naked doll by its hair, puts it back in the drawer and closes it.

'Wait and see,' Rico says.

The old lady comes back in, carrying a plate of bread, her full cup perched in between the slices. 'For you,' she says and puts the plate on the table. The bread's not doing well, the slices are crooked and dry like the cheese we burned, topped with shiny salami with a green tint to it. 'I've always got everything I need,' the old lady says. 'Help yourselves, boys.' She fumbles around between the slices until she's got her cup, then sits down in her chair and drinks.

'Thank you,' I say, taking a piece of bread and pushing the plate over to the others. 'Very nice,' I say, and throw the bread in the crate of coal, 'lovely.' The old lady slurps her grog, her half-blind eyes staring into her cup and then at the door.

'Ten out of ten,' says Mark, taking a piece as well and throwing it in the crate.

We throw the bread over towards the stove; Pitbull misses the coal crate and we laugh at him. 'Your hands are too crooked, you need to calm down with the wanking!'

'Shut up, you're the wankers!'

The old lady shifts side to side in her seat and laughs along with us. 'Oh yes,' she says, 'you can have your fun here. That's right, boys, in the old days...' She coughs again.

'The bread,' Rico whispers. 'We'll chuck it in the stove before we go, alright?'

'Be prepared,' whispers Mark, putting his hand to his head, and I smile 'cause it looks just as stupid as in the Zone days.

Rico nods at Pitbull, and Pitbull gets up. 'Mrs Böhme,

we've got to go now, we've got school in the morning...'

'Yes, boys, yes, it's getting late.' She gets up and drapes the blanket over her shoulders. 'Your money, boys, I'll just go and get it...' She hobbles into the next room, followed by Pitbull.

'What's he...?' Walter gawps at me.

'Don't ask stupid questions, carjacker!' I push his chest and he blushes. We down our drinks. We hear the old lady crashing about in the next room.

'Now he's giving it to her,' Mark says, grinning.

'You shut your mouth!' Rico's finger is right in front of Mark's face.

'Alright, keep your hair on.' Mark plays around with his mug handle, tilts and pours, the apple korn glows golden in the bottle and a few drops run over his hand onto the table. We look over at the door. Pitbull comes back in. He's clutching a bundle of notes with a crooked smile on his face. There's blood on his hand.

No. We look over at the door. The old lady comes back in. She's clutching a tenner with a few coins in her other hand. 'Here we are, boys, for being so good!' She puts the money down on the table for us and laughs and coughs and drops back down on her seat. Rico looks at me and I take the money and put it in my pocket. She's paid an extra five marks on top.

Rico takes a breath and raises his hand like a conductor. 'Thank you, Mrs Böhme,' we chorus. Pitbull's standing behind the old lady, and he waves and grins and rubs his thumb against his forefinger. I can feel myself smiling, and I look past him.

The old lady's almost vanished into her chair, breathing and wheezing like she's about to drop dead. 'You will come back, won't you, boys? You'll come back again?'

'Sure,' I say. 'We will, we'll be back, happy to help, Mrs

Böhme.'

'It's so cold,' the old lady says and gets up again. 'I need it nice and warm in here.' She hobbles into the hallway, jangling keys. Mark and Walter squat down at the stove and burn the slices of bread. We go out to the hall. The keys have fallen down and the old lady's kneeling by the front door, feeling the floor for them.

Mark picks up the keys and holds out his arm to her. 'Up you get, Mrs Böhme.' She pulls herself up and leans against the wall. Mark unlocks the door.

We shake hands with the old lady before we leave. 'There's so many of you,' she says. We walk down the stairs; the old lady stands in the doorway and waves. 'And you'll be back, won't you? I've always got a nice grog!' We hear her locking the door. The light in the stairwell goes off but we don't turn it back on again, walking down in the dark.

Then we stand in the yard and look up.

'There's the Big Dipper,' Mark says and smiles and points up at the stars. The light's still on in the old lady's kitchen, then it goes out suddenly.

'She's off to bed now.'

'D'you think she'll have a wash first?'

'Right, how much did you get?'

'A hundred,' says Pitbull, taking out a note. 'We'll have to break it.'

'A hundred,' Walter whispers, gets out his cigarettes and treats us to a round. We stand in a circle around Pitbull and hold each other's shoulders and look at the blue banknote held in his trembling paws. We head for the fence.

'Shut your bloody mouth, you dirty bitch!'

'What's that?' We turn around.

There's a light on two floors below the old lady, and

that's where the shouting's coming from. 'Whore! You whore! You dirty fucking slut!'

'It's the drinkers,' Pitbull says. 'I can hear them all the way from my place sometimes. They're... they're poor bastards.' He's breathing through his mouth, his cheeks flushing, and we move in closer to him.

'Come on, Pitbull,' Mark gives the fence a quick kick, 'let's go back over to your cellar.'

There's a bang; the balcony door is jerked open. 'Help! Murder, murder in Germany!' A woman leans over the edge. It's dark but I can see her long hair.

'Come inside, you cunt! I'll kill you, you stupid bitch!' Someone's standing behind the woman, trying to pull her inside.

'Let go of me, let go of me, I'll jump, I swear I'll jump!' She's already halfway over the edge but she can't jump, the guy drags her back and across the balcony, inside the flat. The door slams, 'Murder in Germany!' and then quiet.

'That bastard's gonna beat her to death.' Pitbull throws his fag on the ground, not even half-smoked.

'Jeez, leave them be. I'm going back over.' Mark crawls through the gap in the fence to Pitbull's backyard. It's still quiet up there but then there's a crash, something crashes and clangs and splinters as if the guy's got a few mates up there, or his brothers, but nobody screams.

'I'm going up to teach that shithead a lesson, shut him up for a while.'

'It's not worth it,' Rico grabs him by the shoulder. 'Don't do it. You'll only make trouble. Let's go over and share out the money. A hundred and fifteen marks, come on!'

Pitbull takes a step aside; Rico's hand falls off his shoulder. He looks up at the building. No more crashing. The woman screams again.

'Nah,' says Pitbull and puts his hands in his pockets, 'I'm gonna go and take a look, I've heard it often enough, I can't stand it, you know, when some bastard... you know...'

And I do know, 'cause I know his parents. Pitbull's had a handle on his father since the thing with his dog, but we don't talk about that.

'If you're going up, I'll come with you and keep an eye out.'

'Nah, Danny, don't, it's my business, don't worry. I'll give that bastard a quick seeing to, won't take long, you'll see!' And then he runs off. Inside the building, he turns on the hallway light and we see him walking up the stairs through the window. Everything's quiet again in the flat.

'Fuck,' says Walter. 'He's off on one again. Why didn't you stop him? What do we do now?'

'Nothing,' Rico says. 'Give him the money, Danny.' I dig in my pocket and give Walter the fifteen marks. 'Go and get some crisps and a nice bottle from the two gays, but not Goldblatt, alright, something good. And cigarettes. Better get a move on, they're closing soon.'

'And you two?'

'Go on, off you go. We'll see you in the cellar.'

'Hey, Rico, I'm not a pussy, I'm staying here!'

'Nobody said you're a pussy. I know you can throw a punch. But if Pitbull doesn't manage, up there I mean, then two's enough.'

'But if you need help,' Walter crosses through the gap in the fence, hardly needs to bend down 'cause he's so short, 'if you need me, just call, alright!'

'Course,' says Rico, 'we'll just call.'

I hear Walter's footsteps over in the next backyard.

'Three minutes,' Rico says. 'What d'you say, we'll give Pitbull three minutes.' I nod. The woman screams, very short and very high.

'What is all this crap,' I say. 'First the crazy old lady, and now this...'

'You know how it is, Danny.' He lights two cigarettes and passes one to me.

I look up; clouds in front of the stars and I can't see the Big Dipper. 'Nah, Rico, let's go up there.'

'Maybe you're right, Danny.' We throw our cigarettes away and walk inside. The stairwell is quiet too.

'Does no one else live here?'

'I don't know, Danny.'

The door to the flat is open and we hear Pitbull's voice inside. 'It's alright, it'll be alright, everything's fine now.' We walk down the hallway. In one room is a big bed, with Pitbull sitting on it and the woman lying next to him. Her head's on his lap and he's stroking her hair. I knock on the door frame and he turns around slowly. 'Oh, it's you.' The woman is crying, her face covered in blood. Her blouse is torn with one breast hanging out, not a nice breast, a drinker's breast, and there are all these scratches on it.

'Where's the guy?' Rico asks.

Pitbull points his thumb at the wall. 'Next door.'

'Shit,' I say. I'm scared he's killed him. We'd have to cover it up and that wouldn't be good.

'Leave me alone,' the woman mumbles, and I see a few broken teeth under her swollen lips – the drink or her old man – 'just leave us alone.'

'It's alright,' Pitbull strokes her hair. 'You don't need to be scared anymore, it'll be fine.'

We go next door. The guy's not visible; perhaps he's underneath all the crap. All the drawers in the big wall unit have been pulled out and the stuff that was in them is all over the floor. There must have been food on the table; the remains are piled in with all the other crap. And bottles, more bottles than upstairs in the old lady's place, but almost all broken. There are two shoes in one corner; the feet of a man hidden under a blanket.

'Rico...'

'Seen it.' The rubbish crunches and splinters under our feet, we crouch down by the man and pull the blanket away carefully. The guy's face is barely recognisable; Pitbull's done a thorough job. Now the guy moves, something's working away in his throat like there's a fist in there, now he makes noises like he's gargling, and out of his mouth comes all this blood and stuff that looks like sick, smells like it too. 'Oh shit,' says Rico. 'Turn his head to one side.'

I turn his head and more runs out of his mouth. There are a few little white stones in the mush; I pry his lips apart with my fingertips, almost all gone at the top and a few missing at the bottom as well. 'What d'you reckon, Rico, is he gonna die?'

'Nah, he's just knocked out. We'll get him in the bathroom to start with, clean him up a bit, then we'll take care of Pitbull and the bastard's old lady.'

'Shit,' I say. 'They'll lock him up for this.'

'No one's gonna know, Danny, you think anyone here called the... and anyway, it was them that did it, they won't remember it in the morning.'

'Maybe you're right...'

'I am, Danny.'

'He certainly deserved it, the bastard.' I grab him by the collar with one hand and by the hair with the other, and drag him out of the corner. Rico takes his feet and we carry him into the bathroom. The guy babbles something or other; maybe he's coming round. 'Shut your bastard mouth,' I whisper. I take a quick look into the room with the big bed; Pitbull has put his head on the woman's head. The bathroom door is closed and Rico kicks it open 'cause he doesn't have a hand free. We lug him to the bathtub and prop him up so he's kneeling in front of it. Rico turns the water on and I push the broken face under the stream. Rico rinses it carefully, his hair as well and then his neck, first with lukewarm water and then he turns the mixer tap to cold and I have to hold onto the guy and I press my chest against his back 'cause he's moving more now and swaying and mumbling something.

'Hold nice and tight!' Rico gets up and grabs a towel. 'His nose is gone,' he says, dabbing the guy's face with the towel. 'Maybe his jaw as well, but that's not that bad, as long as nothing's happened to his head.' Rico knows that kind of thing; he's a pretty good boxer. We lay the guy out on the floor. His shirt's wet and Rico takes it off. The guy's all quiet now, but I can see his chest moving up and down under his T-shirt. He's got an eye tattooed on his upper arm, crying blue tears; it's a prison tattoo, I can tell right away. I used to know a guy when I was little, he had a blue tear tattooed underneath his real eye.

'Shall we leave him here?'

'No, Danny, not on the cold tiles.' We drag him back into the hallway and lay him on a rug by the front door. Then we go back to Pitbull. He's kneeling by the bed, leaning over the broken woman; he pushes her breast back under her blouse and buttons it up. She's breathing calmly and it looks like she's asleep, but one eye's open and she's looking at us. There's almost no blood on her face now; Pitbull must have wiped it off.

'That bastard,' says Pitbull, 'that bloody bastard!'

'You know how it is,' Rico says and squats down next to him.

'Yes, I know.' Pitbull gets up. 'She can't get away from the arsehole.'

'It's almost always like that,' Rico says.

'Yeah,' says Pitbull. He goes to the door, sits down on the floor and leans his head on the wall. I grab my cigarettes and chuck one at him. He nods, smiles and lights it up. 'Could have saved myself the trouble, eh, Danny?'

'I dunno.'

'There's no point, Mark's right, they're alkies, they'll just go on like this forever.'

'It was an OK thing to do,' I say. 'The guy really needed it, the bastard.' We sit down on the floor next to Pitbull and smoke. It's quiet in the flat, it's quiet in the whole building; all we hear is a few cars out on the road.

'Where are the others?'

'Over in the cellar,' I say. 'In your cellar. We've got crisps and a couple of bottles.'

'My idea,' says Rico. 'It's not that late yet.'

The woman starts snoring on the bed. It smells of booze when she breathes out.

'The guy,' says Pitbull and turns his head very slowly to look in the hall.

'It's fine, Pitbull, he's just asleep, he's just having a little nap.'

'I didn't mean to,' Pitbull says, and I see his body going limp as he collapses against the wall, 'I didn't mean all this.'

'No,' Rico says, 'you did the right thing, you hear? He needed it, believe me, he really needed it, the mean bastard. Nah, Pitbull, he's a wife-beater, the worst there is.'

'Yeah,' I say. 'Rico's right about that.'

'I wouldn't want to fight you, you're a real fury.' Rico puts his hand on the back of Pitbull's neck and presses his muscles. 'In the ring, I mean, you'd be a real fury.'

'Really?' Pitbull smiles.

'Definitely.' We stub out our cigarettes on the soles of our shoes, even though the carpet we're sitting on is covered in burn marks, and we get up. We open the window and throw our fag ends down into the yard.

'You go ahead,' I say to Pitbull, 'drink one for us, we'll put this arsehole to bed.'

The guy's still lying on the rug, not moving, but now his legs twitch a bit like he's running in his dream. We push Pitbull past him to the door and then out into the stairwell. He turns on the light, standing right under the bulb; he looks very old now even though he's only sixteen. 'Rico, Danny...'

'What, Pitbull?'

'Don't put him in with her, don't put him in the bed next to her, OK?'

'Don't worry, man. And don't drink everything up without us.'

He smiles, then he goes down the stairs. We close the door. We drag the guy down the hall into the bedroom and put him in bed next to his old lady. She's still snoring; now she rolls around a bit and puts a hand on his leg. The guy's starting to come round and he garbles something into the mattress. She curls up and presses against him.

He's started bleeding again and the sheet turns red underneath his head. 'Rico...'

'It's just his nose, Danny, it'll stop on its own.' There's a blanket at the bottom of the bed and we cover them up. We go in the bathroom, rinse out the tub, and Rico grabs the bloody towel and throws it on the bed. I take a chair leg out of the other room, rub the bloody towel on it a bit and throw it in the hall, right outside the bedroom. Rico nods. 'Let's go, Danny.' We slam the door and run down the stairs. We run across the yard, over to Pitbull's cellar. On the way down we hear music, techno.

'You took your time!' Walter plonks a bottle of whiskey on the table and Pitbull gets glasses out of the old cupboard. Walter's bought Full House; the label shows a group of men playing cards.

'What's this crap, Walter?'

'What?' He unscrews the top and sniffs at the bottle. 'Rico said a nice bottle, and this is a nice bottle. Full House isn't bad, right, Rico?'

'Sure, it's the best.' Rico grins and winks at me.

We sit down around the table and Pitbull fills the glasses. 'To us.'

'To you,' we say, and Pitbull smiles. We drink. Mark grabs a big bag of crisps, squeezes until it pops open at one end and chucks it on the table. We drink another round.

'Here's to Paul,' Rico says.

'To Paul,' we say. We drink another.

'Your lady,' says Pitbull, 'tell us about your lottery girl, pipsqueak. Is she really fit?'

'Yeah!' Walter almost yells. 'I told you! We'd make a really good couple, I'm gonna get her, I swear!'

## II. Competition

We're drinking at the old lady's place. Pitbull hasn't come this time, he said he's never going in the building again 'cause if he hears those drinkers yelling and the arsehole lets loose again, he'll go down and finish him off.

We've brought Paul along; he's got the latest *Praline* and he's flicking through it. The old lady doesn't notice there's a new boy with us, she doesn't know our names properly even though we're always telling her. We've fetched up some coal and done some shopping and kept half the change. She wants to give us a tenner for the coal as well. Rico comes out of the money room. He looks over at the old lady drinking in her armchair, and then he sits back down with us. Sometimes the old lady's all quiet and listens to us, but I don't think she gets much. 'We can't take as much today,' Rico whispers. 'There's hardly any left.'

'We've got something already anyway,' I whisper, patting my shirt pocket with the money in it.

Paul looks at us over the top of his magazine. 'Never overdo it, or people start to notice.'

'Smart arse,' says Mark.

'He's right, though,' says Walter. 'It's like with women, if you go after too many at once it all goes wrong.'

'Oh, yes,' the old lady laughs, 'with the girls, you've got to take them out dancing, boys... oh dearie me!' She jumps up, falls back into her seat and tries again. 'The grog, my grog's burning.' There's a stench of booze coming from the kitchen; the stuff must be boiling over. The old lady gets up and hobbles out. We hear her rummaging around the kitchen.

Mark picks up the apple korn and drinks out of the bottle. 'Shall we take this with us later, for the cellar?'

'No,' says Walter. 'Not her booze, we said we wouldn't.' We hear the old lady laughing in the kitchen. She comes back in carrying a big mug that steams up her glasses. She's still laughing and she sits down with her big mug in her armchair. She arranges the blanket over her legs. The grog spills over her hand onto the blanket but that doesn't bother her. We raise our glasses and drink. Walter tops up his cup, the apple korn shines golden in the bottle and he holds it up to his eyes and moves it to and fro.

'So how's it going with your lottery girl in the Black Hole?' I can see his eyes all blurred through the glass of the bottle and the apple korn.

'Shit!' He slams the bottle down on the table and we

grin. 'There's some guy there now, some old bloke from round that way, every Wednesday, a system player, ten slips, a hundred and twenty rows of numbers, she chats to him every Wednesday, he thinks he's better than the rest of us with his ten lottery slips!'

The doorbell rings. We exchange glances. Mark jumps up and runs to the unit with the radio on it. The doorbell gets drowned out 'cause Mark turns the music up, a brass band with accordion. The oompah channel's on, the old lady likes all that. She puts her grog down and claps her hands. 'You've put music on!' she shouts. She sways her head and her legs twitch under the blanket.

Rico walks slowly across the room and looks out in the hall. 'Light's on,' he says. 'They're up here already.'

'It'll be Jochen,' Mark whispers next to me, 'It bet it's her stupid Jochen.'

'It can't be,' I say. 'He's not coming 'til next week, she said.'

'She doesn't even know what time it is.'

Someone beats a fist against the door and even the trumpets and the accordion can't drown it out. 'The cops,' Paul whispers, pressing the *Praline* to his chest. 'I bet it's the cops.'

'Jesus, shut it!'

'What's that, what's that noise?' The old lady gets restless, looks around the room, and I see her half-blind eyes moving behind her dark lenses.

'It's on the radio,' I say, 'because of the weather.'

'Winter,' the old lady says, 'I don't like the winter.'

Someone hammers on the door again and I cough loudly, and Walter and Paul join in to drown out the noise.

'Bad cold,' says the old lady. She picks up her grog and slurps up half the cup.

Mark and Rico run out to the hallway and gesture for

me to go with them. I go after them, and Walter gets up too. 'You stay here,' I say. 'Make sure she doesn't come out.' Walter nods and pulls the bottle of apple korn over to where he's sitting.

'Where are you off to?' the old lady yells. 'Don't go yet, stay a bit longer!'

'We're still here,' Walter says behind me. 'They're just going for a smoke. We don't smoke inside, here.'

'No,' says the old lady, and now she laughs again, 'not under my roof, you don't! I have my rules, I make sure of them!'

Mark and Rico stand by the door and take turns looking through the spyhole. 'Who is it, then?' I push Mark aside and press my eye to the peephole. There are three guys with big heads outside, looking at the door. One of the heads is shaven, and I spot scars on his scalp. The guy's wearing a green bomber jacket with steel toe-caps and an evil look. The others are both in trainers. They don't look as dangerous and can't manage the evil look, even though they're trying.

'What d'you think, Danny?'

'Never seen 'em before.'

'Maybe some of Engel's people,' Mark whispers.

'Nah, I'd know them. But the skinhead, he might be from the old roller rink...'

'That's what I thought,' says Rico.

'Fuck,' Mark whispers.

The skins in the next neighbourhood meet up outside the old roller rink. They say some of the Reudnitz Right hang out there as well, RR, their tag's on every third building in Reudnitz and other parts of Leipzig East and even Engel doesn't bother them, even though Engel's a real force to be reckoned with, he knows people from the red-light district. Pitbull knows a few of the skins but

Pitbull's not here. They ring and bang on the door at the same time and shout: 'Open up, Mrs Böhme, it's only us, Mrs Böhme!'

'I've had enough of this,' Rico says. 'I'm gonna have a word with 'em.' I look around the hallway; there's a broom in the back corner and a big metal-tipped umbrella hanging on the coat rack. Rico opens one of the hatches in the door and looks out through the mesh. 'Oi oi, Sieg heil, what's the problem?' The skins leap back, and for just a moment it looks like they're Sieg heiling.

'Shit, who are you, what're you doing here? Open the door, will you!'

I plant myself next to Rico, and Mark opens the other window in the door. 'Buzz off!' he says, and I can see his legs are trembling a little bit, but that's normal, it's the same with me before the dance starts, every time.

'This place is taken,' Rico says. 'It's not your territory, she's our old lady.'

'Listen, you,' says the skin, tapping the mesh in front of Rico's face, 'don't act the hard man! We've been onto this one for a good while now, see, so you pack your bags and get going!'

Rico opens the door and goes out to the competition. Mark and I stand behand Rico on the threshold. He builds himself up in front of the skin, a hand's width between their two faces. 'So you want stress, do you?' Rico says quietly, and we hear the oompah music all the way from the back room. 'So you're gonna spoil our night, are you, bonehead? I'll break your nose for you if you want, right now.' He lowers his forehead and touches it between the guy's eyes, gently. That's Engel's method, and Rico learned a whole lot from Engel when he only just lost to him. The skin takes a step back. The other two just stand there and look at us; I've got my eye on the one on the left, 'cause I've seen Mark's watching the other one.

'Shit,' says the skin, 'you don't know who I am, do you? You know Kehlmann? If I let him know, you'll have twenty men running you down, you won't know what's hit you. And you too, you fuckwits!' He nods at Mark and me.

'OK,' says Rico, and raises his left hand slightly, he's got a great left hand, I've seen it in action a few times now, in the ring and on the streets. 'Alright.' He walks back a few steps and turns around to us. The guy could get him in the kidneys, but he doesn't.

'There you go, told you,' says the skin. 'And now fuck off.'

Then it all goes quickly: Rico turns back round, jumps the guy, grips him by the neck with his right hand, slams him against the wall and gives him his left hook. I try to be quick too and grab my man by the shoulders and ram my knee in his belly, but he's already a way away from me and all I get is his hip. The stairwell light goes off. A fist hits my ribs, below the shoulder, and I hear the boom all the way up to my head. *Muss i denn, muss i denn!* The music wafts all the way out to the stairs, I'm scared the guy's got a knife and I lash out at the darkness and hit something soft, probably his throat by the way he screams, and I hear him going down. Someone turns the light back on, it's Mark's back, the guy's pressing Mark against the wall and punching him in the face. *Muss i denn...* Mark manages to turn away and the fist rams the wall. He's taken a few punches, I can tell by the red marks on his face. Rico's still got the skin by the throat and I jump up to Mark's one and knock him to the ground from behind. Mark is straight on him and punches him with both hands in the chest and the head, almost in time to the music. *Zur Städtele hinaus...* Rico's skin fights back, he's the one with the evil look; he yells something and slams his right fist against the back of Rico's head, but Rico just sucks it up and plants his left hook in the guy's side. He goes down and shuts up. Got him in the liver. We move back to the doorway as the guys get slowly to their feet and back off towards the stairs. The skin's clutching his side, spit running down his chin, but he still starts up again. 'I'm telling Kehlmann. We'll get you!'

'Jesus, I can't believe it!' Rico jumps on him again and slams his left fist right in his face. The skin stumbles back and goes flying down the stairs, but just a few steps 'cause the other two grab him. They pull him back up; his nose is bleeding. 'Don't you get it?' Rico yells. 'If anyone else comes, your Kehlmann or whatever, and if anymore of your lot turn up, I'll finish you off, I'll break your fucking face, you get it? And I know enough people round here!' He moves towards them but then stops, 'cause they turn around and run for it.

'Jesus, are you crazy, what's all the noise, the old lady's pissing her pants!' Walter's in the doorway. 'And she doesn't want to listen to music anymore.'

'You missed it all as usual, Little Walter.' Mark sits down on the stairs. He's got a red mark under his left eye and one on his forehead.

'But you told me to stay inside and watch out for the old lady. I'd have joined in, you know that!'

'We know, we know,' I say. 'It's fine, Walter, someone had to keep an eye on her, that's important too.'

'Yeah, like I said. Who were they?'

'Just a couple of skins,' says Rico. 'You go back inside, we'll be right there. You can fill our glasses.'

'Right, Rico.' Walter turns around and walks down the hall.

Rico and I sit down next to Mark on the stairs. 'Everything OK?'

'Yeah,' he says, 'Nothing I'd shit my pants over. The bastard got lucky, that's all.' He runs his hand over the red swelling underneath his eye.

'Yeah,' I say, 'just beginner's luck. You'd have dealt with him without me.'

'I would've, yeah,' says Mark. He gets out his cigarettes and gives us one each.

'Hey, Rico,' I say, 'd'you think the guy was serious? About the skins, I mean.' The light goes out and I watch the red tip of his cigarette.

'You scared, Danny?'

'Nah, just asking.'

'Maybe Pitbull knows them,' Mark says. He switches the light back on and presses his eye to the cold wood of the bannister. 'Maybe he can sort something out. He used to hang out at the roller rink, right?'

'Jesus, you two. Give it a rest! You think I'm scared of those fuckwits? We wiped the floor with them. Did we finish them off?'

'We did,' I say.

We put our cigarettes out on the stairs and throw them down through the bannisters. We go inside and lock the door. We sit down at the table and drink. The music's still on but much quieter, and the old lady's glad we're back. She rummages in a drawer and brings a few photos over to the table. One of them is of a woman holding up a little kid, and she looks beautiful and she's smiling. 'Mummy and Jochen,' it says on the back. 'My Jochen,' the old lady says. 'He's very little in this one, I can hardly see him.' She leans over the table until her glasses almost touch the picture. We pass the photos round and drink a few more glasses of apple korn. There aren't many photos, and most of them are of the old lady back when she was young, and Jochen. I get up and go to the window; the street's empty.

The old lady says something and laughs, then she puts the photos away again.

'We'd best be off now, Mrs Böhme.'

She hobbles to the door.

We like going to the old lady's, it's better than at home or out on the street, no parents, no cops. We've turned off the bell 'cause all sorts of competition comes over, not just the skins. Even two of Engel's people came once, and we couldn't just beat them up. We gave them forty of the old lady's money to bugger off. Friedrich's people tried it on a few days ago, even got into the flat. Since Maik's been gone, Friedrich's been the head of their little gang, but they're all wimps, we could smash them back when we were kids. We had to drag them out and down the stairs and give them a bit of a slapping in the backyard so the old lady didn't notice. Half the neighbourhood's going to the old lady and trying it on, but she's our old lady and it's our coal and our money, and we look after her and don't let anyone in.

## III. Excursions

We're drinking in the cellar; only Pitbull's outside in the corridor, puking his guts out. 'Listen to him!' Mark yells, laughing.

'Barf, barf, barf, barf,' we chant, and Pitbull retches and hollers everything out. He mixed apple korn and brandy in a litre jug, but it wasn't a good idea. There's a few bottles left on the table and between them a screwed up tenner and a few coins: what's left of the money we got at the old lady's.

Walter's lying on the sofa, pressing a bottle of vodka to his chest with both hands. We've been drinking all evening and he's pretty far gone. 'I can't believe it's so shit with that girl, it's so shit.' He unscrews the lid of the bottle and the vodka spills on his jumper.

I get up and go over. 'Give it here, will you?' I take the bottle off him, drink some and then pour some in his mouth. He coughs, and it sounds like he's about to vomit. 'Jesus, go out to Pitbull!'

'Are you crazy, you shithead!' He jumps up, wipes his mouth, walks a few steps and lies back down again.

I sit down on the edge of his sofa and wedge the bottle between the cushions by his head. 'So what happened?'

'Nothing, nothing happened, Danny.' He closes his eyes and rubs his forehead against the bottle.

Mark and Rico come over. 'Did you fuck her at last?'

'You shut your fucking mouth!' The bottle smashes against the wall, vodka and shards splashing all the way over to us.

'Are you fucking crazy, you dirty bastard!' Mark grabs him by the collar and lifts him up. Rico just grins and picks up his cigarette. He wants to put it in his mouth but he drops it again.

'Leave it.' I push Mark away.

'Jesus, it's true, he's mental!'

Rico goes to the table and gets a full bottle of apple korn. 'Alright, take it easy,' he says, and sits down. He opens up the bottle, takes a swig and passes it to Walter. 'Now tell us all about it, Little Walter.'

'Don't call me that.' He pushes Rico's arm aside.

'So she messed you about?'

'Yeah, she did!' He's shouting again. 'That stupid slut, stupid bloody West German slut.'

'Don't get wound up,' says Mark. 'That's just women for you, they mess you about. You ask Paul.' He turns around, but Paul's been gone for half an hour. He has to go home at eleven or his mother locks him in the next day. He doesn't stand a chance with the girls round here – they don't go wild until after eleven.

'I thought it was going alright,' I say.

'It was going alright.' He rolls over on the sofa.

Pitbull comes back in. We turn around to him. He's pretty white in the face, with water running down his chin. 'All a bit too much,' he says.

I pick up a mini bottle of clear korn off the table and open it up. 'Come here,' I say, 'so you smell better!' He comes over slowly; I take a swig and hand him the bottle. He takes out a tissue, pours some of the liquid on it and wipes his mouth with it, then he takes a glug, gargles and stumbles against the wall.

'Why aren't you listening?' Walter yells. 'You never listen to me properly!' His head sinks onto the arm rest. 'I love her so much.' He's totally smitten and nothing embarrasses him now.

'Shit,' Rico whispers, 'he's making a complete tosser of himself over that girl.'

'I heard that,' Walter leaps up, 'I heard what you said, you stupid bloody show-off. So what, I don't care if I look like a tosser!' He grabs the apple korn out of Rico's hand and downs half the bottle, then throws himself back on the sofa and presses his face into the grubby cushions.

'Hey, no taking the piss,' I say. 'We all stick together. And now tell us what happened!' And he tells us. And we listen, and when we can't help laughing we turn away, and only Pitbull, sitting on the floor by the wall, breathes really loudly and belches a few times, but that doesn't bother Walter.

'... and then I took her out for a walk. To Stünz, to the park, there's this new café there. No, not the caff with the drinkers, a nice place right by the lake. And she held my hand, she took my hand, jeez, her skin was so soft.' He holds the bottle of apple korn up to his face. 'But that was it. Jesus, she drove me so crazy before, her hand and all that. She says I'm too young, it won't work...'

'How old is she?'

'Twenty-eight, she says. 'But I'll be sixteen soon. I wanted to hot-wire a car for her to take her out to eat, you know, but nah, she doesn't like that kind of thing.'

'Let me give you a tip,' says Rico. 'You need to drink her right out of your head!'

'But I love her so much.' Walter looks through the bottle.

I see Pitbull getting up and lurching over to the hifi on the shelves. 'Drink her out of you,' he yells. 'Drink her right out!' He fumbles around with the hifi. It takes a while and then he manages, and the bass kicks in, and then a beeping and screeching and in between a bit of a tune, acid techno.

Mark turns the light off. 'Fire 'er up!' he shouts. And Pitbull fires her up. He turns the volume all the way, then he turns on the strobe. He saved up for it for ages and only bought it last week from the electronics Vietcong, when we gave him money from the old lady. Pitbull wants to make his cellar into a proper techno club, but that's not gonna work 'cause it's where he lives.

I see Walter getting up and lurching around the cellar, no, he's dancing. He's cradling a bottle like it's his lottery girl, and now Mark gets up too and moves in the flashes of the stroboscope, I see his arms jerking and his grin, his arms and his grin, I bet he's taken something again. Then Rico dances too, moving like a boxer, bobbing and weaving round the cellar and moving his shoulders and arms, left – left – right, and he ducks and feints, and in the flashing of the strobe he's faster than Oscar de la Hoya, and even that fucking Gentleman Henry Maske wouldn't stand a chance. He dreams of going professional, but we know it won't work out, and he knows it too. He's pretty good in the ring but there's better than him, and apart from that he drinks and he never says no, but on the street, on the street he's the greatest. I'm dancing now as well, and Pitbull staggers around between us, raises his arms with his eyes closed.

Someone turns on the light. Pitbull's father's standing in the doorway. He's only wearing a white vest and trousers and I can see the tattoo on his shoulder, the same one my father had, Chemie Leipzig and above it the club's emblem, the curly C with the green whistle. Pitbull's old man might support the right club but he's still an arsehole. He goes to the shelves and pulls out the hifi plug. 'Jesus, Stefan, are you mad, boy, we can hear this rubbish all over the building!' He's had a skinful, I can tell by his eyes.

Pitbull leans against the wall. 'Piss off, arsehole!'

'Don't you talk to me like that, boy, don't you... Come upstairs now, or... Hey, I'm telling you!'

'Or what, Dad? Or what? That's over, Dad!' Pitbull walks towards him but he can hardly stay upright.

The old man sees that Pitbull's drunker than he is and grabs him by the collar. 'You're coming upstairs right now! And you lot can bugger off, go home, just go home, will you?'

I plant myself in front of him, Rico next to me, and Mark comes towards him as well. The old man stinks of booze. He takes a few steps back and grabs Pitbull's arm. 'Come upstairs with me, Stefan.'

'Let go of him,' I say. I reach for Pitbull's shoulder and pull him back to us.

'He's my son,' the old man says, 'and I'm taking him with me. Look at the state of you boys!' He's talking like he's got a perfectly clear head but I can see his face working and his mouth twitching. 'The boy's had enough. Be sensible, you're his mates, aren't you?'

'Pitbull's staying here,' I say, and I put my arm around Pitbull's shoulder. He really has had about enough, and he hangs onto me, and I hold him tight.

'No,' says the old man. 'Please...'

'Go on, bugger off!' Mark claps his hands in front of the man's face. 'Buzz off! Go upstairs and beat your wife!'

Pitbull's dad's face twitches like mad. It's Rico's turn now. He taps him on the shoulder, all gentle, and says: 'By the way, you can forget doing that to Pitbull's mum from now on! I hear our Pitbull's been giving you what you deserve, and you know what for... Dad!'

Pitbull's old man is quiet now, staring at the wall and looking pretty done in. He turns around and leaves. I hear his slippers dragging along the cellar floor.

'Right, Pitbull,' I say, 'we gave your old man what for, eh?'

'Yeah,' says Pitbull, still holding onto me, and I take him to the sofa. 'Poor Dad,' he whispers as he lies down, but I pretend not to hear. Mark switches off the strobe. We sit down next to Pitbull and smoke.

'Where's Walter gone?' asks Rico.

'Must have gone for a wazz,' Mark says, 'or a puke. He was here a minute ago.'

Pitbull gets up and goes outside, slowly. He does his best not to sway. 'I'll go and have a look.' We hear him walking around the cellar, then there's a crash. He's holding a bottle of fizzy water when he comes back in. 'From the neighbours,' he says. 'From their cellar.' He drinks a swig and tips the rest over his head.

'What about Walter?'

'He's not outside.'

'He must have gone, Danny,' Rico says. 'He was so pissed, he'll be making trouble, he'll be getting in the shit, I bet!'

'Me too,' I say. 'I know where he is.'

'He tell you where he's going, or what?'

'Nah, Danny can see the future, you know that.' Mark laughs.

'He's been mooning over that stupid cow for days,' I say. 'That's where he'll be, at the newsagents.'

'But it's closed now.'

'Right,' I say, 'exactly.'

Rico stands up. 'You sure, Danny?'

'Pretty much.'

'Then we'd better get over there, he'll get in trouble otherwise, he's so pissed they'll pick him up right off.' He puts on his jacket and sticks a bottle of apple korn in the inside pocket. We've been drinking a lot of apple korn since the old lady gave us a taste for it.

'A tenner,' says Pitbull, 'a tenner, Danny, or I'm not coming.'

'Are you shitting me?'

'Nah, Danny, I mean a bet. I don't think he'll be there, he could be anywhere, see, bet you a tenner, Danny.'

'OK, a tenner.' We shake on it.

Rico stands next to us and chops our hands apart with the side of his hand. 'The bet's on,' he says, and then we head out. Pitbull wants to take his junior axe but Rico says he won't need it. Pitbull runs his hand over the sheath and puts it back in the cupboard. Then he does a quick search of the sofa cushions to make sure there isn't a lit fag end on there, 'cause the last sofa got half-burnt that way. It only smouldered away but the fire brigade came anyway 'cause the whole building filled up with smoke.

We wait by the back door, listening to Pitbull putting

the three padlocks on his cellar door. We take the shortcut across the backyards. We pass the old lady's house. All the windows are dark and the drinkers are quiet, probably beaten each other into a stupor. We climb over dustbins and crawl through gaps in fences. Then we're back on the street, heading for the trade fair where the newsagents is. Most of the wing mirrors on the parked cars are bent or have come off entirely. Walter's left a trail. 'Nice work,' says Rico. We stop in front of a nice blue Golf that's totally fucked: the front and side windows kicked in, and the roof and the bonnet look like someone's been jumping on them. 'Better cross over,' Rico says. 'If the cops come they'll say it was us, they know us too well.' We cross over to the opposite pavement.

'Fuck the po-lice,' Mark shouts so loud that it echoes along the road. 'I haven't beaten anyone up for ages.'

'Shut up and cross over.' Mark grins, then comes over to join us.

The street's pretty dark 'cause most of the streetlamps are broken. That wasn't Walter though. Flashing blue lights. The cops are coming. We jump into a doorway, the door's open, and we watch the cops through the window from inside. 'Hope they don't see us,' says Mark.

'But it wasn't us,' Pitbull says.

'You gotta prove that to them first, though.' Rico takes the bottle of apple korn out of his pocket and hands it round. A cop car stops by the fucked up Golf, two uniforms get out, talk into their radios and write something on little pads of paper. They walk along the road; Walter probably dinged a couple more cars.

'Maybe they've already got him in the back of the van,' I say.

Rico stands on tiptoe. 'Can't see anything. No, don't think so.' The cops get back in and drive slowly down the road.

'I think I knew one of them,' Mark says. 'Southeast Copshop.'

'You must have beaten him up one time,' says Rico. 'Right, you cop-killer?' We laugh. Rico passes the bottle round again, then he opens the door carefully and looks outside. 'We can go,' he says, 'they've pissed off.'

We stick close together and keep going towards the trade fair. Rico passes the bottle around as we walk, and even Pitbull drinks some, slowly getting back on track. 'If the cops get him,' he says, 'I mean, before he gets there, I mean, if he even wanted to go there, the tenner's mine.'

'Hey, don't be an arsehole,' I stop and dig my elbow in his side. 'That's bad luck, don't say that kind of shit, you know how crap it is down the station!'

'Don't touch me, Danny!' Pitbull nudges me back. 'Little Walter'd be proud if they took him down the station, you know he would, he's just as stupid as us!'

'Shut it!' I tug at his jacket and shove him up against a wall. But he's right, we are proud if we end up down the station. We even argue about who's been put away more often and who's had the most warnings, but we don't stand a chance against Rico and old Fred.

'Jesus, get it together, you two!' Rico yells, and Mark goes between us. 'Forget that shit, this is about Walter!'

'Yeah,' I say, 'yeah,' says Pitbull, and we shake hands. Rico hands us the bottle and we empty it. Pitbull smashes it against the wall. 'Riot!' he yells. We laugh. We turn our heads, we look at the sky, we look at the night, we're alone and we're not scared of nothing. We light one up and then we go on walking.

'There he is, over there!'

'The Black Hole,' Pitbull whispers, and we go quiet, and our footsteps echo back off the buildings. There are only a few lights in the windows, some of them red, and we look at each other and grin, 'cause loads of whores live in the Black Hole and work from their flats. Walter's newsagent's is in a little lean-to on the side of a big block that looks pretty decrepit and half empty, like almost all the buildings round this way. We throw our cigarettes away and inch over to the shop window. 'Looks normal,' Pitbull whispers, and tries the door. 'I told you, he's not here.'

'The back door,' I say. We walk around the shop. But the back door looks closed too. I give it a shove – it's not locked, and now I spot the broken lock and the splintered wood on the door frame. 'Come on!' I say. I spark up my lighter and walk into the shop, the others close behind me. My foot hits something and I bend down; it's a bottle of brandy, a quarter full. I hand it to Rico.

'From the cellar,' he says. 'Goldkrone.' He unscrews the cap and takes a slug.

'Give it here,' Mark whispers beside me. We share what's left. Goldkrone's way better than Goldblatt, the kind the old lady drinks. Then there's Goldene Aue, but they only make good korn. Ahead of us is another door, that one open too, and behind it I can see the shop window. I flick off my lighter; there's a streetlamp on outside.

Behind the door come a couple of steps and I stumble; Pitbull grabs me by the jacket. 'Jeez, keep the noise down!' He's angry 'cause he owes me a tenner now.

There's a sound. Mark clicks on his lighter. 'Leave it off,' Rico whispers. 'They'll see us from outside.' We step carefully across the shop floor. Walter's flat out on the counter. He's not moving and it looks like he's asleep, but he's whimpering. He's crossed his arms over his chest and there's a whole lot of lottery slips on top of him and beside him, plus a couple stuck to his wet face.

'Jesus, Walter,' I whisper. 'Get up!'

'He's past caring.' We stand around him in a circle. Mark takes out a tissue and wipes the lottery slips off his face. He smiles underneath the slips.

'This is where I shagged her,' he whispers. 'She's so gorgeous, Danny.'

'Sure,' I say. 'Course she is.'

'Where is she, where is she now?' He wriggles onto his side and shuts up. I take off my jacket to cover him.

I turn back to the others; they're combing the place. 'Look, scratch cards!' Mark calls. He plunges both hands into a see-through plastic box and throws the loose cards up in the air like confetti. Pitbull stuffs his pockets full of chocolate bars from a shelf next to the till.

The till's open but Rico's swearing at it. 'Nothing in there, not a penny, that stingy bitch!'

I go over to him. 'Hey, let's just grab Walter and get out of here. If the cops come it'll be breaking and entering.'

'Scared, are you, Danny?' Pitbull's leaning against the counter eating a Kinder egg.

'I told you before to keep your trap shut!' I slap the little plastic toy out of his hand.

'Hey, you wanker, what was that for?' He bends down and picks it up again. 'It's like a bear-cat, girls are really into them!'

'Jeez, dial it down a bit,' Rico puts his hands on our shoulders. 'You're right, Danny, we'd better get out of here.'

''Cause of Walter,' I say, 'I just wanna go 'cause of Walter, he's done in, he needs to get home.'

'It's shit here anyway,' says Mark, stuffing scratch cards into his pockets. 'Not even any fags.'

'Nah, she does have fags.' Rico points at a steel cabinet mounted on the wall above the till. 'But we'd need a crowbar or something.'

'A car and a chain would do it,' Pitbull says with a grin, and I grin too, and even Rico raises a bit of a smile. We're thinking of that number with Fred a few months back when we ripped a cigarette machine out of a brick wall using his car. Fred was so wasted he didn't stop, and the vending machine was dangling off the back of the car for miles and making a hell of a noise and banging into all these parked cars until the cops came and we had to run for it. Only Fred stayed in the car, like he always does.

'Look, *Praline*, *Das neue Wochenend* and all the girly mags.' Mark's at the magazine rack, rummaging through it.

'She could at least have some proper porn,' says Pitbull. 'I'll take a couple anyway, for Paul, you know, not for me, just for Paul.'

'Right,' says Rico, planting himself in front of Walter, who's still all quiet underneath my jacket. 'Let's get going.'

'Wait, wait a sec!' Mark's kneeling on the floor collecting up the scratch cards. 'We can make a packet on these!' We squat down next to him and stuff our pockets. 'Twenty-thousand top winnings,' Mark says. 'Imagine winning twenty grand! Come on, Rico, you take a couple, scratch something useful for once!' We laugh and head over to Walter, I take back my jacket and we lift him off the counter.

'No!' He screams and kicks his legs. 'No, don't take me away! I love her, you bastards!' He roars like some kind of animal, and I put my hand over his mouth. He tries to bite me, I take my hand off him, he roars again and Rico punches him on the chin, just a gentle one but in exactly the right spot, 'cause he goes quiet instantly. We drag him out behind the shop and then out onto the street.

'Wait, wait a sec,' says Pitbull, and we stop. 'We can't

get him all the way home like this. He might be small but he's heavy.'

'Run out of strength, have you?' Rico says. 'I'll carry him on my own, just say the word.'

'What about a car?' Mark says. 'There's a few over there.'

'Are you mental?' I say. 'Not today, not now. Remember the cops back there.'

'Be right back.' Mark heads back into the yard.

'No cars,' I call after him. 'You hear me, no cars!'

'Come on, let him, if he wants to get one.' Rico lays Walter down gently by the kerb. 'It'll get us home quicker, won't it?'

'Or maybe not,' says Pitbull.

But Mark's not getting a car. He comes back out from the yard pulling a little metal handcart. 'Not bad, eh?'

'Where'd you get that from so quick?'

'Found it,' he says with a grin. We pat him on the back, pleased, only Rico looking over at the parked cars. We manoeuvre Walter onto the cart and Mark takes the drawbar and pulls. Walter's legs drag along the pavement but that doesn't bother him.

'We should've got a car,' Rico says. 'Would've been way easier. And faster.'

'What, faster than this?' Mark yells, and then he breaks into a run with the cart. It moves pretty quickly, Walter's legs bouncing off the paving stones.

We run alongside the cart. 'Come on, put your foot down!' Mark runs faster and faster, and as he goes into a corner the cart jumps out of his hands, swings onto the road, tips over, and Walter rolls all the way to the strip in the middle. We laugh. We lean against the wall of a house, laughing. Walter's bedded down on the road, one arm under his head. Mark gives us all a cigarette and then we drag Walter off the road and back onto the handcart. We wheel him home.

The front door is open and we lug him up the stairs. He lives on the fourth floor; we swear all the way up, but only quietly so we don't wake the neighbours. We search his pockets but we can't find his keys. Rico rings the doorbell three times until we hear his parents inside, then we lean Walter's back against the door and run down the stairs. We wheel the cart into the middle of the crossroads and walk home. We walk together 'cause our roads aren't far apart.

'What about the money?' Mark says. 'What'll you do with the money?'

'What money?'

'If you win something, I mean. We've got a couple of hundred scratch cards, we must have good chances...'

'I'll get my cellar converted,' Pitbull says. 'And a garden, for new dogs...'

'A boxing ring. My own ring. Punching bag and that. Just for me. Or a car, a legit one.'

'You can't drive until you're eighteen.'

'So? I'll get one anyway.'

'Twenty grand and I'm out of here, I swear...'

'It's all bollocks, no one ever wins. It's a scam, just a scam.'

'Hey Rico, what d'you reckon, when shall we go and see the old lady again?'

'We only just went there yesterday. Next week, maybe next week.'

We're at the junction of Oststrasse and Martinstrasse. Rico holds out his hand and we put our hands on top of it.

'See you in the cellar tomorrow?'

'See you in the cellar tomorrow.'

We're drinking at the old lady's place, Mark, Paul, Rico and me. It's Friday afternoon and we're bunking off school 'cause the holidays start in a few days anyway. Walter didn't come along. He's been hanging out with the crazy carjackers from Mühlenviertel. All they do is hotwire cars, every day, every night, and they don't care about anything else.

'We always used to go dancing,' the old lady says, showing us the photos she's shown us a few times before. 'My Horst,' she says, and she runs a hand over the photos on the table. 'My Horst must be here somewhere.' We give her the photo of their wedding, a young man and a young woman in white, and she holds it up close to her eyes.

'Same name as your old man, Danny,' Mark whispers.

The old lady takes off her glasses and puts them on the table. Her left eye is dark and clouded over; it looks like painted glass. 'Haven't seen him for a long while now. Haven't visited him for a long time now.' She gropes around the table again and we hand her her glass. She's drinking brandy and water 'cause she only drinks after four, really, she told us. 'The taxi's so expensive, see, I don't have much, boys, you know that.'

'Taxis are bloody expensive,' Rico says, and we nod. Paul's flicking through his *Praline*; he shows us the Girl of the Week. The old lady looks as well but there's no way she can see anything, even though the Girl of the Week's got huge breasts and she's holding them in her hands to turn us on.

'The tree, though,' the old lady says, wobbling her head. Seems like she really does only drink after four, 'cause she's already pretty far gone. 'He's got a lovely tree, though.'

'What tree's that?'

The old lady gets up and goes to the shelving unit. She uses her stick even though it's only a few steps. She opens a drawer and rummages around with both hands. She leans down to see something, her head almost inside the drawer. She tugs something out, a golden picture frame, and brings it over to the table. In the frame is a photo of a tall tree, an oak or something, and a bit beside the tree is a gravestone, its inscription not really legible. Mark leans forward and his shot glass tips over, but it's empty. The old lady's head wobbles to and fro, touching Mark's shoulder. 'That's where I laid him to rest. Picked everything out myself.'

'Where is it?' Rico asks. The old lady goes to grab the frame but Rico takes it and looks at the picture.

'A long way away,' the old lady says. 'I can't go there anymore. Out in the North Cemetery, that's where he is.'

Rico holds the picture up. 'I'll drive you if you want. I've got a car now, remember I told you?'

I look at him, tapping my forehead. 'Are you mental?' I whisper.

'Would you?' the old lady says, trembling so hard the shot glass she's holding dances on the table. 'That'd be nice.'

Mark stands up next to Rico. 'Right, Mrs Böhme, we'll drive you there now! Then you can see your Horst again. And Rico's got a car, brand new, a lovely new model!' Mark puts his arm around Rico's shoulder; they both look at me, showing their teeth as they grin.

'But I haven't got anything to wear,' the old lady shouts. She's only wearing her grey nightshirt, with a blanket around her shoulders.

'That doesn't matter,' Rico says. 'Just put your good coat on over the top, that'll do.'

'Yes,' says the old lady, 'yes, that's what I'll do,' and she gets up and hobbles into the bedroom, then we hear her opening and closing cupboards in the kitchen.

I fill my glass from the bottle of brandy. 'Jeez, Rico,' I say. 'You really want to get a car? It's only lunchtime.'

'Easy now,' says Mark. 'Let the professionals get on with it.'

'Shut it, you!' I knock back my brandy and fill the glass again. 'It takes you half an hour to crack a car door!'

'Hey, Danny,' Rico says, 'we can go without you if you don't want to come.'

'Don't take the piss!' I knock back my brandy and fill the glass again. 'I never said I wasn't coming.'

'Nice one, Danny, that's more like it!' Mark pats me on the shoulder and then he and Rico go to the door. The old lady meets them halfway. She's got her coat on already and she's wearing a little red hat.

'Ready in a sec, Mrs Böhme,' Rico says. 'I'm just fetching my car. Five minutes, Mrs Böhme.'

I hear them out in the hall, then at the front door, and then they walk down the stairs.

'I'm so excited!' The old lady picks up the bottle and fills her glass to the brim. 'You have a drink as well, boys, it's cold out.'

'It's not that cold, Mrs Böhme,' I say, pushing the bottle over to Paul. 'Alright, Paul?'

'Alright,' he says, and he rolls up his *Praline* into a tube and looks down it at me.

'Come on,' I say, 'have another.'

'Alright,' says Paul, pouring so much brandy in his glass it overflows. He lifts it carefully and drinks it.

'Cheers,' I say.

'Yes, cheers.' The old lady's sat down in her seat, clutching her stick with both hands. I get up.

'Hey, Paul, wanna come with us to the graveyard?'

'Alright, why not?' He looks at me through his telescope.

I go out to the balcony for a smoke. The backyard is full of shadows 'cause the sun's on the other side of the building. I lean over the edge and look down at the drinkers' balcony, empties everywhere. I throw my half-smoked cigarette between the bottles and light up a new one. The doorbell sounds quietly from inside. Someone runs down the hall, must be Paul. I take a few more drags and then squash the cigarette in my fist before I throw it away. The heat hurts my skin a bit and I spread my hand along the cold edge of the balcony. Then I go back in. Rico's coming out of the kitchen door. 'There you are!'

'Hey, Rico, if they pick us up, I mean I don't care about the cops and that, but the old lady, 'cause of the old lady I mean...'

'Jesus, Danny, stop saying they'll pick us up...' He comes up close to me and puts his hand on the back of my head. 'If we're fast enough no one'll notice, we'll just put the car back where we got it from, you know the score, it's easy, and the cops...'

'That's not what I meant. You know me, I'm not bothered about the cops.'

'Course, Danny, I know that. We're the greatest.' He laughs, and it makes me laugh too; he puts his arm around my shoulder, and we go out in the hall.

The old lady's by the door, putting glasses and a bottle of brandy in a fabric bag. Mark takes the bag off her, saying: 'That's much too heavy, Mrs Böhme, let me take it.'

'Nearly ready, Mrs Böhme,' Rico says, heading into the old lady's bedroom. I put on my jacket. Rico comes back out, pats his breast pocket and grins. 'Expenses,' he whispers.

We head down the stairs. Mark and Rico run ahead

while Paul and I link arms with the old lady. 'Nice and slow, Mrs Böhme.'

Mark and Rico have got us an Opel Kadett – they're the quickest to crack. The car's parked half on the pavement, next to a Golf Two and a Wartburg.

'Why didn't you just take that one?' I ask.

'Too conspicuous,' Mark says. 'You know that, man – a couple of streets away's always better.'

'Four doors would have been more practical,' I say, tipping the passenger seat forward. Paul gets into the back and slides over to the window.

The old lady's standing next to the car, holding onto the open door. 'What a nice car,' she says, 'what a nice car you've got.'

'Ready in a minute, Mrs Böhme,' I say, sitting down next to Paul. 'Come on, Mark, get in the back!'

'I'm driving on the way,' he says, with a pat on the car's roof.

'Forget it.' Rico walks around the car and opens the driver's door. 'You look too young, I told you before. Not today.' Mark sits down next to me and tips the front seat back again. 'Bollocks to that! Too young, I'm not too young. I look at least eighteen!' Rico's fumbling with the wires but the old lady's still on the pavement. 'Come on,' Mark yells, knocking on the window, 'in you get.'

'No rush, it's all part of the service.' Rico gets out again, walks around the car and helps the old lady into the passenger seat. 'See, better than a taxi!' He slams the door. The old lady leans her stick against the dashboard and reaches for her little red hat, which is all wonky on her head. Rico needs a few sparks to get the car started, and then we're off.

'Nice car,' Rico says, changing gears and accelerating like a real chauffeur, only without the cap.

'I bet the cops have got it on their list by now,' Paul says next to me. He usually keeps out of things like this, just watching us get into trouble, mostly 'cause of his mother but also 'cause he's more into pornos.

'Nah, they're not that fast,' I tell him.

'You can drive, Rico,' Mark yells, 'there's a green arrow!'

We're at a red light and Rico's indicating right. 'Calm down, I'm just looking to see if anything's coming.'

The old lady's very quiet; I can see her dark glasses in the rear-view mirror. She hasn't fastened her seatbelt, so I lean forward, pull the belt around her and click it into place. She doesn't move and for just a moment I think she's dead, 'cause she's old enough to die, but then I see her fingers clenching around the grip of her walking stick. I slide a bit closer to Paul and lean my forehead against Rico's headrest. 'Rico,' I whisper, 'if they see you with her in the front, it's like an alibi, you know... She's your gran, you're taking her out for tea.'

'Yeah, my gran,' Rico laughs 'cause he lives with his gran, but she's not quite as old as the old lady. Another red light, and Rico lets the car roll to a standstill. We're well out of our neighbourhood and out of the east, driving through the north part of town on the way to the graveyard. Rico knows his way around the whole city; he's often out and about at night.

'Cops!' Paul slides around on the back seat and puts his hand on the window. I press his arm back down. A few yards behind us is a cop van, and even though I can't make out the cops in the van, I get the feeling they're watching us and talking about us.

'What d'you think, Danny, turn off?'

'Don't know, Rico. Might be better.' Rico indicates, moves into the right-hand lane and turns off onto a side street. I see the cops indicate too but we're faster than them. Rico turns off again, left and then right.

I can't see the cops anymore, maybe they weren't after us at all, but Rico parks the car anyway, pretty quick and better than a driving instructor. 'Lie down!' We duck down and disappear from view.

Only the old lady's still sitting upright, wobbling her head. 'Are we there yet?'

'No, Mrs Böhme, not quite.'

We lie on the seats, listening. Paul's head bumps into my knee. 'The cops, Danny,' he whispers. 'The cops.' But the cops don't come, and all's quiet on the street.

We sit back up, grinning. 'See, the cops don't stand a chance!' Rico starts the car and we're off again. Mark takes the bottle of brandy out of the old lady's bag. He drinks and passes it to me. Paul has some too; he goes to hand the bottle to Rico but Rico shakes his head.

Then we're at the North Cemetery on the edge of town, and Rico parks the car right outside the gate next to a few others. 'Everything's fine,' he says, and then he gets out, walks round the car and opens the old lady's door. 'Here we are, Mrs Böhme.'

'Oh yes,' she says, raising her head and sniffing like a dog. 'Smells different, smells really different.' Rico holds out his arm for her and she gets out of the car.

Mark folds the front seat forwards and we all crawl out before I slam the door. 'Shall I lock it?'

'Nah, Danny, don't bother. Who's gonna steal a car outside a graveyard? I'd only have to open it up again afterwards.'

'I'm happy to pop it open again,' Mark says, showing us his screwdriver.

Paul and Rico link arms with the old lady; we walk through the gates. 'And where exactly is the grave?'

'By the chapel,' the old lady says. 'A little path at the back left. A tree, there's a big tall tree.' We walk along the main path towards the chapel. The old lady stumbles, her hat falls on the ground, Paul kicks it up in the air with the tip of his foot, catches it and puts it back on her head. There are a few people standing around between the graves on either side. We pass the chapel. 'Wait,' the old lady says, 'not so fast.' She stops to rest on her stick. She's breathing heavily and her face is blotchy.

'Let's hope she doesn't die on us,' Mark whispers.

We take her to a bench and fill one of the shot glasses she brought along. There are only two; we drink out of the bottle. 'Thanks, boys,' the old lady says, holding the glass up, and Rico tops it up again. The old lady takes off her glasses and blinks at the sun. I get out my cigarettes and hand out a round; we smoke and look at the graves around us.

'Back there,' says Rico, 'that looks like your tree.'

'Where d'you mean?' I look around.

'Over there by the wall.'

'My tree,' the old lady says. 'We'd better keep going, boys.' She drops her glass and Paul picks it up and cleans it on the bag before he puts its away.

Then we're standing at the grave, supporting the old lady; she's really heavy suddenly. *Horst Böhme, 20.08.1912–13.02.1984*. The grave's very small, looks like an urn grave, with just a bit of greenery growing on it. She reaches for the stone and we let go of her. She goes right up close and strokes the inscription.

'Where's my drink?' We hand her a full glass. 'And the other one too, please, boys.' We fill the second glass and she pours it on the greenery before she drinks the other one. 'Another,' she says, 'another one, boys.'

Paul wanders around between the graves, coming

back with a couple of flowers. He puts them on the grave, but the old lady doesn't see; she's staring at the stone and drinking. The bottle's almost empty now and we take the glasses away from her. 'Horst,' she says, 'my good old Horst, my husband.' We smoke another one, and then we take the old lady back to the car.

# THE BIG FIGHTS

It was the days of the big fights. Rico's big fight was long over and he hadn't set foot in the ring since then, but whenever Sir Henry Maske, Rocky Rocchigiani, The Tiger or chubby Axel Schulz boxed on TV and Rico wasn't in the youth detention centre or in jail, 'in the box,' he called it, we'd sit in front of the TV at Goldie's bar, and he'd fight along with them. 'The Tiger's good,' he'd say. 'He's got bite, he knocks everyone out.' But what he liked best was watching Rocky fight, Graciano 'Rocky' Rocchigiani, 'a mongrel,' Rico said, 'he's a mongrel from the streets just like me, he burrows right into you, eats you up and spits you out.'

And then Rocky wanted to make a meal of World Champion Maske, 'the fucking Gentleman,' as Rico said, and he'd put a couple of notes on Rocky with some guy he knew from inside, 'cause the odds were nine to one. Against Rocky.

We went back to Goldie's 'cause he had the biggest TV in the neighbourhood. We got there more than an hour before the fight 'cause we wanted to prepare ourselves, 'get warmed up,' Rico said, 'just get a bit warmed up, don't want to get in the ring cold,' and 'cause we wanted the best seats, but Goldie's stayed pretty empty as usual. There were just a few local drinkers in there and almost all of them supported Maske, we could hear them talking about it at the other tables.

'That fucking Gentleman,' Rico said. 'They all love him round here just 'cause he comes from the Zone.'

'He's a ladies' man,' I said, looking around, but there weren't any women at Goldie's; just Schäfer's old lady, already resting her head on his shoulder and breathing so heavily we could hear it at our table, but she wasn't a proper woman.

'Bollocks,' said Rico. 'Ladies' man – he's a wimp. Rocky's a ladies' man. You know, he's got... what d'you call it...?'

'Character,' I said. 'Charisma.'

'Right, exactly, that's exactly what I mean, Danny. His face, he's a fighter, a proper fighter. That's what the ladies like.'

'Another beer, Goldie!' yelled Schäfer's old lady two tables down. She was back with the living again, sitting straight as a rod next to Schäfer and staring at the TV up on a shelf screwed to the wall by the bar. There were ads on, and I bet she couldn't wait for the Gentleman to come and dance around the ring for her.

'Another round over here,' Rico called, waving at Goldie. I emptied my beer and pushed the glass to the edge of the table.

'You put a lot on him, didn't you?'

'Doesn't matter, that's not what it's about. Honour, Danny, you get it, honour. He came up from the streets, just like...'

'You and your streets, Rico.'

'Man, you know what I mean, fought his way up, Danny, or are you on that fucking Gentleman's side now?'

Goldie brought our round, beer and clear korn, and he rapped his knuckles on the table before he went back to the bar. 'Any minute now, eh, lads?'

'A while to go,' said Rico. 'But he's warming up now, Rocky's warming up. Boom, boom, boom, right, left, right, left, straight to the mitts.' Rico moved his hands in mid-air while I held onto his beer glass. Rico was still pretty fast, but Goldie didn't see it, 'cause he was back behind the bar. 'Right, left, right, left,' Rico whispered, his hands dancing, 'quick little jabs, quick little jabs...' Then he stopped and leaned his head against the wall, his eyes closed. 'You know what, Danny, I used to like boxing.'

'I know. I know you did.' I raised my shot glass. 'Here's to Rocky,' I said, 'and... to Leipzig's Rocky.'

He opened his eyes, smiled and picked up his glass. 'Leipzig's Rocky... Jeez, Danny, you...' We clinked glasses and knocked back the korn. 'You'd have made a good boxer and all, Danny. Remember that Chips guy... you really messed him up back in the day...'

'Don't, Rico.' I didn't like talking about the Chips thing; I dreamed of it often enough.

Rico smiled and nodded. 'Back in the day, Danny, back in the day,' and he drank a mouthful of beer.

The ads had finished and we saw Maske, the Gentleman, in his changing room, planting long straight-arm punches on his trainer's mitts. 'He does have long arms,' I said.

'That's the only long thing he's got,' said Rico, and we laughed. Then we saw the full hall and the empty ring, bathed in spotlights, then the commentator said something, but Goldie hadn't turned the sound up yet, and then we saw Maske in one of his old fights. He was boxing a guy who didn't even come up to his shoulders, and every time he tried to get up close to Maske he ran into his long right jab. 'Get in there,' Rico yelled, punching the air as though that might make the guy any better, when really he'd messed it all up months before, 'you gotta get right in there, kid!' He took a mouthful of beer and dismissed the other boxer with a gesture. 'He was a fall guy, Danny, way too small, didn't stand a chance... he's doing it wrong, he needs double cover, gotta get up close to the man, half distance, in-fighting, you get it?'

'Like Eismann,' I said, 'like the Ice Man.'

'Yeah,' said Rico, picking up his glass and downing

it, 'like Eismann back then.' He lit one up and blew the smoke into his empty glass.

I put my hand on his arm but he moved it away. 'Sorry, Rico.'

'It's alright, Danny, no problem. It's over. Done and dusted, Danny. Don't bother me now.' He stretched his arms out along the back of the seat and smiled at me. I nodded, took a cigarette and tapped the filter against the box.

'Eismann,' Rico said, leaning back and laughing. 'Eismann can blow me.'

Steffen Eismann was a good boxer over in Grünau, from the West Leipzig Boxing Club, and Rico's last fight had been with him, and we never usually mentioned Eismann in front of Rico. Eismann boxed in the Saxon Amateur Championships and he'd even been to the German Championship, where Rico wanted to go, and Rico was good, every boxer in Leipzig knew that, he was training at Motor Southeast at the time and the famous Boxing Development Centre Leipzig wanted him 'cause he'd beaten the best amateurs in his weight division, unofficially, in the city's boxing clubs and at competitions as well, and the only one left was Eismann, and Eismann was good, 'The Ice Man's got fire,' they used to say, 'The Ice Man burns bright,' but Rico wouldn't take their word for it.

'See that man,' Rico said, pointing his cigarette at the TV, 'the black one, Danny? He's messed up, used to be a star, Iran Barkley, the Blade, used to be really sharp.'

'He beat him to a pulp,' I said. 'Maske beat him to a pulp.' The Blade's face flashed across the screen for a moment, his upper lip curled up almost to his nose, which was as wide as a fist. The Gentleman had done a good job back then.

'Used to be a star,' Rico said, 'three times world champion, knocked out the Hitman, third round. Goldie, another round!' I didn't know who the Hitman was but I didn't ask. 'He was a fall guy for Maske,' Rico said 'Just a body, poor guy. They served him up on a silver platter, Danny.'

'I thought he was good?'

'A while ago though. Half blind, he was half blind against Maske. Detached retina. The Blade's gone dull, Danny.' He smiled, resting his chin on his arms.

Goldie brought our round, rapped on the table again and asked: 'Any minute now, eh, lads?'

Rico looked at his watch. He had to pull his sleeve up 'cause he was always wearing jumpers these days, even though he still had muscly arms, but maybe he didn't want everyone to see all his tattoos, even though he used to be so proud of them. 'You can turn the volume up, Goldie, it's starting soon.'

Goldie said 'OK,' and went to the bar and fiddled with the remote. I picked up my shot, wanting to clink glasses with Rico, but he'd already knocked his back, and he slammed his empty glass down on the table.

'Fire,' his whispered. 'Rocky's got fire, Rocky burns bright,' then he got up and went to the toilet.

He'd been to the gents a couple of times already since we got to Goldie's, and I'd tried to look him in the eye afterwards every time, but he'd noticed and turned his head away. And this time he turned his head aside when he came back, when I wanted to check his pupils, but he wasn't fast enough and I saw they'd shrunk right down.

'Goldie,' Rico called, 'Goldie, turn the sound on!'

Goldie was squatting in front of the bar, picking up the remote batteries. 'In a minute, any minute now. My hands are a bit shaky today.' I saw Rico's hand trembling as well, his whole arm trembled as he raised his beer glass to his mouth.

'Goldie,' yelled Schäfer's old lady two tables over, 'Goldie, the Gentleman's coming!' I looked up at the TV, but it wasn't the Gentleman striding slowly with all his retinue down the long, long path through the crowd to the ring, it was Graciano Rocky Rocchigiani, hiding his head under a black hood, and his face wasn't visible either 'cause he held his head down and looked pretty fucking dangerous. 'Henry,' screamed Schäfer's old lady, standing up, 'my Henry.'

'Rocky, for fuck's sake, it's Rocky, not your fucking Sir Henry!'

Schäfer grabbed his old lady by the arm and dragged her back down to the seat. The drinkers at the other tables laughed. The TV went off.

'Goldie, Jesus, Goldie!' Everyone was shouting now, and Goldie was squatting on the floor in front of the bar, manhandling the remote. Rico pushed his glass away and got up. He was quiet now and his arms had stopped trembling as he picked up a chair and walked very slowly between the tables to the bar.

'Rico,' I said, 'Rico...' but he didn't smash the chair down on Goldie, he put it down in front of the TV, climbed up on it so his head was right in front of the screen, and pressed a few buttons.

'It's alright,' said Goldie, 'I've got it.'

The TV went on again and the volume went up. 'In the red corner, wearing black, weighing seventy-eight point nine kilograms...' Whistles. More and more whistles getting louder and louder, so loud you couldn't hear the ring announcer, Michael Buffer, flown in especially from the US of A. More whistles and boos as Rico put the chair back at our table and sat down on the seat next to me, but Michael Buffer gave it all he had and Rocky, in the spotlight, bent his upper body and jumped up and down a little. 'Ladies and gentlemen, from Berlin, the challenger and former super middleweight champion of the wooorld ... Graciano ... Rocky ... Rocchiiiieee – giaaaa-niiieee!'

'Rocky! Rocky!' Rico stood up, raised his arm and clenched his fist, his sleeve slipped down and I saw the tensed muscles of his lower arm moving underneath his tattoos. He was still in good shape, even though he hadn't been training for a long time now. 'Goldie, another round, quick!' Goldie ran behind the bar like he was Rico's trainer and had to fetch his refreshments before the first bell. The ring wasn't clear yet but the hall was quiet, only a few people whistling.

'And now, as a professional he has a perfect record of twenty-six victories without a loss, including twelve KO's...'

'Fall guys,' Rico yelled next to me, 'all of them fall guys!'

'Ladies and gentlemen, from Frankfurt/Oder... presenting the undefeated light heavyweight champion of the wooorld... Gentleman... Hen-ryyyyyyyy Maaaaaskaaa!' Cheers. Clapping. 'Henry, Henry!' And Schäfer's old lady had got up again and all, never mind Schäfer tugging at her. 'Henry, Henry!' Rocchigiani and Maske stood face to face as the referee, his head between them, spoke the last instructions into the microphone, '...You've received your instructions in the dressing room... Good luck to you... shake hands.'

'It's all in bloody English,' Rico said. 'I can hardly get a word of it.'

'Good luck, he said.'

'Yeah,' said Rico, 'good luck, Rocky.'

Rocky was squatting in his corner now, gloves on the rope, stretching his upper body. 'Seconds out for the first round!' The bell rang and the fight kicked off. Goldie brought our beer and shots, Maske tapped a long right jab onto Rocky's cover, and Rocky sought distance with his right hand too. 'Get in,' said Rico, and knocked back his shot and held the little glass in his fist, clenched so tight I was scared it might break, 'get inside, Rocky,' and as if he'd heard it, Rocky got inside. He pushed up against Maske with his double cover, got in close to the man, dug in, and then right, left, right, left, quick jabs to the body, and then, to finish off, bang, a left uppercut to the chin that made Maske jerk his head back. 'Nice,' Rico yelled, 'nice one, son!' 'Surprising left-hand strike,' said the commentator. And Maske was surprised too, his long right passing by Rocky's head, then he stopped still for a moment, moved his torso and took a step back before he tried again to hit Rocky's head with his jab but only met his peek-a-boo cover. And again, Rocky went into half-distance and then into infight, and again he gave Maske's head a shaking with two uppercuts. 'Watch out, Henry, watch out, my lad,' yelled Schäfer's old lady, wheeling her arms, and her Henry had got careful and was trying to keep his distance by jabbing away, and then suddenly a right-left combination, pretty fast, but it all bounced off Rocky's cover. 'That's Maske's strong point,' the commentator said once Schäfer's old lady'd finished yelling, 'those abrupt, fast one-two punches.'

'They're not even landing,' Rico shouted, 'keep it up, son, keep that cover up, he's not even touching you!' But Rocky was landing punches again, back in close, swinging away from Maske's right jab and coming back with a left uppercut. They stood head to head, a tangle of limbs, and again Rocky's right and left hooks shot from below into the tangle. 'He's not backing off,' Rico whispered beside me, 'Maske's not backing off, and Rocky's landing punches. He's gonna get him, he's really gonna beat him. He's gonna beat him, I swear.' And we'd all thought the same, back then, no, we'd known it, that he'd get him, beat the Ice Man, beat the guy who they said had fire, burned bright, and we'd have put even more money on it, if we'd had it, on Rico blowing out Eismann's fire. And it was a home game for Rico, 'cause the fight was in the old gym at Motor Southeast, and half the neighbourhood had shown up and all these guys from Grünau, and even a couple of trainers from the famous Boxing Development Centre Leipzig were there, and almost all of them had put a few notes on Rico or Eismann, most of them on Rico. Engel's buddies from the red-light district were taking the bets that night, and when I saw them counting the notes and stuffing them in A4 envelopes, I wished I was the postman so I could piss off to the station with the cash and board the next train to Paris, but the only direct trains went to Poland or Prague, and anyway my mate Rico, no, my brother Rico was fighting Eismann, and that was his big chance.

'Eat him up,' Rico yelled beside me, 'eat him up!' and I saw Rocky punching from the half-distance, right, left, and Maske jumping back 'cause at least one hand had hit hard. I nodded at Rico and he clenched his fist. 'Yes,' he said, 'yes!' I drank a mouthful of beer. 'Back, Henry, get back,' Schäfer's old lady screamed so loud it made the glass vibrate in my hand, and when I turned around I saw Goldie sitting at their table next to her, so close their heads were almost touching, infighting, and I knew Goldie hadn't had a woman in a long time, and I knew as well that he sometimes took one of the lady alkies home with him when he was really lonely, after he closed up, and I knew as well that he didn't give a shit whether she was Schäfer's old lady, 'cause Schäfer hardly picked up on much anymore. Goldie liked to nip the odd korn behind the bar, and at some point even Schäfer's old lady transformed into a beautiful woman with long legs and small thin hands, and the way it looked between them right then, she already had.

'Both landing blows, my arse. You hear that, Danny, he said they're both landing blows!'

'Who did?'

'The TV guy, aren't you listening, the stupid TV commentator. Rocky's landing, Rocky's the only one landing anything!'

'Yeah,' I said, although I'd seen Maske's right hook hitting home, 'Rocky's the only one landing.'

The bell rang, round one was over, ads.

'These days, life is more of a risk. Even a normal accident can cost you your existence...'

'Bloody ads,' Rico said, 'can't see the number girls.'

We'd had number girls as well back then, Estrellita and Anna. We'd given them a shitload to drink and they stripped off practically naked. Rico got up. 'What d'you think, Danny, round one to Rocky, right?'

The insurance guy on TV was talking about immediate payouts or something, and I said: 'Round one to Rocky,' and Rico nodded and headed for the toilet. He'd won the first round against Eismann as well back then. The fight was scheduled for five rounds 'cause it wasn't official, 'cause then it would've been three rounds, and they weren't fighting by amateur rules in the ring either.

'Just for the honour,' Rico had said, 'a matter of honour. I'll finish him off, don't matter if it's five or three.' But maybe three rounds would have been better for him, 'cause he liked a drink and sometimes he took a few pills as well, mind you he'd given up both a few weeks before the fight and he was hardly smoking either. But everyone wanted to see five rounds, and Eismann's people from west Leipzig were up for it too. 'Ali was supposed to do five rounds,' the guy who owned the sports bar by Motor Southeast told us, the place right next to the old gym, 'back in the day, against Stevenson, Teofilo Stevenson, the world's best amateur, he was practically professional actually.' And Rico dreamed of going professional too, one day, 'then I'll give up all the shit, no more booze, no more pills, no more fags,' and what was five rounds compared to twelve, anyway?

'Round two,' said the commentator, and it had been going a few seconds. Rico sat back down next to me, and again his pupils were tiny, and I didn't get how he could watch the fight with his pupils so small. And again there was a lot of action in that second round, Rocky went up close with his double cover, 'Get in there, get right in there, son,' he got some good hooks in like in the first round, and Maske landed a few hits now, but Rocky went marching in and wouldn't let off. 'Go on,' I yelled, 'sock him one!' And Rico went marching in and wouldn't let off. He'd been above speed the whole first round and caught Eismann a couple of times, once he'd even got him on the ropes and battered away at him, left, right, left, right to the head, neither of them wearing head guards or shirts 'cause it wasn't official, left, left to the body and then a right to the head so hard Eismann's mouth guard went flying, and Rico was fair, he stepped back and the referee interrupted the fight so Eismann could put his mouth guard back in once his trainer had given it a quick rinse. Rico was playing with Eismann in the first two rounds, and maybe that was his mistake, 'cause at the end of round two it came back at him. Rico threw a long left at Eismann's head, but Eismann's right cross went above it and caught Rico right on the corner of his chin, he buckled for a second, doubled up and then stepped back. And now Eismann was on the march and stuck close and slammed shitloads of straights and hooks at Rico's head and a couple at his body. 'The Ice Man burns bright, the Ice Man's got fire,' and now we believed them. But it was still Rico's round 'cause he'd been clearly ahead for the first two and a half minutes and hardly let Eismann touch him, and I was certain he wouldn't get knocked out in the last few seconds of round two, 'cause Rico could take a whole lot and had never gone KO, except once against Engel, but that wasn't in the ring, it was in some back-yard in our neighbourhood, and anyway he'd nearly had Engel, as well. They'd slogged away at each other for ages until Engel knocked him out with his knee. Engel wasn't a boxer, and he always said himself he'd be a dud in the ring 'cause they had rules there, but he was a big name on the streets and he'd wiped out some of Leipzig's best fighters, and hardly any of them had held out as long as Rico, and none of them had got him that close to KO.

'Rocky's round,' Rico said, writing '10-9' on the beer mat in front of him, underneath the '10-9' from round one.

'Might be a draw,' I said. 'Maske had a couple of good responses.'

'Nah,' said Rico, 'forget it, don't even start on that one, if it's a draw they give it to the champ, you must know that, and Rocky got the better hits in.'

'Yeah,' I said, 'Rocky hits better,' and Rico nodded and patted me on the shoulder like it was us scoring the rounds and not the judges.

Goldie brought us another round 'cause he'd spotted our empty glasses. He bobbed and weaved between the tables and chairs and drinkers with his full tray, ducking down so he didn't obscure the screen. 'Here we go, lads!'

We nodded at him, then raised our glasses and drank our shots, and Rico shook the last few drops out of his glass into his beer. And then, in round three, everything was like in the first two rounds, and Rico drew a little line on his beer mat every time Maske's head jerked back after one of Rocky's hooks.

'He's a hook man,' Rico said once the round was over, 'a real hook man, hardly any straights, but he doesn't need them for that fucking Gentleman.'

Rico had never been a hook man in the ring, never one to get in close, he was strong up close, and he had a strong hook, but he'd won the first two rounds against Eismann with his long straights. And he was right back on track at the start of round three, once his trainer had pepped him up in the break, and it looked like he'd taken the Ice Man's hard punches at the end of round two well enough, 'eaten them up,' as he said. And it looked like Maske had eaten up Rocky's punches no problem too, 'cause in round four he was right back on track as well. He was keeping Rocky at a better distance with his long jab, moved around more than before, threw punches from a backwards move, scored with quick right-left blows, 'Fight, Rocky, fight!' and Rocky fought and tried to get close up and aimed his fast hooks at Maske's head and chin, but he didn't hit home as often as in the first three rounds. And in round five, too, Maske tried to dominate the fight, and he got a couple of good hands in. And now the handful of drinkers at the next tables, who'd been drinking silently so far, perked up as well, maybe Schäfer's old lady had woken them up with her screaming and clapping. 'Henry,' someone called out, 'come on, Henry, show us where you come from!' 'You show that bloody Wessi, Henry!' I looked at Rico but he just pressed both fists against the table and stared ahead at the screen with his tiny pupils. 'Show him how the East throws a punch, Henry!' And Schäfer's old lady clapped her hands and it echoed so loud and dull around the room it was like she was spanking old Schäfer. But Schäfer was sitting all quiet next to her, gazing at the empty shot glasses on the table, the fight long over for him. 'Rocky showing first signs of fatigue?' the commentator asked at the end of round five, 'cause Rocky had dialled down the speed a bit, but, as if he'd heard it, he dug right into Maske and his hooks hit home again, and for a moment he had Maske in the corner and rained down punches on him. No, he wasn't tired, not by a long shot, and now Rico got up again too, holding his beer glass in his outstretched hand, and yelled: 'Don't let him get you down, don't let him, show 'em who you are, show 'em you're still here!' And I yelled too: 'Keep it up, man!' 'cause Rico was getting tired. He'd led the first half of round three, chased Eismann round the ring with his long straights, but then in the last minute Eismann was suddenly back, and again it rained down on Rico, Eismann's right cross over and over, catching Rico full on. The gym had quietened down as people sensed the fight was in the balance. And then Rico was on the floor, I'd never seen him on the floor before, only against Engel and that didn't count, and once when it had been him against fifteen skins, or was it only ten, it had been in my backyard and I'd been hiding on my balcony and watching through a hole in the wall, but Rico didn't know that. '...three ...four ...five...' The referee had his hand right in front of Rico's face, and Rico was back up at seven. He moved his shoulders, shook his head and squinted out at the crowd, and when he saw Mark and me and Little Walter, still there back then, and the others, he tried to smile. His mouth guard had slipped a bit and he put it back in properly, then the referee cleared the ring, and now Eismann wanted to prove himself. He stormed at Rico with his head down, Rico bobbed back and tried to counter, catching him a few times, but Eismann didn't seem to feel it, just ate it all up and landed doubles on the body so hard I could hear them from where I was. Rico buckled for a second, dropped his cover a way, and Eismann's fists were right there, the Ice Man burns bright, the Ice Man's got fire, and again Rico was on the floor. This time he came straight back up, he knew they weren't playing by amateur rules and the referee wouldn't take him out of the fight; he raised his right glove and shouted something, and the crowd cheered and yelled. 'Give it right back, show him you're still here!' The refugee was by him, took his arms and tapped them to his chest, Eismann came out of the neutral corner, the ref yelled 'Box!' but the bell rang, and the round was over. Eismann's round.

'What d'you reckon to round five, Danny...?'

'Not sure. He got some good hits in again at the end, Rocky, I mean. Maske's hitting a lot of cover.'

'Yeah,' said Rico, 'Rocky's cover's bloody good.' Round six was already on, but Rico was looking more at his glass than the screen now. He'd leaned back with his hands jammed between his legs, like he was cold. 'You know what, Danny, I really bloody liked boxing.'

'Yeah, I know.' I leaned forward and looked him in the eye. His pupils had got bigger again, the shit had made its way to his brain at last and it had him in its grip. Rocky landed a combination on Maske's head, both hands hitting, but Rico didn't see it.

'You were a good boxer,' I said. 'You should start again.'

'No,' he said. 'I can't anymore.' He put his right hand on his left arm and moved it up and down. 'You know that, Danny. You know all that.'

'No,' I said, and he kept on rubbing, not stopping until the round was over. 'Goldie,' I called over, 'Goldie, two whiskeys, Jack Daniels!' Goldie nodded as he passed with a huge cocktail glass, complete with umbrella and straw, and put it down in front of Schäfer's old lady. 'Before your memories fade,' the ad blasted out, 'hold onto them with the new Samsung Camcorder.' They filmed Rico's last fight as well, Karsten's brother brought a video camera along, not a Samsung, some cheap make from the Vietcong, and after the fight Rico had taken the tape and smashed it, but my memories hadn't faded yet, and I'll never forget Rico down on the ground in the third round, and he went down again in round four as well, even though he'd gone into the round throwing everything he had at Eismann and got Eismann up against the ropes. He'd stopped relying on his long straights, his combinations, his technique, he went at the man like a little Mike Tyson with mighty swings and hooks, he wanted to knock the Ice Man out, no, beat him to a pulp, he wanted to get him on the ground, and he did get him down, but the Ice Man got up again. Rico had hit as hard as he could, sometimes he roared as he punched, not just expelling his breath with a whistle like most boxers, he'd roared as if that would hit Eismann even harder, but the Ice Man got back up again. Goldie brought over our whiskies. 'So, lads, happy with the fight?' He rapped his knuckles on the table. 'Yeah,' I said, and I saw Rocky land an unexpected left hook on Maske's chin. 'Ooh,' said Goldie, 'that hurt.'

'It did,' Rico said and looked up. Maske went straight into a clinch, slinging both arms around Rocky's torso and leaning his head on Rocky's shoulder.

'I guess you're rooting for Sir Henry now,' I said, nodding over at Schäfer's table, where Schäfer's old lady was getting to grips with the giant cocktail.

'No,' said Goldie, and wiped his nose with a trembling

hand, 'just trying to be a nice guy.'

'You are a nice guy,' I grinned, and Goldie went back to the bar. I raised my whiskey glass. 'Right, here's to our fight.'

'To our fight,' Rico said, moving the glass in his hand, the ice cubes clinking, and then he drank. I knew Rico loved Jack Daniels and I knew it had got him back on his feet a good few times when he'd been in a bad way, 'cause Rico used to steal shitloads of the stuff from the supermarket and then sell it to the Silver Slope, and he'd drunk a few himself, with me, with the others, and they were good memories for him 'cause he'd been on top form back then, and I hoped good old Jack would help him again now, 'cause Rico was in a bad way. He was looking over at the TV again but still sunk down next to me in his seat.

'Come on, Rico, it's nearly round eight and your Rocky's doing well, really well!'

'My Rocky?' He put his glass down and smiled.

'Our Rocky,' I said.

'Did he score, Danny, did he win the rounds on points?' He picked up the beer mat where he'd written down 10-9 four times.

'Yeah,' I said, 'he got every round, almost every round. Five, six, seven. You saw it.'

'Was it close, Danny?'

'Well, the Gentleman wasn't bad in round six.'

'The Gentleman,' he dismissed him with a wave, 'that fucking Gentleman. They'll give it to him if it's close, you can bet on that, Danny.' He sat upright again and sniffed at his glass, the dregs at the bottom. 'Jackie,' he said, 'it's the good stuff, Danny. Thanks.'

'Nah, come on, I know you love the stuff.' I put my arm round him and shook him a couple of times, and he laughed. Round eight was on and Rico was back on track, looking over at the TV with his eyes screwed up. But it wasn't a good round for Rocky, he was looking tired and not punching as much, and his hooks often landed in mid-air. He was bleeding under his left eye. Rico's left eye had bled too, 'cause that was where Eismann's right cross had hit him over and over, and when Rico went running into Eismann with his head down in round four, he gave him plenty of his blood before he knocked him to the ground, and at first I thought Eismann was bleeding too, but then Eismann got back up and I saw that his brows were pretty swollen but still in one piece. Rico opened up Eismann's right eyebrow a bit later with a headbutt, everyone round the ring had seen it was a headbutt, everyone but the referee. He let them go on, and then Rico got Eismann on the ropes again and gave it to him pretty bad, but Eismann just wouldn't go down again.

And wouldn't go down either when Rocky caught him on the chin with a right hook, now, in the ninth round, and then pushed him up against the ropes. He'd just wiped his fist over his bleeding eye and stared amazed at the blood on his glove, and maybe that'd made him mad, 'cause now he got Maske, still on the ropes, with another right, and then a powerful left hit the other side of Maske's head, Rocky's punch, and Maske doubled over and bounced off the ropes, and Rocky tried to finish him off. 'He needs to grab now, he needs to cling now,' the commentator yelled, 'he might go down now.' But Maske stood, swaying but standing. And Rico was standing too, shouting so loud his spit splashed out of his mouth: 'Knock him down, come on, knock him down, just knock him right down!' Rocky tried everything but Maske stayed standing. 'Is Rocchigiani going to use up all his strength on these punches?' the commentator asked. Rico sat back down. 'No,' he said, 'no, not Rocky, Rocky's gonna eat him up,

Rocky's better than...' he looked at me. He picked up his beer glass and downed it. He was still fighting his fight against Eismann, over and over again, and he was fighting another fight too, Pitbull had told me, and he ought to know, and I'd seen his tiny little pupils when he'd got back from the toilet before, but I still didn't want to believe it. I knew Rico necked the odd pill now and then, but more... it couldn't be more than that. 'We're in the last minute of round nine, and it's been looking bad for Henry Maske...'

'Henry, please, come on Henry, please!' Schäfer's old lady was screaming, and it sounded almost like she was crying. The big cocktail glass in front of her had tipped over and the swill was all over the table. '...he was defenceless in the corner,' said the commentator. 'Defenceless,' Rico said next to me, moving his body a little side to side. He was looking up at the TV, his mouth open, but I knew he was somewhere else. He was standing in front of Eismann, who was bouncing off the ropes, could hardly keep his cover up, we were in the last minute of round four. And Rico was giving it all he had, but Eismann stood. The hall yelled and jeered, I was right by the ring and Walter, Little Walter, still there back then, was gripping my arm so hard it hurt, and I yelled too: 'Knock him down, come on, knock him down now!' And Rico gave it all he had but Eismann stood. He managed to bob away on wobbly legs, he went into a clinch and came through with a couple of uppercuts, Rico pushed him away and now he hit him with his right jab, he'd changed his delivery, that was his speciality, but it was too late. Eismann had come back and countered now, and then the round was over. And although they still had one round to go and Rico might still have been ahead, I knew as he was shrunk on the stool in his corner and his trainer was pepping him up and wiping his chest and face with a wet sponge that he'd lost. 'In the tenth,' Rico yelled next to me, 'he'll knock him down in the tenth!'

'Could do,' Goldie said, setting down two beers and two more whiskeys on our table, 'could well do.' He looked tired now and pretty wiped out, maybe he was sad 'cause Schäfer's old lady had knocked out his nice cocktail. But Rocky didn't knock Maske down in the tenth either, 'cause Maske had recovered in the break and tried to keep Rocky at a distance with his jab, and now Rocky didn't get through as often as in the ninth, maybe he really had exhausted himself like the commentator said. But Rico believed in him, he wouldn't give up, 'You'll get him, you're gonna get him Rocky, down him, knock him out!' and when the round was over and Rocky hadn't downed him and hadn't knocked him out, he said: 'In the eleventh, he'll have him on the floor next round!' And in the hall, too, back then, Engel had called out from the ringside when the break was almost over: 'In the next, you'll have him on the ground next round!' Engel would probably have been happier for Rico to get wiped out in the ring, but his friends from the red-light district had organised the betting and Rico was the favourite, though a lot of people from out west had put money on Eismann, and if Eismann won, the bookies would make a loss.

The eleventh round went to Maske. 'Now,' I said, 'now the Gentleman's fighting properly, he... he was boxing, did you see how he started brawling? He doesn't want to lose, lose his title and that.' Rico was restless now, sliding up and down in his seat. He knocked back his whiskey and then started rubbing his left arm again with his right hand. 'The twelfth,' he said, 'if Rocky gets the twelfth he'll steal that fucking Gentleman's title.' He stood up. 'Where are you going, they're starting again.' 'Just to the toilet, Danny, just popping to the bog.' He made a move, but I grabbed him by the sleeve. 'Don't go, Rico, stay here. Please.' He stopped, looked down at me and then smiled, and for an instant it looked like he'd sit back down with me, but then I saw it wasn't a smile at all, his face was twitching and quivering, and then he tore his arm away. 'Jesus, Danny, what's your problem, I'm just going to the toilet, man!' I watched him go. The last round began. Both came out of their corners, the referee stood between them with outstretched arms, then he started the fight. I'd thought they'd pile into each other straight away, but they just stalked one another, and it took ten, fifteen seconds before they threw the first punches. They were both barely landing, surely tired and almost out of strength, but when they went into a clinch and then fought up close, Rico took two or three punches. Rico stumbled, badly rocked, everyone could see, and then Eismann finished him off, left, right, left, right, chin, temple, nose, brow. Rico was down, lying on his belly and moving his legs, he wanted to get back up, crawled a bit on all fours, grabbed at the ropes and collapsed again, and the referee counted.

'Ah fuck me, he's got him now!' Rico leapt up, I hadn't noticed him coming back from the toilet, and Maske was stumbling around the ring on bent legs. Rocky took it straight to him again, and he fell backwards onto the ropes. He forced himself past Rocky somehow, to the middle and backed up, but again Rocky caught his head, left uppercut, and Maske stumbled and fell against Rocky's torso and held onto him for support. 'You've got him, you've got him! Send him down now, send him down, down to the floor!' 'No,' Schäfer's old lady screeched, 'no, no, no!' A glass cracked and smashed – never give her another cocktail, Goldie. Maske stumbled sideways into the blue corner and Rocky punched and punched. And then down went Sir Henry. 'Come on, count,' I yelled, 'count him out!' But the referee didn't count, 'cause Rocky had shoved the Gentleman away when he wanted to lean on him, and the Gentleman just let himself fall, wiped out. 'Timewaster, get up, you timewaster! Don't shove, Rocky, punch, punch, punch!' One more minute. I'd got up too and Rico grabbed my arm. 'He's got him, Danny, he's got him, he's got the round, they've got to give it to him!' 'Fuck the judges,' I yelled, 'now he's gonna knock him out, knock him right out!' And Maske stumbled round the ring but he just wouldn't go down. He tried to counter, slow-motion blows, and Rocky just ducked down under them and slipped in his right, and Maske fell against him and hung off him, and Rocky punched and punched. 'Get back, Rocky, step back, then he'll fall!' But Maske didn't fall, he stumbled, clung, stumbled back, but he didn't fall. 'Come on, Rocky, another twenty seconds!' 'Run, Henry, run away,' Schäfer's old lady screamed, 'watch out, watch out for yourself!' We laughed. 'Yeah, Henry, run away before he eats you up!' And Rocky wanted to eat him up, he kept on hitting, but then the bell rang, and the fight was over. 'It's going to be interesting what the judges decide,' the commentator said. Both boxers put their arms in the air and went to their corners, Maske stumbling more than walking, and his trainer came towards him and caught him and held him. 'Rocky's enjoying the cheers,' the commentator said, and we were cheering too, clapping and yelling 'Rocky! Rocky!' and raising our glasses, 'Goldie, another round Goldie, a thirteenth round!' and we laughed and Schäfer's old lady yelled: 'Henry was much better, Henry looked much better!' and then the ads came on and we sat back down.

'Gonna be a close call,' I said, lighting one up.

'Yeah. Not like me and Eismann,' Rico said and smiled and patted me on the shoulder. 'He knocked me out, he really knocked me out.' He was still smiling, and now it looked like he'd finally made his peace with his last fight through Rocky's big fight, put it behind him, 'eaten it up,' as he said.

'No,' I said, 'not like you and Eismann.' And he'd still finished Eismann off back then, even though he'd lost. He'd been back on his feet at nine and leant on the ropes, but it was too late, and the referee waved both arms around in front of him and took him out of the fight. But Rico just pushed him away, stumbled towards Eismann waiting in the neutral corner, and before Eismann knew what was up, Rico had given him two or three headbutts, right on the nose, and Eismann's blood was in his face, and then he slammed his elbow into Eismann's throat right under his chin, and Eismann was on the floor and didn't get up. I climbed in the ring, all sorts of people climbed in the ring, 'Rico,' I yelled, 'Rico...' but he didn't hear me and he was kicking Eismann on the floor, curled up.

Goldie brought our beer and shots. 'What d'you think, lads,' he said, rapping his knuckles on the table, 'who's won?'

'Rocky's two points ahead,' Rico said, 'I'd even give him 10-8 for the last round.'

'Close call,' said Goldie.

'Yeah,' I said, 'it was a close fight.'

'They've got to give it to him,' Rico said, 'they've got to. But he should have knocked him out, should have sent him down. Like I did with Engel back then.'

'Engel?'

'Yeah, Danny, Engel! In your backyard, the... that return fight, you know...'

'Yeah, Rico, you had him on the ground.' I smiled, 'cause there'd never been a return fight, not with Eismann and not with Engel either, 'cause Engel might have been the best fighter in the whole city, and only somewhere in Rico's dreams, or in the other dreams when he'd necked something, had he ever beaten him.

The ads were over. 'The judges' verdict,' the commentator said. The referee was with the two boxers, embracing each other now, then he went between them and held them by the arm. Everyone in the bar had stood up, staring at the TV, all quiet. 'Ladies and gentlemen, we go to the scorecards. Judge Scarla scores one seventeen to one eleven, judge Mühmert scores it one sixteen to one thirteen, judge DeCasas scores it one sixteen to one thirteen ... for the winner and... still... light heavyweight champion of the wooorld... Gentleman Hen-riiiieeee Maaaaaskaaa!' The referee tugged Maske's arm up high. Graciano Rocchigiani turned away.

'No,' Rico yelled, 'no!' he picked up his whiskey, knocked it back and threw the glass at the wall below the TV, so hard the shards came flying back to our table. 'You bastards, you fucking bastards!' He punched the air, kept punching at nothing with both fists, left, right, left, right, so hard that his sleeves slipped back and I saw the red dots inside his left elbow. He always said he gave blood, they paid good money for it, and I wanted to believe him.

'There's only one Henry Maske, there's only one Henry Maske!' one of the alkies chanted, growled it like an animal 'cause he'd been smashed and empty for years now, but Rico seemed not to hear him.

'You cheats, you fucking cheats! Rocky, Rocky, my money!' He was still punching at nothing, left, right, left, right, punching and punching and not stopping.

'Rico,' I yelled, 'Rico...' I climbed in the ring and pulled him away from Eismann. He turned around and hit out at me, but it didn't land. He stumbled and fell onto the ropes and went down on his knees. He stayed that way. 'Rico,' I yelled, 'Rico...'

It was the days of the big fights, and he'd lost them all.

The guy whose nose I'd broken, they called him Chips. It wasn't his real name, but everyone called him that, Rico'd told me. But he didn't know whether they called the guy Chips 'cause he liked chips – all he knew was that Chips was a famous fighter over in Paunsdorf and I'd got ketch-up all over him. 'You can be proud of yourself,' Rico said. 'No one's ever beaten him, I heard.' But I wasn't proud of beating him, or maybe a bit 'cause I'd done it like in the movies, with my forehead. He'd been standing in front of me and I'd grabbed him by the shoulders and lifted him up, 'cause he was a good bit shorter than me, and slammed my forehead in his face. That was actually Engel's meth-od, Engel used it pretty successfully, he was famous for it, and Engel was bound to be angry when he heard I'd cop-ied him. There'd been a cracking sound and Chips had screamed, and his blood had splashed on my face.

'Nice one,' Rico said. 'You were really good, you gave him what for.' I nodded – it hurt to speak. 'I don't know anything about the others,' he said, 'but they were all Paunsdorf heavies. Maybe I'll find something out.' I nod-ded. He held out his cigarettes to me. 'Wanna go out, Danny, have a smoke?' I nodded. I took a cigarette and I wanted to stick it behind my ear, but I couldn't, there wasn't room, so I dropped it in the pocket of my gown. I sat up on the edge of the bed and looked for my slippers on the floor with my feet. Rico pushed them over. I nod-ded again to say thanks. 'Jeez, Danny,' he said, 'can't you talk anymore? Say something, you're scaring me!'

'Look, pussy,' I whispered, and every word hurt my jaw and my voice box.

'Where, Danny? Where's the pussy?' I raised my arm cautiously and pointed at the big pane of glass in the wall with the nurse sitting behind it. 'You kidding me, Danny? She's old, old like gold.'

'Don't matter,' I whispered.

Rico grinned and then came over. I put my arm round his shoulder and he pulled me up, then we walked across the room to the door. The nurse was standing out in the corridor. 'You can't do that...'

'Just a bit of fresh air,' Rico said. 'You'll get him right back...'

'Bedrest, he has to stay lying down, it's nearly time for his blood pressure!'

'Be OK,' I whispered, and then we walked down the corridor to the door.

'I'll tell the doctor!' she called after us.

'That's what they're all like,' said Rico. 'Always telling on you.'

'She's OK,' I whispered. 'Nice soft hands.'

'Hmm, she didn't look that bad, without the glass. But you can't even have a decent wank, can you? They can see everything!' He laughed.

'Idiot,' I whispered. He pushed the glass door open with a careful foot, then we were out in the grounds and sat down on a bench. I fished out my cigarette and he gave me a light. I coughed and dropped the cigarette. Rico picked it up off the ground, blew on the filter and stuck it back between my lips. I just let it burn down, not smoking it, 'cause my lungs were hurting.

'What d'you think, Danny, when are they going to let you out of this place?' I held up three fingers. 'Three weeks?'

'No, man, days!'

'That's alright then. You'll be fit again that quick?'

I shrugged. 'Getting better every day,' I whispered. 'Talking, too.'

'No, no, you stay quiet, Danny, save your voice, you don't need to say anything.'

I nodded and stroked my throat; the bastards had stepped on it a few times once I was down on the ground.

'Hey Danny, those guys, I'm gonna find them, I swear!'

I shook my head. 'Don't bother, Rico...'

'No, Danny! They just go and beat you up. They could have killed you, and you're my mate... my brother.' He'd stood up and punched the air. I smiled, and even that hurt. 'Hold up, Danny, I've got something for you.' He reached into his jacket pocket and took out a knife, a black switch-blade with a silver button. It looked just like mine. 'That's a surprise, eh?'

'Is it...'

'No, Danny, no, it's not your old knife, the cops have got that one still, you know that. But look, I stole it from the same shop, just this morning!' He put the knife in my hand, I pressed the button with my thumb, there was a click and the blade stood. No, it wasn't my old knife, even though it looked exactly like it and felt exactly like it in my hand. I'd left my old knife in some guy's shoulder, one of Chips's men, in the middle of his tattoo, 'cause the guy was only wearing a vest. It was a badly done tattoo, some kind of demon head with a wonky nose, and I'd spoiled it for good with my knife.

'My tattoo, you fucker, my tattoo, you've messed it up!' But I hadn't meant to stab it, I wanted to get him in the belly, but he caught my hand and batted it away when my knife was almost in him, and the blade only went into his shoulder. The guy wasn't bad, I surely wasn't the first to come at him with a knife, 'Go on, stab me,' he kept yelling, 'stab me, you fucker!'

'Jesus, Danny, watch what you do with it!' I nodded and flipped the blade back in and dropped the knife in the pocket of my gown. 'You're a fighter,' Rico said and put his hand on my arm, 'you're a real fighter, Danny. Better than me.'

'Nah, come on, Rico.'

'I'm telling you. So d'you like the knife?'

'Course.'

'For the nights, Danny, so you're not scared.'

'Thanks,' I whispered. I felt my throat and my head trembling and I couldn't do anything about it. 'Lie down,' I whispered, and the cigarette fell out of my mouth.

'Course, Danny, I'll walk you back in.' He took my arm and laid it over his shoulder. We stood up and went to the door. Everything was blurry again and I saw some things double, two doors, two nurses telling us off, that was the concussion, 'traumatic brain injury' the doctor had said, but once I lay down and pulled up the covers, everything was alright again. 'Need anything else, Danny?' Rico sat down on the chair by the bed. 'Shall I get you anything else, bottle of korn or a couple of beers?'

'Thanks, Rico, that's nice of you, but...'

'Shall I get Anna to come in?'

'No, Rico, no.' I shook my head and all these stars danced around the room, I closed my eyes but they were there too, in the dark.

'When you're fit again, Danny, we'll go back to training, you hear, like we used to. I've got a fight soon, a big fight, and... and I'll need a good sparring partner, the best, Danny, the best...' I heard him getting up and heading for the door. 'Shall I come back tomorrow?'

'Yeah,' I said.

'Will do, Danny, and I'll tell the others.' I moved my head very slightly, but he probably didn't see. 'Right, Danny, I'm off... Look after yourself.' I heard his footsteps in the room, then he opened the door. There were voices in the corridor, emergency ward, jaw surgery, I wasn't the only one who'd got messed up. 'Alright, Danny, see you tomorrow.'

'Yeah,' I said, raising my arm, and I clenched my fist. He closed the door. I pulled the covers up over my head and breathed into the fabric. I turned on my side and felt the knife in my gown pocket. 'Piss off!' I screamed. 'Leave me alone, fuck off!' but they weren't scared of my knife even though I had the blade out already and was stabbing at the air. They weren't scared of my knife and I couldn't understand it, 'cause if I caught them in the belly or the throat they might die, but they just laughed and came towards me. There were too many of them, at least ten, and now I understood I'd have to stab one of them, maybe two, for them to leave me alone. Then they'd have to call an ambulance and I could make a break for it. Where were Walter and Mark? I turned around but I couldn't see them. Why weren't they helping me? I hadn't seen them since the guy'd kicked me in the face, just like that, not saying anything even though he was a good bit shorter than me. 'Why?' I'd yelled. 'What the fuck was that for?' and he'd kicked me again, right on the chin, but I didn't feel it and I yelled: 'Why?' I didn't even know him, never seen the guy before, but he kicked again, and this time I caught his leg and hung onto it, then punched him with both hands. He turned away, I punched his back with both fists, I let go of his leg and he plunged to the ground. 'Why?' I was holding something in my hand, it was my knife. Suddenly there were ten or twelve guys all around me. 'Go on, stab me, stab me, you fucker!' And I stabbed. The knife stuck in his shoulder, he screamed and I was still holding the grip. I wanted to pull it back out, I still needed it, there were so many of them, but I couldn't, I just couldn't. I let it go, the blade wasn't even halfway into him and it fell on the ground. I screamed. The covers were gone. 'Don't worry, Mr Lenz, we just have to take your blood pressure.' The nurse looked down at me; she had big eyes. Blue. 'Yeah,' I said, sitting up and holding my arm out to her. She rolled up the sleeve and put on the cuff. 'How are you feeling? Still got a headache?'

'Alright,' I said.

The blood pounded in my arm, she read off the measurement, 'Getting better,' then she let the air out of the cuff. 'How's your throat? And your jaw, is it still very painful when you talk?'

'No,' I said as loud as I could. 'It's getting a bit better.'

'Open your eyes nice and wide.' She took a little torch, leaned over to me and shone it in my eyes. 'Good,' she said and switched the light off. 'Turn over on your front, please.' She undid my gown and felt my back. 'We'll have to treat the bruises again later.' She stroked my back and then felt my neck. She did my gown up again, picked up the blood pressure machine and went to the door. 'We'll come and get you in an hour or so.' She opened the door. Then I saw her behind the glass. A little lamp was on there at night, and they watched me or read the paper or a book. On the first night, when they'd brought me in, I was put in a big room with other people in it, they'd stuck diodes on my forehead and my chest, and there was a blood pressure machine on my arm that switched on automatically every fifteen minutes and stopped me from sleeping, and if I passed out it brought me back round.

I sat up and took the glass of water from the bedside table. I was tired but I didn't want to sleep. My chin was so swollen I spilled half the water when I drank. I poured water in my hand and wiped my face. There were five cigarettes and a lighter on the table; Rico must have put them there. I took two cigarettes and the lighter and then got up. I pulled out one of the crutches from under the bed where I'd hidden them before Rico arrived, and hobbled to the door. At the window, I stopped. The room behind it was empty and I could see into a room like mine on the other side of the space, a man lying in bed there, his legs hanging from ropes, and his head was a big white ball. I opened the door and hobbled down the corridor to the toilet.

Everything was quiet. I stood in front of the mirror and turned on the tap. The black marks under my eyes had got bigger, they had blue edges now, blending into the dark red of my swollen cheeks, and my cheekbones had gone green at the sides. But they weren't my cheekbones anymore, my jaw, my cheeks. The swellings weren't normal swellings now, it looked like their fists had got stuck in my face and grown into it. And they hadn't just used their fists, in the end they'd come with fenceposts, torn up somewhere, but I could understand that 'cause I'd had an iron bar first that I'd found by a building site. They stood in front of me and I just thrashed at them. They screamed and scattered, for a moment everything went differently, me chasing them. But there'd been no point to that either, even though I got a couple of them, there were just too many of them. I bent down over the sink and held my head under the running water. I wanted to go home. My mum had visited me, didn't recognize me at first, and then she hadn't stayed long. I turned off the tap and looked back in the mirror. Mark had looked about the same once. Four or five guys had got him, over in Mühlenviertel. There were always so many of them. I lit a cigarette. Then I went up to the window, opened it and sat down on the windowsill. I leaned the crutch against the wall. Across the way was the high-rise, twenty floors of hospital wards, a hulk. A man in a white coat and glasses walked past the window.

He looked at me and I blew smoke after him. It was afternoon, the sun still shining, and a couple of patients were taking a stroll in the grounds, some of them smoking. We'd visited Mark back then, and later we'd got hold of one of the guys who'd done him over and done him over, with KO spray so he'd tell his people about it. Why were there always so many of them? Why wasn't it like at boxing, man versus man? Why were there always so many of them jumping you? I thought of the backyard where me and Walter had lain in the dirt because Engel's people had got hold of us, I thought of all the battles over the last few years. And I thought of the guys we'd done over.

I opened the door and hobbled down the corridor to my room. 'Mr Lenz, your back!' The nurse was in the room. I had to sit down on a wheelchair – ridiculous, I could walk! – and she pushed me along the corridor, around the corner and then through a door and down another corridor, then into the lift, second floor, and down more long corridors, meeting doctors and other messed-up people.

Then it was night, all was quiet, and the little light was on behind the glass. I didn't want to sleep so I watched the nurse sitting at the desk behind the glass, reading the paper. There was a thermos flask next to her. Sometimes she got up and looked in my room or at the man whose legs were suspended on ropes. Sometimes she disappeared and I heard her out in the corridor. Rico's knife was by my pillow, I could reach for it any time and let the blade loose. Chips wasn't here and none of the others I'd got either, Rico had asked around, and the doctor had told me as well. They were probably all back home; I'd tried to mess them up good and proper but it hadn't worked, and a broken nose and a stab wound to the shoulder weren't enough for a few days in hospital. But there'd been that other guy, and I wished he was blind now, at least in one eye, and I'd done my best when I'd stuck my fingers in his face like a V. All I hit at first was the bones under his eyes. My other hand was round his neck, I felt his voice box but something made my hand go limp so I couldn't press hard, and I stuck the V in his face again, my fingers hitting something soft this time. I bored and pressed, and he screamed so loud his screams went inside me... And there they were again, I heard them outside in the street and in the driveway. He'd been the fastest of them, but now he was lying underneath me. I'd been too exhausted to run any further, but I wanted to mess one of them up before they got me. The guy thrashed around and screamed even louder, and now his fingers were in my eyes, like I was lying on a mirror, but I just pushed his hand away with my head. I pressed him to me and turned on my back so he was on top of me. I couldn't see them but they were standing around us in a circle. I put my legs on his back, grabbed his head and banged it against my forehead, over and over. I couldn't feel anything. 'Take him away, get him off me!' He wept and my face got wet, maybe I'd really messed up his eyes. 'Please, please,' he wept, 'get him off me.' They tugged at him, couldn't get at me otherwise, and I pressed my legs around his back so hard he went quiet. They worked silently too. All I heard was their footsteps and their breathing. Now they got their feet in at my sides and on my head. A piece of wood rammed into my neck, I couldn't breathe, and I screamed. I was amazed at how quietly I screamed. My strength was gone, and I let go of him. They pulled him off me, I saw a few stars in the sky and the windows of the buildings, dark.

'Are you in pain?' asked the woman behind the glass. 'Are you alright?' She'd switched on the intercom and I leaned my head against the glass.

I nodded. 'Yeah,' I said. She got up, the newspaper on

the desk was yesterday's, the door opened and I walked back to bed, slowly. 'Mr Lenz!' She was standing behind me now, her hand on my shoulder. 'Mr Lenz, if you need anything...'

'No,' I said, 'everything's fine.' I sat down on the bed and looked at her. 'Just dreaming a bit, didn't watch out...'

'I can give you something, for the pain. Then you can sleep.'

'That's nice of you,' I said. 'But it's OK.' I lay down in bed and she covered me over.

'You won't need this!' She reached for the knife and laid it carefully on her palm.

'Watch out for the button!' I said.

'I'd better take it...'

'No, please, leave it here.'

I reached for her hand.

'You might hurt yourself, Mr Lenz... You're not allowed to...'

'Please... please leave it here!' She was holding the knife, and I gripped her hand and looked at her.

'I'll put it in the bedside drawer. But you'll have to promise me you won't...'

'Yes,' I said, letting go of her hand. 'Please don't take it away.'

She opened the drawer and put the knife in it. 'We'll leave this closed, Mr Lenz. And don't show it to anyone. You won't need it!'

'Thanks,' I said.

'Good night.' Then she was back behind the glass where the little lamp was on. I put my hand on the bedside table and tried to sleep.

'Danny, they held us back, there was nothing we could do!' Walter paced the room. I wasn't mad at him, he was far too little, they'd have beaten him to a pulp. 'Danny, I tried, honest! The bastards held me back!'

'They wanted to have a party with you, you know?' Mark was on the chair by my bed. Rico was there too, standing over by the glass, watching us silently, he had nothing to feel bad about, he hadn't been there, but he'd have helped me even if they'd beaten him to death, I was sure of that.

'Your knife,' Mark said.

'What about it?'

'He held it to my throat, the bastard.'

'Who did?'

'That wanker with the tattoo, the one you... here!' Mark tipped his head, leaned down to me and showed me a thin red line. 'He would have slit it.'

I nodded. 'If I hadn't fought back... they'd have given me a quick kicking and that's all.'

'Don't talk crap, Danny!' Rico came over to us. 'You did right. Like a professional!'

'Yeah,' said Mark. 'All on your own, you... If he hadn't had the knife I'd...'

'Shit, Jesus, Danny, I'm so sorry!' Walter was standing on the other side of my bed, and he put his hand on my arm.

'It's alright,' I said. 'It wouldn't have helped, you'd only have ended up in here and all.'

'Danny, you know the windows...' Mark had got up and Rico sat down on the chair.

'What windows, Rico?' I knew what windows he meant, but I didn't want to talk about it.

'Thing is, Danny, I went by there yesterday and there were at least seven shop windows smashed. You had an iron bar, didn't you?'

'Yeah, I did.' I whispered again 'cause my throat and

jaw were hurting again.

'Was that all you?'

'Yeah, it was.'

'Not bad, Danny, not bad. But they'll book you for that, it'll be pricey.'

'What did you do it for?' Walter asked, sitting down on the edge of the bed.

'Alarms,' I said.

'Right, I get it,' Rico said. 'You're clever, Danny, a real professional!' He patted me on the shoulder and gently on the neck. 'They didn't have any though,' I whispered. 'Not one alarm went off.'

'And you'd smashed seven shop windows!' Mark clapped his hands. 'You're an ace, Danny!'

I nodded. 'Still gonna be pricey.'

'Yeah,' said Rico. 'You can bet the fucking judge won't get it. It's a street thing, a war, the fucking judge won't get it.'

'Yeah,' I whispered.

'Those bastards,' Mark said. 'They wanted to have a party with you!'

'And they did,' I said.

I didn't tell them I'd almost got away, I was a good runner, did sixty metres in 7.6 seconds in P.E., I'd lost them, but then I'd found the iron bar and run back. I wanted to show them. I couldn't just run away, those bastards still had Walter and Mark. I couldn't just run away and leave them back there, that wasn't on. The bastards had jumped us, just like that, I didn't know any of them, but now I wanted to show them what for. 'Come and get me,' I yelled. 'Come and get me, you bastards!' I couldn't see them anymore, I was all alone in the street, walking in their direction with the iron bar. And then they were back, a good way away, walking slowly towards me in a row in the middle of the road. 'Come and get me, you bastards,' I yelled. 'I'm gonna beat you to death!' There was a crash, a big glass shard stuck to my chest. Another crash and I pulled the bar out of the window, my hand bleeding.

'No,' I said and leaned my head against the wall. 'Not one fucking alarm...'

'Usually all you have to do is touch a car and it starts beeping,' Walter said. But I hadn't just smashed the windows to call the police – I wanted to scare the guys, and everything happened automatically: first the iron bar to the windows, then thrashing the bastards with the bar, then flinging the bar at them, then grabbing one guy and pressing his head against the wall; everything just happened, I ducked down and ran back and forth between them, 'I'm gonna kill you, you bastards!'

'And then people came,' I said.

'Who came?'

'Out of the buildings.'

'Did they call the cops?'

'No, they jumped on me, 'cause of the windows.'

'Jesus, what bastards, what fucking bastards!'

'Danny, I swear,' Mark was almost yelling, 'if he hadn't had the knife to my...'

'It's over,' I said.

'No,' said Rico. 'It's not over. It's never over. I'm gonna get a few of them, believe me, Danny! It's never over.'

The nurse knocked on the glass and put a finger to her lips. Rico went over and ran his tongue up the pane of glass in front of her face. We laughed. She turned away and went to the door, then we heard her footsteps fading out in the corridor. 'Now you've got rid of her,' Walter said.

'No,' said Rico. 'She's just gone to get a few more nurses. Gang bang, you get me?' We laughed.

## ALWAYS PREPARED

The last time I saw Rico before he had to go away, he was standing up at the window and waving at me. He looked really small. I'd rung the doorbell downstairs but his mum wouldn't buzz me in. I took a few steps back into the road, looked up at Rico and put my hand upright on my head in the Pioneers' salute. 'Be prepared,' I whispered. I could see Rico laughing, up at his window. Just for a second, and then I saw Rico's mum. She drew the curtain across the window. A car honked behind me. I got back on the pavement and headed home. I walked down the road to the park, then I stopped again and turned around. I could still see the window on the third floor, where the curtains were closed now. Rico had laughed when I'd done the Pioneers' salute in the middle of the road. He'd laughed even though he had to go away the next morning. 'Off at six thirty,' he'd told me the day before. 'Taking the train – exciting, eh?' And even then, he'd tried to laugh a bit.

I walked through the park, our park. It had rained that morning and it still smelled wet, and the rain dripped from the trees. There was our tree, the one so tall we could see the school and the graveyard from the top. We'd always met there in the afternoon, when we didn't have Pioneer manoeuvres or recycling collection. Later, Rico stopped going to the Pioneers and I'd sometimes see him sitting in the tree on his own when I walked to the meeting places or to school, or usually when I ran, 'cause I was late, 'cause of the stupid neckerchief I could never do up properly. Rico didn't have a neckerchief anymore. He'd burned it. He'd burned it here in the park, I'd been with him. Now I saw the sandpit with the little climbing frame to the left of the path where he'd hung it up and burned it. And I'd been with him. At first I'd thought he was just kidding, and then he'd got out the matches and set it alight. 'Are you crazy?' I'd yelled. 'Jeez, Rico, stop it!' But it was too late, he was on his third match, and all that was left on the climbing frame was a burnt scrap. Rico took it off and threw it in the sandpit.

'Right,' he said, looking at me.

I had a funny feeling in my belly. I sat down on the edge of the sandpit and stared at the burnt fabric. 'Jeez, Rico,' I said. 'Why did you...?' But I knew why. Rico had told me everything. About his father, the officer, who'd sometimes be sitting at the table in his uniform when I went round to visit Rico.

Rico's father wasn't there anymore. 'He's got some stupid cow in Berlin,' Rico had told me. When they asked us what we wanted to be when we grew up at Pioneers, when Rico was still going and everything was fine, or in Homeland Education, Rico had always said 'officer.' Not soldier – 'officer'. And even when we met up after school, Rico used to wear his Pioneer outfit: dark blue trousers, white shirt with epaulettes, the blue neckerchief and even the cap, that was his uniform, but that was all over now.

I walked faster, looking down at the path 'cause I didn't want anymore pictures in my mind. Rico's going away, I thought, Rico's got to go away, Rico's a difficult case, Mr Dettleff said, and then I started counting the puddles on the path, and then I saw Maik. He was sitting on a bench, up on the back of it with his feet on the seat, and there was a wooden club next to him, and on the bench was a mesh shopping bag with a couple of empty deposit bottles in it, bottles of spirits, thirty-five pfennings' deposit each over at Böhland's recycling yard. Maik looked at me and said: 'Hey, Danny, hold on!'

I stopped in front of him, leaned one hand on the back of the bench and said: 'Alright, Maik, what's up?'

'Peace, Danny,' he said, and tapped one foot against the club so it fell over. 'No fights today. Take a seat.' I sat down next to him, glad he wasn't starting trouble. I'd often got in fights with Maik and I'd almost always lost. Maik was a big lad, the tallest boy in our class, and two years older than us 'cause he'd had to repeat the year twice. I didn't actually mind him but he often hung out in the park with his friends, and then we usually got into fights. Maik spent all day outside, even in the winter, 'cause his father drank, everyone knew. There was always trouble at home, sometimes you could hear the yells a few doors down, and that was why he went home late, sometimes not until night-time. Most of us at school had respect for Maik, 'cause he lost his temper easily and then hit out. Rico was the only one Maik was careful about, Rico knew how to box, his father had taught him and one time, he'd given Maik such a black eye that everyone thought it had been Maik's drunk dad.

'You know,' Maik said next to me on the back of the bench, 'it's rubbish about Rico.'

'Yeah,' I said. My head was resting on my hands and I looked over at the grass on the other side of the path.

'You know,' Maik said, 'I don't know how to say it, but I feel really bad. I wanted a boxing match with him, a real boxing match, we'd agreed. And, Danny, it was wrong what we did, I didn't want it like that.'

'What?' I asked. I didn't know exactly what he wanted from me, but I had an idea and I hoped he'd keep his stupid mouth shut.

'You know what, but it wasn't my idea, I swear, it was Friedrich's, he wanted it. And it's not the only reason he has to go away. I know how bad it is there, my brother...' I didn't know Maik had a brother. He wouldn't stop talking, and I wished I hadn't stopped and sat down with him, wished I'd just gone home.

'Danny, I don't think it's just because of... Rico went crazy, and his dad, well, the divorce, you know, and then his three sisters...'

'What do you want, Maik?' I yelled. 'Jeez, what do you want? Stop talking crap about Rico!'

'Danny, Danny, alright, keep your hair on, I just wanted to say I'm sorry we told on him, and it was Friedrich's idea. I gave him a bit of a punching, Danny, I gave him a couple in the face.' I remembered Friedrich's eye swollen shut a few days earlier.

'What are you sorry about?' I said. 'What did you tell on him for?' I knew now what Maik meant but I wanted him to say it out loud. I'd felt guilty, thought I should have denied everything, should have defended Rico and maybe taken the blame myself, at least a bit. But I hadn't.

'The thing about the neckerchief,' Maik said now, at last. 'You know, Danny, you did as well, but I shouldn't have told, but it was Friedrich's idea. And anyway, he did burn it.' Actually, I'd always known it was Maik who'd told them, him or his friends. They'd seen it somehow, probably from the tree, and then told on him. But I'd admitted everything too, sitting there in the Pioneer leader's office with them all standing around me: the headmaster, the Pioneer leader, Mrs Seidel, Mr Singer with all his badges on his jacket.

'You pig,' I said, and I stood up and planted myself in front of Maik. 'You stupid tell-tale pig, you stupid dirty swine!' I shoved at him with both hands, as hard as I could in the chest, and Maik fell off the back of the bench, and when he went to stand up again I threw myself on him, pressed his head to the ground with one hand and punched him in the face over and over with the other. 'You pig, you tell-tale traitor!'

No, we were still both perching on the back of the bench, saying nothing and staring at the grass on the other side of the path. Two boys had stuck fence posts in the ground and one of them stood in between them, as goalie, and the other came over to us. 'Wanna play?'

'Piss off,' said Maik. 'Or I'll make you!' The boy didn't reply, just moved on.

I stood up now too. 'It's all crap,' I said, 'but you're still a traitor.' Then I headed across the grass to our road.

'You talked as well!' Maik yelled after me. A ball rolled in front of my feet and I kicked it as hard as I could, so hard it flew onto the pavement and rolled from there into the road. 'Such an idiot!' I took no notice. All I wanted was to get home and listen to loud music or turn on the TV, 'cause I could hear their voices again in my head, all standing around me up in the Pioneer leader's office.

'We have witnesses, Daniel!'

'And we know you just stood by and watched.'

'Rico's a difficult case,' Mr Dettleff the Pioneer leader said. 'His behaviour's not worthy of a Young Pioneer, and you know it.'

'And there's no excuse for it.'

'It wouldn't be the first time, either,' said Mr Singer, and I stared at the badges on his jacket, one of them had a fist clenched around a flaming torch. 'Rico's not a good influence on you, Daniel. And apart from that, Rico's character displays damaging tendencies, and I don't think,' Mr Singer looked around the room and everyone nodded, 'and I don't think we can tolerate it any longer.'

'It's best you tell us exactly what Rico did in the park,' said Mrs Seidel. 'And that you couldn't prevent it.'

'We don't understand why such an exemplary Pioneer as yourself would still be keeping company with Rico, after all he's done this school year. He's exploiting your friendship, Daniel!'

'It's in your interest, what with you taking the Council of Ministers Certificate this year.'

'And think of the talent competition, Daniel. We're sure you'll represent our school just as well there as last year.'

'And Rico can only harm your future plans!'

'You don't want to let your parents down again, Daniel!'

'And you did want to prevent it!'

'Yes,' I said. And then... and then I told them everything. I went up the stairs. I looked for the key in my trouser pockets. It wasn't there. Maybe I hadn't taken it out with me, left it in my bedroom, maybe I'd lost it along the way. I rang the doorbell. It was Sunday afternoon and I had to go to school the next morning. Without Rico.

My mum opened the door. 'There you are, at last,' she said. I took off my shoes.

'The head of the class council reports: Class 6b is all present and correct!'

'For peace and socialism: be prepared!' said Mrs Seidel by the backboard.

'Always prepared!' we chanted, touching our hands to our head in the Pioneer salute.

'Sit down, class,' Mrs Seidel said. We sat down. She peered at us over her glasses. She said something: 'Text book... page... From the beginning...' but I wasn't listening properly by then. I opened up my reading book without looking at which page I was on, and stared at the desk in front of me. Katja sat there but the chair next to her was empty, Rico's old place. My mum had told me to forget about him, everyone had told me that, but I couldn't.

'A mandarin is golden green, fat and round like a fist.'

'And do you eat it like an apple?'

'It's a magic fruit, Leka, like a miracle herb.'

Katja was reading aloud in her lovely voice.

'...and when you eat it, it makes you dance, yes, dance!'

'And perhaps sing too?'

I looked at Rico. He'd put the book aside and had his head down, silent. 'The Red Army in the Fight against Hitler Fascism' was our homework title, and it'd been Rico's turn to read, but he'd just stopped.

'Come on,' said Mrs Seidel, 'don't you want to go on reading?'

'No,' Rico said. 'No, I don't want to talk anymore crap about Soviet soldiers. No.' Rico was sitting next to me and I kicked him under the table. 'No,' Rico said again, slamming the book shut so loudly I flinched, 'No,' and then he threw it on the floor, in the middle of the aisle between the desks.

'Stand up,' Mrs Seidel said, very quietly. We could hear football players shouting outside on the pitch, and between them the P.E. teacher's whistle. 'Katja,' Mrs Seidel said, 'I'm leaving you in charge for five minutes. Class, read the rest of the text. Rico, come to the front!' Rico walked very slowly up to the teacher's desk, then he had to open the door and go outside. Mrs Seidel was behind him.

'Maxim doesn't want to lose his valuable load. All they need to do is fire grenades, and then the children will never get to see mandarins, Maxim thinks. The enemy swings back into position.' I watched Katja's lovely throat moving as she read. She'd made him sit there, next to Katja.

'Perhaps she'll have a beneficial influence on Rico,' Mrs Seidel had said to me.

And I'd tried to persuade him: 'Rico, come on, go back to normal, please, everything will be alright,' but it had been no use, and I wished his father had come back to them, sitting at the table in his uniform when I went round to visit Rico...

'Daniel!' Mrs Seidel was standing in front of me, her glasses slid down to the end of her nose. 'Daniel, for the third time, please read the next section. You're not concentrating properly these days!' I flicked the pages of my reading book, trying to find the right place. Katja turned around to me and moved her lips.

'Sorry, Miss,' I said quietly. 'I was... I'm on the wrong page.'

'Daniel,' Mrs Seidel said, just as quietly, 'see me after class. Maik, you read up to the end and then summarise.'

Maik began to read, very halting and slow: 'Leka... swallows a seg-ment of the ma-gi-cal fruit. He swings up to the window. Holds on tight. Sings: Look, two robins, red of breast, all alone in their wee nest.'

## THE RETURN

Rico was back. He was supposed to stay away for longer, but they'd let him off what time was left. Now he had to go to a social worker every week and tell her all his problems, if he had any. 'Rico, you're clean, aren't you?' I asked him.

'The old lady's great,' he said. 'When to see her yesterday, first time. Blonde but it looks dyed. Tits not too big, no, not too big. She had this tight top on, Jesus, you know where I've been. She wants to get me turned on. Yeah, right, Danny, she's hot for me...'

'Bollocks,' I said. 'You're kidding yourself 'cause you've not had anything for over a year, or did you go gay in there?' I nudged him on the shoulder and he dropped his beer glass just as he was about to drink.

'Jesus, shut it!'

He'd been back for four days but he'd only got in touch with me that day. I was a bit disappointed, but I'd invited him out anyway. We'd gone down to the Tractorist 'cause the beer was cheap there. Goldie came over to us. 'You'd better get the next round in, then, butterfingers,' he said to Rico, taking the empty glass.

'Hey, hey, hey, enough of the stupid comments!' Rico held his finger up to Goldie's face.

'Calm down, keep it nice and calm. I'll bring you two korns, alright?'

'Thanks, Goldie, yeah,' I said. Rico wiped the puddle off the table with a beer mat, then fingered his shirt pocket. A couple of cigarettes fell on the floor. I bent down and picked them up. I put one between his lips and lit it up. 'Alright, jeez,' I said and took one for myself.

'Have you not got any of your own?' He slid around in his seat, blinking.

'Rico, come here!' I put my hand on the back of his

head and pulled him closer. 'You're not inside anymore, you hear, everything's back to normal. You're back home. Look at me, it's me, Danny, you can look everyone in the eye out here!'

'Sorry,' Rico said with a grin, and the corners of his mouth twitched, 'I'm not quite back properly. It'll be OK, I'll be OK. Here, help yourself.' He put his pack of cigarettes on the table and opened it. 'Danny, you know, inside, they were so important...'

'I know,' I said.

Goldie put two korns down on our table. 'Listen, Goldie,' Rico said, 'I didn't mean it before...'

Goldie smiled. 'Nice to have you back... welcome back.' He went back to his glasses and bottles.

We drank our shots. 'To you,' I said.

'Yeah,' said Rico.

A woman came in and went up to the bar. She looked pretty good, short skirt and plenty of skin on display up top. 'Jesus,' said Rico, 'it's November.' We both stared at her skirt and her legs and her half-naked back, but she didn't feel anything and didn't turn around. She sat down on a bar stool; Goldie didn't have a mirror behind the bar.

'She's a professional,' I said.

'Nah, rubbish,' said Rico. 'She's on the pull, she's looking for someone for the night, my God, you know how much I'd...'

'Not so loud, she'll hear you.'

'I went round to Anna's yesterday but she's gone, don't know where, no one knows anything, and Janine won't let me in anymore, you know, 'cause of that thing...' I didn't know exactly what he meant by 'that thing' – maybe that night he'd wanted to drive her to an Italian restaurant in a stolen car, even booked a table and I bet there was a guy playing violin like in a movie, but then she had to spend all night down the station with him, Leipzig Southeast, 'cause Rico had nicked some kind of open-top model, I think it was a Porsche. 'I borrowed it,' he'd told her, and of course the cops had noticed him in that car. No young lad in Leipzig East drives an open-top Porsche.

'Look, man, look, she turned around, she's just looked at me!' I looked over at her, but all I saw was her sipping at a glass of red juice, probably Goldie's best wine. 'What do I do now? I'm out of practice.' He ran his hands through his hair and slid around on his seat. He was actually always good with women, and he'd been the first of us to get a girl in bed, but on a park bench over in the East Woods, he'd told me. He'd met her at the Apple Club and she must have necked too many pills 'cause afterwards she tipped over in the snow, 'cause it was winter, and he had to break into a car and put her in it so she didn't get too cold.

'I'm gonna chat her up,' Rico said. 'I'll just go over and chat her up.'

'Wait, wait. What are you gonna say? Hello, I just got out of jail...'

'I'll think of something. I'll just have a quick drink and then I'll go over, I'm telling you!' But it was too late. A guy came in and I knew right off that he was there for her. He'd dolled himself right up, purple suit with a blue tie, and gold bracelets glinting down by his cuffs. His fake Rolex was hanging halfway off his hand so everyone could see it. He sat down next to her and said something to Goldie. Then the guy had a rose in his hand, I hadn't seen where it came from, maybe he was a magician and whipped it out of his sleeve. 'Look at that bastard of a pimp,' Rico said, putting out his cigarette even though he'd only smoked half of it. 'That pimping bastard comes in here and takes my woman away!'

'He really is an arsehole, Rico, but don't make a fuss,

she's his girlfriend, that's all.'

'Fuck, you know how I hate guys like that, dressed like poofters and taking our women away!'

'Leave him alone, Rico, you've only just got out!'

Rico blinked and said, 'Yeah, true.'

I called Goldie over and ordered another two beers. 'D'you know that guy, Goldie?'

'Nah,' Goldie said. 'But I'll bet he's buying himself a new one, if you get my meaning...' He went back to the bar and I saw him messing around with fruit and a couple of bottles. He'd done a cocktail making course a few years ago 'cause he wanted to keep up with the times; we called Goldie's cocktails in their big glasses with straws and umbrellas 'exotic fruits,' but that didn't make them any better.

'You know what, Danny, I don't give a shit about that bitch, but I feel kind of... all alone. I'd like to lie next to a woman, you know, just look at her...' Rico drew circles on the table with his finger, first anticlockwise and then clockwise. I tried to look him in the eye but he was somewhere else, and I knew where. And I knew as well that he'd go back there some time.

'Rico,' I said, putting my hand on his arm, 'let's get out of here, we gotta celebrate you being back. Come on, I know this place, the girls'll dance buck-naked just for us, you know, only the best!'

Rico looked at me and smiled. 'Yeah, sounds good. I can't even remember what a woman looks like, without...' We emptied our beers, talking about old times. We didn't talk about Mark. Rico knew he was dead, I'd written to tell him, but I didn't want to start on that now, Rico had smiled and that was a good thing. Maybe later, in the strip club, he'd ask me how it all happened, but I didn't know what I'd say then and it wouldn't be the right place for it either. We paid up.

We stood outside the Tractorist for a last cigarette, 'cause the night bus into town only went once an hour. 'I think I left my lighter in there,' Rico said. 'I'll be right back.' He chucked his cigarette away and went back inside. I watched the door closing behind him.

Rico came back out. 'Step aside,' he said. The pimp guy came crashing out the door, his jacket off, his sleeves rolled up and showing off loads of cheap tattoos, probably trying to scare Rico. I could just read 'Ramona' as he raised his arm, but he ran straight into Rico's fist. Rico used to be a good boxer, but the guy didn't know that. His back slammed against the wall and he slid down it. I didn't see any blood on his face, but his nose wasn't the same as before. Rico didn't move. He stood in front of him, looking down at him. The pimp rolled to one side and leapt up again. There was blood coming out of his nose now, but not much.

'I'm gonna fuck you up, you bastard,' he yelled. His voice was so high it hurt my ears. 'I'm gonna kill you!' He ran at Rico again, but Rico just stayed put, catching him again with his left fist, a punch out of nowhere, and this time Rico rammed his right in after it, hitting the back of his head when the guy was half-down.

Rico stepped towards him. 'Leave him,' I called. 'That's enough now, let's get out of here!' Rico didn't even look over at me. He squatted down next to the pimp and searched his pockets. 'Rico, come on, don't do anything stupid!' Then the fear came over me: What if he was dead? Maybe he'd fallen badly. But the guy was leaning against the wall again, his head swaying.

'Do you know who I am?' he muttered.

'I don't give a fuck,' said Rico. 'Danny, come and have a look what this bastard's got here!' He was holding a little bag, probably coke or heroin or some shit like that.

'Give it back,' I said.

'Don't worry, Danny, I don't need it anymore!' He stuffed it down the front of the guy's trousers. 'So, you gonna call the cops, shithead? If you make trouble, I tell you, I don't give a fuck about anything, I'll slit you open.' Rico took out a tissue and wiped the blood from under the guy's nose. We headed over to the bus stop. Rico was crazy and it was getting worse and worse. Maybe he'd been away too often, even as a child. The bus came and we got on.

The bar was round and there was a cage in the middle, on a little pedestal. The music wasn't too loud, dancefloor and techno, and a woman was dancing in the cage. She had nothing on, clinging to a pole in the middle of the cage, and her breasts bobbed up and down against the pole. We walked along the bar looking for a good spot. 'Not here,' Rico said. 'Too many people here.' We walked past tables with little candles on them, people were sitting at some of them, but I couldn't make out their faces. The room was in semi-darkness, just a few spotlights above the cage, trained on the woman. There was a light on her breasts now; it trembled a bit and then disappeared.

We sat down at the bar, right underneath her breasts. She turned around and the light was on her back.

'She's still wearing her knickers,' Rico said.

'Maybe she'll take them off.'

'I thought you'd been here before?'

'No, Paul told me about it, he's often in here.'

'Paul,' Rico said, stroking his hair down. 'I almost forgot about him. How's he doing?'

'He's alright,' I said, and waved the barmaid over; she didn't have much on either. 'Go round and see him, he'd be glad to see you... Two large beers, please!'

She was right in front of me and I looked at her bra and half of her breasts. She had two flowers tattooed around her navel, not roses, they had blue petals, and her belly was slightly curved, and I saw the flowers moving as she breathed. 'We've only got small beers.'

'That's OK,' I said, 'we'll take two small ones, then.'

'A round of applause for Chantal, charming Chantal, all the way from Paris, ooh là là! And now the queen of Leipzig, our lovely, sweet, blonde... Barabella!'

'That's not a name,' Rico said. He lit a new cigarette from the butt of the last one, looking at the cage, which was empty now. I felt someone walking along behind us but I didn't turn around. The barmaid put two beers down in front of us. She smiled. She leaned forward and I looked at the little triangle between her breasts. I ran my finger over the wood of the bar, I felt her ribs beneath her skin.

'My God, will you look at her, Barabella, my God, she's gorgeous!' Rico ran his hand over his eyes. Barabella was kneeling in her cage, her head and upper body lowered so that her blonde hair covered her whole body. She moved her head and shoulders to the music and the blonde curtain parted slightly, and we saw her breasts. I looked aside to where the barmaid was standing, drinking a little bottle of Coke. She had short dark hair and the rest of her wasn't as voluptuous as Barabella either, but I looked at her until she turned away and started cleaning glasses. Barabella had stood up now, her panties had disappeared and we looked at her blonde pubic hair. 'It's dyed, it must be dyed, my God, that looks gorgeous, have you ever had a blonde?'

'No,' I said. My beer was all gone and I took Rico's glass. Barabella turned around and stuck her arse out in our direction, rubbing it with both hands. Rico looked for something in his trouser pocket, his keys fell out and he bent down and picked them up. Barabella held her pants in her hand and swung them in front of her breasts, then squatted down and put them back on. She reached for the pole, rubbed her back against it and gradually straightened up. Then she stalked along a kind of catwalk out of the cage and onto the bar. She danced along the counter in little steps. A few people came forward and stuck notes in her knickers. I didn't want to see their faces, so I looked at their hands, briefly touching her hips and thighs before they stuck the money in. Barabella came dancing over to us slowly, she was wearing fluffy red shoes with a bobble on the front, and I took my hand off the bar. She stopped in front of us, one foot right next to the ashtray. I looked up; she had long nipples that pointed up at the ceiling. All I had left was a hundred and a whole load of coins, but I couldn't give her them. Rico's hand was on her hip now, and he was sticking a tenner into her panties with the other. 'Wait,' he said and rummaged around in his pocket again. She smiled and moved her torso. Her navel wasn't as nice as the barmaid's. Rico touched her thigh and her pants before he put the money in. It was twenty marks, and for that he touched her knee again as he pulled his hand away. Barabella went on dancing, then got down from the bar and went through a door at the end of the room. 'Another round of applause for our swinging blonde Barabella!' I turned around and saw the announcer. He was standing behind us right by the wall, on a little platform. There was a desk in front of him with tech stuff on it, and he was holding a mic and waving his arms around as he spoke. 'And now, a warm welcome for our exotic jungle beauty, Li Dong Kallam!' A little Vietnamese woman walked past us and went through a door into the bar. She was holding one of those brown women's cigarettes and she dropped it before she got in the cage. The barmaid stepped on it. She was wearing white trainers. 'Two beers,' I said.

'And two double Jack Daniels,' Rico added, looking at the cage where the Vietnamese girl was dancing with her bra off. She'd probably taken it off before she climbed in the cage. She wasn't moving properly to the beat, and she looked small and unhappy, although she was smiling.

'I thought you were skint, Rico?' He put his hand in his pocket and pulled out a roll of banknotes. He waved it in front of my nose, grinning at me. I could see the Vietnamese girl looking over at us and stumbling even more as she danced and pressed her little breasts to the bars.

'You got it from the guy, that pimp...'

'Nah, Danny, I didn't take everything off him, 'cause of the girl in the bar, you know, so he could pay the bill, right, and 'cause of Goldie as well.'

'That guy might mean trouble, who knows who he knows...'

'Rubbish, stop worrying about it, I know enough people, and anyway, we wanted to celebrate!'

The barmaid brought the beer and whisky. I picked up my glass and stared at the ice cubes. 'To you,' I said.

'To you,' said Rico. We drank. 'I drank something inside once, the Russians made it out of bread and apples and that. Yeah, it was called samogon, I think.'

I didn't want to hear anymore jail stories. I'd heard too many from other people. The Vietnamese girl came out of her cage. She was wearing high heels, tripping along the bar. Her left foot bent to one side as she danced past an ashtray. She stumbled, raised her arms and almost fell off the bar. It looked pretty good to the music, but still no one came to give her any money for it. She danced back the way she'd come, not stumbling this time, and an old man went over to her, white hair, patted her hip and stuck a note in her panties. 'Shit,' Rico said next to me. 'She's lonely, really lonely.' He got up and walked over to her. Holding his roll of money in one hand, he pulled a couple of notes out. The old man was still standing there looking up at her. Rico tapped him on the shoulder and the old man turned around and walked slowly back to the tables. Rico stuck his money in the little Vietnamese girl's panties; the old man's note was on her other hip. She smiled and climbed down from the bar. She stroked Rico's face and pressed her little breasts against his shirt, then whispered something in his ear. I saw Rico leaning his face against her hair. He stroked her back with one hand but then pulled it away again, quick. She pattered around in front of him, laughing, then she crossed the bar to a small door. She leant her head back as she walked, like she was looking at the ceiling, stuck her little breasts out and walked really slowly 'cause she didn't want to trip.

Rico came over to me. 'She was kinda great,' he said.

'Did she want you? She's hot for you, right?'

'Oh, she just said she'll do it for fifty and she'll be in Kremer Chaussee after midnight...'

'That's a brothel, it's crap, it's not worth it!'

'She'll give me a discount, fifty, but full service, if you know what I mean!'

'She's just trying to get you through the door, man, you don't really wanna go there, do you, it's really shitty there, Kremer Chaussee's a right dump!'

'You ever been there, Danny?'

'Been outside to take a look, but inside... nah.'

Number 5 Kremer Chaussee had been the first brothel in town, opened in spring 1990. Actually it was a normal block of flats in the north of town, you could walk up and down the stairs and the girls stood waiting in the open front doors and looked at you. Walter'd told me that once, and he said the black girls lived in the basement and on the ground floor, the Asian girls in the middle, and the German girls up the top. That was probably crap, though – I'd asked him what the Polish and Russian girls did but he didn't know about them, and sometimes when I was in the north of town I'd stood down outside number 5 Kremer Chaussee and looked up at the red curtains at the windows.

'Hey,' Rico said, grabbing my shoulder, 'Jesus, you know I need a woman, properly, you know, not just to look at, I want to do it properly again, flesh and blood!'

'OK, it's your night,' I said. 'I won't leave you on your own. If you want to go over there, go and meet her... Let's have another drink first.' I didn't know how much money he'd taken off the guy; the wad was getting smaller, but it must still have been well over a hundred.

The music got quieter and the announcer started up again. 'A round of applause for lovely young Carmen, turned sweet eighteen just last week so this is only her fifth time here with us!' And then she came in, walked past us, just strolled across the bar and climbed into the cage. Her name wasn't Carmen, and the old days weren't over.

Rico dug me in the ribs. 'Jesus,' he said, 'look who it is!' I didn't answer. I stared into the cage and at her breasts, the breasts she never used to show me even though I'd have done anything for her, anything, and not just for her breasts.

'That arsehole's telling lies,' said Rico, 'total porkies. Carmen! What a load of toss, and wasn't she a bit younger than us and all, is she eighteen already?'

'I think so. It's ages ago. You know, the thing with Fred,

it's so long...'

'Shit. It's so long ago.'

I nodded.

'Inside, Danny, you know, time just...'

'Yeah,' I said.

'Hey, weren't you really into her, Danny?'

'Leave it, Rico, it was all... just don't.'

'Estrellita,' Rico said, 'Little Star, yeah, that's what we... no, that was you, it was you called her that.'

'Be quiet,' I said, but he went on talking, about her and about back then, the old days that were somehow never really over, and I stopped listening, I smoked one of his cigarettes and looked over at her in the cage. She was a good dancer. She moved her body right in time to the music, she'd always been a good dancer. She still looked beautiful. Something in her face had changed though; I didn't know what. Back then she'd just disappeared, from one day to the next, no one knew where she'd gone. Someone told me later she'd met some guy from the West, some bigmouth who'd talked crap about the good life and all that. Now she was back here, and she was dancing for us. She'd looked so fragile back then when she'd come out of the coma, after over a month. We'd visited her in hospital and I'd sat down on the edge of her big bed and held her hand, for over an hour, 'cause she was so cold. Her face had been pale and her eyes had been white too, with tiny pupils. She looked at me but she was looking somewhere else, it looked like she was searching for something. Maybe she was still there, part of her. She stood on the bar in front of us and waggled her hips. Her panties were stuffed with notes. I tried to look her in the eye again but she turned her head. Rico rummaged in his pocket and added a twenty to the notes covering up her navel. I put my hand on the tip of her shoe. Now I looked her in the eye, she looked over at Rico, and then she smiled. She turned to the side slightly and ran one hand over her breast.

'It's... it's really nice to see you again,' Rico said. 'Will you have a drink with us, after?' I looked at her teeth as she moved her lips.

'Applause, a round of applause for our teen star! Carmen's young, she loves dancing and she's guaranteed to come again!' Carmen got down from the bar and walked past us to the little door at the back of the room. She put her bra back on as she went, stopping for a moment and fiddling with the fastening at the back. Rico got up and went over. He stood behind her, said something in her ear and then did up her bra. Estrellita turned around to me, laughed and then disappeared through the little door. Rico sat back down next to me.

'What did you say to her?'

'I said she's got nothing to be ashamed of and that you're glad to have seen her naked at last. Am I right?'

'You're an idiot.'

'But listen, Danny, it's crazy, it's really... I mean, I don't give a monkey's what she does, but here of all places!'

'It's better here than Kremer Chaussee, at least.'

'Hey, Danny, don't tell her anything about the little Viet girl... What d'you think, d'you think Estrellita would give me a... You wouldn't mind, would you? Nah, we'll go to Kremer Chaussee later on, that little girl's got me all...'

I nodded. I picked up my glass. I thought of the women standing and waiting there, outside the front doors. I thought of Estrellita's front door, where I used to wait some nights until I fell asleep on the stairs. Estrellita stood in front of me and said: 'So how's it going?'

'Alright,' I said.

'Mmh, yeah,' said Rico.

'Let's go to a table,' she said. 'Better than sitting here.' She was wearing black trousers now and a dark blue T-shirt.

We left the bar for a table in a corner. Rico lit the tea light with his lighter. 'Romantic,' I wanted to say, but then I didn't. I sat down in an armchair, Estrellita and Rico sat side-by-side on the sofa. It looked red, dark red, but it might have been brown or purple as well. Not enough light. 'You're a good dancer,' I said.

'Yeah,' she said and gave a quick smile and then looked at the table. The barmaid came over with a bottle and three glasses; I looked closely – it was a bottle of bubbly, some brand I didn't know. 'It's on me,' Estrellita said. I watched the barmaid walk away; her panties had slipped out of place.

The fabric of Estrellita's black trousers looked expensive. 'Making good money,' I said.

'Yeah,' she said, fiddling with her glass. I picked up the bottle and poured for her.

'Fill it right up,' Rico said, holding his glass out to me. 'It's really good stuff.'

We raised our glasses. 'To you,' I said to her.

'And to money,' said Rico, grinning. We drank. The wine was sweet and I felt it hit me after only a few sips.

'What are the others up to?' she asked.

'Not many of them left,' I said. She nodded. I didn't know if she'd heard about Mark's death, but Walter had been gone a few years now and Fred had disappeared as well, first to jail and then somewhere else.

'A girl's gotta pay the bills,' Estrellita said. 'I've always liked dancing. It might not be what I used to want, but Danny, I earn good money here, I can put some aside. I'll give it up one day, obviously, you know...'

'Sure,' said Rico. 'That's right, everybody's gotta pay

the bills!' He slammed his fist down on the table, so hard the bottle tipped over and I had to grab it. Wine foamed out of the top, I whisked my glass underneath it, and Rico leaned forward and drank the rest.

'And it's fun too,' Estrellita said. 'I've always liked dancing.' She gave a quick smile and then looked at the table. Rico budged up closer to her. He topped his glass up again and downed half of it.

'What were you doing, I mean while you were away for those years? No, you don't have to tell us, it's rude to ask. Me, I'm just the same as before. I'm not one to get knocked down, no, not me. You're beautiful now, Estrellita!'

'No one calls me that anymore.' She looked over at me. I looked at the floor, then back at her eyes. There was something different about her face but I didn't know what.

'Your Danny,' Rico said, patting me on the back, 'he's getting married soon, wife and kids, you know, and then he'll be out of the picture!'

'Bollocks, don't talk crap!'

Estrellita laughed and topped up her glass. 'Remember how we used to get beer, by the crate? Even I had to help carry it!' She looked at her fingernails, which were very long and varnished black.

'You with your little paws,' I said, taking her hand. She pulled it away.

'Most of that bloody beer was out of date, and they gave me a full rap sheet for it!' Rico slammed his fist on the table again, not as hard this time, so only the glasses clinked. 'That's where all the shit started!'

'Stop it,' I said. 'It's all crap, stupid talk! No one remembers what days what started!'

'Look,' said Estrellita, pointing over at the cage. 'That's Ramona, she's had a boob job. D'you like the look of them? They're real hunks of meat!' We looked in the cage. There was a woman dancing there, small and petite, only her breasts were pretty big. The woman danced slowly around the pole; she probably couldn't dance any faster 'cause her breasts were too heavy for her little body.

'Yeah,' said Rico, 'you're the real thing!' He stroked her shoulder, his little finger resting on her breast. She looked down at his hand and placed it back on the back of the sofa.

I stood up. 'D'you drink whiskey, Estrellita?'

'Course, you know that.'

'I'll get three on my bill.'

'But get Coke in it, Danny, I don't drink so much these days, have to take care of myself!' She ran a hand through her hair. I went over to the bar. Behind me, I heard Estrellita's laugh and then Rico's voice. I walked faster, hearing only the music now. I leaned both arms against the counter. The barmaid came over but I looked past her at the bottles and glasses. 'Three Jim Beams,' I said. 'One of them with Coke, please.'

I'd always liked Jim Beam better, it was softer than Jack Daniels, Rico's favourite. Plus, the bottle cost a couple of marks less at the supermarket, but that didn't actually matter 'cause we never paid for it anyway. 'Might as well nick the good stuff,' Rico used to say, but it was way harder whenever I went for a fifty-mark bottle of Dimple's, 'cause the bottle was this extravagant shape and the corners pressed against my belly down my trousers and sometimes even gave me bruises... 'Your whiskey, here you go!' I looked at the barmaid's face, a different face now, I looked at her navel and the blue flowers had gone, just a long fold right across it. Shift change, I thought, and picked up the glasses, two in one hand, I balanced them carefully and walked back to our table. I couldn't find it at first and saw a man sitting there on his own, drinking a blue drink out of a tall thin glass. Then I saw Rico's cigarette packet on a table, but the sofa was empty. I sat down and waited. Maybe they'd popped into Estrellita's dressing room, if she had one, maybe he'd talked her into it and was giving her one in some corner or other. I'd always imagined she wouldn't let anyone have her, or at least only one guy a month, 'cause I wanted her for myself. But that was all over now, other girls came along, like Anna, who could have been her sister, to look at. There were lots of girls like her round our way, but every one of them had something special. I drank my whiskey and got up, shaking the ice cubes into Estrellita's glass. I needed a pee.

I didn't find the toilets right away so I asked one of the huge bouncers, who smiled at me like he was gay and pointed them out. I walked past the Ladies; the door was half-open and I closed it. I opened it quietly again 'cause I'd heard Estrellita's voice. I can't believe it, I thought, he's giving her one, he's giving her one in the fucking toilets. I looked in but didn't see anyone, then I heard Rico's voice from one of the three cubicles. I heard someone coming down the corridor behind me, went in and eased the door shut. The room and the washbasins looked clean.

'Go ahead, help yourself to a bit more!' That was Rico. I heard something crackling and crinkling, then there was a sound like someone sniffing up snot.

'Yeah,' said Estrellita. Then I heard the sound again, very long this time, and I knew it.

'Good, eh?' Rico said. 'It's pure stuff, got it straight from the source.' You stupid bastard, I thought. I'd looked away for a moment and he'd gone and emptied that guy's pockets. Estrellita laughed. Her laugh echoed around the Ladies, bounced off the walls, and Rico said: 'Not so loud, someone'll come in!'

'Not in here, Rico, the girls go backstage. Give us a bit more, Rico, go on. And then we'll go back in, yeah? 'Cause of Danny, I mean, or he'll notice.'

'You and your Danny.'

I heard Estrellita snorting more of the stuff, making noises that sounded like quiet moans. 'Stop it, Rico, don't. Not like...'

'Why not, Jesus, why the hell not, Estrellita, come on...'

I heard her shoes clattering on the tiles. 'No, Rico, shit, stop it, I don't want to, stop it!'

'Alright, fine, if you say so. They've just let me out, you know. I only just got out.'

'Oh Rico, but I don't want to, no, sorry, but everything's different...'

'Just let me have a little feel, just a feel, you know, just let me touch!'

'Jesus, Rico, stop it, please, let go of me or I'll run out of here, please, Rico, stop it!'

I stood there listening to them. I thought for a moment whether to kick the door in and drag Rico out, but no, I'd never do it, even if he didn't stop. I'd go out to the bar, drink another whiskey there and wait. I'd put Rico's cigarettes in my pocket so nobody nicked them, and I'd light one. Estrellita was crying now. 'It's alright,' Rico said. 'It's alright. I'm sorry, I'm really sorry, I didn't mean to, I'll stop, hey, I'm sorry...' I'd never heard her cry before, but she was quiet again now. 'I'm sorry, jeez, I didn't mean to. In there, you know, in... in there, hey, stop crying, come here, let me wipe that up, no more tears now. You're so beautiful, you know, no need to be scared now. I'm back to normal, Estrellita, I'm back to good old Rico.' She sniffed a bit, not drugs this time. 'Look,' said Rico. 'Want some more? Go on, take a bit, it's straight from the source. Don't be like that, give us a laugh!'

And she laughed, I really heard her laugh.

I opened the door and left. I walked down the corridor, then I remembered I needed a pee. I turned around and went to the Gents. A man was standing at one of the urinals so I stood two urinals down. He made a huffing noise and I heard him splashing very loudly, then he was done and went out again. I washed my hands. There were no paper towels left so I wiped my hands on my trousers. I went back into the main room. I saw them straight off, sitting at our table drinking whiskey. Rico was sitting in my armchair and I sat down next to Estrellita on the sofa.

'Where've you been so long?' Rico asked.

'Just for a pee.'

'We thought you'd buggered off with one of the girls. Shit, where are my fags?'

'Here.' I took them out of my shirt pocket and put them down in front of him. Rico looked over at Estrellita, then gave her a cigarette.

She slid closer to me and rested her head on my shoulder. 'You know,' she said, 'everything used to be so different.'

'Yeah,' I said, looking Rico in the eye. He looked at me for a moment, his mouth twitched, then he stared into his glass.

'Gotta go in a minute,' Estrellita said, and I felt her voice in my shoulder. 'Gotta go home, done so much dancing today. I'm tired...'

'You get a good night's sleep,' said Rico. 'You go on home and have a good sleep.'

'Done so much dancing,' she said, smoking and blowing the smoke past my shoulder. She kept her eyes closed, and I picked up her whiskey and Coke and drank it. Then she suddenly stood up. 'I've got to go now. Working again tomorrow.' She leaned down to me and I kissed her goodbye on the cheek. She did the same with Rico, and I saw his hand scratching away at the chair's arm. 'And you'll be back, right, you two?' was the last thing she said, and then she walked across the room, past the cage and the tables with the tea lights.

'D'you think she's got a boyfriend?' Rico said, watching her go. 'I didn't want to ask...'

'Me neither.' We smoked. The music was on in the background and all the songs sounded the same.

'...and here comes our very French little Cha-Cha-Chantal, with all her charms – straight from gay Paree!' I stood up.

'Where you going?'

'To the bar, one last one and then I'll pay my tab.'

'Alright, but then... come on, Danny, we'll take a taxi to Kremer Chaussee, to that little Vietnamese girl. There'll be someone for you too, I've still got money left, Danny, I'll pay for it, it doesn't matter anyway!'

We went over to the bar.

The taxi stopped. Rico paid and we got out. The taxi driver grinned and said: 'Have fun then, lads.' Rico slammed the door on his grin.

The taxi moved off, the sign on the roof lighting up a few yards away, and we saw it drive down the road and then disappear. 'How does that bastard know where we're going?' Rico said. It had turned cool and we did up our jackets. We'd got him to drop us off in a side street a few hundred yards away, not right in front of the building.

'There's nothing else round here,' I said. 'He put two and two together.'

'True, it's the back of beyond out here.' The street was dark, just a few lamps on, and there were no lights in any of the windows. We set off slowly. 'Here,' Rico held his pack out to me. 'Have another smoke.' We walked past a shop. The door had been kicked in and the window plastered with posters. I read: 'Boom Rave'.

'You excited?' Rico asked.

'No,' I said.

'Most people think about fucking in the autumn, more than in summer,' Rico said. 'You know why?'

'No,' I said.

'It's 'cause of the dark, 'cause it gets dark so early and all the leaves fall off the trees. That makes people sad and they start wanting a woman.'

'I dunno, really...'

'No, it's true! There it is, up there!' The dark street turned onto Kremer Chaussee, and ahead of us, right on the corner, we saw number 5. The windows were hung with red curtains, shining out into the night.

'Let's hope it's not too busy,' I said.

We crossed the road to the door, which was big and black, and I'd reached out for the handle when Rico said: 'I'm dying for a piss, come on, we'll just have a quick one...' We walked to the next building and peed on the wall.

'Hey, Rico...'

'What?'

'Oh, nothing.'

We went in. Right after the front door were a couple of steps and a landing, and behind that we saw more stairs leading up. We undid our jackets. On the landing was a chair, and on the chair was a huge guy. He looked like a bad guy in a film, wearing a black sleeveless T-shirt, his face covered in scars, and his arms were so puffed up there was room on the left one for a dragon breathing fire, and there was a skull on the other side, grinning even though it was up in flames. The giant had his head down, only looking up to nod as we passed him. The first front door was right by the staircase. It was closed, with a radio on inside, turned up pretty loud; we could hear the weather report.

'Hey, Rico,' I whispered. 'Give us some of that cash.'

He stuffed a fifty and a tenner in my shirt pocket. 'That'll have to do,' he said. I turned around to the giant, still sitting silently on his chair and looking like he was asleep. We walked up the stairs. Rico stopped again and leaned over the bannisters. 'Hey boss, I'm looking for a little Asian girl...'

'Third floor on the right.' He spoke very quietly. The really dangerous ones never make a lot of noise. We went on up. First floor. The two front doors were open. There were two women in the doorway on the left: a tall black one in a white bra, and the other one was pretty short and pale and looked really young. The little one was wearing a leather collar and boots, and the little of what she had on was leather as well. Outside the other door, a blonde was sitting on a stool. She was forty if she was a day, but she still looked good. She wasn't wearing a bra; maybe she'd have been better off with one, but when she saw me looking at her breasts she stood up. She came towards me, put her hand on my back and pressed me against her, and I felt her bare breasts through my shirt.

'Come on,' she said. 'Come on, come inside, I'll do it so good, I'll give you everything I've got.' She pulled and tugged at me. She kept hold of my arm, and when I stopped and turned back round to Rico, her hand clenched around my arm, and she started fumbling with my flies with her other hand. 'I'll treat you so good,' she said, pressing herself against me, 'I'll blow you so hard, come on in, come quick, I need it right now!' I saw the other two women standing with Rico, the black one behind him stroking his back, the little one rubbing her head against his chest. She had studs on her leather collar.

Rico extracted himself and then ran up the next flight. 'See you downstairs, Danny,' he called, and then all I heard was his footsteps. I put my hand on the blonde's shoulder, we went inside and walked down the hallway. I looked into a room where a woman was sitting on the floor by a sofa, leaning her head against the cushions. She was naked. She stared out at the hallway, right past us, not seeing us.

'Come on in,' said the blonde, opening a door at the end of the hallway. We walked into a small room. She went over to the huge bed, took off her panties and sat down on the edge. She put her hands on her knees. 'You like what you see? I'm so hot for you. Take off your clothes, quick!' She stood back up and came towards me. She stood close and unbuttoned my shirt. She took my jacket and threw it on a chair. It hung off the back for a moment and then fell on the floor. The blonde went over, bent down and picked up the jacket, patting it before she returned it to the back of the chair. She smiled and sat down on the chair and rubbed her breasts with both hands. 'Come on,' she said. 'I'm so hot for you, come and touch me, come here, I'll blow you real good.' I went over to her. She undid my belt and I stoked her breasts. 'A hundred,' she said. 'I'll treat you real good for a hundred.' I gave her Rico's sixty, then I checked my trouser pocket and gave her the rest. She took the money and went to a low chest. Then she lay down on the bed. 'Come on, come on then!' I'd taken everything off, and I lay down next to her. I stroked her thighs, then I leaned over her and licked her breasts. 'Hey,' she said, 'hey, kiddo, that costs extra! I'll give you a blow job and then you fuck me, but tongues cost extra.' I rolled back onto my side. My hand was still on her thigh. She'd propped herself up and bent over me and rubbed her breasts on my chin and my lips. 'Twenty,' she said. 'Gimme another twenty and then you can go down on me! Come on, my sweet little pussy's waiting for you!' She grabbed my hand and pressed it between her legs for a moment. She was shaved and I felt her stubble against my skin. I went over to my jacket for the money. It was the last I had on me. I gave it to her and she went back to the chest. I lay down and looked at the sheet as she bent over and opened the drawer. There was a condom by the pillow.

I walked back down the stairs. As I passed the other room, I looked in. She was still sitting on the floor in there, naked and staring at the wall through the open door. The giant was standing next to his chair, smoking a cigarette. 'Has my mate come out yet?' I asked him.

'No,' he said, blowing smoke in my face.

'Mind if I wait here for a bit?'

'No. But only ten minutes, then you leave.'

'It's cold out. Hey, could you lend me one, you'll get it back from my mate...'

'Don't worry about it.' He gave me a cigarette and then handed me his lighter. I leaned against the wall to smoke. I searched my pockets but all I found was a few coins. Someone came down the stairs; I could tell it wasn't Rico by the footsteps. It was a pretty thin bloke but his shoes made a lot of noise. He said goodbye as he left but the giant didn't answer. He trod his cigarette out and sat back down. The radio was still on inside the flat and I tried to listen to the music. 'See you soon,' someone said inside the flat, right by the door, and then the door opened. A man came out and walked past me but I didn't look at him, I only looked at Estrellita, standing in the doorway and fastening her bathrobe.

'How's business upstairs, Spud?' she called.

'Alright,' the giant said.

'I'll leave the door open. Gimme a sign if punters come, gimme a call or something!'

'Yeah, yeah.'

She hadn't seen me; she went back inside. I saw the green bathrobe in the hall, then it vanished through a door. I turned around and walked past Spud, outside. I sat down on the kerb and chucked my cigarette away. I did my jacket up. The night was cold and I could see lots of stars.

I heard the door opening behind me. Rico sat down next to me. We stared at the dark buildings across the road. A taxi drove past, the sign on the roof lit up. Rico leapt up and waved it over. 'Let's go home, Danny.'

We got in and Rico told the driver our addresses. The car pulled off. We didn't speak on the way.

I lay in the dark, staring at the ceiling. Down on the street, I heard a car driving off. Must have been the cops. I was ashamed. Of my mum. Because she'd cried. She'd already had tears under her eyes as she stood outside the front door in her nightshirt with a cardigan over it, and the two cops brought me up the stairs. They hadn't taken the handcuffs off even though I'd said to them a couple of times: 'Take the bloody cuffs off, I'll be home any minute.' The bastards wanted me to stumble up the stairs with my hands behind my back, and then I stood facing my mum with my shoulders bent back and my head down, them behind me, and I felt in my back that they were grinning in their spinach-green uniforms.

Once the cops had left my mum really started crying, filled a glass, went back to bed and carried on crying. I'd heard her through the wall until not long ago, but now she was quiet. Maybe she'd fallen asleep. She hadn't said a thing to me, not a word. Mark's dad had probably gone ballistic again, maybe he'd hit him, and Mark would be lying in bed crying, no, he was lying in bed smoking a cigarette. He'd locked his bedroom door from the inside and was laughing at his dad. There wasn't a dad for me. I got up and felt for the light switch. My face was sticky. I took off my outdoor shoes. I'd only taken my jacket off, before, and laid down on the bed and blocked my ears. I went down the hall to the kitchen. The floorboards creaked slightly and I heard my mum breathing in her room. The door was ajar; I closed it carefully. Mum was asleep, and that was good 'cause she had to go to work at the fish factory at six thirty. It was the only fish factory in Leipzig 'cause it was a long way to the sea. I stood in the kitchen and turned on the light. I locked the door; the key was always on the inside. We didn't have a bathroom but the tenants before us had put in a shower cubicle where the pantry used to be. They'd buggered off to West Germany just before 89; otherwise they'd never have given up the flat, 'cause of that shower. There was only one other shower in the building, down at Wolfert's place, and sometimes the woman from upstairs came round to take a shower. She'd have a drink with my mum as well then. Once, she came when my mum wasn't in and we shagged in the shower, four times, and my skin was really dry afterwards. She was 48 but it didn't matter. We didn't let the woman next door use our shower; she had too many cats.

I saw my face in the mirror, above the sink by the door. I was all white, only my eyes were red, I hadn't cried, no, it must have been the drink and the smoke and the night. My left eye was black. I had blue eyes, more grey-blue, but under my left eye was blue too and a bit swollen. In the mirror, I saw a bottle of Nordhäuser Korn on the kitchen table. I went over. It was open, the lid next to it. The alcohol had almost completely left my head, taken away by the bloody cops. I screwed the lid on the bottle and put it on the shelf. The black eye wasn't that bad, it'd look impressive, especially at school. My mum had stuck my timetable to the fridge. I took it off when one of my friends came round. I went back to the sink and washed my face. There was piss on my face. Old Wolfert's dog howled on the ground floor. It must have been around three 'cause the dog always howled around then, luckily not for long though, 'cause then the old man went out in the backyard with him and smoked a couple of cigarettes. The dog howled again, sounded almost like a wolf, and then went quiet. The American Indians believe the last thing we'll hear on earth before it breaks down forever is a wolf's howl. I read that once. I loved Indians, I wanted to get one tattooed on my upper arm, or better on my lower arm so everyone could see it, by this inker Rico knew from jail. Next week, probably. I took off my jumper and dried my face on it, 'cause I didn't want to use the old towel. I looked in the mirror again; my arms were a bit thin but I looked pretty good in my tight vest, even though it was a bit grubby. Mum's cigarettes were on the kitchen table, Cabinett 100s, and I took one out of the pack. I couldn't find a lighter so I turned on the gas cooker. I opened the balcony door and went outside. Down in the backyard, in the corner with the bins, I saw a shadow with a little red dot where the old man was standing and smoking; I couldn't see the dog. I flicked the ash down, went back inside and stood in front of the mirror with the fag in the corner of my mouth. A rebel, I thought, tensing my arm muscles. If Estrellita could see me now. I threw the cigarette in the sink and sat down at the table. I started getting undressed. I'd called her earlier, from the station. I'd yelled the place down until they let me make a call. Three of them had dragged me to the phone, 'cause I'd tried to kick one of them 'cause he wouldn't take the handcuffs off until we got to the phone, and he had his fucking paws on the back of my neck.

No one had answered at first, and then her dad picked up. 'Hello?'

'Hello, I'd like to talk to Little Star!'

'Who? There's no star here, you arsehole!'

I could hardly understand him, but it wasn't the connection.

'Listen, you, just go and get her right now, or I'll come over and...'

He'd hung up but I kept hold of the receiver and went on talking. 'It's me, Estrellita, no, don't be scared, no, you don't need to come and pick me up, I'll be right back, don't be scared...'

I turned on the water in the shower. I held my hand under the jet, then I turned the water back off and switched the boiler to five. I took one of mum's cigarettes; the gas was still on and I lit it. I felt the flame's warmth on my face and hair. I ran a hand through my hair, feeling hard blood at one spot. I sat back down at the table, smoking and waiting for the water to heat up.

'You little bastard,' said the cop right behind my head. He'd grabbed me by the hair and he pressed my face into the piss, my piss. 'You little bastard think you can just go and piss here? I'm asking you: Are you at home here?' I said nothing. I pursed my lips and breathed into my own piss. He let go of me. I felt and heard him standing up and taking a few steps back.

I lifted my head out of the puddle. I turned around. 'You know what?' I said, and I was glad there was piss under my eyes, but that bastard wouldn't have seen my half a dozen tears anyway. 'It's about time you gave your boyfriend a really good seeing to again.'

The other cop was standing in the corner, smoking. The pervert took a step towards me. 'Get up,' said the cop who was smoking. 'My colleague's going to take you to make a statement.' The water was warm. I pissed as I showered. The toilet was in the stairwell, one flight down. I wouldn't have peed in the waiting room if they'd have let me go to the toilet.

They'd taken us to give blood first, three cops holding onto Mark. 'Get that fucking needle away from me!' Then Mark was gone and I went into one of the waiting rooms with them. There was a window in the wall with cops sat behind it, on the phone. I'd seen two uniforms in the corridor, shoving a Vietcong around. The guy had his arms behind his back, we all had our arms behind our backs, I felt kind of good about it, I was better than James Dean, even though it hurt, and the Vietcong had nothing on except a pair of way too big underpants. He yelled something in his language, his voice high and shrill like a woman's, and I whispered: 'It'll be alright, mate.'

I turned off the water. I went out on the balcony and took a towel off the washing line. I looked down at the yard and the buildings on the other side; no light in any of the windows. I was scared of jail, things could move so fast. I went back inside, sat down and shut my eyes. And then I heard Mark singing. 'Two, two, the lily-white boys, dressed all in green, O, Cops are bastards, pigs are cunts,' and then he yelled the last line, 'And evermore shall be so!'

I took the cigarette Mark had stuck behind my ear before they'd taken him away, and lit it. He'd put one behind my other ear as well but that one was gone. Then I sang along: '...Cops are bastards, pigs are cunts, And evermore shall be so!'

'Danny,' Mark yelled through the walls and the halls and the doors, 'we're gonna get 'em, the bastards!'

Someone took the fag out of my mouth. 'You old enough to smoke?'

'Course,' I said, and the pervert took my fag over to the big silver ashtray in a corner and put it out. Mark was quiet now. There were typewriters hammering everywhere. I lay on my bed smoking. I didn't have an ashtray so I flicked the ash in an empty Coke can, which gave off low hisses.

My alarm clock said it was 4:08. I'd have to get up for school in two and a half hours. I thought of the big chemistry test coming up in second period, and I hoped I'd manage at least a C. I didn't give a shit, really, but it'd make my mum happy. It had all been a bit much recently, with the cops and all that, so many green nights. She'd had to go to court with me once, and she'd been so ashamed she'd left her cigarettes at home, 'It makes a bad impression,' she said, and she took my cigarettes away too and didn't give them back until after the trial. I only got a few hours' community service, but my mum moaned and groaned all the way home on the tram, which made me feel pretty bad, and then she still bought me a new pair of trousers in town. 'Don't you ever do it again, my boy, don't ever do anything like that again, please.'

'No,' I said. 'Never again. Never again, Mum.' But there was more trouble not much later, and my mum was really angry and probably sad too, when she had to come down to the cellar, and it wasn't just her that came down, it was everyone from the building, 'cause I'd turned off their electricity. 'Why... why do you do it, why don't you ever think of me, why are you like this?'

I wanted to tell her about Engel, who was waiting out in the street, the best and most famous street fighter in Leipzig East, a guy even the skins over in Grünau were scared of and who wanted to smash my face in with his ice hockey stick, I wanted to tell her Rico would knock him out later, but she wouldn't have understood. Engel was a brutal piece of shit, and if he didn't have his ice hockey stick with him (they said he used to be a hockey ace back in the Zone days) he'd break his opponent's nose with his forehead. I didn't actually have any beef with Engel, but he was a Lok Leipzig fan – they were called VfB Leipzig now and about to go up into the Bundesliga, actually Engel wasn't a real fan, he only went to matches for the punch-ups – and I hated Lok, me and my friends went to Chemie, that was my problem. 'Out, out, Chemie bastards out!' he'd yelled over in the park this one time, and I'd leant out the window, 'cause I'd had a bit to drink, and shouted as loud as I could: 'Shut your filthy mouth, you Lok bastard!'

My lips got warm; the cigarette was smoked down to the filter. I heard my mum in the hallway. She unlocked the front door and went down to the toilet. I took a new cigarette out of her pack; I'd taken it into my room. Sometimes, when my mum went to the toilet in the night, she had a smoke afterwards. I got up, picked up the pack, put another two cigarettes on my bed and went in the kitchen. I heard Mum coming back up the stairs, making noises as she walked 'cause her knee hurt sometimes. I put the pack on the kitchen table and dashed back to my room. I turned off the light and lay down on the bed. I heard mum walking around the flat, then she was back in the hall and opened my door. The light behind her made her nightshirt transparent and I stared at the wall. 'My cigarettes,' she said with her hoarse night voice. Then she shut the door again. I lit one up. It was always the same – I was supposed to feel guilty, and sometimes I did.

'Mum,' I'd said, 'Engel... Engel was outside, he would have beat me to death, I swear...'

'You and your crap,' she'd screamed, 'you and your crap! Don't you see? Why don't you see it?'

And she was right, in a way, Engel was dirt, and I was scared shitless of Engel, and he wasn't on his own, and if the two other guys hadn't been there I might not have been so scared, and I'd have gone up to Engel, nice and slow, and said: 'Hey, arsehole, you ready?' But I climbed over fences, over bins and backyards, until I got to our yard, and then my key was missing, the fifth time in a year. I stood outside the locked back door and heard their voices, really low, from the street side of the building. I climbed into the cellar through an open window. The cellar door leading to the stairwell was locked too, and now I heard their voices clearly.

'He'll turn up, that little wanker.' I heard a sound as well, a kind of knocking, probably their ice hockey sticks drumming against the ground or the wall 'cause they were impatient to get stuck in. If Rico'd been there we'd have faced up to them and caused plenty of damage, even if we hadn't beaten them. Rico always says: 'If you can't beat 'em, break 'em as much as you can.' He was training every day now, boxing his fists bloody in Pitbull's cellar so he could properly break Engel. And then... the fag fell out of my hand, the Coke can was gone and I put it out on the windowsill. The fuses, I unscrewed the fuses. It was nearly midnight and my mum was watching TV, everyone in the building was watching TV. I screwed the fuses back in and then out again. SOS. Get me out of here, you old farts. And then... and then... 'Shhh,' whispered Estrellita by my side. 'Forget Engel, forget the cops, let's get out of here, let's just stop, no more green nights and we'll never, never come back to all this crap.'

Dad fills up his glass again and downs it in one. 'Ahhh!'

'Here's to Chemie,' yells the bald man. 'Here, another fizzy drink.' He gives me a bottle of raspberry-red lemonade. 'Ernst Thälmann's sweat, the real thing,' he says. Dad laughs. What rubbish, I think. 'Salt sticks, salt sticks, lots and lots of salt sticks,' the bald guy yells and tears open a packet and shakes the sticks straight onto the table, some of them falling on the floor. No one tells the bald guy off 'cause it's his house. It's right by the East Woods, fifteen minutes away from our flat, if I run. I call it the doll's house 'cause it's so small, and it's all just for him. Dad often goes to see the bald man, and he stinks of booze when he comes home, and Mum tells him off. The bald man always goes to football too, we met him today after the match and he gave us a lift on his motorbike. 'No,' he said, 'I'm not driving you home, you're coming to mine, just for an hour, Horst, we need to celebrate!' Then he put me in the sidecar and fastened me in and pulled the tarpaulin up to my chin. Dad sat behind him and held onto his shoulders. The bald man drives slowly 'cause his motorbike's very old.

The bald man's wife comes in and gives me a plate of bread and butter. She's very pretty with long black hair that smells good, but she's not his real wife, Dad told me, she just cooks for him and he lets her sleep in his bed 'cause she hasn't got one of her own. Dad likes her, I can tell by his eyes when he talks about her. I eat my bread and butter. She's put too much salt on it. The doorbell. 'It's open,' the bald man yells, bits of salt sticks flying out of his mouth.

'Watch where you spit,' Dad says. He's smoking again, like he always does when he has a drink.

Two men come in. They're carrying a crate of beer. One of them has hair almost as long as Baldie's wife's. 'Here you are, jeez, we're dying of thirst here!'

'Took us a minute,' the long-haired man says. 'You brought your son, Horst?'

'Course I did, he's a Chemist too, aren't you?'

I blush. 'Dad,' I whisper, tapping him on the knee, 'we've got to go home.'

'Oh,' Dad says, 'we've got a bit of time, don't you worry. We'll just say the trains weren't running, what with the cops and the aggro.'

'Glöckner's coming by later. He'll know about it, I bet, the aggro, I mean.' The long-haired man takes four beer bottles out of the crate and puts them on the table. 'I heard things really kicked off, especially at the station in Leutzsch.'

'Berlin bastards,' Baldie says, opening his beer and passing on the bottle-opener.

The long-haired man's friend reaches into the crate as well and takes out a bottle. He comes over to me and holds it up to my face. 'Here you go, kiddo, drink one for Chemie!'

'No thanks, I've got a drink,' I say, holding up my fizzy drink.

'Hey, hey, hey,' Dad gets up. 'Watch it, the boy's only eight! Who are you, anyway?'

'Just kidding, just kidding around! Klaus, I'm Klaus, you know me, I was here the other week...'

'Alright... Klaus,' Dad says.

'Here's to victory, to Chemie,' calls Klaus.

'To victory, to Chemie,' they all shout, and they drink their beer. I don't join in the shouting. I drink my fizzy drink.

Dad picks up the korn bottle and fills the little glasses.

'And now,' he says, 'let's drink to our Hansi. We wouldn't have won today if it weren't for him!' He raises his glass and says again: 'To our Hansi!' I raise my bottle but nobody's looking.

I'm happy. Hansi's my favourite player. But Weiss, Weiss was just as important today. He was through on the Union goal. 'Please, please, score,' I whispered. I saw Dad's lips moving, but then all I saw was the ball flying towards the goal and the goalie flying to the ball with his arm outstretched. I stretch out my arm. 'Please, please, go in!' It's already in, it's well in now. The goalie's flat on the ground and the ball rolls back out of the goal. I hold my ears but I join in the cheering as well.

I'm standing on my seat, laughing. Dad takes my hand, shakes it and laughs and cheers. 'Glöckner's coming, Glöckner's here!' The doorbell. I get up and go in the kitchen. Baldie's wife is at the kitchen table, buttering bread.

I stand behind her 'cause her hair smells so good. She turns around. She smiles. 'Alright, kiddo?' she says, and I get a shock 'cause she smells of booze as well. There's a half-full glass on the kitchen table. 'Did you have a good time at the football?'

'Yes,' I say.

'Danny's your name, isn't it?'

'My name's Daniel.'

She strokes my head.

'Your hair's so long,' I say, and I blush.

'You're sweet,' she says, and she laughs a bit and strokes my head. 'You sit down on that chair and tell me a bit about the football. I'm not allowed to go, you know, he doesn't want me there. But I don't really want to. All those people, you know.'

'It's good at football,' I say. 'I go with my dad. He knows

everyone there.'

'Oh yes, your dad,' she says, and takes a sip from her glass. 'And you won today, didn't you?'

'Two-one. And now we won't get relegated.'

'Winning is good,' she says, slicing a big salami. 'He gets in a mood when Chemie lose, Baldie, I mean... then he's not as sweet as you!' She wipes at her eyes, like Mum when she's chopping onions, then she strokes my head again.

'Leitzke got the goal,' I say. 'And first it was Weiss, 'cause Union was in the lead.'

'And how old are you?'

'Eight. It was a bicycle kick. A real bicycle kick.'

A man comes in the kitchen. 'Anything to eat, you two?' He's got a blue teardrop underneath one eye, even though he's grinning. I've never seen blue tears, but this one's only tattooed on. He's wearing a short-sleeved shirt and his arms have all these pictures and words on them, 'pussy, fight,' and they even come out of his collar and wrap around his neck.

'You again, Glöckner,' Baldie's wife says. 'Come to nick some food as usual, have you?'

'Better than going in the nick,' Glöckner says, and laughs. He grabs the salami and bites into it. Then he cuts off the part with the bite in it and eats that bit. 'Maria, Maria,' he says, stroking her back, right where her hair ends.

'Stop it,' she says, and nods over at me.

'Oh, Horst's lad, Danny.'

I don't know how he knows me. I want him to leave Maria alone. 'Glöckner!' That's my dad. 'Come back in here. Tell us more, about the aggro!' Dad's standing in the doorway. He's holding a beer bottle and smiling at Maria. Glöckner goes over to him. 'We're going home soon,'

Dad says to me. 'Going home any minute, kid.' His cigarette falls out of his mouth and he picks it back up. They go in the other room; I follow them. There are loads of beer bottles on the table. I look for my fizzy drink but it's gone. The air's so full of smoke it makes me cough, and I go over to the window and open it. I lean my head on the windowsill and breathe the fresh air. Outside the window is a little garden but there's nothing growing there, just a few bushes, and behind them I see the road. I could get up on the windowsill and then climb out and run home. It'll only take a quarter of an hour, if I run fast. Mum's cooked and dinner will still be warm, I bet.

'...and then, and then?' Dad calls out. 'Did you get the bastards?'

'Well, then they all got on the train,' says Glöckner, 'and we chucked stones after them, it takes a while for the train to get moving, you know. But I think we got a couple of them, broke a few windows, they went straight through...'

'Jeez, it's their own fault though, coming to Leutzsch and then starting argie-bargie...'

'That's the last we'll see of them,' says the long-haired man, raising his glass. 'No more league, premiere league forever!'

'Danny, what are you doing over here?' my dad says. 'All on your own, standing around on your own...'

'Dad,' I say, looking out of the window, 'we've got to go home...'

'Course, Danny, just another half hour, you're having fun, aren't you? With the Chemie lads, come on kid, it needs celebrating. Has no one got a fizzy drink for the boy?'

Glöckner comes out of the kitchen and hands me a bottle of lemonade. 'Come here, kiddo,' he says, and rolls up his sleeves to his shoulder. 'Come and have a look at some pictures!'

'But none of your dirty stuff,' Dad says. I know he'd like a tattoo as well, the Chemie logo on his arm or his shoulder, he says he knows someone who'll do it for him, 'for a bottle of booze.' Mum doesn't want him to. She says it's banned and he'll get AIDs from it. I ask her what AIDs is and she says it's something new, something like cancer – that's what Grandad died of when I was little.

'Who's Pussy?' I ask.

'Oh, you know... an old girlfriend of mine, but look at this one, the snake with the knife!' The snake is blue with black eyes. It's curled around a knife and it looks more like a sock, but I don't say that to Glöckner.

'Is that your wife?' The woman's lying down on his shoulder with nothing on and crying blue tears like Glöckner.

'Used to be,' he says. 'Not anymore, no, not anymore.' Maria's standing next to me, looking at Glöckner's arm.

She puts a tray of sandwiches down on the table. There's a bottle of korn in between the sandwiches. Dad pushes in front of Maria. 'Look,' he says, putting his beer bottle down. 'These are real muscles, unsullied!' He rolls up his sleeves and shows off his muscles. Dad's strong, he builds machines, every day.

'Arm wrestling,' Glöckner shouts, clapping his hands. 'It's still two-one to me. And it'll soon be three-one!'

'Alright, Glöckner,' says Dad. 'The winner gets to kiss Maria!'

'You're like kids, you are,' she says, blushing. 'Aren't you ashamed of yourself, Horst?' and then she goes up to him and whispers, but I can still hear it, 'In front of your boy.'

Dad and tattooed Glöckner fetch two chairs from the

kitchen and sit down at the table. Baldie comes from somewhere or other; he looks tired and he pushes the glasses aside. 'On you,' he says, kneading Dad's shoulders. 'My money's all on you, Horst!'

The long-haired man and Klaus scoot their chairs up closer to the table. Their faces are all red and they're sweating. 'Hey, Baldie,' says Klaus, and I can barely understand him 'cause his voice is so slurred, 'a tenner on Glocki, you on?' He takes a whole load of coins out of his pocket and jangles them onto the table. The bald man goes to the wall unit and moves aside a picture of a boxer; I've only just noticed it; I'll have to have a look at it before we go.

Baldie puts a note on top of the coins. 'Bloody small change,' he says, kneading my dad's shoulders again. Glöckner takes off his shirt, he's wearing a vest underneath, and I count four patches of skin on his chest and shoulders that haven't got pictures.

'Show us, Glöckner, show us what you've got,' Klaus calls out. He raises his bottle to his lips but half of it runs down his chin to his jumper.

Baldie fills up two little glasses and puts them in front of Dad and Glöckner. 'Down in one,' he says, 'and then you start.' They're already in position, the palms of their hands touching, and now they clench into each other.

'Nice and slow, Glöckner,' says Dad, sliding around on his seat. Dad's going to win, I think, Dad's going to win 'cause he's strong. They both pick up their shot glass with their free hand and drink. Dad slams his on the table with all his might.

'Hands behind your heads,' Baldie yells. 'Put your free hands behind your heads!' They both raise the other arm and put their free hand on the back of their necks. They're pressing and pressing like crazy, Glöckner's arm's even fatter than before, and the naked woman on his shoulder moves up and down.

Maria's standing behind Dad, and now she leans down to him so her hair falls on the back of his neck. I hear Dad's teeth grinding. 'You're not gonna get me,' he whispers between his teeth. Glöckner doesn't say anything. His face goes red and his arm moves slowly towards the tabletop. Dad's gonna beat him, I think, yes, I know he is. His arms aren't as big as Glöckner's but they've got more strength in them. A whistle comes out of Glöckner's mouth that sounds like 'Nooooo,' then the back of his hand slams against the table.

'Yes!' Baldie shouts, and I laugh.

'Happy, are you?' Klaus gives me an angry look. 'That's my tenner gone though.' I'm still laughing, someone's stroking my head, must be Maria, and Dad picks me up by the shoulders and puts me down on the table. Glöckner's sitting in an armchair, drinking a new beer. Now it looks like his blue teardrop is real.

I get down from the table and stand in front of him. 'Don't be sad,' I say. 'You've got such pretty pictures.'

'Oh, I'm not sad,' he says. 'It's two-two now.' Baldie's in the chair next to him, his chin on his chest. He's smoking with the korn bottle gripped between his legs. A bit of ash falls on his jumper. I go over to the wall unit, to the picture of the boxer. He's holding his gloves right in front of his chin so you can only see half his face, but the top half looks like Baldie, except the man in the photo has blond hair.

'Maria,' Baldie shouts behind me, and then again: 'Maria, where've you gone?' Maria doesn't answer, and Baldie's quiet again now. I turn around. The long-haired man and Klaus have got playing cards on the table and are talking quietly to Baldie.

Glöckner gets up and goes over to them. 'Oh, leave him to it,' he says. 'Let's have a round of cards.'

'Come here, kid,' Longhair calls. 'We'll teach you a thing or two!' I walk over to them. My father's gone. He has to pee a lot when he drinks beer.

'I know how to play skat,' I say. I sit down on the sofa next to them.

Glöckner passes me the cards. 'You're the dealer. You can join in the next round.'

'Having a nice game, are you, Danny?' Dad's standing in the kitchen doorway. He's got a cigarette in his mouth and he's tucking his shirt in. 'We're going home soon,' he says, 'going home any minute.'

We're walking through the East Wood. Dad's holding my hand. He's swaying, pulling me side to side. It's already getting dark and I think of Mum. She's standing waiting in the kitchen. Dinner's cold.

# ZEITHAIN JUVENILE CUSTODY CENTRE

After the judge, the public prosecutor, the clerk and the witnesses had left Courtroom 23, I stayed in my seat and stared at the wall behind the judge's desk. There was a brown stain there, the size of a hand, I'd been looking at it all the way through, I could see it every time the judge moved her head. The woman from the Youth Offending Team was still in the room; I watched her putting her papers in a green satchel, then she came over.

'Daniel, Danny, you know you can actually...'

'Blood,' I said quietly, staring past her at the stain.

'What? I mean, I think we can...'

'It's blood. That stain over there, it looks like blood.'

She turned around and looked at the wall. Then she looked me in the eye. I didn't want that; I lowered my head to the papers in front of me and started folding them up.

'I think there was no other option today,' she said. 'And I did keep telling you. So it's not a bad thing that...'

'It doesn't bother me,' I said, packing my papers in the red leather briefcase I'd borrowed from Paul. 'It doesn't bother me at all, you know.'

She was leaning her elbows on the desk between us, not taking her eyes off my face. 'But you have to go today... later today. Shall I come with you to the station to pick a train?'

'No,' I said. 'There's plenty of time.'

'Have you got the list of what you need to take with you?'

'Yes. I'm not a little kid.'

Her gaze passed me by. I turned around. There weren't any stains on the wall, it was perfectly clean and white. They'd recently done the building up, everything was new and modern-looking, except the judges and the public prosecutors and the cops and all the other court people were just as mean as before.

'You shouldn't have been late,' she said.

'Yes.' I looked at her hands, propping up her chin. I'd known her for two years now. I'd promised her every time that I'd never do stupid shit again, never. But things went differently, every time.

'And you shouldn't have,' she said, and I felt her breath on my neck even though there was enough space between our faces, '...well, it's up to you what you do with your... what you do. But for the judge, it was... it didn't make... a good impression, Daniel.'

'School,' I said. 'You mean school.'

'Yes,' she said, 'school.'

'Probation's alright,' I said. 'Could have been worse.' I leaned back in my chair and tapped the cigarette box in my breast pocket.

'And the four weeks, Daniel?'

'Four weeks, a month, that's nothing.'

She shook her head, just for a moment, and then straightened up. 'I don't want to see you back here again! Alright, Daniel?'

'Yes,' I said. 'That's it now, really. Honest.'

She held out her hand across the table, and I shook it. I knew her hand would be cold; it was cold every time. Must have been some blood pressure thing, and she wasn't that young either.

'I'm off now,' she said. 'Are you sure you don't want a lift? It's cold outside.'

'No, I'll just get the train.'

'If you're not there by this evening it'll only be worse.'

'I know.'

She went to the door, then turned back. 'Never again,' she said. 'You hear me?'

'Yes,' I said, standing up. 'Really this time, never again.' Did she smile as she turned and left?

My mum came home as I was packing my bag. That was exactly what I'd been afraid of, sitting on the train and looking out at the run-down houses and factories on either side of the line. Almost all the buildings you could see from the train were run-down or derelict, and the snow didn't make it any better; it looked like a whole gang had been on a rampage around Leipzig with hand grenades and machine guns.

She's gonna shout, I'd thought. And she shouted. That was nothing new; I just went on packing. 'Aren't you ashamed of yourself, boy?' she shouted. 'First school and now this. You and your crap. You and your crap. If your...'

'Don't you bring Dad into this!' I shoved my bag aside, straightened up and stood facing her. 'Don't bring Dad into it!' How small she was. She turned on her heel and left my room. She slammed the door but it didn't bang; I'd seen it coming and put an old T-shirt in the way. Dad had sometimes slammed doors when he'd been angry. I went on packing. A few pairs of pants, shirts, two jumpers, T-shirts, socks. 'Laundry facilities available,' it said on the list the judge had given me. I went through the kitchen to the clothes horse and took off a pair of trousers.

Mum was standing at the sink, washing up. She was all quiet now. I walked back past her, and as I was behind her she turned around suddenly and yelled in my face: 'Aren't you ashamed? Why aren't you ashamed of yourself? With your crap!' I took a few steps back and leaned against the wall. 'Why won't you stop?' she shouted. 'You like it, don't you? Why?'

'No,' I said. 'That's not true.'

'Why do you never think of me?' She was quieter now.

She stood in front of me and pressed her little fist against my chest. 'Why don't you ever think of me?'

'I do. It makes me mad as well. I messed up. I'm sorry... Mum, I'm sorry.' Please, I thought, please don't cry now.

But she shouted. 'Over... and over, and over again, it's always the same!' I slid past her, my back to the wall, and ran into my room. I heard her voice through the door. 'Over and over, always the same.' I lit a cigarette and opened the window.

It was afternoon, getting dark now. A few flakes were coming down outside the window, and I quickly flicked the ash out so it didn't fall so alone. There was an off-licence across the road; I saw people going in and out; I even heard bottles clinking in one man's bag.

I picked up Paul's red briefcase and opened it up. 'Individuals arriving under the influence of alcohol will be refused admission,' it said on the list. I screwed it up and threw it at the wall. Then I picked it back up and stroked it smooth, 'cause it had the map on it and I wouldn't find my way without it, even though Rico had told me a lot about Zeithain. There was a knock.

'Come in,' I said. Mum was in the door.

'Don't go getting up to anything in there,' she said. She was holding one of her long cigarettes and it looked like she was wagging her finger at me.

'No,' I said. 'Course not, you know that.'

'And do you really have to go today?'

'Yes,' I said.

'Do you know when the trains leave?'

'No,' I said.

'I'll give them a ring for you,' she said. 'The station, I mean.'

'Thanks, Mum.'

Did she smile as she turned and left?

At first, I'd thought about calling Paul so he could take me to the station. He would have carried my bag, I bet, and then he'd have waved, and he might even have run alongside the train. But I didn't want that.

Mum had gone to lie down, and I walked quietly down the hall. There was a fifty-mark note by the phone and I put it in my pocket. I took Mum's key out of the lock and laid it on the telephone table by the door. I went out, stood for a moment outside the front door, then I locked up.

I walked to the stop. It wasn't snowing anymore. I looked at the lights of the supermarket, Christmas decorations still in the window. There was a Vietnamese man next to the supermarket, holding a big plastic bag from the Karstadt department store, and I went up to him. He was wearing a fur jacket and must have had at least three jumpers underneath, 'cause his upper body looked huge but his legs were really thin. He'd pulled his scarf up to his nose. 'Golden,' I said, 'a carton.'

'Golden,' he said in a high voice into his scarf, then he reached into the bag and took out a carton of Golden American 25s. 'Golden,' he said again, and his scarf moved; perhaps he was smiling. He had mittens on and the carton slipped out of his hand. I caught it. 'Twenty-two,' he said. 'Usually twenty-five.'

'OK,' I said, giving him the fifty.

'Nothing smaller?' I shook my head. He pulled one mitten off and dropped it in the bag. He took a twenty and four two-mark pieces out of his pocket. He counted the money into my hand, and I put it away. 'You alright?' he asked.

'Yeah,' I said. 'I'm fine.' His scarf moved again and I walked over to the tram stop. I was still holding the carton, so I stopped and put it in my bag. I sat down on the bench underneath the shelter, then I got up again 'cause it was so cold. A girl came and stood next to me. Her face was all red and she rubbed her hands together. There were little white clouds of steam in front of her mouth, and when I looked at her and tried to make eye contact, she looked away.

The tram came and I got on. The girl stayed put, probably waiting for the number 22. I sat down by the window; the glass was misted over and I wiped it with my sleeve. The train pulled off and I looked at her face and the little clouds in front of her mouth.

'Single or return?' asked the woman at the counter.

'Just a single please.'

'Change at Riesa,' the woman said, 'arrival 21:16. The connection to Zeithain is at 21:28.'

'Bit late,' I said as I paid. 'Got to make the curfew.' I knew there was a big army barracks in Zeithain as well. She looked at me and nodded and gave me my change.

The train stopped. I'd been standing by the door with my bag for ten minutes, looking out through the window at the night and the lights as we passed them. I opened the door, had to tug two or three times before the lever moved, and then I got out. I looked at the big round clock directly above me. 21:15. I went to the station concourse. Through the open door, I saw a little kiosk with a couple of men standing outside it, drinking beer. There was a tall table between the men, a fat woman leaning against it. She had a little bottle in front of her. Green – must have been peppermint liqueur. A man with a grey beard had rolled up his sleeves despite the cold. His lower arms were covered in blue tattoos and I saw dots, lines, letters on his hands as well. Perhaps he'd arrived from Zeithain one day and had to change trains and wanted to get a beer to toast his freedom, and then got stuck here. I turned and went over to one of the timetables. My train was due on platform six. I went down the stairs and then through the tunnel.

I sat down on a bench. It was cold and damp, but that didn't matter now. It had started snowing again. There was no roof over the platform, just a waiting room in the middle, but I stayed put and watched the snowflakes melting on my jacket. I got out a cigarette and lit it. The flame went out a couple of times; I had to shield it with my hand. I stood up and started pacing, from one end of the bench to the other. A voice on the tannoy said: 'Now arriving at platform six...' A drawn-out screech drowned out the announcement. I picked up my bag and walked slowly to the edge of the platform. The train was there. I went to a door and opened it. I put my bag inside, then I threw my cigarette on the tracks and got on.

The conductor was standing next to me; she looked at me and said: 'Get off at the next stop.' She was still looking at me once I'd picked up my bag and gone to stand by the door like before, waiting. She stood next to me, holding a lamp with one green and one red light to her chest. She was a bit flat-chested and not very pretty either, but she was looking at me. The train slowed and then stopped. She reached for the door handle and I pushed her hand aside. Just for a moment I felt her skin, then I opened the door and got out. She went down onto the two steps, looked along the train and then waved the lamp, the green light now on. 'Down that way,' she said, pointing at a road behind a little fence, 'left, and then keep going straight.'

'Thanks,' I said. 'Thanks a lot.' Did she smile as she turned and closed the door?

The jail was in the middle of fields. Big and square. And dark. Just a couple of spotlights yellow against the walls.

It was still a good way off. I stumbled through the snow and looked at it, the jail. I'd often dreamed of the place at night, and plenty of guys had told me about it, not just Rico.

I bumped my bag against a gate. It was locked. It was only a small gate, maybe two metres high, like the wire fence. Behind the fence were a few parked cars, and further back, but still a good way away from the jail, in the middle of the snow and illuminated by spotlights on high masts like the real jail but much smaller, was a low building, maybe two storeys, and that was Zeithain Juvenile Custody Centre, just like Rico had always described it. He'd been there a few times, two weeks, three weeks, four weeks. If they gave us more than a month they'd send us a few metres further to the real jail, and Rico had been there as well not long ago, and now he was over in Torgau for a few months.

There wasn't a doorbell on the gate so I threw my bag over the fence. It was a bad shot, bouncing off the fence against my chest. I looked around. They must have had cameras somewhere, and the guys on the monitors must have laughed, if they'd seen it. I took a few steps back and threw the bag again, then I climbed up the gate. At the top, I stopped and looked at the custody building, which had two stone table tennis tables in front of it, with a dark cat sitting on one of them, right in the spotlight; perhaps it was warmer there. I jumped down from the gate and grabbed my bag. I walked past the table tennis tables, the cat blinking green at me, and then there was a tall thin man at the door to the custody centre; he called something and came towards me. He was wearing a tracksuit and waving his arms around. 'Oh boy, you can't do that, you can't just...' I put my bag down in the snow and searched my jacket for my admission papers. 'Hey, hey, no trouble!'

'No,' I said. 'I'm supposed to...' I held the paper up to his face. He took it, moved into the spotlight and read it through. He turned the page over and looked at the other side but that was empty, and then he folded it up and handed it back.

'Alright, come with me, then.' He turned and went to the door, but then he stopped and ran to the table tennis table. 'There you are,' he called, grabbing the cat. 'There you are, my girl. It's cold outside, much too cold for you.' He clutched the cat to his chest and walked past me and vanished, not looking at me, through the door. I stood beside my bag and drew a circle in the snow with my foot.

'You staying outside, are you?' A blonde woman in uniform was leaning in the doorframe. She was holding an unlit cigarette in one hand and a lighter in the other, and I stared at the rubber truncheon by her hip. I grabbed my bag and went over to her.

'Bit late, aren't you?'

'It was only this afternoon when they... they only told me this afternoon.'

'Never mind.'

We went up the stairs, me directly behind her. She didn't look bad, considering she worked in a jail. The guy in the tracksuit came towards us. 'I'm off, Ina, have a good shift.'

'Safe home.'

'Oh, the cat!' He was already down by the door but he turned back. 'The cat's upstairs. I gave her some food.'

Ina laughed. 'You and your cat.'

'It's much too cold outside. And it's snowing, coming down again. Night.'

We walked on and I heard the door closing. 'I'll take you to Mr Fischer, he'll do your admission.'

No, she really wasn't bad looking, and she must have

had her reasons for working in jail. 'You're beautiful, Ina,' I said, slipping in front of her and stroking her epaulettes and resting my head against her neck; she was a bit taller than me.

'Do you think so?' She leaned against the white wall of the corridor we were in and ran her hand over my hair, still wet with snow. 'Do you really think so?'

'Yes,' I said, and I was so tired and I held tight to her and pressed my head against her neck, 'really beautiful.'

'What's your name, I asked!'

I looked through a big window onto the stairwell. Through another window, I saw a long white corridor with lots of doors with numbers on them. 'Daniel Lenz,' I told the man behind the computer, 'Daniel Lenz, date of birth 20.11.1976, Leipzig.'

'ID?' said the man behind the computer. 'I need your ID card and your admission slip.' I took out my wallet and gave him my ID and the slip, which had a few wet spots on it now.

'I'll be heading down again then,' Ina said behind me.

'Right-O,' said the man, and by the time I turned around she was gone, and I just saw her for a moment through the glass, out on the stairs.

No, she really wasn't bad looking, and I remembered Rico telling me something one time, about a blonde woman in jail, in Zeithain Juvenile Custody Centre, who'd driven him crazy. 'Outside, just a one-night stand at most,' he'd said. 'Tops! But inside, Jesus Christ...'

'Undress and stand up straight.'

'What...?'

'Coat, trousers, jumper, shoes. You can keep the rest on.' He tapped my details into the computer. Next to the monitor was a giant electric typewriter, and as I took off my jacket and laid it over my bag, the man nudged the keyboard with his elbow and the thing started juddering away. 'Over here, on the chair,' the man said. I picked up my coat and put it on the chair, then my jumper, I took off my shoes and trousers, took the change out of my trouser pockets and hid it in my fist. 'And put your money on the desk,' the man said, 'all of it. Wallet as well.' I jangled the money onto the desk and emptied my coat pockets as well. 'Your socks,' the man said, looking at me over the top of the monitor. I took them off and put them in my shoes. The lino was cold and sticky under my feet. I looked through the big window onto the corridor and the doors. The man was still typing, rolling the mouse across the desk and grimacing at the screen; maybe he was having trouble. He opened a drawer, took out a sheet of paper, rolled his chair over to the typewriter and inserted the page. He typed very slowly and each keystroke echoed; the others must have heard it in their rooms 'cause I didn't think they were asleep yet. I looked down at myself, glad I was wearing a good pair of pants. The man got up. 'Cigarettes?' he asked, and began searching my coat.

'A carton,' I said, 'and half a pack.' I pointed at the desk.

'Put the carton with them.' I opened my bag, took out the carton of Golden and put it on the desk. He'd finished with my coat, shook my jumper a few times, then the trousers, patted them down and fingered the legs and stroked them very thoroughly like they were a woman's legs. He moved onto my shoes, knocking and pressing them, even looking inside my socks, and I was annoyed I'd put on a clean pair. 'Pass me the bag, please. Any other luggage?'

'No,' I said, pushing the bag over to him with my foot.

'You can get dressed again,' he said, then crouched down and began to rummage. He unpacked everything, folded and turned it over, he felt up my toothpaste tube, opened it and sniffed at it, and he still wasn't finished by the time I was dressed. I leaned against the wall. 'Take a seat,' he said. 'You can sit down.' I went over to a chair, sat down and looked at his back and the truncheon by his side. 'You can smoke if you like. There's an ashtray next to the machine.' His voice sounded dull; his head was almost inside my bag. I scooted the chair closer to the table, lit one up and blew the smoke in his direction. He packed my stuff back in the bag and zipped it, then picked it up and put it down in front of me. 'Right, Mr Lenz.' He took my cigarette packet, removed the lighter and shook the cigarettes back and forth in the pack. Then he swept up the carton of Golden, felt it all over and took out a few packs. 'From the Vietcong, eh?' I nodded. 'I'll lock these away. You can have one pack a day, maximum.' I nodded. He pushed the carton aside and counted my money into his hand, then counted it again. And again. '19 marks 60, is that right?' I nodded. He put the money back in the desk and picked up my wallet. 'Have you got any other cash with you?'

'No,' I said, but he still went through all the compartments in my wallet, then he picked up my ID card, which was still by the monitor, and put it back behind the little window; it took him a while to get it back in place.

'Would you like to buy more cigarettes while you're in custody?'

'Yes,' I said, 'if possible.'

'How much does your ticket back cost?'

'8 marks 20.'

He counted out eight marks and two ten-pfennig pieces onto the desk in front of me, put it in my wallet and then took it over to a metal cupboard at the very back of the room. I heard drawers opening and closing. I put out my cigarette. There were three filters in the ashtray, one a bit red, blood or lipstick, and I moved it to and fro with mine. The man was in front of me, holding a little black bag, into which he dropped my wallet. He picked up my keys from the desk as well and jangled them a couple of times, before he put them in the bag. 'I'll seal this in a minute, but first you have to sign a few things.' He sat back down at the typewriter and put the bag down beside him. 'Cigarettes,' he said quietly as he typed, 'one carton. Cash...' I leaned my head against the glass and closed my eyes.

We were outside a door. The man reached for the ring of keys attached to his belt by a chain, found the right key and opened the door. He went in and turned on the light. 'Wait here.' I saw shelves piled with sheets, others holding jugs, plates, mugs. He took out two blue-checked duvet covers, a brown blanket and a sheet. He came back to the door, handed me the stuff, and I folded it over my arm. 'You can go ahead to 18.' I looked at the numbers on the doors as I walked down the corridor. There was a window at the end, but all I saw in the glass was my reflection and the dark bars behind it. I put my bag down outside room 18 and leaned against the wall. I heard the warder's footsteps behind me. He put a brown plastic jug, a mug and two plates and cutlery on top of my bag, then he unlocked the door and switched on the light. I pushed the bag past him into the room with my foot. 'Ten minutes,' he said. 'Lights out in ten minutes. Good night.' He closed the door. He locked it. Once, twice, three times. He stood outside the door for a moment, then I heard his footsteps fading.

I looked at the window, but again all I saw was my reflection. In front of the window was a table with two chairs, and next to it a cupboard. I went to the bunkbeds and threw the sheets on the top one. There was an ashtray on the table, and I lit a cigarette. I put the plates in the cupboard as I smoked. I balanced the cigarette in the ash-tray and took off my jumper. I went to the door. Next to the door was a button; if I needed the toilet, I could open the window and stand on the table or press the button; there wasn't even a sink in the room. I knew the button from the drunk tank at Leipzig Southeast. They had a sort of intercom in the drunk tank as well, but if I rang here they'd have to come and ask me what I wanted. A drawn-out beep out in the corridor. I leaned my head against the door. And then they came.

I heard them outside the door. It took them a while to draw back the bolt and unlock the door. I took a few steps back. The door slammed against the wall, they grabbed me and knocked me to the floor. They were too fast; I hadn't got any of them. I was too tired and all my strength was gone 'cause I'd been banging on the bell and the door for an hour. First I'd just rung normally, but they wouldn't answer me, not even the bangs, I banged until my fist bled, then I threw my body against the door, over and over, and now here they were at last. One of them sat on my back and pressed my head to the floor. Something in my face was bleeding, must have been my nose, the guy on my back had grabbed me by the hair and was smearing my blood on the tiles. I pulled in my legs and got him on the back with my heel. The guy yelled something, the other one caught me on my side, and I yelled into the floor. Then my hands were behind my back and I felt the steel on my bones. I shouted and bucked, my foot landing on his shin. Then they stood over me and I could see their shoes coming closer in slow motion before they hit me. I crawled to the wall and rolled underneath the cot.

I heard them outside the door. I heard them in the corridor. I heard a child's voice in the corridor. 'Just need a quick...' A couple of doors opened and closed, the key jangled, footsteps, more doors, then quiet. I went over to the table. The light went out. I sat down on a chair. The spotlight beam fell on the table before me. The cigarette in the ashtray had burned down and I lit a new one. I pushed the table aside a bit and scooted my chair closer to the window. I saw the lights of the cars. I leaned my forehead against the glass. It steamed up in front of my mouth and I drew a D with my finger, leaned back and watched it disappear. I opened the window, threw the cigarette down in the snow and ran my hands down the bars a few times before I closed the window again. I undressed down to my pants and T-shirt, put my clothes on the chair and pulled the duvet and pillow down into the light to put the covers on them. Then I threw them back up, climbed the ladder a bit and tucked in the sheet. I lit a cigarette, put the ashtray beside the pillow and lay down. I blew the smoke into the spotlight beam touching the wall above me, watching it move and tear apart. The last time I'd slept in a bunkbed was on some school trip, but I hadn't smoked back then. I'd always wanted to sleep at the bottom, 'cause I was scared of falling out of bed if I had a bad dream. I wasn't scared now.

She was standing in the middle of the room. I hadn't heard her unlocking the door. The spotlight beam was on her uniform and she was standing perfectly still in the middle of the room, right by the table, and looking at me. I reached my hand out for her. 'Please,' I whispered, 'stay here, please.' She came over to me, stroked the cover and put one foot on the ladder. I touched her shoulder, her hand was on the cover. 'Please,' I whispered. But she moved her hand away and took a few steps back. She shook her head. She didn't smile as she turned and left the room.

The warder was standing in the middle of the room. I hadn't heard him unlocking the door. The spotlight beam fell through the window onto his uniform. It wasn't the one from the night before. He jangled his keys in his hand and looked up at me. 'We're moving you over to 23 later,' he said. 'We've got to budge you up a bit, we're filling up on the weekend.' He went to the door. 'The showers are next to the clothing store.'

'Alright,' I said into the cover. He'd left the door ajar and I heard him unlocking the other cells. I looked at my watch, quarter past six, I looked at the window and the lights of the cars, far away. I got up, climbed down the ladder and turned on the light. I took some clean clothes, a towel and my leather washbag, then I put on my flipflops and went to the door. The corridor was empty. I walked past 23, stopped for a minute; the door was ajar but it was dark and quiet inside. I went on. There was a boy standing in the corridor in front of me. He was wearing bright Bermuda shorts, his top half naked, and I immediately saw the big scar across his chest – probably a carjacker, most of them had some kind of scarring from crashes; Walter and Fred had put their heads through a couple of windscreens as well. The boy looked at me for a second, nodded and then walked ahead of me to the showers. He'd draped his towel around his back and was holding a little bag and a huge bottle of shampoo, with a bear on it juggling brightly coloured balls. The boy was a good bit shorter than me, but he had pretty big arms. Maybe he was a fighter as well, and the scar was from a bottle or a knife. He held the door open for me and then went to one of the sinks. He looked in the mirror and ran a hand over his face. 'You're the one who arrived last night, right?'

'Yeah,' I said.

The boy washed his face and I saw his eyes moving in the mirror, watching me. There were four showers; I went to the last one and turned on the water. It was cold so I let it run for a while. 'Takes a minute,' the kid said. He'd spread shaving foam over his face and was scraping away at it with a disposable razor. I held my hand under the stream; the water was gradually warming up. I turned to the wall, undressed and hung my clothes and my towel on a hook. I took my shower gel and turned the water on further. I stepped under the shower and closed my eyes as I washed. I thought of the woman upstairs who I'd shagged under the shower a couple of weeks before, four times, even though she was over forty.

I turned off the water. I took my towel off the hook. The boy who'd been shaving was gone. I dried myself and got dressed. I gathered up my stuff, went to a sink and brushed my teeth. The mirror was misted over and I wiped it clear. Two boys came in, both with pretty short hair, almost skinheads. One went to the sink on my left, the other was on my right. The skin on the left was pretty big, not just his arms. He had an SSS tattoo on this shoulder, the letters like lightning bolts. I knew those symbols, 'Skinheads Saxon Switzerland', they were famous, especially round Dresden way. I'd heard they had pretty good connections to Leipzig-Grünau, where the skins lived. 'Shitheads, Semen-Eaters, Shit-for-Brains,' this punk I knew from school told me, 'cause he'd got his face kicked in by the SSS at some punk meetup in Dresden.

The short skin on my right washed his face, then leaned over to me. 'Got here yesterday, eh?'

'Yeah,' I said. I spat the foam in the sink and rinsed my mouth.

'Bit late in the day, eh?' The SSS one turned to me, his belly hanging halfway over the sink. I gargled.

'You a bad boy, are you?'

'Not that bad,' I said, holding my toothbrush under the tap. The fat one grinned. I watched the smaller one in the mirror; he'd started to shave, even though his face was smooth as a baby.

'How old are you, kid?' The fat one leaned on the sink and grinned over at me.

'Less of the kid,' I said. 'My name's Daniel.' I saw the other one stop shaving. Foam slapped into the sink in front of him.

'Alright, how old are you, Daniel?'

'Eighteen,' I said; actually I was still seventeen.

'And you're not a bad boy?'

'I am if I have to be.'

The fat one was still grinning, and now I smiled too, though I didn't know if it was the right thing to do. I saw the little one grinning as well and going back to shaving.

'How long have you got?'

'A month.'

'Ah, maximum penalty.' He turned to the mirror and ran a hand over his short hair. I packed my stuff in my washbag, took out my watch and put it on.

'So, d'you like it here?' The fat one slurred his words 'cause he was brushing his teeth now, foam running down his chin.

'Don't know yet.' I wrapped my towel over my shoulders and walked past him.

'Hey,' he said and turned to me, 'I'm Klaus.' He held out his hand, and I took it and pressed it as hard as I could, 'cause he was squeezing like he wanted to break my bones.

'What kind of fags you got with you?'

'Golden,' I said.

'From the Vietcong?'

I nodded.

'Nah, then I don't want to swap.'

'See ya then,' I said.

'See ya.'

I went back to my cell. The doors in the corridor opened, boys with towels and washbags came towards me.

I carried my bag, plates and bedding over to 23. The light was still off and someone was sleeping on the top bunk. The boy's feet poked out the bottom of the cover and I could hear him breathing. I cleared my throat loudly, then I coughed, but the boy just went on sleeping, even when I turned the light on. 'Have you got all your stuff?' The warder was in the door.

'Yes,' I said, sitting down on the bottom bunk. The warder nodded, looked around the room, and then he went out in the corridor and I heard him locking 18. The room stank. Maybe it was the feet up above my head, but probably the boy just slept all day and never opened the window. I went over and opened it now. It was getting light outside. The gate I'd climbed over the night before was open, and there were loads of cars parked outside the gate and in the yard.

'Jeez, what's all this, you want me to freeze to death, man, shut that window, will you!'

I turned around. The boy had pulled his feet in under the cover and was tossing from side to side; now he sat up. 'Jeez, it's so bright and all, turn it off...' He had pretty short hair and his face was red and furrowed by acne scars. 'You're here already,' he said. 'Didn't think you'd be coming 'til after lunch. They told me already, see, asked me earlier if I'd mind and that...' He stretched and punched the air. 'Right,' he said, 'time to get up!'

He climbed down the ladder and I took a step back. 'Everything OK?' I asked.

'Always,' he said, and came down. His top half was naked and he was wearing pants with two holes in the arse. 'No need to stare like that,' he said. 'They're not mine. Jail pants. All jail clothes. They came to get me, see.' He held out his hand to me. I waited a few seconds before I shook it. 'André,' he said. 'That's my name.'

'Daniel.' He was so thin I could see every bone, not just his ribs, and I had to watch out he didn't spear me with his collar bone, which stuck out of his back.

He walked barefoot to the cupboard and took out a towel. 'Jail towel. Look.' He held it up to my face and showed me a little label in the bottom corner: Zeithain JCC. 'Not bad, eh?'

I nodded. 'Yeah.' He rummaged through his things and brought out a big cake of soap. 'Jail soap?' I asked.

'Right.' He laughed. 'They came to get me. Didn't get to do any packing. Didn't have anything anyway, see.' He laughed again, and I was glad to see his teeth were still pretty intact. He wrapped the soap in his towel. 'My toothbrush, though, that's mine, that's my own, not from the jail.' He took it out of the cupboard. 'And my toothpaste. Wanna know where I got them?' I lit a cigarette and saw him squinting over at my pack. 'From Schlecker,' he said. 'I nicked them right off the shelves, nicked them a few days before. Not bad, eh?'

'Yeah,' I said, and watched him walk out to the corridor with his stuff, grinning. There were a couple of faded scars on his back, criss-crossing, like some bastard had given him a whipping. Someone laughed outside, then someone else, then he came back. 'My shoes,' he said quietly, pulling them out from under the bed, and now I knew why the room stank so badly. 'Shit happens,' he said, and gave me a wonky grin.

We ate our breakfast. They'd locked the door again. We'd left the window open and we sat at the table and ate bread and jam. The jam and margarine were outside, on the narrow window ledge on the other side of the bars. 'They all do it like this,' he said. 'It's almost like a fridge.' I nodded. He'd given me some of his bread 'cause they handed out breakfast rations in the evening.

'I've only been here two days myself,' he said, and a piece of bread fell out of his mouth. 'But I've been paying attention. 'Cause it's important. You gotta pay attention, or it won't work out.'

'Where you from?'

'Leipzig.'

'What part?'

'Connewitz.'

Connewitz was where the crusties lived, and the way his clothes looked, he'd been living with them in the squats or on the street. I knew a few guys from Connewitz, but I didn't ask after them.

'What about you?'

'Reudnitz,' I said.

'Rough part of town,' he said.

Rico would have punched him in the face for that, though he was right enough, but I didn't say anything. He got up, went to the cupboard and took out a slice of salami. 'I had this outside yesterday but this bird came for it. Really big one, a black one. But they can't get at the margarine, it's too big, see.' He put the salami on a slice of bread and spread jam on top. 'Proper food at last. You a big eater?' He'd been chatting away and he didn't stop, even though I was hardly answering. 'I don't usually eat much, see.'

'I can tell.'

He looked at me, bit into his salami and jam, and then he laughed. 'Oh, I get it. Yeah, I'm a bit thin. Don't usually get much to eat.'

I poured myself a mug of tea. It was cold and sweet.

'Bromide,' André said.

'You what?'

He laughed. 'You don't know it, huh? It's stuff they put in the tea. For hard-ons, see, so you don't get a hard-on.'

'Bollocks!'

'No, it's true, it's so you don't get horny, it's the same tea as in the big jail, I swear!'

'Hmm, maybe.' I remembered Rico telling me something like that. He was turning into a real jail specialist, a jailologist, as they said round our way, and now he was inside too, in Torgau. 'I couldn't fuck,' he'd told me. 'When I got back, you know, I went round to Janine's and I couldn't get it up. They poisoned me, the bastards, in there, they poisoned the bloody tea.' I drank up my cup and screwed the lid back on the jug.

'Hey, Danny...'

'Yeah?'

'You don't mind if I call you Danny, do you...?'

'You can if you like.'

'So Danny, I dilute my tea with water, you know. So I can still get it up, once I'm out of here, see.' He grinned, clenched his fist and pushed his thumb underneath his index finger.

'Bet you get all the ladies, eh?'

'Course I do, what do you think?' He stabbed his knife around in the jam and licked it. I pushed my plate aside and closed the window. 'Hold on, Danny, I've gotta put my stuff outside first.'

I pulled the ashtray closer and lit one up. He put the jug

on top of the cupboard and blew the crumbs off the table.

'Hey, Danny...'

'Yeah?'

'Have you got one spare for me, Danny? I've got tobacco, I'll roll you two later...'

'Nah, that's OK.' I handed him my pack and he fumbled one out and lit it.

'A ready-rolled at last. Thanks, Danny, you're alright!' He grinned at me with the cigarette in the corner of his mouth and then leaned forward and opened the window. 'Just wanna put my stuff outside, I'll close it again in a...' I nodded. He took the margarine and jam, put them out on the window ledge and jammed them under the bars. 'Yesterday,' he said, shutting the window, 'yesterday I dropped my jam. It slipped through the bars. I rang the bell and went down with the warder but it was broken. I got a new one though, not bad, eh?'

'Yeah,' I said. I put my cigarette out, picked up the pack and lay down on my bed.

'Good idea,' he said. He dragged on the cigarette until the red almost disappeared into the filter, then he put it out. 'Hey, you've still got loads of tobacco left!' He came over to the bunks and climbed up the ladder. He rummaged around on top, the mattress wobbling above me, then he came back down holding a pouch of tobacco. 'Up there, see,' he opened the bag and sniffed at it, 'no one can find it up there. You're honest, aren't you?'

'You taking the piss, or what?' I sat up.

'No, no, sorry, I didn't mean it like that. Course you're honest. I can tell just from looking at you.' He went over to the table, took my cigarette butt from the ashtray, broke off the filter and crumbled the leftover tobacco into his pack. 'I do this everywhere, Danny. Makes it go further. I'm not embarrassed, it makes it last longer.'

'You're a real ace.' I leaned my head against the wall and looked past him at the window.

'You've gotta be a bit clever, you know.' He climbed back up the ladder.

'You've got a lot of scars, haven't you?'

'Acne, I had really bad skin, it was really bad.'

'On your back.'

'Oh, those. Old stuff. That was back then...' He threw his shoes down. I heard him moving around up there, the mattress above me wobbling. There were a few names written on the wall next to me, and lines and numbers. Marko was here, Ronny was here, Thomas 21, Mario King. Next to a matchstick man was 'André', the writing not yet faded. Maybe he'd slept in the bottom bunk the first night, then he'd got scared they'd come in and get him, him and his tobacco. He'd heard the wardens' footsteps outside in the corridor, then he'd taken his bedding and tobacco and climbed up to the top and still been scared.

'Hey,' I knocked on the bedpost. 'How long have you got left, anyway?'

'Eighteen days. What about you, Danny?'

'Thirty,' I said.

'It's good we're not on our own anymore, right Danny?'

'Yeah, it's better.' I heard him tossing and turning up above, the mattress moving, then he was still again. I took my shoes off and put them next to the bed. I lit one up. The ashtray was still on the table, but I didn't want to get up. I flicked the ash under the bed. I heard him breathing above me. 'Hey,' I called quietly. He didn't answer. He'd gone back to sleep.

'Coffee,' the warder said, looking down at me. I was lying in bed, smoking. We'd had lunch a couple of hours ago and the dirty dishes were still on the table. 'Clean that up,' the warder said, pointing at the plates with his key.

'Will do,' I said, 'right away.' When he turned his back, I made a gun out of my finger and thumb and shot at him. Eight times, 'til the clip was empty.

I got up and took my plate, cutlery and the empty aluminium tray the food had come in. 'Hold on a minute,' André called down, but I was already out in the corridor. The doors to the cells were open and all these boys were heading for the washroom and the toilets with their dirty dishes; a couple of them turned round to me. I looked at my dishes and waited for the boys to finish at the rubbish bins. Then I cleaned my stuff in the sink. They looked at me again, it was pretty quiet, just a few of them talking, and someone laughed loudly down the corridor.

I walked to the door. A Vietcong came towards me, maybe my age. He was wearing a wife beater so everyone could see the symbol tattooed on his shoulder. He saw me looking at him and walked right up close to me, banging his shoulder against my chest. 'Watch it, Vietcong,' I whispered, but he went on walking. Maybe he was a cigarette king, and I didn't want any trouble with them, but he can't have been a big player 'cause you got a whole lot of years for illegal cigarettes. Rico'd told me there were loads of Vietcong in the jails in and around Leipzig. André came out of 23 with his dishes, grinned and said something, but I blanked him. I put my dishes in the cupboard, then I went to the rec room. I saw the others had brought their mugs and a plate so I went back. Outside the door to the rec room stood a fat woman with curly hair and big glasses. A couple of boys were standing around talking to her. I joined them.

'So did you bring good cake?'

'Of course I did,' the woman said. 'Like last week.'

'And is there still some of that stollen, the Christmas stollen?'

'Yes,' said the woman. 'There's still a bit of stollen left.'

'That's what I want,' said a pretty short boy who only looked about twelve or thirteen. 'I've been waiting all week for it.'

'It was only four days ago,' the woman said. 'I was just here on Sunday.'

'Still,' the boy said, looking around at us with wide eyes, then he went in the rec room. He came back, stood behind the woman and held two fingers up above her head so she couldn't see them, and waggled them. He grinned, then he stuck his tongue out and pretended to lick her back all the way up to her neck. The others laughed and I laughed too, and now the woman laughed as well. The boy bent down, sniffed at her arse, waggled his hand in front of his nose, grinning, and we laughed, then he went back in the rec room.

'You're new, aren't you?' She looked at me and rubbed her hands together like she was cold.

'Yes,' I said.

'Only got here yesterday,' one of the boys said; he was tall and thin and leaning against the wall on his own and he had yellow drinker's rings under his eyes. 'In the middle of the night. Woke us all up.'

'You must like a good kip,' I said, and saw his eyelids twitch above the yellow circles. 'Need your beauty sleep, do you?'

The others grinned; the woman went to the door. 'Coffee's on its way...' she said. 'Nearly ready.'

We filed in. 'Hey, tell me,' I tapped one of the boys on the shoulder, very gently, 'who's this coffee lady anyway?'

'She's from Clink,' the boy said, turning round to me, and now I recognized him, the little skin from the showers that morning.

'And what's that?'

'Wouldn't you like to know.'

'Come on, just tell me.'

He stopped. 'They go to the proper jail first, see, with cake and coffee and that, all donations. Then they come here.'

'Right.' I patted him lightly on the shoulder again, and he nodded and went over to one of the tables.

'Shit, I spilt my stupid tea.' André was behind me in the doorway. There was a wet patch on his trouser leg.

'Pissed yourself, have you?' I said loudly. Someone laughed.

'No, no, just the cup, just knocked over the stupid cup... Hey, Danny, shall we sit together?'

'But don't get me wet, OK?' Someone laughed again. We went over to the tables. André walked so close behind me I could feel his breath on the back of my neck.

The woman came round again and poured us coffee. There was another woman there who looked almost the same, except she didn't have glasses and was going from table to table with a tray of cake. I sat at the two skins' table; the smaller one was called Frank, he'd just told me, and he raised his coffee cup to mine. The skins were in a good mood, especially Klaus, who'd swiped a couple of boys' cake and almost eaten it all. André sat next to me.

'My stollen, where's my stollen?' The clown from before was following the cake woman.

'There's something for everyone,' the cake woman said, holding the tray up high when he went to grab it.

'But my Christmas stollen,' the little clown complained, even though Christmas had been over a while now, but maybe he'd been here at Christmas, or they didn't have it at home where he lived.

'Sit down on your arse, kid,' someone called. 'You've had enough.' We laughed. The coffee woman walked round the tables and topped up our mugs.

'Hey, Daniel, gimme a bit of your streusel cake...' Klaus held out his plate.

'Sure, you can have it. It's too dry for me anyway.'

'Too true,' said Frank. 'My old man, my old man's a baker, he makes streusel cake, really good stuff. In our village...'

'What village are you from then?' I asked, breaking my cake in two and putting half on Klaus's plate. Klaus grinned and nodded at me.

'Round Dresden way,' said Klaus, dropping crumbs on the table as he talked. 'That's the best area. Your village is 100% German, right, Frank?'

'Course,' said Frank.

'Leipzig,' I said. 'Can't get better.'

'You tell that to him over there, the tall one,' Klaus nodded at one of the tables by the wall. 'He's from Dresden. Pretty hard number.'

The guy really did look pretty hard; his nose had been punched flat and didn't fit into his narrow face. He was at least a metre ninety-five, and the others at his table didn't even come up to his shoulder; it looked like they were his little brothers and he had to look after them 'cause their mum was gone. 'He's a Dynamo fan,' Klaus said, 'a real heavy number. I fancy a bit of a match with him. Me and him, just the two of us, outside in the yard, bit of a match, that'd do the trick. He's alright, though, Danny.'

'What do you mean, a match? Football, or what?'

'Are you dumb, Danny, are you dumb? You know, a bit of a knockabout, throw a few punches, you know. He's a Dynamo fan!'

I blushed and felt like everyone at the table was staring

at my red face. 'Right,' I said, 'I know what you mean, a bit of a match, couple of punches, I just didn't hear you right.'

Klaus looked over at the giant and pushed his mug around a bit. 'Me and him, you know, that'd do the trick, just a bit of a match, that'd be a great fight. But he's alright, Danny, really, he's a Dynamo fan, see?'

'Right,' I said. I hated Dynamo, almost as much as Lok Leipzig, 'cause back in the Zone days they were paid by the cops, Dresden People's Police, and what I hated most of all was Dynamo's fans, 'cause almost all of them were hools or skins. The giant over at the table wasn't a skin, his hair was pretty long actually, almost down to his shoulders. He looked about thirty but he couldn't be, not in a juvenile custody centre; it must have been the drinking and fighting that made him old, and most of the boys I'd seen in here so far had fucked-up faces.

'Anyone want more coffee? There's still some left, I can... you can finish it off.' The coffee lady put the jug on our table. I took it and topped up Klaus's cup first, then mine and passed it on. A boy grabbed it and filled his mug. He'd been quiet the whole time, pretty small kid, and whenever I looked over at him he looked down at the floor.

'Hey, leave some for me!' Frank reached for the jug but the silent boy pulled it away.

'You... you've had... loads,' he stuttered a tiny bit but you could hardly hear it. 'I want some now.'

'What? You cheeky little bedwetter! That what you are, eh, a bedwetter?' We laughed.

'I'm not, you arsehole, no I'm not!' He stood up. 'Tea! I told you before, it was just tea! It spilt on my bed, I knocked the jug over, you arsehole!' I could see André grinning next to me.

'Stank of piss, though, your wet patch,' Frank said. 'Or

did you piss in the jug?' We laughed.

'It wasn't piss!' the boy said in a high voice. 'It wasn't bloody piss!'

'Hey, hey, hey, less of the stress!' Klaus had stood up and his big hand was on the boy's shoulder. 'Everything's fine, nobody's saying you wet the bed at night.'

He'd spoken really calmly and quietly, like you do with a dog, but the boy kept getting louder. '...that arsehole said so. But it was tea, just tea, just tea! I'm not a bloody bed-wetter!' He'd screamed the last words, and everyone in the room went quiet and looked at him.

'Bedwetter,' said someone at one of the tables. (It wasn't the giant, 'cause I had my eye on him.) The boy started yelling, grabbed his coffee cup and chucked it across the room and then threw the jug after it. Then he wanted to jump up and start some kind of shit, but Klaus had him by the collar. He pulled him over the table and held onto him with both hands and pressed him to his chest and dragged him past the tables to the door. The warder came his way. He'd been leaning on the wall, drinking coffee and watching us.

'No problems,' Klaus said, 'no problems here. I'm taking him out.'

The boy was screaming and crying into Klaus's T-shirt. 'Tea, it was just bloody tea!' Then they were out in the corridor. The warder followed them out.

'So how d'you like it here now?' asked Klaus.

'It's only for a couple of weeks,' I said. 'You hardly have time to get settled in before they send you away again.' I lit one up and looked at the tiny notches on my lighter: five days.

'Right,' said Klaus. 'Couple of weeks is nothing.'

We had a free hour. We were sitting at the table in his

cell, playing cards. We were playing 31, Frank, Klaus, André and me, and we'd got the bedwetter in on it as well, 'cause it was more fun with five players.

'I'll be glad to get home,' said André.

'I thought you didn't have a home,' I said.

'Well, yeah, you're right I s'pose, I haven't got a proper flat or anything, but I can go to the homeless project for a shower and a meal and that...'

'Stop talking and swap cards,' said Klaus.

'Nah, I reckon I'll pass. Yeah, right, I'll pass.'

'Jesus Christ, get your head fixed! We said no passing.'

'Alright, then I'll close.' He put his cards face down in front of him and started rolling a cigarette. He licked the paper, rolled the cigarette a few times in his hand, and before he lit it he used one of his cards to sweep the tobacco crumbs off the table and back in the pouch.

'Alright then, what have you got?'

We all slammed our cards down on the table.

'Twenty-nine,' said André. He'd won again, and he picked up our matches from the middle of the table. 'I'm good, eh?'

'It's just stupid luck, not skill!'

'I'm still good.' He shuffled and dealt a new round. We smoked and played.

Only the bedwetter didn't have any cigarettes. I passed him my pack. 'Go on, help yourself.'

'Thanks.'

'Speak up, we won't bite!'

Frank gave him a light. 'Go on, kid, take a good drag, that'll make you grow big and strong.' We laughed, and he smiled too now. He put our matches in the middle. We played.

The bedwetter put down a ten. André picked it up, put down an eight and slammed his cards down on the matches. 'Thirty-one,' he yelled. 'I win again!'

'Jeez, shut it, will you!'

'Christ, you... you...' Frank slapped the table. 'Why d'you go and give him the bloody ten?'

'But I needed a seven,' said the bedwetter, drawing on his cigarette and coughing a bit. 'Seven, I... I needed a seven. I had... had three!' He showed us his three sevens.

'Not much use to you now.' Klaus gathered up the cards, shuffled and dealt. We put our matches in the middle. We turned around. Ina was standing in the doorway. She wasn't quite as gorgeous as on the first day.

'Want to join in?' Frank looked at her over the top of his three cards.

'Don't forget,' she said, her hand on the hip where the truncheon was, 'locking up in fifteen minutes.' She turned and left very slowly, crossing the corridor to the opposite cell, and we looked at her arse as it moved with every little step. There were twenty-six on the table; I put my cards down and took them instead. Klaus threw down the Queen of Hearts.

'Shit,' said Frank, taking it and holding it up, 'every night I wait for her to come in and give it to me, give me a real rough ride, but she'll come, right, Klaus?'

'Christ, shut the fuck up!' The two of them shared a cell. We went quiet now. We'd put our cards away. André rolled a cigarette and I lit one up too. Klaus stuck one between the bedwetter's lips. 'On the house,' he said. We smoked.

'You know what I'm scared of?' said Frank. 'If they lock me up for real, for longer, I mean, a year or so, and then no girls for a year, only blokes...'

'You'd love every minute,' Klaus said. We laughed.

'Nah, don't... but really, jeez, you know, I've got an old lady. I've got a proper lady. Been with her two years now, more than that. You know, I see her everyday, see, and I fuck her every day as well, obviously...' We laughed. 'And then just blokes. Shit, and what if she left me, by the time I got out, after the year, I mean...'

'My last girlfriend,' André said, crumbling the tobacco out of our extinguished cigarettes into his pouch, 'my last... lady, I lived with her in a squat. It weren't bad, I had a room just for me, all to myself, so I could, every day I could...' He grinned and I kicked his leg under the table. He didn't notice, just went on talking, and he didn't see Klaus putting his cigarette out real slow and staring at him. I knew the whole story, he'd told it to me the night before, and maybe I should have told him what the score was here, 'cause it looked like he hadn't worked it out yet. '... they're not bad, those crusties and their squats. And then... and then this guy stole her off me, a fash, don't know where she knew him from. This stupid fash stole my lady, a stupid fash, can you...' That was as far as he got, though. I'd kicked him in the shin a few more times, he must have had bruises by now, but maybe I'd been hitting the table leg, or he was into that kind of thing. Klaus had stood up. His big hand was on André's shoulder.

'What's that? Say it again! Who stole her off you? Am I going deaf? Hard of hearing? Who stole her off you? Am I not hearing properly? Am I going crazy?'

'Come on, leave it out, they're locking up in a minute.' Frank stood up next to him but he just shoved him away.

'I think I'm going crazy. Say it again, go on, loud and clear: Who stole your girlfriend off you, you fucking crustie?' His hand wasn't on André's shoulder anymore, it was on his T-shirt and now round his neck.

'I'm sorry, I didn't mean...' André wanted to get to the door but Klaus had him by the throat.

'Sitting right here next to me and he goes and says that!

Come on, say it again, I want to hear it again! I'm hard of hearing, see, I want to hear it again: Who – stole – your – girlfriend – off you?' He had André pretty firmly by the neck, and now he pressed his head back with the other hand.

I stood up. 'Listen, no listen, Klaus...'

He didn't let go as he turned to me. 'You. I bet you can tell me who stole your mate here's girlfriend. I didn't quite get it, see.'

I knew that game. If I told him he'd punch me in the face. Mean skinhead game. Stress-maker game. Seen it often enough. 'Oi, what you looking at, what you staring at?' 'I'm not looking!' 'You mean I'm ugly? You saying I look shit? I've got shit on my face?' And then a couple of punches.

'He's not my mate,' I said. 'But just leave it now, they're locking up in a minute, give him a quick slap and be done with it. They're locking up in a minute, come on.' He gave him a couple of quick ones. Punches. A short left hook to the edge of his chin. Not too hard; he didn't want to leave a mark. He let go of his throat; André stumbled into the wall and slid down it. He covered his face with his arm but Klaus had stayed put and wasn't finishing him off, and André got to his feet. His legs gave way and he had to try again; he looked like he had a glass chin, but that fat skinhead could really punch.

'I'm sorry,' he said, walking back towards Klaus, 'I didn't mean it like...'

'Fuck off,' I said, 'get out of here, you crustie, out, jeez!'

He turned and went to the door. 'Your bloody tobacco!' Klaus picked it up and threw the pouch in the corridor. It was still open and half the tobacco fell out mid-air and sprinkled down to the ground between us like brown snow. The bedwetter laughed. I saw him take a cigarette out of Klaus's pack and light it.

'Look at that crustie!' He pointed his cigarette at the corridor, where André was squatting, sweeping up the remains of his tobacco with his hand and stuffing it back in the pouch.

'We'll talk about this again, crustie,' Klaus called.

'Listen,' I said, 'it's not...'

'You keep out of it, man. You a crustie too, are you?'

I made a note of where the chair was, then I went right up to him. 'Hey, I'm not a fucking crustie, you'd better remember that!' He took a step back, and when I thought he was about to hit me or grab me by the throat like André, he held out his hand.

'Alright, Danny, you're not a crustie, I know that, but that stupid fuckwit out there made me mad!' He turned to André. 'Dirty fucking crustie!'

I took his hand and pressed it. 'He's an idiot, that's all,' I said. 'Don't take him so seriously. He's a poor bastard, he'll water your shoes if you hit him too hard, you know, poor bastard, gets beaten up all the time, you'll only make a mess of yourself.'

'Yeah, yeah, you're right. But fuck, he shouldn't go talking so much shit. In my cell, yeah, in my cell! I'm gonna give him another one, he hasn't had enough yet, I'll give him another one...'

'Lockup time!' Ina called out in the corridor.

'See ya tomorrow, then.' I patted Klaus on the shoulder.

'Yeah, alright. And give that dirty bastard one from me, give him a good one from me!'

'If he opens his mouth, maybe.' I went to the door. Klaus said something else but I was already in the corridor.

'Locking up time!' Ina was standing outside the office, jangling her keys. I smiled at her as I went to 23. I smiled at her until my face hurt. Once I passed her I turned around and walked backwards and kept on smiling, but she took no notice, jangling her keys. André was in the top bunk. He'd rolled up against the wall under his cover and I could only see his feet. I lit one up, took the ashtray and lay down. I knew she'd come in again, that was the rules, to check: are the children all in bed? I heard her in the next-door cell. I got up again and opened the window. It was almost dark outside, not snowing. I went back to the bed and smoothed my hair straight. I leaned against the wall, blowing the smoke to the door. Then Ina came in, looked around, nodded, went out again and locked up.

'Do you want to do some work, Lenz?' The warder was in the middle of the room. I hadn't heard him unlocking the door.

'Work?' I sat up on the edge of the bed.

'One of us is driving to the shops. If you want... It'll go in your report.'

'OK,' I said, standing up. 'At least it'll get me out of here.' I put on my shoes.

André was leaning on the wall in the top bunk, looking down at us. 'Can I...'

'Not today,' said the warder, 'we only need one person.'

We went out and he locked up. 'Wait, my coat.' He unlocked the door again and I took it out of the cupboard. I put two cigarettes on the table before I went back out. I followed the warder to the staircase. Through the window, I saw another cop (we usually called them cops, even though they weren't proper cops, didn't even have guns) sitting behind the computer and smoking.

'Wait here.' He went in to him, said something, the cop at the computer nodded, looked at me through the window and nodded again. My cop came back out and I followed him down the stairs.

'Hey crustie,' I called over. 'Get up!' I took off my coat and hung it in the cupboard. It was a bit wet from the snow in Riesa.

We'd crossed the car park to the superstore, the cop in plain clothes and me ahead of him with the stack of empty plastic crates, I was just a normal guy going shopping with his dad, I lowered my head, all the snow, but when we got back in the green jail van and I sat behind the tinted barred windows...

'Jesus, crustie, get up!' I slapped the bedpost.

'I'm not a crustie.' André leaned against the wall and looked down at me.

'Is it your birthday today?'

'No, why, what d'you mean?'

'Course it's your birthday, crustie!'

'Hey, Danny, don't be so mean. Why are you...'

''Cause I've brought you a present.'

'A present? What present?' He was halfway down the ladder already.

'Wait and see, something special...' I undid my flies and reached into my pants.

He stopped. 'Jeez, Danny, what the...'

But then I had the 0.2-litre bottle out; there was a pube stuck to the label and I blew it away quickly. André jumped off the ladder and ran over.

'Jeez, watch it,' I said. 'Don't make me drop it.'

'Wow, Danny, where d'you get it from?'

'Found it,' I said, grinning. I sat down and put the bottle on the table in front of me.

'Come on, tell me, Danny, go on!'

'I went shopping with the cop, see...'

'Jeez, if they'd...'

'I'm far too good for that.' I laughed and held up the

bottle. 'Crate of fruit, see, I had it in a crate of fruit...'

'But Danny,' André said, 'we're gonna share it, right?'

'Jeez, are you taking the piss, I told you it's your birthday. You think I'm gonna get a bottle and then down it all on my own?'

'Sorry,' he said quietly. 'I didn't mean...'

'It's alright.' I put the bottle back on the table and pushed it back and forth.

'Hey, Danny,' André said, 'shall we just...'

'Nah, we'll do it later when we're locked in again. We've got free time in a minute anyway.'

'Danny,' he said, 'I'm not going out of the cell today. I'll stay here and act like I'm asleep.'

''Cause of Klaus?'

'Yeah.'

He'd stayed in bed for four days, hadn't even taken a shower and I had to lend him my deodorant so he didn't smell so much. I got up, took a few steps back and admired the bottle. 'Probably better. You stay here. He'll calm down again though. I had another word with him. He's not even that angry anymore. Already gave you one anyway.' I leaned forward and ran my finger down the bottle's neck and slim shoulders. 'But there was nothing I could have...'

'I know,' he said, standing up next to me and admiring the bottle.

We sat by the window and drank. It was afternoon, getting dark. I'd poured the korn in our teacups, it wasn't very much, ten cl each, that was two and a half double measures in a bar. 'Cheers,' I said, raising my cup. We clinked our cups together. We drank in sips and I kept the korn in my mouth for a long time before I swallowed it. It was only Goldene Aue, but now it tasted better than proper Nordhäuser Korn.

'I bet you're a really good shoplifter,' said André, taking one of my cigarettes. I'd opened the pack and put it down by the bottle.

'Not bad,' I said. I lit one up as well and looked out at the car park. The gate was still open, and now I saw a long green bus on the road, heading slowly our way. 'Lightning speed,' I said. 'One swipe. I was only at the booze shelf for a second, the guy, the driver, he must have been a cop as well, he kept his eye on me all the time.'

The bus drove slowly across the car park. I opened the window. It was still snowing; a few flakes fell into the room. 'Toothpaste,' I said. 'We'll put toothpaste in our mouths later, or they'll smell it.'

'Right,' said André. 'Otherwise we'd be in big trouble.'

The bus drove slowly through the gate. We were stood up now. Clutching our cups, we looked out at the bus. It didn't have windows on the side, just portholes like on a ship. And behind the portholes, there were faces. I raised my cup. The bus drove slowly past us, heading for the jail. Once it got there, a big gate opened and two red lights flashed on either side, on the wall. I saw hands and faces behind the portholes. I closed the window. There weren't any curtains to close. We hung our towels in front of the window at night, 'cause the spotlights outside in the yard shone all the way into our beds. I drank up and sat down.

The Russians' cell was across the way, on the other side of the corridor. The door was almost always closed, even in our free hour, and the two of them only sometimes stood by the window at the end of the corridor, with their backs to us. The Russians didn't talk much, and we didn't talk to the Russians either. The Russians were fucked up, you could tell by their faces, they were all white and their eyes were red and swollen, with big black circles underneath. The two of them looked like brothers, the same faces, constantly looking like they were about to cry (why do Russians always look like they're suffering?) but one of them was a good bit shorter than his brother, and he had three scars on his neck that were just as white as his face, neatly burned in with a cigarette. The Russians had loads of cigarettes with them, Ernte 23 and some Russian brand I'd never seen before. Early in the morning, when I went for my shower, they headed for the office to collect their day's packs. They waited for the rest of us to finish in the showers, then they went to the washroom in their big slippers, with brightly coloured towels. I'd seen scars on their arms, in neat rows, but they weren't from cigarettes. The Russians were pretty fucked up, and when they stood by the window with their backs to us, I could see their insides churning and their bodies aching. They couldn't stand still, they jagged from left to right, their legs gave way and they leaned on the windowsill 'til the jiggling reached their arms too. The Russians were even more fucked up than the guy from cell 30, the one who was all yellow in the face, especially under the eyes, and was getting yellower and yellower. He drew his head in so far, his shoulders almost touched his ears, and it took him a week to stop trembling and start playing cards properly. When it was his turn, he'd jerked a card out of his hand so hard we'd flinched and the bedwetter ducked when he was playing along, and then the card in his hand trembled across the table, and it took a good while for him to put it down properly.

We didn't play cards with the Russians; we didn't talk to them either. They didn't speak good German anyway, I could hear that when the wardens were in their cell. They had high-pitched kids' voices, but their faces... their faces, like OAPs in a home. I'd done a couple of years of Russian, started in the Zone days, but I was never good enough for the Russian Language Olympics; Katja had always gone, my Katja.

'Khorosho,' I said quietly at night when I couldn't sleep, trying to remember. 'Ochen khorosho. Skolko tebe let?'

I heard André turning over in the top bunk, the mattress moving. 'What's the matter, Danny?' He'd leaned down and his head hung dark beside the ladder.

'Russian,' I said, 'it's Russian. What's your name? Skolko tebe let?'

'Nah, André said above me. 'How old are you, that means.'

'Really?'

'Yeah. I used to be pretty good at Russian. My mum knew this Russian guy, you know.' His head vanished again.

'Right,' I said. 'I've got it now. Kak tebya zovut? Yeah, right, it's kak tebya zovut. What's your name?'

'Yeah,' said André, 'that's about it, that's about it. And then: menya zovut André.'

'Yeah,' I sat up and leaned against the wall. 'And how are you, that's kak dyela, I think.'

'Right, right, Danny, kak dyela. Menya zovut Igor. Igor lyubit fut-bol.'

'You said Igor loves football, right?'

'Right. Hey, Danny, shall we have a smoke?'

'Sure.' I waited for him to come down the ladder and go over to the table, then I got up. I pulled my T-shirt down over my pants 'cause I had a hard-on, I'd had it for an hour, it was starting to hurt but it wouldn't go away. Never mind the bromide. I sat down at the table. André took down one of the towels and the glare of the spotlights fell on the table. My cigarettes were next to the ashtray; I took two out of the pack and handed one to André, who'd already started rolling. We smoked. My hard-on was gone. 'Ochen khorosho,' I said.

'You know what?' André said. 'I'd really like to have a chat with them, just a bit of a chat, you know, to see if I can still speak it.' He got up and hung the towel back over the window 'cause the light was shining right on his face. 'Might be nice, eh, Danny?'

'Maybe. But I don't think it's worth it, they're fucked up, you can't talk to them, they need their medicine, you know?' And the Russians didn't have any medicine, that was why they were fucked up, really fucked up, even worse than the yellow-faced guy in cell 30, everyone knew it.

'The Russians,' Klaus said when we were playing cards in his cell. 'Those fucking Russians are going cold turkey.'

'Yeah,' said André. 'You can tell, it's heroin, it's stuff you get...' He looked at us, then he shut up again and put a card down. He was still bricking it that he might talk too much, even though there was no more trouble with Klaus. He'd apologised to him over and over, but Klaus had given him another one anyway, in the belly, right to the liver, Klaus knew what to do and the cops might have seen something if he'd gone for the face. André had dropped to his knees, almost puked, and the bedwetter had counted him out like in the ring. Once he could talk again he'd apologised to Klaus again, and then everything was alright.

'They should put them in a cell with the Vietcong,' André said now, quietly. 'The Russians, I mean.'

Klaus had won the round and picked up the matches. 'That Vietcong, I'd watch out for him. I'm not scared of him or nothing, I'd finish him off, I'd beat the shit out of him. But I heard...' Klaus leaned forward and lowered his voice. 'I heard he's really good at karate or kung fu or something. He's like a hard man, for the cigarette kings, you know?' The bedwetter shuffled and dealt.

'The other day,' Frank said, 'I saw the Vietcong showing off one of his kicks in the dining room, he got his leg right up over his head.'

'Anyway, the Russians,' Klaus said, 'they're fucked up. It's not even worth dusting them up a bit. At least they keep their mouths shut though...'

'No one understands their Russki foreign, anyway,' said André.

I got up. 'No cards for me,' I said. 'I'm going back over. I want to get some more tea and it's locking up time in a minute.'

Klaus looked at his watch. 'We've got a few minutes. Sit back down, Danny.' It was a good watch with a golden strap and he was proud of it and showed it off to everyone, but you could get watches like that on every corner in Leipzig from the Vietcong. I didn't say that to Klaus though.

'Nah,' I said. 'I won't bother, Klaus. We'll play again tomorrow.'

He said something else but I was already out in the corridor. I went back to 23 to pick up my tea jug. The door to the Russians' cell was closed but the Russians were by the window at the end of the corridor. They almost always stood there when we had a free hour, with their backs turned to us. Once, they weren't there, probably lying in bed sweating through their mattresses, and I'd leaned on the windowsill and looked outside. But there was nothing there, just roads and fields.

The cops were in a bad mood. Probably annoyed 'cause

Ina wasn't working and they couldn't look at her arse when she strolled down the corridor. 'Five minutes,' the cop said. 'Locking up's in five minutes, then I'll chuck you out.' We were in the rec room, playing Monopoly. I had Bond Street, and there was a brothel on Bond Street; I'd only just built it for a lot of money. Now Frank had landed on the brothel and had to pay. And he paid.

'Good shag,' he said. 'All the specials, blow-job, oral, all that. I had a black girl, more like pale brown. Man, was her pussy on fire!' We laughed. He handed me the notes and I put them in my chest pocket with the rest. The place was making me a mint.

'You and your black bitches,' said Klaus. 'You know who's the best fuck? The Viet babes, the Vietnamese girls, right?' He patted the Vietcong on the shoulder. 'No, honest, your women, they're... well, beautiful.'

'Yeah,' said the Vietcong. He spoke pretty good German, even though he didn't talk much.

'Five minutes, I said! And clean up those houses as well!' The warder looked at his watch and then went out. We'd written on the little houses with felt-tips, most of them had a B for brothel, I had almost all of them (three brothels made a high-class establishment), and Klaus had built two big amusement arcades over on Piccadilly. There were a couple of bars as well, and Frank had a green house with a big C on it where he was growing grass.

The bedwetter rolled the dice, landed on one of my brothels and paid. 'You can't get it up anyway,' said Frank. We laughed.

'Shut your mouth!'

It was the Vietcong's turn. He rolled the dice. He landed on the booze factory, but he owned it himself. The yellow-faced boy would probably have liked to have it but all he had on his streets was a couple of cheap bars. The cigarette factory wasn't sold yet, but the Vietcong would get that too, I was sure of that. He rolled the dice again 'cause he'd thrown a double. He landed on Chance and took a card. 'Go to jail,' he read slowly. 'Go directly to jail. Do not pass Go, do not collect 400 marks.'

'That's tough,' Klaus exclaimed. 'You're... you're double in jail!' We laughed.

'Maybe,' said the Vietcong, putting his piece in the Jail corner, 'maybe they want me to go over, to the big jail, you know...' We laughed.

'Right,' the bedwetter called out, spitting as he spoke. 'Miss three turns in Zeithain!' We laughed.

'Locking up time!' The warder was out in the corridor but we took no notice. We laughed and laughed and couldn't stop. We slapped the table so hard our pieces tipped over and we had to pick them up again. The two warders were in the middle of the room now. 'Time's up,' one of them said. We weren't laughing anymore.

André rolled the dice. 'Five,' I said. 'Come on into my brothel!'

'Shit,' he said, unfolding his money and paying.

'You know what you are?' Klaus said. 'A pimp, a proper pimping bastard!'

'Right,' I said, lighting one up. I put my open pack down on the board. 'Help yourselves, business is booming.' Everyone took a fag. I got out my lighter, they leaned forward, and I lit them all up. The warder turned off the lights. It was almost dark outside now, and we blew the smoke into the glare of the spotlights falling through the window.

'Time's up! Locking up time! Clear up and get back to your cells!'

I could see the yellow-faced guy trembling, but that wasn't 'cause of the cops; he had it bad in the evenings, dreaming of all his pubs and bars. Klaus put a pile of notes down on the table. 'Another arcade and a brothel for Oxford Street.'

'That was the last brothel,' said Frank, who was in charge of the money and the houses.

The two warders were standing right by the table now. 'Go back to your cells, there's no point in this, it'll all go down in your reports!'

The Vietcong rolled. He was out of jail again and just about to reach the cigarette factory. He rolled a six, four plus two, but that was one too many. 'That would've been great!' André said. 'Straight out of jail to the fag factory!' The Vietcong nodded.

'Buying your way out of jail, that's cheating,' said Frank. 'It's stupid!' The Vietcong had bought the parole card off the bedwetter for three thousand, and that was the only reason why they'd let him out.

'Clear up the game and go to your cells. That's it, that's the end of the discussion!'

'We're not discussing anything,' Klaus said. 'We're just finishing our game, that's all.' One warder stood right behind him. The other cop reached for the dice. André wanted to grab them but all he got was the hand now holding the dice. He gripped the cop's hand with both of his. He pulled and tugged at the hand, the cop tipped forward onto the table, we leapt up, money, brothels and arcades spilled on the floor, André let go of the hand, ducked down and crossed his arms in front of his face.

The other warder was behind him now and had him by the collar. 'That's enough now! Back to your cells! Right now!'

The dice-thief had righted himself again, his face bright red, and there were a couple of houses and pieces stuck to his yellow cop shirt, falling off one by one. 'You want me to report you, do you? You want something else on your record? You want to go next door, do you, want to go straight next door? You're welcome to stay longer, you can stay a week longer!'

'Sorry,' André said quietly. 'Sorry, sir... I didn't mean... I didn't mean to...'

'Before,' the warder said, holding his forefinger up in front of André's face. 'You have to think about that beforehand!'

The other warder pointed at the door. 'In your cells! You all go straight to your cells, boys!'

'Men,' said the yellow-faced guy, trembling and blinking. 'I'm a man, not a boy!'

'Go to your cells,' the warder said again. 'Or I can give them a call next door and get them to clear you out!' His hand was on the grip of his truncheon.

André was still facing the dice-thief, his head lowered. 'André,' I called, 'come on, get over here!' He looked at me and then at the warder. I went over to him and pulled him by the shoulder to the door. 'Come on, let's go, we'd better get to bed or Daddy's gonna tell us off!'

'No,' the warder said. 'You stay here.' André walked back to them. I stood by the door; the others walked past me into the corridor. 'The same goes for you, get back to your cell!'

'I'm just waiting for my mate!'

'Get out, he'll be right with you, he just has to do a bit of tidying up in here.' André gave me a wonky grin; I nodded at him and went down the corridor to 23. Klaus waved from the doorway of his cell. I saw the yellow-faced guy, the Vietcong and the bedwetter duck into their cells. The other doors were already closed; it was twenty minutes after locking up time. I went into 23 and sat down at the table. I heard the warder jangling the keys out in the corridor. He took a quick look in my cell, closed the door but didn't lock it. I sat in the dark, lit one up and watched a man walking across the car park to his car. He got in, turned the key – the engine took a while to start – then he drove off in the direction of the station. I opened the window and threw my cigarette down in the snow. There was new snow again, from the night before. I lit a cigarette, laid my free hand in the snow on the window ledge and then held it against my forehead. I stood up and turned on the light. The warder was outside the door; I took a step back. André came in, the warder behind him. He looked at me, then he closed the door and locked it.

'Everything alright?' I said.

'Sure,' said André, giving me his wonky grin. 'I made right tits out of them, didn't I?'

'Yeah,' I said, 'you did.' I passed him my pack and he took one out.

'Hey, look what I've got here.' He reached into his pocket and put two dice down on the table. 'He dropped them, the cop that stole them, the one I made a tit out of, dropped them, the idiot.'

I patted him on the shoulder. 'Nice one.'

'They were bricking it, right, Danny? When we all jumped up, they were bricking it.'

'Yeah,' I said, 'they were. Definitely. The way you laid him down on the table, it was great, that was.'

'Really?' He grinned.

'Yeah,' I said. 'Like a professional.'

We rolled the dice all evening. They turned off the lights and we rolled the dice in the glare of the spotlights out in the yard. We were still rolling them when the others started banging on the walls and then the doors. Someone mooed, someone else crowed like a rooster. The corridor rang with sound. We put the dice aside.

We banged on the walls. And then on the door. We beat along to the others' rhythm. I heard the warders' footsteps out in the corridor. The keys jangled. We ran to our beds and lay down. A couple of cells were opened up – voices, footsteps – and then locked again. Then they came to us. The door slammed against the wall – voices, footsteps – we stopped breathing and pressed our heads into our pillows; they left again. We stayed where we were and tried to sleep.

Yard exercise. We stood outside, smoking in a circle round the table tennis table. It was snowing. A couple of guys chucked snowballs over the fence to the car park. The warder watched us, smoking as well. The giant was talking at me. I'd told him I was a Chemie fan a couple of days ago, and he hadn't left me alone since then. 'How about it, Daniel? A bit of a match, just the two of us? Come on, tomorrow morning, before our showers. Just two or three minutes, someone can keep time! Man, I haven't done a round with a Chemist for ages, just three minutes, get a couple of punches in.'

'Nah,' I said, 'let's not.'

'Man, why not, for fuck's sake? I thought you were a Chemist!'

'Yeah, I am. Started going with my dad back in the day, you know. And don't think I'm scared or anything. But fighting over football, just for fun, nah, I don't fancy it, I don't like all that these days.'

'It's the greatest,' the giant said, rubbing his hands. 'Man, you don't know what you're missing, a match over football, it's better than a woman, better than three women. Fucking, you know...'

'Yeah, I know what you mean. But better than women? Nah, I don't think so. I was there back then, against BFC...'

'Right, the dead guy. That was the cops' fault, though, not us, nah, that weren't us.'

He went quiet and lit one up, then he held his pack out to me. I took one and he gave me a light. A snowball landed right in front of the giant on the table tennis table. He took no notice. He was staring over our heads at the proper jail; he really was pretty tall, at least a metre ninety; he could probably see over the gate and the wall if he stood on tiptoe. 'Over there,' he said. 'I've got a lot of mates over there. It's not like the old days. We used to punch the cops in the face if they disturbed our matches. You know, I even used to know a couple of cops, they'd come along to match when they were off work, and they were real hard-hitters. Scarf round their head, you know, so the other cops wouldn't recognize them.'

'And you,' I said. 'You're a clever lad, aren't you, you don't get caught, do you?'

'Right, I am.'

'You're lucky they put you in here with us, though. You're too old for this place.'

'I'm soft in the head,' he said, looking down at me. 'They said I'm soft in the head. I'm not ready yet. Not mature enough. Otherwise I'd be over there next door and all.'

I threw my cigarette butt in the snow, took two out of the box and handed him one. He nodded and lit it. 'Those bastards went and said I'm like a kid. Shit, I'm one of the best back home in Dresden. Profesh, you know, at the football, I mean. And the bastards go and say I'm a kid. Juvenile law. It's a load of bullshit, man!'

I looked up at him; his nose was beaten pretty flat but he looked normal apart from that. 'Four weeks' custody. And probation, just bloody probation. Juvenile custody, shit. I'm twenty-four, I am.' He looked back at the jail where his mates were inside.

'I got probation as well,' I said. 'Two years.'

'Not bad,' the giant said, grinning.

Klaus came over. The bedwetter trailed after him, wearing a red hat with a blue bobble on top. Klaus stopped in front of the giant and boxed him lightly on the chest. 'Alright, Dynamo?'

'Yeah, I'm alright,' said Dynamo, looking down at him.

'So does Danny want a match with you at last?' Klaus said.

'No, he doesn't,' said the giant.

'Probably better,' Klaus said, and patted me on the shoulder. 'Chemie stinks.'

'Shut your fucking mouth,' I said, pushing his hand away. 'You and your fucking SSS.'

No, I just thought it.

'Watch it,' said the giant. 'Or you'll have to do a match with Danny, tomorrow morning before showers. You can go in my cell. Three minutes, one round, no one'll notice. I'll keep time.'

'Nah, forget it,' said Klaus. 'Then Danny'll have to say he fell down the stairs or rammed his head on the bed-post. Anyway, we're mates, aren't we, Danny?' He put his arm round my shoulder.

'Yeah,' I said, 'we are.'

Someone opened a window. We turned around. On the ground floor, behind the bars, a guy was standing in his cell, looking out at us. 'Look, it's one of the day release guys,' the bedwetter said, pointing.

Klaus pushed his arm back down. 'Are you crazy? Want a fist in the face, do you? Don't stare at the guy like that, Christ!'

The day release prisoners lived on the ground floor. When I smoked by the window in the morning, I could see them leaving for the station or the bus stop. They came back in the afternoon and stayed in their cells. One of them went by bike, even when it snowed.

'They haven't got it so bad,' I said. 'Better than next door. They can go out, they've got jobs...'

'And girls,' said Klaus. 'I bet they've got a girl in town. It's definitely better than next door.' We smoked and looked at the jail.

'I was in proper jail once,' the bedwetter said. He bent down, picked up some snow and made a snowball. 'Not for long though. And not here. It was in...'

'Ah, shut it!' Klaus knocked the snowball out of his hand. 'Don't talk lies. You wouldn't be here, they'd have... they'd have spent all day messing up your face if you wet their beds... What a big fat liar.' We grinned.

The bedwetter had crouched down and was stabbing at the snow with his hand. The giant nudged him with one foot. 'Come on, up you get, you gangster.'

The bedwetter got up; he'd made a new snowball, it was balanced on his hand, and he rocked it back and forth like some kind of animal. 'I've got thirteen things on my record,' he said. 'All cars. No need to laugh – I'm the best back home.'

'Not bad, kid,' said the giant, grinning. 'You're a right gangster.'

And I grinned too and said: 'Not bad.' The bedwetter smiled. He threw his snowball up in the air and caught it again.

'Bullshit,' said Klaus. 'That's nothing to show off about. Cars – that's kids' stuff. ABH,' he punched his other hand. 'ABH, GBH, that's the premiere league!'

'You're a big strong boy, are you?' the giant said, looking down at him. 'Pack a punch, do you?'

'Noses,' said Klaus, 'I kept breaking noses. That costs

you, see. But I always aim for the chin, see, I aim right at that point, right there on the chin. And then I mash up their noses, every time.'

'That never happens to me, I punch down, from one side and down,' he punched the air, right next to my head. 'On the cheekbone, that can take a bit of a punch. Or on the forehead, right on the skull above the nose, that takes care of 'em, that takes care of 'em nice and quick, take my word for it.' He showed Klaus his fist, dangling it in front of his face. 'From the top, like this, then they don't see it coming, see?'

'Not bad,' said Klaus. 'Me and you, a match, what d'you reckon?'

'Hm, maybe.' The giant lit one up and held his pack out to Klaus. The bedwetter fished his lighter out of his pocket and wanted to give Klaus a light, but it fell down in the snow. He picked it up and blew it clean but it wouldn't spark. 'You know who I would match with?' said the giant.

'With our Vietcong? Hasn't he gone home now?'

'Nah, the new guy, the debt collector. If he is one.'

'Yeah,' said Klaus, 'I bet he's worth it, he looks like he'd put up a proper fight, the debt collector, if he is one.'

'Ask him, then,' I said.

'Nah, maybe later.'

The debt collector was standing over by the window, one arm leaning on the bars, talking to the day-release guy. Maybe he wasn't a debt collector, but the others said he was. He was a big enough guy. He wasn't quite as tall as the giant and not as wide as Klaus, he was that tough kind, not an ounce of fat, I'd seen him in the showers. He had a whole load of tattoos, especially on his back. The others said he'd been inside for a few months before he came, but there'd been a new trial or something and they'd let him off the rest and given him a month in custody instead. They said he'd done a deal with the judge, he had a whole load of money, he was a debt collector, wasn't he, and anyway they said the old lady in the robe had the hots for him, but it was probably all bullshit. He'd worked for the Vietcong, apparently, but we couldn't ask our Vietcong 'cause he'd been back out for a few days now.

'What did you do, Danny?' They looked at me. The bedwetter had taken his hat off and was playing with the blue bobble.

'Oh, you know, this and that. Bit of cars, bit of knocking about, lifted a bit of stuff, that kind of thing.' They nodded. 'And... a couple of counts of tresspassing.'

'Tresspassing? What d'you do? Broke into a couple of houses?'

'Nah. Club. We had an illegal club. In a factory, you know, and then it's trespassing.'

'Not bad, Danny. A proper club.' They nodded and looked me up and down. The giant held his pack out to me, even though my fag was still alight. 'So how was business?'

'Alright.' They nodded again and looked at me. Then we shut up and smoked. It was still snowing and we cupped our cigarettes in our hands. The snowflakes melted on our faces.

'He got probation and all,' the giant said, pointing at me. His finger was almost as long as my arm. I smiled and wiped the snow off my face.

'Good lad,' said Klaus. He pointed at the jail. 'Over there. You know, one day.' I nodded.

'Rubbish,' said the bedwetter. 'I'm not going to jail. You won't see me here again.'

'Not here,' said the giant, 'nah, not here.' We laughed.

'Couple more minutes,' the warder called. We lit up

another one.

Klaus turned around. 'Oi, crustie, come here!'

André had been standing by the door on his own the whole time; now he walked slowly over to us. 'I'm not a crustie,' he said, stirring the snow with his foot.

'Nah, 'course not.' Klaus laughed. André got out his tobacco and started rolling. He went from cell to cell every day, collecting the butts out of the ashtrays. 'Tobacco rescue,' he called it.

'Forget that shit, you can have a ready-rolled.' Klaus gave him a cigarette. 'Only crusties roll their own.'

'Thanks. I'm not a crustie, though.'

'Anyway, tell us, number one: What did you do?'

'Do? Nothing. I didn't do nothing, honest.' He raised his shoulders and took a step back.

'Hey, don't start bricking it,' Klaus patted him on the shoulder; I saw the bedwetter grinning and showing his teeth, one canine missing like Pitbull – I only just noticed it now. 'I just wanna know why they sent you here.'

''Cause of the bollards, that's why!' I turned away. I'd heard the story a couple of times now. The day release guy had closed his window and the debt collector was standing by the warder, smoking. Now he threw his cigarette on the snow and stepped on it. '...and then we ripped the bollards out.'

'Bollards, what bloody bollards?'

'Around the trees, you know, round the parks, see? We ripped them out and chucked them at the cars. More than twenty of us.'

'Proper riot, eh?' The giant grinned.

'Yeah, and then we went for the cops, then the cops came, and we went for the cops with the bollards. We totally trashed their van!' He'd told me the story a couple of times, but it was news to me that they'd gone for the cops.

'Time to go in,' the warder called. 'Locking up time!' He opened the door. I strolled over to him.

There were boys all over the yard, standing alone or in groups, smoking. Someone barged into me, some boy was in my way, and I shoved him aside. 'Oi, watch it, you weirdo!' I took no notice, just carried on walking.

'Hey, Danny, wait a minute!' I turned around. There they came, Klaus, André, the giant and the bedwetter. They had to go back home in a few days. I still had more than two weeks to go. We chucked our cigarettes in the snow, then we went up the stairs.

'You've got post, Daniel!' I nodded, got up and followed the warder to the office. He went in; I stayed outside the door. 'Come on!' He held the door open and then went to the desk, where there were a few letters and parcels. 'From your mother,' he said, and gave me a greeting card with an apple on it, with a worm peering out and grinning. 'Lousy times,' it said underneath the apple. 'Your mother sent twenty marks, do you want me to add it to your cigarette money?'

'Yes,' I said.

He nodded and wrote something on a list. 'I need an autograph.' He put the paper on the desk, tapped it with one finger, and I signed without reading it. The warder took the list and went to the cupboard.

I opened up the card. 'Hope you're not doing too bad. From Mum.'

'You can go now.'

'OK,' I said, and I opened the door and went out in the corridor.

'What did you get?'

'Ah, nothing.' I pressed the card to my chest. I went into my cell and closed the door behind me.

'What you got there?' the new guy asked, from up in the top bunk. 'What you got there, Danny, got something nice, something from Mummy?' He laughed.

'None of your fucking business.' I lay down and ripped the card into tiny pieces, which I put in my pocket.

I was sitting at the table having breakfast. It was my last breakfast. I'd packed my bag the night before and stowed it under the bed. The new guy was sitting next to me. He ate like a pig, and I looked past him out of the window. 'Good breakfast, is it, Danny, Danny, Danny?' That was his thing to wind me up, and he knew I'd keep quiet 'cause there'd been trouble with the warders again, just before Klaus went home. They knew I was on probation, they had my files here, and the judge had given me conditions, how I had to behave and all that, I had it all in writing at home in my probation plan. And I didn't trust them: juvenile court, judges, prosecutors, cops. And it wasn't just the warders, the cops, the trouble; I was tired, I didn't want any fights or arguments, not in here, 'cause I knew, back home, in Leipzig, in our neighbourhood, it'd all start off again.

The new guy went on eating, his face shiny; the new guy didn't wash. He'd been in my cell for a week now but he hadn't once taken a shower. The cell stank and I kept opening the window all day, even though it was so cold outside. I pushed my plate away and lit one up. I looked over at the jail, then at the car park. There was a guy pacing back and forth. Now he walked to the gate and stopped. I leapt up and leaned out the window. 'Paul,' I yelled, 'Paul, up here!' He hadn't heard me; he walked back to the parked cars. I grabbed the new guy by the throat. 'Come on,' I said. 'Lean out the window and whistle! You're so good at whistling!'

'Are you crazy!' He jumped up and grabbed at me. I batted his arm away, not letting go of his throat and pressing his head to the wall. I could have leaned out the window and kept on calling 'til Paul heard me, but no, I wanted the new guy to whistle. And he could whistle right enough, he'd whistled plenty of times when I wanted a bit of peace and quiet, he'd put two fingers in his mouth like my dad used to at football, and whistle. I couldn't do it.

'You lean out the window and whistle. Is that clear? I said, is that clear!' The new guy aimed a short left hook at my face; I turned my head away and he didn't hit my cheekbone properly, just grazed it. I let go of his throat and gave it right back to him. I got him a few times in the belly, right where his liver was, and when he shoved me away and came towards me, I punched, left – left – right, around his hips, on the kidneys; I'd got that tip from the debt collector.

'You can't see a thing,' he'd said. 'No marks. And it finishes them off nice and quick.' The new guy leant back against the wall, holding onto the cupboard. I pressed my forehead against his face and bumped him, just a quick one, above the bridge of his nose.

'You're a fighter, are you? A real hard man, are you? The greatest in your shitty little village!' He'd told me about his village every night, what a hero he was there, how many girls he shagged there, how the cigarette kings used his dad's barn as a stash...

'You're crazy, you're all-out crazy!' He didn't yell; he spoke quietly, and I saw he was almost crying.

'Whistle, or I'll beat the shit out of you!' I twisted his arm so hard he went down on the floor, and pushed him over to the window. 'Whistle, I said, just fucking whistle, or Paul'll just leave again!'

And he whistled. He leaned out the window, put two

fingers in his mouth and whistled. I stood next to him. 'Paul,' I yelled, 'Paul, up here, it's me, it's me, Danny, Daniel!' And the new guy whistled.

Paul turned around; he shaded his eyes and looked up at me. He walked through the gate to the custody building, he waved and stopped under the window. 'Danny,' he called, 'it's me, come down!' like he was standing outside my house and I was late. I combed my hair, put on my jacket, then I ran down. 'Danny,' he called, 'when are you coming?' He was still waving; now he lowered his hand and put it in his pocket.

'Might take a sec, Paul, might take a minute!' I pushed the new guy aside and picked up some snow from the window ledge; I made a snowball and threw it down at Paul. He jumped out the way. We laughed.

'I'll wait, Danny, I'll wait in the car. Right 'til tonight, I don't care!'

Paul was the only one of us who had his driving licence. He was a bit older than us, just turned eighteen, and his mother had paid for his driving lessons 'cause she was scared he'd do it like us and drive without a licence. Paul waved again, then he turned round and went back to the car park. I closed the window. The new guy was sitting on the top bunk. I lit one up and paced across the room.

'Jesus, what was that all about? You're crazy...'

'Shut your fucking mouth,' I yelled, punching the ladder, 'shut your mouth, for fuck's sake, or I'll come up there!' My cigarette was broken and I put it out in the ashtray. The new guy was quiet now, looking down at me wide-eyed. I lit a new cigarette and lay down. Three days ago, the new guy and his two mates had stood by my bed. 'Danny, Danny, Danny,' the new guy chanted. 'Don't get in a huff!' I looked up at the mattress above me. Their eyes were on my face; I turned to the wall. 'Danny, Danny, Danny, don't get mad now.'

'Shut your fucking mouth,' I yelled. 'Shut your fucking trap!'

'I didn't even... I'm not saying anything...' I ran to the window. The new guy was leaning against the wall, his pillow pressed to his chest. I spotted Paul in the car park, smoking and walking around between the cars.

'Hey, listen,' I said. 'You're gonna keep your mouth shut, right?'

''Course, Danny,' the new guy said, and he put the pillow in front of his mouth.

I nodded and looked out the window again; Paul was still there. 'Course, Danny,' the new guy said again, through the pillow.

'Alright, hard man, alright.' I put out my cigarette. There was a pack of cards by the ashtray; the new guy had brought them. I picked them up and lay down in bed. I heard the new guy breathing up above. I took the cards and played the Queen of Hearts game. She was always on top when I lifted the cards. It worked with any other card but I loved the Queen of Hearts.

'Don't be mad, Danny, Danny, Danny,' the new guy said. I chucked the cards on the floor. 'Don't be sad, Danny. It's just a game.' They laughed. But it wasn't a game anymore. They'd cheated me. They'd ganged up on me and screwed me in every round. They'd given each other signs, laughing, they'd played their sevens and aces so I always had to take a card or miss a turn. Every round. Every day. The three of them stuck together, 'cause they came from the same area, somewhere near Meissen. 'No one gets into my village,' the new guy had said one night. 'There's a barrier and a gatekeeper, you have to show your ID to prove you live there. No one gets in, no strangers.'

He'd told me all sorts of other crap and I was glad to fall asleep, but usually I lay awake a long time, not only 'cause the new guy was talking crap. 'I was there in Rostock,' he said. 'We set light to the Vietcong, I threw a Molly myself. I used to be a skin, see, a proper skinhead, they were all scared of me, even the cops!'

'Yeah,' I said, and I pressed my head against the pillow and tried to sleep. Ina was in the middle of the room. I hadn't heard her unlocking the door.

'Take your plates out, sheets as well. Then come to the office.'

'Yeah,' I said, and I looked at her arse as it moved at every step out of the room.

*Zeithain JCC,* it said on the round piece of metal hanging like a label on the zip of the small black bag containing my valuables. Ina took a pair of pliers out of a drawer and cut through the wire. The piece of metal fell on the table. I put my hand on it, picked it up and pocketed it. Ina gave me my wallet. I opened it and counted my money. 'Nothing goes missing here,' she said.

'I know,' I said.

She gave me my keys. 'Sign here, please.' She handed me two forms. 'One's for you.' I signed, folded one of the release certificates up and put it in my breast pocket. 'You can go now.' I stood up and picked up my bag.

'You didn't apply for travel expenses?'

'No,' I said. 'Paul's outside.' She nodded. I looked through the window into the corridor.

She held the door open for me. 'Go on, then, off you go.'

'Yeah,' I said and walked slowly past her. 'Maybe we'll see each other again sometime.' She smiled. I went down the stairs. At the bottom, the warder was sitting behind his glass; he looked at me, nodded and pressed the buzzer. I crossed the yard to the gate. My shoelace was undone; I put my bag down, crouched and tied it. I turned around, saw the bars, faces in a few windows.

'Danny, that took a while!' Paul was standing by his car; it was his mum's red Peugeot.

'Thanks for coming.' I shook his hand, my other hand on his shoulder.

''Course, Danny, 'course I've come to get you.' He opened the boot and took my bag.

'How d'you know I'm here? I didn't...'

'Your mum, Danny, your mum told me.' He slammed the boot shut and we got in the car. 'Why didn't you let us know?'

'Oh, you know, it was only four weeks...'

Paul stalled the engine, started again, and we drove off. We drove past the fields the Russians had loved so much. 'Does your mum know about the car?'

'Yeah,' said Paul. 'But if she hadn't given it me...'

'You'd have taken it, eh? Or a different one.'

Paul nodded and strained his eyes on the road. It had started to snow and he switched on the windscreen wipers. 'Bloody winter,' he said. Paul had never broken into a car. He'd only ever stood and watched when we got down to it with Fred. We'd let him behind the wheel a couple of times, but we had to talk him into it, and he always drove so slowly and carefully we were scared the cops would stop us for it.

'For you, Danny,' said Paul, 'for you I really would have...'

'I know you would, Paul,' I said.

'Oh yeah, my mum says hello.'

'Thanks,' I said. I knew he was lying. I knew his mum.

'Hey, Danny, was it... was it... Oh, nothing.' A sharp

bend; Paul went down into second gear.

'What, go on.'

'You know, whatever you ask, was it... it wasn't bad in there, was it?'

'It was only four weeks, Paul.' I lit one up and rolled the window down a crack.

'Got one for me, Danny?'

I handed him mine and lit myself a new one.

'But we can't smoke that much, 'cause of my mum, you know...'

'Course,' I said. 'We'll wind the windows right down for a bit once we get into town.'

A sign said *Leipzig 42 km*.

'So it wasn't hard, wasn't bad?'

'No, Jesus, I just told you. Like a holiday camp, it was like some stupid summer camp.'

Paul opened his window and chucked out the half-smoked cigarette. I could have told him something, about the giant, about the new guy I'd roughed up just before, or about the epileptic who was probably just crazy and had smashed up his cell a few days ago. Or I could have told him how a couple of boys had dragged the epileptic under the shower and... he stood screaming in the corridor, the water running down him.

'Bloody hell!' Paul braked sharply and went down a gear. 'Why's that bastard there stepping on the brakes like that!'

'Maybe there was an animal on the road.'

'In the middle of winter, Danny?'

'A cat, maybe it was a cat, or a fox.'

'Hey, shall we go out for a drink tonight? I can let the others know. Maybe at Goldie's or somewhere.'

'Course,' I said. 'Course, why not.'

She wasn't there when they let me out. I stood outside the big gate, my bag on the snowy ground, and then I saw Paul running towards me.

'Danny,' he yelled, 'Hey, Danny!' We hugged and I looked over his shoulder at the car park.

No, she wasn't there, and it was winter again, and last winter she'd said goodbye to me here. We'd hugged so long I couldn't breathe, and I'd only let her go once the tears had gone from my eyes.

'Alright?' Paul asked.

'Alright,' I said, still looking at the car park where she'd stood in the snow last year and I'd imagined I could see her footprints days later, every time I looked out the window.

Her little feet, my God. I'd thought of her little feet every night, her pink-and-white toes that were so small and delicate, like a pixie princess's. I thought of her little feet every night, I could wrap my hand right round them and protect them from the others, I dreamed of her whole little body 'til everything hurt. Sometimes number 72's feet slid over the side of the top bunk and I got a good view of them, and that messed everything up. I felt like breaking every toe on his sweaty feet one by one. 'You know,' Paul said, 'she couldn't...'

'Yeah, yeah,' I said, and then we walked over to the car park, to Paul's car. Paul carried my bag.

We drove back to town. I'd only written to Paul to say when I got out. She knew as well, of course. She'd come to visit often in the first few months. Everything was fine at the beginning. We'd hugged and kissed and touched as much as you could in there. When we hugged, she'd often whispered in my ear: 'Please, don't ever do anything bad again. I don't want to be alone, ever again.'

Then I breathed into her black hair and whispered back: 'I promise, never again, I love you,' and so on, and I'd meant it. Sometimes I tried to imagine we were in a hospital visiting room and I'd just broken a leg and three ribs from falling down the stairs drunk, and I could go home in a week's time. After three months she stopped coming as often, and when she was there she was so different and distant that everything hurt between my belly and my throat and I didn't know what to say to her. She'd ask what the food was like, or tell me about the spring and summer weather, and that was worse than not talking. Sometimes I'd take her hand and put it to my face, and sometimes she wouldn't talk then and she'd look down at the table between us or up at the windows with the bars – how many were there, anyway? – and sometimes she'd say, really quiet: 'Danny, please, I don't ever want to be alone again.'

Then she stopped coming at all, and letters came, and she wrote that she needed time, she had to think everything over, she loved me and so on, and it hurt her to see me this way. My God, it hurt me not to see her.

'Paul, my man, how're the ladies?' I asked, not looking at him. It was getting dark outside, it was afternoon, and I watched the car's headlights touching the street signs. Leipzig 24 km.

'The ladies?' Paul said. 'Perverted, as usual.'

Paul was the porno king of our neighbourhood and perhaps the whole city and maybe nationwide. He was a member of all thirty-two Leipzig video shops and the eighteen in the villages around the outside of town. There was no joint-wrenching sex position, no sexual perversion he didn't know. He'd had them all and seen it all:

golden showers garnished with caviar, Max Hardcore's anal orgies, hot Asian hos, pregnant and horny, seventy and horny, and the only pornos he hated were the ones with kids in them. He said he'd cut off anyone's dick if he caught them at that kind of thing. 'The women have to want it,' he said, and they all wanted it in his films. We called him Porno Paul, and not many people apart from me knew he'd once had a real woman. We were seventeen and Anna, our nympho who made all our dicks sore, had grabbed Paul at a party one time and locked herself in the outside toilet with him. We all had to piss and puke in the sink or out the window for half an hour, then Paul came slowly up the stairs, his trousers gone, and he said: 'Kinda disgusting.'

Anna was the first and the last. He hadn't had another woman all these years.

Anna. I hadn't loved Anna, or maybe a little bit when we lay down drunk on the roof of her building at night and she rested her head on my shoulder. Anna was crazy and she drank like a fish and did it with every guy in our neighbourhood. She just came round my place one time – my mum wasn't in – and she ripped my shirt open so hard the buttons went flying round my room, and then pushed me on the bed and tore the rest of my clothes off. I couldn't believe how warm it all was. Seven times she rode me, like a crazy thing, she always wanted to go on top, and only sometimes, when she hadn't drunk anything at all, would I go on top of her and she'd go all quiet.

Later, I found out she'd gone down to Pitbull's cellar after those first seven times, and they'd heard her screams three doors down. It didn't bother me when she went to other guys, there was no satisfying her, that's just how she was; there was no point trying to change it.

Much later, I met *her*. Everything was completely

different with her. 'Danny,' she'd say, and I felt her nose on my ear. 'Please, don't ever do anything bad again. You've got to stop all the crap.'

'Yes,' I said, 'I promise, I love you,' and so on, and I'd meant it.

I barely saw Anna, only heard her sometimes in the cellar where Pitbull lived, and sometimes I dreamed at night of the roof of her building, and her head resting on my shoulder.

We were in Leipzig. It wasn't snowing. 'Where shall I drop you off?' Paul asked, squinting at the sludge-streaked road.

'Take me to my mum's. That's my official address. And, Paul, don't tell anyone I'm back.' I looked at the buildings and the streets and the cars by the edge of the road, I saw the streetlamps and the neon ads that hurt my eyes, I looked at the bright empty bus stops we used to smash up some nights, screaming and yelling. I leaned my head against the window. Paul stopped the car.

We got out and he gave me my bag. 'Danny, I'm so glad...'

'Yeah,' I said, patting his shoulder. 'I'll come round and see you.' I turned away and walked across the pavement to my mum's building. I heard Paul slam the door and drive off.

The front door was open, downstairs. I pressed the bell, the third one up on the right with no name next to it, and went up. On the first floor, I turned on the light. Someone had used my time away to change the light bulbs. My mum was standing outside the open door to the flat. She was wearing her good bathrobe and I saw her legs from below through the bannisters. She was holding a glass. 'My boy, my boy, come to your old mum.' She was the first woman I saw, and I wished it had all turned out different.

'Hot sex on cold days. 0173...'

'A taste of class to blow your mind – three spicy ladies.'

'364 days a year! Always open for sexy fun and games! 0170...'

I drank some of my mum's brandy and looked at the small ads in the paper. Mum was in bed, I could hear her breathing through the door, left ajar. I brought the telephone to the table, then I drank two glasses, then I called a couple of numbers. I asked them how old they were, what hair colour, whether their breasts were big or small or medium, how much they weighed – no, not their breasts – whether their pubes were shaved, and so on. It was sort of funny asking that kind of thing, but I had to. One metre 75? OK. Figure not too thin, no, not a Rubens model either.

I took the bus over to Plagwitz, where the big factories were crumbling away. The buses and the streets there were empty at night.

It said 'Meier' on the bell, and I waited until I'd turned the hall light back on five times, and then I smoked another one, even though I wanted to give them up, something else I'd decided on when they let me out. I gave three short rings and one long, like she'd told me on the phone. The door opened and she only looked a tiny bit like *her*, but that didn't matter now, my imagination would do the rest.

'Hello.'

'Hello, come in.'

She was only wearing a kind of bathing suit, and I followed her down the hall into a room with a big bed and red light. There was a table there too, with a little stereo and a CD rack on it, and there were two chairs by the table. 'Take a seat, take off your coat.'

'How much for an hour?'

I was relaxed now and only thinking of her, and the red twilight helped.

'It's 200,' she said. 'That's oral for you, for me if you want, and sex three times, maximum.'

'OK,' I said. 'And the money...'

'Up front.'

I took out my mum's purple purse; I'd borrowed it 'cause I didn't have a wallet, and put my jail money in it. I'd taken out Mum's twenty marks and put the note under the brandy bottle. I gave her three notes, and she said: 'You get undressed, I'll be right with you.'

'Don't get a shock,' I said. 'I've got sixteen tattoos.' She laughed as she left the room, and now I was so relaxed I saw *her* laughing. She laughed her laugh and I saw her teeth.

'What's your real name, Michelle?' I asked when she came back in.

'Cleopatra,' she said, and she laughed her laugh again. I'd got undressed and she was naked as well now, her skin glinting. She sat down in front of me, and when I licked her breasts she tasted of skin cream. I sucked so hard on her nipples I was scared I might hurt her, but she was all quiet. I put a finger inside her, I rubbed my face on her labia, and then I started licking her out. My God, I'd almost forgotten how warm it was.

She sneezed, and then she laughed again, and I leaned back and said: 'Sit down on me.'

'Not so fast.' She reached between the pillows somewhere and pulled out a condom. 'Abracadabra,' she said, and bent down.

I went to Paul's place, number 73 bus to the eastern edge

of town, where strange memories waited for me on every corner.

Paul wasn't there. I'd rung the bell a few times and knocked and called his name, and then I went back down the stairs. The light went out when I got to the ground floor and as I was looking for the red dot on the light switch, I heard it. A faint yowling. It came from the cellar, and then I saw the light reflected on the steps down there, and I don't know why but I immediately thought of Paul. I went down, the door was open, and one of the coal cellars was open too. A lightbulb was hanging from the ceiling, Paul sitting below it right in the middle of the coal, howling. There was a toilet bowl in front of him. He sounded just like a dog howling at the moon or something.

'Paul, Jesus, what are you doing...?'

He didn't look at me. 'Danny, I'm sick in the head.'

'Crap, you're just a bit crazy, like all of us.'

'No. No. I can't do it with women. For years now.'

'I know, but...'

'I'm not gay. Believe me, I'd be glad if I was. I can't do it with anyone. And the others, the others are all gone. Oh God, it's so fucking awful.' I didn't know what else to say. He just sat there in front of the toilet bowl and howled. 'They knocked the building down while you were away. I went over in the car one night and got it.'

Maybe I should have sent him to Michelle-Cleopatra, but that wouldn't have helped; he'd tried it before.

'Come on,' I said, 'we'll go for a bit of a walk.'

# EASTSIDE STORY

I often dreamed of the Eastside when I was away, not every night, no, 'cause sometimes I dreamed of women or of taking the tram all round Leipzig with a one-day pass and a crate of beer, and sometimes I dreamed of Little Walter and the night I saved his life twice over, Walter who just left us anyway all those nights later, and sometimes I didn't dream at all, but there were nights when I knew even before I fell asleep that I'd dream of the Eastside, and then I'd lie awake for a long time, looking forward to it.

And I still often dream of the Eastside and the time back then, and it seems like – even though it wasn't really a year, the Eastside year, and so much came after it and had happened before – like it was the longest part of my youth, or were we still kids? And when I dream of that year or think of it, I know we were the greatest back then. We had a club, over in Anger-Crottendorf. We were the youngest club-owners in town, 'cause we were only 16 or 17 back then. The club was in this old gearbox factory, on the main road out of town, a few hundred metres before the city limits sign. When we climbed on the roof of the little tower, we could see the villages and the East Woods on the other side of the neighbourhood. Behind the factory was a railway embankment, and sometimes we shot our air rifle at the freight trains. We shot at the remains of the glass in the windows too, or we put cheap or nicked beer cans on the windowsills and shot 'til they were drained. From the embankment, a track with an old set of points led through a gate to a platform; we were going to fix it all up and divert the trains, 'cause some of the freight trains carried rows of cars stacked up on top of each other; we didn't shoot at them, 'cause we loved cars.

Sometimes Fred hid his stolen rides in one of the halls. The factory was big, all different buildings with roads and paths between them, like in a little town.

The factory's gone now. They built an Esso garage there, even though there's already a Shell garage in the neighbourhood, over by the old Duroplast state toy and rubber stamp factory. Sometimes I buy beer at Esso when I happen to pass by, and I go and visit Thilo the Drinker, who sits at a little table behind the garage and drinks. He's even there in winter, wearing a woolly hat with a big red bobble on the top and drinking vodka to keep the cold out. He can't get away, he says, 'cause it was his factory all along, he showed it to us, he was there before us, sitting in the cellars and the halls and drinking. Thilo the Drinker sits by a little wall, all that's left of his factory. Behind the wall is a pit where one of the factory's many cellars used to be, and now Thilo the Drinker chucks his empty beer cans in there, vodka bottles in the winter, and the pit's almost full. Thilo the Drinker's always been a drinker but he says he only started when his parents died a few years ago. I get him a beer and a mini vodka bottle whenever I happen to be passing and I go and visit him, 'cause he's right, it was him who showed us the factory, if it wasn't for him we'd never have thought of setting up a techno club in one of the buildings. The bar was already there, he'd built it just for himself, piled up a couple of old lockers across the room and hung a big sign from the ceiling, 'Thilo's Bar'. He'd even got hold of a couple of old bar stools, and behind the bar he'd made shelves out of bricks and boards, a few bottles of spirits on them, candles lit in front. There he sat and drank while they cleared out his parents' flat. They'd had a big pile of debt and the repo man came to collect the furniture and valuables, and that was why Thilo sat at his bar all day long and drank. I think the health department was after him and all, 'cause his dad had died of TB and they wanted to put Thilo the Drinker in quarantine, 'cause they didn't know if he'd caught it. Rico told us that the first time we visited Thilo at his bar, and we tried not to get too close when we talked to him – TB was bad news. He offered us vodka and we drank out the bottle 'cause his glasses looked like he'd pissed in them, and they smelled like it too. We drank out the same bottle as him but that didn't matter 'cause it was original Russian vodka and his TB didn't stand a chance against it.

I can't remember now whose idea the club was, maybe it was Walter, maybe Mark or Rico; sometimes when I sit behind the garage drinking with Thilo the Drinker, I think it was my idea, but actually I know it wasn't, 'cause I only came up with the name, 'Eastside', but that was later.

In those days we used to go to the illegal techno clubs in Connewitz, in old factories or derelict buildings. It was better there than at the Apple, even though the girls had less on there, even in winter. There weren't any mean bouncers at the illegal clubs, and no guys getting aggro when you watched their girlfriends dancing, it was way too dark anyway and all you could see in the light of the stroboscope was arms and legs and sometimes a few heads. The fog wasn't just on the dancefloor, it went all through the corridors and the bar, out onto the street. The cops almost never came. 'Techno's gotta be in a factory or a cellar,' Mark always said back then. He'd started DJing himself, first with two old record players from the Zone, then Karsten's brother got him two belt-drive HTEs, two hundred each. He really wanted two Technics 'cause they were better, direct drive, but Karsten's brother couldn't get hold of them just like that, only for six hundred each, and that was two hundred empty beer crates

Mark would have had to fetch from the Leipzig Premium Pilsner Brewery or round the back of the supermarket and then hand them back in again for the deposit money. He'd started, but the cops caught him at it twice so then he just went for the HTEs. He practiced on them every day, and Walter sometimes had a go as well, and the rest of us listened and drank beer; we weren't allowed to smoke in Mark's room. When his parents kicked up a fuss we lugged the stereo and the record players over to Pitbull's cellar, no one bothered us there, only Pitbull's dad sometimes when he was drunk, but Pitbull already had him under control by then. Pitbull even had a little strobe in his cellar, and this plastic ball with coloured lights rotating on the ceiling that he'd got cheap from the Vietcong electrics guys. Maybe it had started in Pitbull's cellar when Mark or Walter spun some tracks and we turned off the light and the flash of the strobe and the coloured lights were in our beer and korn bottles and we danced drunk around Pitbull's old armchairs, maybe we'd had the idea there, of our own club, our own bar, and the idea was still there once the alcohol, and sometimes a few pills, had left our heads.

'We'll be the greatest if we open up our own club,' said Rico, 'the greatest in the neighbourhood.' And we really were the greatest, even if it was only a year, and not just in our neighbourhood, the whole city came to us... but that was later. And when I sit behind the garage drinking beer with Thilo the Drinker, then it's all still there, the cellar, the illegal clubs over in Connewitz that are long gone now too, the factory, Thilo's Bar...

Thilo the Drinker yelled when Rico climbed on the counter and cut the sign in half with his knife and threw the Thilo part on the ground. Thilo still yells about it these days, and then I get him a beer and a mini vodka bottle and remind him that later, once the club was up and running, we let him stand behind the bar and open the beer bottles and mix our Eastside special cocktails (brandy, korn, Jägermeister, orange juice / korn, brandy, cherry juice / sparkling wine, korn, Coke and a slice of lemon), and then he smiles and he's happy again. And he was happy back then too, even though we took his bar away from him and his air rifle and all, the one he'd hidden behind the bar; he was happy 'cause he wasn't all alone in the big factory, and 'cause we let him help us set it up, build it up, we told him he was like the bar's general manager. And we let him pull the handcart we used to fetch the armchairs and tables and chairs from the local fly-tipping spots. One time, we found this huge sofa that wouldn't fit on our handcart, so we let Fred know and he came along in one of his cars in the night and we heaved the sofa onto the roof, four of us, and then drove to the factory at walking pace; the streets were empty and we didn't see any cops. The cops didn't come until the place was up and running. They came the very first night, to our first party, even though nobody invited them. They must have found one of our flyers, 'Eastside – the new location in L.E.', that we'd distributed all over town, in record shops, bars, discos, at New Yorker when we went in to look at clothes, six hundred flyers, but we didn't get six hundred guests in Anger-Crottendorf, more like fifty, plus the cops. We knew the cops in our neighbourhood, Leipzig Southeast Station, we knew all the cops there, but that probably wasn't why they just said: 'Turn it down and don't make any trouble' and then went away, 'cause actually they knew we were specialists at making trouble of one kind or another. But they must have known the trouble would only kick off if they shut down the party, so they just got back in their cop cars and drove away.

No. There weren't any cops there, that first night at the Eastside, there can't have been any cops there 'cause the big gates to the main road were locked with chains and padlocks, 'cause the public order department had come round a few days before – 'Private property. Trespassers will be prosecuted' – and we only opened the gates for the second party a few weeks later, with a bolt-cutter from Fred's collection, and people had to cross the train tracks from the back to get in that first time.

Sometimes I remember it that way and sometimes it's different, and in some dreams the cops come the first night, every first night, and sometimes I dream they were never there, and sometimes, when I happen to pass by the garage and see Thilo the Drinker, he has to tell me how it was. Then I get him a couple of beers and a mini vodka, 'cause he has to drink to make the memories come back.

'The cops didn't come across the tracks,' he says. 'The cops came through the gates, the second time. No cops across the tracks. Just people. Lots of people.' But only fifty, maybe sixty guests came, stumbling over the tracks in the dark, and sometimes we heard the rumbling and screeching of a train from inside the factory, even though the music was pretty loud, and I think we spent all night terrified that someone would get knocked down, out on the train tracks. But no one got knocked down, even though plenty of people must have popped plenty of pills, but maybe it was because some of them turned round and went home when they saw the dark railway embankment ahead of them and the dark factory behind it with the music booming out. 'It's underground,' Walter said back then. 'Crossing the tracks, watching out for the trains, and then through the mud to the party. It's underground, like at the Idyllic.'

And he was right, 'cause the Idyllic was one of our role

models. The Idyllic was an illegal club out in Connewitz, in an old mansion. The entrance was a narrow toilet window on the ground floor with a big heap of rubbish outside it, that you had to climb up like a staircase if you wanted to get in. There were loads of illegal clubs in Connewitz and the south of town, one of them so fucked-up that the entry tickets warned you it might collapse, and another club really did collapse, luckily on a week night when there wasn't a party on, but no illegal techno club had had such a crazy entrance as the Idyllic, not until we came along and people had to cross the tracks while the freight trains ran all night.

We still broke the gates open for the second party, 'cause it had mainly been girls who'd turned back when they got to the embankment, there were like ten girls at the first Eastside and it couldn't go on like that, we thought back then. And apart from that, the number 73 bus stop was out on the main road and the station wasn't far away, and good connections were important. We had to break open the steel door of the old electrics hut as well, between the gates on the factory grounds, 'cause the pissers from the public order department had bricked up the window we'd used to plug in our extension leads and junction boxes (we were always terrified when it rained, scared there'd be a short circuit, even though we'd protected the cables running across the yard with plastic bags). Inside the electrics hut there was a humming sound and lots of LEDs flashing, and Walter, who knew a bit about electrics 'cause his dad was an electrician, put on rubber gloves when he touched the power connectors. Later, before our fourth party, there really was a short circuit and we had no more power. That was Engel's people trying to sabotage us 'cause they'd opened up their own club, and we had to get hold of a petrol generator from a building site, but luckily there were loads of building sites in Leipzig East back then. But on the night of the second party, it wasn't Engel's people who were the problem, and it wasn't the cops either, who just said: 'Turn it down a bit and don't make any trouble' and then got in their cop cars and drove off.

The Markkleebergers came that night. They smashed everything up, even though we'd done it up better than the first time. We'd copied flyers on green paper, we'd got ourselves even more sofas and invented even more cocktails. We'd borrowed a better sound system, with Technics record players instead of HTEs, and we'd even booked a famous DJ who played sets over in Kleinzschocher, DJ Frog, at the Oasis, Leipzig's first techno club, not an illegal club but just as good. DJ Frog cost us two big ones, but he was worth it, even though he had to leg it a bit early 'cause the Markkleebergers turned up. He must have been scared for his records (and he had a lot of records), his girls (he'd brought three with him, flashy pussies in short glittery dresses), and most of all his car (he drove a Cadillac with two little American flags on the bonnet; we'd never seen such a big long bonnet, and he had to sell the thing later on when petrol got expensive). I didn't see DJ Frog legging it, but someone told me later he'd run screaming across the factory yard – 'Get out of here, for God's sake, fuck off out of here, all of you!' – and a couple of records fell out of his box into the dirt as he and his three pussies legged it. But the Markleebergers left him alone, didn't harm his records, and didn't do anything to his girls either, even his Cadillac didn't get a scratch on it (as they drove off), 'cause everyone in town knew DJ Frog and respected him. The guy had a proper club, with security and all the right connections, and the right connections always led back to the red-light district, and no one wanted trouble with those guys, not even the Markkleebergers.

We had our own kind of security: Rico, who was the boss on the door and took the money, and a couple of guys from Engel's lot, who were suddenly all really nice to us and wanted to help us with anything they could, 'cause we had our own club now, we counted now, we had respect in the neighbourhood, but the Markkleebergers didn't know that, and even if they had known they wouldn't have given a shit. They didn't come from our neighbourhood, they'd come all the way from Leipzig-Markkleeberg, only fifteen minutes on the train, all the way to us to party and drink and dance. But they didn't party and they didn't drink, and they didn't dance either; the bastards smashed everything up: the bar, the furniture, the old TV with Mark's video recorder and the Donald Duck videos we'd put behind the bar, and loads of beer and bottles of spirits.

Luckily, when the trouble kicked off, I'd handed out a whole load of beer, spirits and Coke bottles to the people in the bar room so they could defend themselves, but most of them didn't defend themselves, just legged it, and the bottles went with them. And I could understand them, a bit, 'cause there were at least thirty guys waiting outside in the yard with big sticks and baseball bats. At first there were only ten Markkleebergers making trouble. They'd paid to get in, Rico even let them in for forty marks, group discount, and then they wanted their money back 'cause they didn't like the place.

The building we partied in had three storeys. There was an old washroom on the ground floor where we chucked all our rubbish, the bar room was on the first floor, and the dancefloor was on top, full of people dancing that night 'cause DJ Frog was really good. There were candles everywhere, at least a hundred lit candles, on the stairs, the windowsills, the tables and the bar. The fog machine was pumping full-blast, and the fog spread from the dancefloor down the stairs all the way into the yard. We'd wrapped tinfoil round the old radiators, the pipes on the ceilings and the pillars in the middle of the room, so they reflected the candles and the Christmas-tree lights Mark had borrowed from his parents. In the bar room, the normal lights had red and purple bulbs in them, and Thilo the Drinker had saved his parents' whisky-bottle collection (empty, though) from the repo man and put them on shelves behind the bar, covering the whole wall. We'd put metal lockers around the other walls of the room, pasted with posters and flyers from all different techno parties. The walls of the dancefloor were covered in graffiti artworks done by sprayers we'd got round from the youth club. And the Markkleebergers smashed it all up. A few days before the party we'd smashed a few things up ourselves, broken tables and chairs, thrown a couple of lockers and sofas out the window, 'cause we'd had a bit of a drink and felt like running riot. But that didn't count, it was our club, and anyway we put it all back together again.

Maybe we should have given the Markkleebergers their forty marks back when there were only ten of them, but we were businesspeople, we were running a club, and where would it all end if we started giving people their money back, we already let too many people in for free, Engel's people, Karsten and his brother, all sorts of friends of Fred's, all sorts of friends of Pitbull's, loads of girls we fancied... Or maybe Rico and his boys on the door shouldn't have threatened to beat up the Markkleebergers when there were only ten of them, but we were businesspeople, we were running a club, and if someone made trouble we had to go in hard, and where would it all end if we started going soft. And then they came back, maybe an hour later, and then there were thirty of them. At least.

I can't remember exactly how it all happened that night, all I know is I was suddenly on my own in the bar room, a bottle in each hand, and outside in the yard I heard a whole load of noise and yelling. And I don't remember exactly how I got out of the building, but I did get out somehow without them catching me, and I'd stuffed the money from the bar down my pants, just the notes, and the change was in my socks. And then I stood alone on the street and heard the smashing and crashing from the factory, and I remember to this day that I felt like crying, that I sat down on the kerb and felt like crying. Those bastards were smashing up our dream. The only thing they left in one piece was the sound system and the record players, Mark and Little Walter told me later they'd hidden them in a corner of the dark dancefloor, the power was out 'cause all the junction boxes were broken by the time the Markkleebergers came up the stairs, shone their lighters around the room and wanted to smash up the sound system, until one of them said: 'Better not, it might belong to DJ Frog.' And that's how DJ Frog did help us out a bit after all, even though he was racing home in his Cadillac with his three glittery pussies by then.

Thilo the Drinker sometimes talks about the big counter-attack that night, but there wasn't a counter-attack. We did come back together, Rico was there, Karsten and his brother, Pitbull, a couple of the sprayers from the youth club, and I'd already climbed over the fence to Böhland's recycling yard a few times, right next to the factory, and passed iron bars, clubs and two old car bumpers back over, but once I got back onto the road, in among all the weapons, I was on my own. And then the iron bars and the clubs and the two old car bumpers were on their own, 'cause I ran too, ran as fast as I could when I saw the Markkleebergers coming towards me out of the gates of the factory, our factory. And then the cops came for the second time that night, and it was maybe the first time I was glad they'd come. A couple of days later, Engel's people, Rico, Fred, Karsten and his brother, and a few other guys who couldn't have sat together inside Leipzig's biggest church without punching each other's lights out, they all went over to Markkleeberg, 'cause it was about more than our club, our neighbourhood's honour was at stake. I didn't go with them – Rico said he'd represent the Eastside, 'cause he'd been responsible for the door. We heard a whole lot of stories later about the big retribution over in Markkleeberg. Legend has it the guys' boss was blind in one eye afterwards, but Rico never told us anything.

The Markkleebergers never came back but the cops did, every time, and we got charged with trespassing loads of times, but that didn't bother us as long as they didn't close down the parties. We kept having trouble with some guy or other, and now we had a doctored alarm gun behind the bar and one on the door, 'cause Rico said he'd rather kill someone than let them smash up our dream. And one time, he did almost kill someone, I can't remember exactly what party it was, Eastside 5 or Eastside 6, but we were already pretty well known in town and people came to us from all over the city, only DJ Frog wouldn't do the decks for us anymore, not even for three big ones. But we didn't need him anyway, Walter was pretty good on the decks and Mark wasn't bad either, and there were plenty of guys from the youth club who wanted to DJ for us, would even have paid to do it. Karsten's brother was on the door with Rico now, 'cause we'd had another row with Engel's people 'cause they'd opened up their own club in another one of the factory buildings, even though it was our factory, we'd found it (Thilo the Drinker didn't count), and we'd had the idea to set up an illegal techno club there first. But there was nothing we could do about Engel and his people, even though Rico always said he wasn't scared of no one, in a dark corner with a knife. But Rico didn't have to worry about how to get even with Engel, 'cause Engel's club never went that well, he only had two parties, and no one came apart from his own people. He'd done the place up badly, he had no imagination like we did, he just wanted to show he was the greatest in the neighbourhood. Maybe it was Engel who sent those guys over that night, to rough us up a bit. We had a full house again, the ceiling of the bar room was shaking from the dancers up above and Thilo the Drinker still says the plaster was falling off onto the sofas, but I think he's exaggerating.

Pitbull had to go home to his cellar every couple of hours that night to offload the cash, and when I tell that to Thilo the Drinker these days, he says I'm exaggerating, but I know that's exactly how it was. And I'm not exaggerating when I talk about the guys who made trouble, there weren't thirty of them like the Markkleebergers, there weren't even ten of them, I think there were seven or eight guys, and maybe Rico and Karsten's brother who sometimes did the door at the Apple, maybe they would have dealt with them if they'd just been normal guys, but they were giants. They looked like hooligans, Lok hools, and they acted like it and all. First, they started barging into people in the bar room, but they all just stayed out of their way and didn't say anything, 'cause anyone who looked at the guys knew they were just waiting for someone to say something. And the minute I started thinking they'd given up and fucked off to try their luck somewhere else,

I heard Rico yelling down at the door. 'You stupid fucker, I'm gonna kill you!' I ran across the bar room, down the stairs, and then suddenly there were two of the guys on top of me, a fist in front of my face almost the size of my head, 'No,' I screamed, 'no! What the fuck's this all about, what the fuck?' but they didn't hit me, why didn't they hit me? and then I saw Rico, the gun in his hand, and the gun to a head. I saw that the gun was cocked and Rico's arm was trembling, but the guy with the barrel to his forehead stood there, calm. I wriggled between the two giants, stumbled down the stairs, and then I was by Rico and... All I remember is that there was suddenly a big crush, 'Put that thing down, put the fucking gun down!' and the hools grabbed at the gun, and then I had Rico's arm, and then I had the gun, and they could have finished him off but they didn't. Just two or three punches, Rico hit back, Karsten's brother pushed his way between Rico and the hools, and I yelled like a beast: 'Stop it, please just fucking stop it!' Pitbull came down the stairs with the second gun tucked in the front of his trousers so everyone could see it, and the hools... the hools stayed calm. One of them smashed the window in the entrance door with his bare fist – it was the only pane of glass in the whole building still in one piece. His fist started bleeding and I wished he'd slashed his wrist, but they stopped attacking. They yelled and shouted a bit more and I was fucking scared and held the gun tight and didn't put the safety on 'til they were gone. If one of us or one of them had made a wrong move at that moment, maybe a hectic movement would have done it, some fast step in some wrong direction, there'd have been more blood than just on the guy's fist. Or maybe it was Little Walter who saved the day, 'cause he gave the hools two six-packs of beer so they could fuck off without losing face.

For years after that, Rico still held it against me that I took his gun away that night, 'cause he said he'd had everything under control. But I saw his face when he stood there with the gun and the guy, and I reckon he'd have pulled the trigger. It was only a souped-up alarm gun, but it was right on the guy's forehead and the pressure would have gone straight into his head, and Rico would have gone to jail for even longer than he did, later, when they locked him up again.

Maybe that was another one of the reasons, Rico going to jail, why it all ended with the Eastside. And I think he was glad about it, 'cause he couldn't have taken it, sitting inside while half of Leipzig partied in our club.

But it was the drugs, the bastard drugs that messed everything up, that smashed up our dream, the dream not even the Markkleebergers, the hools, Engel's people and all the cops in Leipzig could put a stop to.

It was Pitbull, it was Pitbull who started selling his shit at the Eastside. He always said: 'We're businessmen now, we have to offer people what they want.' And he was right, there were loads of people who came to us and wanted his shit, and even I used to have a try of it now and then. And then Engel's people came along and screwed down Pitbull's prices and there was more trouble. And then Walter and Mark started taking Pitbull's or Engel's stuff at every party and stopped taking care of the bar and the entrance and the cops, when they came, and later Rico started too, and I popped a pill or two now and then as well, and everything... everything started to get messed up. Engel's people stuck their oar in everywhere, at the bar, on the door, they wanted free drinks, free entry for their girlfriends, and their girlfriends' friends and their sisters, then money went missing and we all accused each other, and everything started to get messed up.

We didn't have clear heads anymore, half of Leipzig was coming to us, we were the greatest, we were famous, not just in our neighbourhood, and every one of us, Rico, Mark, Pitbull, Walter and me as well, we all wanted to be the boss, and everything started to get messed up. The mood at the parties wasn't as good as it was at the beginning either, people were still dancing 'til it got light and the birds started bothering us, but loads of people just sat on the sofas or in their cars and popped Pitbull's or Engel's pills.

And in the end the cops stopped playing along, no more 'Turn it down a bit and don't make any trouble,' they blocked the gates at night so no one could get in, more and more trespassing charges and that scared us, though we never admitted it, they sent plain-clothes men in who caught a few of Engel's people in the act, they threatened to confiscate the sound system if we didn't shut it down, one time they took Rico and Pitbull down to the station, Leipzig Southeast Police Station, and Mark, Walter and I had to keep the party going on our own. The cops didn't want another Connewitz in Leipzig East, in Anger-Crottendorf, 'cause they'd lost control of the illegal clubs there long before. But the cops were part of the whole game, and when we negotiated with them and people saw that the party was saved, when the cops fucked off again, we were the greatest.

Thilo the Drinker always says it was the shit-man's fault it all went kaput, but that's not true, he just showed us how sick and fucked-up and perverted some people in town were, but we knew that already anyway, and actually he had nothing to do with the Eastside, he was just there, in the factory, even though we never saw him. I don't like talking about the shit-man, even though Thilo the Drinker's always going on about him, 'cause I saw his photos. They'd be on the bar or one of the tables sometimes when we got there, along with his letters. There was usually a plastic bag with them, but we didn't give him what he wanted, even though he offered us money for it, in the letters.

And then we lost all of it, 'cause we just couldn't keep going, and we never went back inside the factory, and only Thilo the Drinker stayed behind, alone in his bar until they pulled it all down.

'So, Daniel,' Mrs Seidel says, peering at me over the top of her glasses, 'how are things at home?'

'Alright, pretty good.'

'And are you helping your mum with the housework?'

'Yes,' I say.

'That's good,' she says. 'A Pioneer is always helpful. Especially to his parents...' she adjusts her glasses, '... his mother. Give me your homework book.' I open my satchel and hand it to her. She writes something in it with her fountain pen, not the one with the red ink. 'Show that to your mum, she'll be pleased with you.'

'I will,' I say. 'Thank you.' I put my homework book away again.

'I hear you've been helping Rico to reintegrate into the collective.'

'Yes, Miss,' I say.

'A Pioneer is always helpful,' she says, raising her finger, but I know all that already and I've heard it often enough. 'But he also has to have self-discipline. A Pioneer has to pursue his own achievements and goals with good discipline. Do you understand me, Daniel?'

'Yes, Miss,' I say.

'And we had good reasons to put Rico back to year seven. He has to show us he has the willpower. It's all up to him, only he can do it. He has to achieve his new goals with discipline. And we're giving him an opportunity to do that.'

She looks at me and I see her glasses sliding down her nose, and I say: 'Yes.'

'Don't let yourself get distracted by him.' Suddenly, she speaks very quietly and slants her head so it almost touches her shoulder. 'Think of your goals, Daniel. Make sure you do that.'

'Yes, Miss.'

'Good, Daniel, you can go now.'

I pick up my satchel. Mrs Seidel puts the class register in her bag and then locks the desk drawer.

'Bye, Miss.'

'Yes, Daniel, see you tomorrow.'

I leave the classroom, Mrs Seidel jangling her keys behind me. I go down the stairs. I go down to the playground, past the rear building to the sports ground. Sometimes Rico runs his laps here or up and down the hundred-metre track; it's good for his endurance. Rico boxes in the borough sports group now. The sports ground is empty. I don't know Rico's timetable. We don't see each other as much these days, but that's partly because of the trouble at home.

Two girls are sitting on the grass by the wall, sunbathing. I crawl through the gap in the wire fence and walk home. On the corner after the bridge is the Silver Slope, my dad's local. I stop outside the door. I hear lots of voices and glasses clinking. I hear Dad's voice: 'Hey, Danny, come in for a lemonade. And then tell your mum I'll be right home.' I inch up the three steps to the door, then I open it and step into the semi-darkness of the Silver Slope.

Queen of Hearts, Ace of Clubs, King of Spades and the Old Man. Big stained-glass playing cards are lit up on the wall to the right of the door. I walk past them, looking for my dad. But I can't see him. Not back there either, where two men are puffing on fat cigars; Dad's not hiding in the smoke. Anyway, he always used to sit at the big round regulars' table, where there are four men now, drinking and smoking cigarettes. In the middle of the table is a metal sign that says RESERVED in capital letters. Only the best are allowed to sit there, Dad told me one time, and he was one of the best, but he's gone away now. And here, this is where it happened, but I don't know exactly which spot. Dad didn't tell me, not even when he left the house with his big bag. I kept on asking him, but he wouldn't tell me. 'It's not for you,' he said, 'no, it's not something for you to know about.'

'Oi, kid, what're you doing in here, this place ain't for you.' There's a man behind the bar, holding a scrunched-up white cloth in his outstretched hand. 'You're not allowed in here, not all on your own. Or have you come to pick up your dad? Did Mummy send you?' He laughs. The men at the regulars' table stare at me, and the smoke from their cigarettes burns my eyes. I look down.

'Hey you, hey, come over here,' one of the man beckons. 'Aren't you...? Yeah, right, you're Horst's son, Horst's boy. What are you doing here all on your own, come here.' I walk over to him. I don't know him; he's wearing a hat, a brown leather hat; Dad never wore hats. I stop next to his chair and he puts a hand on my shoulder.

'What's your name, eh, boy?'

'Daniel.'

'Yeah,' he says, 'yeah, Horst's son. So you want to get a look, do you, at where your dad...' He pushes his hat back on his head and rubs his forehead. 'You want to take a look, boy, eh, at where it happened. I'm right, aren't I...?'

'Yes,' I say quietly. They all look at me, silent, and I notice I'm blushing, but it's dark here and smoky and they can't tell.

'You'd better sit down then.' The man with the hat budges up; someone pushes a chair over for me.

I want to take my satchel off and the man with the hat helps me and puts the satchel under his chair, and then I sit in between them and look at the table and draw circles on the table with my finger. 'The best,' Dad said, 'only the best get to sit at the regulars' table,' even though I'm not doing so well at school anymore, but the men don't know that.

'Hey boy, I know you. It's a few years back now. After the football, at Baldie's place, remember...'

I look at the man; he's sitting opposite me and his hair, his hair's much longer than my mum's. That's Longhair, a good friend of Dad's, we sometimes met him at Chemie or afterwards in Baldie's little house. 'Hello,' I say.

'Hello,' says the long-haired guy, and he smiles, picks up his cigarettes and lights one up. 'Your dad, well, your dad... How old are you now, then?'

'Thirteen,' I say, even though it's not my birthday for a couple of months.

'Yeaaah,' the long-haired guy says, breathing out smoke, 'the thing with your dad...' Someone slaps the table next to me, so loud that I flinch and the glasses rattle, and the beer glass next to me foams over: the man with the hat.

Now he gets up and raises his glass. 'To Horst, let's drink to Horst.' The long-haired guy and the other men stand up too and raise their glasses. I stay sitting down.

'No, wait, we can't.'

'Why not, what's up?'

'The boy, come on, the boy...' Holding their glasses outstretched, they look down at me. I prop my head on my hands and blink up at them. 'Dieter, bring the boy a lemonade or something, come on!' One of the men waves at the bar. Dieter is the man at the bar, and now he clanks around with bottles and glasses; I hear his footsteps behind me and he puts a bottle of red lemonade down on the table in front of me.

'Thanks,' I say, turning round to him.

He's holding a full beer glass as well, and he laughs. 'Original Ernst Thälmann sweat,' he says, and now they all laugh. Dieter lifts his glass. 'Men,' he says, and they raise their glasses again. The long-haired guy nods at me, and I pick up my lemonade and stand up. 'Men,' Dieter says again, and they all stretch their arms out even further with their beers, but I hold tight to my lemonade, press it to my chest. The bottle's cold. 'To Horst,' says Dieter.

'To Horst,' say the others.

'To Dad,' I whisper.

We drink. 'Ahhh!' We sit back down, the chairs noisy as they scrape across the floor. Dieter leans against the table next to me. He's got huge hairy hands and there's a long scar on one of his lower arms. 'Listen, boy, the thing with your dad...' I look at him but he stares past me at the table and glasses. '...Well, you know, we... there was nothing we could do. Impossible, there was nothing... well, you know, the cops... the police, nothing we could do, boy, really.' I look at his hands, still on the table next to me, two fingers moving and scratching at the wood.

'Hey, Dieter, bring us another round and a couple of shots.' The hands disappear and I hear Dieter's footsteps behind me, then he starts jangling glasses at the bar.

'And then,' I say, 'and then...?' I look at the man with the hat, I look at the long-haired guy, but they don't say anything, and the long-hand guy starts stroking his glass.

Dieter hums a tune behind the bar; I hear the beer hissing out of the tap. 'Maria, Maria,' Dieter sings quietly behind the bar.

'And why...' I say, looking at the other two; one of them's got glasses, which he takes off now, big square glasses with golden frames; he puts them back on and takes them off again.

'We couldn't do anything,' he says. 'They just... took

him away, just like that.'

'No,' says the man next to him; he's really old and his hair's white. 'No, not just like that. He put up a fight, you know, boy, he defended himself.' He clenches his fist and I see the blue eagle on his arm, poking out underneath his sleeve. Its wings are way too small, like a sparrow's.

'But why,' I say, knocking my lemonade bottle on the table, 'why did they want to take him away, how come they're allowed to do that...? Just like that.'

'It's my bar,' says Dieter, walking around the table with a tray, passing out the glasses. 'But the cops, the cops can do almost anything.' He puts a new bottle of lemonade down in front of me, even though my old one's still almost full. 'It's my bar,' Dieter says again, and he puts the tray down, pulls up a chair and sits down next to me. 'It's my bar...' He pauses, looks over at the counter, and it looks to me like his face is trembling slightly. He wipes his forehead with his big hand, and his eyes as well. 'My place, men, right?'

'Yeah,' say the men, 'your place,' and they raise their glasses to him.

Dieter nods, picks up the last shot on the tray and knocks it back. 'And I say –' he taps the empty shot glass against the table, like I did with my lemonade bottle before. 'And I say, it was that bastard, that stupid bastard, that stupid Lok bastard that started it. Isn't that right, men?'

'Yeah,' say the men, 'that's right,' and raise their glasses to him.

'You're a Chemist too, aren't you?' says the man with the hat, putting his arm round my shoulder.

'Yeah, I am,' I say, and I clench my fist and press it to my chest. The men smile, and I smile as well and don't know why. 'That guy was a police auxiliary,' the long-haired guy says. 'Half a cop. You know what a police auxiliary is?'

'Course,' I say. 'Half a cop.'

The men nod. 'Half a cop.'

'So that guy,' Dieter's clutching his shot glass and I'm scared it might break and cut him, 'so that guy starts talking crap about Chemie, talking shit, the usual Lok bastard.'

'And you know,' the long-haired guy says, 'you know how crazy Horst would... how upset he gets when someone says bad things about Chemie.'

'Yes,' I said. Sometimes Dad would rip the sports pages out of the paper and flush them down the toilet or throw them in the stove in winter, 'cause the newspaper often said bad things about Chemie.

'The last fortress,' says the man with the hat, 'Dieter, we're the last fortress in this whole bloody Lok neighbourhood.'

'True!' Dieter puts the shot glass down and punches the table a few times. 'Dammit, that's true!' He puts the empty glasses on the tray and goes over to the bar. 'And your father,' he calls out, 'good old Horst defended that fortress, you get it, boy, he defended all that!'

'Yes, he did,' and 'That's right,' the men say, nodding. I slide my lemonade back and forth on the table.

'Our honour!' Dieter calls from behind the bar. 'All that, boy!' I turn around to him; he's clenching one fist and pointing his other hand at three green-and-white pennants on the wall above the shelves of bottles. I remember my dad showing them to me once when I got sent to fetch him home, long time ago. Dad told me how often we were champions and cup-winners, long time ago, and one day we'll be champions or cup-winners again, 'but when you're champion,' Dad says, 'when you're champion, you're one of the best in the whole world.'

'Remember that time,' the long-haired guy nudges the old man with the eagle, 'that time in Bautzen...'

The old man smiled. 'Course,' he says. 'I still dream about it these days.'

'What was in Bautzen?' I asked.

'A jail,' the long-haired guy says, 'a prison.'

'Cup final,' says the old man with the eagle. 'Back in 66.'

'Wasn't it 65?' the man with the hat says.

'No, no,' Dieter puts a tray of beer and shots and a bottle of red lemonade on the table, 'he's right, it was 66, you can check on the pennant.' He sits back down next to me and passes the lemonade over. I've got three bottles now, arranged in a row in front of me.

'Your dad,' Dieter says, 'your dad knew all that kind of thing, for Chemie, I mean, dates, team members, all that, he had it all up here,' he taps his forehead, 'no one could beat him, he knew it all, boy.'

'He did,' and 'That's right,' the men say and nod.

'He didn't just have these,' Dieter clenches a fist. 'No, he had it up here and all.'

'You can be proud of him,' the long-haired guy says. 'You can be really proud of him. No need to be ashamed 'cause he's gone away now. He'll be back.' The men nod and stare into their glasses. 'You can be proud, Daniel, you get me, proud!'

I drink up my lemonade and put the empty bottle on the tray. 'And then,' Dieter whispers, and the men go quiet and stare into their glasses, 'and then he'll soon be back. Then he'll be sitting right here... and then he'll get everything on the house. Everything.'

He has to stay away for ten months; my mum cried, she cried for days, quietly so no one in the building could hear. And I still sometimes hear her at night, all dull, like someone's holding her mouth shut. She presses her face into her pillow, I know she does, there are two stains on the pillowcase that look like her eyes.

'How many?' I say, picking up a new bottle of lemonade, holding it up to the light above the table and looking at the men through the red.

'What d'you mean?'

'How many?' I slam the bottle down on the table; the lemonade fizzes over and runs red over my hand. 'The cops... the guys, you said he put up a fight, and...' I prop my head on both hands and stare at the lemonade puddle on the table.

'Oh, right... there were loads of them, Daniel, loads and loads of them.' I see the long-haired guy's hair moving as he speaks. 'Three or four.'

'More than that,' says the tattooed man. 'At least six, probably seven.'

'Seven,' says Longhair, 'seven cops, auxiliaries and that kind of scum. The guy went to get them, he was an auxiliary too, got his mates 'cause your dad gave it to him.'

'Gave it to him good and proper,' says Dieter next to me, 'good and proper. Like a professional. The guy talked too much, talked too much crap, and then Horst just... well, he just lashed out...'

'No, wait, it wasn't like that, that's not exactly how it was.' The man with the hat gets up, waves his cigarette around and a bit of ash falls in his beer, and I see it sinking slowly to the bottom, and the beer starts fizzing and the tiny bubbles dance in the glass. 'You know what, boy, that guy... that Lok bastard hit him first, right, men? Good old Horst... Horst doesn't just lash out, you know, boy, he's a man of honour! The cop hit him first. Shoved him, just went ahead and touched him, shoved him in the chest.

And that's no good, no, not with Horst!' He looks around the table, drinks a mouthful of the beer with ash in it, and sits back down slowly.

'True,' says Dieter, 'you're right, that's how it was. He didn't just lash out straight off, your dad, just pushed him away a bit, just gave him a bit of a shove, that's all. But the guy, the bastard wouldn't let it go. I wanted to chuck him out, it's my bar, my rules, I would have chucked him out, he had another two mates with him, remember, the two guys at the bar, I wouldn't have cared, it's my bar, but Horst, your dad...'

'Wanted to deal with it himself,' the old man with glasses butts in. 'He's a man of honour, your dad. Even gave him a chance: Get lost, you Lok bastard, he said.'

'Yeah. Get lost, Lok bastard,' the men say, and the old man with glasses nods. 'The guy goes and shows him his ID, shows your dad his bloody police auxiliary ID. He didn't give a shit, though, Horst didn't: Get lost, Lok bastard, that's all he said. He was all calm, your dad, had everything under control, no problems, all calm, your dad, uses his head first, that's him, your dad.' The men nod again, and Dieter raps his knuckles on the table three times. I know it's for good luck, and I tap my finger on the back of my chair three times.

'And then,' I ask, 'and then?'

'It was an uppercut,' yells the old man with the eagle, punching the air, 'a lovely clean uppercut! Your dad knocked him so hard the guy lifted off the floor, nearly went flying!' He jumps up and punches the air a few more times, knocks his glass over, but the man with the glasses grabs it so only a little bit of beer spills on his hand and onto the table.

'Watch it, Rudi,' he says.

But Rudi doesn't listen to him, he holds his fist up to

my face and yells: 'An uppercut, boy, he nearly went flying, your dad's the greatest!'

Now Dieter gets up too, propping himself on the table, and he looks down at me and smiles; but he smiles the way dad smiled when he left the house with his big bag. 'No, Rudi,' he says, 'no, you forgot something. You forgot that the guy, the Lok bastard, he threw the first punch. It was a straight right, right from the shoulder.' Dieter's right arm darts two or three times across the table, and Rudi takes a step back. 'Fast as lightning, that bastard, faster than me now, believe you me, boy, but Horst, your dad... he ducks down under it, ducks under it like a professional...'

'Like a professional,' says Rudi, swinging his torso and ducking down a few times, 'and then...'

'And then came the uppercut,' says Longhair, brushing his hair back from his face and tapping at his chin, 'right to the sweet spot. It was self-defence, Daniel, clear as day.' He picks up his beer and drinks. 'Self-defence,' he says again.

'Self-defence,' say the others, and they nod.

'Like Stevenson,' Rudi's torso is still swaying, 'ducked under the punch and then countered. Like Stevenson.'

'Stevenson hasn't boxed for years now.'

'So? He was still the best. Better than Ali.'

'Bollocks, better than Ali! That's just bollocks, that is! Stevenson was just a bloody amateur. Ali, Ali was the best.'

'That would have been a fight! Ali and Stevenson, Ali versus Stevenson!'

'Leave it out with Ali, will you? Have you seen him these days, he's gone slow, slow in the head and the hands. Can't hardly talk properly these days. Too many blows to the head! Aw, leave it out with your Ali!'

They're all talking over each other now and only Dieter

is quiet. He bends down to me and puts his big hand on my shoulder. 'Knocked him out, knocked him out cold. He deserved it, that guy, you get it?'

'Course,' I say. He smells of beer and shots, like Dad when he came home from the Silver Slope at night; I close my eyes.

'It was fair game. One on one. Broke his jaw, but it was a fair match. One on one.'

'Yes,' I say.

'But then... that Lok bastard's mates, and then the cops. It wasn't fair anymore. Your dad went at them, he's a brave man, not scared, you know that.'

The others are still talking about Ali and Stevenson and the big fights, but Dieter tells me about Dad's big fight, and I keep my eyes shut and feel his hand heavy on my shoulder. '...We couldn't do anything, nothing we could do, they already had him. He fought back like a man, landed a couple more punches, we wanted to go between them, it's my bar, my rules, we wanted to go between them, but it was... we're not cowards, boy, I'm not a coward, but it was too late. You believe me, don't you, boy...'

'Course,' I say, and the hand on my shoulder moves back and forth.

'Come on, boy, come with me, I'll show you... Chemie, our Chemie.' The hand's gone; I open my eyes and see Dieter ambling to the bar. He beckons me and I get up and go over.

'...I'm telling you, that Maske wouldn't stand a chance against Sugar Ray, twelve rounds, I swear, twelve rounds...' I go over to the bar, and their voices quieten behind me.

'Sit down, lad.' I climb onto one of the bar stools (I've never sat on a bar stool before) and put my feet on the footrest attached to the counter. Dieter pushes two crates of beer up against the shelves with all the bottles, climbs onto the crates and very carefully takes the three pennants off their nails on the wall; I can see his arm trembling, then he lays them down on the bar. '...You know what, I haven't taken my pennants down for years.' He strokes the fabric, then pushes them over to me. 'Not for... not for... twenty years, boy.' The pennants are dusty and the white of the team colours has gone yellow in lots of places. I pick one up and hold it carefully in the light. 'That one's from 1951,' says Dieter, 'an original champion's pennant. GDR champion. No, all-German champion 1951, we were better than Kaiserslautern that time.'

I put the pennant back down on the counter, and Dieter runs his finger over the Chemie emblem and the letters and numbers, 1951. 'I was seven years old back then. I went with my dad. How old are you now, Daniel?'

'Twelve. Nearly thirteen though.'

'Oh, I bet you've got a little girlfriend already, haven't you?'

'Yes,' I say. 'But she's gone, she's not here anymore.'

'You must have been too wild,' he says, and picks up another pennant. 'Look at this one, 1964, champions again.' There's a little yellow cup sewn onto the tip of the pennant; I can hardly see it 'cause the fabric's almost as yellow as the cup. I want to tell Dieter he should put the pennant in the washing machine, but he's probably scared it would shrink in the wash. 'There's history in there, there is, that's when we beat the bigwigs, we were the greatest back then, that's not something you learn at school, boy, it's history, proper history...' He puts a shot glass on the bar, takes a bottle off the shelf and fills it up. He looks at the glass for a while, then he knocks it back. 'And why, why's she gone?' He holds the empty glass in his hand and moves it back and forth in front of his face.

'Who?' I ask. I know exactly who he means but I don't like talking about it.

'Your girl, I mean, your little girlfriend.'

'Oh, her.' I put my finger on the little yellow championship cup. 'That's over. She... she was... really beautiful. It's over now.'

Dieter fills his glass again, drinks it all, then picks up the third pennant. 'You know what, boy, with women, it's all complicated.'

*BSG Chemie Leipzig – FDGB Cup Winner 1966*, it says on the pennant. 'Did you go to that one with your dad?'

'No, I was with mates that time. We played against Lok, but not the Lok Leipzig bastards, it was Lok Stendal, they're alright.'

'Another round, Dieter. And shots!' Longhair's stood up and is waving over.

'Right-O,' Dieter calls. He takes four glasses and fills them under the beer tap. I see the beer foaming white and yellow out of the tap, whirling around the glasses, and the beer only calms down when Dieter puts the glasses on the tray, and the bubbles rise up to the foam in long lines. Then Dieter puts four little glasses in a row on the tray and runs the spirits bottle over the top until they're full, almost spilling over. The stuff in the bottle looks like water; Dad drinks brandy, his favourite's Goldkrone, he calls it 'ten to three' 'cause a big bottle costs fourteen fifty.

'Can you get us two large ones as well, Dieter.' One of the two old men comes over to the bar; the cigar's dangling between his lips and it's gone out, but it still stinks all the way over to me.

'You can just call, Frank, no need to come all this way!' Dieter puts the tray back on the bar and fills two glasses.

'You know, Dieter, my lung, my lung!' He coughs and

the cigar wobbles between his lips. He nods at me, then he picks up the two glasses, holds them to his chest and walks slowly back to his table, where the other old man is sitting and smoking. Dieter holds the tray up by his shoulder as he carries it over to the table; it balances safe and sound on his hand, the beer in the glasses not even moving. Next time Mrs Seidel asks me what I want to be when I grow up, I'll say: publican. I lay the three pennants on the bar in a row, pushing the 1966 cup victory in the middle up a bit so that the three of them look like a winners' podium.

'You like them, eh?' Dieter's back, dunking empty glasses in the big metal sink behind the bar.

'Course,' I say. 'They're ace.'

'You can keep one of them,' he says. He picks up a tea towel and dries a glass.

'Really?'

'Course. The cup winner, you like that one, don't you?'

'It's great,' I say. 'But... but don't you need it? Everyone has to see it up on the wall. What if Lok bastards come in?'

'Lok bastards won't be coming in here, Daniel, not since your dad... and anyway, I've had it so long, it wants to see a bit of the world, you know.' He smiles. 'You gotta watch out for it though, Daniel, make sure no one nicks it. A lot of people tried to get that off me, it's an original, that's why I put it up so high. Gotta watch out for it!'

'Course,' I say, holding the pennant in both hands. 'No one's gonna get it off me, never. Thanks, thank you!'

'Course, boy, course, that's fine, you're welcome.' He takes the other two pennants, climbs on the beer crates and hangs them back above the shelves. There's a pale triangle where the cup-winner pennant was, with a nail above it. 'You do it just like this, see, all you need's a nail, and then you can hang it up in your room. Not everyone's got a pennant like that, it's an original. Your dad'll be pleased when he...'

The pennant's far too big for my coat pocket, only the tip fits in, and I tuck it under my jumper. 'Yeah, yeah, Chemie, yeah, yeah, Chemie, yeah, yeah, Chemie is on the up / Yeah, yeah, Chemie is on the up, yeah, yeah, Chemie is on the up!' I turn around. They're singing at the table, they've stood up and they're holding up their glasses. 'Yeah, yeah, Chemie, yeah, yeah, Chemie... Another round, Dieter!' Dieter hold up a finger and starts filling the glasses. I get up and take a few steps back from the bar.

'I'd better...' I say, 'I'd better be going home now.'

'Your mum's waiting, eh?' The glasses clink as he puts them on the tray.

'Yes.'

'In the old days,' he says, walking over to the table, where they're still singing, 'Yeah, yeah, Chemie, yeah, yeah, Chemie is on the up...'

'In the old days she used to come in here with Horst. Long time ago.' I walk alongside him, and when he puts the tray down on the table the men suddenly stop singing. Longhair smiles, brushes the hair off his face and takes his new beer.

'Alright, Daniel?'

'Yes,' I say, 'but I've got to go home now.'

'Tired, eh?'

'No, I'm not tired, but I still have to go. Got things to do.'

'You'll be back, though? You can come back whenever you like.'

'Right,' says Dieter, 'you can come any time, for a lemonade or something...'

'Thanks,' I say. 'I like it here with you.'

The men smile and look at the table, and the man with the hat takes my satchel out from under his chair and hands it to me. 'Bet you'd have forgotten that, wouldn't you?'

'Probably,' I say.

Dieter, Longhair, the man with the hat, the man with the glasses and the tattooed man stand up in a line by the table, and I shake their hands. 'And don't forget, boy, come back soon, your dad, your dad used to come almost every day.'

'I know,' I say.

'Your mum,' says Longhair when I shake his hand, and he leans down to me so that his hair lands on my shoulders, 'say hello to your mum, say hello from Adolf, no, say: from Longhair.'

'I will.'

'...ask her, ask her if... she must be all on her own now...'

'Yes,' I say, 'but I'm here. I help her a lot.'

'That's good, Danny. But ask her... I mean, I can come over, just whenever. Your dad was almost like a brother to me. Ask her, alright?'

'I will.'

He pats me on the shoulder. 'You're a good lad, Danny.' He picks up his beer glass and drinks it dry. 'You will ask her, Danny?' And then I'm at the door, and then I'm outside on the pavement. 'Hey, Danny, wait a minute!' I stop and turn around. Longhair's behind me. He waves and smiles and stops in front of me. He's got a cigarette in the corner of his mouth. 'Hey, Danny...' the smoke comes out of his mouth as he talks, 'you know what, we could go to the football, I mean, to Chemie, Danny, just you and me, that'd be...'

'Yes,' I say, 'maybe.'

'Course, Danny. You ask your mum...'

'She doesn't want me going to football, not since dad...'

'Oh right, right... I bet I can talk her into it.'

'Maybe,' I say. I head slowly towards the park.

'And who's on the up?'

I turn around; Longhair's sticking his head out of the door. 'Chemie,' I shout, and he laughs and waves and disappears again. I walk faster. It's getting dark and I'm thinking of Mum. She'll have cooked something. She's standing in the kitchen, waiting. Dinner's cold.

I run home. School's over and I run as fast as I can, 'cause I want to go to the Silver Slope this afternoon. I've been looking forward to it all day.

Mum told me off when I told her I'd drunk lemonade with Longhair and Dad's other friends in the Silver Slope. 'You're not going there again,' she said. 'Promise me not to go back to that mousetrap. That place did your father no good.' She calls Dad's bar a mousetrap, even though she used to go there herself, Dieter told me, and he ought to know 'cause it's his bar, Mum says mousetrap even though Dad always said, when he came home at night and bumped up against the coats and the shelves in the hall so loud it woke me up in my room: 'The Silver Slope, I tell you, the Silver Slope is golden!'

Mum was really angry. 'But Longhair, Mum, Longhair told me to say hello, he told me specially,' and then she went quiet.

I open the front door and walk up the stairs. Mrs Lieberwitz comes down. 'Hello,' I say.

'Hello, Daniel.' She stops on the landing but I walk up past here. 'How's everything at home?'

'Alright.'

'Now... now don't run away. Tell your mother, if she...'

'Yes,' I say.

'...if there's anything she needs, she can always come to me.'

'Yes,' I say.

'And your father, is he back soon? From his training course?'

'Yes, soon.'

She nods. I keep going up, and I hear her keys jangling by the letterboxes in the hallway.

'A training course, his dad's on a training course,' Mum told everyone. 'Up on the coast, our Horst's up on the coast, and when he gets back he'll be one level below the engineers.' She told everyone in the neighbourhood, and sometimes strangers nod at us in the street or say hello or shake my mum's hand. I put my satchel down and take out my door key. I unlock the door and slam it behind me. Mum's not here yet or she'd tell me off. I take off my shoes and put them on the little shelf. One of my slippers is by the kitchen door and I put it on; the other one's disappeared. I take my satchel into my room and look at the Chemie pennant hanging above my bed; I lean against the doorframe and look at it for a minute or two, then I go in the kitchen. There's a jug of cold rosehip tea on the table. The leftovers from the morning are still in my glass and I tip it in the sink before I pour myself some more. I sit down at the table and drink. I hear Mum outside on the stairs. She makes noises when she walks 'cause her knee hurts sometimes. I go out in the hall to open the front door, but Mum's key's already in the lock. I take a couple of steps back and she opens the door. She stands on the threshold, it's dark in the hall, and she nods at me. She sits down on the chair by the shoe shelf. I see she hasn't got any bags with her, so I put on my outdoor shoes and run down to the letterboxes, where she's left the shopping. It smells of fish. I run back up, looking at the front doors, but it's all quiet in the building. I put the bags on the kitchen table. Mum stands behind me, smelling of fish too. I step aside and she unpacks the bags and puts the newspaper-wrapped fish on the table. She's brought fish home from work every day since Dad's been gone. I go to my room. I lie down on my bed and look at my Chemie pennant. Mrs Seidel and the Pioneer leader didn't see it, 'cause when they came round the pennant was still above the shelves behind the bar at the Silver Slope. If they'd seen it you can bet they'd have a lot of respect for me, 'cause everyone in Leipzig has respect for proper Chemie fans. '...and we know your father was a good, disciplined worker in his collective, and we're sure you know your father wants to reintegrate when he comes back.'

'Yes,' I say.

'And you don't want to make the same mistakes as Rico did.'

'No,' I say. 'No.'

Mum's standing in the doorway. I get up and walk past her into the kitchen. There's a plate of fish and potatoes on the table, and I sit down. The balcony door is open and Mum goes outside to smoke. I cut the herring into little pieces before I choke it down. We've had fish every day since Dad's been gone. Sometimes big fat women from the fish factory come round and bring more fish, and then they stay a bit and drink with Mum, and the flat smells of wine and fish and cigarettes.

'To the army,' Mum says on the balcony, leaning her head against the wall, and my food goes down wrong and I look at her, but she doesn't see me, 'gone to the army, I should have said. Called up again, I should have said... ten months of training, no one believes that...' She keeps jabbing her cigarette in the flower box, even though it's already out. But Dad's up on the coast, on a training course, and even the army can't get him out of it now. I get up and throw the herring and potatoes in the bin. Mum's still smoking on the balcony; she doesn't see me. I pick up the bin and go to the door. I walk slowly down the stairs, trying to be really quiet. I cross the backyard to the big bins and open one up. Full. I open another bin and throw the rubbish in there. At the very bottom of our bin bag there were two broken wine glasses, now on the top of the rubbish. There are still a few dried red drops on the shards. Dad's workmates broke the wine glasses last time they came to visit us. They know Dad's not on a training course and that's why they often come to visit, like the women from the fish factory, and they bring flowers and wine and chocolate. They never did that when Dad was still here. Every time, they talk about what a good worker Dad is, and sometimes they stay really late. I can't sleep then 'cause they start singing sad songs. I slam the lid of the big bin and go back upstairs.

It's evening. I'm standing outside the house, looking up at it. Most of the windows are dark; the only light is on the third floor. I go inside and up the stairs. Before I open the front door I take off my jacket, 'cause it smells of Silver Slope.

'Did you have a nice time?' Mum asks.

'Yes,' I say, and then she smacks me. Her hand was so fast I didn't see it coming. Mum's good with her hands; she has to gut and pack fish at work every day. Bang! And another one. I take a few steps back.

'No,' she says, and then she yells and her hand is back, but I've been watching out for it and she doesn't get me this time. 'Why, boy?' she yells. 'Why do you go there, why do you lie to me, why do you do... your dad!' Her face is bright red and she's breathing loudly, and her shoulders rise and fall. I reach out my hand but then I drop it. 'No,' she yells, 'why can't you see? Why can't you see it? The mousetrap, it's always that mousetrap! And you two and your Chemie, your bloody Chemie!' She sits down on the chair by the shoe shelf and leans her head against the wall. My face is burning; Mum's got strong hands. Mine trembles as I lay it cold on my cheek. Mum's very quiet now. I walk over to her, slowly. 'Why?' she says quietly. 'Why do you do it? Why would you do it?' I reach my hand out again and she lifts her head. Bang! She smacks me again. I stop where I am and look her in the eyes until she closes them. I go to my room. My pennant is gone.

## TATTOO-THILO

Thilo the Tattooist and Thilo the Drinker don't know each other, and that's a good thing 'cause Thilo the Drinker talks a lot of crap and pisses people off and won't stop talking stupid crap at them when he's had a drink, and he's almost always drinking.

Tattoo-Thilo doesn't drink much; he broke the habit in jail. He's been to jail a couple of times even though he's not yet twenty, and he doesn't like people talking stupid crap at him. I don't know exactly what he did time for, but GBH was on the list.

I get my tats from Tattoo-Thilo 'cause he's got a pretty good reputation when it comes to tats, not just in our neighbourhood. Rico told me there are even guys from the red-light district who go to him, and Rico got inked by him as well, but that was in jail. Rico doesn't talk about jail much, but I know almost all tattooists get their training there.

Rico got me my first tattoo when I turned eighteen, 'cause Tattoo-Thilo owed him a favour. Now I've got a lizard on my lower arm, 'it'll never go away,' Mum complains, but it moves when I clench my muscles. I actually wanted an Indian chieftain, I'd torn a picture out of a tattoo mag at Rudi's shop, 'cause those mags are really pricey. Tattoo-Thilo's got loads of tattoo mags at home, must be about a hundred, with whole tribes of Apaches and Cherokees in them, but I didn't know that then.

Tattoo-Thilo can't do Indians, I didn't know that then either, and when he told me at first I thought that he didn't like foreigners. But it's a technique thing. 'It's not like sex,' he told me, 'where it's all automatic, where you learn it on the job.' I guess he doesn't know about the Kamasutra and that, but what he's not so good at yet with Indians is shading. Shading is this really light grey tone where the tattooist has to dig the needle into the skin really carefully in a really special way, and he's still learning that, he told me. And seeing as he's not in jail right now, all his learning takes a bit longer. So he carved me a lizard on my right arm; I mean I'm not into lizards or anything but lizards are in fashion right now, he told me, and he said the favour he owed Rico wouldn't have been enough for an Indian anyway, only for a lizard at most. Now it's squatting on my right arm, 'it'll never go away,' Mum complains, but I don't care about that, the problem is I told everyone, especially girls, I'd soon have an Indian on my right arm, a real chieftain, Sitting Bull himself, and now everyone wants to see it and touch it, and then I roll up my sleeve and it's not even a sitting duck. They get a bit disappointed, especially girls, they don't want a lizard in bed. So I've thought up this story to tell everyone, the legend of the lizard: The lizard is a sacred animal for the Indians, way better than buffalos and bears and better than a warrior and all, 'cause none of their tails grow back if they get cut off. The lizard stands for eternal renewal, not only of tails and limbs.

People like the sound of that, especially men; I haven't managed to convince the girls yet. So I'm getting an ornamental done on my right upper arm, girls are into ornamentals, even though Tattoo-Thilo says the lizard's really lonely and could use a partner, a snake or a spider maybe, but I don't want snakes or spiders on my body. The ornamental's nearly finished, it's even 3D 'cause the black ink doesn't want to stay in my skin and it pokes out in little bulges. Tattoo-Thilo can't finish it off yet 'cause it's got infected and we have to keep taking a couple of weeks off. I'm scared my arm's going to drop off 'cause it's really swollen like I've got huge muscles, which I have, and it's pretty red and a bit blue as well. Tattoo-Thilo says that's normal, and tells me to keep putting butter on it. So I put all this butter on my fresh tats, and my mum tells me off for using up all the butter, and Tattoo-Thilo tells me off as well when he sees my buttered arm. 'That's way too much,' he complains, 'the tattoo needs to breathe!' Tattoo-Thilo complains a lot anyway, especially when he's tattooing. Sometimes he complains 'cause my arm's too hairy and he has to shave it or it gets in the way, then he complains 'cause I bleed so much, 'You bleed like a stuck pig!' and he's always complaining 'cause my arm twitches but I can't help that, there must be some nerves he keeps hitting with the needle. Most of all, though, Tattoo-Thilo complains if I let my pain show when he carves away at my skin. I don't want to let it show, I want to be hard, which I am, but sometimes I just can't stand it and then I breathe out loudly or grind my teeth so loud that it drowns out the buzz of his machine. It's a pretty crap machine, home-made out of a CD-player motor and a dirty sewing needle, but I don't say that to Tattoo-Thilo, 'cause he's named his machine Steffi, some kind of jail thing, he told me. Steffi's an original replica of his jail machine, and I'm pretty glad he doesn't ink me with the same needle covered in the blood of a hundred jailbirds; I bet he tattooed a few murderers in there.

'Not to worry;' Thilo says. 'Hygiene and that's my number-one priority.' That's not true though, hygiene is about his number 42 priority, and I remind him every time to clean up his machine before he sticks the needle in my skin. 'It's still clean, don't worry, still looks good,' he says, and then he goes and gets a knife from the kitchen and scrapes the old ink off the needle. Then he gets a bottle of Stroh 80 rum, fills a glass and dunks the needle in for a few seconds. 'Kills all known germs dead,' he says. I guess he doesn't know there's all sorts of stuff Stroh 80 doesn't kill that can kill you, like AIDs and hepatitis. Hepatitis is hell, especially the C kind, 'cause if you have it you can't drink. I know this girl who's got hep C, but she didn't get it from tats, she used to shoot up and for a while she'd do anything for money or drugs. She's a lovely girl but she's in a right state, and if she didn't have hep C I'd start something with her, 'cause she's clean now, but then again she drinks a lot so she won't be around much longer. There's a couple of guys running round Tattoo-Thilo's place, ex-jailbirds and the kind who'll soon be inside, who look like they've got hep or the clap or some other kind of dodgy shit going on.

Tattoo-Thilo lives in this kind of flatshare, and everyone he shares with has just got out of jail or has to go back in again soon. There's this social worker that looks after them so they don't get up to any shit, a young social worker, quite pretty even, maybe the courts think the young jailbirds would listen to a young social worker more than a dried-up old one. But the social worker's pretty soft and she lets them get away with loads of stuff, sometimes the whole place stinks of hash, and Tattoo-Thilo tells me he sometimes hears her at night with Stabber Number One in the next room.

I can't imagine that, 'cause Stabber Number One's a pretty ugly guy with scars on his face. He says they're from fists, bottles and knives, but they look more like acne scars or pockmarks or something. Stabber Number One knifed an old lady who wouldn't give him her handbag, Tattoo-Thilo told me. He still inks him. He inks almost all the guys in the flat, and the social worker doesn't mind. Sometimes she even stands next to him and watches Tattoo-Thilo inking me, and then I try to stay real calm and smile at her, even when Tattoo-Thilo carves his needle right down to my bones. Sometimes the flatshare jailbirds are there too and they watch me really carefully, and sometimes other mates of Tattoo-Thilo who he's inking come along, and then they all talk among themselves, and Tattoo-Thilo joins in and stops looking at my arm while he's inking, and I hope Steffi can tattoo on her own and doesn't draw a swastika on my skin or a girl with her legs apart or something. Although, a girl with her legs apart would be OK, you could stroke her and you'd never be alone.

If I go to jail – not youth custody, I've been there already, proper jail, the box, like Rico calls it, and I probably will one day, even though I try to mind out a bit – but if I go to jail, to Zeithain or over to Torgau or Alfred Kästner Road, then I'll already know the fixtures, the rules, the warders, the old-timers and the prices for services and specials, 'cause Tattoo-Thilo's jailbirds tell a whole load of jail stories; Rico never liked doing that. My favourite's the story of the tattooed dick, although I can't really believe it's true 'cause who'd get their dick tattooed? But maybe the guy was into pain, and there's nothing else to do in jail, so he went and got a fly tattooed on his bellend. Maybe he wanted to surprise his old lady when he got out, if he had one, and maybe she was into creepy-crawlies, and I bet the fly looked really good when he had a hard-on. 'Must have hurt like hell,' I say, 'cause I'm hurting like hell even though no one's tattooing my bellend, but Tattoo-Thilo wants to show his jailbird buddies how well and fast he can tattoo, and he's running his machine up and down my arm like a madman.

'We numbed it for him,' one of the guys says. 'We kept on hitting his bellend with the back of a spoon 'til it went numb, then you can't feel anything, right.'

'Right,' I said, 'I get it,' even though I don't get it at all, but there's nothing else to do in the box and it gives you crazy ideas.

Sometimes, when the social worker's not in the room, they start doing deals, talking over jobs and break-ins, and sometimes they ask me if I want to go in with them, but I say I play with my own team over in Reudnitz and Anger-Crottendorf. And sometimes they unpack their powder and cut lines all across the table, and sometimes they ask me if I want to go in with them, but I say I can't, 'cause of the inking, 'cause I bleed faster if I'm on something, but really I'm thinking of my old friend Mark who's in such a state 'cause of that shit. Tattoo-Thilo says I'm right about that and he says I bleed too much already anyway, and then he turns off the machine and does lines himself until the table's empty.

Tattoo-Thilo's on the needle himself, and I don't mean all the tats he's done. They're mostly on the left of his body 'cause he's right-handed; he's got a couple of tats on the other side from other jail inkers, and they look a bit better than the ones on the left, his canvas that he started practising on when he was fourteen or fifteen, he told me. Tattoo-Thilo's on the needle. He shoots the shit right in his arm, but only when none of his jailbird buddies or flatmates is in the room, even though a couple of them probably inject as well, but none of them wants to admit it in front of the others – it's a bit more than a few lines; everyone does that. But it doesn't bother him if I'm there when he shoots up. He used to send me out at the beginning, and I always thought he had to do a bit of meditation to prepare for inking me. But once he'd finished the lizard and started on the ornamental, he started injecting in front of me, 'to steady my hand, Danny.' Maybe he doesn't mind his regulars seeing, and maybe he thinks I'm used to needles now. I sometimes even lend him my belt 'cause he hasn't got one, but he'll probably get one of his own soon enough.

Tattoo-Thilo's disappeared, and now I've got a skull with no eyes on my arm, and it's missing four teeth as well, but the eyes are worse 'cause he's had his teeth knocked out, he was a wild and crazy skull, that's what I tell everyone.

Tattoo-Thilo's back in the box, got up to no good, I don't know exactly what, but actually I'm glad of it, 'cause by the end he was shooting up quite a bit, but it didn't make his hand any steadier. But I'm still pretty happy with the tattoos, they look real jail-style, especially the skull, and I only ever walk around the neighbourhood in short sleeves, even if it's cold or snowing, and I wish I'd got my arms done sooner, then loads of people would have had plenty of respect for me, but sometimes I just wish Tattoo-Thilo would come back, and I imagine him turning into a proper artist inside, learning everything and then finishing off my tats and covering me in beautiful works of art, so gorgeous even my mother would stop complaining and all the girls in the neighbourhood would come to me.

## MONGRELS

I was smoking on the balcony. It was after eight in the evening but it was still light. Mum had gone out; there was a work do at the fish factory, some guy's retirement. I stood and looked over at the railway embankment, a freight train passing. I counted the wagons... eighteen, nineteen, end.

I flicked my cigarette off the balcony and leaned over the edge. There were two girls in the playground right next door. They must have just arrived and sat down on the bench by the sandpit. I could see one of them smoking, I could see her legs as well; she was wearing a pretty short skirt, it was still summer. I ran to my room for my binoculars. They were always at the ready 'cause women sunbathed on the grass behind the playground in summer, and when it got really hot they'd show me their breasts. Sometimes I'd call Paul and we'd have a nice cold beer and look at the women and the breasts. The other girl had a cigarette between her lips too now, and I watched her blow out the smoke. I'd never seen them in the neighbourhood; they must have been about fourteen and it was probably their first real summer. I looked at the legs again, adjusted the focus and wished they'd sat on top of the climbing frame. I leaned further over and tried to see down their tops. 'Drop your stupid fag,' I whispered. 'Just drop it and pick it up again.' But the fag didn't fall, and I watched her friend again, who wasn't wearing a skirt but had pretty tight jeans on. I trained the binoculars on the denim between her legs; Paul called it a 'payslip' but he'd never got a salary.

Now she stood up and turned her back on me, and I slapped the wood of the balcony parapet. The bare-legged one had stood up as well. I could count the folds in her skirt, and she flapped her arms around, but she didn't have much up top to bounce around. I saw their lips moving; they were both pretty excited – maybe their boyfriends were on their way and they'd had enough of those losers. Now they threw their cigarettes away, crossed the sandpit and started running. I moved the binoculars over to the railway embankment. Two people running. Not the girls. I adjusted the focus and then I saw Rico's face right in front of me, all contorted. Mark was running a bit behind him and he kept turning round. More people running, one, two, and another two, and more behind them; I took the binoculars away from my eyes. Rico and Mark were almost at the playground now, and there were ten or twelve guys running after them; I counted again – there were fourteen of them. I'd put my cigarettes on the edge of the parapet, and when I went to take one out of the pack they fell down into the backyard. Mark and Rico ran through the sandpit, Mark stumbled and fell down. Rico turned round, ran back to him and pulled him up again. Most of the guys were wearing bomber jackets, red, green, blue; only one was wearing snow camouflage. I knew who he was; that jacket was his trademark. He hung out at the roller rink with the skins and he was a big number there, Kehlmann's right-hand man. He called himself 'the Leopard' 'cause of his grey-and-white bomber jacket, but most people in our neighbourhood just called him 'Birdshit' for the same reason. We'd had trouble with the skins a few months back, but we thought they'd forgotten or they were too scared. Rico and Mark climbed over the low wall between the playground and the backyard. I could hear them now. 'Shit, Rico, they're gonna get us, they'll mess us up!'

'Jesus, shut it, get inside, get up to Danny's!'

I'd locked the back door. About half an hour ago, I'd

taken the rubbish down to the bins 'cause Mum's knee was hurting again and she had to get dolled up for the do at the fish factory, and I'd locked the door to the backyard before I went back up. Down in the yard, they slammed against the door. 'Shit, shit, Danny, open up the bloody door!'

I ducked down behind the wood of the parapet. 'Kick it in,' Mark yelled, 'come on, kick it in!' I stood back up, wanted to run down and unlock the door, I had a doctored alarm gun in my room and a whole load of knives, but it was too late – the first of the bastards were already at the wall and now in the yard. Why hadn't I shouted, yelled like a monster and thrown the plastic chairs and the table and the flower boxes down on the bastards? 'You dirty bastards, you dirty fucking bastards!' That was Mark. I ducked again and looked down at the yard through a gap in the wood. Mark was lying on the ground and two of the bastards were kicking him. Where was Rico? I leaned my head against the wood and punched the concrete floor.

'Wait, stop a minute!' The guy with the snow camouflage bomber jacket was standing in front of Mark. The two who'd been kicking him pulled him up. Where was Rico? The bastards were all over the backyard, and now I saw him. Four of them were holding onto him. The guy with the snow camouflage walked towards him, no, he ran, and he hit Rico in the face mid-step. 'You arsehole,' he yelled. 'You wanted to make like Billy the Kid, did you? Playing the cowboy? You're a boxer, aren't you? You're a real boxer!' The others let go of Rico and the guy swung at him like a madman. Left, right, left, right, Rico went down, why wasn't he fighting back for God's sake, why didn't he get up and knock the guy off his feet? He went down and the guy kicked him in the back. 'Get up, you wanker, I told you to get up! Call yourself a boxer?'

I punched the concrete floor of the balcony. I crawled to the door, had my hand on the door handle, had my hand almost on the gun in my room, but I stayed put by the balcony door and then slid back to the edge and looked down at the yard. Rico had rolled onto his side while the guy kept on beating him, he was covering his face with his arms and pulling his head in to his chest. 'Get up, get up, come on, you scared, boxer? You are a boxer, aren't you, a real boxer!' The dirty bastard was kicking Rico, and Rico was trying to crawl away from him.

Any minute now he'll jump up, I thought, any minute now he'll get back on his feet and grab the guy. He'll finish the guy off, he'll mash his nose to a pulp, no, he'll take him hostage, then the other wankers will fuck off. But he didn't get back up, he just didn't. I turned away and looked at Mark, who was lying by the bins a few metres away. He was struggling to sit up, his face covered in blood too. He leaned his back against one of the bins, pulled his legs up and rested his head on his knees.

'Get out of there,' I whispered. 'Go on, Mark, get out. Go and get help, the bastards aren't watching you.' But he just stayed there, wiping the blood off his forehead. The guy with the snow camouflage had stopped kicking Rico now. He took a few steps back. 'Had enough, have you? I want to hear it, you get it? Come on, say it, boxer boy!' Rico turned around to him and moved his lips. 'What, what's that? Speak up, boxer boy!' He put his hand behind his ear and bent down to Rico. Now, I thought, pressing my eye to the hole in the wood so hard my head hurt, now he'll nut that arsehole right in the face. Rico said something and the guy jumped up, kicked Rico in the stomach, bent down to him again and slammed his fist right in his face. 'Too proud, eh? You're a real proud one! I want to hear it, alright, or I'll mess your face up!'

'I'll kill you, you bastard,' I whispered. 'I'll... one day I'll get you and kill you.' Rico tried to stand up but the bastard kicked him right in the small of his back, and Rico fell face-down.

'I told you, I want to hear it! Had enough, boxer boy, sorry, are you, boxer boy? No more cowboy stuff, you hear, no more acting the big man, boxer boy!' He bent back down to Rico and grabbed him by the hair. 'Take a look at your mate, we're gonna mess that poofter up for real now!' Three of the guys went over to Mark. They'd rolled up the sleeves of their jackets and their arms looked thin from above. Mark turned on his side, pressed his head against the bin and crossed his arms in front of his face. I wished someone in the building would call the cops; I couldn't do it, we had rules. But I knew I was breaking all the rules of the street while I squatted up here, breaking every oath we'd sworn to each other, 'never run off, never leave anyone in the lurch, never give up.'

'Stop,' Rico said so quietly I could hardly understand. 'We've had enough. I'm sorry, I won't ever, just stop...'

'Hey, hey, hey,' said the arsehole in the snow camouflage, 'the boxer boy's giving up! What kind of coward are you, eh, giving up like that! A boxer, Jesus, boxer boy, you're a fucking coward!' He spat twice on Rico, then he pressed his foot into Rico's face and rubbed his sole on it. 'Please,' he said, 'say please!' Rico tried to hit out at the foot but his punches came in slow motion, and the arsehole just pushed his arm away. 'What do you say? I want to know what you say when you're a good boy! You are a good boy, aren't you, boxer boy?'

'Yes,' Rico said through the shoe. 'Please.'

'What? I can't hear you!' He bent down again, hand behind his ear.

'Please,' Rico said, louder now. 'Please stop.'

I turned away and leaned my head against the wall.

'Look, a packet of fags, nearly full!' The bastards had found my fags, and I hunched up behind the parapet and tapped my head against the wood a few times. 'Leave them alone, will you, you bastards.'

When I put my eye to the gap again they were gone. Rico had rolled onto his back and I could see blood running from his face onto his jacket. 'Rico.' Mark crawled over to him. 'Oh God, the bastards.' He grabbed Rico by the shoulder and shook him gently. 'Get up, come on Rico, get up, they'll come back, I bet!'

Rico pushed his hand away. 'Shut up!' He coughed and spat a whole load of blood on the ground. 'It's over,' he said. He righted himself very slowly and then stood up. 'They won't be back. It's over.'

'Those bastards.'

'Stop it,' said Rico, 'leave it, that's enough. Don't talk about them.' He swayed, looking up at me. I looked him right in the eye.

'One day,' he said. '...Shit.' Mark was standing next to him now and his face looked pretty bad, even though he hadn't taken as much of a beating. He put his arm round Rico's shoulder, then they swayed over to the bins and sat down with their backs against them. 'At least they didn't rob us.'

'I told you to stop talking about them.' Rico took out a pack of cigarettes and they smoked.

Ducked down, I went inside and then to the kitchen. I ran to my room to fetch a couple of empty beer cans. I threw them in the empty bin, then I tore up a couple of exercise books and put them on top. I opened the fridge, took out the out-of-date milk and put it on top of the exercise books and the beer cans. I went to the sink and washed my face with cold water. I picked up the half-full bin and went downstairs. I'd forgotten the back-door key, so I ran back up. Then I was down by the door to the backyard, put my ear to the wood and listened, but all was quiet. I put the key in the lock and tried to make as much noise as possible as I turned it. I started to whistle some stupid tune, but then I stopped again. I went outside. They were still sitting against the bins, smoking.

'Shit, what are you doing here? What's... what's... what bastards did that?'

'Danny!' Rico said, and he stood up and held onto the bin. 'Danny, where were you? The door, Danny, the bloody door, why was the bloody door locked?' His eyes were pretty swollen, and his whole face was green and blue and in some places pink and purple.

I put the bin down. 'Why... why didn't you call, Jesus... I'd... I'd have come down, I'd have brought my gun, we'd have finished them off! Who was it, Rico?'

'There was too many of them,' said Mark, still sitting on the floor. 'There was just too many, Danny. Twenty of them. At least twenty.' He didn't look as bad as Rico, just a swollen lip and his nose had taken a hit, and there was blood everywhere.

'But who?' I said. 'The bastards, in my backyard!'

'I got a couple of them,' said Rico, 'I got a couple... we did a couple of them in, right Mark? But there was too many of them, the cowardly bastards!'

'Remember those skins at the old lady's place?' Mark stood up now too, held his fag box out to us, and we took one.

'The skins,' I said. 'You mean those skinhead bastards from the roller rink...'

'Yeah,' said Mark. 'That's the ones.' He gave us a light; their cigarette filters went red as they smoked.

'We gave it to them that time,' Rico said. 'That's what

it's about, that's it, Danny.'

'There was just too many today,' Mark said. 'If we'd had a couple more people...'

'I'm sorry.' I put my hand on his shoulder. 'If I'd known... you know me.'

'It's alright, Danny.' Rico put his hand on mine. 'How are you supposed to know what's going on down... But we fought back, you better believe it. Mark got one right in the face, probably broke his nose.'

'Right,' Mark nodded and licked blood off his lip. 'We'll give it right back to them, right?'

'We got to!' Rico punched the lid of the bin. 'I'll go and have a word with Karsten's brother tomorrow. And Manfred the boxer, he's good, I go to training with him, he knows loads of people and all.'

'Maybe Pitbull can sort it out,' I said. 'He knows a few of the skins.'

'Forget Pitbull. There's nothing to sort out. It's started now, it's too late, Danny. He'd only get it in the face himself. You know how it is.'

'Yeah,' I said. We put our cigarettes out on the bins. Mark took out a crumpled tissue and wiped his face clean, then he passed it to Rico.

'Come upstairs for a minute,' I said. 'You can clean up properly. My mum's out.'

'Bit of cold water,' Rico said, feeling his face, 'bit of cold water'd be good.'

I tipped my rubbish in one of the big bins, then I went up the stairs ahead of them. In the flat, I gave them a towel and they went to the sink in the kitchen, turned on the tap and took turns to hold their faces under the running water. Rico looked in the mirror on the wall. 'Shit, those stupid bastards. I'll give it back to them, I swear I will! I can't run around looking like this. I've gotta go to school.'

Rico had hardly been to school since I'd left, and he'd been in youth detention a few times too, over in Zeithain, and they'd probably thrown him out by now, he just didn't know it yet. I got some ice from the freezer compartment and wrapped it in a tea towel. Rico pressed it to his face.

'And me?' Mark tapped his lip, which was curling up more and more to meet his nose.

'Hold on,' I said, 'I've got something better.' I handed him a can of beer out of the fridge. He pressed it to his lip and his face, then he opened it.

'Hey, Danny, the ice...' Rico took the tea towel off his face and chucked the ice cubes in the sink. I took another two beers out of the fridge, gave one to Rico. He cooled his face and then we made a toast.

'To getting those bastards.'

'To getting the bastards.'

We went out on the balcony to smoke another one. It was getting dark. 'Better watch out for yourself, the next few days,' Rico said, looking down at the yard. 'They're probably after you as well.'

'Right,' said Mark. 'You were there as well, in the old lady's house, remember...'

'Right,' I said. We didn't talk about the old lady any-more 'cause she was dead now, and sometimes we thought it was our fault, what with the thing with the cops...

'But don't worry,' Mark said. 'I know a few people as well, we'll sort it.'

'Right,' I said, 'yeah.'

'I guess we'd better be going, then.' Rico finished his beer and crushed the can.

'No rush, don't be in such a rush, Rico!' Mark leaned over the parapet and looked down at the yard. 'What d'you reckon, think they're still here somewhere?'

'Nah, they're gone,' said Rico.

'I can come with you,' I said. 'Right, I'll come with you. I've got my gun, haven't I. And a couple of knives. There'll be blood if they come back again.'

'Don't bother, Danny, it's alright.' Rico patted me on the shoulder. 'They know where you live, and if they see you...'

'I thought they were gone, Rico, for fuck's sake!' Mark chucked his fag-end off the balcony and I could see his face twitching.

'They're gone,' said Rico, 'no need to piss your pants.'

'I'm not scared, I'm not pissing my pants, I'm just careful, man!'

'You're right, Mark,' I said.

I put my doctored alarm gun in the waistband of my trousers and walked Mark and Rico down to the front door. It was almost dark now, and most of the streetlamps on my road were broken. We stood in the doorway and looked carefully in each direction. 'The coast's clear,' I said. 'But I can come with you for a bit anyway.'

'Nah, don't worry, Danny.' We shook hands. They walked down the road. Rico turned around again. 'And watch out for yourself, Danny. I'll come over if anything comes up.' They sped up and kept on looking around, then they went round the corner. I closed the door and went back up.

I'd waited three days for Rico. I'd gone to school early, taken detours, I had two knives and my gun on me every time I left the house. I'd talked to Mark on the phone and he'd told me the skins had got Walter as well, just because he was one of us. They'd only knocked him about a bit, probably 'cause he was pretty small and they were scared they might break him if they gave it to him like with Mark and Rico.

Now Rico had turned up at last, had rung the bell downstairs and was waving at me from the pavement. I opened the window. 'Come down, Danny!'

'Door's open,' I shouted back. 'You come up, my mum's still at work!' I saw him head back to the front door. I closed the window and then I heard him coming up the stairs. My big Russian knife was on the telephone table by the door. It was actually a bayonet for a Kalashnikov, the Russians had sold it outside their barracks for ten marks after the Wall came down. I'd have preferred a Kalashnikov but they wouldn't sell me one.

Rico knocked. 'Open up, come on!'

'Alright, I'm coming!' I put the newspaper over the bayonet and then I opened the door. Rico shoved past me into the hall. His face still looked pretty bad.

'Quick, Danny, lock the door!'

'Jeez, what's the matter?'

'Danny, you gotta do me a really big favour.'

'Calm down a minute, Rico, sit down a minute. What's happened?'

He pushed the chair aside and paced up and down my room. 'It's shit, it's a pile of shit, but there's no other way.'

'Is it your probation? You want me to make a statement?'

'No, Danny, no. You know, you know what it's about.'

'The skins? The bastards?'

'Yeah, yeah, yeah!' He lit a cigarette. 'Where's the ashtray?'

'Use that empty can.'

'You heard about Walter?'

'Yeah, I did.'

He flicked his ash into the can, and somehow he dropped his cigarette and it fell in. 'Shit, I can't believe it, why haven't you got a proper ashtray, Danny?'

'Hey, calm down a bit, Rico.' I pushed him over to the chair and he sat down. He took another cigarette and gave me one too.

'Danny, you gotta come down with me.'

'What d'you mean, come down with you?'

'Listen...' He was holding the cigarette, not lit, and rolling it between his fingers. 'They were down there. Round the corner. I'm supposed to get you to come out, or else... Danny, you got to go down so they see I'm doing what they want, then you pretend you've noticed them, and you bugger off. You're a fast runner, Danny!'

I had the fag between my lips and he gave me a light. 'You're fast, Danny!'

'You're kidding me!'

The filter broke off his cigarette; he put it on the desk and scooted his chair closer to me. 'Danny, you're my best mate... I need a bit of time to get everything sorted. We have to play along, you get it, until we... like Estrellita, Danny, your little star...'

'What about her?'

'Negotiate, Danny, you get it, I need a bit of time, you just have to buy me the time, then I'll get those bastards, then we'll get them, I swear! We have to act like we're giving up, you get it, it's all part of my plan, Danny. You gotta help me or they'll do me in again!'

I rolled back a bit on my desk chair.

'Danny, we gotta hurry or they'll notice something!' I got up and went over to him. I stood in front of him, and he looked up at me. Then he looked down.

'Alright, come on then,' I said.

'Thanks, Danny, thanks, I'll never forget this.' His hand was on my arm and I went out in the hall with him. 'All I need is a bit more time, Danny, and you're such a fast runner they'll never get you!'

I put on my jacket.

'We gotta negotiate now,' he said. 'Diplomacy, you get it, and then we'll get them for real later on.'

'Just be quiet, OK?' I took the knife out from under the newspaper.

'No, Danny, no, leave that up here. You won't need it.' He pulled my hand away from the knife. I nodded.

'Danny, believe me, in a couple of days I'll have it all sorted, I'll have enough people together, and then we'll go for them. Us two right at the front Danny, you get it? Couple of days, just a couple of days.' I nodded and he rested his forehead against mine. 'Run across the grass, they've got a car. You're fast, Danny, I know you are.' I locked the door behind me and we went down the stairs, slowly.

I opened the front door downstairs; we stopped in the doorway.

'How many are there?'

'About a dozen, maybe. At most.'

I looked at my watch. It wasn't yet five and it wouldn't be dark for another four hours. We shook hands, then I stepped out into the street. Rico walked a bit behind me.

'Rico, something's fishy,' I yelled. 'They want to beat me up. You won't get me, you bastards!'

And then they came. The guy with the snow camouflage bomber jacket leading the pack. Rico grabbed at me, held me by my jacket and then let go. 'Run, Danny,' he whispered. And I ran. I ran around the side of the building, across the playground and then the grass. I didn't turn around for the first hundred metres, I knew it would cost me precious time, and fear just made my legs weak. I didn't look over my shoulder 'til I was almost at the embankment. They were still there, maybe twenty metres behind me. And now my stomach started burning, from the fear, and it went down to my legs and wanted to make them weak, but I was a good runner, I ran sixty metres in 7.6 seconds at school. There was a little wooden fence along the embankment, but I knew where there was a gap and I crawled through. I ran up the embankment, stumbled across the tracks, no train came, and I ran back down the other side. I turned around, heard them behind me at the fence, and I wished all the trains in Leipzig would come along right that moment. I was in a patch of allotments, on the main path that led right along the embankment to Stötteritz station. Ahead of me, behind a fence in one of the allotments, was some gardening arsehole, staring at me. He said something but I went on running. 'Stop, you fucker!' That wasn't the gardening arsehole; the skins had caught up. I ran faster. I ran sixty metres in 7.6 seconds at school, but I had problems over long distances. I tried to breathe evenly.

I turned around; they were about thirty metres behind me now. They'd got slower and were running side by side across the whole of the path, and in the middle at the front was a grey-and-white blur, that was the Leopard, the one everyone called Birdshit. Ahead, the path took a bend and led back to the road. They couldn't see me behind the bend, just for a few seconds but that would have to do. Buildings. I ran to the first door. No handle, just a knob. The next door was open; I jumped inside the hallway. I ran to the back door: closed. I heard their footsteps outside the house. I ran up the stairs to the fourth floor. I ran really quietly, and the stairwell was quiet too.

I sat down on a step. I rested my head on my knees, opened my mouth and let my spit run. I choked a few times, but I didn't puke. I'd often run away from some guys or other, but it still wiped me out every time. In the flat next to the attic doorway, someone rattled pots and pans. I leaned against the banisters and closed my eyes. But then they came in, and I heard them on the stairs and jumped up. I kicked in the attic door, there was a fire extinguisher and I yanked it off the wall. I ripped off the safety wire and shot a cloud of mist at them, fogged up the whole stairwell. There were two buckets of coal outside the flat door; I picked up a couple of briquettes and chucked them into the fog. Someone yelled, I ran back into the attic, there was a pile of junk, and I dragged an old bedstead onto the stairs...

'What are you doing here, what on earth are you doing?' A woman was standing over me, her big head looking down at me.

I jumped up and almost fell down the stairs. 'Shit!' I grabbed hold of the bannisters and looked around. No one else there; I must have been daydreaming.

'Do you live here? Are you the Simons boy?'

'No,' I said, instantly annoyed with myself for saying no.

'What are you doing here then, why are you sitting here? Why don't you go home?' The woman was about forty, wearing an apron; the door behind her was open and the stairwell smelled of cooking.

'I can't go home right now,' I said, trying to look like a nice boy.

'In trouble with your parents?'

'No, there's these boys outside, they want to beat me up, so I came...'

'You're lying, I don't believe you. They keep smashing the cars round here... sometimes they smash everything up.'

'No, no, please. I don't do that kind of thing, I'm just scared of the boys. They want to break my bones.'

She rubbed her hands against her apron. 'Well, you

don't look like one of those criminals...'

I smiled.

'How old are you?'

'Fifteen,' I said, 'and the others, the others are all older, they hang around outside my school, they stole my money once, and my mum went to the police and...'

'Your mum did the right thing. And now they want to beat you up?'

'Yes,' I said. I was sweating, the sweat ran down my face and I wiped my eyes like it was tears.

'You can come in for a minute if you like. You can have something to drink and we'll look out the window and see if the boys are still there.'

'They've all got skinheads,' I said, wiping my eyes even more so they went really red.

'Come on then, but take your shoes off.'

I put my shoes next to the mat and went in after her. We went along the dark hallway into the kitchen. There was a big saucepan steaming away in there, the water boiling over and hissing in the gas flame. She picked up two potholders and put the saucepan on the kitchen table. 'My husband gets home soon,' she said. The saucepan steamed in her face; she brushed her hair off her forehead and turned around to me.

'I'll be gone in a minute,' I said, rubbing my right foot against my left leg.

'Hold on,' she said, 'we've got a bit of time yet.' She stirred the saucepan with a big wooden spoon. 'We don't want those boys to get you, do we?' She went to the window and opened it. She moved a couple of flowerpots aside and leaned out. 'There's some over there, running around. Come and have a look.'

She stepped aside and I went to the window. 'Where?'

'There, right back there.' She stood behind me, leaned

over me, and I felt her breasts, pretty heavy on the back of my head. She took my hand and pointed it down at the street. 'There. Is that them?'

'Yes,' I said. They were at the other end of the road, almost at Stötteritz station, and again I could make out their chieftain's grey-and-white bomber jacket; he must have been almost invisible in winter. A green Golf was driving at walking pace ahead of them. The windows were wound down, a head with no hair the size of a rubbish bin on the driver's side, Kehlmann, and I saw a girl on the passenger's seat, recognized her dark shoulder-length hair. I turned away. 'Yes, that's them.'

'There really are a lot of them,' she said, and her breasts moved against the back of my neck.

'Yes,' I said. 'They'd have beaten me up. Thank you.'

I turned around to her; she went to the kitchen table. She picked up the saucepan and drained it into the sink. A few potatoes fell out and she put them back in the pan. I closed the window. When I turned back round she was in front of me again. 'Do you want something to drink? You must be thirsty.'

'Yes,' I said. 'Thanks.' She smiled, stroked my hair and my ear, then she went to the fridge. She filled a glass of Coke for me. She handed it to me and I drank. She stroked me again.

'You're a nice boy,' she said. I put my glass down and stepped up close to her. She pressed herself against me and I stroked her back. She pushed me away, took off her apron and put it on the table, next to the potatoes, then she walked backwards into the hall. It was dark there, no windows, and she unbuttoned her blouse. I stood in the kitchen doorway, holding onto the frame. 'Come here,' she said, 'come here, please.'

She fumbled behind her back and when I got to her,

she took my hand and laid it on her bare breasts. Her skin was rough, and they were huge and swung to and fro when I stroked them, and her hands were on top of mine and she said, 'Please.' Then she was quiet, and I stroked her face and my hand was wet. She leaned against the wall, trembling. I let her go.

'I'm sorry,' I said, and I walked to the door and heard her breathing in the dark.

I lit up a cigarette. I stood on the stairs and smoked; the building was quiet and I walked down slowly. I stopped by the letterboxes and waited a couple more minutes before I went outside.

The street was empty, they must have given up, and I headed for Stötteritz station 'cause they were probably waiting outside my house. Only the S-Bahn went to Stötteritz station now, but in the old days the trains to Thüringen stopped there, there was a proper ticket hall and it was still open but you couldn't buy a ticket there, it was just full of tramps, drinking. I looked at my watch, ten to six, a long time to go before it got dark. There was a little van outside the old ticket hall where the alkies in the station got their drink. I had a couple of marks on me and I needed a beer or too after all the stress. The van was called 'Ralf K's Corner'; Ralf was an ex-jailbird, you could tell by the dots tattooed on his hand. He sold sausages and chips as well, but most people bought beer and hard stuff from him, and he must have made a fortune when the trains to Thüringen were still stopping there. His van looked pretty dirty inside and I'd heard he slept in there as well, and sometimes you saw light behind the sales flap at night.

'I'll have a beer.'

'You sixteen yet?' Ralf grinned and put a can of Grafenwalder down on the counter for me. 'One fifty.' He had Holsten for two marks as well, but if you just asked for a beer you got Grafenwalder. Most of the alkies went for Grafenwalder. I gave him a couple of coins. He nodded and I put my beer on one of the two tall plastic tables and lit a cigarette. There was a bit of sausage in the ashtray. I opened the beer; foam ran over my hand. The beer was ice-cold, that was the only good thing about Ralf K's Corner. One of the alkies came out of the ticket hall. He walked like he'd shat his pants, clutching three empty beer cans, and he chucked them in the rubbish bag. He went up to the counter; something dripped from his beard.

'Another three beers, boss.' The boss nodded, opened the fridge and gave him three cans. A train crossed the bridge behind me and stopped on the platform with a screech. A freight train rumbled across the second bridge, a little way down the road. I wanted to count the wagons like when I was a kid, but it was gone already. Behind Stötteritz station was a freight station with big loading cranes that worked day and night, making loads of noise and lit up by a kind of floodlight. Fred and I had gone in for a couple of canisters of diesel one night a while ago, 'cause he was driving a Volvo diesel at the time. They stored all this fuel for the trains in steel drums and giant tanks. I emptied my beer and threw the can in the rubbish bag. The tramp had gone back inside the station.

'I'll have another one, please.'

'At your service.' I put the money on the counter and he nodded and opened the fridge. It was full of Grafenwalder cans, just a few red Cokes and green Holsten Pilseners on one side. 'Here you go, nice and cold.' A hand grabbed my shoulder as I reached for the can. I didn't turn around. I knocked the beer off the counter, jumped aside and bumped into the table so hard it fell over, then I ran past the station building to the tunnel leading to the platforms.

'Hold onto him, the fucker!'

The tunnel was dark and stank of piss, and I hoped they wouldn't get me in there.

They got me over at the freight station, between two goods depots. They'd split up into two groups and chased me across the whole place, and now I was trapped. As I ran, I'd passed a couple of orange railway workers, but they didn't seem to give a shit what happened at their station. Now the bastards came at me from both sides, real slow; no need for them to run anymore, they had me. No, I didn't give up that easy. I ran to one of the depot doors, it was locked, I threw myself against the door but there was no point, it was metal. I turned to face them, felt the metal behind me through my jacket. They stopped in a semi-circle around me. Kehlmann wasn't there; that bastard was probably sitting in his car nearby and touching up his girl, or cutting her hair.

The skin with the snow camo bomber jacket came towards me. It looked like he wanted to deal with me all on his own, not like with Rico, but then I didn't have Rico's reputation. He just came up to me with his arms dangling, and I waited until he was right up close and then I punched him. I wanted to get his nose 'cause it looked like it'd been broken a few times before, but the bastard was really fast. His head twitched aside and then he had me all of a sudden and slammed my head against the door. It didn't hurt that much though; much worse was that I'd missed him. Boom. Boom. Boom. With every punch he landed I saw an orange that got bigger and then smaller and then disappeared. 'Arsehole,' the guy squealed, 'look at me when I'm talking to you, you fucker!' He let go of me and I slid down the door. I drew up my knees and peered between my arms at their bald heads above me.

Only four or five of them had hair combed back with gel, fashion-conscious skins. 'Look, the poor kid's scared!'

'You're the greatest, arsehole!' I said, and tried to get up. Someone kicked me in the stomach, further down would have been worse but I still tipped over and couldn't breathe for a minute. I managed to get my arm underneath my chin before my head hit the ground somehow, but no, it wasn't the ground, there were legs all around me, luckily most of them wearing trainers and not army boots or steel toe caps, fashion-conscious skins. Dong! Boom! Boom! But mostly dong! Dong! Dong! More oranges in the dark. 'You bastards,' I screamed, 'you stupid fucking bastards!' I clutched my arms around my head. Someone pulled me up and shoved me against the wall. I opened my eyes, they were standing round me in a semi-circle again like nothing had happened, maybe they'd planned it all in advance, their movements and that, like a dance group. I stood up. I shook my head a few times, was I bleeding? Then I walked slowly up to the arsehole, who was standing in front of me again and grinning.

'Want another chance, do you, fighter?'

'Go on, finish him off, finish him right off!' A couple of the bastards started clapping, a couple whistled, and that, that was much worse than the dongs and the oranges. Everything was blurry, there must have been tears in my eyes, no, just sweat probably.

'Please,' I said, raising my hands, 'stop, please! I've had enough.' But I hadn't had enough, I was a shitty little liar, 'cause now I had him by the head with both hands. But the bastard had almost no hair and my fingernails dug all these bloody gouges into his scalp. He jerked himself away, I put my fists up in front of my face like Rico had showed me and blocked a couple of his punches, and it was only the stupid tears... no, the low sun shining in my eyes was to blame;I only got him once, and only on the shoulder.

Dong! Dong! Boom! Then I was down. The orange was a big red ball now that wouldn't go away and bounced up and down. It couldn't just be the one guy, they were all having a go at me. Then they stopped suddenly. I stayed down, my arms around my head, not moving. I felt the blood warm on my face and then on my neck.

I couldn't hear them anymore. I rolled on my front, opened my eyes and saw blood dripping onto the ground in front of me. I raised my head slowly; they were gone. Ten or fifteen metres away from me was a green Golf. I half-straightened up but then I collapsed again; the bastards had done a thorough job. I heard the door of the Golf opening and then slamming shut again. I clenched my fists, crawled to the wall and leaned against it. Estrellita was standing in front of me. I closed my eyes. 'Why,' I said. 'Jesus, why?'

'Poor thing,' she said, 'poor Danny.' She was next to me and whispering and breathing in my ear. I felt her wipe my eyes and face with a tissue. 'My poor little mongrel.' She stroked my hair and I opened my eyes.

'Why,' I said, grabbing her hand, 'why that arsehole skinhead?'

'Poor little mongrel,' she whispered again, and with her free hand she gently slapped my fist gripping her arm.

'Why? That arsehole messes us up, and you...' She wiped the blood off my face and pressed the tissue to my mouth.

'Everything's alright, my poor little mongrel,' she whispered, putting her cool hand to my forehead, 'I'm here.' She stroked me like I really was her dog.

A car door opened again. 'Come on, babe, let's go!'

'No,' I said, 'no, fuck that arsehole, fuck that wanker,

we'll get him, I swear!'

'Quiet,' she whispered, stroking my forehead. She stood up.

'Come on, babe, leave that little shit alone.' She went to the car, and before she got in she looked back at me once and raised her hand, just for a moment. I saw that it was covered in blood. Kehlmann came a few metres towards me. 'You can thank her that you're still alive!' He had a cigarette in the corner of his mouth, and now he flicked it five or six metres, right onto my chest. The guy had great aim, must have been pretty good at darts, but I'd still have put money down against him. I'd have flung all my darts right in his eye. He slammed the door and then I heard them driving away. Estrellita's tissue was still stuck to my neck; I threw it away.

I rolled onto the cobbles. The stones were cool, perhaps they'd stop the swelling from getting too bad. I noticed I was crying, and I tried to stop. I turned on my back, nice and slow. The sun was above the depot and between the cranes. The place was empty. I got up. I was dizzy. I took out my cigarettes; the box was squashed and the fags were broken. I lit a half up. I felt my face; it seemed to be alright, still. There was just a little cut where my hair started, and my nose wasn't broken either, maybe just fractured. I thought of Rico and was glad they hadn't done me in as badly as him. I thought of Estrellita and... I spat blood on the cobbles and pressed my teeth with my tongue; the top right incisor was a bit wobbly but it had been like that before. They told stories round our way about kerb stompers, guys who knocked you out and then lined your front teeth up on the kerb and stomped on your head. And they said a couple of skins had done it with a skateboarder and his skateboard, and the guy's teeth got stuck in the wood.

I threw my fag away and zipped my jacket right up. I walked back to the road. I saw the big cranes moving their arms; they looked even better at night in all the spotlights.

'You and your crap! You and your crap! It's always the same, over and over, always the same!' Mum was yelling in the kitchen. 'You... you... don't you see, why don't you see? A criminal, you're like a criminal!'

'Please be quiet,' I said, 'just stop, please!'

She'd been doing overtime all week and now it was Friday and she'd been drinking. I'd had blue and purple bruises under my eyes for a few days, but she'd only just noticed.

'It's my flat,' she yelled, waving her little hand around in front of my face. 'When are they coming then, the police, when are they coming to pick you up at last, you... you... a criminal, that's what you are!' She turned around and leaned on the kitchen table with both hands.

'Mum.' I stood behind her, touched her shoulders.

'Go away,' she said quietly. 'Just go away.' Them Mum was silent, lowered her head and breathed loudly.

'It's not my fault,' I said, 'the eyes, I mean, I can't help it, I didn't do anything this time, really! They just beat me up, loads of them, for no reason!'

'You and your crap! You and your lying crap!' She yelled again and I took a few steps back. She leaned over the kitchen table and yelled at the wall. 'Don't you see? And the neighbours, the building, boy, if the police... if the police come again. The way you... the way you look... like a brawler, like your father, get out of here, you, just get out!'

'But the police aren't coming, Mum!'

'Strike you dead, that's what they ought to... criminal... strike you dead.'

I went to my room and fetched my cigarettes. I put on my jacket. I heard Mum punching the kitchen table, I knew that sound. Her handback was hanging up in the hall. I took a tenner and two two-mark coins out of her purse. Mum was yelling and cursing in the kitchen but I'd stopped listening. I left the flat, slammed the door behind me and ran down the stairs. Mum was yelling pretty loudly and I could still hear her downstairs as I opened the front door.

It was evening, the sun already behind the houses. I went to Pitbull's, cutting across the backyards. I didn't look up at the old lady's window when I passed her place. Someone had mended the fence to Pitbull's yard so I had to kick two new slats out. The back door was closed; it was almost always open 'cause we'd often meet up in Pitbull's cellar. I went to the cellar window, it was light inside. I tapped my foot against the frosted glass a few times. The window opened and I saw Pitbull's head. 'Oh, Danny, it's you.'

'Why's the door shut? Let me in.' I squatted down by the window and looked at him. He was pale, looked like he'd had a good few already.

'I can't, not right now. I can't let you in.'

'Why not? You got a girl down there?' I knew he didn't have a girl with him. His head wobbled back and forth, and I'd have smelled the alcohol even if he hadn't been breathing.

'I'm sorry, Danny, but you know, they... they came round, I used to hang out with them, back in the day. And now... and now...'

'Why, Pitbull? Why didn't you do something? You know them, you said it yourself! They, they beat us up really bad, and you just sit tight down there and do nothing!'

'Believe me, Danny, I'm really sorry, I do what I can,

you know, but, jeez... Rico, he'll come up with something, he'll get something together. Like he always does, Danny.' He tried to smile but it didn't work. I stood up and looked down at him. I could see the sofa against the wall behind him, where he slept when there was trouble upstairs. He slept there almost every night.

'For fuck's sake, Pitbull, if we stick together, you know, if everyone brings a couple of people along, we can do it!'

'No, Danny, no, there's too many of them, believe me, the Reudnitz Right, you know them. I'll sort something out with them, we'll talk to them, a bit of negotiating, you get it, and everything'll be fine again!' My foot was in front of his face; I turned around. 'Hey, hold up, wait a minute!'

I walked across the yards back to the street. I walked to our park. The table-tennis area was empty. Fred was in jail, the others were hiding from the skins, and Estrellita... I sat down on a bench, on the backrest. I smoked one, then another, and waited for the night. I looked over at the sandpit with the climbing frame where I'd played with Rico back in the Zone days. Our tree was gone now. They'd chopped it down a few years ago 'cause it got diseased and the leaves stopped growing. I smoked a few more cigarettes, then I got up. Maybe Mum had gone to bed now, but she'd probably gone on drinking. I headed for Connewitz; it was a good way to walk but I had plenty of time.

I gazed up the dark outside wall. The windows were boarded up, the front door too, and through its broken windows I could see a pile of junk in the hallway. I took the mini brandy I'd bought at the garage out of my pocket and drank a sip, then I went round the back. This was where the crusties lived, I knew that from Werner, who was a crustie and lived here too. I knew him from school, my new school, and he'd lived in our neighbourhood for a long time even though crusties weren't popular round our way, but everyone had respect for him 'cause he'd been the first crustie in Reudnitz after the Wall came down, or that was what he said at least, and as well as that he knew the Antifa, and they steamrollered everyone. I climbed onto an old car and from there onto the back wall. Werner had told me how to get in the house once, if I wanted to pay him a visit without getting beaten up. The crusties were nervous, especially at night, 'cause sometimes the skins came over from Grünau and attacked their houses, or they tried to. 'If you're ever in trouble,' Werner had said, 'you come to me, I can help you out, any time.' Werner was alright, we were almost mates, even though he was a crustie. I'd taken him along to Pitbull's cellar once and he almost got in a fight with Pitbull but we got in between them. He was a punk, a crustie, they weren't popular round our way, but he'd stood by me when I'd had all that trouble at school and they wanted to chuck me out. Then he'd chucked it all in himself, left school and our neighbourhood and moved here, and I admired him for that.

There was gigantic fridge in the middle of the backyard. Maybe the crusties had thrown it out the window or off the roof when the skins wanted to raid the house; Werner told me once they had whole sets of furniture up on their roofs. I didn't put my lighter on. There had to be a ladder somewhere leading to the first floor. I stood still and gave my eyes time to adjust to the darkness; not even the moon was out. There was a big circle of rocks on the ground; I bent down, the ash was still warm. 'Hello,' I called quietly. 'I'm a friend of Werner's.' No answer. Not a sound. I went up to the house. The back door was bricked up, with the ladder in front of it. I climbed up. The window was ajar and I pushed it open. I climbed into the stairwell and lit up my lighter. I walked up. I passed a toilet, the door off its hinges, leaning against the wall. I tried not to look in the toilet bowl. There was a front door open on the second floor and I shone my light into the hallway. 'Hello, is anyone in?' There were at least ten crates of beer along the wall; I went closer, they were empty. I went on to the third floor. 'Werner, it's me, Daniel!'

I beat my fist against the door. The handle was gone and I looked through the hole where it should have been. Everything was dark inside, he wasn't there, he'd told me he lit fifty candles at night in his flat. He'd also told me where he hid the door handle. I went down a flight of stairs to the window. The glass was broken and I reached carefully past the shards to the outside window ledge. A good hiding place for a door handle. 'Come and visit me,' Werner had said as he got on the tram with his backpack and a plastic carrier bag, and left our neighbourhood. 'Come whenever you like, I'd be glad to see you.'

'Course,' I'd said, 'next week maybe, probably!' That was a few months back now. His mum had sent Child Services and the cops after him, but they hadn't found him.

I opened the door to the flat. Right next to the door was a table with a couple of candles on it. I lit them. There was an old sofa against the wall so I sat down on it. I didn't know which room was his; he shared the flat with other crusties and I didn't want to go rummaging around or they'd be mad when they got back. Those guys knew the Antifa, and they steamrollered everyone. I put my mini brandy on the floor; it was almost empty, but I had plenty of fags. I lit one up and watched the candles and the shadows. There was a spider on the wall; I was bloody scared of spiders. I knew this girl from the corpse-fuckers, she was really into spiders and had a whole load of them at home in some kind of tank. She'd been pretty drunk and I'd been looking forward to banging her all night, even though her perfume stank like shit, corpse-fucker perfume, but the stupid spiders had messed everything up.

Footsteps on the stairs. I drank up my brandy and shoved the bottle under the sofa. I got up and went to the door. The guys' boots were making all this noise, and I hoped they had Werner with them 'cause crusties were usually drunk, and then they were trouble. I lit a new cigarette and leaned against the doorway. Then they came. There were three blokes and two girls. The guy at the front was holding a candle. He had a skinhead, just a few dyed red locks of hair flopping over his forehead at the front.

'Hello,' I said.

'Shit, who are you?'

'Werner, I'm looking for Werner, he's a good mate of mine.'

'And what are you doing in here?'

They were right in front of me now; the other two guys looked like proper crusties, with mohicans, boots and loads of metal on their clothes and in their faces. The girls were quite pretty but their clothes and dyed hair messed it all up. Mohican Number One came right up close to me. He didn't smell, not of sweat or booze, and that surprised me. 'I asked you: What are you doing in our flat?'

'Werner told me to wait here, he told me where the door handle is, he told me to wait in the hallway. Where... where is he, Werner?' I left the cigarette in the corner of my mouth as I talked and put my hands in my pockets, and the smoke burned in my nose and eyes.

'You fash?' Mohican number two came and stood next to Mohican number one.

'No. Do I look like one?'

'What's your name, fash?'

'Listen, I'm not a Nazi, I'm just looking for Werner, he's a mate of mine.' I took my hands out of my pockets. The guy with the red hair pushed in front of the two Mohicans. I stepped back and raised my left fist to chest height. If I knocked over the table with the candles...

'Hey, hey, it's alright. Everything's fine.' The guy with the red strings of hair raised both his arms and showed me his palms. 'You gotta understand, we're always on guard, the skins, you know, the skinheads.'

'I'm not a skin.' My cigarette had fallen down and I lit myself a new one.

'So you're looking for Werner?'

'Yeah,' I said and held out my pack. He nodded and took one. He was something like the boss, probably, 'cause the two Mohicans stood behind him giving me dumb grins.

'You're a friend of Werner's, are you?'

'Yeah,' I said, 'from Reudnitz, Leipzig East. Werner comes from round my way.' The guy grinned and I blew smoke in his face, then I gave him a light.

'Reudnitz,' said the guy. 'Right, that used to be Werner's manor. Tough part of town.'

'It's alright,' I said. The girls walked past us and sat down on the sofa. They whispered to each other and gave me dirty looks, probably fancied a shag but now I was there, messing everything up.

'You're in luck,' the guy said. 'I'm in a good mood tonight.'

'Me too,' I said.

'OK, you need to go to HERA, it's a bar, Werner's doing a shift there tonight.'

'Where is it?'

'Down the road a bit and then left.'

'OK,' I said. He looked at me and nodded, then I walked past him to the stairs.

One of the two Mohicans rammed me with his shoulder. 'Watch it, fash,' he whispered.

'Fuck off and die, crustie,' I said, but I was one flight further down by then. I climbed down the ladder and crossed the dark yard. Someone in the house laughed; they were probably getting down to it now, getting turned on.

I climbed over the wall, walked down the road a bit, then I stopped and looked around. I was in the middle of the crusties' part of town. It wasn't a proper neighbourhood, just a few blocks of derelict buildings they'd squatted. There was a huge white cloth hanging from a building right in front of me, they'd probably sewn ten sheets together, with a big red A on it. Cars hadn't driven down here for ages, and the cops only came once a year. A couple of times, Fred had parked his cars here and hidden out when they were after him, there were loads of backyards and a few empty factories, and sometimes the crusties built barricades to wind up the cops.

Ahead of me, a huge campfire was burning in the middle of the road, with a horde of punks sitting round it. A couple of them looked over at me and I nodded at them and walked past. 'Hey lad, want a drink?' The fire crackled and snapped, and when I turned around there was a guy behind me with a bottle in his hand. 'Come on, lad, have a drink.' He was much older than the crusties from before, he had a straggly tramp's beard and the rest of him looked like a tramp as well, I could only tell he must be a punk by his clothes and boots, or he had been once. There was a police truncheon hanging from his belt, maybe he'd nicked it, but you could get them in weapons shops or from the Vietcong. 'You a tourist, are you?' I made a grab for the bottle; he pulled his hand away. 'No, no, lad, you gotta sit down, sit down and have a drink.' The guys round the fire looked at me, a couple grinning, almost all of them had a bottle in their hand, and I went ahead and sat down between them. My heart was making plenty of noise but they couldn't hear it 'cause the fire crackled and snapped pretty loud. The tramp put more wood on, leaning so far forward I hoped his beard would catch alight, then he sat down next to me. He handed me the bottle and I drank a mouthful; the stuff tasted like finest hair lacquer. 'You a tourist, lad, are you?'

I coughed. 'No,' I said, 'no.' The guys looked at me and grinned, and then they drank out of their bottles, almost in synch, like they'd planned it all in advance.

'So you're not a tourist,' said another guy whose face looked pretty messed up; maybe this was some kind of club for run-down crusties. 'But I bet you've got a bit of spare change for us, eh?'

He slurred his words and wobbled his head and clapped in front of my face a couple of times, but I still said: 'No, I'm just a poor bastard myself,' even though I was scared they'd roast me on the fire.

'Ah, but you can spare a few cigarettes for me and my mates.'

'Couse,' I said, 'course I can.' I took one for myself and then handed my pack to the guy. He took one out and passed them on. There weren't many left in there anyway and I'd picked up a new pack at the garage.

'And have you got a light, tourist?'

'Course.' I wanted to get out my Zippo but it was too pretty, shiny silver in the night, so I reached into the fire, took a pretty big ember between finger and thumb and passed it really slowly to the guy, who held his cigarette up to it. He patted me on the back and I lit my cigarette on the ember, cool and collected, before I threw it back in the fire. The tramp passed me the bottle and I drank a mouthful. 'I'd better be going;' I said once I could speak again, but they took no notice as I got up; they were staring at the fire and drinking.

The music came out of the open front door, sounded almost like the Nazi stuff Pitbull used to listen to. I went in. There were candles all over the floor and the steps. The door to the ground-floor flat on the left was open, and now a couple of crusties came out. They barged into me, but they were out of it, I could tell by their eyes. There was a sign above the door, HERA, and someone had drawn a big anarchist-A and a dancing man next to it, but it didn't look good. There was a rusty street sign screwed to the wall by the doorbell: *Hermann Albrecht Strasse*. I lit a cigarette and headed into the flat. There was a lot going on inside: at least twenty crusties dancing and chanting along to the song, and behind me I saw the bar and even more crusties. They barged into me and shoved me aside, one of them jumped against my back; it was their way of dancing, and I joined in for a bit: I rammed my shoulder into one guy's back and gave him a few elbows in the ribs and the neck, and the guy turned around and grinned and jumped about in front of me. I shoved my way through towards the bar – no, all the cops and all the skins in Leipzig would never get the crusties out of here, not with the way they danced, like other people fighting in the street. A ladder was propped in the middle of the room and I looked up at the ceiling; there was a huge hole and through it I saw tables and legs. A woman climbed up the ladder wearing a skirt, but it was one of those long ones that come down to her shoes, so you couldn't see anything.

Werner was behind the bar opening a beer with his

teeth; that was his speciality. He'd showed it to us in Pitbull's cellar that time, and even Pitbull, who'd wanted to beat him up a few minutes before, even he was impressed. A couple of days later, one of Pitbull's top teeth was broken. 'It was my old man,' he'd said, but I knew better.

'Alright, Werner,' I said, rapping my knuckles on the counter.

He spat out the bottle-top and slammed the beer down so hard on the bar it foamed over. 'Jesus, Danny, that's crazy, you're here!' He pulled back his hand and we high-fived. 'Have a drink!' He pushed the bottle of beer over to me. 'Great, Danny, it's great that you made it.' He bit another bottle open and we clinked them together.

'Great to see you, Werner.'

'And you, Danny.' We drank.

'You're in good shape,' I said, although his face looked pretty messed up, and I punched him on the shoulder. 'Great to see you, Werner.' He nodded and smiled and ran a hand through his green hair.

Next to me at the bar was a thin guy with a shaved head, playing nervously with his braces and raising and lowering his shoulders. 'My beer, Werner, I wanted a beer, you were...'

'Right, coming, coming right up.' Werner bit one open for him, and the guy dropped a few coins on the bar and headed off. 'Jesus, Danny, I never thought I'd see you again.'

'Oh, you know, lots going on, lots of stress, lots of stress. You know our neighbourhood.'

'You can say that again!' He smiled again. He put his bottle to his lips and downed half of it in one. We sometimes used to do drinking competitions after school or in the breaks, and he'd always been faster, except for a few times when he let me win and pretended his beer went down the wrong way, 'cause he knew I was pretty proud of my drinking skills. 'Have they chucked you out yet?'

'What d'you mean, Werner?'

'Out of school, did you make it yet?'

'No, still undecided.'

'You know what, Danny, I'm glad to have seen the back of that place. Those bastards messed us up good, didn't they?'

'Yeah,' I said, 'they did.' I lit a cigarette and passed him the pack. He took one and I gave him a light. He didn't actually smoke but he had a practice one sometimes, for smoking joints.

'Hey, Werner...'

'Yeah, Danny?' He leaned against the counter and blew his smoke over at me. 'What's up, Danny? Go on.'

'I'm having a bit of stress with my mum, you know. You know my mum, right?'

'A bit.'

'You know, Werner, I don't want to go back... just for tonight, you know...'

'You can stay at my place, you know that, I told you that, didn't I? I've always got a spare bed, for you, always.' He held out his bottle and we clinked them together again.

'Thanks.'

'That's alright, Danny. You can stay longer if you like.'

'Five beers, Werner.' A couple of punks popped up next to me and Werner shoved the bottles over to them. Then he took another two bottles out of the crate behind the bar and bit them open. He spat out the tops, and I saw that his front teeth weren't in such great shape anymore.

'Jeez, Werner,' I said, running my finger over my top lip. 'Just use a bottle opener.'

'No, Danny, no. It's not the bottles, that was a couple of

skins.' He tapped his front teeth and grinned.

'Yeah,' I said, 'fucking skins.' I had him now. I took a cigarette, leaned over the bar and lit it on a candle, so the flame lit up my swollen left eye. 'Yeah, yeah,' I said, 'those fucking skins.'

'Woah, Danny, what have you got there, that doesn't look good.'

'Oh that, nah, that's nothing, nothing much. You know our neighbourhood, full of boneheads. Nah, we've got it under control, Werner.' I raised my bottle to him and drank.

He pushed his bottle aside and put his hand on my arm. 'Danny, you know if you're having stress with skins, you can always come to me. I know people, you know that, right...'

'Yeah, I know. But you know us, me and Rico and the others, we'll get it sorted. We know all sorts of Chemie bruisers and that... we'll get it sorted. There's just a lot of them, skins, you know, it's hard work.'

'That's what I'm saying, that's what I'm saying, Danny. I've got a few debts to pay back round that way, anyway. They're not Engel's people, though, are they?'

'No, they're...'

'Not that I'm scared, Danny, we'd finish them off as well. Antifa, you know.'

'I know you're not scared. You're a Reudnitz lad, aren't you?' He laughed and we clinked bottles and drank.

'It's just the wankers from the roller rink,' I said, and wiped my mouth.

'I know the bastards,' said Werner, 'they're no problem.'

'But I don't wanna get you mixed up in anything.'

'Listen, Danny, we're mates, aren't we?'

'Course.' I leaned over the bar to him. 'OK, you're a crustie, but you're a real mate.'

He smiled. 'We gotta stick together, Danny, against the skins.'

'Yeah,' I said, 'you're right there.'

Four crusties next to me. 'Four beers, Werner, and four korns.' Werner nodded and opened the bottles. This time he used a bottle opener and I was glad of it, 'cause it hurt my fillings to watch him bite off the tops.

'Listen, lads, my mate here... my mate here...' They looked at me. Didn't look friendly. '...he hates boneheads, he's an absolute skin-hater. He might not look like it,' he winked at me, 'but he cleaned up good and proper over in the east the other day, right, Danny?'

'Right.' I turned to the crusties, took a deep breath and made my shoulders really broad inside my jacket.

'Well, there were quite a lot of them though,' said Werner, filling four shot glasses and spilling korn all over the bar. 'They're a real problem these days, the skins, you know what I...'

'Cleaned up,' said one of the crusties, a guy with a shaved head who looked like fash himself, but with a bit of metal in his face. When he leaned forward to grab his beer, I saw he had a gun in his waistband, but it wasn't a doctored alarm gun like I had.

'Right,' said Werner, 'it's almost as bad over there as in Grünau, with the skins, I mean. We've gotta... I mean it's about time we...'

'Cleaned up,' said the crustie with the metal in his face. 'Where is it exactly, skin-hater?'

'Reudnitz,' I said, and I lit a cigarette from the candle. 'Near the centre, the old roller rink.'

The guy with the metal nodded, and the three other crusties at the bar nodded as well and then drank some of their beer.

'We know the ones,' said the guy with the metal. 'RR.

Small-fry. Cost you two crates.'

I nodded. I'd get the crates with Rico or Mark from round the back of the Leipzig Premium Pilsner Brewery. Sometimes it was out of date, but the crusties wouldn't notice that, they usually drank Sternburg or Grafenwalder and thought Goldkrone was the world's best cognac.

'Two crates,' I said. 'No problem.'

'It's worth it, Danny,' Werner patted me on the shoulder, 'definitely worth it.'

'When d'you want us there, skin-hater?'

I looked at my cigarette and shrugged. 'Dunno. Whenever you've got time.'

'Wait a minute, wait a minute, lads.' Werner filled another two shot glasses and pushed one over to me. 'Contract,' he said. 'Let's drink to it first. We can make the appointment later.'

'You're right, Werner,' said the guy with the metal in his face, picking up his glass. The three other crusties at the bar took their glasses too. They hadn't said anything so far, maybe they were off their faces and miles away, maybe they talked really quietly and I hadn't heard them 'cause the music was so loud, and they kept quiet now as well as we raised our glasses. 'To cleaning up,' said the guy with the metal in his face.

'To cleaning up,' said Werner and me, and the three crusties nodded and then moved their heads really slowly like they were looking around, but their pupils were so tiny they could probably hardly see anything, and I hoped they didn't just daydream about being tough guys. But even the skins over in Grünau were scared of the Antifa.

'The appointment,' Werner said, 'me and Danny'll talk about that, it'll all go though me, lads. You've got a phone at home, right, Danny?'

'Course,' I said. 'Mum's got all the mod cons.'

He grinned, and the four crusties grinned as well. 'But no going back on it,' said the guy with the metal, and the way he looked at me, I knew what he meant. 'It's a job, you know, cleaning up, cleaning up the skins, you know...'

'Hey, don't worry about it,' said Werner. 'Danny's a man of honour, don't even think he'd go back on his word.' He put his hand on my shoulder, and I nodded.

'See you soon, then,' said the guy with the metal, and then he took his beer and went over to the dancers jumping up against each other and yelling along to the music. It took the other three a while to notice he was gone, but then they went after him.

'Professionals,' said Werner. 'The one with the gun's from the Antifa, an old fighter, and there'll be more like him as well.'

'Thanks,' I said quietly.

'Ah, shut up, Danny.' Werner grinned and dug his hand into his green hair. He turned round to the shelf full of bottles, took one and put it down on the bar in front of me. 'You like whiskey, don't you, Danny?'

'Course. You should know.' He might be a crustie and know his way around illegal things, but I'd taught him after school how to nick booze in supermarkets and shops. I was pretty good at it and I'd been proud he was such a good learner.

He took two tumblers and half-filled them. 'Ah, Danny, I'm really looking forward to it, the contract, you know, victory...' He held the bottle up. 'Got this one myself, Danny.' He winked at me and smiled, but there was no reason 'cause it was Full House whiskey, the cheapest you could get. There were four men playing cards on the label, but that didn't make the stuff any better.

'Jesus, Werner, Full House?' I said. 'Have you forgotten everything I...'

'Oh, come on, Danny, it's not that bad.'

I smiled and drank. The stuff hadn't even gone all the way down before it came back up again, and I had to dilute it with plenty of spit and swallow it back. I rinsed it down with beer and lit one up.

'You not in shape, Danny?'

'Bollocks, why d'you say that?'

He passed the bottle over and I topped up my glass, blew smoke inside it and breathed it in before I drank. 'Been a tough day, Werner,' I said, and I leaned so far over the bar that my head almost touched the wood, 'with my mum and all that, you know.'

He put his hand on mine but I pulled it away. 'Danny, you can stay with me as long as you like.'

'Nah, Werner, thanks, but it's just for tonight. You know, I've gotta get back to the neighbourhood...'

'I know.'

We drank, and Werner served the crusties. Loads of guys started coming to the bar and ordering beer and shots, a few girls as well, but I wasn't into punk girls, and even if there were a couple of pretty ones, their clothes messed everything up. Werner bit the bottles open and filled the shot glasses, the crusties talked at him and patted him on the back, the girls too, he was the king of the bar and I bet he could get every punk girl into bed. Round our way they said the crusties all fucked each other any which way, free love and all that, that was why there were so many of them, and that was the only thing we envied them for.

'Help yourself,' Werner called, spitting out a bottle-top and taking money from a couple of punks, 'you can have the whole bottle if you want.' I nodded and filled my glass again. The stuff didn't taste all that bad now. That's how it was with gut-rot, once you'd downed enough of it.

I lit one up. 'Got a spare one, do us a favour and spare one?' There was a guy next to me, his hood pulled down low over his face, holding a big red pen in his hand and moving his torso side to side like a boxer.

'Course,' I said, and handed him the pack, 'cause the guy didn't look quite compos mentis and I didn't want his pen in my eye. He took two and put one behind his ear. The guy didn't look like a crustie, normal hair, normal clothes, just a tattoo on his neck like a kind of pin-code.

'I'll do you a picture, return the favour.'

'That's OK,' I said.

'No, no, I'll do you a picture, I love drawing.' He leaned on the bar, took a piece of paper out of his pocket and started drawing on it.

'He's got stuck, Danny. Not quite with it.' Werner tapped his forehead as he filled a couple of shot glasses, spilling half of it on the bar. I looked at the guy but he seemed not to have heard, 'cause he just went on drawing.

'How d'you mean?'

'You know, stuck on a trip, LSD, he can't come down, always away with the fairies, you know. Got stuck.'

'Right,' I said, 'I've heard about that.' The guy'd finished now and he passed me his picture. There was nothing on it, just circles and dots and lines. 'Nice picture,' I said, and poured another whiskey.

'This,' he said, pointing the pen at one of the circles, 'this is us.'

'And the others?'

'Stars,' he said, 'just a few stars.'

I visited Werner again later, a long time later. He wasn't there. No one was there. The windows of his building were bricked up and the building with the bar had disappeared altogether. When they'd beaten up the skins

I'd promised to come by often, but it didn't turn out that way, even though I owed it to him. I just didn't get out of my neighbourhood, only to court or to youth custody or to jail, and anyway the crusties weren't all that popular round our way. But they still talk in our neighbourhood about that time when a horde of punks came from the south of town to Leipzig East to clean up the skins at the roller rink. I never saw Werner the bottle-biter again.

## SHOTS

We got to Chemie late, Rico and me, that Sunday in the year after the Wall came down, when we played BFC Dynamo. It was the last season of the GDR League, even though the GDR didn't exist by then. BSG Chemie Leipzig didn't exist anymore either, we were called FC Sachsen Leipzig now, and a few months before that we'd been called FC Green-White Leipzig for a while, but we didn't understand why, we believed in Chemie and we were Chemie, forever. BFC wasn't called BFC either anymore, they were FC Berlin, but we didn't care, we hated them either way.

We got to Leutzsch late that day 'cause my parents had just got divorced, Dad lived somewhere else now, and I went to the Silver Slope for lunch with him every other Saturday, and that Sunday as well, I'd sat with him in the bar looking at my watch (under the table so he couldn't see), 'cause I was supposed to meet Rico on the corner at one.

'Come with us,' I said, 'like the old days, Dad, against the Berlin bastards...'

'No,' he said, and he smiled and knocked back his shot, 'even if it is the Stasi bastards, I'm never going back to Leutzsch, that's all over for me, Danny.' Dad drank quite a lot when I went for lunch with him, actually he drank the whole time I was eating, and when Chemie were playing and he didn't want to come and stayed behind on his own, and when I got out my green-and-white scarf and went off he drank even more.

'Berlin bastards,' he said now, as I put on my green-and-white scarf 'cause it was almost one o'clock. 'Wipe 'em out, the Stasi bastards, they cheated us all the years, all those years. And say hello to Leutzsch from me, Danny.'

I sat back down and told him all the news from Chemie, and there was plenty of it: new players, new chairman, new kit, we even had a different name, and that's why I got to Rico late, and he'd been waiting on the corner for ages and was a bit angry, 'cause he'd seen our 13:12 train crossing the bridge and the next one wasn't for another twenty minutes.

'We'll be at least fifteen minutes late,' Rico said once we were heading for Leipzig Central at last. 'D'you know how much can happen in that time?'

'Yeah,' I said, 'one-nil for us, two-nil for them, you never know before the game.'

'D'you have to sit watching your old man drink for so long?'

'Yeah, I do.' I rested my elbows on the window ledge and looked out at the old factories in the industrial estate we were stopping at.

'Sorry, Danny, I... I didn't mean it like that.'

Rico had been living with his gran for nearly two years now, and he couldn't stand dads since his had buggered off, but he couldn't stand his mum either 'cause she hadn't been able to deal with him. He couldn't stand all kinds of people, and that was why he liked going to Chemie so much, 'cause everyone there couldn't stand the others, especially if they came from Berlin. Rico tugged and jerked at his green-and-white scarf, wrapping one end around his hand. 'What d'you think, Danny, you reckon we'll make it into the top league?'

'Dunno, don't think so, we need eight more points for second place. And last week... against Dynamo Dresden, I mean...'

'You're right. Seven-nil, beaten seven-nil. I just... I was just... oh, you know, top league would be great, but second league of the Bundesliga, that's be great too. Top league, Danny, Bundesliga, I just... I was just...'

'Dreaming,' I said, and we laughed. The compartment went dark 'cause we went through the little tunnel.

'Bundesliga!' Rico yelled right by my ear, and I jumped up.

'Jesus, leave it out.'

'Give you a shock, did I?'

'No, you didn't. I just wanted to get up in time.'

We pulled into the station and Rico looked at his watch. 'Twenty minutes, Danny, if we run at the other end we'll be in the stadium in twenty minutes. Hey, where are you going?'

'Just wanna look outside.' I left the compartment and headed for the door. The train jiggled a bit, I stumbled down the corridor and held onto a grip, then it braked with a screech and I heard loud-speaker voices from outside. 'Arriving... platform 22... continues... via... 13:46... fast train to Halle/Saale Central... platform 19... for Leutzsch.'

I tugged at the door lever. It was stuck but Rico shoved me aside and yanked the door open. 'You got no muscles, Danny.'

'Yes, I have.' I gave him a shove and he jumped onto the platform.

'Hey,' he said, 'there's people coming.'

'Course,' I said. 'We're at the station.'

'No, look.'

But before I could look, I heard them.

'Berlin, Berlin, we're hardmen from Berlin!' Many voices, still far off, but coming closer. 'Berlin, Berlin, we're hardmen from Berlin!'

'Shit, Danny, shit, look!'

I put a foot on the steps and leaned out of the train. And then I saw them: 'Hooray, hooray, BFC rules OK! Hooray,

hooray, BFC rules OK!' a hundred, a hundred and fifty, no, it must have been more, the whole station was full of them and the first of them had reached the platform. 'Hooray, hooray... Berlin, Berlin, we're hardmen from Berlin!' A whole load of burgundy scarves, Dad used to call them 'bloodhounds'. I could spot the first of them already, skinheads, huge skinheads marching in the front row.

'Shit,' said Rico, and I held onto the grip with both hands, 'BFC bastards.' He stepped back, stumbled and leaned against the train next to me. 'Danny,' he whispered, 'Danny, we're in the shit.' He backed onto the first step up to the door; I saw his legs trembling. I couldn't even feel my own legs.

'Chemie bastards out, Chemie bastards out!'

'The scarves, Rico, our scarves!' I grabbed him by the shoulders and shook him, 'Rico, Jesus, Rico, we gotta go!' but Rico just sat down on the bottom step.

'Chemie bastards out, Chemie bastards out!'

Their voices bounced off the big station dome, I wanted to bugger off, duck back inside the train and jump off again at the front and cross the tracks somewhere, but Rico... now he jumped up suddenly, 'Bloody BFC bastards, bloody Stasi club!' He shoved me back on the train and slammed the door behind him. That was Rico all over, the best welterweight in town (under 15s), that was what he called himself and we believed him, and anyone who'd seen him in the ring believed him, and now I believed him again. 'Come on, this way, get rid of the scarves, take your scarf off!' He'd already stuffed his scarf under his coat and was tugging at mine, but I'd wrapped it round my neck twice 'cause it was so long, and Rico ran and dragged me along by my scarf. I ran as fast as I could along the corridor, but Rico ran faster and the scarf was like a noose around my neck, I couldn't breathe, but now I got it off at last and Rico stuffed it under his coat. I heard the door opening behind us, 'Chemie's going home in a fucking ambulance!' we ran further, out the window I saw the crowd on the platform, I saw a man stuffing a green-and-white hat in the bin in a compartment, then we were at the very front, right behind the driver's compartment, and Rico yanked open the toilet door, and then we stood in front of the sink with three empty beer bottles in it, and we didn't breathe and we saw our pale faces in the mirror. Rico locked the door.

'Leave it open,' I whispered, 'leave the door open!'

'What, are you crazy?'

'No, then they'll think it's empty, you know, like fare-dodging.'

'Forget it, Danny, they're not conductors, I'm not letting those bastards in here. They'll finish us off.'

'But... but we're... we're just kids, Rico.'

I smiled in the mirror. It looked terrible.

'You might be, Danny, but they don't care, they'll still give us a kicking.'

'Will they find us in here? They won't find us, will they, Rico?'

'Dunno.'

I squatted down by the sink and Rico leaned against the door. The toilet stank really badly, someone had shat all up the bowl and not flushed it all away, but there was nothing we could do about that now 'cause the flush was so loud. We heard the crowd marauding along the train, 'Fear and loathing – BFC, fear and loathing – BFC!' and I really was afraid, and Rico must have been afraid as well, even if he was the best welterweight in town (under 15s), 'cause there weren't any Chemie fans who'd protect us, no fence and no police to keep the Berlin bastards off our backs like in the stadium, and we'd heard the stories about the hardman BFC fans they called *hooligans* now, Dad had told me all about them, and he'd told me they ruled every football stadium in the country, except in Leutzsch, at Chemie. But we weren't in Leutzsch yet.

The train jerked a few times and then pulled off. Rico looked at his watch. 'Five minutes late,' he whispered. 'Those bloody BFC bastards.'

The chanting started up again, like they'd heard him, and something smashed nearby. 'We're gonna smash up Leutzsch, we're gonna smash up Leutzsch...'

'Only a Leutzscher is a Deutscher,' Rico whispered, clenching his fist.

'Yeah,' I said, 'yeah, but what do we do now?'

'I don't know, Danny.' He slid slowly down the door and squatted next to me. 'We'll be there in a few minutes, Danny, we'll wait 'til they've all got off and then we'll sneak over to the stadium somehow, to our terrace.'

But I knew it wouldn't end up like that, 'cause something smashed again, this time right outside the door, footsteps, voices, someone tried the handle. 'Jesus, open the bloody door or I'll piss in the corridor!'

We jumped up; Rico took one of the beer bottles out of the sink. 'Alright, keep your hair on, mate,' he yelled, 'just coming. Won't be a minute.' He pulled the scarves out from under his coat, stepped on the foot pedal for the flush, and stuffed the scarves in the shitty toilet bowl. 'Rico, no!' I grabbed for my scarf, my Dad had given it to me, but it was too late, it disappeared down the drain and then I saw the sleepers underneath us for a moment before the hole closed again.

'Come on, take a bottle, Danny.'

'Shit, Rico, we don't stand a chance.'

'We're Berlin bastards, come on, we're BFC bastards,

Danny.' He pressed a bottle into my hand, then went to the door.

'No, Rico, don't open it, maybe he'll just piss in the corridor and then bugger off.'

'They'll knock the door in, Danny.'

I stood right behind him; he undid the bolt, then opened the door. 'Alright, mate, here you go.' And he was right, the guy really would have knocked the door in, and he wouldn't even have needed both fists, he had a head the size of a rubbish bin, and no hair on it. 'Watch out, mate,' said Rico, waving his beer bottle, 'some nasty Chemie bastard's shat all over the bowl.' The giant grinned for a moment, then shoved us in the corridor and slammed the door behind him. 'See,' Rico whispered. 'Told you it'd work.' I nodded and looked at his back and heard the voices and the chanting and the smashing of bottles coming from the carriage ahead of us.

The corridor was empty. I looked out the window; we were passing through Möckern, the train slowing. 'Now,' I said, 'we can get off now,' even though I knew Rico didn't want to get off, even if he was afraid just like me, 'cause he was the best welterweight in town.

'No,' said Rico, 'no, not now, what about our scarves, come on, we'll keep it up, we'll get to Leutzsch, we're not giving up, we'll get to the stadium, to Leutzsch, Danny, we'll shit on BFC...'

The toilet door opened on the giant fiddling with his belt, then he shoved us aside and swayed down the corridor to the next carriage. Glass crunched under his feet, I only saw it now, pale glass from the window in the compartment door, and in among it lay green and brown shards from beer bottles. 'Listen, lads,' the giant stopped and turned around, 'come with me, it's better to stick together, with the cops and that, it's better.' He slurred his words, I could hardly understand him, and his big head wobbled around as he spoke. 'Gotta stick together, gotta look after you, lads. For BFC, all together, all together for BFC.' He smiled and leaned his head on the wall.

'Right,' said Rico, 'all together, all together for BFC.' The train stopped; I saw the big Möckern sign right outside the window. Rico headed after the giant, 'Come on, Danny, get moving,' the train moved off again, and the sign disappeared. The giant yanked the compartment door open, a few shards of glass fell on his bomber jacket... and then we were right in the middle of the BFC bastards, clutching our empty beer bottles with both hands.

They'd quietened down now, we just heard singing and shouting from the other carriages now and then. 'We're gonna smash up Leutzsch, we're gonna smash up Leutzsch, we're gonna, we're gonna, we're gonna smash up Leutzsch...'

'Five minutes,' someone said, 'five more minutes to Leutzsch.' I peered between the people to the windows, saw the little river alongside the train and beyond it the Leipzig-Möckern allotment gardens. Five more minutes to Leutzsch.

'To victory!' said a man next to us, raising his beer bottle.

'To BFC, to victory.' Arms holding beer bottles rose out of the crush, 'to BFC, victory for Dynamo, come on lads, drink up, everything's allowed here.' Rico raised his beer bottle at the guys next to us and I pretended to drink out of my empty bottle too. The dribble at the bottom ran into my mouth and I choked it down. The giant was standing a few metres away from us, and he smiled down and winked at us. The train slowed, someone yelled, 'Leutzsch! I can smell it, we're in Leutzsch!' and then everyone pushed their way to the broken door, along the corridor and past the toilet, I dropped my bottle and grabbed Rico by the arm, bellies and backs, arms and legs blocked us in and tore us along and shoved us ahead, shards crunched beneath our feet, 'Hooray, hooray, BFC rules OK!' the doors were yanked open while the train was still moving, the first ones jumped onto the platform and onto the tracks on the other side, the giant roared something behind us like an animal: 'Let's get going, let's get going,' and as the train stopped with a screech Rico and I stumbled outside, and we were in the middle of the BFC fans still, all storming out of the other train doors and dragging us along.

Rico had grabbed my arm now, so hard it hurt, but I didn't care, I didn't want to be on my own, we ran down the stairs, don't fall down whatever you do, all the legs, they slowed down in the tunnel, 'Hooray, hooray, BFC rules OK!' A couple of men pissed against the wall even though the tunnel already stank really badly of piss, bloody BFC bastards, 'We're gonna smash up Leutzsch, we're gonna smash up Leutzsch, we're gonna, we're gonna, we're gonna smash up Leutzsch...' My sleeve had slipped and I saw my watch – we'd been playing for ten minutes already. We went up the stairs and out of the tunnel, past the station building to the street.

Rico let go of my arm, stood on tiptoes and jumped up a few times. 'Shit, Danny, we're...'

'What?'

'Berlin, Berlin, we're hardmen from Berlin...' Some guy yelled right in my ear and I ducked, I couldn't see the station, the houses, the street, only men, only BFC, there were army boots next to me and I saw how small my feet were. Rico stumbled and fell into my arms.

'We... we'll never get out of here, Danny...' I held onto him. A few boys our age, maybe a bit older, were a couple of metres ahead of us, laughing and clapping and chanting along. 'Chemie, Chemie, we shit on your Chemie!' But we were Chemie, we wanted to get to Chemie, we wanted to get to our Dammsitz terrace where I used to sit with Dad when I was little, we had to get to the main entrance, but on either side, far away above the crowd, I saw the treetops of the Leutzsch Woods, hardly any leaves left on the branches, it was autumn already, we held each other's arms and walked with the BFC fans, with the BFC bastards, if Dad saw me now, to the side entrance where the away fans went. We held each other's arms and stayed quiet, even though they kept yelling and chanting all around us, 'Berlin, Berlin, we're hardmen from Berlin, Chemie, Chemie, we shit on your Chemie!' Rico clenched his fist and I pressed mine against it. He smiled and leaned over to me. 'Only a Leutzscher is a Deutscher,' he whispered in my ear.

'Only a Leutzscher is a Deutscher,' I said quietly. I could see the stadium now, the clubhouse and behind it the standing terrace, green and white from the Chemists' flags and scarves, and above the standing terrace the scoreboard: Home 0 – Visitors 0. At least everything was more or less OK there, still.

I bumped into the man in front – no going further. Ahead of us, they were yelling, 'ACAB, ACAB... Pigs in shit, like Chemie, pigs in shit, like Chemie...' They were pushing and shoving from behind, we were wedged between bellies and backs, then suddenly we moved forwards again, we ran a little way, then the crowd jammed up again, and then the first men started backing up, and then the first men turned around in front of us and ran towards us, and we turned around and ran as well, and when we looked back we saw swathes of white smoke above the crowd, right in front of the side entrance.

'ACAB, ACAB, shit like Chemie.' A couple of guys running next to us had tied scarves round their faces, 'Tear gas,' someone yelled, 'tear gas.' And now I felt a biting and stinging in my nose, but maybe I was just imagining it, it had been way ahead of us, but when I looked over at Rico he seemed to have tears in his eyes, but maybe it was just sweat running down his face.

'Shit,' I shouted, 'let's get out of here, let's get out of here, Rico!'

'Where to?' he yelled, 'where can we go?' And he was right, the cops were behind us, and in front of us and on either side the BFC mob, pushing us along back to the road, past the station, we were running slower now, no one was yelling now, no one was chanting now, they were marching in silence to Pettenkofer Strasse, that was where our Dammsitz terrace was, and we... we were marching along with them.

'Danny, Danny, listen.' Rico had his hand on the back of my head and his face was right by my ear. 'When they've passed our terrace, by the entrance, you know, if they want to get to the away terrace, then... listen, will you, just listen!'

'Yes,' I said, 'yes, Rico, yes.'

'Please, Danny, we've got to make it.'

'Yes,' I said. 'Yes, we got to.'

'... then we'll make a break for it, to our terrace, to the Dammsitz terrace, Danny, you hear! We'll push our way through somehow, Danny, we'll just sit down on a garden fence or something, we'll wait 'til they're gone, it'll be fine, it'll work fine, yeah. Chemie, Danny,' and he whispered even lower, 'just think of Chemie, Danny.'

'Yeah,' I said, 'yeah, Rico.' And I thought of Chemie, and I thought of our Dammsitz terrace, of the green-and-white fans there and the high fences that would keep us safe, but we didn't get to the Dammsitz terrace even though we could see the top of it, 'cause we slowed down even more on Pettenkofer Strasse, then there was no going forwards, and again I saw guys with scarves covering their faces, or their hoods pulled low like boxers entering the ring, running through the crowd. Hands stretched up holding bits of paper, entry tickets, they were entry tickets, 'We want in, we want in!'

'Cops,' said Rico next to me, 'there must be more cops.'

'We want in, we want in!' But we guessed the cops wouldn't let them in 'cause again, everyone backed up, and then suddenly everyone was running every which way, some back, others forward, yelling, but I couldn't understand what they were saying and we just stood there, and then we saw the cops, helmets with the visors down, shields and clubs, edging towards us in a line.

'Let's get out of here,' I shouted, 'come on, out of here!' And Rico went for it, but he went the wrong way, he went straight for the cops, he didn't run, he walked really slow towards the chain of cops; there was a man lying on the ground at the edge of the road, another pulled him up and kicked out at a policeman clubbing him, now the cop had coshed him with the club; the man turned away and the cop whacked him on the back.

More swathes of white smoke drifting over the road and people running in the mist, and Rico just walked towards them. 'Rico,' I screamed, 'Rico!' but he didn't even turn round. I ran after him, I caught him by the shoulder and held onto him.

'Danny, the stadium, we gotta get into the stadium! To our Dammsitz, Danny!' Tears running down his face, and again I felt that biting and stinging in my eyes and nose and held my arm in front of my face.

'Forget it,' I yelled, 'jeez, forget it!' I dragged him away,

away from the cops and the tear gas, and now he looked at me, his eyes really big, he wiped the tears away with his sleeve, shook his head and looked around like he'd just woken up. And then we ran after the crowd, towards the station. I turned back round; the cops were standing behind the fog, forming a wall out of shields.

I ran into something and fell down. 'Watch it, son!' My knee hurt and Rico squatted next to me. I looked up at a man standing by a car. 'Everything alright, son?'

'Yes,' I said, and the man punched the car's side window with his bare fist, once, twice, until it shattered, then he kicked off the wing mirror, climbed on the bonnet and jumped on the windscreen with both feet, then he ran across the car roof and down the other side. There was crashing and splintering everywhere as they all started in on the parked cars. They danced, yelling over the roofs, ran up and jumped at the doors, 'We're gonna smash up Leutzsch, we're gonna smash up Leutzsch, we're gonna, we're gonna, we're gonna smash up Leutzsch,' and now they really were. I got up even though I had no strength left and wished I could just stay put, and I walked slowly with Rico along the middle of Pettenkofer Strasse, the road we'd walked so many times with our scarves that were now on the tracks somewhere, covered in shit, and the Berlin bastards rampaged from one car to the next on either side of us, the rest of the mob ahead of us on the main road, smoke rising from there now, not white tear-gas clouds like behind us, but black fumes, and I smelled burnt rubber. The crowd scattered and spread across the main road, some ran to the station building, and now I saw the burning police Lada tipped on its side at the edge of the road, and a bit further along was a Trabbi in the same position, but not on fire. We ran onto the pavement and squatted down by a wall. 'Shit,' I yelled, 'it's like a war.'

Rico pressed himself against the wall, all quiet, staring at the burning car. There was a green police van outside the station but there weren't any cops in it, there weren't any cops visible anywhere, only Berlin bastards jumping up and down on the van's bonnet, one of them holding a green cannister. A bench came flying out of one of the station windows, the crashing and splintering so loud it was like it had landed right next to us, but actually there was crashing and splintering all along the main road and in and outside the station, the green van burning. And then... then came the shots.

Maybe we could have got out of there earlier, we probably could have got out earlier, people were running up and down the street anyway and no one would have cared if we'd run the other way, down the road and over the big bridge where the trains ran underneath, to the tram stop or somewhere, just got out of there. Maybe we should have got out when fifty or sixty or more hooligans started picking up stones from the tracks in the station, running past us and heading back to the police chain on Pettenkofer Strasse. But we didn't run away, we stayed hunched by the wall and slid closer together and watched the first lot take a run-up and sling stones, huge rocks, saw more and more stones flying and more and more hooligans with rocks in their hands storming into Pettenkofer, then some of them came running back, we slid along the wall on our knees and looked down Pettenkofer, we saw the hooligans still throwing stones, we saw the police shields, we pressed ourselves even tighter to the wall, everything suddenly seemed very near, too near, and still we stayed, and I don't know why, we stayed put, maybe we were scared to get up and run away and be back in the middle of them, have to get past them, and then we heard the shots: Bang! Bang! Bang! Pause. Silence. And then again: Bang! Bang! Bang!

like fireworks on New Year's Eve, a thin, high snapping sound that bounced around the street, almost like an echo.

The crowd scattered, some lying on the ground, everything was so near again, and I saw Rico tipping over onto the pavement and putting his hands on the back of his head like he'd been hit, and I fell on top of him and screamed: 'Rico, Rico, Rico!' and felt his body with both hands and held him tight and felt him trembling, or was that me? 'They're shooting, Danny, they're shooting, they're shooting, they're shooting.' I rolled off him and raised my head. A couple more stones flew at the cops, and again: Bang! Bang! Bang! some lying on the ground, screams, I'd never heard screams like that, then they ran past us, a white sweater, two men had him on each side and dragged him, 'cause his legs had given way and his knees jolted across the ground, a red pattern on his sweater and a clenched fist on it, his fist, red as well, scrunching up the fabric. I stood up. I stumbled against the wall and grabbed hold of it. Rico was still on the ground, punching the pavement with both fists. 'They're shooting, Danny, they're shooting... they can't just... they're shooting.' But they weren't shooting now. The crowd ran past us, back to Leutzsch station, some lying on the ground and moving their legs and writhing, and the cops walked slowly up the street. Some of them held long black guns with the barrel pointing downwards by their hips.

A few days later, I saw the dead boy's photo in the paper. Shot in the lung. He was only a couple of years older than us. There were lots of injuries too, some in Intensive Care, almost all bullet wounds, and we'd lost the game as well, four-one. We didn't go up into the top Bundesliga in that last season of the GDR League, or to the second league either, we had to go down to the North-Eastern Amateur League, southern branch, but sometimes we still dreamed.

We carried on going to Leutzsch, Rico and me, and we got ourselves new scarves, but it was never the same as before that Sunday, in the year after the Wall came down, when we played BFC Dynamo.

## RETURN, GOODBYE

There were a lot of scores to settle when Rico got back from *there* after almost two years.

They wouldn't let him back in our class, he had to go down to year seven, even though I'd been looking forward to it like crazy, and maybe we could have sat next to each other again, but Mrs Seidel would never have let us. Rico had a score to settle with her as well, with her and Mr Singer, with Mr Dettleff the Pioneer Leader, with his dad the officer, who lived in Berlin now, and with his mum as well, who'd let them send Rico there. He lived with his gran now and he didn't have any scores to settle with her, he got on really well with her, 'Old folks, Danny, the really old ones, they're almost like us, like kids, you know,' but what chance did he stand against the other adults? None, and he knew it. Alright, he'd made all sorts of plans, 'At night, Danny, that's when it was worst. Well, not that bad, don't worry, Danny, you know me, but at night, at night, Danny...' He knew where Mrs Seidel lived and at first he wanted to set fire to her flat, 'Just a little bit, Danny, just to give her a shock,' but I'd talked him out of it, 'Then her car, at least, Danny, just smash it up a bit to wind her up, so she can't drive it to the seaside,' but he didn't smash up her car 'cause he knew it would have just made it all worse, and he never wanted to go back *there*. He couldn't do anything about the adults but the other kids didn't stand a chance against his rage. He was boxing in the juniors club now, and sometimes he trained out at Motor Southeast, under 15s, even though he wasn't yet thirteen, but he was pretty tall and strong for his age, 'Press-ups, Danny, press-ups every day, and sometimes at night, the nights, you know, the nights, boom – boom – boom against the wall,' and when he was in the ring, with his head guard, mouth guard and jersey and the giant red boxing gloves on his fists, it seemed like it wasn't one of those poor bastards he was fighting, it was his dad the officer, or Mr Dettleff the Pioneer Leader, and they didn't stand a chance against his rage.

But outside the ring you didn't have to stop after three rounds and there weren't any rules, and Rico still had plenty of scores to settle. The first one was with Friedrich. Friedrich and Maik had taken over the park with their gang, our park, and I'd been waiting a long time for the day Rico came back, 'cause I knew it would be our park again then. But Rico didn't go for Friedrich in the park, he wanted to get him at school so everyone could see. 'Respect, Danny, respect, you know, everyone has to see that I'm back!'

He attacked him at breaktime, round the back by the bins – that's where Friedrich and Maik and their gang spent their breaks, 'cause the teachers couldn't see them there, and that was their bad luck in the end. We'd met before school to plan it all out, Rico, Mark, Walter and me, and Stefan had come too even though Rico didn't like him much. 'What does he want here, Danny, why d'you bring him, that biter, huh, Danny?'

'Stefan's alright, Stefan stands by us, and we need every man we can get!' And we really did need every man we could get, 'cause Friedrich had a few friends in year nine and we had to keep them in check while Rico dealt with him. 'And Maik, what about Maik? He's really strong.'

'Forget Maik. I've beaten him before, remember Danny, he won't want another go, I had him on the floor two years ago, he won't want to go down again, believe me.' And he was right, it all went according to plan, Maik really didn't want to go down again, and I wouldn't have got him on the floor, that was for sure, but he had respect for Rico, 'cause Rico was a boxer. And he felt guilty 'cause he thought it was partly his fault they'd sent Rico *there*. And maybe that's why he held back when we rushed them at breaktime. Even Little Walter wasn't scared, he had a couple of pebbles in his clenched fist so he could punch harder, 'cause Rico had egged us on before: 'We want to show them I'm back, we want to show them no one starts trouble with us!' And we forced Friedrich's gang back, only Maik stayed a few metres away with his arms dangling by his sides, while Rico got down to business with Friedrich. He had him by the neck with his left hand right away and gave him a right in the stomach and Friedrich bent double and fell against Rico and put his arms round him like he wanted to say hello, welcome back Rico. 'Give it to him, Rico, wipe him out!' And Rico wanted to keep going and get him down on the ground like he'd got Maik down two years ago...

'Are you crazy, boys? Stop it right now!' Katja came along. My Katja. Katja the head of the class council. She just strode towards us, past the bins, her head high and her arms waving like she was a teacher, and with the pretty lines on her forehead and her white Pioneer shirt with her chest stuck out underneath it, she really looked like a teacher.

'Katja,' I said, 'Katja, you keep out of it, please.' But she took no notice, even though I'd said please and she liked it when I asked her for something, she just strode past me straight over to Friedrich and Rico. Friedrich was still hanging on Rico's shoulders and Rico's fist was in mid-air right in front of Friedrich's head, but they didn't move, and when Katja stopped in front of them, hands on hips, he dropped his hand. 'Stop it right now, I said!' And they really did stop, first Friedrich stepped back, ducked down, his hand on his belly, and then Rico did too. Everyone had respect for Katja. Alright, she was a girl, but she was head of the class council and sometimes, in assembly, she held a little speech up on the stage.

'Katja,' I said, 'it's just a bit of fun.'

'Don't you interrupt me, Daniel Lenz.' She placed herself between Rico and Friedrich, looked from one to the other, and the pretty lines above her nose and on her forehead got deeper and deeper. 'If you don't tell me right now what's going on, I'll have to report you.'

'Katja,' I said again, 'it was really nothing.'

'...and you as well, Daniel Lenz.'

The year-nine boys grinned over at me, and I blushed and looked at the ground and saw Katja's legs and her blue Pioneer skirt that she wore almost every day. She had five of them at home in her wardrobe, she'd shown me when we were revising Russian.

'Who started it?'

They both looked at the ground, silent.

'You tell me now what was going on, and then we'll sort it out.'

'It was just a bit of fun. Right, Friedrich?' Rico raised his head and smiled and smoothed his shirt.

'Right,' said Friedrich. 'It was really just a bit of fun, Katja. Rico was just showing me how to do boxing.'

'Rico Grundmann,' said Katja, looking up at him.

'Yeah,' said Rico, 'so?'

The bell rang, the first bell, ten minutes to go until class. Katja shook her head. 'Rico,' she said so quietly I could hardly hear her, 'be a nice boy, please,' and the guys from year nine stopped grinning, they turned round and walked slowly back to the playground, Friedrich and Maik behind them.

'I am a nice boy,' Rico said, and he smoothed his shirt again and did up the top button. Then he came over to us.

'Come on, Danny, let's go inside.' I saw Little Walter open his fist and drop the pebbles.

'You lot go ahead,' I said. 'I'll come in a minute.'

And then I was alone with Katja by the bins; she was still standing where Rico and Friedrich had started fighting, and I walked over to her and went up really close.

'Daniel Lenz,' she said.

'Katja,' I said, brushing the end of her red neckerchief off her shoulder. 'Everything's fine, right?'

'No,' she said, and she held onto my hand, 'no, Daniel, you're supposed to watch out Rico doesn't start anymore trouble.'

'I am watching out,' I said, 'I am watching out, Katja.'

'Promise me, Danny.' At last she was calling me Danny again, and I stroked her neckerchief.

'I already did.'

'No, Danny, properly. Pioneer's honour.'

'Alright, Pioneer's honour,' and I raised my hand, which she was still holding. 'Pioneer's honour,' I said again, and put her hand on my face.

She smiled. 'Daniel Lenz.' She pulled her hand away and I bent my head down to her. The bell rang, second bell, only five minutes to go before class. She stepped back. 'We mustn't be late, Danny!'

'Please,' I said, 'stay here a minute, Katja, just a minute.'

She laughed. She took my hand and pulled me to the playground. 'Daniel Lenz,' she said, and I squeezed her hand and felt her little fingers.

Rico was standing by the door to the rear building. 'Come on, Danny, let's go.' I let go of Katja's hand and stopped with Rico and watched her walk in through the door and run up the stairs. She didn't turn around, and I saw her legs and her blue skirt through the railings.

'Man, Danny, what's up with you, leave her.' He gave

me a light punch on the shoulder. 'What's so great about her, Danny, what do you like about her so much? She only messes everything up for us with her bossing about.'

'Yeah,' I said, and then we went upstairs, Rico to the second floor, me to the third. The bell rang, longer this time, and breaktime was over.

I watched out that Rico didn't make trouble like I'd promised Katja, but it was pretty hard. Rico was still keen to mess Friedrich up, and he wanted to get Maik back on the floor as well, 'It felt good that time, Danny, always feels good when you get a man on the floor.'

'But he's scared of you, Rico, he knows you're way better than him.'

'True, Danny. But you know, him telling on me back then, that was out of order. I've still got a score to settle, Danny.'

'He's really sorry, Rico, he told me afterwards. He's got a brother, you know, he was in a home as well...'

'Where was he, Danny?'

'Oh, come on, you know...'

'Don't ever say it again, Danny, I don't ever wanna hear it again, it's a shit word.'

'Sorry, Rico.'

'It's alright. But you know, a tell-tale like Maik...' He wouldn't let it go, and I knew I couldn't stop him from beating up Maik and Friedrich, and he'd probably find a few other candidates, 'cause he'd had a whole lot of rage inside him since he got back.

'But Friedrich did keep his mouth shut when your little Katja...'

'She's not my little Katja.'

'Yes she is, come on, Danny. I know what's up. Head of the class council, Danny, she's not for you.'

'Katja's alright, she's... she's...'

'See, I'm right, aren't I? Your little Katja.'

'Stop going on about Katja, Rico. What's up with Maik?'

'Yeah,' he said. 'Maik and Friedrich, we'll get 'em both. You're in, right, Danny?'

'Course,' I said, and I looked at the ground and saw Katja's legs and her blue skirt.

Rico wanted to beat Maik up first 'cause he couldn't get his hands on Friedrich anymore, he'd stopped coming to the park and the kids from year nine looked out for him at school, and Katja kept close to Rico at breaktime, and sometimes, when she saw me playing table tennis with Rico, she smiled at me.

'Why are you so worried?' I asked her when we walked home from school together. 'About Rico, I mean. I thought you didn't like him?'

'Daniel Lenz, don't say that.' She took my hand and pulled at my thumb. 'Rico's part of the collective, even if he's in year seven now. And anyway, he's your friend, and you...'

'And me?'

'Daniel Lenz.' She laughed, and it was so beautiful that I stood still, and she pulled at my thumb. 'Come on, Danny, come on.' We went on, but I walked really slowly 'cause we'd almost got to her house. We stopped there, her standing outside the door and playing with her keys. 'Hey, Danny...'

'Yes?'

'Shall we... shall we go for a walk one day? Maybe to the East Woods. Maybe next week. Just the two of us.' She played with her keys and looked at the ground.

'Yes,' I said, 'that'd be nice.' She smiled, and she jangled her keys with one hand, and with the other hand she tugged at one end of her red neckerchief.

'Hey, Danny...'

I took a step towards her.

'Daniel Lenz,' she said, and she leaned forward and touched my mouth with hers for a moment, then she turned, unlocked the front door and ran up the stairs.

I didn't tell Rico anything about that when we went over to Maik's house later to catch him coming out; Maik spent a lot of time outside. I didn't talk about Katja to Rico, 'cause he didn't want me to hang around with her. 'She's one of them, Danny, she's not for you, head of the class council, Danny, you get it, she's really not for you.'

'Stop going on about Katja,' I said, and he really did stop complaining about her; we were outside Maik's building.

'And now?'

'We're going in, Danny, so he can't escape out the back way.'

'What if he's already gone out?'

'It's not his time, Danny, it's not three yet. His old man usually gets in around three. I've taken care of everything.'

'Are you really gonna beat him up? Think about it.'

'Jesus, Danny, don't keep trying to change my mind. He deserves it, of course I'm gonna beat him up. What's the matter with you? It's just 'cause of your little Katja, isn't it, Danny, she's turning you soft, admit it!'

'Don't talk crap, she's not turning me soft, she's not doing anything to me!' I went up to the front door.

'Wait a minute, Danny, wait!' I crossed the hall to the stairs and waited there.

'Not here, Danny, he'll see us here when he comes down. Better to wait back by the cellar door.'

And we waited by the cellar door, we leaned against the wall and listened to the sounds in the stairwell, but Maik didn't come down. We squatted on the floor and waited and listened, and then someone came down the stairs, Rico rolled up his sleeves and moved his shoulders and head to loosen up, but it was just an old granny and we let her pass. We went on waiting, it was half three already, but Maik didn't come. 'He's gone out already, let's go.'

'No, Danny, we'll wait, we'll wait a bit longer.' I could see him clenching his right hand into a fist, opening it and closing it again, opening it and closing it again. 'We'll wait a bit longer, Danny.'

'We could ring the bell, Rico, and then we'll know if he's still in.'

But we didn't need to ring the bell. We knew Maik was still in 'cause we heard him screaming. We couldn't hear what he was screaming, even though it was only two floors above us, 'cause he screamed like a stuck pig, then a door slammed, and then it went quiet again.

'Shit,' said Rico. 'Let's go up!'

'Wait, jeez, wait!' I held him by the shoulder. 'That's his old man, he must be in trouble with his old man!'

'He's stealing all my hard work, that arsehole. Let's go up!'

And he went up, and I followed him. And I knew he wasn't going up there 'cause Maik's dad was taking all his hard work off him. And he must have met plenty of kids in the home ('Sorry, Rico, I won't say it again') who'd been ground down by their dads.

We stopped outside the door on the second floor. It was quiet, but then we heard a dull thud from inside, very low, and then a groan, just as quiet. Rico rang the bell. He was a good boxer but he knew he wouldn't stand a chance against a grown-up, but he'd had a whole lot of rage inside him since he got back. He rang again, and no one answered again. He put his fist on the doorbell and the ding-dong, ding-dong, ding-dong drowned out the slaps and thuds and groans from inside. Rico drummed his other fist against the door. I looked around, looking for something to help Rico with when the door opened, 'cause Maik's dad went crazy when he'd had a drink or two, and he almost always had a drink or two, everyone in our neighbourhood knew that. There was a bucket of coal by the neighbours' door, and I stepped aside to get closer to it when the trouble started, even though I was scared and thinking of Katja, but I couldn't leave. And then the trouble started.

'Bloody hell,' Maik's old man roared from inside, there was a bang, the door was yanked open, Rico jumped back and jerked his fists up, but Maik's old man stood perfectly still in the doorway, just swaying a little bit and leaning his shoulder on the door frame. 'What do you kids want?' he slurred.

'Come to get Maik,' said Rico, and I eyed the bucket of coal.

'Maik can't come out. Bugger off.' He stepped back and was about to slam the door, but Rico had his foot in the way; he was pretty fast. He was standing right in front of Maik's old man now, I saw him making himself taller, balancing his weight on his tiptoes like in the ring and lifting his shoulders, but he still only came up to the man's chest.

'Are you deaf, boy? Take your bloody foot out of my door!'

'We've come to get Maik,' Rico said again, louder this time, and I could hear his voice trembling a bit.

'He's not in, I told you!'

Maik's old man was roaring again, and I thought he could smell the booze as he roared it out, and now Rico roared as well: 'Yes, he is!'

'Piss off or I'll swipe you one!'

'Rico,' I whispered, 'come on, Rico, let's go!'

But he didn't hear me, and when I looked in his eyes, all glassy and fixed now, he didn't even wink, and I knew he didn't care what happened next.

'Haven't whacked Maik enough yet, eh?'

'You little bugger, I'll give you a slap!' Maik's old man raised his arm and stumbled towards Rico; he held his head lowered and he ran right into Rico's fist, which looked really small in the middle of that big face. Rico was a good boxer but he couldn't just knock a grown-up over, and that one punch couldn't get Maik's old man on the floor either, but Maik jumped on his back from behind, we hadn't heard him coming, and his old man stumbled into Rico's fist again, but even that wouldn't have sent him down, except when Rico leapt aside Maik's old man lurched further forward, his hand still raised, and slammed his head against the stair post. He grunted, went down, rolled onto his back and stayed put and went quiet.

Maik was standing in the door, his face red, his nose bleeding. 'Why d'you do that?' He went to his old man and squatted down beside him.

'Listen,' said Rico, 'if you're gonna get fresh...'

I threw the coal back in the bucket. 'Come on, let's get out of here, quick.'

'Easy,' said Rico. 'I just want a word with him.' He went over to Maik and squatted next to him. 'Listen, your old man...'

'He wanted to slap you around,' Maik said quietly. 'He wanted to slap you around, Rico. That's not allowed, no, that's not allowed.'

'No,' said Rico. 'It's not allowed. He's not allowed to hit anyone.'

Maik stood up and went to the door. 'Bernd,' he called, 'Bernd, come here.' Only then did I see that the red marks on his face were handprints. Big hands. Blood dripped out of Maik's nose onto his shirt, but it didn't seem to bother him. A boy was standing in the door. He had a long face, his mouth was open, and he stared at Maik's old man, who was still lying there all quiet. 'My brother,' Maik said, 'this is my brother.'

Rico nodded at him. 'Alright, Bernd,' but Bernd was silent even though his mouth was wide open.

We dragged Maik's old man into the front room and put him on the sofa. Maik jammed a bottle of booze in between his old man's head and the cushions. Maik's brother stood next to him, his bottom lip drooping, and stared at us. Rico wiped his hands on his trousers, then went to the table and sat down on a chair. 'You know why I'm here, Maik?'

Maik nodded. 'You can go now, Bernd,' he said. 'Go back to our room.' Bernd backed to the door, then we heard him legging it across the hall. 'Rico,' I said, looking at Maik's old man, who was moving his feet, 'Rico, let's go.'

'You know why I'm here, Maik?'

'I'm not scared,' Maik said.

'I know,' said Rico. 'You're not even scared of your old man.'

'I'm not scared,' Maik said again.

'Are you sorry?'

'Yeah,' said Maik. 'I didn't want to tell on you. My brother, you know, Bernd...' He swayed and held onto the wall with both hands. 'I'm not a tell-tale, Rico, I just... I'm sorry.'

'Alright.' Rico stood up. 'Come on, Danny, let's go.'

'I'm sorry, Rico.' Maik turned away as we walked past

him, 'cause his face was wet now.

'Listen,' Rico stopped at the door. 'If you like we can box a round or two, properly, I mean, in the ring.' Then we went down the stairs, and it was about time, 'cause Maik's old man's legs had started moving faster and faster on the sofa, like he was chasing us in his dreams.

I didn't tell Katja about any of that when we went for our walk in the East Woods. I only told her what a good influence I was on Rico now, that he was really integrating into the collective with my help, and she was glad to hear it. I'd bought us ice creams up at the Palace Theatre, and now she wiped my face with a tissue.

'Don't wriggle, Danny, you're all covered in ice cream.'

'So are you.'

'No, I'm not.' She wiped my mouth with her tissue, and even though there really wasn't any ice cream on her face, I ran two fingers over her lips.

'Don't, Danny.'

'Why not?' I said, tugging gently at a strand of hair behind her ear.

'Why are you always so wild?' She pushed me over to a bench and we sat down.

'Don't know,' I said.

'I do,' she said, and she tapped her finger on my shoulder a few times until I held onto it. 'Let go, Danny.'

'Only if you come with me.'

'Where to?'

'I'll tell you when we get there.'

'To the lake?'

'No, not the lake.'

'Come on, tell me, please.'

'If I tell you, you won't want to come.' I let go of her finger and she shifted up close to me, so close her hair touched my ear.

'I will, Danny. If you're there, I'll come with you. Then I won't get scared.'

'Do you get scared, Katja?'

'Sometimes.' She shuffled even closer and put both hands on my shoulder.

'Come here a sec,' I said, and I leaned over her and undid her red neckerchief.

'No, don't take it off.'

'You look much better now.' I put the neckerchief in her jacket pocket. She smiled and blushed as red as the fabric.

'Hey, Danny...'

'Yes?'

'Did Rico really burn his that time?'

'Yeah.'

'Is he sorry now?'

'A bit.'

'That's good, Danny.' She leaned on my shoulder; she was really heavy.

'Do you like boxing, Katja?'

'Don't know.'

'Come with me, then.'

We stood up and I took her hand. We walked very slowly through the East Woods, over to Motor Southeast where Rico trained.

It was Friday afternoon and he was doing a couple of training matches, he'd told me. 'You can come over if you want, see me dancing.' And he really did dance, he danced across the ring, around his opponent, and he punched and punched. We stood at the door to the gym, Katja behind me, holding onto my arm.

'Come on,' I said, 'let's go up closer.'

'I don't know, Danny.'

'But look, Katja, look how he's dancing.' And Rico's fists were dancing on air as well, he was hitting his opponent any way he wanted. Left - left, on the headguard, and then right, in the middle of his face. Left to the body so his opponent dropped his cover, and then right to the headguard, and another right to the middle of the face. And then he danced away again, ducked under his opponent's fists, danced around him and punched and punched.

'Watch out, Rico, slow down, slow down, lad,' called the trainer, who was standing at a long bench by the ring where a few more boys were sitting, all of them looking at Rico in the ring. And Rico danced and punched again, he didn't slow down, and now he had the guy on the ropes, and now the guy sat down on his arse. 'Stop,' the trainer called. 'That's enough now, Rico. Come down, both of you.' Rico helped the other boy up and they climbed out of the ring. The trainer went up to them, put both arms round them and talked to them, quietly. I pulled Katja over to an empty bench under a set of wall bars on the other side of the ring.

I was suddenly scared Rico would complain about Katja, and I put my arm round her and pulled her close and held her tight. But he didn't complain, he looked at us and jerked both his arms up and knocked the big red gloves against each other. 'Hey, Danny,' he called. 'Watch this, you two, I'll show you something, you and your little Katja, my special guests.' He laughed and knocked the gloves together. The trainer walked round the ring and looked over at us. 'He's my brother,' Rico called from the ring and jumped up and down in his corner and knocked the gloves together, 'and she's the head of my class council.' The trainer nodded and climbed into the ring to Rico and his opponent. I'd let go of Katja and now I was just holding her hand, behind the bench so no one could see.

'Are they having a proper fight, Danny?'

'Course,' I said. 'But's it's just training.' But Rico fought like it was the GDR championship in his weight and age division, after the trainer, standing between them with his arms spread out, opened the fight. Rico rushed up to his opponent, head lowered, and hit a volley of body hooks to the jersey, then he danced a few steps back, let his left fist fly, over and over again, and to finish off he slammed his right fist to the boy's headguard. But his opponent wasn't bad, 'Counter, Ralf, counter,' called the trainer right next to them, and he countered and caught Rico once, twice with his right hand, hitting straight over the top of Rico's left. Katja squeezed my hand. 'Don't worry,' I whispered in her ear, touching it very slightly with my lips, 'Rico's good.' And Rico really was good, he was getting better and better, he worked away at the guy with his jab, he didn't let him anywhere near, he gave it to him left - left - right, so the guy stumbled against the ropes and yanked his fists up in front of his face. 'Slow down, Rico, slow down!' called the trainer, but it was too late, the guy stumbled and sat down on his arse. 'Danny,' Katja whispered next to me, 'Danny.'

'Don't be scared,' I whispered. 'He'll get back up.' She squeezed my hand behind the bench, and Rico danced around the ring and laughed over at us.

And then it was goodbye. We'd been to the East Woods again and we were walking home. We passed the swimming baths, heard screaming and sometimes splashing behind the fence when someone dived off the three-metre board.

'Hey, Katja...'

'Yes?'

'We... we could... go swimming one time, I mean,

maybe at the weekend.'

'Oh, Danny, no, I'd rather not.' She'd tied her neckerchief back on, and she wrapped one end around her finger.

'But I can show you my dive, head-first, straight as a rod!'

'But my legs, Danny...'

'What's the matter with your legs?'

'Oh, they look terrible. I've got really thin legs, and they're so white.'

'I don't think so,' I said. 'Don't talk rubbish, Katja!' I stood in front of her. 'Stay there a minute.'

I put my hands on her shoulders, then I took a few steps back and looked at her white socks and the white skin under her blue Pioneer skirt. 'No,' I said, 'can't complain. You're lovely. You're beautiful, Katja, and your legs are too.'

'Oh, Danny.' She took my hand and we walked on. When other children came towards us we let go of each other, only for a minute, and then we held hands again and walked close, side by side. We'd almost got to her road. 'Hey, Danny...'

'Yes?'

'We can't go swimming, we really can't.'

'Then... then let's go to the cinema. The Palace Theatre's showing *My Name Is Nele...*'

'I've seen it already, Danny.'

We stopped outside her house. She let go of my hand, went to the door and leaned her head against the glass. 'Daniel Lenz,' she said. I ran my hand over her hair and she turned, fell against me and held me tight. 'I don't want to, Danny, I don't want to, but we're leaving tomorrow.'

'Who... who's leaving?'

'For the West, we're going to the West, Danny.' She

pressed her face against my shirt and I felt her voice inside me. '... to the West, Danny, we're leaving... leaving the country.'

'And... and you?' I asked, even though I knew what it meant, going to the West, lots of people were going to the West, and there were a few empty seats in our classroom already. Leaving. Never coming back.

'Daniel Lenz,' she said, holding me tight. She didn't cry, she was head of the class council...

'No,' I said, 'don't leave, you're not allowed!'

'Look out for Rico, Danny, and you, don't you get in anymore trouble please, promise me.'

She really wasn't crying, and I bit my tongue and said: 'Alright, I promise, Pioneer's honour.'

She let go of me and backed towards the door. 'I'm sorry, Danny.' I went to hold onto her, didn't want to let her go, but she leaned forward, and I stopped, and she touched her lips to mine, just for a moment. She smiled and it was so beautiful I had to hold onto the wall. She undid the top button of her collar and untied her red neckerchief. 'Here, Danny, I won't need this anymore.' She folded it neatly and put it in my chest pocket. I still wanted to hold onto her and I wished we were grown up and could hug and kiss for ages and ages, like the grown-ups in films.

But there was no goodbye. And she didn't give me her neckerchief either, even though I often imagined it and dreamed of it. She was just gone and never came back. She used to sit in front of me, and one morning her seat was empty. Mrs Seidel didn't say anything about it and didn't mention her, none of the teachers talked much about the empty seats in the classroom but we still knew their parents had taken them to the West. Those stupid idiots had just taken Katja away from me. I had a score to settle with her parents, even though I knew I'd never get a chance.

Rico consoled me and said I'd see her again someday, 'Believe me, Danny, she'll be back, I came back too, believe me, Danny, she'll come back one day,' but I knew I'd never see her again.

Rico couldn't come. He was over in Zeithain again, with almost a year left to go. Maybe he'd have got a day-release pass, not that that was likely, but I hadn't even written to him. I could have visited him, with his gran or on my own. I'd have had to apply for a visitor's pass first and then we'd have sat at a table together, with his gran or on our own, and then I'd have told him.

But I hadn't done all that, even though I would have had time, and now Mark was in his urn. The grave was covered in so many flowers and petals you couldn't see the snow, and now they put the little urn in the hole in the middle of the grave. There was a little hill of earth next to the grave. The grave was small too, so small I was scared there wouldn't be room for the big wreath we'd got him.

We stood at the very back of the queue, which wasn't all that long, and I stood on tiptoe and looked over the other people's heads. There it was, our wreath, and it didn't look that big anymore on the small grave. We'd wanted to lay it ourselves, but one of the cemetery staff had taken it off us before we went in the chapel where the urn was, and the family and the other people. Pitbull didn't want to let go of it, 'It's our wreath,' he said, 'what d'you want with it?' but I'd put my hand on his shoulder and he'd calmed down and let go of the wreath and kept his eye on the guy until we were in the chapel and took off our hats. We'd put them on especially, so we could take them off again.

'Remember at Walter's?' Pitbull whispered next to me. The people ahead of us took a couple of steps and then stopped again. 'Remember his parents, his mum screaming...' I put my hand on his shoulder and he went quiet again.

I felt Paul's shoulder against my arm. I looked at him.

He was white in the face. He gave me a wonky grin. 'You go first, Danny,' he whispered. I looked at Pitbull; he nodded. There were two people I didn't know ahead of me. I looked across the cemetery, you could see the fields from here, black and white, snow and earth, and then it was my turn and I looked down at Mark. Two cemetery staff were standing by the grave holding little buckets, one full of petals, the other one with earth. I dropped first flowers and then earth on Mark's urn. Weren't you supposed to take three handfuls? I looked at the urn again and moved my lips, then I turned around. A little way off were his parents and his sister next to them; I hadn't seen her for years and I couldn't even remember her name. She was pretty short and thin, and she swayed on her thin legs. Mark had told me once that she had a kid already. I bit my tongue and walked over to them.

I stood in front of his mother, and when I held my hand out to her she hugged me. She pressed her face to my neck. I didn't know what to do with my hands so I put them on her back, carefully. I felt her heart, but perhaps she was trembling. Pitbull was behind me. I stepped aside to Mark's dad and held my hand out to him as well. He shook it for a long time. 'Thank you for coming,' he said quietly.

'Of course.' And then I said, even though I didn't want to, 'He was the best.' Mark's dad smiled and I saw his face working. I nodded at Mark's sister and held out my hand, but she turned away. Behind me were Paul and Pitbull, and I walked slowly back up the path and watched them shaking Mark's dad's hand and distorting their pale faces, and then I looked past them at his grave. The two cemetery guys were still standing there with their little buckets, but no one else came to throw earth and flowers on him.

'What now?' Pitbull and Paul were next to me.

'Let's get out of here,' I said.

'Yeah,' said Pitbull, 'let's go and have a smoke.' We walked up the path between the graves and I turned back round, and then again, and I stumbled and Paul held onto me. One of the cemetery guys was holding a spade now. We walked to the exit.

'Did you see his neighbours?' asked Paul.

'I don't know his neighbours.'

'No, Danny, I mean the stones...'

'One of them was called Limburger,' said Pitbull.

'Like the cheese,' said Paul.

The snow was piled in tall heaps beside the path.

'Shame Walter's not here as well,' Paul said. 'Then he wouldn't be so alone, you know, Mark I mean, then they'd be...' A couple of old women came towards us. They had red faces under their headscarves and hats and they were carrying little buckets with bouquets and fir branches in them.

'They'll be buried as well soon,' said Pitbull, and we laughed quietly. We walked through the big gate and stopped at Paul's car. Pitbull got out his cigarettes and passed them round. Then he took a mini-bottle of korn out of his coat pocket.

He drank a mouthful and passed it to Paul. 'Nah, I'm driving, thanks.'

'Rubbish, you've got to drink a sip to Mark!' Pitbull pressed the bottle to Paul's chest. Paul looked at me.

'Go on,' I said. 'Don't piss your pants over a little sip.' Paul took the bottle and downed half of it, and I yanked it away from his mouth. Korn ran down his chin. He grinned, then he coughed, and it sounded like he was about to puke. I drank, then I said: 'To Mark.'

'To Mark,' said Pitbull and Paul, and I poured a bit on the snow and passed the bottle to Pitbull. 'Put it away, they're coming.'

Mark's parents were walking slowly along the main path. The others followed two or three metres behind them. A guy was walking next to Mark's sister now with his arm round her, and it looked like he was dragging her along. He was wearing black, like most of them. We weren't wearing suits, just black shirts that we'd gone to buy together before. We'd gone into town with T-shirts under our coats and bought the shirts at New Yorker ('In New York,' as Pitbull said), they were cheapest there, and we'd put them on right by the till. We'd left our jackets open even though it was so cold, so everyone could see our black shirts.

Mark's mum was standing in front of us. We threw our cigarettes in the snow. 'Come back to ours, won't you, we're having a cup of coffee and a bite to eat.' Her face was swollen and red, like she'd taken a few punches.

'Yes, of course,' I said. 'Thanks.'

'You were his friends... you always helped him.' I nodded. Mark's father put his arm round her and led her to the car, opened the passenger door and put her in the seat.

Paul searched his pockets, swaying a bit; he never could take his drink. He dropped his keys and picked them up again. He brushed the snow off them, then he unlocked the car and we got in. We drove along a country road; the cemetery was a little way outside of town. Paul didn't drive as safely as usual, he drove way too close to Mark's parents' car in front and almost crashed into it a couple of times as we followed them.

'I'd rather go for a drink,' Pitbull said behind me.

'We will,' I said, 'later. We're going to his mum's first, she wants us there.' I saw his face in the mirror. He had huge black rings under his eyes and I knew where they came from.

'Shall we go to the Green Pastures?' Paul asked, and braked with a screech; he went down to second gear.

'Watch it, will you!' I put my hand on his arm.

'Sorry, Danny, I'm a bit down.'

'Me too,' I said, 'but you don't have to get us killed.'

'It's alright, I'll watch out,' he said. Rico always used to say that when he'd driven us to visit Walter at the cemetery in a stolen or semi-legal car, 'cause he'd usually been drinking or taking something. I'd prayed every time that we'd get home alive, or only slightly injured, even though I didn't know God and didn't believe in him either. Walter used to believe in God, only a bit in the end, but it hadn't helped.

'You think he can see us now?' Pitbull leaned forwards and his head was alongside mine.

'Don't know,' said Paul. He was driving normally now.

'No,' I said. 'Mark's gone, just gone for good.'

'I don't want to be cremated,' said Pitbull. 'Better to decay nice and slowly in the earth, eh, Danny?'

I didn't answer, hoping he'd shut up.

'Remember at Walter's, Danny, he must have looked really gruesome but he didn't get cremated.'

'He did,' said Paul, 'he did burn, really.'

'Would you please just shut up, both of you,' I said quietly; I wanted to shout it.

I saw Pitbull's face in the mirror; he leaned back and looked out the window. We drove past the Leipzig Premium Pilsner Brewery and I saw his lips moving. I wound the window down and we took deep breaths in, through our noses. A tangy smell of hops, a bit like tea only way better.

Then we got there; we parked right behind Mark's parents. 'Great parking space,' Mark's dad said as we got out.

'Yeah,' said Paul, 'big enough for two.'

A car pulled up on the other side of the road and Mark's sister, her boyfriend and an old woman got out. Mark's mum waved at them, then they came over to us. 'I'm so glad you...' she said, 'Mark's best friends, he'd be so glad, he's so glad.' I looked past her at the ground-floor windows with no net curtains; that was where Big Paula used to live, the first woman Mark ever shagged, a few days after his fifteenth birthday, but his mum didn't know about that.

She turned. 'Come on, Mum.' She went to the old woman and held out her arm for her. Mark's sister and her boyfriend walked past me to the front door.

'Come on, then,' said Mark's dad, holding the door open. We went upstairs.

We were standing in Mark's room. 'I'll leave you alone in here for a minute,' his mum said. 'You can take a look around.' She stopped at the door. 'I'm glad you're here, I'm sure he's glad... I'll make some coffee. You can come in the living room when you're done.'

She went out and closed the door. We could see the backyard through the window. There was an ashtray on the windowsill. It had a fag-end in it. Paul went to the table with the decks and the mixer. Behind the record players, on the wall, were a few old Eastside flyers. 'I thought he'd stopped DJing,' said Paul, leaning forward to look at the flyers on the wall. 'I thought he'd sold his equipment.'

'No,' I said. 'He wanted to start practising again when he was clean. He wanted to get clean, one day.' I nodded, turned and looked at Pitbull.

'Right,' he said, 'he wanted to do it, that was the most important thing, he told me.'

'They haven't changed anything in here,' Paul ran his finger over the desk and looked at the dust on it. 'Everything's the same as before, right, Danny?'

'Yeah,' I said, 'everything's like before.' The only thing they'd done was make the bed, and put a blanket over it. I went to the window. There was a birthday card on the windowsill, next to the ashtray. I opened it. A miniature speaker somewhere in the card beeped the tune of 'Happy Birthday'. I closed it quickly.

'What was that?'

'Just a stupid birthday card. Let's go.'

'Not yet,' Paul said. 'Just a minute. It's Mark's room, Danny, we won't get to see it again.' He went to the wardrobe and opened it. 'Even his clothes are still here.' He took out a sweater and sniffed at it.

'Don't overdo it,' said Pitbull.

'Come over here,' Paul held the sweater out to him. 'It smells of Mark, that's what Mark used to smell like. Remember that funny deodorant he always sprayed all over?'

Pitbull took a sleeve and now they both sniffed at it. 'True,' said Pitbull, and he breathed in through his nose, sniffing like a dog. 'Smells like Mark, yeah, that's him alright!'

I looked out the window. We'd had a barbecue down there one time, when Mark's parents were on holiday. We'd built a huge bonfire but not until we were all drunk. We'd ripped all the planks off the fences 'cause we needed firewood, and then Rico got an axe and started on next door's bike shed, but someone called the fire brigade and they brought the police along.

'Come here, Danny, go on, have a smell of it, don't be like that, it's just... it's just what's left of him!' Pitbull took the sweater, came over to me and pushed it in my face.

'Are you crazy!' I grabbed him by the shoulders but then I let him go again. They were right, the sweater really did smell of Mark, just like he always used to smell, a bit of his funny spray-on deodorant, a bit of fabric conditioner, a bit of cigarettes and a tiny bit of sweat. 'Stop it, will you?' I said. 'I've got a cold anyway, I can't smell anything, put it away.'

Pitbull turned around and put the sweater back in the wardrobe. 'Come on,' I said, 'let's go and have coffee.'

Paul went to the door. 'Wait,' said Pitbull, grabbing my arm. 'You know what to say to them...'

I stopped and turned to him. He let go of my arm. 'What d'you mean?'

'The shit, Danny, you know, we tried to talk him out of it, we tried to the very end to talk him out of it, you know, Danny, his parents, if they ask...' I nodded.

Next to the windowsill, on the bedside table, was a black eight-ball and a yellow number one, his favourite billiard ball, 'the golden one,' he used to call it, 'the yellow one brings good luck.'

Paul was stood by the door, pressing the handle up and down. 'Coffee time,' he said, 'let's go and have coffee.'

'I tried to talk him out of it,' I said, tapping my finger on the wall by the door. 'Yeah, I tried it, you know, at least I tried...'

'Right, Danny, I know that, you did.' Pitbull walked past me to the door. He pushed Paul out of the way and opened it. 'Come on,' he said. 'Let's go and have coffee.'

Mark's mum was in the hall. 'Come in the front room,' she said. She held the door open for us and we walked past her. Mark's dad was sitting at the top end of the table. He was smoking a cigar, Handelsgold brand, I could smell it, and he had a full shot glass in front of him.

Mark's sister's boyfriend sat next to him, and on the other side was Mark's gran, wobbling her head. I hadn't seen any tears in her eyes at the funeral; maybe old people don't have many tears left, and I hadn't cried either.

'Sit down, go on.' Mark's dad picked up his shot glass and drank it down and pointed his cigar at the empty chairs. 'Plenty of space. No one else is coming.' We sat down. I sat next to the old lady; she didn't smell good even though she'd used a lot of perfume. A baby started crying somewhere in the flat and Mark's sister's boyfriend got up and left the room. The baby cried and cried, the old lady mumbled something, and Mark's dad nodded. Mark's mum came in, put a huge pot of coffee on the table and went out again. 'Go ahead and smoke if you like,' said Mark's dad, 'go ahead. You can smoke in here today.' Pitbull took out his pack and offered it around. 'He smoked a lot,' said Mark's dad, 'twenty a day, or thirty. Every day. I know that.' The ash fell off his cigar; he picked up the ashtray and blew it in carefully, then he passed it over to us. 'Want a round of shots?'

'Sure,' said Pitbull.

'Anke!' Mark's dad yelled, turning to the door. Mark's mum came in, carrying a tray of cups and a plate of cake, and put it down by the coffee. 'Anke!' Mark's dad was still yelling even though she was right next to him now, stroking his shoulder.

'What, what's the matter?'

'Glasses for the boys, Anke, just a couple of glasses for the boys. No one else is coming now.' He still spoke pretty loud, and we put out our cigarettes and looked at the table.

'I'll get them in a mo,' said Mark's mum, and she took the cake and the milk off the tray and handed out the cups. 'I'll get them in a minute.' She picked up the empty tray and stroked Mark's dad's shoulder with her free hand. He looked up at her for a moment, then he drew on his cigar, which was almost smoked up now, and blew the smoke at the coffee cup in front of him. 'I was just going to get some anyway,' Mark's mum said. 'We've got to drink to him, eh, got to drink to him.'

'Yes,' said Mark's dad quietly. 'Yes, we do.'

She went out and then we heard her opening and closing cupboards in the kitchen. Mark's sister and her boyfriend came in; she was carrying the baby, it wasn't a real baby anymore, almost a little kid, maybe two years old, and it looked huge in front of her little head and narrow shoulders 'cause it was wearing a big bulky suit. They sat down. Mark's sister sat opposite me and stared past me.

Mark's dad tapped his cigar butt a few times against the ashtray. 'Lads,' he said, 'we'd better stop smoking now, the baby...' Mark's sister smiled and patted the kid's head.

'Of course,' I said. 'It's bad for children, smoke and that.' Mark's sister wasn't smiling anymore.

Someone coughed in the doorway. A grey-haired woman was buttoning up her coat. 'I'll be off then,' she said, and she raised her hand and then dropped it again.

'No,' Mark's dad said, very loud again. 'Come on in, have a drink with us, you have to have a drink with us, you have to drink to him, to our boy... you have to...'

'The cake,' said Mark's mum, who was standing behind the woman now with the shot glasses, 'I got the cake specially... you were so kind... with the babysitting.' She edged past the woman to the table, put the glasses down and pulled a chair out for her. 'Here you are,' she said, 'take a seat, please.' The woman came slowly over to the table, undoing the top buttons of her coat and nodding at us, then she sat down, smoothed her coat and looked at her knees. Mark's mum picked up the coffee pot, walked around us and filled the cups. 'Cake,' she said, 'help yourselves to cake. It's fresh from the bakers. I got it this morning. It's still fresh.' She put the coffee pot down, picked up the shot glasses and distributed them. 'From Hauke's,' she said. 'Hauke's Bakery. You know it, don't you?' She put slices of cake on Pitbull's, Paul's and my plates. 'Eat up, go on, it's good cake.'

'Yes,' I said, 'Hauke's.' I smiled. Mark and I used to go there for cake scraps from round the edges of the trays, in the Zone days when we were little.

'To our boy,' said Mark's dad, 'one last drink to our boy.' He'd stood up and was holding his shot glass in front of his face, he'd filled it way too much and the liquid dribbled down his hand. 'One last time,' he said, and he stretched out his arm and now the shot glass was so far away from him that the liquid dripped on the cake plate, 'one last time, to our boy.' I saw the big baby grab at the cake, and Mark's mum picked up the bottle of Goldkrone and walked round the table, 'cause our glasses were empty.

'At least it wasn't like at Walter's,' Pitbull said, waving the landlord over. 'Another three large ones.' The landlord nodded and took away the empties. 'Remember how Walter's mum screamed?' We were in the Green Pastures 'cause we didn't want to go to Goldie's; he'd have told us off for not telling him about Mark and the funeral, and anyway Mark had liked the Green Pastures better than Goldie's.

Everything was new: the tables, the wallpaper, the bar – and the landlord was different as well. Roman had been out of the picture for a good while so we had to take more money out with us 'cause Roman used to give us plenty of drinks on the house. The landlord brought our beers; at least he was faster than Roman.

'To Mark,' I said, raising my glass.

'To Mark,' said Paul and Pitbull, and then we tapped

glasses and knocked them on the table before we drank. We'd drunk to Mark at the graveyard already and then at his parents', but that wasn't enough. We were sitting in the same corner we'd always used to sit in; we could see the pool table from there.

'They should have bought a new one,' I said. 'It was already pretty fucked up before.'

'It was good enough,' said Paul, 'you could still play on it...'

'You never could play anyway,' Pitbull tapped his finger on the table. 'You always had to get home to Mummy in time, forgotten that, have you?'

Paul stared down at his beer. 'No, that's not true. I did play sometimes, sometimes I got to stay out longer.'

'True,' I said. 'You did play sometimes. You weren't that bad, actually.'

Pitbull got up and went to the toilet.

'Danny,' Paul shifted up closer to me. 'You mustn't hit him, OK? It's not his fault, believe me.'

'Why would I hit him? He's my mate, isn't he?'

'Danny, you know he used to... the shit, you know, Danny.'

'Shut up,' I said, 'shut up.' I took a cigarette. I smoked and looked over at the pool table.

I heard Pitbull's footsteps behind me, then he patted me on the shoulder and rapped his knuckles on the table. His belt-buckle was still undone and he did it up before he sat down. 'Still stinks like it used to,' he said. He grinned and wiped his nose with his hand.

'How about a korn?' I asked.

'Sure,' said Pitbull, 'Sure,' said Paul.

'Three korns,' I called out, but the landlord didn't turn round.

'Four,' said Pitbull, 'order us four.' I called again; this

time he heard me and nodded.

'Why four?' I said, but I knew why.

''Cause of Mark, right, one for Mark, you know!'

'Are you gonna tip it on the floor, like at the graveyard?'

'Nah, we'll leave it on the table. Like if he was here, you know. That's what you do.'

I nodded. The landlord brought the shots and marked scores on our beer mats. Paul pushed one of the glasses over to the empty chair. 'And a beer,' he said. 'What if he wants a beer?'

'The shot'll do,' I said.

'No, Danny, Paul's right. He can't have a shot without a beer. Like in the old days, you know.' Pitbull turned to the bar. 'Another beer, please, mate!'

The landlord nodded, got a beer glass and held it under the tap. He was really good, way faster than Roman. I looked past the bar to the regulars' table; the same guys were sitting there drinking as in the old days. I recognized the old guy from the Zone, the one they used to call Salomon, with his long yellowish beard. He'd had a clean shave for years, fresh every morning, but one day the beard suddenly appeared and they told us his wife had died.

The landlord came and put the beer down on the table. Paul pushed it next to Mark's little shot glass. 'And now,' Pitbull said, 'we'll make a toast with him.'

'Careful,' said Paul, tapping his shot glass against Mark's. 'Don't want to knock it over.'

I laughed. 'Yeah, he'd have liked that.' I touched glasses with Mark first, then with Pitbull and Paul.

'To you,' said Pitbull, looking at the two glasses and the empty chair. I closed my eyes as I knocked back my shot. Mark had liked Jägermeister or brandy best, but we'd got him a korn.

'Have you been there?' Pitbull took out a cigarette and put it next to Mark's shot glass.

'No,' I said, 'I haven't been there yet. And stop all this shit!' I picked up the cigarette and lit it.

'That wasn't for you, Danny!'

'I said stop all your shit, that's enough!'

'And why haven't you been, are you scared or what?'

'No,' I said. 'But what's the point of me going there?'

'I walked past one time,' Paul said, leaning over the table and inserting his torso between us. 'I only stopped for a bit though. The door's nailed shut now.'

'You can get in round the back,' said Pitbull, 'through the cellar window.'

'You've been there, then,' I said, trying to look him in the eye, but he closed his eyes when he noticed, and then he looked down at the table.

'Yeah,' he said.

'And did you see anything, was it worth it?'

'I sat down on the stairs, Danny. That's where he was sitting. It was funny, kind of funny.'

'Did you see anything, did the cops leave anything...'

'It smelled,' he said. 'Alcohol. There were stains on the stairs, they'd cleaned up. Alcohol, Danny.'

'You know,' said Paul, 'sometimes I imagine it, I can't help it, how he looked then, at the end, I mean, when he'd been dead... I can't help it, sometimes I imagine it, it just comes into my head.'

'Yeah,' said Pitbull. 'Same here. You know, I sometimes even dream of him. Drinking together, like the old days, you know. And sometimes he says things to me, says stuff...'

'No wonder,' I shifted my chair a bit further from the table. 'No wonder he's angry with you, I mean.'

'What are you talking about, Danny? He's not angry

with me, he's not. Why would he be? No, Danny, you can't...'

'Oh yeah,' I said, 'I almost forgot, you tried to talk him out of it, right. You said so before, I almost forgot that, Stefan...'

'Pitbull, my name's Pitbull, alright!'

'You were always great at that, talking him out of it.'

'No, Danny, you can't say that... no, you can't just say something like that!' He stood up and his finger was in front of my face, right in front of my mouth, I could have bitten it off.

I pushed my beer glass away and smiled at him. 'See?' I said. 'Now we're talking.'

Paul was standing behind Pitbull now, and he put his arm round him. 'Come on, Pitbull, sit back down. Danny doesn't mean it like that, do you, Danny?'

'No, Danny, you can't say that!'

'Look,' Paul said, taking his arm off Pitbull's shoulder, 'look over there, the old bloke!' He turned and pointed at the door. All I was looking at was Pitbull's finger, though, still right up in my face.

'Stefan,' I said, 'you see, now we're talking.'

'The old bloke,' Paul called, 'remember him? You remember him!'

'Leave it out, Paul,' I said. 'No one's interested in your old bloke.'

'But it's Harry,' Paul said quietly, sitting back down.

And it really was Harry. He came over to us and knocked on the table. 'Hello there, gents,' he said. His jacket was undone and I saw the butt of the gun he wore in his waistband. 'No arguing, gents,' he said, 'no arguing.'

Pitbull sat down. 'We're not arguing, Harry,' he said, looking over at me.

'Hey, Harry,' I said, pointing at his belly. 'Put your gun

round the back.'

'No, I won't,' he said. 'I want everyone to see it. Harry's not chicken.'

Harry really wasn't chicken, 'cause he wasn't quite compos mentis. He'd been running round with that gun for years, a real one, you could see the bullets in the barrel, and he'd showed it to us often enough. He used to come in the Green Pastures almost every night, and he'd bought us plenty of drinks.

'You lot haven't been in for a while,' he said.

'True,' I said. 'Not since Roman... And you, you're still in here, just like the old days?'

'Right, almost every day. Always around six. Like the old days, it's my time of day, you know.' He walked round the table and sat down on Mark's chair. 'Oh, did you know I was coming?' He picked up Mark's shot and knocked it back.

'Are you taking the piss?' Pitbull slapped the table. 'You taking the piss, Harry?'

'What's the matter, Stefan? I'll get the tab, you know me.'

'Pitbull, the name's Pitbull!'

'Oh, I forgot, sorry. What's up with you lot? You haven't been in for ages.'

'It's alright, Harry,' I said. 'Everything's fine, don't worry.'

'It was really boring without you.' Now he started drinking Mark's beer, and I saw Pitbull clench his fist.

'Just leave it,' I whispered to him. 'There's no point.'

Harry put the glass down. He leaned back. 'You'll be back in more now, you're back now, are you? And the others, you'll bring the others along!'

'Course,' I said. 'Why not.'

Harry liked drinking with young people best, even

though he was over sixty. He wasn't a perv or anything, he just wanted a bit of a drink and a chat, but one time he'd partied with a couple of guys from the youth club, they'd had their girlfriends with them, and when they were drunk Harry'd started playing round with them. He denied it later, 'It was them,' he always said, 'they wanted to get old Harry turned on,' but anyway he'd got a real kicking out of it, and he'd had the gun out with him ever since. Now he put it down on the table.

'Put the thing away, Harry,' I said.

'Nah,' he said, 'nah, I'm not chicken. Bruno knows I look out for him. Right, Bruno?' The landlord walked past us with a couple of glasses, and he nodded and smiled even though there was a gun in the middle of the table. 'Harry's got a grip on it,' said Harry, and he took a cigarette out of his pack. He was smoking Davidoff as usual; they were the best. He held the pack out to us. 'Help yourselves, gents.' Pitbull took one of his own and lit it up. I took two of Harry's Davidoffs and handed one to Paul.

'I'm playing today, don't take it the wrong way but I've got to pop off in a minute.' Harry put his gun away again. I could see the butt. I looked over at Pitbull. The cigarette in the corner of his mouth bobbed up and down, he blew smoke over the table and I looked him straight in the eye, and he lowered his head.

'You know what, Harry,' I said, 'since Roman's been gone...'

'Yeah, yeah, good old Roman, our Russian bear.' The landlord brought our beer and shots. 'Bruno's alright, Bruno's got a grip on it, right Bruno?'

Bruno smiled. 'Course,' he said. 'Going well.' He went back to the bar.

'It was better with Roman,' Harry whispered, 'but don't tell anyone, gents – he's behind bars, our Russian bear's locked away.'

'What?' I whispered. 'Still for that same old story?'

He nodded, winked at me and raised his shot glass. 'Here's to Roman, to our Russian bear.'

'To Mark,' Pitbull said quietly, but Harry didn't hear.

'When does he get out?' I asked.

Harry coughed. He held his hand in front of his mouth and then wiped it on his jacket. 'Don't know. No idea. It's his own fault. Agathe, no, Agathe was alright. She was a good woman, he shouldn't have done it.' He played around with the butt of his gun and hummed to himself. 'Agathe, Agathe, you always were smarter...' Agathe had been Roman's wife, until he attacked her with a knife when he was drunk. He only nicked her on the arm but they locked him up anyway, and 'cause of the bus driver he'd wanted to kill a few weeks before and almost did kill. Roman was crazy, but only when he'd had a drink or two, and he'd almost always had a drink or two. He called us his kids, 'kiddies,' he'd say, 'Herrrrre, my kiddies.' He rolled his Rs like a Russian, but he wasn't one. He'd been there, he said. And when he talked about Russia he'd bring us shots and beer, and we almost never had to pay 'cause we were his kids.

'Look at this,' Harry said next to me. 'I kept it.' He rummaged around in his jacket and took out his wallet. He opened it, put a couple of notes out of the way on the table, and then he handed me a folded-up piece of paper. I saw Pitbull lean forward and look at the money; Harry put it away again. I unfolded the paper; it was a newspaper article about the bus driver thing. Next to the article was a little photo of Roman. He'd been really proud back then and stuck it to the bar. And we'd cut it out of the paper as well and showed it around.

'Look!' I said, holding up the article. 'It's Roman, our

old Roman!'

'Seen it,' said Pitbull, 'I've seen it before.'

'Remember that time he punched Mark in the balls,' I said, looking at Roman, 'just for fun...'

'No,' said Pitbull, 'it was 'cause he'd got fresh. Mark opened his big mouth, talked crap about the Russians, that was it.'

'Right,' I said, 'that was it.'

'Yeah,' said Paul, 'and then he couldn't play pool.'

We laughed. Paul leaned over the table. 'Show us the photo.'

'But don't get it dirty,' said Harry.

'No need to shit your pants over some stupid photo.' Pitbull lit one up and blew the smoke over at Harry. He liked Harry, actually, they'd often sat and drunk together and told stories.

'You can tell straight off,' Paul said, tapping the picture of Roman, 'you can see he's not quite right. That face. Like an animal, like a wolf. The sideburns right down to his mouth, it's crazy!'

'If he heard that he'd break your arm,' said Harry.

'Right,' said Paul, 'he would.' Roman's arms were as big as our legs and covered in tattoos and scars. The biggest scar was in the middle of his right hand; he said he'd nailed it to a table with a knife to impress some Bulgarians he was doing business with. He'd kept on telling us, and he'd even showed us the table where the thing with the Bulgarians happened: a little round wooden table under the awnings outside the bar, and in the middle of the table was a notch and Roman had carved 1971 into the wood next to it. Fred had stood by that table for ages and then put his hand on the notch.

'It was boring without you, gents,' Harry said. 'But you'll be back in again, now?'

'Course,' I said. 'Course we will, Harry.'

'And when you see the others, your mates I mean, Rico and Mark and little... Walter was his name, right, when you see them, and Fred, you will see them, won't you?'

'Course,' I said. 'They're our mates.'

'Well, you say hello to them from old Harry, then!'

'Course,' I said. 'Yeah, I will.'

He drank his last mouthful of beer and then got up. 'Gents,' he said. 'I've got to go over to the regulars for my game.' He knocked on the table.

'No rush, Harry,' I said. 'We'll be here for a bit, we'll see you later.' He knocked on the table again, then he went over to the regulars' table. We used to sit there sometimes and drink and play poker dice with Roman and the old blokes, or skat or bullshit or some other card game.

'Thank God he's gone,' said Pitbull. 'I don't mind the old bugger, but he turns up and drinks Mark's drinks, just knocks them back.'

'Why didn't you tell him, Danny? About Mark, I mean.'

'It's none of his business, Paul,' Pitbull said. 'You did right, Danny.'

'I could have told him, actually.' I looked at the empty glasses by Mark's seat. 'Harry liked all of us, Mark as well.'

Pitbull stood up. 'Gotta put that beer away,' he said, grinning, and then he went to the toilet. I got up as well.

'Danny, don't, Jesus, wait, don't do it.'

'I just want to take a piss,' I said.

I walked past Paul and he held me by the arm. 'Please, Danny,' he said, 'please don't hit him.'

I took his arm and put it back on the table. 'I don't want to hit him.' Paul looked up at me, his lips moving; I headed for the toilets. I walked past the regulars' table, where Harry was playing poker dice with a couple of men. He shook the cup, the dice clattered, he grinned and nodded at me. I opened the toilet door. Pitbull came towards me. He was grinning too and his face was all red.

'The beer in here makes you piss like a horse, eh, Danny?' I stopped in the doorway. He wanted to pass me but I put both hands on the doorframe and wouldn't let him through. He took a couple of steps back. 'What are you doing?'

I heard the dice clatter in the cup; I closed the door. 'What you said before, Danny, you didn't mean that.' The toilet was small, just a urinal and a stall, and it stank exactly like it used to.

'See?' I said. 'Now we're talking.' I stood in front of him, and he leaned against the wall.

He used to be good in the old days, not as good as Rico but pretty good, he'd been a biter as well, and there were plenty of people who were really scared of him, but he'd been out of shape for years now. He wiped at his nose. 'Don't be like that, Danny. You don't mind, you don't mind a line or two.'

'No,' I said, 'I don't give a shit, actually.'

'Now and then, Danny, you know me. You never used to be like that. Remember that time, with Hasenhof...' He grinned again, Hasenhof was in my dreams, and I stepped up closer to him. He was a bit taller than me and my forehead was level with his nose.

'Why d'you do it, Stefan? Why did you do it?'

'What d'you mean, shit, I told you to call me Pitbull, what d'you want?' He shoved at my chest with both hands; Dutch courage. I stumbled back a few steps. In the old days he'd have thrown me against the door. I stood in front of him again. 'Danny, stop, stop or you'll be in real trouble! Come on, I don't want this!' He'd got up his courage, and I grabbed him by the throat with one hand.

'Why did you do it? Tell me it's not true, tell me you didn't sell it to him!'

'Please, Danny, please!'

'You did it, Stefan, didn't you, you sold it to him.'

'No, Danny, no!' My hand was on his Adam's apple and it moved slightly when he spoke. 'He was my mate, he was my best mate, my brother, Danny. You too, Danny, you are too.'

'Then why did you do it, why did you sell it to him?'

'You can't say that, Danny, you can't say it. He was my mate.'

I went to the towel dispenser and pulled out a piece of paper. I gave it to him.

'Why are you like this, Danny, why are you so mean to me?'

'You know why.'

He went to the sink and I saw his face in the mirror. He pushed his sleeves up, his arms were really thin, no, he'd been out of shape for years now.

'Listen, Pitbull,' I said. 'How about a round of pool? Just the two of us, one round. You used to be really good.'

He turned round to me, water dripping off his face. 'You really want to?'

'Sure, why not.' He took another paper towel and dried his face.

'But don't be angry with me anymore.'

'No,' I said, 'you're my mate.'

He smiled. 'One more go,' he said, 'just a little nose. Just for the game, you know.' He took a baggie out of his pocket and shook a little heap on the back of his hand. 'Don't look like that, Danny, don't stare at me like that.' I turned away and heard him snorting. 'You go ahead,' he said. 'Get the table set up.'

'But you're coming...'

'Course I'm coming, where else would I go?' He laughed. I went out.

The regulars were still playing poker dice. Salomon, the old Zone guy, was holding the cup in both hands and shaking it like a cocktail mixer. I went up to the bar. The landlord was writing something in a little book. 'The balls for the pool table,' I said.

'Just a sec,' he said, writing numbers in the book.

I turned round. The old man at the regulars' table was still shaking the dice. 'Get on with it,' someone yelled.

Paul was sitting all alone at our table in the back corner. I waved at him but he didn't see. 'The balls,' the landlord said behind me. I turned back to him and he handed me the little open box holding the balls. 'Eight marks for an hour.'

'OK,' I said. I took the balls over to Paul. An hour used to only cost six marks, in the old days. I heard footsteps behind me, probably Pitbull. I put the balls on our table. Paul looked at me, then he picked up the yellow one and rolled it slowly across the table. Pitbull was standing next to him now; he took the one and put it back in the box.

'Me and Danny, we're playing now, like we used to. Right, Danny?'

'Yeah,' I said. 'Let's see if you're still any good.'

'Haven't played for at least a year. But I'll still be good enough to beat you, Danny.' He laughed, then he picked up the balls and went over to the pool table.

'Come on, Paul,' I said. 'Bring a chair, you can watch.'

He put his cigarettes in his pocket and picked up his beer. 'I was scared you'd make trouble, I thought you two would...'

'See?' I said. 'Nothing happened, don't worry so much.'

'Don't be angry with him, Danny. He didn't want it, he didn't know...'

I took my beer glass; Pitbull's was empty. We went over to Pitbull, who was already leaning over the pool table. I put my beer on an empty table by the window. Pitbull had set up the balls and was taking the black triangle away again. He put it on top of the big lamp above the pool table. 'Time to get serious,' Pitbull said. He took a cue from the rack on the wall.

I took one too, I held it under the light, twisted it, then I took a different one. 'Point was a bit wonky,' I said.

'They're all a bit out of whack,' said Pitbull. 'They're the same ones as before.' He took the cue ball and put it on the dot. 'I racked up, so I'll break.'

'No, that's not fair,' said Paul. 'You're only playing one round, right?'

'We'll see,' I said.

'I racked, I break,' Pitbull said again. He chalked his cue, then he put the chalk back on the edge of the pool table. 'Remember, Danny? That's how we always used to do it.'

'Go on then.'

'No,' said Paul, 'it's not fair, if you're only playing one round it's not fair. I'll toss a coin.' He dug around his pocket and took out a five-mark piece. 'Heads or tails, Danny?'

Pitbull leaned his cue against the table. 'That's stupid, with a whacking great five-mark piece. Hold on, we'll do it differently.' He walked past us to the bar. I saw him talk to the landlord, who gave him something, and he came back to us. 'Might as well do it properly!' He was holding a pack of cards, and he put it on the pool table next to the cue ball. 'And just so you don't think I'm cheating, Danny, you can shuffle.'

'You do it,' I said to Paul. He picked up the cards and shuffled them. He held one fan of cards in each hand and pushed them together, he made the shabby pack dance between his fingers, pulled it apart like an accordion, slid two piles of cards into another, three or four times, he smiled and put the cards down on the felt. 'Off you go, then.'

'You go first, Pitbull.' He turned over the top card.

'Jack, jack of spades,' said Paul. I took my card. 'Eight, eight of hearts,' said Paul. 'You break, Pitbull.'

'That's what I said – I rack, I break.'

'Pub rules,' said Paul, 'as usual.'

'As usual,' said Pitbull, and he picked up the cue ball and put it down a bit to one side of the dot. He chalked his cue again, then he leaned down and slammed the cue ball, without aiming much, onto the left side of the triangle, right between the second and third balls. That was his shot, he always did it when he started the game. Almost every time, he got a striped ball in the left centre pocket, and now all fifteen balls rolled around, the triangle collapsed, and only the yellow stripe ran calmly to the right cushion and from there to the other side, to the left centre pocket. That was his shot; when he played it too hard he pocketed the cue ball on the top left, but it had worked again this time. It was a Green Pastures shot that only worked when Pitbull had racked up and we played by our pub rules. 'Stripes,' said Pitbull, walked around the table and aimed at the next one. The green stripe was right in front of the top left pocket, and the cue ball was well placed, right behind it, a bit away from the cushion. Pitbull squeezed one eye shut, moved the cue back and forth a few times between finger and thumb, and potted it neatly.

'Granny shot,' I said.

He took a few steps back and looked at the table. 'So? Watch this, though, look at this one!' He knocked the red right on the arse, but he didn't hit it gently enough and it rolled up to the cushion a bit above the right centre pocket and stopped there. 'Shit, I slipped, did you hear that, Danny?'

'Shit happens,' I said, and picked up my cue. I looked at the table. My red spot was by the bottom left pocket, but the cue ball was pretty far away and a couple of spaces were so tight I wasn't sure I'd get it through them. I walked round the table. I leaned over and looked between the balls. I put my hand on the baize and placed my cue.

'Remember playing that ten-round match with Mark, Pitbull? He wiped the floor with you, eight-two, wasn't it?'

I shut one eye and looked down the cue and the cue ball all the way to the red ball in front of the pocket. I had to catch it slightly on the arse. 'Seven-three,' Pitbull said behind me. 'It was only seven-three. And I beat him almost every time after that.' The cue ball rolled between the others, it was really pretty tight, it hit the red right in the spot on the arse where I wanted it, and sank it. The red didn't go fluidly into the pocket, it heeled a bit before it fell, and we heard it rolling through the table down below. The balls used to get stuck sometimes in the old days, and we had to lift up the table after the game, three of us 'cause it was so heavy, to get the balls back out the big opening at the front.

'Nice shot, Danny,' said Paul.

I went over to the empty table with my beer and drank it down. 'Three beers, three shots,' I called to the landlord, who was walking between the front tables with a tray. He nodded.

'Come on, Danny, shoot.'

I lit one up, took a few drags and put the cigarette in the ashtray. I went to the pool table, chalked my cue. I leaned over the table. My yellow one was a tiny bit below the right centre pocket, quite near the cushion, I had to tap it really gently, and I did tap it really gently. It twisted in and rumbled through the table's insides. 'Two-two,' I said. Pitbull was standing next to me now, smoking as well. 'Look,' I said. 'There under the cushion, Mark's burn mark. Remember how Roman got all worked up?' I put my finger on the little black hole in the felt.

'Shup up and play, will you!' I potted the blue two, it wasn't a hard shot but I hadn't paid attention to the cue ball and it banged into the black eight, which rolled slowly down to the left pocket. 'That won't go in,' said Pitbull, and he was right. He still had a good eye. The eight stopped by the short rail. I walked round the table, then back again. My spots were all at the top, the cue ball was down by the eight and I couldn't play any of them directly 'cause Pitbull's stripes were in my way. I cushioned the cue ball on the right, just gently, it touched my purple ball, the seven – I'd forgotten the numbers of the colours long ago – and then it stopped.

Pitbull's turn. The barman put the beer and shots down on the empty table. 'How's it going?' he said.

'Fine,' I said. I drank a mouthful and watched Pitbull walk around the table a few times, moving his head from side to side and ducking like a boxer.

'You're a clever one, Danny,' he said, running a finger down the edge of the table. 'But if this goes well I'll get mine anyway.' I'd positioned the cue ball so he couldn't play his striped red directly, still up in front of the right pocket. He had to play against the bottom rail, Mark had always liked playing those cushion shots, 'cause when they worked out and the ball fell, you were the greatest. And Pitbull was the greatest, even as the cue ball was still heading for his red I saw that he'd pot it. 'Yes!' Pitbull punched his fist in the air. He picked up his shot glass and downed it. He was in a good mood again, he'd probably forgotten me grabbing him by the throat in the toilets.

'Almost as good as Mark,' I said.

'Shut up, Danny, I was always better than Mark, and you know it!'

'When did you and him last play?'

'Don't know, must be about a year ago, probably longer.' He wiped his mouth and walked slowly back to the pool table. The chalk squeaked as he twisted it against the tip of his cue.

'And when did you last see him?' He was already leaning over the table and aiming at the striped orange, probably wanted to play it into the left centre pocket, and now he straightened up again.

'What's this about, Danny, you said you were gonna stop.'

'I'm just asking.'

'That's not fair, Danny,' Paul said. 'Pitbull's got to concentrate.'

'I just asked him.'

Pitbull bent back over the table and took his shot, but he didn't sink the ball. 'It's your chatting, Danny, that was you, that was.'

'Listen, if it bothers you when I do a bit of talking...'

'Alright,' he said, 'it's alright, Danny.'

I played the purple solid but I didn't hit it properly; I was out of practice. Pitbull played the striped orange again for the left centre pocket, but he was a few centimetres short and it bounced back from the corner. 'Ah, shit!' I'd seen his arm trembling as he shot, just a little bit, but it was enough. I drank my korn and went to the pool table. I chalked my cue.

'Remember when we caught you cheating that time?'

'I never cheated,' said Pitbull. 'I don't need to.'

'You knocked it in with your hand, but Mark saw you.' I slammed the purple solid into the bottom left pocket, straight past the eight. I only had three balls left on the table, and I potted the blue straight off.

'You must have been practising secretly,' said Pitbull. I played the brown to the left centre pocket, but the angle was too small and it bounced off the cushion and rolled into the bottom half. Pitbull played his striped green but he couldn't sink it, it stopped right in front of the pocket. 'Just lined that one up for next time,' he said. I only hit the cushion as well, but I was in luck, the orange ball rolled in a clean straight line into the opposite pocket. 'Lucky fluke,' said Pitbull.

'Part of the game.' I downed a mouthful of my beer. Only my brown ball was left pretty much in the middle of the table. The cue ball was up by the cushion, I could try to knock the brown on the arse and play it into the centre pocket, the left one, 'cause it was closer to that one, but then I'd have had to pot the black in the other centre pocket, and that was tough. It was still down by the bottom left pocket.

'You know what, Pitbull, I played with Mark this one time, a while ago now, and he was so wasted, you know, it wasn't alcohol, he was so out of it he could hardly even hit anything.'

I shot really carefully, and my brown ball rolled past the centre pocket, touching the eight really gently, but that didn't matter 'cause it still fell in the pocket and rolled through the inside of the table.

'Eight off the cushion,' said Paul. 'Not bad, Danny.'

'Top right,' said Pitbull. 'Go on then, Danny.'

'And you know where he went after that?'

'Who, Danny, come on, play your shot!'

I played the eight so that it rolled up from the bottom left pocket to where I wanted it. It bounced off the short rail, ran back across the table a bit and stopped.

'Mark,' I said. 'I mean Mark, of course.'

I hadn't watched out; the cue ball was gone, I heard it rolling underneath the table. I'd probably put too much energy in, and it had rolled into the right centre pocket. I would have lost, but we were playing by our pub rules.

'He went round to see you, Pitbull. Wanted a top-up. Your turn!' I took the cue ball out of the opening and put it on the dot.

'Danny,' said Paul, 'Danny, don't, not now!' Pitbull was standing in front of me. His mouth was open and I saw his broken tooth.

'Go on, your turn!'

'Danny,' he said, 'stop it, Danny!'

'It doesn't matter,' I said. 'Everyone knew. Only his parents didn't know.'

He was holding his cue, and the tip was up by my chin.

'Danny,' he said. 'Please, I just want to play pool.'

'Go on then! I'm just talking, don't mind me.'

He turned away and picked up the chalk. 'It's not like it was anything bad,' I said, going over to my beer. 'That's just how it was.' He potted his brown ball. It was a safe shot and he'd played the cue ball with such power that it bounced off the brown, jumped up in the air and banged back down on the felt.

'Great momentum,' said Paul. 'Nice one.'

'But you know,' I said, leaning on the wall, 'that time a month ago, you could have said no that time, you know what I mean. He was already in a bad way.'

Pitbull played the striped orange off the long cushion into the opposite centre pocket.

'Good shot,' I said. He didn't turn around; played

his stripe. It looked like he hadn't aimed properly, just whacked at it, 'cause it bounced to and fro off a couple of cushions, bumped the eight, which rolled back down the table, and just about made it into the right centre pocket.

'He'd been in hospital, you knew that, didn't you? You knew that, Pitbull.'

He couldn't pot the green, he only pocketed the cue ball, and he leant his cue against the pool table. 'No,' he said, 'no, Danny, I didn't know that.' I walked past him; he wanted to put his hand on my shoulder but I turned away. I put the cue ball on the dot. The eight was below the centre pockets and I had to knock the cue ball off the top short cushion to play it. I hit the eight just about on the arse and it only rolled a little way. I knocked into Pitbull's cue, it fell over, and I picked it up again. I handed it to Pitbull. 'Go on then,' I said. 'You've only got one to go.'

'I need a piss,' he said. 'I need the toilet again.'

'No,' I said, pressing the cue to his chest. 'It'll be over in a minute anyway.'

He leaned over the table and I saw his arm trembling as he aimed. It sounded like his cue had slipped but he still potted the purple ball.

'Top left,' I said. 'Finish it off.'

'Danny,' he said, 'Danny, I really didn't know. He begged me. I didn't know he was shooting up.'

'The hospital, you knew he was in there to dry out, we wrote to him.'

'No, Danny, no, you weren't there then, you were away, just like Rico.'

'Leave Rico out of it.'

My beer was all gone; I couldn't see the landlord. The eight rolled off the top cushion to the middle of the table. Pitbull came over to me, stood next to me and drank up his beer. 'Listen, Danny, I really didn't know he was shooting up, otherwise I wouldn't have...'

'What?' I looked at Paul. He was still sitting on his chair, his head leaning on the wall now, and it looked like he was asleep.

'You know what, Danny...'

We looked at the pool table. The cue ball was a little bit away from the bottom cushion; if I caught the black at the right angle I'd win the game.

'Why, why did you do it, Stefan?'

'Leave it, Danny. He would have got it somewhere else, you know that, Danny. He'd just have got it somewhere else.'

'Maybe.'

I took my cue and went to the table.

'No one knows if that was it,' Pitbull called after me, 'if that was what finished him off... if it was mine. No one knows how much other shit he had inside him. You listening, Danny?'

I looked at the pool table; the felt was pretty wrinkled in places and there were loads of stains on it, but the balls still ran pretty smoothly.

'Three beers, three shots!' That was Pitbull. I looked for the chalk. It was under the pool table; I picked it up. There were a couple of coins down there too but I couldn't reach them. I tried to pull the money closer with my cue.

'Jesus, Danny, what are you doing down there?' I saw Paul's legs on the other side of the table.

I had the money; it was a mark and three ten-pfennig pieces. I got up and put the coins on the edge of the table. 'Here,' I said, 'for petty cash.' I chalked the cue, then I bent over the table. The cue wouldn't run properly between my fingers, and I wiped my hand on my trousers. I bent back down and aimed.

I heard the landlord walking past behind me and

straightened up again. 'Alright?' he asked.

'Yeah,' I said, 'everything's fine.' I waited for him to put the full glasses on the table and the empty ones on his tray and head back to the bar. Then I slammed the eight into the top left pocket. I walked past Paul and Pitbull to the rack on the wall and put the cue away.

'Danny,' said Pitbull, 'that was my pocket, you must have slipped, you slipped.' He put out his cigarette and drank a mouthful of beer.

'The game's yours,' I said. 'But you shouldn't have done it, with Mark.'

'Danny, what... why won't you just leave it?'

I stood in front of him. 'Go home, Stefan.'

'Hey, Danny, that's... and my beer, what about my beer, and my shot...'

'Go home. Just piss off.'

Paul pushed between Pitbull and me. 'Hey, Danny, leave him, leave him be...'

I shoved him aside. 'Did you not get my meaning? I told you to fuck off. That was our last game.'

His mouth was open and I looked at his broken tooth. 'Danny, why... My beer and my...' I picked up the shot glass and emptied it over his shirt.

'No, Danny, no.' Paul tugged at my arm but I just shoved him away. Pitbull backed up to the wall and held onto it. I was scared he'd start crying.

'Don't forget your jacket,' I said.

Paul was standing next to me, his lips moving. 'Daniel,' he whispered.

Pitbull backed over to our table, where his jacket was still over the back of a chair. 'It wasn't me that killed him,' he said quietly. He bumped into a chair and turned round. I looked at his back and his black shirt. Now he put his jacket on over it.

'No,' I said, very quiet, 'it wasn't you,' but he couldn't hear me 'cause he was on his way to the door. Paul raised his hand and then lowered it again. Pitbull opened the door; he looked back over at us and then he went outside. I saw the door fall slowly shut.

The regulars were still playing dice at their table at the front, clattering the dice cup and laughing. I lit one up and held the pack out to Paul. He shook his head. I went to the pool table, took out the balls and put them back in the case. There was one missing. In the old days, we'd sometimes taken balls with us as souvenirs, from other bars around the city, but only from automatic tables otherwise they noticed straight away. We kept the balls in our bedrooms, and Pitbull had one in his cellar as well. I walked around the pool table, feeling in the pockets. It was in the right centre pocket, had to be that striped purple Pitbull had potted last, but I could only reach it with my fingertips. I took the cue ball and slammed it into the pocket, then both of them rumbled through the table's innards. I took them out at the bottom and put them in the case with the others. 'Hey, Paul,' I said, walking past him to the bar, 'can you take our beer back over to the table?' He nodded.

'I win!' yelled Harry at the regulars' table, waving at me. 'You've brought me luck, gents!' He picked up the dice cup and shook it by the side of his head. I smiled and nodded at him.

The landlord was filling a glass at the pump. I put the case down on the bar. 'The balls,' I said.

'Finished already?'

'We'll have two Jägermeisters, then we'll get the tab.'

'Pool separate or divided by two?'

'I'll get it.'

He took a Jägermeister bottle out of the little fridge and filled two glasses. 'You can take them right now.'

'Sure,' I said, and walked slowly over to Paul, a glass in each hand.

'Five minutes,' the landlord called over. 'That OK?'

'Yeah,' I said. A couple of drops of Jägermeister ran cold over my left hand.

We were standing outside the bar. It had been dark for hours now. 'Look,' Paul said, 'a taxi!'

'Forget it,' I said. 'It's not far.'

'True.'

We walked slowly down the road to the railway bridge, past the allotments. It was snowing a bit, and when I looked up 'cause I wanted to see the Big Dipper, icy flakes fell in my eyes and I wiped them away with my sleeve. Paul gave me a cigarette, already lit. I turned back again; the lights of the bar were there between the trees' branches. The Green Pastures was on the edge of town not far from the East Woods, only a few metres from the *You Are Leaving Leipzig* sign. In the old days, we'd sometimes kicked in the allotment fences and ripped out the fence posts on our way home. One time, Rico had climbed over a garden fence and chucked a few plastic chairs over to us on the pavement. Pitbull had taken two back to his cellar, one was on Mark's parents' balcony. Cops hardly ever came past here.

The street was empty and I crossed to the other side. 'Hey, Danny, wait for me!' I turned around; Paul was still on the opposite pavement. 'We've gotta go straight on.'

A train crossed the bridge, a freight train, no lights. 'It's a short cut,' I shouted 'cause the train was so loud, and I turned into the little dark road directly along the railway embankment, called Embankment Way. 'Come on!'

He ran across the road; I heard his footsteps behind me. 'It's not a short cut, Danny, it's dark as hell, you can't see a thing!' There weren't any houses here, only allotments, and most of the streetlamps were broken.

A car came towards us, 'Jesus, watch it, arsehole!' driving almost on the pavement, and the mirror brushed against my arm.

'I told you, Danny.'

'We always used to come down this way,' I said.

'Right,' he knocked on a garden fence. ''Cause no one heard us here, or saw us.'

The two Rottweilers barked. They always barked when someone came past, had done for years now; they must have been ancient. They lived on an allotment on a little hill by the embankment; no one knew who they belonged to. We'd seen a car parked outside the allotment a few times and guys lugging stuff in and out, probably dog food or gold or drugs. People told all sorts of stories in our neighbourhood about those two dogs, and the treasure in the allotment. 'Bloody mutts,' said Paul. 'Remember when Pitbull wanted to set them free?'

A car headlight in my eyes. 'Dip your lights, arsehole.'

'With Pitbull just now, Danny...'

'No, Paul,' I said.

On the corner ahead of us was the green-and-white illuminated Lotto sign.

'I know where you want to go,' said Paul. 'I don't want to, Danny. No.'

'Come off it,' I said, laughing. 'I don't want to go in there, don't worry, I don't want the lotto millions.'

'No,' said Paul, 'I know you don't.'

We'd always told each other, on our way home from the Green Pastures, that they kept the millions in there, down in the basement of the Lotto company, in big safes.

'I know where you want to go, Danny. But I don't want to go in there. I can't, I've had enough for one day.'

'You don't have to come in with me, but I owe it to... I have to, you get it.'

'Course, Danny. If they knock it down or someone moves in, then that's it, you can't ever see it again. But don't be mad at me, Danny, I can't, not today.' He took a deep breath and lit one up.

'Hey, Paul, I've even got flowers.'

'Flowers? Really, Danny?'

'Yeah, look.' I stopped, reached into my inside pocket and took out the little wooden vase of plastic flowers I'd nicked off the big family table in the Green Pastures once we'd paid our bill; that table was always empty anyway.

We walked on. We walked past the Lotto company and then down the road to the Nazi house. It was a detached house, empty for years now, probably 'cause it was right by the railway embankment. The Nazis used to meet there for drinking sessions for a while, but by the time we'd taken over the house all that was left was their swastikas and slogans on the walls.

There was a little wall in front of the house with broken glass embedded in the top, but the shards were blunt. We stopped outside the gate.

'Hey, Danny, I'll come in with you if you want.'

'You don't have to if you don't want to, Paul. I get it.'

'Then I'll stay here and wait for you and make sure no one's coming.'

'You can go home if you like, Paul, you don't have to wait for me.'

'No,' he said. 'I'll wait, you know me.'

I patted his shoulder, then I put my hands on top of the gate, braced my feet against the metal and pulled myself up. I sat down on top of the gate, then I jumped down on the other side. A path led to the house; I walked past the door and round the back. 'Through the cellar window,' Pitbull had said before. I stopped and listened. Something snapped in the bushes; we'd often seen cats here. One of the cellar windows had no glass left in it. I squatted down, pushed my feet through, and held onto the window frame. I felt a piece of glass against my hand, I let go, then I was standing in the cellar. I flicked on my lighter; there was a door ahead of me and a black spider on the wall next to me. I jumped aside. 'Fucking creepy crawlies!' My voice sounded really quiet and dull in the cellar room, even though I'd screamed.

There was a mattress in the corner and someone was lying on it. I got out my flick knife, it clicked, the blade was out. 'Hello?' I said. I held my lighter in my outstretched hand, my fingers getting warm. I stood in front of the mattress; the only things lying on it were a sleeping bag and some rags and blankets. 'Jesus, Mark,' I said quietly. I put my knife away. I knocked the mattress with my foot; perhaps he'd slept here, or perhaps the stuff belonged to some tramp. I reached into my inside pocket and got out the little vase of plastic flowers. I went back to the door and then up the stairs to the ground floor. I stopped there, lit one up and left my lighter off to cool down. I sat down on a step and looked into the hallway. The doors to the rooms were gone, and a little light fell in through the windows. The ceiling above me was slanted; it must have been the staircase up to the top floor. Mark had died on that staircase. I looked at the floor of the room in front of me, a square of yellow light. I lit a new one from my finished cigarette, picked up my flowers and stood up. I walked slowly down the hall to the stairs. Through the window, I could see the wall and the road, car headlights moving along the wall beside me, then disappearing.

I walked up a few stairs, then I stopped and leaned on the banisters. He'd been sitting on one of these steps, his chest on his knees, his arm still tied, and he'd put his hands together like he was praying. That's what the cops had told his mum, and she'd told me on the phone. It had come to him here on the stairs, he'd just stayed put and then his chest sank forward, and the last thing he'd seen had been these stupid stairs. He'd sat like that for a long time, two or three days – his mum wouldn't tell me. Some tramp had found him, then. He'd called the cops, anonymously, and the bastard probably cleaned Mark out as well 'cause they hadn't found anything on him, no money, no papers, no cigarettes, no drugs. Only the empty syringe one step down, he'd got it out somehow, probably didn't want to cark it with a needle in his arm. I sat down. I chucked my cigarette down the stairs and lit up a new one. 'Why didn't you go up on the roof?' He'd only have had to climb up the little ladder to the attic, then opened one of the hatches... We'd laid on the roof some summers and drunk. Mark had always showed us the Big Dipper, and if he'd gone out on the roof to cark it – did he know it was coming? – he'd have seen it, his Big Dipper, and maybe then he wouldn't have carked it.

I stood up, flicked on my lighter and went up the stairs. Pitbull had mentioned a stain but I couldn't see one, and it didn't smell of alcohol anymore, either. There was something; I stopped and leaned down. Someone had carved something into the wood. 'Stefan was here'. I ran my hand over the letters. I put my flowers next to it, pushed them aside a bit so they wouldn't cover the name. Then I scored a capital D next to the flowers with my knife. Then I walked back down, slowly. I opened a window on the ground floor; there was a swastika on the wall and underneath, it said RR, Reudnitz Right. I lay my arm along the window and looked out at the night. Then I climbed on the window ledge and jumped out. I went to the gate.

'That you, Danny?'

'Yeah,' I said. I climbed over to Paul.

'So?' he asked.

'What, so?'

'Hey, Danny, I'm going in there too, maybe tomorrow, you know, but not in the middle of the night.'

I nodded. We looked at the dark windows again, then we went home.

It was the last time I'd studied with her, and by the time I ran out of her house and slammed the front door behind me and kicked it so hard she'd hear it all the way upstairs in her flat, it was almost dark.

I was a bit tired, and I looked down at the pavement as I walked. It was covered in dog shit, which was hard to spot in the dark. It was the shittiest street in the whole city; everyone who lived there had a dog, or two dogs.

I'd been studying all day. I'd revised for our big chemistry exam, I hated chemistry, and I hated the girl I'd been revising with too. She'd rested her breasts on the table and stared at me greedily over her horn-rimmed glasses while she taught me the formulas and all that stuff. She was the only girl who loved me, really loved me, and she wasn't pretty, no, and I wished we could have studied in the dark, using Braille.

My mate Mark was standing on the corner. 'Hi, Danny,' he said.

'Alright, Mark,' I said, and then we slapped our right palms against each other, and then we crossed our hands like arm-wrestlers. Mark clenched his fist and I tapped my fist against it. We laughed.

'Come on, Danny,' said Mark. 'I'll get us a couple of beers from the garage, I've got a bit of cash.' He took a twenty-mark note out of his pocket and held it up to my face.

'I dunno,' I said. 'I was going to go home.'

'Aww, you can still go home later. What's that you've got with you, anyway?' He knocked his foot against plastic bag I'd leaned against my leg, with all my revision stuff in it and a bit of salt from her tears in between the books and papers. She'd put her head down on the formulas and the exercises and cried all over them so the ink ran, 'cause I'd said before I left that we'd never be together, never, and that I never wanted to study with her again if she didn't stop being in love with me (I was terrified one of my friends might find out somehow).

'But you're my rebel!' she'd called down the stairs after me.

'OK,' I said to Mark and moved the bag aside. 'A beer or two, but just quickly.'

'Course,' said Mark, and then we walked over to the garage. Mark was already swaying a bit.

We lay on the roof of the warehouse on the factory grounds right behind the garage. Mark had bought cigarettes as well, Golden American 25s, and I tried not to cough. I'd only been smoking properly for a couple of months, before that I hadn't inhaled, until the others had noticed and laughed at me. I looked over at Mark, a bit jealous that he could light up one after another, and between puffs he spat all over the roof through the gap in his front teeth. Mark had started smoking at fourteen.

I looked out at the dark buildings of our neighbourhood, blue light flickering in some windows. Somewhere out there was my mum. Perhaps she was waiting.

'Look,' Mark said next to me, 'the Big Dipper.' He pointed his cigarette at the stars.

'Great,' I said, flicking my cigarette off the roof. It landed just in front of the edge, though, and I watched it for a while, a little red dot.

'And you know what else it's called?'

'No. What?' I stroked the roof, tarred paper still warm from the day, and imagined little Estrellita lying next to me instead of Mark, and we'd – no, nothing dirty, we'd do that later in my room – we'd just lie side by side, out feet touching.

'The Big Bear. I like that. A really big furry black bear. Like Big Paula!'

'She's not that big. Only round the top.'

'What? You too...? Come on, spill it.'

'Nothing special.' Big Paula lived downstairs from Mark, and sometimes, when we came down the stairs at night, she'd leave her flat door open a crack. I'd shagged her once, with my eyes closed, and I'd tried to think of Estrellita but Paula was just too big, she moaned and groaned like a man, she lay underneath me and I didn't have to do anything 'cause every time she breathed in and out I moved up and down.

I opened up a new can and gave the old one a shove so it rolled down the roof.

'Come on, have a look, the two ends there, the four stars, they really look like a cunt. It's a V, like a classic fanny-shaped V.'

'Like V for vagina.'

'Alright, clever-dick, that's not what I'm talking about. Don't you learn anything at your posh new school? There's cunts everywhere up there! Use your imagination, Danny, that's what it's all about!'

'Alright, Mark. I'm a bit distracted.' I stroked the tarred roof and drank a mouthful of beer.

'I know, Danny,' his hand was on my shoulder. 'Your mind's on that little slut. Jesus, Danny, forget her!'

'Estrellita's not a slut, OK!'

'Jesus, Danny, Jesus, the girl's a nutter, you can ask anyone. And you're the only one she won't shag. She's messing you up!'

I drank a mouthful, I drank half the can 'cause I didn't want to answer, 'cause he was right, she was messing me up, 'cause I thought about her everywhere, even at home on the toilet and in my dreams. But she didn't want me the way I wanted her, 'I'm too bad for you, Danny, you're so good, you're so sweet, you're like a brother to me, Danny.' Sometimes I thought all the crap I got up to with the others was a bit because of her, 'cause I had to let it out somehow. And when I told her about the green nights, and sometimes she came with us, then she'd say: 'Danny, my poor little mongrel.'

'She's a little bitch,' said Mark, and there was a hiss 'cause he opened a new beer. 'Forget that dog, she'll only run away from you, and maybe she'll bite you and all.'

'Don't talk about her like that, OK?' I tapped my finger on his cheek but he just turned his head away and laughed. 'No, Mark, you can't talk like that!'

He laughed. 'Alright, Danny, alright,' and I saw him holding the can above his mouth and pouring the beer in. I tried it too but half of it ran over my chin and onto my sweatshirt. I wiped my face on my sleeve, a siren wailing somewhere, the cops driving through the night. 'Listen, Danny, they're playing our song.' He crushed his can and chucked it off the roof. I heard it hitting the ground, it wasn't loud. 'Hey, Danny, I know...' Another hiss, and I took a new can and hissed as well 'cause I had to keep up. 'Your new school I mean. I was really scared you'd get a big head, Danny, you'd forget...'

'Oh, come off it, Mark, you know it's only 'cause of my mum... I only went there 'cause of my mum!' ('Do something right, boy,' my mum had kept saying. 'For once in your life, do something right!' And I'd promised her 'cause she had to pay for the bus window I'd broken when I was drunk.)

'But Danny, all those idiots there, all those swots, Danny, they'll talk you round, you'll forget where you come from, no, I was really scared. 'Cause, Danny, you're one of us, aren't you, you belong with us.'

The siren was still wailing somewhere in the neighbourhood, somewhere in Leipzig East, and Mark said again: 'They're playing our song, Danny.' I nodded but he didn't see. He held the can over his mouth and the beer glugged in. I took a swallow as well, then another, and I looked at the Big Dipper up above us. Next to it was the moon. There was a bit missing on one side and it wasn't quite round. The one end of the dipper really did look a bit like a fanny, actually an irregular triangle, but never mind... Mark's cunt constellation. And now I was seeing Estrellita's little constellation up there, even though I only knew it from my dreams.

'Give us a fag, Mark.' He put two cigarettes in his mouth and lit them, then he stuck one between my lips. We smoked and looked at the stars.

'A dog!' Mark yelled. 'Did you hear that, there's a bloody dog coming!'

I jumped up, my beer can fell over and rolled down the roof, really, a dog barking, not far away, definitely on the factory grounds, and it was coming closer.

'They're coming,' yelled Mark. 'It's security guards, they're coming!'

'Jesus, no need to shout,' I whispered. 'You'll only get us in trouble!'

'What do we do, Danny, they must have seen us!'

'Come on, let's get down! Over there, the tree, we'll climb down and leg it!'

'No, Danny, we can't. If we go down that way the dog'll get us! I bet it's not on a lead! No, Danny, no, something else!'

Mark was scared of dogs, really terrified, 'cause the Rottweiler at Böhland's recycling yard had bit him in the leg one time and then in the arse, back in the Zone days when we wanted to nick bottles and paper one night and cash it all in again the next day. He still had the scars to prove it, and his leg and his arse nearly rotted away back then 'cause he couldn't tell anyone and we'd treated his wounds ourselves with korn and lighter fuel.

'Come on, look, the hatch!' said Mark. I saw the beam of a torch in the dark yard in front of the warehouse. The dog had stopped barking. We'd stopped breathing. I saw a second beam of light, now they crossed; the dog barked again. 'Come on!' Mark whispered behind me. He crawled up the roof to the hatch.

'It probably only opens from the inside,' I said, 'cause I didn't want to go in there; all we'd done so far was trespassing, that was a couple of hours of community service if they caught us, but I guessed, no, I knew, that we'd get up to some kind of crap down there in the warehouse. The dog was barking like crazy, it sounded like two dogs now but that might just have been the echo in the yard.

Mark had got to the hatch and was jiggling it and pulling and pressing it. 'I've got it open! I've got the bloody thing open! The bolt, those idiots didn't do it up properly!' He flipped the hatch carefully back onto the roof and put one hand inside the dark square. 'A ladder, Danny.' The dogs were only barking now and then down on the ground; I looked at the open hatch and now it seemed like something wonderful was waiting for us inside the warehouse.

Only Mark's head was poking out of the hatch.

'Listen, Mark, promise me...'

'What, Danny?'

'If we go down there...'

His head disappeared and his voice came dull out of the hatch: 'Jesus, Danny, it's like in Mühlenviertel, remember that?' In Mühlenviertel, I thought, the bloody Zone policeman caught us red-handed. We'd met up in the old buildings and factories before they got pulled down, Mark, Walter, me, Paul, Pitbull, who was still called Stefan back then, and Rico as well, once he got back.

I looked down at the yard. The dogs had stopped barking and the beams of the torches had gone too, we could have buggered off down the tree, just like that, but I didn't say anything. Mark's head popped up again. 'The beers, Danny.'

'Shit!' I crawled back to the edge of the roof.

'Come on, come on,' Mark called quietly.

'Yeah, yeah.' I grabbed the bag of beers and stood up.

'Jesus, are you stupid, they'll see you!'

'Calm down, they've gone,' I said loudly. I felt my heart beating all the way to the tip of my tongue.

'You're a nutter, Danny.' Mark vanished in the hatch again. I climbed after him. I reached onto the roof and pulled the hatch towards me, I saw the starry sky again, the Big Dipper had disappeared and taken the moon with it, then I closed the hatch. Darkness. I searched my pockets for my lighter. I heard a strange sound below me, something slipping away, the iron ladder vibrated and then I heard something hit the ground further down, and then nothing. I stared into the darkness, seeing nothing, and then I saw Mark's head in a pool of blood, still attached to his body but his body was all twisted, especially his arms and legs. 'Bloody hell, shit, bloody fucking shit!'

'Mark,' I whispered, 'is it bad? Don't mess about!'

Mark groaned quietly out of the darkness, and then I had my original storm-proof Zippo that I'd only just nicked two weeks before from the Vietcong stall outside the supermarket, and I flicked the wheel, it sparked, the wick burned, and the flame grew slowly bigger. The ladder ended a little way below me, then there was nothing for a few metres, and then there was a white VW van right underneath the hatch and the ladder. With Mark lying on the roof. He moved one leg and I knew straight away there was nothing wrong with him. Mark was a hard guy, and the doctors praised his hard bones. One time, a couple of guys with bats beat him up so bad, the left side of his head was swollen up like he had a second one growing out of it. He showed us his hospital admittance slip later: suspected fractured skull, jaw, cheek and nose, but there'd been nothing wrong with him, just bruises and swellings. His whole body was still in one piece except for a missing tooth at the front, and he was really good at spitting through the gap. We'd visited him in hospital back then; the white bed was way too big for him. When I went to take a photo of him and his second head, he grabbed the camera out of my hand (luckily that was nicked as well, from Karstadt that summer) and threw it against the wall with a yell, chucked it so hard that screws and springs went flying round the room and other patients started limping out of there. 'I never want to see what those bastards did to me again!' (We got one of them later on, or Mark thought he was one of them anyway. He sprayed half a bottle of CS gas in his face and the guy couldn't stop crying.)

'Jesus, Danny, what a crock of shit!' Mark was kneeling on the van roof, feeling his body. 'All in one piece,' he said. 'I'm all in one piece. As usual. Man, Danny, remember those guys with the bats...'

'Yeah,' I said, and tapped my cheekbone.

Mark had sat up straight and got out his original stormproof Zippo I'd given him two weeks before. I'd nicked three of them; Rico had the other one. 'Look, now I really need it at last!' Mark was more of a matches man, 'cause he'd heard one time that some guy from our neighbourhood had had his lighter explode in his hand and it blew off three of his fingers. Our lighters couldn't explode, though, they were made differently with a little sponge inside that stored the fuel. But he still hardly ever used my lighter, 'cause, as he said, 'you got to save something like this for best.'

'Right,' he said, shining the light up at me. 'Now you've got to get down here and all.'

'Shhh! Be quiet a minute!'

'Why, what's up?'

'Shut it, mate!'

We both shut up. No footsteps, no voices, no barking. Everything was fine.

'OK,' I said. 'You better catch the bag first!'

'Wait, wait!' Mark put his lighter down next to him on the van roof. I chucked him the bag of beers. Mark caught it but not properly, and the beer cans fell out of the bag on his head and on the van roof and down onto the floor. The lighter went out. 'Watch it,' Mark shouted. 'Can't you do anything right?'

'You're the one who can't catch!' I climbed down slowly until my legs were dangling in the air above Mark's head.

'Come on, just a bit more, then you can put your feet on my hands!' I hung off the last rung. 'Oh man, you've got shit on your shoe!'

'Jesus, just take the other foot then!' Then I was standing next to Mark on the roof of the van. I flicked my lighter back on. We stretched out our arms and waved our original storm-proof Zippos in front of us but it was still too dark, we couldn't see the treasures that must have been all around us.

'Let's have a beer first.' We slid down the front window onto the bonnet, and hopped down from there. The flames of our lighters had comet tails. We each picked up a can from the floor; mine was open a bit and had foam dripping out. We said 'Nastrovye' and tapped our cans together, then we drank.

'Give us a fag, Mark.'

We smoked and exhaled the smoke with a low whistle; girls always liked that, not that there were any girls around.

'Right,' said Mark. 'Now we need some proper light.'

'Hold on, hold on. Let's see if there's any windows first. Don't want them to see us.'

'Good one, Danny.'

There weren't any windows. We couldn't see the night's lights from outside anywhere, the flames of our lighters didn't reflect off any glass. Most of the walls had shelves along them, up to the ceiling. There were boxes all over the place. In one corner were these dark workbenches with all this stuff on them, and next to them was a big iron door we'd seen from outside. 'Hey,' I said, 'how are we gonna get out of here?'

'No problem, mate, we'll work it out. There must be a door we can kick in somewhere, I bet.' He went over to the van, which was really exactly in the middle of the hall. 'You'll never find a light switch in here,' he said. 'But I'm gonna turn some light on for us.' He bent down and pushed up one trouser leg. There was a rubber band round the top of his sock, and between the sock and the rubber band was a little leather holder with a screwdriver in it. 'Watch this, Danny, watch and learn!' He inserted the screwdriver carefully into the lock on the van's door. 'You gotta get a feel for it,' he said. Then he started moving the screwdriver slightly.

I knew Mark wasn't really good. He was better than me but I'd never have admitted it, even though I wasn't as car-mad as the others. I wasn't a good driver either, Fred had let me drive a couple of times and I'd stalled the cars at some crossroads every time, and knocked off loads of mirrors as well, and once I bumped into someone so we had to get out of there really quick, but the cops never caught us. 'You're a lucky bastard,' Fred had told me, 'even if you drive like shit.'

'Shit, this crappy door!' No, Mark was no good at cracking car locks. He was still in training with Fred & Co., still a novice but he liked to act like a big professional.

'Shit, shit, shit, the bloody thing's stuck!'

No, he wouldn't manage it and we'd have to use brute force, that was always the safest bet. Someone had showed me not long ago how to open up a Wartburg with a kind of karate kick, slamming your ankle on a certain spot on the roof above the driver's door so it popped open. I took off my jacket and wrapped it round my right hand. I shoved Mark aside and put his burning lighter on the floor next to us. I pulled back my fist and thought of Engel, who'd wanted to beat me up a few days ago, and my fist rammed into the side window but there were only a few cracks in the glass, I punched again as hard as I could, and then the window broke, just a few jags of glass round the edges.

'Aww, Danny, that was my van, Jesus...' I put my jacket back on; little bits of glass fell out of it. I reached through the side window and opened the door. I felt the jags of glass through my jacket.

'Come on,' I said. 'Let's turn the light on.' I turned around. Mark was gone. I saw his light over by the shelves. I got in the car and switched on the parking light. I sat down and leaned back. My head was pretty hot and I tried to get all the blood back out of it. I laid my hand on my forehead. There was a cigarette jammed behind my ear. I couldn't remember putting it there. I smoked it anyway. I blew smoke against the windscreen, closed my eyes and thought of the Magic Vietcong, 'cause since he'd cast a spell on me I kept finding fags everywhere when I thought I'd run out. I'd had a funny relationship with the Vietcongs anyway, since I (and the others) started nicking all sorts of stuff from their stall outside the supermarket. We'd heard they'd lopped four fingers off some guy's hand over in Grünau with a samurai sword, all they'd left him was his thumb, after he'd tried to nick a couple of cigarette cartons out of their hiding place. But I still kind of liked the Vietcongs; they sold cigarettes for two fifty a pack! And their women! They had gorgeous little bodies, and someone told me once, 'You can buy yourself a Ming vase, fifty a pop,' and I'd started saving up a few times, but I kept spending all the money, beer, korn, pool, and I'd got myself a pair of binoculars as well. But it would have been shit to pay for a woman, probably, and I'd only feel sorry for them anyway, they were so tiny...

A bang. Hailstones flew in my face. No, glass shards. Mark grinned at me through the second broken window. He was holding a stone; now he threw it away. 'Now we're quits, Danny,' he said. He opened the door and sat down next to me. He dumped two beer cans on the dashboard and lit up a cigarette. Mine was finished and I flicked it out the window. 'Where'd you get that fag, I thought you didn't have any?'

'Didn't I tell you about the Magic Vietcong?'

'Come off it, not that crap again! Tell that to the kids at your posh school! You just forgot how many were left in the pack.'

'I didn't!'

'That don't matter, Danny! Come with me, I've had a bit of a nose around while you were taking a kip.'

'I wasn't taking a kip! Let me have a drink first, Mark.

Those dogs before, I bet they heard us. Did you know they can hear five times as much as us... five times louder, you get it?'

'Smartarse!'

I saw the two beams of the headlights touching the iron door. 'Come on, then,' said Mark. We put out our cigarettes on the windscreen; the empty beer cans we chucked out the broken windows. Then we got out of the van and slammed the doors; a couple of bits of glass fell by my feet. 'Right,' said Mark. 'It's basically just crap, all this stuff in here.' We went over to the shelves on the walls. There were all these tools on the shelves. And loads of cans of white paint for walls. We had our arms up to the shoulders in the shelves, digging and delving, chucking all the crap on the floor.

'Maybe they put all the good stuff at the top,' I said. 'We need a ladder!'

'God, why does everything always have to be so complicated, ladders and climbing and all that. Shit, I can't see a ladder anywhere.'

'Ah, it doesn't matter. What's gonna be up there anyway, apart from stupid tools. They're not even electric.'

'Shit...' But then I saw the big boxes in front of the opposite shelf. 'Look, Mark, look at that, boxes, a whole pile of them!' I got there first and I grabbed a cardboard box out of the middle, sending the pile down. A couple of boxes fell on Mark, who'd squatted down to rip one open.

'Danny, you gotta be kidding, it's a monitor, a real computer monitor!' Mark held it over his head with both hands and waved it around like a football trophy. He put it down carefully, then he ripped open a few other boxes. 'We're the greatest, Danny! We'll get the lot of them out of here. We can get good money for these, definitely! The kids at your school, Danny, those idiots need these!'

I'd sat down on one of the boxes, and he grabbed my arm and shook it. 'Jesus, Danny, don't sit on it, they're fragile! Don't sit around, up you get, come on, help me out with this, man. Out, we'll get all of them out!'

'Alright, Mark, keep your wig on.' I stood up.

'Hey, Danny, if you're scared or whatever, I can do it on my own!'

'What, me?' I tapped him on the shoulder. 'You know I'm never scared!' I squatted down and stroked the curved glass of the monitor. It was very cold.

Mark counted the boxes. 'Thirteen, Danny, thirteen of them. Jesus, work it out, fifty each, or better a hundred! For your school swots, Danny.'

'They're not my school swots.' I thought of the big chemistry test the next morning. Shit, my bag of books! I'd left it up on the roof. The test was important, our reports were due soon and I'd promised Mum I'd pass, this one last time at least, but now everything was starting to go wrong. I needed a piss and I walked over to one of the dark corners.

'Hey, where you going?'

'Taking a slash,' I said.

'Hold up,' Mark ran after me and stood facing the shelves a few metres away. I heard splashing.

'Don't piss so loud,' I said, and then I saw I was pissing against a little door. It was moments like that I believed in God, who Little Walter kept telling me about. I loved kicking doors in. Not long before, we'd kicked in a couple of hundred doors in an old tower block in Grünau that was due for demolition. 'Hey, Mark, I've found our way out.'

'For real?' He came over to me, doing up his flies. 'Not bad, Danny, you've got everything ready, eh?' He pointed at the puddle in front of the door, glinting in the dark. 'All we have to do is kick.' I punched my fist against the door; it was metal. 'Tried the handle yet, Danny?'

'No.' I tried the handle. Locked.

'We don't want it to be like in a film, Danny, you break it down and it was open all along!'

'Hey, Mark, how are we gonna get all of them out of here? Two or three each'd do it.'

'No, Danny, no, don't mess everything up. All of them, you hear Danny, all of them! And if you're scared...' I moved back, took a run-up and kicked my right foot as hard as I could against the door, but it didn't even move; I did another run-up and rammed my shoulder against the door but there was no point, it was harder than me, and I ran back again... 'Hey, Danny, wait a sec, wait a sec, there was a crowbar somewhere, wasn't there, on the shelves somewhere!'

'If you say so. But I'd have got it open anyway, for sure.'

'Sure, Danny, course you would.'

We went over to the shelves and looked for the crowbar. We even found two, like the guys who owned the place had left them there just for us. We squatted in front of the boxes on the floor again and drank our last beer. Mark gave me a cigarette. 'If we take two each,' he said, 'that's three goes, and then I'll come back for the last one as well.'

'And where will you...'

'Maybe in Pitbull's cellar...'

'Nah, not at this time of night. His old man'd lose his rag again.'

'The station, Danny, the freight station...'

'I dunno...'

'Come on, Jesus, it's not that far, and no one'll ever look there. Down in the cellar with the oil drums!' He picked up a monitor, stroked the curved glass, then held it up above his head. Then he dropped it.

'Shit, what was that?' It had hardly made a sound but the screen was shattered, and the grey plastic casing had a crack at the top.

'I don't believe it, you're kidding me!'

'What's up, Mark?'

'Look at that, Danny! Look at what the bastards wrote on it. They're lying, they're taking the piss!'

'What, Mark, what does it say?'

'Look at it, Jesus, take a look at it... those bastards!' He kicked the casing, twice over. I bent down and saw a white sticker with a big red D on it, and underneath the D it said in little black letters: 'Defective, 07.92'.

'What if it's not true?'

'Jesus, Danny, forget it, that's crap, why would they write it then?'

'But what if only one of them's broken, did you... We've still got twelve.'

'You reckon?' He squatted down and ripped open one box after another. I looked down at him, drinking my beer. There was no point helping him; he was like a raging beast. 'Nothing! Fuck! They're all defective, broken, all fucked up, for fuck's sake, why did you get my hopes up, you stupid wanker, it was obvious they'd all be fucked, what kind of a coincidence would that be... defective, defective, defective.' He hurled the monitors at the shelves and against the wall. 'Crap!'

It was so loud I knew that they'd come for us, here or outside, and I started adding up the damage. Was it criminal damage if you broke broken computer monitors? Mark had checked all the boxes now and was kneeling by the pile of rubbish, gibbering something. His cigarette pack was a few metres away from him. I picked it up, lit two cigarettes and pushed one between Mark's lips. He slid aside and leaned his back on the door. 'That's where I pissed, before,' I said. He slid over to the shelves. Something fell over.

'What the fuck?' he said. He was holding a bottle. 'Jesus, it's Goldkrone!'

He put the bottle to his lips. I grabbed it off him and drank. We went to the van and sat down inside. Mark hotwired it and reversed a few metres, then turned on the radio. We found Leipzig's golden oldies station, 'the very best oldies, morning, noon and night.' We drank. 'You're tuned into Master Mario's Sixties Soiree,' said the radio man, 'for all of you out there in the dark night or snuggled up under the covers...'

'Gay,' said Mark.

'It's just coming up to one,' said the radio man.

'Congratulations,' said Mark, and then he beeped the horn. 'Gimme my fags, Danny.'

I picked up his pack from the dashboard and handed them to him.

'Listen,' he said, 'I've got a surprise, it's actually for the weekend, for me, you know, but we can do it now, Danny, 'cause it's great right now, Danny, the night and that, right?'

He fished around in his pack; a few cigarettes fell on the floor and I started picking them up.

'I was saving it for the weekend, just for me, you know, but... Man, come on, look at it, will you?'

I raised my head and put the dropped cigarettes down on the dashboard. My head was spinning. He was holding something between finger and thumb. I couldn't see it properly, so I moved my head slowly towards his hand. That little bugger had a pill in his hand. Now I could even make out the symbol stamped on it, it looked kinda like a... little star. Mark grinned at me and said: 'We'll share it,

Danny. I got it from Karsten, fifteen marks. Mates' rates.'

I leaned back, drank a mouthful and nodded. 'Right, Karsten.'

Karsten was only a year older than us but he did a bit of dealing now and then. His big brother was a bouncer at the Apple and Karsten kept the punters in there topped up, the ones his brother let in. 'Broken noses are no good for trade,' Karsten told his brother when there was trouble on the door or inside the club. We went to the Apple a lot, 'cause it was in the next neighbourhood and the music wasn't bad. Pretty good techno. On the radio, a guy who sounded like Elvis was singing 'Why Do Fools Fall in Love'. The techno was better and harder in the illegal clubs in Connewitz, but the girls wore less at the Apple, even in winter, and we were the greatest 'cause we knew Karsten and his brother...

'You really think it's a good idea, Mark?'

No, it couldn't be Elvis, the guy sounded like the tape was stretched. 'Why ... oho hohoho why do they fall in love...'

'Course,' said Mark, holding the pill up so close to my nose I was scared it might go up one of my nostrils when I breathed in, 'half each, Danny, like brothers, Danny, it'll be amazing.'

I nodded. 'So have you done it before?'

'I'm not a virgin anymore, Danny.' He grinned and rolled the pill back and forth between his finger and thumb. 'Have you?'

'Course.' I nodded and took a mouthful of brandy. 'Couple of times. No big deal.'

'The colours, Danny, the colours...'

'Right,' I said, 'the colours.'

Mark grinned and I saw him swaying in his seat.

'Give it here,' I said. 'I'll break it for us. You'll just drop it, you and your shaky hands.'

'Shaky hands? Don't take the piss!' He gave it to me anyway. He put it on my open palm, right in the middle.

'Like blood brothers,' he said. 'Two equal halves.'

'Wait a bit,' I clenched my fist around the pill. 'We'll have a smoke first, ratchet up the tension, you know!'

'You're such a dick.' Mark put the cigarettes from the dashboard back in his pack; he lit two of them. Two filters burning.

'Wrong way round,' I said. He grinned, threw them out the window, lit up two new ones and gave me one. He smoked fast, almost as fast and greedy as the jailologists outside the supermarket, the ones with blue-black tattoos even on their faces, who never stopped jigging their legs even when they smoked and drank beer.

'Finished my fag, Danny, let's go!'

He flicked the fag-end out the window and slid around on his seat.

'Calm down, Jesus, I'm still smoking.'

I felt the pill inside my fist. If I pressed hard we could snort white dust up our noses. I flicked my cigarette out the window. I drank a mouthful of Goldkrone.

'Sorry, Mark,' I said. 'I can't do it today.' I took another drink.

'What's up, Danny, what d'you mean?'

I held up the pill. Mark screamed. I watched the pill for a moment on its way through the hall. Mark's fist hit the headrest beside my face. Rico had told me all about boxing and taught me one or two tricks. Mark punched at nothing again, and fell forward onto my knee. 'You dirty bastard, I'll kill you!' I held onto his head. 'You fucking bastard, you fucked up my pill, Danny, why?' He tried to punch me again, but I held onto his head.

'Mark, come on, you're my mate...'

'What kind of mate, what kind of friend would...'

He caught me on the shoulder but he had no strength left. 'Fifteen marks, you arsehole!' I felt his voice through my chest, on my ribs. 'Let go of me, you wanker!'

'Mark, listen, no, listen, I don't want us to neck that pill...'

'We can't now, can we, you stupid bastard!'

'We're too drunk, you know...'

'You might be, you arsehole.'

'It'd mess us up, you get it, it'd mess us up, the Goldkrone, mate, no, I don't want that. The money, I'll get you the money tomorrow!'

'Nick it off your mum, you arsehole!'

'I'll get it, I swear, I promise, and then we can take it, just the two of us, you know, at the disco or up on my roof. But not today... Sorry.'

'Up on your roof, yeah?'

I let go of him and he slid back over to his seat.

'Right, up on my roof. No one's been up there yet, not even Rico.'

I held the bottle out to him. 'Come on, let's just have a bit more of this and then get out of here.'

He lashed out at the bottle but I didn't have to pull it away; he didn't mean to hit it.

'But only if we go up on your roof... with a pill...'

'Course, I said so, didn't I?'

'That was still a mean trick, Danny.'

'Mark, you know that guy of Pitbull's, the Berliner, he's on H.'

'So? That's his problem.'

'Mark, that's what I'm scared of, I don't want us to ever...'

'You're crazy, me and H...'

He took the bottle. He wiped his face with his sleeve before he drank.

The van speeds across the hall. A shelf tips over. The windscreen is gone. Mario announces the best golden oldies. All the singers sound like Elvis. We honk the horn. I piss out the window while the van loops around the hall. There's someone at the door. 'They're coming,' Mark yells. They're coming. There's glass in our hair.

## BOY RACER

### Round One

We were really nearby when it happened. We were drinking at the Mushroom, Rico, Mark and me. I don't know why we were drinking at the Mushroom that night, 'cause we didn't drink there a lot, even though the beer was cheap. We usually went to the Green Pastures or to Goldie's place, the Tractorist, but maybe we had some kind of inkling that night, and we'd been drinking in Pitbull's cellar before, and sometimes when you're in your cups you see the whole truth before your eyes, and sometimes even a tiny little bit of the future, but if we'd seen what was going to happen we'd have gone looking for Walter all over the neighbourhood, all over town, and if we'd found him we'd have locked him in Pitbull's cellar, even if Pitbull didn't like it 'cause he lived there, didn't he, or we'd have taken him to Leipzig Southeast Police Station and asked the cops to chain him to the radiator with the 8, he'd been there before, he'd have leant his head against the wall and maybe got a bit of sleep.

But we didn't have a clue and we didn't see a thing, Rico, Mark and me, we were just drinking in the Mushroom. We were supposed to meet up with Paul but he didn't turn up, probably in trouble with his mum again. Pitbull had had trouble with his mum as well, she'd attacked him with a bottle 'cause we'd made so much noise drinking, and now Pitbull was lying down in his cellar and having a rest.

'I don't get it,' Rico said. 'Paul's old lady's a control freak, she always has to plan everything. When he's allowed out, when he gets home. She needs to leave him alone. She needs to get herself a new bloke instead, get laid.'

'Would you go for her?' Mark asked. 'Just for a shag, I mean...'

'Jesus, Mark!' I said. 'She's his mum!'

'She's not that bad, Danny, she's not forty yet. Maybe a bit dried up, who knows. She needs a young man to get her juices running, you know, she's really horny, I swear, the way she looks at me...'

'Mark, come off it, stop talking about his mum like that!'

And he did stop and he shut up and looked over at the door, 'cause it jerked open and there was Paul. We raised our glasses at him, and it was only then we saw something wasn't right. He was swaying on his feet and holding onto the doorframe, and his face was as white as a brand-new football.

'Walter,' he said, 'Walter...'

And maybe at that moment we sensed something, 'cause we all put our glasses down at the same time, like in slow motion, and then we stood up and went towards him, towards the door, not saying a word.

'Oi, where you going?' the landlord yelled from behind the bar. We didn't drink at the Mushroom that often and he didn't trust us not to skip out on our tab. Rico crumped up a twenty and threw it on one of the empty tables. Not many punters in the Mushroom.

'Walter,' Paul lurched from one side of the door frame to the other and I grabbed hold of him.

'What's up with Walter?' He pulled me outside, took my shoulders so hard it hurt, and shook me. 'What's up with Walter?'

'Gone. Dead, Danny.'

Rico shoved me aside and grabbed Paul by the collar and lifted him up a bit so their faces were touching. 'Don't talk crap, you hear me, don't play games, boy, don't play games.'

'I'm not playing around,' Paul whispered and raised his arm, trembling, and pointed over at Prager Platz, which we called the Czech red-light district, 'cause the lonely girls of the neighbourhood met up on the little patch of grass by the junction and walked up and down and stared after every guy, 'cause they didn't want to be lonely, even though most of them were too fat or too thin or had something else wrong with them. And now we saw the fire's light by the junction, four hundred metres ahead of us. I broke into a run.

'Danny,' Rico yelled after me, 'Danny, wait!'

But I didn't wait, I ran ahead to Prager Platz, to the Czech red-light district, where there weren't any girls sitting on the benches dangling their thin or fat legs for us, there was a car burning there, smashed into a tree. I ran faster and I was almost there and I saw the people standing around on the pavement and in the middle of the road. I heard the muddle of sirens far away. Cops, ambulance, fire brigade.

'Walter,' I yelled, 'Walter, get out!'

But Little Walter was already out of the car, lying on the ground four or five metres away, and the flames couldn't do anything more to him. I ran over to him, it was so hot where he was, and I pulled him further away from the burning car. I knelt down by him, and then I yelled and jerked my head back and looked up at the sky, no stars to be seen, 'cause his face was all black and covered in blood, and he had no hair left. His clothes were in rags, the blood, I didn't want to see the damn blood, but then I bent down to him and put my hand under the back of his head. Now Little Walter moved, just a tiny bit, he moved his head in my hand. I looked for his eyes, where were his eyes? Now one of them was open, blue in the black face.

'Walter,' I said, 'Jesus, Walter...' He moved his lips and I pressed one ear, careful now, to his mouth.

## Round Two

We were really nearby when it happened. We were drinking at the Mushroom, Rico, Mark and me. We were playing 31 'cause Mark was no good at skat, but he won almost every round at 31. 'It's a game of chance, for fuck's sake,' Rico said.

'It's skill,' said Mark, putting his thirty and a half down on the table and winning the round. We were waiting for Paul, whose mum had probably locked him in again. She'd heard Pitbull was inside over at Zeithain for a few weeks for some crap or other, and since then Paul had been in a kind of youth custody of his own, but it probably didn't bother him 'cause he had all his girls with him in all his mags and films.

'I'm out of matches,' Rico said and put his cards aside. 'Skint.'

'I'll lend you some,' I said.

'Nah, don't bother, Danny, I've lost enough already. I don't want to get in debt.'

'I thought you were such a big gambler,' Mark was counting his matches. 'I thought you were champion of the jail.'

'Shut it!' Rico put his hand on Mark's heap of matches and clenched his fist, cracking the matches inside it.

'Hey, leave it out! That was two beers!'

'You'll get them, as long as you don't talk crap.'

But Mark didn't get two beers from Rico, he'd won all his matches for nothing, 'cause the door jerked open and Paul lurched towards us, and we knew straight off that something wasn't right.

'What's up, Paul, what's up? Did you make a break for it? You in trouble?'

'Walter,' he whispered, and now we saw he was trembling, 'by the Czech red-light district, the tree, the car...'

We leapt up and ran past Paul to the door. 'Oi, pay up!' the landlord yelled from behind the bar. There was often trouble at the Mushroom, 'cause sometimes the drinkers didn't pay their tabs, or they started punching each other's lights out until the cops showed up. We ran ahead to the junction in silence, to Prager Platz, which we called the Czech red-light district 'cause the most gorgeous girls in the neighbourhood met up there, and most of them were gagging for us. I ran the fastest, but not 'cause of the girls. There weren't any that night; there was a burning car there. Dense black smoke, so thick you could hardly see the flames. A security guard was jumping around the car, now he went down on his knees and crawled away from it, something running out of his mouth.

'Walter,' I yelled, 'Walter!'

Maybe Paul was wrong, maybe someone else was in the car, burning up, there were plenty of joyriders in our neighbourhood, almost every young lad in Reudnitz, Anger-Crottendorf and the other parts of Leipzig East was into carjacking, we did it too, but when I looked into the flames and the smoke I knew, I just knew it, it was suddenly in my head that he was in there, burning up.

'Walter,' I yelled, 'Walter!'

It was a pale red VW Jetta, they were his favourites 'cause of the woman from the lottery shop he'd been in love with, she used to drive one. I ran towards the flames, I felt the heat and I stuck out my hand, the smoke burned in my eyes.

'Danny,' Rico yelled after me and he held onto me,

'Danny, stay back!' He had me by the shoulders and I pulled and tugged and wanted to go to Little Walter, but Rico wouldn't let go of me. Far away, I heard the muddle of sirens. Cops, ambulance, fire brigade. Now I saw Mark too, squatting next to me and puking. And it was only now I saw the people standing around on the road and the pavement gawping at the burning car.

'Fuck off,' I yelled, 'piss off, you bastards!' I tore myself free from Rico and ran towards the stupid gawkers and raised my fist, but Rico was quick, he grabbed me by the shoulders from behind again, put his arms round me and held me tight.

'Danny,' he whispered, 'it's too late, Danny.' The sirens were close now. Rico let me go and I fell to my knees and crawled to the pavement and leant against a wall. Flashing blue lights. The fire brigade was there. 'He won't have been alone,' Rico said next to me.

'No,' I said, 'he won't,' and then I leapt up again and ran screaming towards the burning car, the firemen standing around it now, but Rico was behind me and grabbed at my legs, and I stumbled to the ground. I stayed down, pressing my face to the street.

## Round Three

We were drinking at the Mushroom, Rico, Mark and me. We didn't drink there a lot but the Mushroom wasn't a bad bar, it had style, even the toilets were clean, and a lot of the neighbourhood's drinkers started their rounds there, and now we were drinking in the Mushroom as well, 'cause Walter had burned up nearby. We'd read about it in the paper, 'cause on the night it happened we'd been drinking in Pitbull's cellar. He'd smashed a car into a tree, over at the junction by Prager Platz, which he'd always called the Czech red-light district 'cause the neighbourhood girls met up there on the weekends before they went out for the night, and sometimes Walter had driven up and down there in a jacked car, but I don't think he ever pulled. There'd been three other guys in the car, joyriders from Mühlenviertel, and they'd burned up too with Walter. The security guard who'd got to the burning car first had said in the paper that they'd still been alive, only just, and he'd wanted to get them out, but he hadn't stood a chance against the flames.

'I don't believe that,' Rico said, 'nah, I don't believe it. They'll have been doing 120, 130, they must have died right off. You can bet they weren't wearing seatbelts.'

'Rico,' I said, 'Rico, stop it.'

'Alright, Danny, alright.'

He knocked back a double korn, and then another one; we'd ordered ahead. Walter had been dead three days, and we'd been drinking three days. We started in the morning and I was glad they'd chucked me out of school a few months before, 'cause now, now that Walter was gone, I wouldn't have gone back anyway.

'I'm not gonna hotwire anymore cars,' Mark mumbled. 'And I won't get in anymore cars. It's over, you hear, over.'

'Yeah,' I said. 'All over.' I waved at the landlord. 'Another round!' The landlord looked over at us for a while from behind the bar, before he nodded and went to the beer pump. Maybe he remembered Pitbull was one of us, and Pitbull couldn't go in the Mushroom anymore, there'd been some incident and Pitbull had paid for it with a month's youth custody over in Zeithain, where I'd been not long ago. But Pitbull wouldn't have been able to come to the Mushroom with us anyway, he'd been drinking and smoking dope and puking, and now he was having a lie-down in his cellar.

Mark rested his head on the table. 'He... he believed in... God and that, Walter... Remember, back in the day, he used to go to church with his mum.'

'Didn't help him, though, did it?' I said.

'No, it didn't. Remember... remember how we used to laugh, about his church, I mean.'

'Yeah,' I said, 'I remember.'

The landlord brought our round, and then we shut up again and drank. The landlord had put the radio on, and we shut up for three songs and drank and stared at the table. 'You guys coming, then?' Rico asked, lighting one up.

'Mühlenviertel?' Mark raised his head off the table. Rico nodded.

'We've got to do something,' I said.

'Got to,' said Rico.

'Got to,' said Mark.

'What about Paul?' I said.

'He won't make it, I bet.'

I nodded. His mum probably hardly let him out the house now that Little Walter had driven himself to death.

'Control freak,' said Rico, swaying back and forth, but he still knocked back another korn, 'his old lady, his mum, I mean. Control freak. Worse than in the box.' He slapped the table and laughed. I'd never heard him say the word 'prison', he always said 'box' or 'jail' or 'inside', and he'd never said 'children's home' in the old days either. 'Chickened out, that coward,' Rico grabbed for his beer, almost knocked it over, and I wanted to help him but I missed as well. 'Too chicken to go to jail, that coward, he'd have had to go inside, one day. Too chicken, and now he's in the box for ever.' He laughed again and slapped the table and swayed.

'Rico,' I said, 'please...'

'The bill,' Rico yelled and waved at the landlord, working the beer pump behind the bar. 'Our tab, Jesus, get a move on.'

And then we went over to Mühlenviertel. We were swaying and our legs kept giving way, and we held onto each other. We were pretty far gone, but we still got hold of a few of the carjackers Walter ended up hanging round with. We beat the shit out of them, until we started sobering up. Then we picked a whole load of flowers from the allotments next to the new blocks, and then we swayed over to Prager Platz.

Estrellita was stretched out on one of the benches, right next to Walter's tree. She stared at us and put one arm under her head, all quiet. We covered her up with our jackets.

We lay the flowers around the half-burnt tree and stayed until morning came.

# MEETINGS

We had meetings every Monday, to plan the week ahead. We met in the pirate ship or in the old building in Mühlenviertel. It was the last old building; they'd torn down all the others and were building new ones. The neighbourhood officer from the People's Police had banned us from playing in the old building, he'd come to our class and explained all sorts of risks and dangers, and Mrs Seidel had warned us plenty of times as well but we met there anyway. Walter didn't come to our meetings anymore; he went to church with his mum instead. Sometimes he went to church on Sundays as well, and we laughed at him for it.

'No,' he said, 'Mondays aren't proper church, it's different, we go marching on Mondays.'

'Round and round the church, or what?'

'No, all the way round town.'

It was Monday again now and he wasn't there, he was marching all the way round the church and the town with his mum, and we were planning the week without him. We were in the old building, Mark, Paul, Rico and me, up on the fourth floor, 'cause the pirate ship wasn't safe anymore, the lads from the toy factory hung out there now, and Mark had seen the neighbourhood officer's car in the backyard not long ago.

'That means trouble,' I said.

'I don't care about him,' Rico said, punching his fist into his open hand. 'I'm not scared of him!'

'You don't care about anything.' Paul stood up and went to the window.

'Hey, shut up, you!' Rico'd had a short temper since he'd got back, but we didn't talk about that. They wanted to take him out of school again, even, but Rico wasn't scared of that, he was pretty good at boxing, and he said they needed him for the city championships.

'Listen, is it true what they...?' Mark looked at Rico.

'Go on, spit it out. Don't wet your pants!'

'Well, they say you bit him, Mr Dettleff, I mean.'

'Oh right, people are saying that, are they?'

'Right,' I said. 'All around school. Even my mother knew... all around the neighbourhood!'

Rico smiled. 'Really?'

'It's true,' Paul sat back down on the floor with us. 'He even had a plaster on his nose, Dettleff did.'

'He can't have,' Rico said. 'I didn't even nip him...' He was still smiling. 'Well, maybe a tiny bit. He pulled his nose away, he was terrified, and he left me alone after that.'

'And your comic,' I said, although I knew the story, he'd told it to me a couple of times before, and he'd lent me the comic as well. 'Was it really *Captain America*? Where did you get it?'

'My gran, you know that. She's allowed to go to the West.' Rico took out a box of matches and lit the candle stuck to a saucer in the middle of our circle. It was afternoon, and not much light came through the window. There were little golden stars on the candle – it was Walter's candle, he'd made it at his church one time, and he'd stuck the stars on it himself.

'But I'm not a biter,' said Rico. 'Stefan's a biter, I'm a fist man!'

Stefan had bitten three times and they were threatening to give him rabies injections, but he went on biting whenever someone wound him up or he had a fight. There were other biters at our school and they threatened to give all of them rabies injections, but they'd never done it.

'So listen,' I said. 'What's the plan?' I took out the homework diary where we wrote down everything we planned. Usually, nothing came of the plans and everything turned out differently, but that didn't matter.

'It's the trade fair soon,' I said. 'We can go there again. I think it's next week.' I marked a cross at next Monday with my fountain pen, and wrote 'Trade fair' after it.

'I'm not coming,' said Paul. 'Can't do Monday.'

'You're just scared,' Rico said.

'Right,' said Mark, 'scared to get in trouble with Mummy!'

'I'm not scared, I'm just busy.'

'Leave him alone, if he can't come he can't come.'

'Rico and Mark,' I wrote in the book. 'Probably not Paul.' 'Anyway, it's better if there's only three of us, otherwise people will spot us.'

'What if Walter wants to come?'

'No, no,' said Rico. 'He can't do Mondays, he goes to his church, he goes on his march.'

'We could go on Tuesday,' Mark said. 'He can come on Tuesday, we'll go in two groups, me and Rico, you and Walter, we'll sneak in separately, you get it? One group across the tracks, one group under the fence.'

'We'll see,' said Rico. 'I'll think about the best way.' He knew his way around the trade fair, he'd been there almost every day in the spring and he'd brought back loads of plastic carrier bags, and some of them even had stickers and pens and little toy cars in them. He'd taken us along one time, and we'd got stickers and plastic bags and pens at the booths, but the teachers had confiscated most of them at school 'cause we'd shown them around, and the headmaster locked them all in the safe in the secretary's office, which had lots of comics in it and my Chemie scarf (the headmaster was a Lok supporter).

'What about football?' I asked. 'Chemie's playing on Saturday.'

'You're going with your dad, aren't you?' said Paul, and Rico hit him on the leg.

'Trade fair maybe Tuesday,' I wrote in the book, then I flicked back to Saturday.

'My dad doesn't go anymore,' I said.

'I'll come with you,' said Rico. 'You know I will.'

'Saturday's tricky,' said Mark. 'We're going away.'

'Scared, are you?' said Paul. 'Too noisy for you at football?' Paul's mum usually worked on Saturdays, so he had time all day.

'Chemie with Rico and Paul,' I wrote in the Saturday space. 'Meet 12.30.'

'I always come, usually,' Mark said. 'You know me, Danny, I'm a Chemist too.'

'Course,' I said. 'You just can't always make it.'

'I haven't got much money though...' said Paul.

'We'll see to that,' I said. 'Wednesday: collect deposit bottles,' I wrote in the book.

'I need a pee.' Mark got up and went into the next room.

'Go one room further,' I called out, 'or it'll stink!'

'Too late,' said Mark, and we heard splashing.

Rico got out a cigar. 'From my gran,' he said. He leaned forward and lit it on the candle. He blew out the smoke and coughed, then passed it on.

Mark was by the window. 'Come over here, look! All the police, all the cops heading into town!' We got up and went over to him; Paul gave him the cigar. The panes were dirty; someone had drawn a naked woman in the grime. Rico opened the window. I shoved Paul aside and leant out. 'Watch it, Danny,' Mark said behind me. 'What if they see you?' The whole of Leninstrasse was crawling with police cars and vans, moving towards the city centre slowly, flashing blue lights, but no sirens.

'You see that?' Rico said. 'They've blocked the road, no more cars.'

'From Southeast,' said Mark, squeezing in between us. 'They're coming from Southeast Police Station, on Witzgallstrasse.'

'Not all of them,' Rico said. 'It can't be, there's too many, there must be some from out of town.'

'Barracked police,' I said. 'I've heard about them, they live outside town, they're like the army. Cops in barracks, you know?'

'Did you see that? There's dogs looking out of that van.'

The cars moved along Leninstrasse, past the old allotments and Peace Park, and then turned off. I could see the trade fair tower in the town centre, the big double-M on the roof shining red and blue and rotating like a carousel. 'There's gonna be trouble,' said Rico, closing the window. 'I bet there'll be violence.'

'Where's the cigar gone?' It was outside on the window ledge, and Rico opened the window again.

'Leave it open,' I said. 'It's stuffy in here.' The cigar had gone out; we lit it again and sat down in our corner.

'What about Walter?' Paul said. He sucked on the cigar, tipped his head back and blew smoke rings. Mark grabbed at them and they broke up. 'He's there now, isn't he?' said Paul.

'His mum's with him, he'll be fine.' I pinched the cigar out of Paul's hand. The ash fell and I brushed it off my trousers.

'There's loads of people there, I've heard,' said Mark, 'loads and loads, more than at the football.'

'Really, more than at Chemie?' I passed him the cigar.

'Hey, don't smoke it all up!' Rico took it out of Mark's

mouth; it dropped and he wiped it with his thumb.

'My mum was there as well, last week,' said Paul.

'Really? Your mum?'

'Course, right after work.'

'Oh right, that's how come you stayed so late, 'cause Mummy wasn't in.'

'So what, at least my mum went on the march. I bet your parents didn't!'

'My gran's too old,' said Rico. 'She can't do that kind of thing.'

'My mum has to work late,' I said. 'And it's dangerous as well.'

'It can't be dangerous,' said Rico, 'not if even Walter goes...'

'And my mum!'

'If Little Walter's there, we've got to go too,' said Mark. 'Just to have a look, at least...'

'What, right now?' Rico stood up.

'No, on Monday, I mean next Monday, it's too late now. We've got to get there at the beginning, you know...'

'What about all the police?' I said.

'That's why, Danny,' said Rico. 'There's something happening, something's really happening.'

'But it's church, it's those crazy churchy people.'

'Maybe, Danny. But if they're marching, there must be a hell of a lot going on.'

'Right,' said Mark. 'I saw it on telly, lots of girls there, really crowded, you can touch their tits and that.'

'I don't think you can,' Paul said.

'You don't have to. You're not ready yet!'

'Yes, I am! The other day, Sandra... in PE...'

Mark leant against the wall and laughed.

'Don't laugh! You can ask Danny!'

I flicked forward to Monday and crossed out the

trade fair. 'Go into town with Mark, Rico and Paul,' I wrote in the homework book. 'Trade fair Tuesday or Wednesday,' and then I drew an arrow down to Tuesday and Wednesday.

'Listen,' Mark got up and went to the window. 'Listen to that!' There were bells ringing somewhere.

Rico put the cigar down on the saucer with the candle. 'The churches,' said Rico, 'it's the churches.' We went to the window and looked out at the steeples and tower blocks over in the town centre. The ringing got quieter, then a bit louder again, some of the bells sounding high and bright, others ringing lower, and a couple of times it seemed like the bells of another church had joined in; there were loads of churches in Leipzig, not just in the centre. It was almost dark outside now, and we could see blue flashing lights where Leninstrasse went around a bend.

'Sounds spooky,' said Paul.

'What, that bit of bell-ringing?' said Mark. 'What's so special about that?'

'And Walter's right in the middle of it.' Rico leant on the window ledge. 'I wouldn't have thought he had it in him, with all those cops.'

'You were laughing at him a minute ago,' said Paul, stepping back from the window. 'You were all laughing 'cause he goes to church on Mondays now.'

'Listen, kid,' Rico didn't turn round, just went on looking out the window. 'Don't talk rubbish. Don't talk crap!'

'But it's true, you were all...'

I nudged him and he shut up.

'Danny, did you write it down? For next Monday, I mean.'

'Course I did, Rico.'

'It's important, Danny. You keep the minutes.'

'Course, it's all in here.' I patted the homework book.

Rico closed the window. 'So we're on, next week!' He held out his hand and we piled ours on top. 'Agreed,' he said.

'Agreed,' we answered.

'Marching,' I wrote in the homework book. Then we blew out the candle and went down the stairs.

'I've got a flag at home,' said Mark, 'from Mayday, a Pioneers flag...'

'No, I don't think that's right.'

'No, why? They've all got flags on the telly.'

'For peace,' said Paul, 'it's for peace, my mum...'

'Yeah, so? Mayday's about peace as well!'

On the ground floor, we climbed out through the window of the outside toilet. 'I won't fit through there much longer,' said Paul.

'Right,' I said. 'What with all your muscles.' We laughed. We looked around, the street was still empty, and then we went home.

'...next door to the Duroplast State Toys and Rubber Stamps Factory. And we know who was there!' Mrs Seidel went quiet, looking down at us from the stage in the school hall. Next to her was Mrs Minkusch, the teacher from 9b, and behind them, in a row, sat the headmaster Mr Singer, the Pioneer leader Mr Dettleff, Mrs Lorenz, 9c's teacher, and the neighbourhood officer from the People's Police. His Wartburg was parked outside the school next to the teachers' cars, it had been there since that morning, and we knew there was going to be trouble. Rico had found a big nail and wanted to puncture his tyres, but he couldn't get the nail in the rubber. Then he wanted to scratch the paint but the teacher on playground duty had started looking over funny, and we'd taken the nail off him. He was sitting two rows behind me; they'd gone to get him especially, 'cause actually he'd gone down a year, they'd made him go down after he came back after almost two years, even though he'd had school in there too, every day.

'I can only repeat,' Mrs Minkusch said in her squawky voice. 'There will be consequences. PC Lansky from the People's Police would like to add a few words.'

PC Lansky stood up, took off his hat and put it on his chair, smoothed the trousers of his green uniform and positioned himself between Mrs Seidel and Mrs Minkusch. 'Dear Thälmann Pioneers of classes 7A, B and C. I've talked to you before about the risks and dangers of playing in old buildings and going to places where you're not allowed to go. It's very important to abide by these rules at the moment, and I know most of you do.' He took a deep breath; a few chairs creaked and I turned around to Rico, Paul and Walter; Mark was at the very back. They were looking at the floor, only Rico gave me a wink. He was sitting right by the big window with the view of the sports ground. There was a class doing laps down there, I could see their brightly coloured PE kits, three running at the front, the rest a good way behind them, and the PE teacher standing alone in the middle. '... there are some, unfortunately, who... there are some who never learn, and that's why we have to... that's why there have to be consequences.' He took another deep breath, he'd got muddled up again, no, it wasn't a good talk, I'd been up on stage a few times at school talent competitions and recited poems or stories, I was good at it 'cause I spoke so loudly and clearly and 'cause I had a good memory – that came from playing skat –and I was way better than PC Lansky. Now he'd finished and he went back to his chair, picked up his hat and put it on his knee. I'd been hoping he'd sit on it.

Mrs Seidel stepped forward. She was holding an open folder in her hands, pretending to read from it. 'The following pupils, please stand up: Walter Richter.' A chair creaked behind me. 'Daniel Lenz.' She looked past me over the top of her glasses. I stood up. 'Mark Bormann. Rico Grundmann.' I thought of Katja, the head of the class council. She would have given me a lovely telling-off but she wasn't there anymore. 'Paul Jendroschek.' Stefan, Stefan had betrayed us, even though we'd taken him to the pirate ship, twice now. 'Stefan Schulte.' No, it couldn't have been him, or else he'd have made a deal with them.

'Rico Grundmann, come to the front.' The headmaster had stood up and was now next to Mrs Seidel. All the other teachers had stood up as well, and the neighbourhood officer, and Rico walked slowly up to them. The headmaster gave him a written reprimand, and they all looked very serious and pursed their lips as the headmaster spoke. It was the worst punishment at the school, the only thing that came after it was expulsion, but Rico still grinned as he got down from the stage and walked past us, and he held up the piece of paper his parents were supposed to sign, but his parents had gone and he lived with his gran and she signed everything without reading it, he'd told me, 'cause her eyes were bad.

'Daniel Lenz, come to the front, please.' I heard Rico sitting back down behind me, and I went to the front. I stood facing Mrs Seidel, my hands on the seams of my trousers. She looked at her folder. 'Daniel,' she said, 'I hereby award you the Council of Ministers' certificate for outstanding school performance.' I bowed and she handed me the red leather folder with the gold GDR emblem and gold curlicues on it, with the certificate inside.

'Thank you,' I said. 'Thank you, Mrs Seidel.' I went back to my seat, no one looking at me 'cause I'd just got a written reprimand from the class teacher, which wasn't as bad as Rico's from the headmaster but it was bad enough. I held the sheet of paper in my hand; I wanted to fold it into a paper aeroplane and fly it across the school hall.

'Walter Richter, come to the front, please.' I sat down and Walter walked past me. I smiled and winked at him, but all I saw was a twitch of his mouth. Walter looked really small up on the stage, and Mrs Seidel told him the same thing she'd told me. How did they know where we met up, how did they know about the pirate ship? They always knew everything, and I couldn't understand it. Then it was Paul's turn, then Mark, and Stefan went last. I looked out of the window. The class down there had finished their laps and sat down on the grass by the wall, the PE teacher waving his arms around in front of them.

Stefan walked back to his seat and only the teachers were left on stage. 'Pioneers!' That was Mr Dettleff; Mr Singer was right behind him and it looked like he was whispering something in his ear. 'Dear Thälmann Pioneers of classes 7A, B and C, I'm sure you know there are lots of meetings going on in our city, marches by individuals threatening our socialist order and safety. And I'm sure you also know that taking part in these marches and meetings is banned. Pioneers! I call on you to be watchful and not to support these individuals threatening our socialist order and safety in an irresponsible manner. These marches and meetings are putting down our socialist achievements, irresponsibly threatening our socialist order and... Pioneers!' He faltered, red in the face, his mouth open.

Mr Singer put his big hand on Mr Dettleff's shoulder. 'You all know the pedestrian bridge by the Tin Can,' he said calmly in his deep voice. A couple of idiots in my row said yes or nodded. 'That bridge is sought out and crossed during the meetings and marches. There are hundreds of people, incited by irresponsible individuals, perhaps thousands. That bridge,' he paused, holding up a finger, 'that bridge, however, was not built for so many people, and the individuals inciting them know that. The bridge could collapse, and if they go on bouncing and jumping on the bridge to provoke our People's Police, and shouting their shameless slogans, it will collapse! And you can imagine,' he paused again, finger raised, 'and you can imagine there will be many injuries and certainly also fatalities. And that's just one example of the irresponsible actions of these rioters and disturbers of the peace.' He turned round to the other teachers, and they nodded and pursed their lips and looked very serious.

Mr Singer put his hand back on Mr Dettleff's shoulder, and again it looked like he was whispering in his ear. 'Thälmann Pioneers,' said Mr Dettleff, 'please stand!' We stood up. 'We'll close this meeting with the salute of the Young and Thälmann Pioneers: For peace and socialism: Be prepared!'

'Always prepared,' we chanted, and put our hands to our foreheads in the Pioneer salute. The teachers did the Pioneer salute too and even the constable, who'd put his hat back on. Then we filed out of the door.

We didn't meet at the pirate ship anymore, we met by the sandpit at the park, like we used to. It was a Monday but we didn't have a meeting and we didn't plan for the new week; that was over. Walter was in town with his mum, and we wanted to go there too even though at school they'd said it was banned, but we'd agreed on it. I was sitting up on the back of the bench with Rico, waiting for the others. 'Maybe they're not coming,' I said. 'Mark got in big trouble 'cause of his reprimand.'

'What about you, Danny?'

'It was alright.'

'They're pretty mean, eh?'

'Yeah, they are.'

'What d'you think, Danny, who was it that told on us?'

'Don't know. First I thought it was Stefan, but they got him too, even though he only came twice.'

'No, no, Danny, it can't have been Stefan, he'd never tell tales.'

'He wants to come to the trade fair with us on Wednesday – what d'you think, Rico, can he?'

'Don't know yet. He'll have to pass a test first, I'll think of something.'

Someone was crossing the grass in our direction. It was Stefan. He was carrying a little canvas shopping bag.

'How's things?' he said.

'Alright.'

'You going into town?'

'Maybe.'

Stefan put the bag on the bench.

'What you got there?' Rico tapped the red fabric with his foot.

'Don't kick it please. It's my camera, it's fragile, it'll break if you're not careful.'

'What did you bring that for?'

'If you lot are going into town...'

'Who told you we're going into town?'

'Mark, it was Mark told me. He can't make it today. His dad, you know... So I thought maybe I could come with you...'

'Show us your camera, then,' I said.

He reached cautiously into the bag and took it out. 'It's from photography club, I'm in the school photography club.'

The camera was big and black with little silver buttons, and there was a huge flash stuck on top.

'They always pick the photo of the month, and I've never won. But if you're going into town...'

'I never knew they let biters join the photography club,' said Rico.

I elbowed Rico.

'No,' said Rico, 'I don't mean it like that, I think it's good...'

'I'm not a biter anymore,' Stefan said. 'I haven't bitten for ages, that was when I was little.'

'It's alright,' I said. 'We've got to go in a minute. Put your camera away.'

I got up.

'What about Paul?' Rico asked.

'He's not coming,' I said. 'Forget it, he didn't even come to football.'

'Chicken, they're all chicken, just 'cause of a stupid reprimand!'

'I'm not chicken,' said Stefan.

'No, not you.' Rico crossed the grass, heading for the tram stop.

'Come on then, you two!'

Stefan picked up his bag and we ran after Rico.

When we got to the road, there was Mark. He was leaning on his flagpole, which was really a broom handle, the flag rolled up around it; he grinned and waved at us.

'There you are, you did come!' Rico patted him on the shoulder.

'Course, we agreed. I sneaked out, you know, my old man...'

'And you brought the flag!'

'Course, I said I would, we'll be the greatest!'

Stefan was standing on the kerb behind us. 'Can I

come with you anyway?'

'Course you can,' said Rico. 'You've got to win your prize, haven't you?'

'Stay like that, that's great!' We were standing in front of Saint Nikolai's, the forecourt so crowded with people we could hardly move, but Stefan still wanted to take a few photos of us. He'd climbed on a low wall; we waved at him and Mark swung his broom handle – he hadn't unrolled the flag yet, it was held in place with two rubber bands, 'Don't want to unroll it too soon,' he'd said, 'not until it starts, not until the bells ring, or else the surprise will be wasted!' There was a flash, Stefan fiddled with his camera, then he got back down.

'Pretty crowded, eh?'

'Yeah,' I said. 'Way more than at football.'

'You go to Lok too, do you?' said Stefan, stuffing the bag in his pocket and hanging the camera round his neck.

'Are you taking the mickey? We're Chemists!'

'Oh. I didn't know.'

'Everyone knows that!'

The bells began to ring and the people came out of the church, there was a huge crush and we moved off with them towards the opera. It was getting dark and the cops' blue light flashed in the side streets. 'Danny!' Mark was a couple of metres ahead, waving at us with his flag. He'd unrolled it at last; it was a big triangular Pioneer pennant with the Pioneer emblem on both sides, and underneath, it said in big red letters: *For peace and solidarity between the nations.*

I squeezed through the crush, Stefan and Rico right behind me. 'We'd better watch out a bit,' Rico said. 'Don't want to lose each other!'

'See?' said Mark. 'It's better with a flag, they've got one

too.'

Ahead of us, two men unrolled a banner, stuck it over two broom handles – they were probably out of flag poles all over town – and held it up. *We are the people*, it said on the banner, and I laughed.

'Look, Rico, you seen that? We are the people.' Rico laughed as well; one of the men turned round and Stefan took a photo of him. The man turned away, covered his face with his hands.

'The people,' Rico laughed, 'I'm the people too, you get it, Danny, Volk-mann?' We were on Goethestrasse now, walking past the opera. The church bells were still ringing, probably a signal, 'cause even more people joined us now from Karl-Marx-Platz. There were three trams held up at the stop; they couldn't get any further. We walked in the middle of the road, and there were policemen next to their cars on the pavements, some of them with dogs. 'Is that all?' said Rico. 'Just that handful of cops?'

'There'll be more,' said a man next to us. He was holding a candle; now he lit it. 'You lads stay here in the middle, don't go to the outsides.' He wasn't holding the candle straight and wax dripped onto his jacket. 'Do you want one?'

'One what?'

'A candle.' He took one out of his pocket, he had more in there, I could see them, and he lit it from his candle and gave it to Stefan.

Rico took it from him. 'You've got to watch out for your camera.'

'A flag and a candle,' said Mark. 'We're the greatest!' He held onto the very bottom of the broom handle and waved the flag above our heads.

'Thanks,' I said to the man, but he was already ahead of us. I saw candles lit up all over the crowd now; the guy was probably some kind of candle distributor.

'It's like a lantern festival,' said Stefan. He turned around and took a few photos of the people behind us.

'Watch out,' said Rico. 'You don't want the cops to get you.'

'No, why would they? I've got my membership card from the photography club.' He put his hand in his inside pocket and pulled out a little laminated card. It had his passport photo on it, with a stamp and a signature, and on the back of the card was a safety pin, which he used to fasten it to his jacket.

'Man, take that off,' said Mark, still swinging his flag. 'It's embarrassing!'

'No, I'm from the newspaper and I'm allowed to take photos, photography club!'

'He's a biter,' Rico whispered in my ear, and grinned. We'd reached the station forecourt. There were cops everywhere now, outside the station and across the road, lined up in front of their cars, wearing helmets, and their shields were like a wall. 'Water cannons,' said Rico. 'Look at that, it's worse than at football!' There they were, down the side of the station, like tanks.

'Oh shit,' I said. 'What if they start using them?'

'Don't think they will,' said Rico. 'Too many people.'

Stefan took a photo; he'd turned off the flash and twisted the lens. 'Night shots,' he said. 'Blue light and candles, they'll be great pictures!'

We were walking slower now, the crowd dividing around the tram stop in the middle of the road. 'Up there!' Stefan called out, aiming his camera at the station. 'There's people on the roof, walking around up there! It's the police!' He stood still and fiddled with his camera, but I grabbed his shoulder and pulled him along with us. There were trams all over, empty, with their lights on.

'Listen, what are they chanting?' We couldn't get any further, we stopped, and Mark propped himself up on his flagpole.

'We are the people! We are the people!' It was coming from somewhere at the front of the crowd, but now they started chanting around us as well: 'We are the people! We are the people!'

'Those blokes from before,' Rico yelled, 'the ones with the poster, that's them, they started it!'

Mark joined in now: 'We are the people!' and swung his Pioneer pennant again. Next to us were two fat women; they looked at Mark's flag, one of them pointed a finger at it, they laughed. 'We are the people! We are the people!' Then we moved on. We walked around the trams, their doors wide open, a couple of drivers sitting on the steps in the doorways and smoking; some of them waved. The cops walked alongside us on the pavement and the road. 'It's crazy,' said Mark, 'there's hundreds of them!'

'So what?' said Rico. 'There's thousands of us.' Stefan got onto one of the trams, stood in the doorway and photographed the cops.

'Here,' Mark yelled, 'us too!' We lined up in front of him, me in the middle, Rico held up his candle, Mark swung his flag, I put my arms round their shoulders.

'There's too many people,' Stefan called out, 'they're walking across the picture!' But now they were pressing from behind, someone shoved me in the back, the crowd was moving faster. Stefan jumped off the tram, stumbling, I pulled him up. Someone yelled 'Pigs!' but they were still standing on the pavements, maybe it was them pressing from behind, from the station.

'Stay together,' called Rico, 'just stick together!' A few people beside us held hands or put their arms round their neighbours' shoulders, and we moved closer together too now, me holding Mark by his jacket and Rico by the arm. Ahead of us was the Blue Wonder, the big blue pedestrian bridge by the big silver department store that everyone only ever called the 'Tin Can'. The bridge was packed with people, banners hanging down from the sides, and loads of candles on the railings. 'Look at that,' said Rico, tugging at my arm. 'It's like Christmas.'

'Free electi,' Stefan read and took a few photos. 'What's that mean?'

'There's more letters, you idiot, free elections!' said Mark, waving his Pioneer pennant at the people on the bridge.

'We are the people!' they were calling up there now, and it looked like they were jumping up and down. 'We are the people!' they chanted next to us, and stopped. We were right in front of the Blue Wonder now and it really was wobbling a bit, almost like Mr Singer had said. They were chanting 'We are the people!' under the bridge now too, there was so much noise, and on top of it they were bouncing up and down.

'If you don't bounce you're a Club supporter,' Rico called, and laughed, 'If you don't bounce you're a Club supporter!'

Mark and I joined in, 'If you don't bounce you're a Club supporter!' – that was what Chemie fans always chanted on the tram on the way to the game, and they'd jump up and down and make the tram wobble. We jumped up and down too, and a few people next to us started jumping as well. 'We are the people! We are the people! If you don't bounce you're a Club supporter!' Stefan stood in front of us, taking his photos. Rico's candle had gone out; his hand was all covered in wax. He searched his pockets but a woman held her candle out to him and he lit his again. Then we moved on, we walked underneath the bridge;

there was a water cannon on our left.

Stefan put a new roll of film in his camera; he photographed the water cannon and then looked up and tapped me on the shoulder. 'Hey, Danny, what d'you reckon, will it really collapse?'

'Rubbish,' I said. 'You don't believe that crap Singer told us, do you?'

He nodded, 'Yeah, that's rubbish,' and looked up again. He walked faster now, squeezing between people, and then I saw him standing on the pavement in front of the bridge with his camera. He was up pretty close to the cops, and I waved him back over.

'Are you crazy, you can't snap them, you'll get in trouble.'

'I don't think so, Danny, photography club.' He tapped the membership card pinned to his chest.

'It's all kicking off,' Rico said next to me. 'Here we go!'

'Why, what d'you mean?' But then I saw it, a big old building with columns ahead of us, I knew the place, I'd been past it on the tram a few times, but there hadn't been any cops and water cannons and tanks outside it then.

'A tank,' said Rico, 'crazy!' There were even cops on the balcony above the columns, wearing machine guns on belts around their necks like Stefan with his camera, one of them watching us through binoculars. On the roof of the building were spotlights, their beams sweeping across the crowd. Now they passed over us; I held my hand in front of my eyes and turned away.

'It's like in the war,' said Mark, and Stefan photographed the building.

'It's a police tank,' Rico said, 'not an army one.' He knew that kind of thing; his father had been an officer. We stopped. The people around us turned slowly towards the building and the cops, holding up their candles and banners, and then the chanting started back in, first quiet, somewhere at the front, then louder and louder: 'We are the people! We are the people!' and then, much faster and in a different rhythm: 'Free elections! Free elections! Free elections!'

The cops were getting nervous, you could tell, they weren't standing still in a single row anymore, they were moving their shields and inching forwards. The one on the balcony had put his binoculars down and had a walkie-talkie in his hand, bigger than his head.

'Who lives here?' yelled Mark, 'Shit, who is it that lives here?'

'The mayor,' said Stefan.

'Rubbish,' said Rico. 'It's police, really high up, secret service!'

This one guy had climbed onto a car at the side of the road. He waved his arms around and yelled so loud we could hear it from where we were: 'Stasi out, Stasi out! Stasi, Stasi, Stasi, out, out, out!' A few cops went running towards him but two men leapt out of the crowd, dragged him down from the car and disappeared into the crush with him.

'What Stasi, who's that?' Mark yelled.

'Police,' said Rico, 'secret service!' The water cannon moved towards the people, the little tower on top turning, cops with dogs alongside it; I could hear them barking.

A few people positioned themselves in front of the cops, holding a big banner with the words *No violence!* A cop pushed his shield into someone's face, the man fell to the ground, holding onto the banner, it was a woman, two cops picked her up and dragged her away. 'No violence! No violence!' the crowd was yelling now, and I saw Rico yelling along with them, Rico the boxer. But the cops didn't listen, just started bashing away at the other banner-holders.

'Come on,' Mark yelled, 'let's get out of here!' He took his flag down, rolled it up and jammed the broom handle under his arm. They were pressing from behind, everyone running to the right side of the road, and the cops and the water cannon stayed put.

'Large-calibre machine gun,' said Rico, pointing at the tank. 'If that goes off, we're all toast.'

'They can't do that,' I said, 'they can't, they can't just shoot at the crowd...' I turned around; the building was a little way behind us now but there were still people walking past it; the *No violence* banner had disappeared.

'Told you,' Mark unrolled his flag again and held it up above his head. 'The tank's just for show, probably not even loaded. For peace, we're marching for peace!'

'Oh yeah, peace?' said Rico. 'You saw, no violence!'

'You and your peace,' I said. 'You're the only one walking around with peace on your flag!'

'Don't put down my flag! Over there, look, freedom, that's almost the same!'

'Too many people,' Stefan said, putting another new film in his camera. 'They were all in the way, too many people in the picture. Did you see the police, they just...'

'If my dad was here,' I said, 'he'd show them...'

'Course,' said Rico, 'he'd beat them black and blue!' He put his hand on my shoulder and I nodded. Ahead of us on the left was the town hall; it looked like a castle.

'The middle,' said Rico, 'we've got to get closer to the middle!'

He was right, we were almost on the pavement, and we tried to squeeze back into the crowd but they were stumbling towards us from ahead, pushing and shoving us onto the pavement, the cops must have been wielding their clubs on the other side, we were in the middle of a load of people suddenly standing in a little side street, blocked at the other end by three police cars, like a dead end. 'Back to the march!' a man yelled, throwing his candle away; Rico held tight to his. It was only ten or twenty metres, I could see the banners and the candles and the people's heads, and now they chanted again, 'We are the people!' but now there were cops between our little group and the big, big march.

'What's going on?' Mark yelled, gripping his broom handle in both hands like a club. At the end of the road, I saw a truck with an open tarpaulin; they must want to get us in there, but why?

'What do we do now?' yelled Rico.

'Photography club,' said Stefan, and he stepped back and lifted his camera, there was a flash, 'I'm allowed!' A few people tried to get out between the cops but they didn't stand a chance, the cops just pushed them back with their shields.

'Into a building,' yelled Rico, 'let's get into a building!' He threw his candle at the cops, it bounced off a shield, and Rico ran to one of the buildings. Mark dropped his Pioneer pennant and ran after him, and Stefan just stood there photographing the cops.

'Stefan, come on!' I yelled. Someone bumped into me, I stumbled and held onto a wall, people ran back and forth in the road, some of them jolting at door handles, I couldn't see Stefan anymore and I ran to Rico, who was standing by a big door; he'd got it open somehow.

'Come on, Danny, in here!' It was dark in the entranceway and we felt our way along rubbish bins to the backyard. Someone flicked on a lighter; there were other faces beside us, not cops. We ran across the yard and then into the building ahead, the door was open. 'No,' said Rico, 'not that way, we won't get out there, up to the roof,

Danny.' He ran back out to the yard, I grabbed Mark by the shoulder and pulled him along.

'Shit, Danny, they're gonna get us.'

'No, calm down, Rico can do it!' Rico was on top of a low wall, and from there he climbed onto a shed roof.

'Come on then!'

'Give us a leg-up,' said Mark. 'Please, Danny, I can't get up there!' I heard the trampling of boots and screaming out in the street. I braced my hands for him, he put one foot on top and climbed onto the wall. Then I pulled myself up, Rico held out his hand, and then I was flat on the roof next to him and Mark.

'Stay put,' said Rico, 'make sure you stay down!' Light in the entrance and then in the yard, torches, cops' flashlights. Then light in the stairwell, proper light, then screaming and trampling of boots on the stairs, they'd caught them, we could hear, and now I saw a cop in the stairwell window, holding a man by the shoulder and shoving him along. Then they were in the yard, more screaming, someone was crying! I pressed my face against the tarred roof until my nose hurt, then they were gone.

'Stay down,' Mark whispered, 'boys, stay down, perhaps they're still waiting!' The light went out again in the stairwell. There really were still some there 'cause there was a clang, but it was just a woman leaning out of her window on the second floor. I could see her white hair. Another window opened two floors up from her.

'They gone?' a man said.

'They're gone,' the old woman said, 'all gone now.'

'I was going to let one in,' said the man, 'but there's no point...'

'No,' said the woman, 'they'd only knock our door down. Hard times...'

'Yes, hard times,' the man said.

'Oh well, maybe it'll all be over soon.' The old woman coughed.

'What, over?' asked the man.

'Oh, you know, I'm just saying.' She coughed again.

'It's one of those things,' said the man.

'Good night,' said the old woman.

'Night,' the man said, and closed his window. The old woman stood there coughing; she was wearing a white nightshirt. She coughed again, then she spat out the window; she must have coughed up a bit of her lung. She closed the window, drew the curtains and turned off the light. I rolled onto my back.

'Look up there,' said Mark. 'The Big Dipper.'

'Stefan,' I said.

'Oh, he'll be fine,' said Rico. 'He's got his photography card.'

I smiled, and then I laughed 'cause they couldn't see me, but not too loud. 'Him and his photography club.'

'No,' said Rico, 'they'll let him go, or they'll give him a lift home, that's not bad either, a thirteen-year-old, they can't keep him... That was his test, he's one of us now.'

'Right,' I said. 'Then he can come to the trade fair.'

'Who knows where they'll lock him up. Come on, look up. And next to it, that's the Little Bear, that's what it's called.'

I patted Mark on the shoulder. You're a real star-spotter!'

'Hey Danny,' he said. 'Do you get it?'

'Get what?'

'What it's all about. Today, I mean, the march.'

'Not really, no.'

'That they just went right into the crowd... I wouldn't have thought they'd do that!'

'They go into the crowd at football as well, don't they?'

'True, Danny, but not as bad as that.'

'Quiet,' Rico whispered. We heard footsteps on the stairs, the door opened, and someone walked quietly across the yard to the entrance. Maybe the man had hidden someone in his flat after all, or the old lady or someone else from the building.

'What d'you think would happen if they find out we were here, Singer and Dettleff? And Mrs Seidel. They always find everything out.'

'They can't do anything,' I said, 'not with so many people. They can't all be rioters.'

'It's people like them,' Rico said, sliding closer to us, 'it's them they're marching against. And against the cops, of course, against them as well.'

'I'm still gonna get in trouble,' said Mark. 'My dad, you know, I was grounded.' Mark stood up. 'Shall we go? It might not be that bad if I don't get home too late.'

'But have a good look first,' said Rico, climbing onto the wall. 'If they're still here we'll have to get out across the yards.' We climbed down the wall and crossed the yard to the entrance. The big door to the street was still wide open and we took a good look to either side, but everything was empty. We stepped out. The street was dark, no blue light now, only two streetlamps on and the rest broken.

We walked to the main road and that was empty as well; two cars drove past. 'Cops!' Mark ducked against a wall. But they carried on, no flashing lights. There were a few candles on the ground, with spots of wax beside them. 'My flag!' Mark bent down. It was all dirty and crumpled; he picked it up and stroked the fabric and the broom handle. He found a rubber band in his pocket and rolled up the pennant.

'Leave it undone,' said Rico. 'Then if they catch us, we

can say we were at a Pioneers meeting.'

Mark grinned. 'See, my flag!' We walked along the main road to the tram stop on Karl-Marx-Platz. The square was covered in candles as well; I picked one up and put it in my pocket. We were all alone on the pavement, Mark swinging his flag.

'Hello, have you got any giveaways?' We were at the trade fair, going from one booth to the next, Stefan, Rico, Walter and me. Mark was grounded again, this time he hadn't managed to sneak out, and Paul couldn't make it either. Stefan had brought his backpack and it was almost full. He was something like a hero for us now, 'cause the cops had caught him and put him on the back of the lorry like the other prisoners, and we were a bit jealous but we didn't tell him that. All we told him was that that had been his test to get in the gang, and he was one of us now.

He'd brought his camera again and was photographing the booths. The cops had confiscated his films when he was at the station but he'd hidden one roll in his underpants and he wanted to win the photography club prize with it.

We went through halls three and four to hall five, where the cars were, proper cars, not just Skodas, Ladas and Wartburgs. They even had Mercedes and VWs. Stefan had pinned his photography club card to his jacket again, 'For good luck,' he'd said, 'cause he'd shown it to the cops and then they'd given him a lift home to his parents.

'Us four in front of the Mercedes,' said Stefan. 'That'd be a great photo!'

'For your prize?'

'No, I'm gonna get the prize for the photos of the Monday meeting. This one's just for us, to remember it by.'

‘Go on,’ said Rico, ‘ask that guy there if he’ll take a snapshot for us.’

‘Better not,’ I said. ‘What if he calls security...?’ There were no cops inside the halls, they just patrolled outside, but there were guards and security men and they could get you in real trouble ’cause you weren’t allowed in the trade fair until you turned sixteen.

‘Rubbish,’ said Rico, ‘look, he’s doing it!’ The man was already holding the camera, it matched his black suit. Stefan showed him something about the flash and the buttons, then he came over to us and we lined up in front of the Mercedes and held hands. There was a flash. We smiled.

# JOB CREATION SCHEME

We were working in the youth club over in Mühlenviertel, Mark and me, 'cause they'd given us sixty hours each. That was a lot, although we knew a few guys who'd had to do a hundred, but we hadn't expected it any other way 'cause we'd got thirty the last time and fifteen before that, and before that, case dismissed – they always did that when you got caught for the first time. I actually wanted to go back to the OAPs' home where I'd done my thirty hours, 'cause all I had to do there was wheel meals around on a trolley. And I'd worn a white coat with a name badge like a proper male nurse, and people had called me 'Mr Lenz', and sometimes old men had come and asked me for cigarettes, and sometimes I'd brought them beer or korn or brandy, and they'd given me a bit of pocket money for my trouble. Mark had worked for the council gardening department, he didn't want to go to the OAPs' home, 'Old people are disgusting,' he'd said, and that was true, but it wasn't down to me if someone didn't make it to the toilet in time, or dropped down dead – that was up to the professionals. But they didn't want me anymore, they'd asked me why I had to do community service this time and I'd said criminal damage and they didn't like the sound of that. The woman from the Youth Offenders Team had tipped us off about the youth club, and no one there had asked what we were doing it for.

The youth club was being done up and we did a couple of hours after school and at weekends. It was slow progress; we had another forty hours to go and the judge had only given us a month's time. 'That stupid cow,' said Mark. 'This is taking the piss! She knows we're still at school!' We were painting the wall black, down in the beer cellar; there was a crate of beer left behind the bar and we took a lot of breaks.

'We can get an extension,' I said. 'We just have to put in an application with the reasons, and that.'

'It's still shit, Danny, another forty hours to go!' He dipped his roller in the bucket and then slammed it so hard on the wall it splashed paint.

'Watch it, will you? I thought you wanted to do Painting and Decorating?'

'I don't want to, Danny, I have to!' Mark was doing a pre-training year, Interior Decoration, and after that he could get an apprenticeship as a painter.

'Come on,' he said, 'let's have another beer.'

'What if they notice?'

'I'll give 'em the money, it's not much!' He went behind the bar and popped open two beers. 'Think how much money we're saving them!'

'True.'

'Come here!' He passed me two bar stools over the counter and we sat down. 'It's Saturday, isn't it?' he said, and we tapped our bottles together. It was just gone one but we were on our third beers, and I didn't feel like working anymore.

'You're right,' I said. 'They get everything for free, all our hard work. It's all just community service and volunteers.'

'And Job Creation Schemes,' said Mark. 'They're new, they're doing the patio outside, but there's only two of them. Old geezers.'

'Alright lads, everything OK down here?' Andrea was standing in the doorway. She was the boss at the youth club but she was pretty young herself. 'Had enough?'

Mark leant against the bar and pushed the beer behind his back. 'We're fine,' I said, 'just taking a quick break, won't be long.'

'Isn't it a bit early for beer?'

'It's just the one,' said Mark. 'Just to perk us up a bit.'

She came over to us, inspected the wall and nodded. 'Looking pretty good, you'll get that finished today.'

'Course,' said Mark, 'easy.'

Andrea wasn't bad looking even though she had a kid already, but she lived alone, the others had told us. 'You're in with a chance there,' Mark had said one time. 'You just gotta keep trying, Danny, I bet she likes 'em young.' Andrea lit one up; she smoked f6, 'Eff Sex,' Mark had said one time, 'that's a good sign, Danny,' but I wasn't into her.

She held the pack out to us and we took one each. 'It's OK,' she said, blowing out smoke; she was really pretty actually, 'you've got to take a break now and then.'

'Can't we do something else for a change?' Mark said, lighting his cigarette and giving me a light. 'All this painting.'

'I thought you wanted to be a painter and decorator?'

'Yeah, I do. That's why.'

'OK, listen, I'll send you one of the JCSs, then you'll be finished quicker and you can sand down the stairs.'

'Thanks, Andrea!' He took her hand and patted it; she pulled it away and laughed and shook her head.

She went behind the bar and put an ashtray down on the counter. 'We don't want everyone to see you drinking. Next time, wait until you've knocked off for the day, OK?'

'Yes, Andrea,' we said.

'There'll be lunch upstairs at around two,' she said, and then she crossed the cellar to the door. We watched her go; she really did look pretty good, even though she had a kid already.

'Must be a real arsehole,' said Mark.

'Who?'

'The guy, the arsehole who knocked her up... just

buggers off and leaves her on her own, must be an idiot.'

Someone came down the stairs. A guy in blue overalls and a blue flat cap stopped in the doorway. He said hello and tapped his cap, then came over to us. He stopped again and inspected the wall. 'Looks pretty good, boys,' he said in a low, calm voice. 'Not much more for us to do.' He stood between us and rapped his knuckles on the counter. 'Taking it easy, boys?'

'Course,' I said. 'Course, Mr Singer, got to take a break now and then.' He took off his cap, put it on the bar and looked at me. Mark picked up his beer and drank a mouthful; at first, I thought he wanted to smash the bottle over Singer's head.

'Daniel,' said Singer, moving his cap back and forth on the bar, 'Daniel Lenz.' He looked old, much older than he used to, he had hardly any hair and what was left had gone white. He held out his hand to shake and that seemed to have got smaller as well, he'd had enormous hands and loads of strength in them. He'd been a woodwork teacher, woodwork and metalwork and high up in the party. I took his hand and pressed it as hard as I could, but it was just soft and moist and limp.

'Bormann,' Mark shouted behind him, and Mr Singer jumped. 'Mark Bormann! Hello, Mr Singer!' Mark slapped him on the shoulder. 'Long time no see, Mr Singer!'

Mr Singer looked at Mark's hand, still on his shoulder, and stepped aside. 'Hello, Mark.'

Mark grinned. 'So how are you?'

'I'm fine,' he said, 'I've got work to do, plenty of work.'

'Yeah,' I said. 'We can see that.'

He ran his hand over his bald head, picked up his cap and put it back on. 'And how are you boys? Volunteering as well, are you, always ready to help?'

'Oh yes,' said Mark, 'we learned that from you, sir, you know that, always prepared, always ready to help, right, Danny?'

'Course,' I said. 'A Pioneer is always willing to help. And friendly, and disciplined!'

'A Pioneer always keeps his body clean and healthy,' Mark gulped down his beer and slammed the bottle on the bar. Mr Singer smiled. He went over to the paint buckets and picked up a roller. Mark went behind the counter and put the empty beer bottles in the crate. 'Old Mr Singer,' he said, shaking his head. 'Would you believe it, Danny? If Rico...'

'Don't tell him, Mark. Please.'

Mark nodded. 'He'd give him a right going over, you better believe it, Danny.'

'I know.' I looked over at Singer. He was moving the roller up and down the wall; he had to stretch to reach the ceiling.

'He'd deserve it, though, wouldn't he, Danny?'

'I guess. But remember back then at shooting practice, with the electric rifles, you were really good. Remember that...?' I couldn't help laughing, 'cause I saw us standing at the electric shooting range with Mr Singer, Mark's red neckerchief tied wrong, the ends far too long, but he got every shot...

'Ah, forget it,' he said.

We went over to the wall and picked up our rollers. Mr Singer didn't turn round when we walked past him. Mark started on the opposite wall and I went to the other end of Singer's wall. It was a pretty long wall. I'd just put my roller to the wall and he took my arm. 'Line it up properly, Mr Lenz.' He only called us Mr when we weren't paying attention or were being undisciplined or... 'Use the sights,' he put his finger on the barrel, 'use these two points to set your sights on the third point, the target, and then you'll hit it!' And he was right, I did hit it. Up, down, up, down, then in the paint bucket, and again: up, down, up, down; I heard Mr Singer breathing, it sounded almost like low moaning, I turned round to him, he was red in the face and had taken his cap back off. I worked pretty fast 'cause I wanted to get to him before he'd done half the wall. My paint bucket was almost empty and I opened a new one. Dipped the roller in and brushed it off against the plastic lattice, and then up, down, up, down again... Disruptive tendencies, and aside from that Rico's character displays... disruptive tendencies... admit, admit everything... we know... that... they always know everything... disruptive tendencies... no longer tolerate... the Elbe flows to Hamburg, the Elbe flows to Hamburg... 'The Elbe,' Mr Singer said in his low voice, 'do you know why the Elbe is so dirty? The Feddies, the Federal Republic of Germany, they pump the pollution out of their polluting factories into the Elbe, and that's why the Elbe is so polluted here! And then they lie, then they lie and say it's us, it's us causing the pollution. But we don't pollute the Elbe, the German Democratic Republic doesn't pollute! Only those dirty Federal German factories!' The Elbe flows to Hamburg, I thought, and I dipped the roller in the paint, disruptive tendencies. I'd never been to Hamburg. 'Breaktime!' I put the roller down, paint dripping down my hand. I was standing next to Mr Singer; his face and forehead were shiny.

'Come on up,' Andrea called from the door. 'Lunch is ready!'

'Right then, boys!' Mr Singer wiped his face with a big handkerchief.

'Exhausted, eh?' Mark planted himself in front of him, hands in his pockets.

'I'll be alright,' Mr Singer said. 'I'm used to hard work.'

'Leave him alone,' I said. 'He's just a poor bastard...'

He pulled his cap out of the breast pocket of his overalls and put it back on. He took a silver cigarette case out of his trouser pocket and opened it. The cigarette case had the GDR emblem on it, and underneath it said in capitals COMRADESHIP MEANS COMBAT.

'Help yourself, boys,' he said, holding it out to us.

We looked at him, then we turned away and went up the stairs.

Stefan had a dog now, a Pitbull. 'A Pitbull's not a dog,' he said. 'A Pitbull's a Pitbull. They're special.' And he wasn't wrong, 'cause even though the dog wasn't exactly big, everyone was shit-scared of it. He'd bought it over in Grünau, from these skins who bred Pitbulls in their allotment. Fifty marks, he'd paid, but only 'cause he knew a couple of them. The dog was only six months old and still really little, but it got a bit bigger every week. Stefan had a wall down in his cellar where the dog had to stand, and Stefan drew lines on the wall so we could see how fast it was growing.

The dog didn't have a name yet, he just called it 'Pitbull', but he thought about what to call it every day and probably every night as well.

'Just leave it,' I said. 'Just call it "Pitbull", that's good enough.'

'No, Danny, no, it's not. He needs a name, he's special, he's got to have a proper name.'

He stroked the dog's head, then he picked it up and put it on his lap. The dog rolled on its back and Stefan stroked its tummy. 'Look at his balls, they're gonna be huge.'

I laughed. 'What do you care about his balls, or are you into that kind of thing?'

He went red. 'Shut it, Danny.'

He stroked the dog under its jaw and on its neck, and the dog breathed loudly and grunted and stretched its front legs against Stefan's chest like two arms.

'Hey Danny, we need more dog food.'

'Give him here.' He picked up the dog and passed it to me. I leant back and put it on my chest; it was getting pretty heavy. The dog sniffed at my face. 'Look, he likes me.'

'Oh, he's always like that.' Stefan budged his chair

closer to my seat. We were down in his cellar 'cause that was where his dog lived. 'Hey Danny, the thing with the dog food...'

'Have your parents stopped giving you anything?'

'Come on, you know.' Stefan's parents didn't like his dog, especially his dad, and that was why he spent all day outside with his dog or at friends' places or down here in the cellar. 'I've run out of money but he's got to eat, he's still growing, he needs a lot of food.'

'I can lend you a couple of marks.'

'No, I need more than that, I need a bag or two. Eukanuba's the best, it's got everything in it, gives him real power.'

'Man, d'you know how much that stuff costs!'

'No, Danny, I don't want to buy it. You know that pet shop out in Mölkau...'

'Yeah, the one by the flower market.'

'Right, that's the one, Danny, that's the one.' He went to the cupboard and took out two bottles of beer. The dog jumped off my lap and followed him. 'See, Danny, I've got him trained!' The dog jumped up on his leg and Stefan bent down to it, and it licked Stefan's face with its pink tongue.

'That's disgusting,' I said.

'He's a dog, Danny.' He opened the bottles and gave me one. 'To my dog,' he said.

'To your dog.' We drank. 'So you want to nick it. But a sack like that must weigh ten kilos.'

'I know, Danny. Not from the shop, that'd never work. They store stuff out the back. I've checked it all out, it's only padlocked. All we need is ice spray.'

'And how are you gonna get it out of there? You don't want to take a car...'

'No, we'll use our moped, with a trailer on the back.'

'You're losing it!'

He put his beer down, picked up the dog and held it up over his head. The Pitbull moved its legs and howled quietly. 'I don't think he likes it, Stefan.'

'Rubbish, he's just happy.' He swayed it around a couple of times, then he put it back down. The dog went to its cardboard box and climbed in. 'I think he needs a pee,' said Stefan, getting up. He picked up the leash from the table, stuck two fingers in his mouth and whistled. Pitbull's head poked out of the cardboard box, Stefan whistled again, and now the dog climbed out again and came over to him, slowly. 'Come on, Pitbull, walkies!' Pitbull turned in a circle, howling and trying to bite his own tail.

'Look at that,' I said. 'Look at him!'

'That's normal,' said Stefan, 'he always does that when he's happy.'

Outside in the cellar corridor, the dog pissed on the wall. 'No, not here,' Stefan said, dragging it away. I laughed. The whole cellar reeked of perfume 'cause Stefan kept spraying the places where his dog had pissed so the people in the building didn't tell him off. Now his mum started telling him off for using up her nice perfume. In the beginning, the dog had shat and pissed all over Stefan's cellar every day, but that was Stefan's fault 'cause he left the dog alone when he went to his pre-training year in the morning and he didn't come back 'til the afternoon, which was a pretty long time for a little dog. He'd taken it to college a couple of times. He'd left his books at home and made holes in his bag, and Pitbull curled up inside it and went to sleep. The teachers hadn't noticed anything and Stefan took Pitbull for a walk in his breaks. But one time, the dog crawled out of his bag and ran up to the teacher's desk, and the teacher was shit-scared; it was a Pitbull, wasn't it? Now Stefan had to get drinkers we knew from the bar or outside the supermarket and give them korn and beer to come down to his cellar in the morning and look after Pitbull and take him out to the park when he needed a pee. I did it too when I had time, of course, or Rico or Mark. We were proud walking round the streets or the park with the dog.

Pitbull squatted and took a huge dump on the middle of the pavement.

'I thought you'd got him trained, Stefan?'

'Eh? I have!'

'No, I mean not to shit on the pavement.'

It stank really bad and we moved off, quick. 'I have, Danny. He usually only shits on the grass. He must have eaten something dodgy. So are you in? The thing with the dog food, I mean.'

'Stefan, mate, I don't know. When d'you want to do it?'

'I thought between three and four, when there's hardly any cops around.'

'Course, but what day?'

We'd got to the park and he let the dog off the leash. The dog ran straight to the grass and started jumping round in circles like an idiot.

'What about tomorrow, Danny? Yeah, tomorrow night.'

'Don't know. Don't you want to wait 'til Saturday? They're closed on Sundays.'

'Na, Danny, tomorrow's better. The dog needs food and if we take four or five sacks it'll last a while.'

'Alright, but only if you let me drive.'

'Thanks, Danny!' He punched me on the shoulder, then gave me a cigarette. I smoked carefully, not inhaling most of it, 'cause it still sometimes made me cough. 'Course you can drive.' The dog had found a bit of wood and was chewing on it. We ran over to it. The dog stood up, clenching the wood between its teeth and growling at us. 'Drop it, Pitbull, drop it!' Stefan stood in front of him and lifted up the leash. 'Drop it now, Pitbull!' Pitbull took no notice; he ducked down, bit at the wood and growled even louder. Stefan squatted down and grabbed him by the head. 'Drop it! Dirty!' The dog howled and dropped the piece of wood. 'Good boy.' He picked the dog up, squeezed him to his chest and stroked him. 'Who's a good boy, eh? Such a good boy!'

'You need to give him a name or he'll never do what you say.'

'Course he will, Danny. I've taught him all sorts already, you know that.'

He'd even tried to teach him to shit or at least piss on command, 'cause then he could take him round to people he didn't like, like his teachers for example. They wouldn't let him in their houses, but he could go up to their front doors with Pitbull. 'Do a poo,' Stefan kept saying when the dog shat on the grass or the pavement, and then he'd give him a dog biscuit or a bit of bread, but Pitbull didn't shit because Stefan said 'Do a poo,' he shat 'cause he needed a crap. He'd taught him 'Speak!' as well, and that worked, even if Pitbull only howled and didn't bark properly. 'Speak!' said Stefan, and got a bit of bread out of his pocket. 'Come on, speak, Pitbull!' The dog sat down, raised his head and looked up at the sky, then he started howling but with a couple of barks in between; he was getting better. 'See, Danny, look how good he is at that!'

'Yeah, not bad.' He held the bread out but then he pulled it back when the dog snatched for it. 'Go on. give it to him, he's hungry!' The dog was on his haunches in front of Stefan, staring at the piece of bread, panting, and there was slobber running out of his mouth.

'Watch this, Danny!' Stefan squatted down in front of the dog and stuck the bread between his own teeth. 'Pitbull, come and get it,' he mumbled through the bread. Pitbull tipped his head to one side and looked at him. 'Pitbull, come and get it!' And now Pitbull jumped, he jumped past Stefan's head and grabbed the bit of bread out of Stefan's mouth mid-leap. 'See that, you see that, Danny? What a dog! Come here, you!' Pitbull had choked down the bit of bread and now he ran to Stefan and jumped up on him and licked his face with his long pink tongue.

I squatted down next to them. I stroked Pitbull's head and he licked my hand. 'He really is a great dog, Stefan.'

He smiled. 'Once he's really big he'll look after me, Danny, then no one'll start anything, you know?'

'Right. He already looks pretty dangerous right now.' The dog had lain down on his back, kicking his legs and rolling on the grass. 'But you still gotta give him a name.'

'I know, I know.'

We crossed the grass back to the path and sat down on a bench, up on the back rest. Pitbull sat on the bench as well, by our feet, and panted and watched the people walking past.

'It's tricky with the name, though, Danny. Rico wants me to call him after a boxer, like Tyson or something.'

'Nah, that's stupid. Anyway, Tyson's inside again, I think. He'd only bring bad luck.'

'Every bloody dog's got some dumb name, Max or... Hey Danny, I know this guy over in Grünau, his dog's called Adolf.'

'A skin?'

'Yeah, a skin.'

Stefan gave me a cigarette; we smoked and looked at the grass on the other side of the path.

'Hey Danny, I think I'll just name him Pitbull.'

'If you say so.'

'I bet there isn't any other Pitbull just called Pitbull.'

'I bet there isn't, nah.'

'And anyway, he knows that name already. Right Pitbull?' The dog looked up at us, still panting like crazy – maybe he was thirsty – and it looked like he was nodding. 'Pitbull. Yeah, Danny, that's good. Come on, we'll have a beer to celebrate, at Goldie's.'

'I thought you were skint?'

'You were going to lend me a few marks, Danny.'

'Yeah, for dog food...'

Stefan got up and patted me on the shoulder. 'Come on Danny, you know you want to, just a couple of beers at Goldie's.' Pitbull howled, jumped off the bench and ran onto the grass. 'See, he wants to go to Goldie's and all.'

'OK,' I said. 'But only one beer.'

We crossed the grass; Pitbull had found his piece of wood again and was running ahead.

We were in the East Woods, Rico, Stefan and me, up on the little hill by the old open-air stage, so we could see if anyone came along. Stefan was inflating a blow-up doll. Karsten and his brother had cleared out some kiosk, out in one of the villages. All they wanted was booze and fags, but they'd found the whole lot in a little storage room, the place was some kind of dodgy village sex shop, and now they had all the stuff at home and couldn't get rid of it.

We'd swapped two packs of cigarettes for Mona, to train Pitbull. Stefan was red in the face, his sweat dripping onto Mona's leg. The valve was down on her foot and Mona's breasts and head were still all flat. Pitbull was lying next to Stefan, chewing a branch. 'I can't believe it!' Stefan stoppered up the valve and put the doll aside. 'It's coming out the top, it's leaking out the mouth.' Mona had her mouth wide open, room enough for a fist, but I only put two fingers in. It was all soft inside, with rubber nubs instead of teeth, and then there was a rubber wall, which I pressed aside, and then another one, and then I thought of Rico and all his girls he was always telling me about, and I took my fingers out.

'There's nothing leaking,' I said. 'You just gotta give her a good blow!'

'You guys do it!'

'It's your dog, Stefan.'

He turned Mona on her front. 'Holes everywhere, it's never gonna work.'

I went over to Rico's bag. 'Haven't you got a pump, like for a blow-up boat?'

'Nah, Karsten didn't give me it.'

Stefan opened the valve and went back to blowing.

Rico took out a jumper and a pair of blue work trousers. 'I hope they fit her,' he said.

'And you reckon we can train him with the doll?'

'Right, Danny. Look at this.' He held a pack of dog biscuits in his hand; Pitbull dropped his stick and came over. 'No, no, Rocky, first you gotta practice "Attack".'

'Pitbull,' I said. 'His name's Pitbull.'

'Right, Danny, right.' He ripped the packet open and gave Pitbull a biscuit. 'Wow, you hear that crunching? Good, eh? You'll get more if you attack!'

'Give me one, Rico, I want to give him one too.'

'Only one, though.' He handed me the packet. I took a dog biscuit and threw it down the hill. 'Fetch, Pitbull!' He raced down, nose to the ground, and then he got it and we heard him crunching it up. Then he ran up to me, jumped up and grabbed the packet out of my hand. 'Drop it, Pitbull, no, drop it!'

Stefan took his mouth off the valve and the air hissed out again; he ran over to Pitbull and ripped the packet of dog biscuits out of his mouth. Pitbull growled. Stefan took the leash and raised his arm. 'No, Pitbull, no!' Pitbull took a few slow steps back, lowered his head and growled even louder. I went over to Mona and closed her valve.

Rico walked around Pitbull and stood behind him. 'No,' said Stefan, squatting down in front of Pitbull, 'bugger off, Rico. It's my dog.' Then he growled, he growled louder than Pitbull, he grabbed him and turned him on his back. Pitbull was quiet now, and Stefan raised his hand and slapped him on the balls. Pitbull howled for a moment, wiggled his legs, but then he quietened down again.

Rico came over to me and squatted down. 'He's doing it right,' he whispered, and he put a hand on Mona's leg.

'Bad boy, Pitbull,' said Stefan. 'Bad boy, dirty, bad boy.' He let go of the dog, stood up and stepped back a bit. Pitbull stayed on his back, the white fur on his chest all grubby and his back legs twitching. Stefan was still standing in front of Pitbull, with one hand on his hip and the other one pointing at the ground. 'Stay! Bad boy, Pitbull.' The dog was still quiet, and we saw his belly moving as he breathed. 'Get up,' said Stefan, and the dog got up and walked slowly towards him. 'Alright, Pitbull.' Stefan squatted down in front of him, and Pitbull jumped up and licked his face with his pink tongue. 'Alright, Pitbull. You're a good boy now!' Pitbull howled and turned in circles and tried to bite his own tail.

I picked up Mona; there was hardly any air left inside her. 'So what are we gonna do, how are we gonna train him?'

'Easy,' said Rico, pointing at Pitbull as he rolled on the grass and kicked his legs. 'He's got to learn when to attack and when not to.'

'He's not actually supposed to attack anyone.'

'Like a guard dog,' said Stefan. 'Just like a guard dog, Danny. Then he'll obey every word. Attack and off, you know, Danny, he'll only do what I say.'

He went back to Mona and started blowing her up again. Pitbull jumped around us and howled and barked a bit. We watched Mona's breasts inflating. Rico went over to his bag, took out a bottle of water and opened it. 'Come here, Pitbull, I bet you're thirsty.'

Stefan stopped blowing and put his finger over the valve; the air whistled and squeaked its way out again under his finger. 'Rico, is it fizzy water?'

'No, it's out of the tap.'

'I'm just asking. He's scared of fizzy water, you know, he doesn't get the bubbles.' Then he went on blowing. Mona was almost finished now, her breasts growing out of her right under her neck; only her nipples needed a bit more air, at the front. Rico poured water out of the bottle into his hand and Pitbull slobbered it up. He drank a whole bottle's worth.

'Like a baby,' I said.

'Don't disturb him while he's drinking,' said Rico. 'He hates that.'

'I'm not disturbing him.'

Rico put the bottle away. Pitbull jumped around in front of him, water dripping onto Rico's trousers.

'Done,' said Stefan and stood up. He lifted Mona up and put an arm round her shoulder. 'She's too fat,' I said. 'Better let a bit of air out.'

'How come, Danny? She's just right, got a nice bit of padding.' He put his hand on her hip and stroked her belly.

'The cheeks,' I said, 'take a look at her cheeks.'

She really did have a bit too much air in her, her cheeks were all puffed up and her eyes were protruding. Rico got the trousers and jumper. 'You're right, Danny, too much air's no good. We don't want her to break too quick.'

'How come?' said Stefan, stepping back a bit with Mona. 'She's just right. You'll only mess up her stopper.'

'Come on, give her here!' Rico tugged Mona towards himself, laid her down on the ground and opened the stopper.

'That's enough!' Stefan called out. 'She's fine like that, just leave her now!' He looked down at Rico, who was lying above Mona and fumbling around at her, and for a moment I thought he'd drag him off her, 'cause his fists were dangling on either side and clenching and unclenching.

'It's alright, Stefan,' I said, putting my hand on his arm. 'He won't do her any harm.'

Rico closed the valve, then put the jumper on her. 'Come on, give us a hand.' Her arms were sticking out like she wanted to hug all three of us, and we bent and pressed her into shape until the jumper fitted.

'Be a bit careful!' Stefan said. 'Watch out, come on, you'll break her!'

Mona's mouth was wide open, Rico was lying on top of her and it looked like she was screaming. 'That'll do,' he said. He took a cushion out of the bag and shoved it under the jumper. 'That's for him to bite into.'

We picked her up and leant her against a tree. 'Pitbull, heel! Sit, sit down there!' Pitbull went over to Mona and sniffed at her leg. 'Sit, I said! Sit, Pitbull!' Pitbull sat down in front of Mona and looked at her.

'Look how he's looking at her,' said Rico. 'He doesn't like her. He'll bite her really quick.' Stefan got a dog biscuit and stood next to Mona by the tree. He pressed the biscuit against her belly. 'Come and get it, Pitbull, attack!' Pitbull jumped up on Mona and grabbed the dog biscuit out of Stefan's hand. 'Good boy, Pitbull! Now sit, sit back down again!' Stefan did the same again, and then he stuck a dog biscuit under Mona's jumper. 'Come and get it, Pitbull, attack!' Pitbull went over to Stefan and sat down facing him.

'He hasn't got it yet,' said Rico. 'You should have done it a bit longer, with the biscuit outside her clothes, I mean!'

'It's not gonna work,' I said. 'You're just making the poor dog crazy.' I sat down by Rico's bag and helped myself to one of his cigarettes.

'Chuck one over for me, Danny!' I threw the pack to him but before he could catch it, Pitbull was there. He leapt past Rico, almost standing in mid-air, and grabbed the cigarettes. 'No, dirty, Pitbull, dirty, no, enough! Dirty, that's dirty!' We all yelled at the same time but he ran, the pack of Golden 25s from the Vietcong clenched between his teeth, past Mona into the bushes. We yelled and screamed, and he came crashing through the undergrowth, dashing past us and down to the old wooden stage. Stefan ran after him.

'My fags!' Rico yelled, 'bloody hell, my fags!' Then he started after him as well. Ever since he'd heard that cigarettes were the number-one currency in jail, he'd had no sense of humour when someone messed with his money. 'I better get used to it, Danny,' he'd say sometimes.

Pitbull was down by the stage now, Stefan and Rico still a good way behind him. I went over to Mona. She was still leaning against the tree, staring at me. I picked her up, laid her down carefully and undressed her. I stuck a finger inside her; it felt exactly like her mouth. I packed the cushion, the dog biscuits and the jumper in Rico's bag. I undid the valve and watched her legs getting thinner and thinner, then her breasts went limp and her face collapsed; she'd got old. I stroked her eyes again, then I folded her up and put her in the bag and zipped it up over her. I headed down to the stage; Stefan's jacket was on the grass and I picked it up. 'Stefan! Rico!' I looked down the path between the trees. 'Where are you? Don't just bugger off!' There they were but I could only see their legs, and now they disappeared under the stage. And there was Pitbull. He came out from under the stage and ran towards me.

I put the bag down and squatted. 'Alright, come here, that's a good boy!' Pitbull rested his paws on my chest and licked my face with his pink tongue.

'Nice and quiet,' said Stefan, 'keep nice and quiet.' We pushed our moped along the cellar corridor to the little door leading to the street. Stefan unlocked it. Outside, it was dark and silent. 'Wait,' Stefan whispered. He fetched a board and laid it up the two steps. We pushed the moped out onto the street. We had a Simson S51 with a four-speed gearbox, souped up so it could do a hundred with only one person riding it.

'What about the trailer, Stefan?'

'It's in the backyard. Hold this a mo.' He pressed a roll of wire into my hand.

'What's this for?'

'For the trailer, Danny.' Then he went round the back into the yard.

Quiet footsteps in the cellar. I turned around; Pitbull was in the corridor. He tipped his head and looked at me. 'What's up, boy? Go back to bed!' But he came up to me and sniffed at the moped and them me. 'No, no, you can't come with us, you need your sleep.' I squatted down and stroked his nose, and when I put my hand on his side and stroked his ribs, I felt his heart. It beat way faster than mine. 'We're going to get you some yummy Eukanuba,' I said. Stefan brought the trailer. I stood up and looked at the buildings across the road; all was dark, just a flicker of blue light in the odd window. 'Look,' I said. 'They're watching the same film, see that?'

'It's fuck-film time,' said Stefan. He grinned, 'cause we'd used to love those late-night TV fuck-films until Karsten and his brother got us proper pornos.

He put the trailer behind the moped. It was really a bicycle trailer with a long shaft, and he pushed that onto the luggage rack. 'Give us the wire, Danny.'

'How's that gonna stay put?'

'It'll stay put, Danny. I've done it before.'

I lit one up. I didn't want to see him attaching the trailer. Pitbull walked along the front of the building and lifted his leg.

'Watch out he doesn't run off.'

'Course.'

'Give us your knife.'

I popped out the blade and handed it to him.

'Gotta give it enough leeway,' he said. 'That's important for the corners, get it?'

'Course.'

Pitbull sniffed his way over to the bus stop; I whistled a couple of times and he came ambling back.

'Danny, mate, this is shit, the rear light.'

'What d'you mean?'

'Look at it, you can't see the rear light now. The trailer's in the way.'

'So we just won't have a rear light, doesn't bother me.'

'No, Danny, that's no good, way too dangerous. What if someone drives into the back of us?'

He stepped back and looked at the trailer. Pitbull was walking along the middle of the road; I went over to him and carried him back to the pavement. 'A building-site lamp,' Stefan said. 'I'll attach a building site lamp to the back. To the luggage rack, right, better than nothing.' He turned and went back down to the cellar.

'Jesus, Stefan, forget it, there's no one on the road at this time of night, anyway.' But he was gone. Pitbull was wandering around in the road again; I picked him up and put him in the trailer.

'Found a red one,' Stefan said, putting the lamp on the seat. 'It's better, otherwise someone'll smash into the back of us.' He had a crowbar in the other hand, which he put in the trailer, and then he took a small torch and a can of ice spray out of his pockets and added them. 'Right, Danny. Now we're ready.' I nodded. Stefan wrapped wire around the lamp and attached it to the back of the luggage rack. 'Got a match, Danny?'

'No.'

He bent a bit of wire straight and stuck it in the tiny hole on the bottom of the lamp. It started flashing. 'At least stop it flashing,' I said. He pushed the wire in again and the lamp stopped flashing and lit up red and flickered a bit; the battery was probably running out.

Pitbull howled low. Stefan looked into the trailer. 'Alright, you might as well come with us.'

Rico and I were at Goldie's. We were drinking beer and apple korn and waiting for Stefan and Pitbull. 'Goldie,' Rico called out, 'bring us a beer, he'll be here any minute.'

'And an apple korn?'

'Right,' said Rico, and I saw Goldie filling glasses behind the bar.

'He's got to go to the vet's again,' I said. 'For more injections. Expensive hobby, dogs.'

'Right. But he doesn't mind paying for it. Hardly

drinks beer or anything these days. All his money goes on Pitbull.'

'He's doing it right,' I said. 'A dog like that, it's something special.'

Goldie put the beer and the apple korn down at Stefan's place. 'Is he bringing the dog?' he asked.

'He always brings his dog, you know that,' said Rico.

Goldie smiled. 'Course. Good for him, it's a good dog.' He rapped his knuckles on the table and went back to the bar.

We lit one up and looked at the door. 'I bet he's shitting all over the place on the way,' Rico said.

'Yeah,' I said. 'It's the cheap dog food.'

'What about your pet-shop job?'

'Didn't work out, the place was full of security guards.' I didn't tell Rico the break-in had gone wrong 'cause Pitbull had rolled in shit. We'd stopped for a break in the East Woods on the way there. Pitbull stank so bad we chased him into the lake. But that had only made it worse.

'Those bloody private cops,' I said. 'We'll get them away somewhere next time and then we'll clear out the whole place.'

Goldie brought a bowl of water and put it under the table. 'I bet he's thirsty, it's hot out.'

'Yeah, probably.' I turned and pulled the net curtain aside. 'You don't mind, do you, Goldie?' Goldie wasn't a big fan of fresh air and he only opened the windows just before closing time.

'Go ahead.'

I opened the window; the sun shone on the table. 'Are you crazy? Jesus, it's really bright!' Rico shielded his eyes with his hand. I leant out; someone on the corner was walking a little white dog. I whistled but it was an old man with a poodle.

'Is he coming?'

'No, not yet.' I closed the curtain again but left the window ajar.

'His beer's going flat,' said Rico.

'He'll be here soon.'

'A dog like that,' Goldie said, 'it takes responsibility. It's like a kid, you know? Like, if he goes to the park he has to wait until Pitbull's taken a dump, you know, responsibility, so he can sit here in peace afterwards.'

'You're right there, Goldie.' Goldie smiled, rapped his knuckles on the table and went back to the bar. We smoked and looked at the door. There was hardly any fizz left in Stefan's beer, and we shared it between our two glasses. I leant out the window again. An ambulance passed, blue lights flashing; it switched on the siren at the corner and turned right. 'What's up out there, Danny?'

'Dunno. Ambulance.' I sat back down.

'Probably a fight,' said Rico. 'Someone's got beaten up.' I picked up Stefan's apple korn and drank it.

'Pitbull!'

We looked at the door; there was Mark.

'Quick,' he said, 'quick.'

We dashed over. 'What's up, what is it?'

'He's dead, Pitbull's dead!'

'Where?'

'At Stefan's.' We shoved him aside and ran. We ran to the corner, then we cut across the park to Stefan's. I turned around; Mark must have stayed at Goldie's. The ambulance was parked outside Stefan's building. I looked up; the windows were open in his flat, someone was screaming, no, that wasn't Stefan's voice. We ran around the ambulance; Pitbull was lying in the road, his eyes open, and his head was all flat. Blood was running out of his mouth; one canine had broken off. I looked into the ambulance, I looked at the stretcher and all the machines and tubes. An ambulance worker came and slammed the doors. I saw Rico going into the building. I sat down by Pitbull. I put my hand on his white fur. He was still really warm. I stroked his back and his neck, I stroked his eyes and tried to close them, but it didn't work. I stood up. I went to the ambulance worker. 'What now?'

'What d'you mean, what now?'

'Aren't you going to take him with you?'

Someone screamed inside the building.

'That's Animal Rescue does that,' he said. 'But he's dead anyway.'

'What's going on up there?' I pointed at Stefan's building.

'No idea, someone said it was an emergency, child fallen out a window or something.'

I saw Rico go in through the door and run up the stairs. 'Police?'

'Don't know,' said the ambulance worker. Someone screamed inside the building; now it was Stefan's voice. I went to the door. A cop car came down the road.

'No, no. Let go...'

I looked up at the building. Stefan's dad was hanging halfway out the window, a hand around his throat. I ran inside. The cops stopped beside the ambulance. There were two kids in the corridor. 'You've got a key, right?' The bigger one took the little one by the arm and pulled him away. I took a few coins out of my pocket. 'The key,' I said, pressing the money into the bigger one's hand. 'Just for a minute!' He gave it to me, on a long string. I went to the front door; the cops had got out and were talking to the ambulance worker; I locked the door behind me. Then I hung the key around the boy's neck. 'Don't open it, go and play out the back!' I ran up the stairs. There was a crash up above, someone screamed again.

The flat door was open and there was a chair on the floor outside it. I went in. I ran down the hall, saw Stefan's mum sitting in the kitchen, her face swollen up and all sorts of bottles on the kitchen table. 'Alright?' I said, but she didn't look at me.

'An accident,' someone yelled. I went in the living room; the glass in the door was smashed. Stefan's dad was on the floor, Stefan was sitting on him and pressing his face in the shards. Rico was sitting on the sofa and the glass coffee table in front of him was broken too, a few bottles lying on the floor as well.

'Come in, Danny.' Rico was smoking and holding a beer.

'An accident,' Stefan's dad screamed, kicking his legs, 'believe me, son.' Stefan punched him in the head but he went on screaming. I looked over at Rico but he'd put the bottle to his lips and was drinking, looking at the ceiling. I stood behind Stefan, and when he pulled back I grabbed hold of his arm. He yelled, I'd never heard him scream like that, he jumped up, and his other fist was right by my face.

'Stefan, it's me, Danny! Come here!' I put my arm round him and pulled him away from his dad.

'Danny,' he screamed into my shoulder, 'Pitbull!'

'Yeah, I know.' The doorbell rang from downstairs. I went to the window; I stumbled over Stefan's dad and held onto the windowsill. The cops were outside the front door, waving up at me. Pitbull was a little white mark down on the road. I closed the window. The doorbell rang again.

Stefan's dad tried to get up. 'Stay down, you!' Rico called from the sofa. 'You get back down, you bastard, you dog-killer!'

'Dog-killer,' Stefan said quietly. His face was shiny and snot was running out of his nose. Rico picked up a bottle of brandy off the floor and handed it to him. Stefan opened it and drank a big gulp, then he threw it at the wall by the door. 'Pitbull!'

He launched himself back at his dad, but I stood between them. 'Stefan,' I said, 'that's enough now, there's no point now, you've already done him in.'

Stefan stumbled to the sofa and sat down next to Rico. 'Pitbull,' he said quietly. 'He's got to go in his box now, he's out in the sun.' I heard footsteps on the stairs, and I went down the hall and closed the door to the flat. Stefan's mum was still sitting in the kitchen, now with her head on the table, in amongst the bottles.

I went back to the living room and stopped in the doorway. 'Stefan, mate, how did it...?'

'It was him,' Stefan said quietly. 'He threw him out.' Stefan was still on the sofa, now looking really small, almost disappearing into the cushions. His dad had sat up and leant against the wall. One of his eyes could only blink and there was lots of blood on his face, and here and there I saw Stefan's toothmarks.

'An accident,' he mumbled. 'I wanted to... wanted to hold onto him.' The cops knocked at the door.

'You shut your mouth, shut your fucking mouth. Mum told me what happened!' He picked up a bottle and threw it at his dad. It only hit the window, scattering more shards. The cops knocked louder. Stefan got up. 'I've got to go to Pitbull. I have to... They'll take him away, they'll take him away from me if I don't.' He walked past me into the hall.

'The cops,' I said. 'The cops are outside.' But they were already in the hall, Stefan's mum had opened the door, she was talking to one of the cops and the other came in the living room.

'Take the boy away,' Stefan's dad slurred, 'take him away with you.'

'Completely wasted,' Rico said. 'The old man's completely pissed, fell on his face, you know?'

The cop stood in the middle of the room and looked around. 'Names and addresses,' he said, taking out a pad.

We buried Pitbull over in the East Woods. Everyone was there who'd known him: Mark, Walter, Paul, Rico, Fred and his brother, Karsten and his brother, Thilo the Drinker, Hasenhof the mentalist who wanted to come along to everything, and even Goldie came along; he'd closed his bar for a couple of hours. Stefan had put Pitbull in a cardboard box, his head on a cushion Walter had brought along, made of red velvet and belonging to his mum.

We buried him up on the little hill; Stefan wanted it that way. 'He always liked it here. He can see everything from here.'

It had taken us almost an hour to dig the hole deep enough 'cause the earth was all full of roots. We'd asked Goldie to say a few words like at a proper funeral, 'cause we thought he'd be best at it 'cause he had did own bar, but all Goldie said was: 'He was a good dog, something special, I knew him well. And we won't forget him... no, we'll never forget him.' And then Stefan threw a bit of earth and some flowers down on Pitbull. By my turn, all you could see was his head, and then we filled in the grave. Everyone hugged Stefan and said something like 'Sorry for your loss' or 'Chin up' or 'He's in dog heaven now,' and Stefan nodded and waited 'til we'd all shaken his hand, and he looked pretty done in. We smoked another one, then we walked down the hill back to our neighbourhood. Goldie promised a round of drinks. I walked next to Stefan.

'Listen, Stefan...'

'No,' he said, 'no.'

'Stefan,' I said, 'you'll be alright...'

'Never,' he said. 'Pitbull, call me Pitbull, I told you.'

'OK, Pitbull.' I put my arm round him. We walked through the East Woods, not talking much until we got to Goldie's bar.

Hasenhof is in my dreams. 'Hasenhof,' said Rico, 'drink.' And Hasenhof drank. Then we gave him a dab of speed, and since he was in such a good mood he necked a pill as well.

'Hasenhof,' I said, 'you're the greatest.' Hasenhof laughed, and since he was in such a good mood he strolled over to the ladies sitting on the sofas and armchairs in the bar room, some of them lying on them. Actually, he didn't stroll over, he danced over to them, 'cause Little Walter was on the decks, two record players on an old school desk, laying down the latest techno tracks. Hasenhof danced over to the ladies, and by that point he must have forgotten who he was and what he looked like. His name wasn't really Hasenhof at all, it was Hof, David Hof, but we called him David Hasenhof or just Hasenhof, 'cause of that good-looking David Hasselhoff the girls all fancied, and the Hasen bit meant hare, 'cause Hasenhof had a harelip, all the way up to his nose. His nose looked worse than all Rico's boxing mates' noses put together, broken a few times in a row and grown back together all wonky. His whole face was wonky 'cause he'd got the shit kicked out of him like a kiddy-fiddler in jail, even though he was still pretty young. Hasenhof was a poor bastard, in care in the old GDR days, and after the Wall came down he lived rough. They said in our neighbourhood his dad was one of the two gay guys in the corner shop by the Silver Slope and had disowned him 'cause it hurt him to think of Hasenhof coming out of a woman thanks to him, and looking so ugly.

He'd tried everywhere but no one wanted him, not the Mühlenviertel carjackers, 'cause he had such clumsy hands and the cops would have recognized him even in the dark, not Engel's people, they beat him half-dead when he wanted to do business with them, they were dirty bastards, really they were, and when he shaved his head and tried to join the fash at the roller rink, they gave him such a beating he looked worse than before. We were the only ones who helped him a bit, and Rico took care of him, especially.

'Hasenhof,' said Rico, 'Go on, my boy, you show 'em!' And Hasenhof gave it everything he'd got, still moving his body to the beat by the time he was surrounded by ladies on the big sofa we'd driven over from the dump on the roof of Fred's car one night. He laid his head back, his arms round two pairs of shoulders, and they were really nice shoulders, lots of bare skin down to their breasts. The ladies didn't notice at first who it was pawing at them, and I saw Hasenhof's hands moving between their backs and the sofa, probably feeling the little chains of their backbones. Maybe, I thought back then, maybe he'll get lucky and he can lie down in between them, 'cause the two of them were out of it, I could tell, and Hasenhof was out of it too, and that would have been the greatest for him, just to stroke the skin on their backs. The flash of the strobe made his wonky face a bit better-looking, but he was out of luck, the ladies recognized him anyway and dragged themselves off to another sofa, even though they were so out of it they could hardly walk, and later, when morning came, Hasenhof was still lying there, on his own, asleep.

I can't remember whose idea it was to have a bit of fun with him then, maybe it was me, and when Hasenhof's in my dreams he says it was me, but I think Rico started it 'cause Hasenhof was his, he took care of him and helped him a bit, 'cause he'd been in a home just like Rico, but we never talked about that. It must have been the drugs to blame, speed and pills and all that shit, and the alcohol too of course, when Rico started having a bit of fun with Hasenhof. It was in the Eastside days, towards the end when the shit started messing everything up. But maybe it was one of Engel's people who'd started having a bit of fun with Hasenhof, and then Rico had joined in to show that Hasenhof didn't mean anything to him, that he was just as hard as Engel's people; he probably would have beaten up anyone who'd tried to punch Hasenhof or something, but it was just a bit of fun and no one wanted to harm Hasenhof. And he was sleeping so nicely, probably dreaming of the girls. And a few of the girls joined in when we started sticking pretzel sticks in Hasenhof's hair. Then there were a few sticks in his ears, and a couple of really long ones sticking out of each nostril. Then we wrapped a turban of bog roll around his hair and a long, long tie around his neck, or maybe it was a kind of noose. We wrapped up his whole body in toilet roll, so he looked like a mummy. But Hasenhof went on sleeping. And then there was the pen, I don't remember where it came from, 'From you,' Hasenhof says in my dreams, but I've never had one of those markers, it must have belonged to the sprayers from the youth club, a big fat black marker pen, that ink that doesn't come off glass or metal, it was one of those pens they used to draw their autographs on trams and trains and shop windows. But we drew on Hasenhof, drew on his wonky face. A moustache on his split upper lip, 'Hitler!' Pitbull yelled, 'Look at little Hitler!', teardrops under his eyes, giant bogies under his nose with the pretzel sticks still poking out, and we did his forehead and then his hands as well. And Hasenhof went on sleeping. And we were laughing. Everyone had a go with the pen and got to play the artist, one of Engel's people signed his name on Hasenhof's cheek, and then, when there was hardly any space left on Hasenhof's face and hands and we'd scribbled on his bog-roll bandage as well, Rico suddenly yelled 'Stop!" and threw his beer bottle at the wall. He stood in front of Hasenhof and shook his head and looked down at him, like he hadn't seen all of it before, like he'd been asleep and not Hasenhof, who was still asleep and only moved his painted head every now and then.

'Fucking hell, Danny, what's all this for?' Rico shook his head again; the shit was probably wearing off by then.

'He's your brother, is he?' said one of Engel's people, and at first I thought Rico would smash his face in, it looked that way and all. Rico shifted his left foot forward, his left fist loose at his hip, and I saw his shoulders moving underneath his shirt, he was wearing a smart white shirt with little roses embroidered on the chest – we were running a club so we had to look like club-owners, even if the place was illegal – but Rico didn't smash Engel's man's face in, he collapsed all of a sudden and fell next to messed-up Hasenhof on the sofa.

'Don't overdo it,' he said, and he grinned and patted Hasenhof's face, 'let's not overdo it.' But it was too late, we'd already had so much fun with Hasenhof that we couldn't overdo it anymore; pretty much the only thing we hadn't done yet was set him on fire. And then Hasenhof woke up and started laughing, don't know why, and the pretzel sticks fell out of his nose. He puked up behind the sofa; Pitbull had given him too many pills. All the toilet paper was covered in puke, and that's how he walked home, right then, to some Youth Welfare place he was kipping in at the time. He probably didn't notice what was wrong with his face 'til the next morning, and I don't know if he ever got the ink off, 'cause I never saw him again after that. Hasenhof jumped out of a fourth-floor window, a few weeks later, New Year's Eve. Maybe he'd been at a party and they didn't want him there, or he'd taken too many pills again and thought he could fly – a lot of people thought that back then when they'd necked too much.

Hasenhof didn't die straight away, they kept him on life support in the hospital for a few more days even though there was no point; he didn't want to come back. And when Rico came back out of jail, where he'd seen in the New Year, I told him the story, 'cause he was the only one in our neighbourhood who'd tried to take a bit of care of Hasenhof.

I saw Rico's face working, and then he turned away and lit one up. And then he shook himself and blew smoke in my face, wanted to be a hard man, and said: 'We should have drawn wings on him.'

Rico had to go away again soon, to the box; that's what he called jail. The cops hadn't caught him but the people in the bank had seen him, and the cameras had probably filmed him as well.

'You can just fuck off out of here,' I said. 'Get out of Leipzig. Lay low somewhere.'

'There's no point,' he said. 'They find you. You know that.'

'Yeah,' I said.

'I need a few more days, Danny, I just want to sort a few things. I want to live it up one last time. With girls and that, you know.'

'Why don't you try it?' I said. 'Try it anyway. Hey, I can lend you money, I've got work now, you can go to Poland or the coast. Or head for Berlin, you can get work on building sites and you can bet they won't look for you there. You can stay here if you want. Stay with me, you can stay as long as you like!' I had a little flat now, two doors down from my mum, right next to Goldie's bar, and Rico had been sleeping on the sofa for a few days.

'No, Danny,' he said. 'It won't work, Danny. I don't want to run away, I'm not a runner, you know me!'

'You can always stay here, you know that, I owe you...'

'Forget it, you don't owe me nothing, don't even start that!' He put the pillow under his head and laid one arm along the back of the sofa. He'd been lying there all day and smoking and drinking beer, and he didn't want to get up.

'But Rico, maybe they're not even looking for you, maybe they won't find out you were in on it.'

'They got Karsten's brother, he's bound to talk, you know Karsten's brother.'

'Yeah,' I said.

'There's no point, Danny. They've got photos and probably fingerprints. I'm on file, aren't I.'

'Yeah,' I said. I was on file as well. Rico threw his smoked cigarette in the beer can and popped a new one open. A hiss, foam dripped on his hand, and he licked it off.

'I'm just lying around here, aren't I? If they find me here you'll only get in trouble. Don't forget your probation!'

'They can't do anything to me...' I said.

'You know, it's not that bad inside, I can deal with it.'

'Yeah,' I said, and I took the beer can from him and drank. It was the cheapest beer, Ratskrone, Goldie had brought over two-dozen cans. Rico hardly left the house apart from when he went to Goldie's, and he was the only person who knew Rico was at my place.

'There's no point anymore,' he said. 'There's no one here anymore, they're all gone or dead. I'll go inside again, Danny, it's not that bad, one more time, clean break, you know.'

'They'll give you a couple of years.'

'I know, Danny.'

I drank another mouthful of beer and then passed him the can.

'It's not so bad in there, Danny. It's no better outside, anyway.'

'And the ladies?'

'Well, yeah, I'll miss girls, you're right. But hey, I want to live it up one last time before they lock me up, dip my wick one last time!'

I nodded. He smiled and clenched his fist and stuck his thumb underneath his forefinger.

'We'll do it tomorrow, Danny, I've got something lined up. A couple of women, one more time.'

He threw off the cover and sat up. He was wearing a vest and I could see the 'Eastside' tattoo on his chest. I had it on my lower arm and I wore long sleeves for work, even now in summer. He took his beer over to the window. He opened it and leant on the window ledge. 'Chuck us a fag, Danny.' I picked up his pack and threw it over. He caught it, put it down on the window ledge and lit a cigarette. 'Look,' he said, blowing smoke out of the window, 'the cops.'

'Where?' I leapt up.

'It's just a normal patrol, Danny.' He leant out the window and waved.

'Jesus, Rico, don't!'

'They're just patrol cops, Danny. Remember those cops, those bastard cops...'

'Are they looking for you yet, what d'you reckon?'

'Don't know. If it was in the paper, though.' He turned to me and smiled. He was proud of it, I knew that, he'd cut out the article and put it in his special folder he kept with him in his holdall. I'd taken a look at it when he was down at Goldie's, drinking in the back room. He had a few photos in there; one of them was of a gang of us: him, Pitbull – still called Stefan back then – Walter and me standing in front of a Mercedes, holding hands and laughing; it had been at the trade fair, autumn 89. Rico had Walter's and Mark's death notices in the folder as well, one of our old school magazines and his release papers. He'd stuck the newspaper clipping to a piece of card and put it inside clear plastic. He was proud of it, even though everything had gone wrong on the break-in and they'd caught the other two.

'A swingers' club, Danny.'

'What swingers' club?'

He came over to me, putting on his shirt. 'I just said,

I want to live it up a bit before they take me in.' He went down the hall to the bathroom and I heard him using my deodorant.

'D'you know how much they cost!'

'A hundred, if you don't bring a girl with you. But don't worry, Danny, I'll pay for you! I've got a few debts to collect.' He walked past me to the window; his beer was still there and he downed the rest. He must have emptied half the spray can 'cause I could smell him all the way across the room.

'I don't know, Rico, what would I do there?'

'Jesus, what d'you think? Come on, it'll be great! They have all these girls there, old women, young women, and they're all gagging for it!'

'I don't know, Rico, I bet it's always really crowded...'

'You bet it is! That's the whole point, Danny! They have all these girls there, and they're all up for it!' He picked up the newspaper, unfolded it and flicked through the pages, then he showed me the page with the sex ads and the professionals' numbers, the one before the sports section. 'Here, Danny, that's where we're going! Swingers and Couples Club Super 6!'

'See, they bring their blokes along with them.'

'No, no, they have a singles night as well, and then they have all these girls there, and they're all gagging for it!' He folded the newspaper back up and slammed it on the table.

'I don't know, Rico.'

'Don't leave me on my own. One more time, just the two of us. The drinks are free, Danny, you can down as much as you want, and the girls, Danny!' He leant over to me and put his hand on the back of my head. 'Just the two of us.'

I nodded. His hand was warm and trembling. I didn't

know if he was clean; I'd searched his stuff when he was down at Goldie's, drinking in the back room, but I hadn't found anything. 'OK,' I said. 'I'm in.'

'Tomorrow night, Danny, we'll show 'em, we'll show the girls, we'll be the greatest, they're gagging for guys like us. Are we men? Are we great guys?' He rolled up his sleeves and flexed his muscles. He was still in shape, even though he'd stopped training way back.

I looked at his tattoos. 'Course,' I said. 'Course we are.'

'Couple of things,' he said, 'I've just got a couple of things to sort out first.'

We were playing skat in Goldie's back room. It was the afternoon and we wanted one more drink and then Rico wanted to sort his things out before we headed over to Industrial Park West; that was where the Super 6 swingers' club was. We were drinking beer and korn, like we used to, but not too much, 'Otherwise we won't get it up later,' said Rico.

'You gotta get it just right,' said Goldie, 'it's tricky, you gotta have exactly the right amount, a tiny bit too much and you can't make it go. But if you get the right dose you can drive the ladies crazy!' Goldie was good with women, even though we hadn't seen him with one for years now. He used to have a pretty one, back when we were sixteen, she couldn't keep her pants on when she'd been drinking, and Rico had been to bed with her a few times; he was good with women back then too, but Goldie didn't know that.

'Eighteen,' said Goldie.

'Got it,' said Rico.

'Twenty,' said Goldie.

'Yeah,' said Rico.

'Twenty-two?'

'Got it.'

'Twenty-three?'

'Got it.'

'I'll pass,' said Goldie, and then Rico passed as well, and I had a shit hand too, and we played a round of rejects but Goldie had the worst cards, so he won in one go. 'Almost a virgin,' he said, and he grinned and collected up the cards. Rico took a cigarette and slammed the pack on the table. He was out of luck today, even though he was good at skat. He'd been world champion in jail a few times, he'd told me.

'You'll get lucky tonight though,' said Goldie, picking up the bottle and filling Rico's shot glass again. 'It's always like that, no point playing when the ladies are waiting.' Rico nodded and knocked back the korn. 'I better go,' said Goldie. 'Punters, I think.' He stood up, rapped his knuckles on the table and went to the door. He didn't open it all the way, just squeezed through the gap and closed it again. Goldie was scared someone would see Rico in his bar and grass him up, but his bar was always empty at that time of day, even though he opened it up a couple of hours earlier. Glasses clinked outside.

'I bet he's just washing up,' said Rico. 'There's no one here. No one comes anymore. Remember back in the day...'

We filled our glasses again. 'To the ladies, tonight,' said Rico.

'To you,' I said, and he smiled before he drank.

He went to the door and opened it carefully. 'There *are* people in, two old geezers.' I put the cards in a pile and shuffled. Then I played the Queen of Hearts game; she was always on the top when I picked up the cards. You could do it with any card but I loved the Queen of Hearts. 'They're cops,' Rico said quietly by the door.

'Nah, you're kidding?' I put the cards away.

'No, Danny, they're two cops, plain clothes!' I got up and went over. 'Stay there, he's looking, that bastard cop's looking at me.' I stayed behind Rico; he closed the door, leaving only a tiny gap. 'They're looking for me, Danny, they want to take me in. No, no, not today, not today!'

Now I saw one of them walking over to the bar and saying something to Goldie. He didn't look like a cop, even though he was smoking a cigar and wearing a brown leather hat. 'He's not a cop,' I whispered. 'I think I've seen him before, around the neighbourhood. He's just some punter.'

'No, Danny, no.' Rico whispered so quietly I could hardly understand him. 'They're cops, you see what they're drinking?'

I squeezed in next to him, my head so close to his that our ears touched. 'I can't see, Rico.'

'Coke, that one cop's got a Coke, and the other one...'

'I can see it now, it's a bottle of beer, Rico, just a normal beer. He's not a cop.' Goldie gave the guy a box of his free matches, and he went back to their table.

'Non-alcoholic,' Rico whispered next to me. 'It's non-alcoholic beer. A small bottle. Danny, the only small bottles Goldie has are alcohol-free.'

And now I saw it too and I worked it out: Coke and non-alcoholic beer, they had to be cops. 'Shit, Rico, you might be right. They really might be cops.'

'They are!'

'But maybe they're just driving...'

'Forget it, Danny. Not today, they're not getting me today. The girls, Danny!' He closed the door carefully, then he went to the table and put on his suit jacket. Actually, it was Goldie's suit jacket but he'd borrowed it for that night, even though you probably walked around buck naked at Super 6. I'd bought us two pairs of pants that morning, really good ones, twenty marks each; first I wanted to nick them, but those days were over. Then I'd taken them round to my mum's and sprayed them with her nice perfume. Rico opened the window and climbed on the radiator. 'Come on, Danny, let's get outta here!'

'Rico, hold on!' But he was outside already and I went to the window and leant out. He was down by the bins, patting Goldie's jacket clean.

'Come on, Danny, get a move on!' I climbed backwards onto the windowsill, held onto it and climbed onto the bins and then down to him. 'Come on, Danny, let's go!' He pulled at my arm and we went down the road to the supermarket and then past the supermarket to the station.

'Now what, Rico? It's only half five.'

'Now we're going to pick up a bit of money, Danny.'

Rico rang the bell but the bell didn't work. Rico knocked, twice, three times, but not a sound came from inside. 'Come on,' I said. 'There's no one in.'

Rico hammered his fist against the door. 'Uwe,' he yelled, 'open up!' He kicked the door but there was still no sound inside.

'Come on,' I said, 'let's just go.'

'No, he's always in at this time of day. He's just bricking it! Uwe! Uwe, it's me!'

But Uwe didn't open up, and I couldn't blame him, even though I didn't know Uwe. 'OK, there's no point, Danny.'

'That's what I'm saying. Let's go. Hey, shall we get an ice cream? They do the best ice cream down at the Adria.' But Rico didn't want to go to the Adria, he kicked the door in without warning, without taking a run-up, he'd been a good boxer back in the day and he'd learned karate as well, and if Uwe had been standing behind the door...

'That bastard's really not in,' said Rico, walking into

the hall.

'Rico, don't!'

'D'you know Uwe?' Rico stopped to inspect the lock.

'No.'

'See, then let me do my thing. That bastard hasn't even locked up properly, he must be in.' There was a chair by the door; Rico lay it on its side and kicked one leg off it. Footsteps on the stairs. I went inside the flat and closed the door behind me.

'Jesus, Rico, what's your plan?'

'I need to sort something out, and you never know with Uwe!' He held the chair leg like a club and walked slowly down the hall to the kitchen; the door was open and he glanced in. He waved me over and shook his head, then he pointed at a door at the end of the hall, with a big poster on it, some girl with not much on and the sun setting red behind her. I propped the front door shut with the broken chair, then I went over to Rico, who had his ear to the poster, right between the girl's breasts like he wanted to hear her heart beating. 'That bastard's hiding in here somewhere,' Rico whispered. 'He's bricking it, and when Uwe's bricking it...' He handed me the chair leg, 'Hold this,' and then he took off his suit jacket and hung it on a row of hooks with only a brown hat on them, the exact same kind of leather hat the cop had been wearing at Goldie's.

'I bet they weren't cops,' I said.

'Who?'

'You know, those guys at the bar.' Rico took the chair leg from me, pressed the handle and yanked the door open.

The room was empty, no furniture, just a mattress with bedding and a chair. 'The bastard's not in.' Rico nudged the mattress with his foot. There was a plate on the chair and that was empty too. 'That bastard owes me three hundred, Danny!'

'You can see he's got nothing.'

'He's got cash, Danny, he bought skag in jail, shit-loads of the stuff. And outside as well.'

'From you?'

'From me.' Rico knocked the plate off the chair, then went back to the hall.

'You're an arsehole, just like Pitbull!' I said.

Rico stood in the doorway, tapping the chair leg against his mouth like a big finger. 'Hey, Danny, shut up, don't say that, you'll mess up our big night. Please.'

'You know how much I hate that shit since Mark...'

'I know.' He got out his cigarettes and held the pack out to me.

'No, not now. I'm trying to give up.'

'Later, though,' he said and grinned, and then he came over and put his hand on my shoulder. 'You've got to smoke later when we... the girls at Super 6, Danny!'

'And the cash?'

'Don't you worry.' He looked at his watch. 'We've still got time. I've got other options. Shall we get hold of a car first?'

'I don't know, Rico.'

'Right, Jesus, your probation. Sorry, Danny, I forgot. Bad enough me going back inside, eh?' He turned around and went down the hall to the kitchen. I heard him getting glasses and running the tap.

'I'll be fucked, come here, Danny!'

I pushed the broken plate shards aside with my foot and then went in the kitchen to Rico. He was standing right in front of the window and the cooker was next to him, and in the little gap between the cooker and the wall was a guy, his eyes closed and his mouth open.

'Is that Uwe?'

'Yeah,' said Rico, 'that's Uwe.'

Uwe was wearing a T-shirt that said 'Security', and there were blue and red dots up his arms in a nice neat line.

'Is he dead?'

'Nah, probably not, he can take a lot.'

It was only then I saw the syringe in a little brown baking tin with a spoon and all the other crap next to him. 'He's dead,' I said. 'Like Mark.'

'No, Danny, he's doing great. Take a look at him.' Rico took a cigarette and crumbled a bit of tobacco onto his finger, then held it up to Uwe's open mouth. A couple of tobacco crumbs moved, a couple fell off his finger. 'See, Danny, he's doing great, I told you.'

'Arseholes like him can take anything, and Mark...'

'Jesus, for fuck's sake, will you stop messing up our night? Just the two of us, Danny, girls, free drinks...' He stood up and took my head between his hands. 'One more time, Danny.'

I tried to nod but he was holding my head really tight; he still had a whole lot of strength even though he'd stopped training way back. 'Yeah,' I said. 'Alright, Rico.'

Uwe moved, his foot knocked against my leg, his torso tipped to one side and his head banged against the cooker. Rico let go of me and leant down to him. 'Uwe, it's me, say something! The money, Uwe!'

Uwe opened his eyes and said: 'Nice,' and then he closed them again and his head fell onto his chest.

Rico grabbed him by the chin, lifted Uwe's head back up and pressed it against the wall. 'Uwe, Jesus, it's me. My money! I need my money, Uwe!' But Uwe had gone all quiet again, and it looked like he was smiling.

'The guy's cleaned out,' I said. 'He's got nothing.'

'Uwe's always got something!' Rico raised his arm and I grabbed it. 'You stay out of it, Danny!'

'Just look in his pockets first, Rico, he won't give you anything if you smash his face in. He's cleaned out!'

'You're right, Danny, you're right!' I let go of his arm and he boxed me gently on the shoulder. 'Look, there's a jacket!' Rico pointed at the kitchen table; there was a denim jacket. 'Have a look through it.' He squatted down in front of Uwe and rummaged through his trouser pockets while I went to the kitchen table and picked up the jacket. Underneath it was half a cheese roll with slices of tomato on it, still looked fresh. 'Just small change,' Rico said and showed me a tenner, a few coins jangling in his other hand. Uwe's wallet was in the inside pocket of the jacket. There were loads of notes in there and I took out four fifties and a hundred. 'See, Danny,' Rico was standing behind me. 'I told you he'd have money. Rich parents.'

I gave him the notes and he put them in his shirt pocket. 'Let's see, Danny.' He counted the money in the wallet and took another twenty. 'That bastard's got a couple of hundred marks and hasn't paid his debts. Interest, Danny. This is just my interest.' He pocketed the twenty and the tenner and the change. 'I could take it all if I wanted, Danny.'

'Right, you could, yeah.'

'Nah, Danny, that's not my style. Interest, just the interest.' He put the wallet back in the jacket. 'I'm a man of honour, you know me.' He moved the cheese roll aside and put the jacket on the table. Then he got out a cigarette and lit it. 'Come on, Danny, smoke one with me, for later, for the ladies!'

'OK,' I said, and he gave me his and lit up a new one.

He opened the fridge. 'That arsehole hasn't even got any beer.'

'Shouldn't we put him on the bed, we don't want him to...'

'He's fine, Danny, Uwe can take it, even in jail... But if you say so – he's paid his debts now.' He left the fridge open, went over to Uwe and dragged him out of his corner. The fridge was full of little brown chemist's bottles, and I slammed the door so hard they tinkled. 'Come on then, Danny, you grab one end, it was your idea.' Rico held Uwe's upper body and I took his legs. He was pretty heavy for a fixer. We lugged him across the hall into the empty room and put him down on the mattress. Rico picked up the blanket, shook it a bit and covered him over. 'Right, Uwe, sweet dreams!' We went to the door.

'Rico.' We stopped in our tracks and turned around. Uwe was moving under the blanket, his head rolling back and forth.

'What's up, Uwe?'

'You remember, Rico?' He spoke quietly, slurring his words; Rico went back to him and squatted down; I stayed put and stayed quiet. 'What d'you mean, Uwe?'

'In jail, Rico, remember, in jail...'

'Yeah, Uwe, I remember.'

'That hooch I made, it was good...'

'Yeah yeah, great hooch.' He pulled the blanket up to Uwe's chin and walked past me to the door.

I went into the hall. Rico put on his suit jacket and we went outside and pulled the front door to, but it was broken, wasn't it, and it stayed open a crack. 'Anyone could get in,' I said.

'It's his own fault,' said Rico. He opened the door again, then he took out a jack knife, a quick click and the blade stood, and he screwed around at the lock and the doorframe. 'Get us a bit of card or something.' There was a little carboard box with letters in it in the hall, and I ripped a bit off and gave it to Rico. He pressed it into the splintered wood of the door frame, then closed the door again. 'That ought to do it. No one'll see it now, anyway.' He put his knife away and we walked down the stairs.

'What now?' I asked. 'Super 6?'

He looked at his watch. 'One more thing, Danny. It's on the way.'

'But we've got the cash now.'

'No, not money, I've got to sort something out, won't take long, Danny. With the black brothers.'

'You mean the Rasta bar?'

'No, Danny, not those black brothers. The corpse-fuckers, I mean!'

'Oh, right.' I was glad we weren't going to the Rasta bar 'cause Rico and Pitbull sometimes used to buy grass and hash from the other black brothers and there would have been trouble. It was years ago now but those guys had a good memory for that kind of thing, and some of them were huge, so big even the skins over in Grünau were scared of them. We walked back to the station.

'It won't take long,' Rico said. 'Just this one thing and then the ladies. Jeez, I'm horny already! You too, Danny?'

'Course,' I said.

The black brothers stank. They all used the same perfume; it smelled like they were rotting away and they thought that was cool. The black brothers had a clubhouse over in Lindenau, one stop after the stadium, our Chemie stadium. I didn't know what Rico wanted to sort out but I hoped there wouldn't be any stress 'cause I'd heard all sorts of stories about the black brothers. They carried little wooden stakes around with them, hung on chains round their necks, and they rammed them into people's hearts to sacrifice them, and they liked a nice sacrifice, especially at night in the city's cemeteries. I'd also heard they had some kind of crypt down in their clubhouse, and anyone who went in without permission never came out again, sacrificed as well. 'That's all crap,' said Rico. 'You don't believe that kind of shit, do you?'

'No, course not.'

The door to the clubhouse was open and we walked down the stairs to the cellar. 'You know your way around here, Rico, right?'

'Course, Danny, I've been here before.' We headed through a small door into a bar room; the walls were black, actually everything was black, including the hair and clothes of the handful of guys and girls sitting at the tables, white-faced. There was a big pool table with red felt in one corner, two guys playing; they weren't any good, I could tell. One hit the one-ball on the arse at the wrong angle so it bounced off next to the pocket. 'It doesn't smell that bad,' said Rico.

'Jesus, be quiet,' I whispered, but no one took any notice of us and we crossed to the bar. We sat down on bar stools and Rico rapped his knuckles on the counter. The barman was standing with his back to us, dealing with bottles and glasses at a shelf.

'Two beers,' Rico said, almost shouting, and the barman turned round. He was pretty big and had thick black leather bracelets with silver studs on them round his wrists. There was a chain around his neck but no stake hanging from it, just an upside-down cross, but I bet it was sharpened at one end.

'Alright, Rico?' said the barman, and then he went to a little fridge and took out two bottles of beer. 'Glass?'

'No thanks,' said Rico.

The barman opened the beers with a bottle-opener fastened to the bar with a bit of rope, and pushed the bottles over to us.

'Hey,' said Rico, 'have one for yourself. On me.'

'Glad to see me again, are you?' The barman took another beer out of the fridge, opened it and put the bottle-top down on the counter in front of us. 'Alright, Rico, here's to you!'

'No,' said Rico, 'we're drinking to my old friend Daniel.' He patted me on the shoulder. The barman drank.

'Hey, hey, not so fast, I said we're drinking to Daniel, right, Danny?'

'Yes, you did,' I said.

The barman put his beer down on the counter by the bottle-top. 'Rico, if you're looking for trouble...'

'Come off it,' Rico flicked the guy's bottle-top past him. 'Don't say that. How long did we sleep together?'

'Eleven months,' the barman said.

'No,' said Rico, 'ten months and eighteen days.'

The barman smiled. 'You could be right, Rico.'

'No,' said Rico, 'I am right. So how long were you inside after that?'

'You know that – another three.'

'Was it bad?'

'It was alright.'

'So how's it going, you still clean?'

A black brother came up next to us at the bar. 'Two beers,' he said, and the barman opened two bottles for him; the guy took them and left.

'Why do you guys smell so bad?' Rico said, batting his hand in front of his nose. The barman grinned, the guy with the two beers stopped and turned round to us, and I saw the barman nodding at him to keep going. I just wanted to get out of the place and into Super 6, even though I was scared of that place as well.

Rico had one hand in his suit jacket pocket. 'Hey,' he

said, 'I asked you something. Are you a good boy now?' The barman grinned again and drank from his beer. He raised the bottle to us and we drank too.

'Heard you messed up a job,' said the barman. He put his bottle down, it was almost empty, and gripped it by the neck.

'Who said that crap?'

'I just heard, Rico.'

'I didn't mess it up, don't say that again. It was the other two arseholes!' Rico drank up his beer and pushed the bottle over to the barman. 'Another two. And one for yourself.'

'No thanks, I'm working.' The barman put Rico's bottle in an empty crate by the fridge.

'Another three,' Rico said.

'OK,' said the barman. 'Since you're here.' He opened three new bottles and put them on the counter.

'I didn't mess it up,' Rico said, taking a bottle and holding it in both hands. 'Don't say that, you can't go round saying that.'

'Alright, Rico, that's just what I heard. I don't think you messed it up.'

Rico nodded. 'No,' he said. 'No one can say that; it was the others.' And he was right. But it'd been his idea to do a job on the bank up at the trade fair, with Karsten's brother and some other idiot. Karsten's brother had been inside a couple of times before, he was well known for messing everything up, and apart from that he was high, he was almost always high, even when he was on a job. 'Just because that arsehole couldn't hold the gun properly and had a gas cartridge in the barrel,' Rico said.

And the barman ran his hand over his chin and said: 'They're idiots, Rico, sorry to hear it.'

'It was even in the paper,' Rico said. 'Right, Danny, you

read it too, right?'

'Yeah, I did,' I said. 'A proper article, really long.'

'Not bad,' said the barman. 'You're famous now.'

'Come off it, you're taking the piss!' Then he smiled, took out a cigarette and lit it up. 'Well, maybe a little bit. But not my name, they didn't have my name.' He held the pack out to me and I took one, then he put it down on the bar for the barman. 'Help yourself, on me.'

'No thanks, I've given it up. Just the odd cigar now and then.'

'You're kidding, you used to smoke like crazy in jail.'

'That was different, Rico.'

'Come on, take one, celebrate our freedom!'

'No, you're alright, I've been out for ages.'

'So listen, you know where I live, right? I mean, you know, where I used to live before the bank job.'

'Course, you told me.'

'Come on, have a smoke, for me, do it for me!'

'Hey, Rico, I told you, don't make trouble here. We're mates, aren't we?' He took my empty beer bottle and put it in the crate by the fridge.

'Course,' said Rico, 'course we are. Old jail mates.' He rapped his knuckles on the bar and winked at me. I nodded, picked up my new beer and drank half the bottle in one; I was going to need an empty one any minute, I was sure of that.

'So are you going to take a fag now?'

'No, Rico, that's enough, leave it out!' The barman stepped back, stumbled on something and rested one hand on a shelf.

'Calm down,' said Rico, 'everything's fine! But the fags, why didn't you bring me my fags, we agreed you would, you promised!'

I downed my beer and kept the empty bottle in my

hand. 'The fags,' said the barman. 'You and your bloody fags. We're not in the box anymore, Rico, it's over, you can forget all that crap!' He took a couple of steps back towards us, and that was his mistake. Rico reached across the bar and grabbed him by his top, the guy jumped back again, and Rico was holding the cross and the chain in his hand. He flung it away, it flew past me across the room. 'Rico,' the barman said. 'Jesus, Rico.' Rico's torso was across the bar, I saw the barman clench his fist and hit out at Rico, but Rico blocked the punch with his left arm, his right hand grabbing the barman's hair, it was long enough, and he pulled him in and pressed his head onto the counter next to him.

'Shit,' the barman yelled, 'fuck, Rico, let go!'

'My fags,' said Rico, 'why didn't you bring me my fags? We agreed, in the box, we were mates, you and me, the fags, remember, the fags!' Rico wrapped the barman's hair round his hand and pulled his head right up close to his.

'Rico, please, please stop, I'll give you them, I'll get some out of the machine!'

'What brand, what brand was it?'

'Rico, please... I don't know, I can't remember...'

'You can't remember? Our brand, Jesus, our Ernte, our good old Ernte!'

'OK, I remember now, I remember... let me go!' The guy was sprawled across the bar, his arms dangling on either side, he looked pretty big but now he was wailing like a baby. And now his black brothers came up, but they stayed a few metres away; I could smell them. I shoved the barstools aside and picked up my bottle. A few drops of beer ran down my hand.

Rico pulled the guy up and turned around, not letting go of his head. 'Tell your mates here everything's fine. Tell 'em to piss off.'

'You hear that?' I yelled, knocking over a barstool. 'Buzz off, piss off, or we'll wipe the floor with you. We'll break everything in this place!'

'Let go of him,' one of the black brothers said. 'Just let him go and get out of here. Then there won't be a war.'

'There's no war,' Rico said. 'We're just getting something sorted, won't take long, and then we'll be out of here. Right?' He slapped the barman on the cheek and the barman said yes.

Rico let him go; he wiped his mouth and eyes. 'Everything's fine,' he said quietly. 'Sit back down. Everything's fine.' Rico nodded and gave him another slap on the cheek. The guys walked slowly back to their tables and sat down. 'Why?' said the barman. 'Why are you so mean?'

'You're the one who messed everything up,' Rico said. 'Why did you mess everything up?'

I put my bottle back on the bar; Rico's cigarettes had fallen down and I picked them up and lit one. Rico took the pack out of my hand and put it down in front of the barman.

'One pack,' said Rico. 'One good pack of Ernte. Remember now?'

The barman took one, and Rico gave him a light. The barman coughed.

'And why,' said Rico, 'why did you have to mess everything up?'

'Rico, I'm... I didn't think you'd take it so seriously, one pack, Rico...'

'Why did you mess everything up?' he said. 'You promised. One pack of Ernte, you arsehole, that meant something, inside. It meant something, you know! It meant something!' He picked up his pack, screwed it up and chucked it at the shelf behind the bar.

'Come on,' I said. 'Let's get out of here.' The barman had stepped back again, he was leaning his back against the shelf, Rico's pack right next to him, between bottles and glasses.

'Yeah,' said Rico. We walked slowly between the tables to the door. The black brothers stared at us but none of them stood up. I saw Rico reach into his suit jacket pocket. At the door, he stopped and turned his head, but he just looked at the wall; there was a poster with a huge skull on it and the name of some band; and then we went up the stairs.

He stopped outside the building and sat down on the kerb. I sat next to him. 'I'm tired, Danny.'

'No ladies tonight, then?' He smiled, then he got up again, bobbed and weaved along the pavement in front of me, moving his arms and shoulders like he was boxing. 'No, no, we'll show 'em, we'll give 'em one. The two of us. Super 6, Danny!' I got up too, and he faked a left hook and then hit a right one, which I blocked, but his left hand touched me below the elbow on my stomach; he was still fast even though he'd stopped training way back. We laughed. Rico held up his hand and we high-fived. Then we walked to the station. 'Cigarettes,' said Rico, and pointed at a little kiosk by the railway embankment. 'I need a new pack.'

The Super 6 swingers' club was on the edge of Industrial Park West, in a villa where the industrial managers or the Stasi or someone used to live. I'd seen the building from the train a few times; they always had spotlights on it at night. The factory halls in the industrial park were all empty and crumbling away, but the Super 6 seemed to be doing well 'cause the car park was full, we saw that from a long way off. But as we came closer we saw the price tags behind the cars' windscreens. The little wooden hut wasn't for a parking attendant, it was for the car salesman; it was Friday evening and the shutters were down.

'Look at that!' Rico said, stopping at an old Golf. 'Eight thousand! What a rip-off!'

'They wanna make money, don't they?' I said, looking over at the villa; the spotlights were already on even though it was still light; it was summer and the sun was just going down.

'Hey, Danny, let's have a smoke first.' Rico got out his cigarettes and sat down on the Golf's bonnet. 'Here you go, Danny, a good old Ernte.' I sat down next to him and he gave me a light. 'Jeez, these cars,' he said. 'If I had the money...'

'You haven't even got a driving licence.'

'If I had the money, if the bank had gone right, I'd have got my bloody licence. Then I'd have got myself a car. All legal, Danny, everything legal at last! That'd be great!'

'Right,' I said. 'That wouldn't be bad.' I looked past him at the villa. 'Don't we want to go in?'

'No rush, Danny, no stress. Let's have a smoke first in peace.' He threw away his cigarette and lit up a new one. 'Hey, Danny, the ladies... Since I got out, it's been a while... I'm a bit rusty, maybe.'

'That doesn't matter, Rico.'

'Well, you know, they're hard work, the ladies. It's hard work if you want an old lady, you know? You know what I mean, right?'

'Course, Rico, I know the problem.'

'Back in the day, Danny... you know me, they all wanted...'

'Yeah,' I said. 'You were in fighting form.'

He nodded and drew lines and circles in the dust on the windscreen. 'You know, I think I'll just pop over there for a bit before we go in.' He pointed at one of the old factory buildings and stroked his hair smooth.

'If you say so, Rico. Might be better.'

'What about you, Danny?'

'Nah, I'll be alright. You go. I'll wait here.'

'You got a tissue or something?'

'Course, Rico, got everything I need.' I reached into my trouser pocket and handed him one. I always took tissues out with me when I was with Rico, 'cause sometimes there'd be blood.

'OK... right, I'll be right back.' I nodded and looked over at the spotlights on the building. It was getting dark. Rico went to one of the factory halls, chucking his cigarette away as he walked. His pack was still next to me on the car bonnet, and I took one out.

A taxi pulled up outside the villa and two women got out, one from the front, one from the back; one of them was pretty fat. They went to the door. The taxi drove off again, the sign on the roof lit up now, and then it disappeared underneath the railway bridge. I flicked ash onto the car windscreen; it rolled down and came to rest on the windscreen wiper. 95 PS, it said on the sign. 1988 make, MOT up to... I turned round; Rico was standing behind me. He grinned and looked past me. I picked up his cigarette pack and stuck it in the pocket of his suit jacket. He nodded and we strolled over to the villa. Another car pulled up, not a taxi this time; two men got out, the driver reversed and parked next to a red Lada. The driver got out and joined the other two men. We waited for them to get to the door. We could hear them laughing. I saw Rico reach into his pocket. The men stood outside the door; one of them pressed the bell, they looked at the surveillance camera above the door, one of them waved, the door opened inwards, and they disappeared. We ambled over.

‘Wait a minute,’ said Rico and stopped outside the door. It was painted red and there was a big wooden sign saying *Super 6 – 8 pm to ?* and there was a flower painted on either side of the writing. Rico ran his hand over his lapels. ‘How do I look, Danny?’

‘Hold on.’ I got one of my tissues and wiped off a little black mark from under his eye. I had two mints in my pocket and I gave one to Rico. ‘Fresh breath,’ I said. ‘The ladies love it.’

Rico unwrapped it and flicked the paper on the ground by the steps. ‘You’ve thought of everything.’

‘I have, Rico.’ He looked at his shoes and then squatted down. ‘Jesus, Danny, you could have said something, they’re filthy dirty.’

‘You’ll have to take them off anyway.’

‘No no, gotta get everything right. Gimme your tissue.’ I handed it to him and he spat on his shoes and wiped them. Then he put a hand on my leg. ‘Jesus, Danny, what do you look like, stay still!’ He spat on my trousers.

‘Stop it, will you!’

‘No, you’re not going in like that. Look at this stain here!’ He rubbed at my trouser leg with the tissue, then scrunched it up and threw it away. ‘It’s OK now, Danny.’ I heard him crunching his mint.

‘Shall we go in now, Rico?’

‘Course, I’m just waiting for you.’

We went up the three steps and looked into the camera above the door. Rico pressed the bell; there was a buzz inside, we waited a few seconds and looked at the camera, then the door opened inwards. A woman had opened it. She was wearing a bra and knickers and looked pretty young, maybe twenty, twenty-five tops, and I was glad Rico and I looked older than we were; that was down to the jail and the drinking and all the other shit.

'Come on in,' she smiled. 'New here?'

I nodded. 'Yes,' said Rico, 'our first time.' He spoke very quietly.

She closed the door again. 'Come with me then, let's get you signed up to start with.' She was beautiful; I'd rather have paid a hundred just for her or taken the hundred and taken her out somewhere nice. We stepped aside and she walked past us to a little door on the left of the corridor. She turned around. 'Come on, don't be shy.' It was pretty dark in the corridor, just a little red light in the ceiling; the girl opened the door and I saw her smiling as she disappeared into the room.

Rico nudged me and we walked in after her. 'Her,' Rico whispered, 'she's the one.' She was standing in a kind of office at a desk, leafing through a folder. It was bright in the room; the spotlight fell right on the window. I looked at her back and the straps of her bra.

'I'll need your ID cards.' We gave them to her and she put them down on the desk and wrote our names on a list. She turned around. 'You're Rico, right?'

'Yes,' said Rico.

'Daniel,' she said, putting her finger on my chest. I nodded. 'Claudia,' she said. 'That'll be a hundred each.'

Rico took two notes out of his shirt pocket and handed them to her. She went to a little cupboard, opened a drawer and put the money inside. She walked past the window and the spotlight fell on her back and neck. She shielded her eyes and closed the curtains. 'Do you need a receipt?'

'No.'

She handed us our ID back. 'Then you can get undressed.'

'Right here?'

'No,' she laughed and her breasts moved with her laughter. She went to the door. 'Come with me, I'll show you.'

'Yes,' Rico whispered in my ear, 'you show us.' She held the door open for us and we went past her into the hall. I saw Rico's hand touch her belly; she looked at him and stepped back. She closed the door, then she went down the corridor to another door; we were a few metres behind her.

'You can change here,' she said, gesturing into the room. There were benches and lockers like in a PE changing room. 'Hold on,' she said, and she pushed us aside and went back to the office. 'You'll need a padlock. One locker's enough for both of you, isn't it?'

'Course,' said Rico. 'We're brothers.' We watched her disappear into the office, then we went in the changing room and sat down on one of the benches. 'What d'you think, Danny, you reckon she... you reckon she'd...' There was a big drain in the tiled floor in front of us, and Rico jabbed at it with his foot.

'I don't know,' I said. 'Probably not.'

'Yeah but... Look at how she walks around the place! She's... beautiful.'

'Yeah, she is.'

We heard her steps outside in the corridor and we shut up and looked at the tiles. 'Here's your padlock.' She came through the door and stopped in front of us. She held out her forefinger with a little padlock dangling from it; I took it; the key was in the lock. 'Just pick any free locker. When you're ready...'

'How much do we have to take off?' Rico stood up and took off his suit jacket.

She laughed again, and her breasts moved. 'Everything except your underpants.'

'Right,' said Rico, 'just checking.' He'd put his jacket on the bench and was taking off his shirt. Rico was still in good shape and the needle marks on his arms had healed and were barely visible; it was all a while ago now.

'You're nice and colourful,' the girl said, and Rico stroked his tattooed chest.

'Wait 'til you see my mate Danny, he's got even more, seventeen of them. Right, Danny?' I felt myself blushing and I went over to a locker with the padlock. I opened the metal door and stood behind it.

'When you're ready, come and find me in the office and I'll show you around.' I heard her footsteps on the tiles and then she was out in the corridor.

'See, Danny, she fancies me.'

'Maybe.' I undressed and put my clothes on a shelf in the locker. Rico came over, hung his suit jacket on a coat hanger and took off his shoes, then his socks. 'We should have brought slippers or flipflops. We'll get verrucas. Like in jail, you know...' He put his socks inside his shoes and put them at the bottom of the locker, then he wiped and scratched at his feet. I took my shoes off as well. 'Look at this, Danny, I've got these weird spots on my feet.'

'No thanks.' I closed the locker and padlocked it.

'Hold on, Danny, my fags.' He took them out of his jacket pocket and stuck them in the side of his pants. They were expensive pants and they looked good on us.

'What about the key?'

'Hold on, Danny, I'll put it in my fag box.' He took it back out of his pants and I gave him the key. We went to the door; the tiles were cold and sticky underneath my feet. Claudia was standing outside the office. She had her arms crossed over her chest and she was rubbing her shoulders like she was cold, but it was summer and it was warm inside too. She looked at us; Rico had his hand on his thigh, covering up the little woman with big breasts some guy had inked on him in jail. Underneath the woman it said 'Mum', and next to Rico's thumb I saw her big hat with a blue feather on it.

'I'll just show you two everything,' she said, and she let go of her shoulders and walked slowly down the corridor.

'Gotta make a few adjustments,' Rico whispered next to me, and I saw him fiddling with his underpants. Claudia led us into a big bar room with loads of sofas and armchairs, a few women sitting on some of them, all in bras and knickers, nothing special, I could see that already even though it was pretty dark, just a few coloured lights behind the bar, and four men were sitting at the bar, drinking. The barmaid was squatting in front of a little open fridge behind the bar and I could only see her head and her back in the light of the fridge; then she stood up and put a bottle down on the bar. She was much older than Claudia but she looked pretty good. I looked at the women on the sofas.

'The buffet's over there.' Claudia pointed at two long tables against the wall, next to two plastic palm trees. 'Hold on a mo, won't be a minute.' She put her hand on my arm, then she went over to the bar.

We were standing by the buffet tables; Rico took a tuna open sandwich with an olive on top, pulled out the little stick and flicked it onto the potato salad. 'There's not a lot of ladies,' he said, and helped himself to a tomato. 'Some of them are pretty dodgy.'

'It's early yet,' I said, looking over at the bar where Claudia was, and the barmaid reached her long arms over the counter and stroked her shoulder.

'True,' said Rico, and I strolled along the table and looked at the open sandwiches and salads and other food.

I grabbed one of the palm leaves; the trees were real, growing out of big plastic tubs. I heard Claudia talking behind me; did she say 'Mum'? I turned around and saw her leaning over the bar and touching her forehead to the barmaid's. 'Hey, Rico,' I said, but then Claudia was back and we followed her into all the club's different rooms.

There was a kind of dark room behind a wooden wall that had a hole in it for crawling inside; there was a cage in one room, with leather kit and chains hanging in it; in another room they were already moaning and a woman was screaming even though it wasn't yet ten. 'If the door's open, that means you can watch or join in.' The door was closed and the moans were getting quieter; maybe they'd heard us or they were finished. 'This is our special playroom, but it doesn't usually hot up until later.' The room's floor was laid out with gymnastic mats and mattresses, there were grips and ropes on the walls, and in the middle was a trampoline. She pointed at it and wanted to say something and laughed, and her breasts moved slightly and I wished she'd jump on it naked, just for us, but her mum the barmaid probably wouldn't have liked that.

Then Claudia showed us the swimming pool in the basement; there was a sauna as well but we didn't want to go in. There were two women in the water and Rico elbowed me, but then we saw three men sitting naked on a bench and drinking beer, with the women's bras and knickers next to them. 'Those bloody bastards,' Rico whispered. 'Fat bastards.'

'You'll find condoms everywhere,' Claudia pointed at a little table against the wall with a plastic bowl of condoms on it, and there were two rolls of kitchen paper and a packet of serviettes as well. 'But there's no sex in our pool. Hygiene reasons, you know.'

'Course,' said Rico and grinned. He took his cigarettes out of his pants and lit one up. He held the pack out to me and I took it.

'Do you smoke?'

'No thanks,' she said. 'Not right now. I've got to get back to my door duty.'

'OK.' I nodded and took one out for myself; the lighter was in the box. We went back to the bar.

'There's no smoking in the playroom, though, we don't want any burn marks, or in the dark room. And not in the corridors either, actually.'

'No problem, Claudia,' Rico put his hand on her arm. 'We're going to the bar first anyway.'

Claudia stopped, turned away and pointed at an open door with a staircase behind it. 'There are more social rooms and two playrooms upstairs, where you can make contact...'

'We'll be fine,' said Rico, putting his hand on her arm again.

She took a deep breath and her breasts rose, even though they weren't as big as the woman on Rico's leg had. 'I've got to get back to the door,' she said. 'Have fun.'

Rico's shoulders twitched as he reached out his arm, but she was already at the door to the bar. Rico flicked his ash on the floor, and then he bent down and blew it over to the wall. 'Let's get a drink then, Danny.'

'Sure, honey.' I put my arm round his hip, he grinned, and we went to the bar.

The men who'd been drinking at the bar before were sitting with the women now; we could hear them laughing. 'Two beers,' I said, and Claudia's mum nodded. She didn't look like her mum; maybe I'd heard wrong.

We moved two barstools closer together and sat down. Claudia's mum put two bottles of beer on the bar for us. 'Glasses?'

'No thanks, we'll drink from the bottles.'

'So, is this your first time?'

'Yes.'

She nodded; her breasts were bigger than Claudia's, and her bra covered up less of them. 'So d'you like it?'

'Yes,' I said.

'Nice place,' said Rico, 'and so big.'

'It'll fill up later on,' Claudia's mum said. The ash from Rico's cigarette fell on the bar; he picked up the ashtray and pushed it in with his finger.

'You two are nice and colourful. The ladies like that. I like that.'

'Thanks,' said Rico. 'I'm hoping a few of them are into it.'

'Where did you get them done?'

'Here and there, you know.'

She nodded, then she went to a tray of fruit and started slicing lemons with a big knife. 'Shit,' Rico whispered, 'the best girls have to work here. And back there,' he nodded his head at the sofas where the five guys were laughing with the women, 'they're already taken. We should have just gone to a brothel, Danny.'

I drew the ashtray over and put out my cigarette. 'Don't stress, Rico, it's only just gone ten. And she just said it'll fill up.'

'Yeah, right, they'll turn up, the right ladies, the young girls, you know, the really gorgeous ones, Danny, they're bound to turn up. You know, if they pick me up soon... I've got to have a proper shag, Danny, I'll be gone then, couple of years, you know... couple of years.'

He grabbed my hand and I said, 'Yeah, I know, Rico.'

'Live it up one more time, Danny!'

He squeezed my hand so hard it hurt, but I didn't take it away, and I nodded and said: 'Yeah, Rico, one more party, say our goodbyes,' and he slammed his other fist down on the bar.

'One more proper party!' Maybe Claudia's mum heard

that, 'cause now the music kicked in and she turned the dial on a stereo and the music got louder. 'Copa, Copacabana...'

I knocked on the wooden wall. 'Hello,' I called quietly, but it was all quiet inside. I pushed the curtain aside and then climbed in through the hole, pressing my glass of whiskey to my chest. It wasn't cold 'cause the glass was full to the top, and ice cubes would only have got in the way. I'd ordered four neat whiskeys and poured them in one glass. I crawled across the rubber mats until I touched the wall with my free hand. I crawled into the corner and drew my knees up to my chest and rested my head on my arm. It was warm and stuffy in there, not a good place for a shag. I took a sip. People walked by, out in the corridor. I heard voices, women, men, then laughing. Rico wasn't one of them. He was somewhere, in one of the rooms, shagging. Or maybe he was chained up in the cage, getting his arse whipped. Rico had been going all out, back on fine pulling form even though the women weren't as pretty and young as they used to be. But he was happy enough, he'd grinned and winked at me when he went off with them. 'Don't you want to come with us?' one of the two had asked me.

'Not right now,' I'd said, even though I was horny, and they didn't look that bad and I could tell they were horny too, and Rico nodded and winked at me as well, but somehow... I couldn't. I drank a sip and then put my hand down my pants. 'Just make a few adjustments,' I said quietly, and then I laughed, and a bit of whiskey ran down my hand.

'Hello?' There was a body outside the entrance, a woman's body, nearly naked, I saw it briefly in the light from the corridor and then it disappeared in the dark ahead of me, the curtain fell back into place and I heard the woman crawling over the mats. I couldn't see her and I tried to smell her or feel her warmth but there was nothing, even though she crawled up close to me, and now she sat down and I heard a quiet tinkling, ice cubes touching in a glass. I heard her drink, and now I could smell her, alcohol, something with vodka in. 'Nostrovia,' I thought, and I drank my whiskey. I reached a hand out in the dark and then there was her neck; I felt the short hair at the nape. 'No,' she said, and I heard her crawl away from me.

'Claudia?'

'No, I've got to get back to my door duty. I've got to work.'

'Hey, hold on a minute, don't run away. Daniel, I'm Daniel, the tattooed guy.'

'The one with the woman on your leg?'

'No, that's Rico.'

'Are you alone?'

'Yes.'

'I just want to have a quick drink. No one can see me in here.'

'Stay a few minutes, please, don't run away. Hey, I've got a whiskey.'

'No thanks, I've got my own.' I heard her crawling up to me, sitting down next to me with her back to the wall, and her shoulder touched my arm. 'I just want a quick break,' she said.

'Go ahead,' I said. 'I'm just sitting here, I won't do anything.'

'Daniel,' she said quietly.

'What are you drinking, Claudia?'

'Vodka and tonic. I'm not really allowed, you know.'

'Is it any good?'

'D'you want a taste?'

'Sure.' She felt for my hand and touched my belly; I reached for her arm and she gave me her glass. 'D'you want some of my whiskey?'

'Just a sip, though,' she said, and we both drank. I heard her shudder and then we swapped glasses again. 'Not your thing, Claudia, right?'

'Oh, you know, I prefer vodka, with a mixer. But your whiskey's not bad either.'

'I've never tried it before, vodka and tonic, I mean. It's really good.'

She moved against my arm, and I stayed still and quiet and didn't breathe. 'Hey, Daniel, have you been in jail?'

I felt for her head, wanting to put my hand on it, but then I changed my mind. 'In jail?' I said and laughed. 'You ask funny questions.'

'Because you're... because you've got so many tattoos.'

'It was a while back,' I said, 'and I got most of them before, anyway.'

'But you... you didn't do anything bad.'

'No. Just little things.'

'And your friend?'

'Rico? Rico's alright.'

'Hey, I saw him, he's with two women... they weren't that great, though...'

'I know.' I put my arm around her shoulder and pulled her closer.

'Daniel...' Her hand was back again, this time touching my chest, 'can you feel them?'

'Feel what?'

'Your tattoos. Can you feel them on your skin?'

I took her hand and put it on the other side of my chest. 'Here, there's one here.'

She ran her fingers over my chest, her thumb on my ribs, then on my neck. 'No,' she said, 'I can't feel anything, just thudding.'

'On my right bicep,' I said and moved even closer. 'See if you can feel that one.' I leant over her and felt her turning away, her back in front of my face and her shoulder bumping my nose.

'No, I've got to go back to the door, I can't stay long, just a little break, it's just a little break.'

'You can feel that one,' I said. 'That tattoo's like 3D.'

'Really?'

'No need to be scared. I... there's no need to be scared.'

'I know. You're not a bad boy.' She slid around me and ran her finger over my right arm. Her other hand was on my belly and I was starting to get a hard-on, even though I didn't want to.

'Yes,' she said. 'It's like... like there's something underneath, under the skin... it wants to get out, the tattoo.' She laughed, her mouth touched my back, and I felt her laugh inside me. 'Why's it like that?'

'Bad ink and a bad tattooist. It's all scarred over.'

'What's it a picture of?'

'Guess.'

She ran her finger over my arm and the lines of the tattoo. 'I saw it before. It was... it's like a head, right?'

'The other side, that's on the other side.'

She put her arm around me and stroked my shoulder. 'I can't feel anything there, though, it's all smooth.'

'That was a good tattooist.'

'I've got to go back in a minute. I'm so tired.' She wrapped her arms around my belly and leaned against my back. I felt her breasts underneath her bra, and somewhere behind them, her heart. My foot was tingling, pins and needles, and when I moved it, I touched her glass. I reached behind me and put my hand on her hair.

'You fucking prick, I'll smash your face in, why are you

touching me? You touched me, you bastard!' Rico's voice out in the corridor. I jumped up and the glass by my foot tipped over; wetting my foot.

'Stay here, please. I don't want to go back out yet.' Her hand was on my leg but I crawled to the entrance. 'Please.' She was still in the corner, and her voice was all quiet.

They were shouting and cursing in the corridor, and then came a couple of crashes. I was at the entrance, reaching for the curtain. 'I've got to go to Rico,' I said, but perhaps she didn't hear me, 'cause it was all quiet in her corner now. I drew the curtain aside and crawled out through the hole. The light hurt my eyes, even though they only had red lamps, even in the corridors. There must have been ultraviolet lights as well, 'cause Rico's teeth were shining so white as he yelled, and the other guy's teeth did too; they looked brand new in his wide-open mouth, as Rico held him by the throat.

'No!' the guy yelled. 'Please, no!' But it was no use, Rico landed a right hook on his chin, not pulling back much, right on the spot, down to the millimetre, 'cause the guy's legs folded and Rico let him go. He was still yelling, 'Stupid bastard, you stupid pervs!' and now I saw the other two guys, one of them collapsed on the floor and crying, his underpants gone, trying to turn onto his front and crawl to the wall, and the other one was sliding across the floor a few metres ahead of him towards the door, he had his pants on, still, but they were ripped at the back and his arse was hanging out. In the middle of the corridor was a smashed wooden chair, three legs missing and the back kicked in.

'You fucking pricks, my women, they were my women!' I put my hand on his shoulder, he turned round, his fist was by my face, 'Jesus, Danny, watch it!' the fist passed by my face and slammed into the wall. 'These bastards touched me, you get it, they wanted to just join in!' He punched the wall again. 'This is my night. Mine, you get it! They go and touch me, the pervs. Jesus, what's that about, Danny, what's that about? What the fuck is going on here!'

'It's alright,' I said. 'Let's fuck off out of here, quick!'

'OK, Danny, I've had enough anyway. Don't feel like it anymore. I wanna go home.' I put my arm round him, and we headed for the bar room; I wanted to walk faster but Rico kept turning back round. 'They messed everything up for me, the bastards.'

'They're bastards, yeah, let's get out of here. If the cops...'

'Fuck the cops, Danny, it doesn't matter now anyway.' There were three women and a couple of guys outside the door to the bar, they stepped aside and looked past us along the corridor, and I turned back round. There were people squatting down by the guys Rico had knocked down, now, two women pointing at us, probably the ones Rico had been shagging when the guys wanted to join in. We crossed the bar; Claudia's mum was standing by the exit with a man in uniform. Not a cop; paid security.

'You can't just go,' she said. 'It's not that simple, we've got to sort this out now.' She'd put on a kind of bathrobe, maybe she'd got cold 'cause she was still trembling. The security man was pretty tall and standing right in the doorway, but he wasn't up to much, I could tell by his face, he looked uncertain, and he avoided our eyes.

'No hassle,' I said. 'We just want to go home. You've got our names.'

'Why did you do it?' She shivered and pressed her arms against her chest.

'Me,' said Rico, 'it's just my business. He's got nothing to do with it, you understand?'

The security man took a step forward.

'I said do you understand!' Rico yelled, holding his finger up to the security guy's face. 'Just my business! And I'm going now, or it'll only get worse!'

'Don't make trouble, lad!' said the security man, even though he was pretty young himself, but Rico just shoved him aside, his hand briefly on the guy's neck. But he didn't fight back, he leaned against the wall and I could see his face twitching and working, but he was all quiet now.

'Come on, Danny, our stuff!'

'I'm sorry about this.' Claudia's mum turned away but I stood in front of her. 'I'll pay for it, I'll pay for everything...' She turned away again and went to the bar. The security man walked after her.

'Danny, come on!' Rico was already at the changing room door; he opened it and went in. He was at the locker, tugging at the padlock. 'The bloody key. My fags are still upstairs.' I turned and went back to the door. 'Wait, Danny, I'll do it!' He reached into his pants and pulled out a condom. 'What the fuck!' He laughed and slapped it against the wall. Then he took off his pants, threaded them through the ring of the padlock, grabbed both ends of the fabric and tugged until there was a bang, and the lock was open. They were proper brand-name pants, brand new as well, I'd only bought them that morning. We got dressed and then we walked down the hall to the front door, Rico's hand in the pocket of his suit jacket. At the other end of the corridor were Claudia's mum and the security guard, and behind them in the doorway to the bar was Claudia. She was leaning against the door frame, and now she raised her hand and waved, just quickly, and then turned around.

'What d'you reckon?' I asked. 'Think the cops are here yet.'

'Don't know,' said Rico, taking his hand out of his pocket. 'You don't need to be scared. About your probation, I mean. It's all my business here, I'll tell them that, Danny.'

'I know Rico, no need to tell me. I know.' He smiled and clenched his fist, and I tapped mine against it.

They caught him a few days later, coming out of Goldie's bar. I was standing up at my window smoking. I'd started again; it was his fault.

He didn't do anything when he saw them, didn't even try to run away, he just stood there and held out his hands. He wanted to turn himself in anyway, but he'd kept putting it off. Maybe he wanted it to end like it always did, for them to catch him, 'in the wild,' as he said. They gave him the 8 and led him to the van, and before he got in he looked up at me, nodded at me, and I saw his shoulders move, he must have wanted to wave but the 8 held his arms behind his back. They slammed the door and then I saw him lean his head against the window. I waved at him, but they were moving off.

'So you guys... you guys want to do an interview with me,' said the guy with the glasses who everyone called Fred, who was a carjacker, or that was what Stefan had told us.

'Right,' I said, and Rico and Mark and Walter nodded. 'Right, we do.'

We were reporters; we started a school magazine and none of the teachers minded.

Loads of the teachers had disappeared, just like loads of the kids had disappeared a year or two before 'cause their parents had taken them over to the West. The teachers hadn't gone to the West. When they disappeared, from one day to the next but not all at once, we whispered amongst ourselves: 'They were in the Stasi.'

'But you're not... you're not going to spy on me?'

'No, it's just an interview,' I said. 'For our school magazine, you know.'

'Oh, right,' he said, 'school magazine,' and he laughed.

'It's serious,' I said. 'We print fifty copies.' And it really was serious, 'School magazine project,' the teachers called it, the ones who were still there. They talked about a 'new era,' about 'press freedom' and 'showing initiative,' and they said they'd always wanted something like it.

'Fifty copies,' the guy said. 'What if the cops read it?'

He looked around like we'd brought the police with us. We were in a backyard, between a couple of empty buildings; the carjackers and joyriders met up there, Stefan had told us. He'd also told us the guys nicked loads of sex mags and comics at the shops and hid them in the buildings.

'You don't have to scared of the police,' I said. 'We'll make everything anonymous.'

'How d'you mean?'

'We'll just give you a different name.'

'Can I choose it?'

'Alright.'

'Then... then call me Don, like Don Johnson, you know. And another thing...' He fiddled with his glasses.

'Yes?'

'Don't ever say that again, that I'm scared of cops.' He turned around and went over to one of the derelict buildings.

'And the interview, Fred?' I called.

'I told you to call me Don!' He stopped by a big heap of junk and waved us over. 'Alright, come on then, lads!' We nodded at each other, picked up our pads and pens and our Dictaphone, which was really a tape recorder, and went over. He was a couple of years older than us but he looked like he was in year seven or eight, even when he sat down on an old car seat on top of the junk heap and looked down at us.

'I'm Leipzig's first carjacker,' he said. 'I'm a professional, you better believe it.'

There were empty beer and Fanta crates scattered around and we sat down on them. Rico put the tape recorder on his knees, and Mark and Walter were already scribbling away on their pads even before the interview had started. 'Great headline,' Mark whispered, leaning over to me, 'Leipzig's First Carjacker.'

'Yeah, maybe,' I said, 'sounds pretty good,' and then I gave Rico a sign, pointing my finger at nothing and saying 'Action' – I'd seen that on TV one time. We were real professionals already, we'd done loads of interviews for our school magazine, even with the neo-Nazis from year eleven, the 'bald-heads' as Rico called them, the guys who met at the back of the sports ground, but all they'd said on tape was 'Sieg heil,' 'Foreigners out' and that kind of thing, even though the boss of the gang, Mikloš Maray, the ex-chairman of the school Soviet-German Friendship Council, was half-foreign himself. Rico scooted closer to the rubbish heap and Fred, grabbed hold of the microphone, fiddled with the cable, pressed Record and held the mic up to Fred. I looked at my watch. 'Interview with Don,' I said in a loud voice. '15:43.' Don laughed.

'So you're a real carjacker, Don?' I said.

'A professional,' he said. He took a bent cigarette out of his chest pocket, broke half of it off and threw it away, and lit the other half.

'And... and why do you do it, why do you steal cars?'

'Don't know,' he said, and I saw Walter and Mark scribbling on their pads, 'no idea... What kind of stupid question is that?'

'Hey, hey, hey,' Rico moved the mic around. 'You wanted to do the interview.'

'Alright,' I said. 'Rewind and wipe that bit.'

'Well, you know, it's fun, like, driving around at night, it's, like... you're something special, you know. You... you can go wherever you like, you know, and at night, all the lights...' He leaned forward on the old car seat, smoking and turning his arms in front of him like he was holding a steering wheel. '...All the lights, and no one's around to... to mess with you, like, and Jesus –' he laughed again, 'all the cars now, look at all the cars we've got here now!'

'And the... the police?'

'Oh, the cops.' He gestured, brushing off the idea. He fell back onto the seat and suddenly looked really small. 'The cops can't do anything to good old Don.'

But it didn't sound like he believed it.

'Have they ever caught you?'

'Caught me?' Caught me?' He fumbled his cigarette and threw it away. 'That's all part of the fun, you know?

The cops take you down the station and let you go again. If you're fast, you're good. Are you lads fourteen yet?'

'Yeah,' I said.

'Course,' said Rico, and Walter and Mark nodded.

'Pity. You'd be just right for cars, at twelve or thirteen. You're not criminally respondable yet.'

'What?'

'I mean, they can't do anything to you. I've got a couple of kids in my team. Twelve or thirteen, they can't touch them. But I like to play alone best. I'm Leipzig's first car-jacker, write that in your article. The night and that, all the lights, you know...'

'Are you ever scared?'

'Stupid question. Never.' He shuffled on his seat, and Mark and Walter scribbled on their pads next to me.

'Are you still at school?'

'School!' He laughed. 'The streets... the streets, like, they're my school, write that in your article! I've had enough of school. In the Ghetto, you know...'

'What ghetto?'

'Nah, forget it.'

I saw Rico look up at him and nod. He was holding the mic nice and still now.

'How did you learn how to steal a car?'

'That? That's easy, it's easy as pie. But you do have to get the knack,' he slapped his chest, 'it takes a bit of talent, like, in the wrist, nice and easy with a screwdriver in the lock. You got to get the twist right so it goes quick. If you take too long, the game's up. The cops, you know.'

'And then? Do you use the screwdriver in the ignition as well?'

'No, no!' He laughed again. 'You don't need a screw-driver for the ignition. You just feel under the dashboard, there's these wires there, coloured wires, you rip them out and then make contact, you have to know the trick, spark the ignition, you know, like in metalwork class.'

I took my notes out of my chest pocket, the ones I'd made when Stefan told me about Fred and the carjackers. Stefan knew a couple of them, and that was why he wasn't with us. 'Otherwise they'll think I'm a grass,' he said. 'I'm not a grass.'

'Drugs,' I said, 'what do you know about drugs?'

'Hey, are you taking the piss, this isn't Zoo Station!'

'I don't know. I heard a thing or two.'

'Shit, what's all this bollocks?' He jumped up and punched the air a few times. 'We've got nothing to do with that shit, you get it, and if anyone says we do I'll smash them in!' He punched at nothing again, stumbled and fell back on the seat.

Rico put the mic down and stood up. 'Don't worry,' I said. 'We've got plenty of good headlines.'

'Drugs! You've got a screw loose! Everyone knows good old Fred... shit, good old Don... has nothing to do with lick-and-stick tattoos and all that shit.' He raised his head, sat up straight and lit up a new cigarette, which looked even worse than the first one.

'Lick-and-stick tattoos,' Rico said into the mic, 'bloody lick-and-stick,' and Mark and Walter nodded and scribbled on their pads. No one used transfers or decals anymore, 'cause some of them had drugs on the back that got you hooked instantly, the moment you licked the back. The teachers had told us, and since then I'd stopped collecting stamps as well.

'It's just 'cause you always trash the cars, 'cause you always smash up the nice cars,' I said. 'They say, the teachers and that, they say you take heroin and then you go crazy.'

'Heroin. Shit.' Fred laughed, exhaling smoke. Then

he got up and turned round to the derelict building behind him. 'Steffen! Bring me some drugs!' We looked past the junk heap and Fred to the building. In one of the windows, behind broken glass, a boy was standing now, waving.

Then he was gone again, then we heard him on the stairs, and then he came out the door and crossed the yard to us. He had three cans of beer clutched to his chest and he gave us a stupid grin as he handed them to Fred. The boy looked like the kind the cops always sent home again; pretty young, and the Micky-Mouse T-shirt he was wearing was way too big for him. Walter smiled, 'cause he loved Micky Mouse as well. Fred opened one of the cans, put it to his lips and drank, ten seconds, twenty, and when he lowered the can again, he belched, then he crushed the can and threw it on his rubbish heap. 'You can go now, Steffen.' Steffen was still giving us that stupid grin, then he went back inside. I saw a face behind one of the windows, then two, and then there was a girl, up on the second floor, I could see her long hair, dark, perhaps black. I raised my head and tried to make eye contact, and now she moved behind the glass and put her hand on the broken pane. She was wearing a pale-blue blouse, it had these bright patches on it, looked like... like stars...

'Jeez, Danny, look, look at him drinking!' Rico elbowed me.

'There's a girl,' I whispered, 'really beautiful, a girl, Rico.'

'You're crazy, where would they have a girl here?'

Fred belched, pretty loud, once, twice. 'Is this heroin, is it?' He'd opened the next can, and he drank. He suddenly looked all grey in the face; it must have been the light. It was afternoon and the sun was starting to disappear. The girl with the stars had disappeared, too, when I looked back up at her window.

'This, you get it, this is my only drug!'

'How old are you, Fred?'

'You know, the smashing up part, that's one of those things. You don't need hard drugs, maybe a beer or two. In a car it's speed, you know, that's better than any drug. Better than going with a girl... You lads have been with girls, right?'

'Course,' said Mark, and we looked at the ground.

'It's like in a movie, you know! You, you're the number one, number one, you know, lads! You're it. And then the night. And all the lights. And then really letting loose, and no limits, you know, until the car's trashed. But only sometimes. Not with all the cars.'

'And the people, don't you feel bad for the owners?'

'Oh, well, the owners. I told you, we don't trash all the cars, some of them are still fine afterwards. The people, well, these days, strange times these days.' He grinned and drank.

'Ask about the sex mags,' Mark whispered. He shuffled on his beer crate and held his pad up to his face so I could only see his eyes.

'I wanted to ask something else about stealing... You go out shoplifting quite a lot, right?'

'Right. Cigarettes, booze, beer!' He drank, then he held up the can, shook it, then he crushed it and threw it away. 'We're pretty good at it.'

'So are we.' I turned around to Mark. He still had his pad in front of his face, and I'd only just heard him.

'Shush,' I said.

'Huh, why?' he mumbled through the pad. 'Remember those pizzas...'

'Shush,' I said.

'Let him,' Rico pressed the stop button. 'He's right.

We're not kids anymore.' He stood up and the mic dangled down to his hip. Rico was pretty tall and he had muscles as well, he did boxing, didn't he, and even though Fred was sitting on top of the junk heap he could look him straight in the face. 'Tell us how good you are at the supermarket!'

'That's my job,' I said. 'I'm the interviewer, you're the mic man.' I was also the editor, but Rico didn't like to hear that 'cause he's just missed out in the vote.

'Alright, Danny, alright.' Rico held the mic up to Fred's face and pressed Record again.

'So how do you do it then?' I asked. 'At the supermarket, shoplifting.'

'We've got our tricks,' said Fred, looking over at the house two or three times, where his gang and the girl with the stars were, somewhere behind the windows, watching us, even though we couldn't see them.

'The sex mags,' Mark whispered, 'ask him about the sex mags!' He was getting louder and louder but Fred didn't seem to hear him, just went on talking.

'It's a question of speed. If you're fast, you're good. And tricks, you know, you always need a few tricks!'

'The sex mags, Danny!'

But then Mark didn't want to know anymore about the sex mags everyone said were hidden in the old buildings, 'cause Rico wouldn't let it go, he wanted to be a hard man, didn't he, and he was one. 'We're faster, Don,' he said, switching the tape recorder off again. 'We're pretty good at shoplifting as well, right, Mark?'

'Right,' said Mark, and even Walter nodded and put his pen away, even though he'd never stolen anything, not even from his mum.

'Reporters!' said Fred, and he turned back to the building, put two fingers in his mouth and whistled. I saw two kids at the windows again, and then they were down in the yard, the boy with the Micky-Mouse T-shirt and his brother, or he looked like his brother. They really were fast, not just at stealing. I looked at the windows again, but I couldn't see the girl.

'What's this all about?' Rico pointed the mic at the two boys, who had stopped behind Fred's rubbish heap. Fred stood up, climbed down from the junk and pushed Rico carefully aside, even though he didn't even come up to his shoulders. He really was a carjacker, Leipzig's first carjacker.

'Just a little demonstration. Free of charge, so you can learn a thing or two.'

'Our interview,' I said. 'Don't mess up our interview, guys...'

'You lot want to be proper reporters?' Fred downed the last beer can, crushed it and threw it away. He really was pretty fast, not just at stealing.

'We are,' Rico said. 'What d'you think this is?' He tapped Fred's shoulder with the mic.

'You want a real story? I mean a proper story, straight from the streets, you know, then come with us to the supermarket, you'll get a little demonstration. Free of charge! Then you'll see how fast we are!'

'I can steal faster,' said Rico. 'My hands are faster, you better believe it!' He moved his shoulders like at boxing practice and made his hands dance in the air.

Walter stood next to him, and Mark said: 'We're the greatest at the supermarket!' but Fred just walked past them to his two mates. He whispered with them, then he went to the building and stopped in the doorway. 'Starbright!' He leaned over the threshold and called again. We looked over at the door. Footsteps on the stairs, pretty quiet, and then the girl I'd seen at the window was there. She was wearing a blue skirt that looked almost like the dark-blue Pioneer skirt Katja always used to wear, and her legs, her thin white legs...

She stopped and stared at us, then she went over to Fred, stood behind him, and I saw her hand grip his arm.

'No need to be scared,' he said. 'They're mates.'

'Yes,' I said and nodded, and the others nodded too, 'we're friends.'

She flashed a smile and then started playing with the stars on her blouse. They were made of gold paper and they looked sewn on. She seemed a bit younger than us, maybe twelve or thirteen, even though the stars on her chest were already raised a bit, and not just when she breathed, and she was still breathing fast now... 'Really, don't be scared...'

'No,' she said, and let go of Fred's arm.

He stroked her cheek and his grey face went all red, and he pulled his hand away quickly when he saw us grinning.

'I thought we wanted to go to the supermarket?' said Rico. 'Bit of shoplifting, your great tricks, or are you scared all of a sudden?'

'No,' Fred said.

'Fred's never scared,' Starbright said, and rapped her little fist on his shoulder.

'Course we're going shoplifting,' Fred said. 'I want to show you lot how good we are. Starbright's coming too, she'll sing for us.'

'Sing? Are you crazy?' Rico slapped his forehead.

'Wait and see!' Fred grinned and winked at us, then he beckoned the two boys over and they went off, Starbright a few steps behind them.

'Let's go,' I called, and we ran after them.

'Run!' Mark yelled, lifting up his dad's big black briefcase that he'd collected specially on the way, and slamming it into the sales assistant's chest. The sales assistant screamed and stumbled to one side, 'cause his chest wasn't as well padded as the fat cashier's, who was trying to get out from behind her cash desk and grabbing at me with her short arms. And we ran. Little Walter was already outside, I could see him through the shop window. In front of me, the floor was littered with chocolate bars; he must have dropped them. I ran past the cashiers to the door. Behind the cashiers, right by the wine, Starbright was still singing, folk songs and Pioneer songs, all mixed up and pretty loud and weird, stepping from one foot to the other and sticking out her chest and plucking at her starry blouse and her skirt, and she looked like she wasn't quite right, no, she looked beautiful. A wine bottle had fallen off the shelf behind her and she was standing right in a red puddle. 'Of all of our brave comrades, none was as good and kind...' For a while she'd distracted everyone nicely as we'd stuffed our pockets, but now they'd spotted us. 'A man stands in the forest on just one leg...' The sales assistant was kneeling on the floor, clutching his chest; Mark had done a good job. We ran past him to the door, Mark with the huge briefcase, Rico, Fred and me; I couldn't see Fred's mates anywhere. A bottle of vodka fell out of Fred's jacket and smashed on the floor. I turned back round to Starbright, who was still singing and dancing in the red puddle, and now she smiled at me. Then we were outside and running down the road, to Fred's backyard and the buildings.

'You guys messed up,' he yelled. 'Starbright's singing was so... you idiots messed up!'

'Shut it, will you!' Rico threatened him with his fist, which wobbled as he ran. 'It's your lot's fault, you couldn't get enough...' I turned around. Outside the supermarket were two white coats, holding onto a boy. I could see the T-shirt under his jacket: Micky Mouse. We ran down a side street. The rest of Fred's gang were behind us now. He looked at me and grinned. His jumper had all these lumps underneath. Fred stopped by a Wartburg, it was a new Wartburg with a VW engine. 'Now what?' Rico yelled. 'Let's go! What if they come after us?' But they didn't come after us, the street was pretty empty, and Fred didn't even look around as he stuck the little screwdriver in the lock.

'It's for your story,' he said. 'You can learn a thing or two,' and the door was open while he was still talking. 'A Wartburg, just to get warmed up.' Walter was a few metres away; he took his pen out of his chest pocket and wrote something on his pad. Fred reached into the car and pulled the lever for the back door. 'Come on, men, in you get!' He grinned and held the door open for us like a chauffeur.

'Don't be stupid,' I said, 'it's only a few metres.' But I saw Rico, Mark and even Walter sitting down on the back seat with eyes wide, and I squeezed in next to them. We leaned forwards while Fred fumbled with the wires. A woman yelled in the street. Walter was writing in his little pad and I was sitting half on his lap as we drove off.

Mark spun the combination lock on the briefcase, then opened it. 'Look, we've got more than you!' We were in one of Fred's empty buildings, right up on the fourth floor, sorting our loot. Fred and his mate had eight packs of cigarettes, five cans of beer, two sets of brand-new playing cards and twelve bars of chocolate.

'Hmm,' said Fred, ripping open a pack of Marlboros and lighting one up, 'not bad.'

In Mark's dad's briefcase was a frozen Black Forest gateau. Rico pulled two bars of soap out of his trousers and put them on top of the cake. 'I told you I've got fast hands.'

'Shit,' said Fred, 'five beers, eight lots of cigarettes, cards and chocolate, that's not bad either!'

Fred's mate rolled up his trouser leg and pulled a big tin of herrings out of his sock. 'For dinner,' he said, grinning.

'Good lad,' Fred patted him on the shoulder. 'And if they hadn't caught Steffen...'

'What's going to happen to him?' I asked. 'And the girl...'

'Starbright? Nah, she was just singing, she'll be along soon, there's nothing wrong with singing. And Steffen'll be fine. He's only twelve, they'll just give him a lift home, the cops will.'

'The cops.' We nodded.

'My Steffen's probably got half the supermarket up his T-shirt,' Fred said. 'You guys can stuff your soap and cake!'

'Ten-pack of chewing gum,' I said, pulling it out of my chest pocket and adding it to the soap and the cake.

'Gum!' Fred dismissed it with a wave.

'Come over here.' Mark cleared the chewing gum, soap and cake out of the briefcase. We moved in closer. On the bottom of the case were three sex mags, *Das neue Wochenend, Praline* and some other girly mag.

'Not bad, eh?'

'How d'you do that, huh? I never even...'

'Fast hands!' Mark picked up one of the magazines and flicked through it. We saw loads of breasts and other things. Far away, we heard a siren.

'You think they're coming here?' Walter ran to the window.

'Nah. It's safe here. You want a beer?'

We exchanged glances. 'Course,' said Rico. Fred passed him a can and he opened it. The foam splashed all the way up to his face.

'You need the knack,' Fred said, 'always keep a calm hand.' Rico passed the can around.

We spread the mags out on the floor and flicked through them. 'Look at that one, look at that babe!' We drank, and a bit of beer dripped onto her. The beer was sour and hurt my tongue, and I felt dizzy after three or four mouthfuls, but I smiled and drank.

'She did a good job,' I said.

'Who?'

'You know... Little Star. The singing, I mean.'

'She's special,' Fred said, and he took the beer can out of my hand, drank until it was empty, and threw it against the wall. 'Starbright's something special.'

'Little Star,' I whispered, really quietly so he couldn't hear me.

'She stays here,' he said. 'Sometimes she sleeps here. Her old man, you know, he's a drunk bastard and an arsehole, and then she stays here with me, sometimes, you know...' He opened a new beer, drank half of it and passed it round. He'd gone grey in the face again, but I was used to it now. Footsteps on the stairs, pretty quiet. Little Star was back. Mark shoved the porn under his case.

'Hello,' she said, and sat down in the middle of our circle. Her pretty stars were gone now; she was wearing an Adidas jumper. 'Did I sing nice?'

'Yes,' I said, nodding, 'you did,' and the others nodded too, and she went red.

Fred pulled a little bottle of green minty liqueur out of his pocket. 'Here,' he said. 'Your favourite.'

'Thanks,' and she was still red and she pressed the little bottle of green liqueur to her face. Mark tore open the cake box and put the gateau in the middle. It was still frozen and we broke off big chunks and ate it like ice cream. We opened the chocolate as well and another beer. It was getting dark outside; Fred lit a few candles and we moved in closer and ate and drank and we were happy.

## Acknowledgements

Thanks to Walfried Hartinger.
Thanks to Ursula Bender.
Also to the Saxon State Ministry of Arts and Sciences, the Mühlbeck-Friedersdorf book village and Schachtbaude Schlaitz.

The translation of this work was supported
by a grant from the Goethe-Institut.

This book is printed with plant-based inks on materials certified by the Forest Stewardship Council. The FSC promotes an ecologically, socially and economically responsible management of the world's forests. This book has been printed without the use of plastic-based coatings.

Fitzcarraldo Editions
8-12 Creekside
London, SE8 3DX
United Kingdom


This second edition published in Great Britain
by Fitzcarraldo Editions in 2023



ISBN 978-1804270-28-8

Design by Ray O'Meara
Typeset in Fitzcarraldo
Advance review copies printed and bound by TJ Books



fitzcarraldoeditions.com

Fitzcarraldo Editions